WHERE THE RIVERS MEET

Nicola Thorne is the author of a number of well-known novels which include *The Daughters of the House*, The Askham Chronicles (*Never Such Innocence, Yesterday's Promises, Bright Morning* and *A Place in the Sun*), *Bird of Passage, Champagne Gold, A Wind in Summer, Silk*, and, most recently, *Profit and Loss*. Born in South Africa, she was educated at the LSE. She lived for many years in London, but has now made her home in Dorset.

NICHOLA THORNE

Where the Rivers Meet

Grafton

This Grafton edition published 1997
by Diamond Books
An imprint of HarperCollinsPublishers
77-85 Fulham Palace Rd
Hammersmith, London W6 8JB

First Published in Great Britain by
Granada Publishing 1982

ISBN 0 261 66987 7

Printed and bound in Great Britain
by Caledonian

CONTENTS

This novel centres around a family and a business in a town on the Scottish Borders that exists in fact – and will be recognisable to those who know it – but has been given a fictional name.

Although the author acknowledges her debt to those who assisted her in her background research she would like to emphasise that the business is a mythical one, and that all the characters in the novel without exception are the products of her imagination, so that any resemblance between actual persons living or dead is purely coincidental.

PART I

Consequences of the Peace
1919–1923

CHAPTER ONE

In the last days of July 1918, with victory a little more than three months away, Malcolm Dunbar gave his life fighting with the 7/8th Scots Borderers during a fierce attack on the Hartennes forest near Soissons. So great was the appreciation of the French for the heroism of the 15th Scots Division in the terrible carnage that they at once raised a monument in its honour on which were inscribed the words: '*Ici fleurira toujours le glorieux Chardon d'Écosse parmi les Roses de France*'. Three colonels out of ten battalions involved were killed, and two wounded. among them Colonel Hart of the Scots Borderers.

Malcolm Dunbar's body was never found. With many of his fellow soldiers it lay forever among the roses of France. Subsequently his name would appear on the great arch raised at Thiepval after the war, in memory of those who had lost their lives but who had no known grave.

The only effects of Captain Dunbar that eventually found their way home to his family in Branswick on the Scottish Borders were his soldier's cap, his Bible and a wallet in which were pictures of his family – his wife, Mary, his mother and father, his sisters Juliet. Susan and Margaret and his younger brother Cullum. His son Murdoch was born a few days after the family learned of the father's death.

It was not a memory to celebrate, those sad tense days the previous year when the family were informed of Malcolm's death and Mary went into premature labour. For a time it was not thought she would live and her baby was a puny sickly creature who had seemed destined to join the spirit of his father. It was a memory that haunted Hector Dunbar, Malcolm's widowed father, and one that he forced the family to live with daily. All life had gone out of the house that July day in 1918 and, except for the steady growth of baby Murdoch, it had been firmly kept out ever since.

One year later, almost to the day when the eldest Dunbar fell in France, this memory was responsible for his younger sisters, Susan and Margaret, facing each other, engaged in a battle which, fortunately this time, was unlikely to prove fatal.

'I *am* going to the ball,' Margaret said, her fair complexion lit up by a sudden rush of colour. 'Whatever Father says. To forbid us to go is ridiculous. I bought this gown in Edinburgh and I intend to wear it.'

They both looked at the object that had provoked such unsisterly discord. It hung between them on the wardrobe like a banner proclaiming Margaret's independence. There was not much of it, a silvery wisp of a thing, net over silver charmeuse – a very light-weight rich satin – the waistline just below the bust festooned with silver cords held by posies of silver rosebuds. The sheath skirt was ankle length and a long net train draped below the rest of the garment, almost reaching to the floor. The sight of it had taken Susan's breath away; the daring, the sophistication. But above all was the fact that Father had distinctly said 'no'. Like two Cinderellas they had been forbidden to go to the ball, and that was the cause of their quarrel.

'You think that Malcolm would have wished us to spend the rest of our lives mourning him?' Margaret continued, flouncing to the window, her arms akimbo. 'Do you *honestly* think he would not wish us to celebrate the victory he fought for? The whole country is celebrating; why should not we?'

Susan, her eyes still mesmerized by the dress, sank onto the bed.

'Margaret, how can I explain Father to you when you know him so well? He mourns Malcolm more than either of us knows. Malcolm was the eldest son, the heir. On him

Father pinned all his hopes because, as we know, Cullum was never his equal. Now he feels that, as the ball is to be held almost on the exact anniversary of the day Malcolm died, we should not go to it. I intend to respect Father's wishes – and so does Cullum.'

'Well, I don't.' Margaret turned to face her sister, leaning on the windowsill. 'Father has an obsession about Malcolm; he will never get over it. He has become more and more morose over the years since Mother died. If Malcolm had not been killed it would have been something else. He is depressed, you know it. He drinks too much.'

'Margaret! You mustn't say that!' Susan looked shocked.

'I will say it. Of course he drinks too much! He doesn't pay enough attention to the business. He despises Cullum because he is not like Malcolm, and us because we are women. And now, when we are all just about to have a little fun and break away from the gloom of the war, he forbids us to go to the Victory Ball. I am going, Susan, I tell you. I *am* going.'

Susan gazed at her sister. With her dazzling blue-green eyes, shapely mouth and black hair which curled naturally around her head she was the acknowledged beauty of the family. Now her chin was tilted and her nostrils flared slightly; her eyes were defiant. It was an expression Susan knew well. Margaret had never been very amenable to discipline and, since their mother's death, had more or less got her own way by sheer force despite the well-meaning attempts of those in charge of her education to deflect her.

'You would distress us all, Father particularly,' Susan went on. 'Everyone would talk about you. I *too* am in mourning, don't forget, for Ian.'

'Of course I don't forget Ian, Susan; but he has been dead two years. He wouldn't wish you to mourn him forever.' Margaret went impulsively over to her sister,

11

sitting on the bed beside her, putting an arm round her neck, her cheek against hers. Unlike Susan, Margaret was a demonstrative girl, eager to give and receive affection. Susan's face had assumed that white, tense look it always wore whenever the name of her dead fiancé was mentioned.

Ian Lyall, killed the year before Malcolm at Passchendaele, had been a member of the Lyall family whose mill, in a neighbouring town, was almost as large as those of the Dunbars and the Pendreighs. He had been the same age as Malcolm, handsome, brave, suitable in every way. Susan had been twenty and they were to have married on Ian's next leave. Margaret had never seen Susan weep for Ian; admittedly she had been at school when the announcement of his death came, but even so she heard that no one saw Susan ever shed a tear. She had retired to her room for a few days, taken her meals there and then come down and got on with her duties as the eldest unmarried daughter of the house, acting in place of her mother; a comfort to Father, a scourge to Cullum and a second mother to Margaret.

The sisters sat silently for a moment, each wrapped in her own thoughts: Margaret's rebellious, Susan's nostalgic and sad. Margaret could look forward to the future; Susan always looked back at the past. She twisted Ian's ring on her finger and then she put an arm comfortingly round Margaret's waist. She knew it was a melancholy household for a young girl of nearly eighteen on the brink of life, perhaps already a little in love. Mary still wore black for her husband, and she and her father-in-law seemed to feed on each other's grief; a curiously horrible, almost cannibalistic form of nourishment. They continually pored over pictures of the dead, talking about days that were gone as though life had ended for them as well.

Once the house had been the centre of gaiety and life, young people of all ages breezing in and out at all times of

12

the day and evening. There were Juliet's older friends; then Malcolm's when Juliet left to get married. There were Cullum's rather boisterous crowd of extrovert rugby players and, finally, the chatter of girlish voices when Susan and Margaret invited friends from school to stay.

All that seemed long ago. The entertaining had begun to taper off when their mother suddenly died from peritonitis in 1912, and had ceased altogether in 1918 when they knew Malcolm would come home no more.

'Is not Ruthven Pendreigh the *real* reason you want to go to the ball?' Susan turned to Margaret and saw a dab of bright colour stain her cheeks.

'Ruthven is certainly *one* reason to go to the ball.' Margaret avoided that frank gaze. 'He is not the *only* reason.'

'You have seen a lot of him this summer.'

'Yes.' Margaret regained her composure, boldly returned Susan's look. 'He likes me and I like him. We enjoy the same things. You know we have always liked the Pendreighs, Sue, and Cullum is fond of Netta. He was going to take her to the ball.'

'Well now he says he won't; he is going to respect Father's wishes.' Susan put her hand on her sister's arm, suddenly feeling much older and protective; aware of herself as the mother she had replaced. 'Maggie, take care, dearest, don't wear your heart on your sleeve for Ruthven Pendreigh.'

'My heart is not on *any* sleeve I assure you,' Margaret said, tossing her head. 'I *like* Ruthven, but then I like many others.'

'And they like you.' Susan was careful to keep the envy out of her voice as she got up and straightened her dress, aware of how unfashionable she looked beside Margaret. 'Come, let's go down. I really came to tell you Uncle Andrew is here. He arrived at about three to see Father and they've been closeted in the drawing room ever since.

13

I have a feeling it's about something serious, because he usually says when he's coming and this time he did not. He's staying for dinner.'

Margaret went to her dressing table and touched her hair with a silver-backed brush, peering at her face carefully in the mirror, always conscious of how she looked. 'Is Aunt Lily with him?'

'No, he came alone by train and took a cab from the station.' Susan joined her sister by the mirror and frowned. Admiring Margaret's beauty made her feel dowdy. Her dress was too long, almost down to her ankles, and her hair was coiled in a rather shapeless bun at the back. She had many of Margaret's features, but they were balanced less harmoniously for some reason that no onlooker could really define. Perhaps early grief and responsibilities had made her mouth seem rather prim and forbidding, as though to control an inner turmoil. It was not as full as Margaret's and did not smile so readily, and her eyes, though the same blue-green, did not have that special luminosity and were closer together, making her look rather hard.

Susan had mourned Ian far more than anyone knew, and felt like his widow. She realized she looked like his widow too. Who would look at her now, with all the young men dead or maimed? She was just twenty-two and yet she felt an old woman, soured by experience and embittered by her losses in the war. For not only had she loved Ian, she had been the closest of the three sisters to Malcolm.

'I must get some new dresses,' she said, almost to herself. 'And have my hair cut.'

'I'll follow you when I've finished my hair.' Margaret accompanied her sister to the door and closed it after her, still applying the brush to her short, curly locks. In the old days when her hair was long she had brushed it vigorously a hundred times night and morning; it was a habit that died hard. Father had been very angry when she had returned home from a visit to Edinburgh, shorn of her thick mass of girlish ringlets.

'I am a woman now, Father,' she had insisted. 'And women do not have long hair any more!'

Margaret yearned for womanhood; she had always wanted to be grown up, to imitate her elders. She loved clothes and dancing instinctively and, instinctively too, the admiration of men. She couldn't wait to leave school and enter into the social life of Branswick, such an enticing attraction for adolescents, even though it no longer had the leisure and glamour of pre-war days.

Still brushing her hair she wandered over to the window and looked down towards the Pendreigh house, which stood just below them on the hill where the town's foremost families lived. The Dunbar house, *Woodbrae*, was the largest and the highest, standing on the very brow of the hill. From it there was a wonderful view of the town in the valley, with its twin rivers running through it, the Drume and the Craigie, converging in the centre just before the Dunbar Mill. But the Pendreigh house was very large too and the Pendreighs had more servants and a tennis court, whereas the Dunbar house was surrounded by woods with a long sloping lawn in front.

Yes, she passionately did want to go to the ball, her first grown up ball, and particularly on the arm of Ruthven Pendreigh. Although she had said she liked many others it was not true. She liked Ruthven more. She had known as soon as she came home from school that Easter that their friendship had turned to something deeper. He was in his second year at Oxford and was then going into the family business, hosiery manufacturers like the Dunbars. The Pendreigh Mill was almost as big as the Dunbar Mill. It would be a most suitable alliance; their families would approve. Ruthven was one of the most handsome, eligible young men in the town; he was good at everything, he excelled at sports. He was three years older than she was; that was just about right too.

Margaret Dunbar was not over-modest, but neither was she excessively vain. She knew that her looks were admired; she had a flair for fashion; she was well informed, and she was considered mature for her years. As young Mrs Ruthven Pendreigh she would step into an almost pre-ordained niche in Branswick society, the sort of niche that her mother had successfully occupied for so many years. She and Ruthven would be a popular, talked-about couple; they would help to set the scene and people would emulate them.

It all looked so right, seemed so right, and here and now she could almost predict their lifestyle from the moment she stood on the threshold of Branswick Parish Church in her white bridal gown, her arm in that of her bridegroom, to the day she was finally laid to rest in its churchyard.

It was an exciting prospect, a realizable dream and, moreover, she would be away from the stifling, funereal gloom of *Woodbrae*. Almost drunk with this sudden feeling of anticipated happiness, Margaret flung open the window, taking deep breaths of good Branswick air which, despite the smoke from the mills, was considered salubrious because of its position in the hills.

She always loved the twilight, especially on these hot summer nights when a mist arose from the rivers, partly concealing the valley, and the lights began to twinkle one by one on the Vertig hill opposite where the poorest townsfolk lived, including most of those who worked in the mills. These little pin-pricks of light, one following the other, looked as though one of the old lamplighters was at work, though most of the town, even on the Vertig, had electricity. Yet she could hear the sound of ball on bat and peering out saw that there were four people on the Pendreigh tennis court.

She leaned so far out of the window that she nearly lost her balance. Ruthven had been away – but now he was back. She could see his tall form striking the ball. He

16

partnering his sister Netta, and his brother Dirk was partnering the other sister Moira.

Ruthven was back!

She shut the window and ran over to gaze at herself in the mirror, fastening her hair back with her hands so that it framed her face. Then she dabbed a trace of powder on the very tip of her nose and ran towards the door, leaving it wide open behind her as she raced down the stairs.

'Ruthven is back!' she said, coming to a halt on the threshold of the drawing room. Everyone inside stopped talking and looked at her. The soft beige dress she had put on for dinner had a round embroidered neck and a slightly dropped waistline. Her Uncle Andrew and Cullum got up, but her father stayed in his chair, his hand firmly round a glass of whisky, and pointed to her proudly.

'You haven't seen our Maggie for some time, have you, Andrew?'

'I have not, Hector!' Andrew Dunbar walked over to greet Margaret, his eyes glinting with admiration. 'My, my, you've become a very bonny wee lassie.'

'Not "wee lassie", Uncle Andrew,' Margaret corrected him reprovingly, reaching to kiss him. 'I am a woman.'

'Are you now?' He held her hand and looked at her. 'And who is Ruthven?'

'Ruthven Pendreigh.' Margaret's voice almost choked with excitement. 'He is back. I saw him playing tennis. Oh Susan, did you know he was back?'

'I saw Netta in the town today,' Susan said carefully. 'She said he was due back from the visit to his uncle in the Highlands.'

'Maybe he came back specially to see you.' Uncle Andrew's eyes had a knowing gleam. 'Tell me, do you like this young man very much?'

'I should have thought that was obvious,' Cullum said gruffly. 'She moons about him all the day.'

'I do not, Cullum Dunbar!' Margaret's eyes flashed

17

angrily at her brother, 'I do not *moon*. I *like* Ruthven, certainly; but then we've always been friendly with the Pendreigh family, have we not, Father?' She sat on the arm of her father's chair and kissed the top of his head. Hector's reply was a grunt and he put an arm round her waist and squeezed her.

It was obvious to Margaret that there had been some sort of scene. Susan and Cullum looked tense, and there was a great deal of cigar smoke about and the smell of whisky fumes. Father was red-faced, while Uncle Andrew's natural pallor seemed to have deteriorated into a chalky whiteness and his lips were so grimly pursed as to be invisible. Cullum was standing on the Persian rug in front of the fire, staring at its pattern as though he had just received a severe reprimand. Yet the brothers' anger did not seem directed at him but at each other.

Hector Dunbar was a handsome man, strongly built, with thick white hair and prominent bushy eyebrows. His father had married twice and Andrew was the son of the second marriage, the very antithesis of Hector, being rather short, thin and now bald. He had a severe lawyer-like expression and always wore a pince-nez on the end of his nostrils, which flared a little as though perpetually assailed by a rather unpleasant odour whose source he was unable to trace.

Andrew Dunbar had a law practice in Edinburgh and, although he had never been active in the family firm, he kept an eye on it as a substantial shareholder. He and his wife were childless, the result of a dangerous miscarriage a year after their marriage, but they lived in style and before the war had liked to travel abroad. They very rarely came to Branswick unless it was on some business to do with the family or the firm. They thought it too provincial.

No one particularly liked Uncle Andrew, so they were not sorry he was so seldom seen. They liked Aunt Lily though, who was gay, rather beautiful and very vague. She was considered a bit fast for Edinburgh society, smoked, played cards and had thought for years that women should have the suffrage. During the war she had worked at a convalescent home and was only prevented by her husband from going to France to nurse.

Andrew glanced at Hector who had his nose in his whisky glass. 'You've three very bonny girlies, Hector. You'll soon have these two off your hands.'

Hector scowled and gazed at his glass. 'Who said anything about wanting them off my hands? Cullum, pour another dram would you?'

Cullum quickly took his father's glass and went over to the table on which were several decanters full of various amber coloured liquids.

'Have a drop yourself, Cullum,' his father added kindly, as though to someone half-witted. 'Andrew?'

Andrew looked at his half-full glass. 'I've had enough for the moment, thank you, Hector. Do the girls not take a drink?'

'They do not,' Hector said firmly eyeing them under his shaggy brows. 'I do not approve of women who drink.'

Everyone knew that Aunt Lily drank rather a lot. Andrew twitched his nostrils and adjusted his pince-nez, gazing sternly at his half-brother. 'Times are changing you know, Hector. Women now have the vote.'

'A mistake in my opinion.' Hector took his glass from Cullum. 'It is even proposed to admit them to the House of Commons. What a disaster that will be. I fully agree with what Sir Frederick Bunbury said – that most women had no desire to enter the House or to live under laws made by their own sex. Women are not wanted in politics, or business, or for that matter . . .'

'Oh Father!' Margaret ran her hands through his thick hair. 'You are an old cross-patch today. You know you don't really believe any of that nonsense at all. You are just doing it to provoke us. Well, you won't provoke me, you silly goose.'

Hector's arm tightened round her waist and he drew her

19

close to him. 'Your uncle has got me in a bad mood I'm afraid, my dear. Though I do think that women should be . . .'

'Kept in their place.' Susan smiled, with a trace of bitterness. Now that she was father's housekeeper she knew he did not want to lose her. He never invited any young men to the house to meet her and discouraged her as much as he could from going out, on the grounds that he needed her by him. On the other hand she knew that no such restrictions would be imposed on Margaret. He would like Margaret to marry well and preferably soon and to adorn Branswick society as her mother once had.

'Not at all,' Hector said, releasing Margaret. 'Women have a very important role as the helpmeets of men. I do not think it is their function to engage in public affairs. It is not natural. 'Tis not what the good Lord created them for. There now.' He glanced at the large watch he wore in the pocket of his waistcoat and then at the clock as though to confirm the time. He was a very meticulous, punctual person. 'Now it is nearly time for dinner. I'll just go up and change. Cullum?'

'Yes Father.'

'You'll not mind if I don't change, Hector,' Andrew said, dusting an imaginary speck off his immaculate suit. 'I didn't bring dinner clothes.'

Hector made no reply but got up, banged his empty glass on the table and walked out of the room closely followed by Cullum.

All during the war Hector Dunbar had insisted that standards would not be dropped and the family would always dress for dinner. The women were not expected to wear evening dress, an afternoon dress was acceptable, but the men always wore black ties. The only concession he had made to austerity was that wine was only drunk on Sundays, and the men did not pass round the port and brandy after dinner but left the table with the women. It seemed a symptom of the times.

Hector Dunbar lamented the passing of the old ways and the old days. It had taken him a long time to understand just what the war meant, apart from the appalling losses which no one had considered possible when it had started. When Lord Grey had said that the lights were going out all over Europe, Hector Dunbar came only gradually to realize that he meant it, and that few of the lights would be relit again.

But this evening, in honour of his brother, he had asked wine to be served and the girls were allowed half a glass each and invited to toast the official declaration of the Peace.

'They say the procession in London will be spectacular,' Andrew said, replacing his glass after the toast. 'I would like to have seen the fleet assembled off Southend. Lily wanted to go but we have our own celebrations in Edinburgh. And you too I understand, Susan?' Andrew looked kindly at his niece.

'We have a ball here, Uncle, but Father does not wish us to attend it.'

'But whyever . . .' Andrew grasped his glass and sipped the contents assiduously.

'I do not wish it, Andrew. I want no more discussion on the subject.' Hector tucked in his chin, a habit he had when he wanted to end a conversation.

'It's the anniversary of Malcolm's death,' Susan said quietly, looking at her brother's widow who sat, dressed in mourning as she had for a year, opposite her. 'Father thinks it would be unseemly to attend a dance.'

'Oh I see.' Andrew coughed and glanced at Mary, whose eyes seldom left her plate.

Looking at Mary Dunbar, who was only twenty-four, it was difficult to believe that she was young, or ever had been a pretty if rather ineffectual and inarticulate girl.

She wore a full length high-necked gown of black bombazine and her hairstyle as well as her dress was of the 'nineties. She looked both pathetic and rather ridiculous. Could this have been the young Mary Wattis of Edinburgh whom Malcolm had impulsively wooed and married one hectic leave before his last? Andrew had seldom seen a woman so changed by circumstance.

'I think Malcolm would not have minded,' Margaret said. 'He gave his life for victory, and so did Ian. I think we should celebrate, not mourn. I still intend to go to the ball, Father.'

Hector brought his fist crashing down on the table, then stood up, swaying back slightly as though he were about to lose his footing. 'I say you will not go to the ball. I forbid it. You will bring scandal on this house.'

'We are the only people in Branswick not attending, Father. The Pendreighs will be there and they lost two sons in the war. The Mactavishes lost a sister when the *Warilda* was torpedoed. The Fairholmes lost . . .'

Hector sat slowly, heavily down again and seized his glass by the stem. 'It does not interest me what you say, Margaret. Have I not heard it all before? The Pendreigh twins were killed in 1915, the Fairholme son right at the beginning of the war with the BEF. The Mactavishes . . . oh, what does it signify.' Hector dropped his head and gave a loud sigh, almost a sob. 'It is my son who died last July, my son, my Malcolm. My hope. I will not dance while his memory still haunts me. Nor will I permit you to. You should have more respect. Every day I miss him. Every day.'

'Ah . . .' Andrew leaned back as the maid served him with vegetables. Hector had cut the beef at the head of the table. 'Thank you, Iris.' He looked up at her and smiled. 'That does bring me again to the point of my visit. Do you not think you should tell your family, Hector?'

'No I do not,' Hector said, brushing Iris away. He was drinking heavily and not eating, something which his

22

family had noticed increasingly since Malcolm's death. 'It is none of their concern.'

'But it is,' Andrew said gently, pouring gravy over his meat. 'It is very much their concern. It concerns them all, their way of life, the standards they are used to.'

'We have told Cullum. It does not concern the ladies.' Hector poured from the decanter of wine which stood in front of him.

'I think it concerns them very much,' Andrew said, 'for they all have shares in the business.'

'Business?' Susan looked at her uncle with surprise. 'You mean Dunbars?'

'Aye, Murdoch Dunbar & Son, established 1796. Well, it's now in very bad shape and your father is unaware of it – that is what I have come to tell him.'

'Then I do not think it *is* our business,' Mary said quickly in her self-effacing whisper, putting her knife and fork together. She had the appetite of a bird and consequently the figure of a scarecrow. She was frightened of her father-in-law, whose grief at Malcolm's death seemed so much superior to her own. After all, she had scarcely known her husband, not like a father. How could she, a bride of a few days, compare with the lifetime's love of a father?

'Mary has Malcolm's shares in the firm,' Andrew said patiently, addressing a middle point on the table. 'That is almost a quarter. If Mary sells she will be quite a wealthy young woman and she has her son to think of.'

'*Sell*?' Susan said. 'Sell her shares?'

'Someone wants to buy Dunbars.' Andrew produced a small gold toothpick and applied it to his lower jaw. 'I think it is a very good offer, considering . . .'

'Considering what?' The colour had come into Cullum's face – alone of the Dunbar children he had the reddish hair and florid colouring of his mother, a MacLeish. He was a tall, thickset, handsome man with broad, open features and this dark sandy-coloured hair. But he had

23

very little beard and this fact did, indeed, make him look boyish. Cullum was very much in awe of his father, particularly as he knew his parent found him so wanting compared to Malcolm. He was almost tongue-tied in Hector's presence which made him seem more gauche than in fact he was.

'Well, considering the business is not doing very well.' Andrew looked round to be sure that Iris was no longer in the room. 'Considering that the profit is so small, and next year you might well make a loss and then the terms of acquisition will not be so favourable.'

'There will be no acquisition,' Hector said, 'as long as I am the majority shareholder of Murdoch Dunbar & Sons.' He rang the bell and as Iris came in told her to clear the table and serve the sweet. In the silence that ensued he sat glowering at his brother, thinking how little love he had for him, how different they were and how much he resented his interfering ways. It was true that as the family lawyer he had a large say in what happened to the family and the business; but he, Hector, was the elder brother; the father of a large family. He resented being talked down to and lectured at like a small child by his pompous younger brother, who knew nothing about the hosiery business in which Hector had spent his life; who didn't even *look* like a Dunbar, taking as he did after his mother, a southerner.

'I think you must consult your family,' Andrew said. 'It is their business as well as yours, their future as well as your own. I realize the death of Malcolm has been a severe blow to you, Hector; but you must get over it. It is not natural to mourn like this. It has affected your work. I'm told that sometimes you never appear at the Mill for days on end. There's no control at Dunbars any more and it shows in diminished profits.'

'Everyone has diminished profits because of the war.'

'It's not only the war; and, besides, other companies have been doing very well. Mactavish for instance have

24

opened another mill at Berwick to cope with the work, and Pendreigh . . .well.'

Iris came in with the sweet and once more there was silence until she tactfully withdrew, closing the door behind her.

'What about Pendreigh?' Susan leaned back in her chair. She was pale and had refused a sweet.

'It is Elliott Pendreigh who has made the offer for Dunbars. A very good offer.'

'But we could never sell to Pendreigh!' Susan exclaimed, looking at her father.

'Why not?' Andrew leaned forward, replacing his gold toothpick in its case.

'We have always been rivals. Our family could never survive the shame of selling out to the Pendreighs.'

'It is surely out of the question to sell to the Pendreighs,' Cullum said diffidently. 'We should have to leave the district.'

'Nonsense! I thought you were very friendly with the Pendreighs.' Andrew finished the wine in his glass and delicately mopped his lips. He was a neat, pernickety man with his well pared nails, his gold toothpick and his frequently adjusted pince-nez. He dressed carefully and had a slight paunch. Also the nuances of social life in a small community passed him by completely because he lived in a large capital city and had few intimates, few close friends outside of the law.

'We *are* very friendly with the Pendreighs,' Susan said quietly. 'That is precisely why we do not want to sell them our business. If we did we would be friendly no more. We would be looked down upon in the town for having failed.'

'It's not failure to sell a business! It's good sense. You'll get a lot of money for it; the property is one of the best in the town. Then if you invest your money wisely, I assure you there will be no shame; no shame at all. You will be wealthy, leisured citizens.'

'Who knows what will happen to money with the

25

depressed state of Europe?' Hector murmured. 'The reparations question alone is enormous. We might see happening to the pound what is happening to the mark and the franc. They are falling. It might be valueless.'

'The pound? Here? Nonsense!' Andrew laughed and drew out a cigar. 'May I?'

'Perhaps you and I and Cullum too should pass the port round and talk this over,' Hector said, looking at the women and appearing to include Cullum as an after-thought.

'I think we should be in on it, Father.' Margaret spoke for the first time. 'It is, after all, a very important matter for us all.'

'But how can it concern you, a girl of your age?' Her father's expression softened and he laughed amiably, reaching over to squeeze her hand.

'Our business concerns me, Father, and the Pendreighs concern me. I've always been very friendly with them. I was at school with the girls and my brothers played with the boys. I agree I do not want the Pendreighs to own our family business. I like them too much.'

'Now don't you worry your pretty head about that,' Hector said fondly. 'We are not selling the business to the Pendreighs or anyone else. I shall look closely into the matter and I assure you it will not be necessary. Now, if you will leave us men alone we shall join you shortly in the drawing room.'

Margaret reluctantly got up and went slowly out of the door in the wake of her sister and sister-in-law. There was a large fire in the drawing room, despite the summer heat, because both her father and Mary seemed to suffer from the cold. It was a large spacious room, recently redeco-rated, and furnished with antiques bought when the Dun-bars had built the house in the 1870s. It was a cheerful room and from it there were quite spectacular views of the whole of the town. Margaret went immediately to the window and, as the curtains were not drawn, resumed her contemplation of the town, now fully lit, the smoke from the mills drifting up against a clear sapphire sky. Her heart was now heavy with the news that the Pendreighs wished to buy Dunbars. She knew immediately how much that would alter the situation between herself and Ruthven; a situation that should be based on equality, not on one family buying out the other.

The coffee already stood on the long walnut table by the window and Susan went over and began to pour. She felt decidedly disturbed by her uncle's news, aware of its effect on Margaret, and she also glanced rather anxiously at Mary who, shivering slightly, had pulled a chair up close to the fire as though to protect herself from the cold. Mary got on Susan's nerves, though she tried not to show it. There was something self-indulgent about Mary's grief, about her detachment from the rest of the family and her neglect of winsome little Murdoch. Susan wished Mary would go back to live with her parents. They wanted her to; but Hector didn't want to lose Murdoch, Malcolm's son, and indeed he was never morose or melancholy when the baby was brought to see him. He hugged and fondled him as though he once again held the young Malcolm in his arms. Susan passed Mary a cup.

'You're very silent tonight Mary. Are you well?'

'As well as I ever am,' Mary said in her little voice, giving one of her wan smiles. She took the cup and immediately put it to her lips as though to banish some intense cold that had penetrated her body.

'And what is your opinion of Uncle Andrew's proposal?' Susan's voice grew a little sharp and she glanced at Margaret as she poured her coffee and handed it to her.

'You know I have no knowledge of the business, or any interest in it. I just hope that what is done will be for the best.' Mary moved nearer the fire.

'But you will be quite wealthy if we sell.'

'I do not feel the lack of fortune now.'

Susan sighed with exasperation and taking her own cup

sat opposite her sister-in-law. It was difficult to know why Malcolm had suddenly decided to woo and marry this pretty but pallid girl who seemed to have so little to give, who was so different from his vivacious and energetic sisters. Maybe the secret lay there; that Mary Wattis's passivity, her very insipidity was welcome to such a masculine man, always surrounded by forthright women. His mother had been strong and fiery tempered, as befitted a member of the MacLeish family from the Highlands. What joy had Malcolm got from Mary in the brief time they had had together? Or was it simply that Malcolm had had a premonition, as so many were later said to have had, that he would not survive the war? Was it that Malcolm, out of a quiet desperation unknown to his family, had desired to sow his seed anywhere in the hope that it might bear fruit, create a living reminder of himself?

'If only Malcolm had not been killed none of this would have happened,' Margaret said suddenly, interrupting Susan's reverie.

'How do you mean?' Susan placed her empty cup on a side table.

'You know Father *has* lost interest in the business. It's true that he doesn't go in for days on end. I thought that Walter Russell was managing well; but apparently he is not. There is no one really in charge of Dunbars now.'

'Then what will we do?' Susan looked at her with respect, then over at her sister-in-law who seemed to have no interest in what was being said.

'Cullum will have to leave Oxford and help Father to run it.' Margaret helped herself to more coffee and sat on a high chair next to the table.

'Oh, but that is out of the question.'

'Why is it?' Margaret gazed straight at Susan.

'Well, you know it is.' Susan avoided Margaret's eyes.

'I don't. I think if Cullum were given responsibility it would make all the difference in the world to him. There

28

is nothing *wrong* with Cullum, Susan. He's not defective in any way. He has not done too badly at Oxford even if he has not done too well. What Cullum would like to be is a leisured, moneyed young man of the world, able to chase women and indulge his favourite sports . . .'

'He has done little else at Oxford.'

'Exactly. Well, let him turn his hand to making Dunbars pay and then he can do as he likes. It's his duty to take Malcolm's place, step into his shoes. He is now Father's heir, the surviving male Dunbar, until Murdoch grows up, to run our family business whether he likes it or not.'

Margaret's eyes flashed and she carefully replaced her cup on the table by the window. It was dark now and the lights of the Dunbar Mill reflected in the Drume made it seem twice the size it was. It was their heritage, their birthright, ever since the first Murdoch Dunbar had set up stocking frames in a shop in Branswick High Street at the end of the eighteenth century. Pendreighs had no business there at all and, banished, for the moment, were her excited, erstwhile thoughts of being young Mrs Ruthven Pendreigh, leader of society.

'Cullum has to think of Father, and of us, we women of the family. Yes, you and I, and Mary too.' Margaret suddenly gave one of her brilliant, slightly sardonic smiles which meant that although she might consider Mary strictly in the helpless female role, she didn't think of Susan and herself in this light.

Susan was again reminded of how suddenly Margaret had matured, of how grown up she had become since leaving school at the end of the Easter term. If only women ran businesses how well Margaret would run this one! If only Margaret and Cullum could change sex. Even as a youngster Margaret had been very decisive, knowing just what she wanted and seldom changing her mind. People called these masculine qualities, but there was nothing very masculine about Margaret.

'Well, I think you have a hard task ahead, persuading

Cullum. Persuading Father too.' Susan saw that her sister-in-law appeared to be asleep.

'Not at all.' Margaret's tone was low and decisive. 'We shall show him it is his duty and he will do it. You and I will help Cullum to realize his responsibilities and become a man.' She paused for a moment and gazed once again out of the window. High above the Dunbar Mill, in celebration of the Peace, the Town Hall was illuminated, the first time that such a thing had been known in Branswick. 'Besides, we must never let the name Pendreigh run over the Dunbar Mill.'

CHAPTER TWO

In front of Branswick Town Hall a dais had been constructed on which sat all the important dignitaries of the town: the Provost, the members of the Council, the Headmaster of the Grammar School, the heads of the constabulary and of the fire-brigade, those who were concerned with municipal works and charities. Everyone had fought for weeks for a place on the dais, and now those who had got one sat there looking triumphant and self-important.

Among them, naturally, was Hector Dunbar. Before the war and the death of his wife in 1912 he had been very punctilious in his civic duties; he had been on various committees and bodies, municipal and private, concerned with good works – the relief of the poor, the welfare of the sick, the destitute widows and orphans. Finally he had crowned this life of not altogether disinterested altruism by serving two terms as Provost.

After 1912 Hector Dunbar had resigned from all his committees, deciding that his care for others would be better directed towards himself. Even during the war he had declined any voluntary positions. This had undoubtedly been a mistake as it had driven him inwards, and thus helped to prolong and extend the depression which had overtaken him after his wife's death. It became like an enveloping fog through which blue skies were only seldom glimpsed.

However, this day of 19 July 1919, when the whole of England celebrated the Peace, Hector was there on the dais, well wrapped up despite the heat, with his daughter-in-law, that other chilly member of the family, similarly cosseted beside him. Punctually at ten o'clock he had been driven down the hill in the pony and trap he used for getting around the town, although he always walked to his mill at the bottom of the hill and up again each evening. His son Malcolm had been one of the first young men in Branswick to own a motor car – almost *the* first – yet Hector still thought, despite all improvements that had been made since those early days, that they were contraptions of the Devil. Not only were they smelly, noisy and ugly, but in his opinion there was something unnatural about them. They did not run on rails like trains or trams or have four feet like horses; they were propelled along by a process he found mysterious, having no desire to know anything about the workings of the internal combustion engine, and less intention of finding out. Moreover he felt they were really dangerous. This was odd in a man whose business was based on the powerful machines that drove his knitting frames, which he understood perfectly well and which, as a young apprentice, he had not only been able to operate but also known how to maintain. But how a motor car got up a hill and down again without hurling its occupants to the bottom was something he regarded as a daily miracle and flatly refused to put to the test on himself. Hector Dunbar had never travelled in a motor car and did not intend to.

Branswick bore an air of triumph tinged with sadness that day in July, as its warriors who had returned from the war prepared to march through the streets accompanied by various youthful brigades and voluntary bodies of a quasi-military nature to swell their numbers, and the town band which had been practising for weeks.

The Scots Borderers, which numbered among their fallen Malcolm Dunbar, had mustered in strength, as many as remained, and they were joined by other battalions of Scottish regiments whose bases were not too far afield.

The crowds thronged the streets, stood on the roofs, on balconies and at windows and the young found more dangerous positions, clinging perilously to parapets, clambering up drainpipes or the narrow iron ladders on the sides of the mill chimneys to wave their flags and shout their hurrahs. One boy fell into the Drume from the bridge across it and, although he was able to swim quite well, enjoyed a brief moment of fame which almost eclipsed the procession while the fire brigade were called, dressed in their best uniforms and highly polished helmets, to haul him out.

Although nestling in a dip formed by the Cheviot Hills and the Branahae range, Branswick was not perhaps the most beautiful of towns, dominated as it was by the mills and the myriads of tall smoking chimneys, except in the eyes of those who loved it – above all in the eyes of those returning warriors whose visions had for so long been bounded by the muddy soil of France and the oceans of skeletal blasted trees, and the mangled forms of the dead. Compared to this aspect Branswick was indeed the most beautiful sight on earth and especially this day as, with tears in their eyes, the veterans marched through their native town receiving the acclaim of their fellow citizens.

Handkerchiefs, scarves, shawls were waved; hats, berets and tam-o'-shanters were thrown in the air, hands were raised, and the cheers and cries of those who thronged the streets drowned the rhythmic stamp of marching boots and almost, at times, the stirring noise of the gallant brass band.

Susan, Margaret and Cullum Dunbar had gone down the hill very early to get a good view of the procession. Margaret had woken in the morning already feeling excited and, forgetting that she was now a woman and feeling once more like an excited schoolgirl, jumped out of bed to see what sort of day it was. First thing it had looked as though it might rain, with heavy clouds massing low over the hills. But by nine o'clock when they took their places by the bridge at the end of the High Street, which ran over the Craigie before it joined the Drume, the clouds had dispersed, the sun shone from a clear Scottish sky. The buildings adorned with their pennants, flags and bunting, the white cross of St Andrew on a blue background everywhere, seemed like a town magically transformed into fairyland.

The bridge was narrow so that only one row of sightseers was possible to allow the procession to pass by, and from their vantage point the three Dunbars saw everything from the Regiments of the Scots Divisions that had actually served in the war to the various Boys' Brigades, Corps of Army nurses, firefighters, volunteer militia, and Boer War veterans who came at a snail's pace in the rear.

In the centre of the front row of the dais stood the Provost in his splendid robes, his chain of office around his neck. The Provost was a large, florid man and his robes became him. On either side of him were various officials, among them Elliott Pendreigh who had been in command of the town's militia during the war. Elliott had never fought in a war but he had very much enjoyed pretending to be a soldier, thankful maybe that his age had spared him from actual service at the front. Now as each section passed the dais and saluted, the Provost gave an elaborate bow, as did Elliott Pendreigh who felt that some of the day's glory must surely reflect on him. As the militia passed, people actually turned towards him clapping and he bowed and waved as though in acknowledgement of this tribute to his endeavours.

Sitting some rows behind, Hector Dunbar could not help noticing the antics of Elliott Pendreigh and he despised him for them. The militia had been of little account and the way he was behaving one would have thought that he'd won the war single-handed. Hector tried to avoid looking at him and concentrated instead on his melancholy thoughts, his chin sunk on his chest, until those near him thought he was asleep.

As the procession drew to an end the crowd's enthusiasm remained undiminished, although among those waving and cheering were many who were openly sob-bing. But the sun continued high in the sky and as the last contingent, the veterans from the Boer War, passed the dais the Provost – and Elliott Pendreigh – gave a final wave, the band struck up *Scotland the Brave* and joined the rear of the line that was moving jauntily towards the park at the end of the town, where marquees had been erected and a great free-for-all party was to be held with sideshows and roundabouts for the children and plenty of ale for the thirsty warriors.

The townspeople began joining the rear of the proces-sion and wove their way in an endless, colourful throng towards the park. The dignitaries came down from the dais and got into the coaches that suddenly appeared from side streets where they had been kept carefully out of sight. Gradually the streets emptied and the whole of Branswick converged upon the park.

Margaret was swept up in the crowd and propelled along, laughing, excitedly holding on to Susan's hand as the press of the mass threatened to split them. Cullum had already been carried away in front of them. Suddenly an arm seized her waist and she tried to stop but couldn't, turning her head angrily because even the joy of the occasion didn't permit such familiarity.

'Ruthven!' His moustache brushed her ear and he smiled into her eyes, pressing her again, his hand straying up towards her breast. 'Oh Ruthven it's you!'

'And whom did you think it was, may I ask?'

His black eyes looked very bold and naughty and she rested her hand on his, aware of the fullness of her bosom just above and how close he was to her.

'I thought it might be some rather forward soldier just returned from the war.'

'No, it is I, just returned from the Highlands. I came up for you this morning but you had gone. Your father gave me a very chilly greeting and Mary did not speak to me at all. Have I done something wrong?'

35

There had been a constriction in Margaret's heart when she woke that morning, a sensation for which she did not at first know the cause; but it soon dispersed because then she had remembered that it was going to be a happy day, the town full of thanksgiving for the end of the war. Now she recalled the reason for the momentary unease, the lump in her throat, the tightness in the breast.

'We must talk, quickly.' Margaret glanced behind her to see where the dignitaries were. 'Did you not know?'

'Know what?'

Now Susan saw Ruthven and the smile on her face changed to a frown. Ruthven, thinking it was because of the way he held Margaret, quickly released his grip and nearly lost her again because the crowd carried her along in its impetus, surging forward.

'Know *what*?' Ruthven shouted, some paces behind her, and Margaret stopped, letting Susan be swept on until Ruthven had caught up with her again. This time, seeing the expression on her face, he did not put his arm around her waist. 'What is it, Margaret?'

'I must speak to you. Come on, let's go off here.' Margaret tugged him out of the mainstream of the crowd into one of the many narrow alleys that ran from the main artery of the High Street like little capillaries. They dived between the shops that fronted the High Street, sometimes making a clean break and open to the sky and sometimes running under an arch formed by the buildings above, for many of them were very old. The network of little streets gave the town a quaint charm because the ones that sloped downwards afforded glimpses of the river and the ones that sloped up showed narrow, cobbled streets and tiny old houses that looked picturesque except, perhaps, to those who lived in them.

Lovers often met at night in these alleys, protected by the dark against the eyes of the curious. Margaret, although she had never been among them, knew the reputation the alleys had and was conscious of this connotation as she drew Ruthven into the shade of a blacksmith's building. The smithy doors were closed, the fires cooled, because the smith and his family had donned their best clothes and gone to join those who were merrymaking.

Ruthven grasped her shoulders and looked into her eyes, perturbed by her strange behaviour. 'Margaret, what has got into you? What is it?'

She leaned back against the roughcast wall, breathing quickly. The excitement had made her cheeks pink and there were beads of sweat between her white brow and her waving black hair, little tendrils of which curled around her ears. She wore a green silk dress with a wide collar and a loosely knotted tie that had blown over her shoulder. She was aware of Ruthven's hands on her shoulders and the quick pulse beating in her neck, the thumping in her chest.

'There was a terrible scene last night at the house,' she said. 'Uncle Andrew came and said your father had made an offer for the Dunbar Mill.'

'Oh.' Ruthven dropped his hands, taking the tie with them, and awkwardly he smoothed it and then backed away from her. 'Yes, I know.'

'You know all about it?'

'Father told me yesterday, though I knew he had it in mind before I went away. He thinks it is the best for Dunbars; for your family.'

'The best for *our* family!' Margaret's pink cheeks turned into a fiery, indignant red and her green eyes gleamed. 'How *can* it be best for our family? And you *knew*!'

'I knew he was going to talk to your uncle. He came with me as far as Edinburgh. He didn't know of course what your uncle or your father would say.'

'Father is furious.'

'I can see that; but it makes no difference to us. Does it,

Margaret?' He came nearer again and made a tentative gesture towards her, a placatory, half-familiar attempt to smooth the green silk bow on her front.

'It makes a difference to everything,' Margaret said. 'To you and me and us and our families. We would never sell out to the Pendreighs. Never.'

'But why not? Your father is not interested in the business. It hardly makes a profit. Walter Russell cannot run it by himself. Your styles are old-fashioned and many of your methods ancient. The war has provided a challenge and Dunbars have not risen to it.'

Margaret moved to one side as though made uncomfortable now by his proximity. He had on a brown tweed suit, the jacket belted at the waist, and a tartan tie. He was over six feet tall and more powerfully built than Cullum, with wide shoulders and a leonine head. His nose was long and broad and his thick gamekeeper's moustache practically obscured his mouth, trailing at the corners, clipped just below his lower lip.

Ruthven, who was a year older than Cullum, had enlisted in the Seaforth Highlanders – a regiment associated with his mother's family – in 1918 in the hope of being quickly sent to join his comrades in France where they were in the thick of the fight. But he had never left Scotland and to his chagrin was still in training when the Armistice was signed. He had declined to take part in the Victory parade because he had not been a fighting man, a loss he felt as keenly as Cullum, even more so because he had worn uniform. But, despite the need for men, too many raw recruits had perished in France and Lloyd George had become reluctant to continue sending fodder for the slaughter.

'They will,' Margaret said at last, aware of the decreasing pace of her heart and a new feeling of resolution overtaking her. 'Dunbars will rise to the challenge, don't you worry. Father is not senile and Cullum is going to come into the business.'

Ruthven stepped back, throwing his head in the air, and began to roar with laughter, baring his fine even teeth. The sight so inflamed Margaret that, without thinking, she raised her hand and hit him across the cheek.

Abruptly he stopped laughing and put a hand to his cheek, stroking the rising red weal that Margaret's fingers had left. She looked as though she were going to hit him again and he suddenly caught both her hands in his and drew her towards him. Then he swiftly bent and pressed his mouth against hers, forcing her back against the wall so that, even had she wished it, resistance was quite impossible.

But Margaret did not wish to resist. The sensation of the rough wall against her back and Ruthven so close to her was very exciting. It was a realization of her fantasies – here in this primitive place – and her arms encircled his waist, pressing him to her, so that she imagined that through the thickness of his tweed jacket she could feel his bare skin. One of his hands slipped into the opening of her dress, cupping her naked breast. With a *frisson* of shock she tried to wriggle away; but his body continued its pressure, his tongue insinuating itself between her teeth, his free hand gently continuing to fondle her breast.

Finally he broke from her, withdrawing his hand and putting it to her cheek, stroking that the way he had stroked her breast. His eyes were tender and smiling and she saw quite clearly the red mark she had made on his cheek. It was a strangely sensual sight; she realized that it had made him desire her. Passion sometimes made people want to hurt each other as well as make love.

'Little Margaret,' he murmured, 'you have a terrible temper.'

'"Little Margaret",' she mimicked, trembling slightly. 'I like that!' She put a hand timidly to the red weal and stroked his cheek. 'I'm sorry. I didn't mean it.'

'Yes you did. You were angry because I laughed at your

39

brother. You were quite right to be angry and I'm sorry too. But look what it did to us, Margaret. It brought us together – and we've both wanted that for some time, have we not?'

'Yes.' She smiled, trying not to laugh, and looked up and down the passage. 'But *here* of all places!'

'Aye, all the lads in the town try and catch the lassies here! Well, I caught you.'

'I can't think what our parents will say.'

'We shan't tell them.'

Margaret's happiness suddenly vanished as she thought of the families, of what they had come here to discuss. 'Ruthven, we have forgotten why we came here.'

'I thought you wanted me to kiss you!'

She blushed. 'You know it was not that! Not here!'

'Well, it was as good a place as any. I'm glad it happened, aren't you?'

Yes, she was glad; it was amazing, physical, frightening, but she was glad. She hoped he would do it again; but she wasn't sure she should let him feel her breast. That was very intimate indeed, more intimate than their tongues meeting inside her mouth. It seemed to her a gesture that was both disturbing and positively dangerous.

He put his head down again and she raised her lips willingly, parting them slightly in anticipation. She fastened her hands behind his head and he put his round her waist, and they swayed together almost as though they were dancing. He didn't attempt to feel inside her dress and this made her relax, able freely to press her face to his, to enjoy the deep passion of their first real embrace.

Afterwards she had tears in her eyes and he took out his handkerchief and wiped her cheek.

'I should keep this handkerchief with your first tear.'

'You're very romantic,' Margaret said, trying to smile.

'Why did you cry?' He dabbed at her cheek again and then folded the handkerchief, putting it carefully back in his pocket.

'Because I was so happy and then I thought of Malcolm and the war and all the people who died and I was glad to have this happiness and to be alive, but sorry for them.'

'You mustn't think about the war, Margaret,' Ruthven said gravely. 'We must all forget it because otherwise it will haunt us for the rest of our lives. We must remember it, but only in the right way; as a lesson for us all. Was that the first time you kissed a man?'

She looked at him provocatively, saying nothing, letting her tongue flick over her lips.

'Well if it was you're very good at it.'

'I'm sure it wasn't the first time you kissed a woman.'

'Ah, then it *was* the first time.' He laughed at her, teasing.

'I'm not saying.'

He put out his arms again but Margaret moved out into the alley, smoothing her dress and patting the green silk bow. When she turned she saw he was gazing at her.

'What are we going to do, Ruthven?'

'About us?' He looked surprised.

'About the families. The Mill.'

'Oh that.'

'I really *did* bring you here to talk about that, you know. You don't believe me, do you?'

'Yes, I do really. I was teasing you. Miss Dunbar would never choose to have her first kiss in the lovers' alley!'

'I didn't say it was my first kiss!'

He came up to her and cupped her face in his hands, his deep black eyes staring at her. 'I hope it was, otherwise I am dealing with a very fast lady – which is not what I thought they taught you at the college in Harrogate.'

'Be serious, Ruthven.' Margaret put a hand on his arm but he continued to gaze into her eyes.

'I am very serious, Margaret. I am serious about you. Are you serious about me?'

She looked surprised. 'Do you mean *love*?'

41

He nodded his head.

'I never thought about it. Aren't we young?'

'I'm twenty-one.'

Suddenly she felt rather frightened, as though the whole thing were moving too quickly, rushing away beyond control. Now that reality had caught up with her dreams, she felt unprepared, curiously vulnerable.

'I'm not sure how I feel, Ruthven. I like you very much; perhaps I do love you. I missed you and I think about you. Is that love?'

'I hope so. I've thought about you ever since I saw you when I came home for the vac.'

'But that's only a month ago.'

'It's a long time to think about someone constantly. It's never happened to me before. You know, I look out of my room at night hoping I'll see your outline at one of your windows.'

She started and smiled. 'I do that too.'

'Do you? Oh Margaret.' He clasped her again, hugging her tight. 'We have all the summer together,' he whispered.

'What about the *Mill*?'

He pushed her from him impatiently, though she saw he was still smiling. 'Margaret, I am trying to make love to you and you keep on talking about the wretched Mill.'

'But it is important, it will affect our lives.' She put a finger on his chest, feeling suddenly possessive. Did not such intimacy give rights? Could she not now touch him and hold his hand because their mouths had joined, their tongues had met?

'I know. Let's go to the park and find our fathers. We shall put the whole thing right.'

'How do you mean?'

'We'll tell my father that Dunbars do not want to sell, and that's all there will be to it. You'll see. It will all be over by evening, and tomorrow we can go to the ball.'

A shaft of sunlight that had been edging along the alley

suddenly discovered them and they laughed in its beam at each other – young, happy, on the brink of love. Joining hands, they fled into the empty street, feeling very different from when they had left it a few minutes before.

It seemed as though the whole of Branswick was in the park that day of the Victory procession, the lovely park on the banks of the broadest part of the Drume, just before it entered Branswick. Its spacious lawns and landscaped gardens led eventually to a wood that went for miles along the river and up over the hill where the wealthy members of the community like the Dunbars, the Pendreighs, the Laws and the Mactavishes lived. It was a favourite spot for lovers, that stretch of wood by the river, and Margaret perhaps wished, as she wandered into the park that day with Ruthven, that her first kiss had been in these more idyllic surroundings, with a leafy bower of leaves over her head and the river rushing at her feet.

People by now had out their picnic baskets, had spread rugs on the ground and lay sprawled on the banks of the Drume, enjoying their fare of patties, oatcakes, pies and freshly cooked haggis, all washed down with plenty of locally brewed ale. Dogs scampered about, toddlers teetered to the water's edge before being seized by harassed parents, children of all sizes played with their balls or hoops or queued up for the swings and roundabouts, or stood appreciatively in front of the Punch and Judy shows which enterprising entrepreneurs had erected overnight.

The park had been turned into a kind of fairground with booths, stalls and sideshows offering such sights as a bearded lady, a man only two feet tall, a one-armed wrestler who would take on all comers, a baby with two heads pickled in a bottle, and a lady clairvoyant who claimed she had predicted not only the exact date of the outbreak of the war but also when it would finish. Naturally no one had believed her. There were enthusiastic queues at all these entertainments, most of which

43

catered to the morbidity of the public as such things usually do – they seem to increase the enjoyment; no one quite knows why. There were further queues at the large public marquee where those good citizens of Branswick who had not brought picnics could purchase lemonade, tea, sandwiches and fancy cakes, but no intoxicating liquor. One specially large tent catered to those who had served their country and marched in the procession; here they could partake of free sausages, haggis, pies and strong ale, all of which had been purchased from a victory fund started after the war by the Provost in anticipation of this happy event.

The younger adults who were not entertained by sideshows or picnics by the river made their way, usually in pairs, into the deeper recesses of the forest where they gave themselves up to entertainments of a more diverting nature, as witness a number of rushed marriages followed by the large increase in the population of Branswick nine months after the victory celebrations.

Well apart from the marquees, tents and entertainments provided for the commonalty, there was a smaller marquee with open sides permitting the free flow of air on this hot day. It was singled out by its blue and white stripes, the Scottish colours, by its newness and by its general air of exclusiveness. Had any ordinary Branswickians approached it by mistake they would immediately have known that they were in an area reserved for their betters, those whom they were accustomed to serve, either by working in their mills, their houses or from behind the counters of shops.

Elegantly clad men and beautifully dressed women moved slowly around chatting, or sat at small wrought-iron tables, freshly painted white, drinking champagne and eating tiny sandwiches and other delicacies which they had paid for in advance by purchasing the thick-laid, gold-embossed tickets that looked like invitation cards. There one saw the very cream of Branswick society – the

44

Laws, the Pendreighs, the Mactavishes, the Hendersons, the Turnballs, the Scotts, the Pattersons and the Laidlaws; all those who by virtue of their wealth, ability or position in society had sat on the dais reviewing the victory parade, or who had taken up other places along the route which provided a comfortable view of the spectacle, a chair and possibly more champagne to help while away the tedious hours of waiting.

But of the Dunbars this day there was no sign; indeed, they were prominent by their absence, and everyone assured Margaret they were not there and never had been because it was the first thing that the Pendreighs, the Mactavishes, the Laws and so on had noticed when they surveyed the pecking order as soon as they had entered the marquee specially reserved for them.

'They aren't here,' she said at last to Ruthven, who had joined her in her search, carefully skirting the group of tables where he saw his father and mother, his sisters Netta and Moira, his brother Dirk and numerous other Pendreigh relations and friends, some of whom had come in from the adjoining countryside. 'I didn't know Father meant us to ignore the victory feast as well.'

'Come and see my parents,' Ruthven said, taking her elbow and propelling her forward. 'Look, they're waving at us.'

Shyly, because of their new found intimacy which she could not help thinking others would notice, Margaret approached the Pendreigh clan, conscious of Ruthven behind her. She felt they were now a couple and that all the world must know they had kissed, that he had fondled her naked breast while his thighs pressed urgently against hers.

'Margaret my dear.' Elliott Pendreigh, talking to the Provost's wife, paused for a moment and kissed Margaret's cheek. 'You look very lovely today. Where are your family?'

'I've been looking for them.'

'Your father was behind me on the dais. I tried unsuccessfully to catch his eye. I thought I saw his coach go up the hill as we turned through the gates of the park but I wasn't sure. What a pity. Is he unwell?'

'Not that I know of.' Margaret smiled at the Provost's wife and accepted a glass of champagne from Dirk. 'Thank you.'

'A sandwich, Margaret?' Mrs Pendreigh, who had been a Turnball and knew everyone in the town although her family were not hosiers, offered Margaret a plate, a kindly smile on her lips.

'Thank you, Mrs Pendreigh.' Margaret glanced at her guiltily. 'She knows,' she thought. 'She knows I have kissed Ruthven.' She thought she must look furtive and sly, and she wished that it were not so hot and that her dress, so fresh that morning, did not cling damply to her body. She did not feel at her best, not elegant and cool like the Pendreigh girls and others like them who strolled around giving one another superior smiles and wondering who had the prettiest dress and, of the dwindling number of men available, whose eye they would catch. Women, particularly the older unmarried ones, were suddenly aware after the war of a new competitiveness in angling for the attentions of the opposite sex.

Ruthven poured himself champagne and started talking to his sister Moira, who was engaged to one of the few men who had returned uninjured from the war and had taken part in the procession. George Law had known Malcolm well. They had served in the same battalion and he was one of the last people to have seen him alive, a fact about which Hector Dunbar constantly questioned him, still reluctant to believe he was dead.

'It's a pity your father grieves so much Margaret,' Mrs Pendreigh said fanning herself with a white handkerchief. 'We have all had to come to terms with our grief, you know. Does he think we do not hourly remember our twin boys, Dougal and Hugh? But we have to go on living, for

46

that was why they died.' Mrs Pendreigh took another smoked salmon sandwich. Clearly the memory of her slain twins did not impair her appetite. But then, it had been four years ago and she was a hardy unemotional Scot from the Border whose grief, although no less real than the Dunbars, she would be at particular pains to conceal.

'I cannot explain my father's grief, Mrs Pendreigh,' Margaret said, thinking of Ruthven's passionate kiss and wondering if his mother noticed anything different about her lips. Surely such ardour, such an imprint *must* have left its mark? 'But for him it is very real. He has been sad, really, since our mother died. It is his nature.'

'You are not to attend the ball I hear? Dear, dear, what a pity. Still, Netta had young men queueing up for her – she is *so* pretty is she not? – and Moira has dear George. What a handsome couple they are to be sure.' Mrs Pendreigh gazed fondly at them for a moment.

'But I *am* going to the ball, with Ruthven.'

'Oh, that is not changed?' Mrs Pendreigh looked first surprised, then clasped her hands rapturously together. 'I am so glad. Elliott, do you hear that? Margaret is still coming to the ball with Ruthven. Elliott, dear.'

Mrs Pendreigh was not a fashion-conscious woman. She wore a mauve dress in a style that was distinctly pre-war with a long skirt, long sleeves, a belted waist, a pleated front and a high neck. Her wide hat with a feather partly obscured her face and a parasol was propped by her chair. She was, however, a handsome woman and had given her looks to all her children except, perhaps, to Moira who wore glasses and was just a trifle on the plain side. Today, though, having her man home from the war, knowing he was safe and unhurt and by her side, made Moira almost beautiful and George Law, who was no oil painting himself, seemed very enamoured of her.

Elliott Pendreigh was always surrounded by people, as a busy man of affairs who has much to say and a lot to do. He liked to appear to have a lot to do all the time and he invariably had, even on a day like today when he would be discussing business or politics, local and national, or something to do with his charitable or commercial interests. He would not be discussing the weather, or talking tittle-tattle about people. He wore a grey frock coat and striped trousers, a high stiff collar and a black cravat out of respect for the dead. His crinkly iron grey hair was sparse but he was not bald, and he had long sidewhiskers and a clipped grey moustache. He was a distinguished-looking man and like Hector Dunbar had served twice as Provost. Only, unlike Hector Dunbar, he had not ceased his public duties despite the tragic deaths of his youngest twin sons, but had increased them.

At her call he drifted over to his wife, stopping here and there for a word with this person and that, his head bent attentively, the man of the world attending to so many things.

Winifred Pendreigh put out a hand to stop him in his tracks. 'I said Margaret is still coming to the ball, Elliott. Did you know that?'

'My dear I am so pleased,' Elliott said, looking at Margaret. 'I thought the family were not coming?'

'They are not. Just Margaret.'

'Oh.' Elliott's mouth rounded and he looked thoughtful. 'Does your father know this, Margaret?'

'He knows I want to come; but he does not think I will. However, I am going to.'

'Margaret, my dear.' Elliott put an arm round her shoulders in an avuncular gesture. 'I do think you should not disobey your father. I think it would upset him too much, circumstances being what they are.'

Margaret's face flamed, and she started back, looking round for Ruthven who, seeing her movement, the expression on her face, hurried over to her.

'Ah, Ruthven.' Elliott removed his hand from Margaret's shoulder and placed it firmly on his son's. 'I do not really think Margaret should flout Hector's wishes and

48

come to the ball. Do you? Do you both honestly think she should?' He looked from one to the other.

'I think Margaret should do as she likes,' Ruthven said, embarrassed by his father's gaze. 'She is a woman now, Father.'

'It is not that, my dear boy, although I do like to think of a daughter being dutiful. You know to what I am referring . . .'

'If you are talking about your intention to buy our business, Mr Pendreigh,' Margaret said heatedly, her voice rising, 'my father will not entertain the notion. You need feel no awkwardness about that. Dunbars are doing perfectly well thank you, and intend to go on doing so. You need not feel embarrassed on that account, and I *am* a very dutiful daughter, except when I consider Father unreasonable, as I think he is being now. I think he should be here today, too, rejoicing in the peace.'

She suddenly realized that those around her had stopped talking, maintaining various poses, glasses half raised to their lips, sandwiches wilting in their hands. Despite her consternation, she was reminded of a group of statues, or a gathering captured on canvas by an artist like Renoir or Sisley.

'Margaret, we cannot talk business here,' Elliott whispered hurriedly, aware of the silence round them. ''Tis neither the time nor the place. Nor is it any concern of yours as far as I can see.' He looked severe.

'It *is* my concern.' Margaret carefully placed her half empty glass on the wrought-iron table beside her. 'I know quite well what my family feels; we are of one mind. The only pity is you did not discuss it with my father first.' She was looking square at Elliott Pendreigh, her determined chin tilted, the defiance flashing in her eyes.

It was a pose that Ruthven was beginning to know well and like everything else about Margaret, he found it irresistibly attractive. He thought of her lips melting in his and he wanted to crush her in his arms again. Yet

49

suddenly he felt frightened. He saw in her opposition to her father, her spirited reply to his, a sudden threat to their happiness. Women might be on the way to emancipation, yet they still had their place and that was not to enter a man's world on men's terms. If Margaret started flouting convention and drawing attention to herself she would cease to be regarded as a darling by the Pendreigh family, or welcome as their daughter-in-law, a notion that was not new to Ruthven's mind, yet one that he was carefully nurturing because the time had not yet come to speak.

'I fully intended to discuss it with your father,' Elliott said, his saturnine face flushing with anger. 'It has all got out of hand. I talked to Andrew Dunbar first to sound out his feelings, and when I saw he was not averse to the idea I felt that was the time to approach your father, not before.'

'My dear, this silly argument is spoiling the day.' Mrs Pendreigh's plaintive tone seemed to contain a warning. 'People are listening.'

'I'm sorry, Mrs Pendreigh.' Margaret lowered her voice. 'It was not my intention to spoil the proceedings. But as I am not wanted by you at the ball you can be sure I shall not come.'

'Margaret it is not that, I *do* assure you. We would love to have you in our party. Only . . .'

Elliott went towards her, but Margaret neatly side-stepped him, her hand out as though forbidding him to come near her.

'Only you do not care to defy my father. Yet you go snooping behind his back, hiding from him, from us all, things which are of vital concern to our family. I am quite *glad* not to be of your party at the ball, Mr Pendreigh. Good-day. Good-day, Mrs Pendreigh.'

Margaret, aware that she had been carrying nothing, not a bag or a parasol, felt somehow defenceless, as though she were naked. After all, possessions did protect

50

one. She had been so free, so happy at the start of the day and now disaster had overtaken her – a disaster that had started, surely, in the alley off High Street when she allowed Ruthven Pendreigh to push her roughly against the smithy wall, to kiss and fondle her, to make known in no uncertain way the amorous needs of his nature.

Disaster was going to turn into a scandal which would now having nothing to do with the décolleté, long-skirted evening dress she had intended to wear at the ball. She knew by the way that all eyes were riveted upon her and Elliott Pendreigh that this affair was going to have ramifications in the town far beyond the mere confrontation in a matter of business between their two families.

Boldly Margaret Dunbar smiled at the Pendreighs, at the Laws, the Mactavishes, the Pattersons and goodness knows who else had gathered to gawp. She smiled too at Ruthven, and then she walked slowly towards the entrance of the marquee while those inside seemed to hold their breaths and parted to allow her a passage, astonished that one of their number could so defy convention and cause such a scene in a public place.

The Dunbars were known as conformists. They fitted in. They did not do extraordinary things and call attention to themselves, as some of the better-class Branswick families occasionally did – after all, every society has its black sheep. But the Dunbars were not expected to be among them, to defy the conventions required of those of good breeding. Hector Dunbar certainly was considered eccentric; but his money and his station cushioned him, as it did others. No family was perfect. But eccentricities and peculiarities were more acceptable and tolerable in men; they were frowned on in women who were expected to be well behaved, domesticated and quiescent. They could be spirited and beautiful too of course, as the Dunbar girls undoubtedly were; but this was a bonus not a disadvantage. Spirited and beautiful women must not take advan-

51

tage of their good attributes, but be thankful for them and conform, always conform.

Outside Margaret felt a rush of air and realized how hot it had been under the awning. She mingled with the happy, laughing, celebrating townsfolk of Branswick and it accentuated the contrast between her and her kind, the kind she had left inside the marquee, and the ordinary people whose lives were undoubtedly quarrelsome and argumentative, turbulent and disruptive and not governed by the conventions that hers was.

The war had changed a lot of things, she knew that; but especially it was going to change the position of women like herself who wanted to be free to do the things men always instinctively had been able to do – to discuss business and public affairs, take part in politics if they felt like it.

She had caused a scene; yet she was not ashamed and she was not afraid. The Pendreighs had behaved badly. She had rather this had not been done in public, but it was done.

She knew a lot of people in the town – as a child she had gone to the local school – and as they greeted her she stopped and chatted to them, sauntering along as though she had no care in the world, as though she had not just created a scene which people would talk about for weeks.

She got to the edge of the park and then she heard what she had wanted, fearfully, to hear, because it had been important that he should come after her, terrible if he did not. Then she might have started to feel shame and have regrets.

She turned and gazed at Ruthven as he came up to her, her smile pleasant but slightly distant.

'Go back to your family, Ruthven. I can see myself up the hill.'

'Oh Margaret.' He held out his hands. 'Please don't spoil this day.'

She looked at his hands, but did not take them. 'It is not

52

I who am spoiling it. It is your father who does not want me to join your party at the ball.'

'But you know what he means, how he feels.' Ruthven shrugged and his helpless gesture suddenly chilled her and made her afraid.

'I know that he means to pursue this business, or he would make it all right with my father at once. He would walk straight up the hill and apologize. But he is not going to.'

'No, he does not intend to give in yet.'

'Well, neither do we.' Margaret felt her confidence returning. 'Your father owed it to mine to treat him with more respect.'

'People will say . . .'

'Oh I know what people will say!' Margaret tossed her head. 'But they will soon stop saying it; they will forget all about it and start saying something about someone else.'

'I hope you're right.'

Ruthven looked angry. Was he angry with her? Had she gone too far? Would she ever get him back? She lowered her voice and took a step towards him.

'I'm sorry, Ruthven. I know you're unhappy and I didn't mean to cause a scene. I wanted to go to the ball and enjoy myself. I wanted this to be a happy day. Now I shall always remember the celebration of the peace as a horrible one.'

'But what about us?'

'We shall see each other. All this will blow over. You can still take me to the ball if you want and we'll defy both our families.' She looked at him challengingly.

He spread his hands wide. 'Margaret, you know I can't. You know we can't.'

'I know *you* can't,' Margaret retorted. 'I thought at one moment you would defy your family when you told your father I was old enough to please myself; but you can't, Ruthven Pendreigh. You're just like all the others.'

Margaret gazed at him witheringly, banishing from her

53

mind those passionate burning kisses, that rugged feel of his tweed jacket between her fingers, that masculine smell of him so unfamiliarly close. Then suddenly she turned her back on him, walking very quickly through the gate of the park, up the hill towards home, never once glancing back.

CHAPTER THREE

The Dunbar family fortune was based originally on the manufacture of stockings. The mechanical knitting machine was invented in the sixteenth century by, it is said, a lovelorn clergyman, the Reverend William Lee. The story is that he wanted to please his lady-love, an ardent knitter, and so devised artificial fingers which could knit many loops at once. The machine which Lee eventually perfected could form five hundred loops a minute, whereas a skilful hand knitter might form a hundred. His lady, however, whether out of pique or jealousy is known to have turned him down.

Lee's knitting machine, the principle of which has never changed, consisted of over two thousand parts – needles, sinkers, jacks, slurcock, locker and bar, presser and treadles. It was simple to operate, a sequence of eleven movements constituting the knitting of a single course. The operator sat at the frame, as at a console, using both hands and feet.

Over the ensuing centuries the Reverend Lee's invention underwent several modifications and improvements, but the essential idea remained the same. At the end of the eighteenth century the frame, which up to this time could only knit stockings, was introduced to the Scottish Borders where the proliferation of sturdy sheep on its hills and the plentiful supply of water from its rivers made knitting stockings an attractive industry. And so the hosiery trade was born in Branswick.

In 1787 one Murdoch Dunbar had opened a stocking shop. He hired frames out to journeymen framework knitters, providing the premises and soliciting custom from customers who supplied their own yarn. For many years in Branswick and other Border towns this form of self-employment on the part of the knitters persisted; they hired the frames, were paid for what they produced and worked when they liked, either in the premises of the frame owner, the Master Hosier as he was known, or at home. They paid their own seaming woman and winding boy, and bought their own oil, needles and candles.

Murdoch Dunbar was not the only Master Hosier of his time but he produced a good number of sons, and in time he purchased a mill by the banks of the Drume and went into partnership with his sons as Murdoch Dunbar and Sons. The year was 1796.

Rather than trying to find customers who would provide their own wool and state their instructions, Murdoch introduced an innovation: he decided to have stockings made to his own specifications and sell them on the market. Murdoch also did his own spinning and by the turn of the century he had already established Dunbars as a family of some importance in Branswick.

The Napoleonic wars had caused a great deal of disruption and afterwards there was some depression, but enterprising men still managed to purchase properties and found dynasties, some more successfully than others: some failed and some went from strength to strength like the Dunbars, the Pendreighs, the Laws, the Laings, the Mactavishes and the Lyalls who moved to Selkirk to concentrate on dyeing and spinning.

In 1820 Murdoch Dunbar died and his eldest son, also Murdoch, took his place. In 1826 a broader frame was invented, a 'braid frame' with rows of needles sixteen inches in width, which enabled manufacturers to make knitted underclothing. Underwear as well as stockings now became the basic business of Dunbars; the production of shirts, men's pants and drawers. In a while the introduction of steam to drive the frames, and then the rail link with Edinburgh, caused not only Dunbars to expand but also others whose mills dotted the banks of the Drume and the Craigie.

By the 1860s Murdoch Dunbar and Sons were one of the ten leading hosiery manufacturers in Branswick, one of the survivors of the many who had tried and failed. The firm was then under the dynamic control of James Dunbar, grandson of the firm's founder. His eldest brother, Murdoch, had been drowned while fishing in the Drume at the age of fourteen. It was James who built the large mansion on top of the hill so that he could keep his eye on his business below day and night. Of all the Dunbars up to then James was probably the most astute businessman, assisted ably by his two brothers Charles and Ian. The Dunbars also installed new power frames at the mill which could knit six pieces at the same time.

The workers who had hitherto been self-employed journeymen, selling their goods back to the Master Hosier, were given regular wages which did not fluctuate as the trade did. Finally, with the arrival of electricity Dunbars were knitting woollen goods in many colours which were being exported all over the world. By this time too the meaning of 'hosiery' had shifted almost entirely away from stockings to underwear, both for ladies and gentlemen, heavy and light and in many different wools – shetland, merino, lambswool, llama, alpaca and cashmere. From 1892 Dunbars even made underwear exclusively from silk, but their most popular combination was silk and wool which did not seem so rough next to the skin. They made vests, pants, combinations (called 'dresses'), drawers for wearing under kilts and knee drawers for wearing under trousers, knee-caps, hose, half hose, bathing suits, ladies' nightdresses, cycle dresses, men's nightshirts, sweaters, body belts, bodices, tam-o'-shanters, rugs.

Hector Dunbar was born in 1870. He was the grandson of Charles Dunbar who outlived his brothers James and

Ian and was chairman of the firm until his death in 1895 at the age of eighty. James Dunbar had only daughters and Charles's one son, Murdoch, did not enter the family business, preferring instead to become a banker, a deed for which he was ostracized by the family for the rest of his life, as his defection had put the succession in jeopardy. James had shamed the family by having only girls and Ian could produce no children at all, so it really was up to Charles's grandson, Hector, to carry on the family firm whether he wished to or not.

The young Hector knew what disgrace his father had brought on the family by refusing to go into the business so, in 1886, at the age of 16 he was apprenticed to the family firm while his grandfather was still alive and could keep an eye on him.

When Hector married Isobel MacLeish in 1889 his grandfather was still alive and they didn't live up the hill but in a village five miles out of Branswick. Juliet was born in the village in 1889 and then a son, called Murdoch, in 1891, who died in infancy, followed by Malcolm, Susan, Margaret and Cullum.

Hector's grandmother lived until 1900 and after her death Isobel and Hector moved with their young family to *Woodbrae* on the hill just before Margaret was born.

In the early years of the century Dunbars was doing well with its fine quality knitted undergarments, but Hector didn't have the business acumen of his grandfather. Hector would have liked to be a man of letters, or perhaps a politician. He had been persuaded – forced might be a better word – to leave Fettes where he was enjoying himself and apprentice himself to the business in the yarnstore as his grandfather, great-uncles and great-grandfather had before him. In the absence of any direct heirs from James or Ian, and because Andrew had always intimated he was interested in the law, everyone – aunts, great-aunts, various uncles-in-law, cousins and, above all his father who had defaulted in the first place – made it very plain to Hector where his duty lay. He had thus had no option but to do as his grandfather wished, nay, ordered. Without Hector there would be no Dunbar, no direct descendant of the founder Murdoch, in a firm where there had nearly always been one or two brothers, sometimes more.

Something had gone very badly wrong with the Dunbar genes and it was up to Hector to remedy this sad state of affairs. Consequently he was even married off early, at the age of nineteen, to satisfy an anxious family that he could do his duty further and produce male heirs.

But before this happier event came to pass the young Hector, cushioned from public school, now living with his grandfather, found himself getting up at five in the morning to start work at six with all the other millworkers. It was a far cry from the life he really wanted and although he dutifully carried out his apprenticeship, going through every department and process in the mill, he never learned to love his work, only to endure it. He was not an ambitious man and he did not covet wealth; but in order to maintain his family in the style Dunbars were accustomed to he had to work hard. He worked hard and he hated it; what few pleasures in life he had came from his devotion to his family and, increasingly as he got older, drink. By 1919 this lack of real interest in his business was reaping the consequences.

The other mills in the town had started to go into other fashions: the production of cardigans, skirts, even dresses and jumpers with various fancy trimmings. But, although Dunbars had been among the first to put frilly bits on their underclothes (their lace tops to vests and combinations for ladies were a positive rage in the nineties), they had never really advanced beyond what they were doing in 1901 when Hector and Isobel moved to the big house and Margaret was born. As Ruthven Pendreigh had said, although their quality was still second to none, they were old-fashioned; some of their equipment needed replacing and their styles changing. Orders were dropping while other houses, like the Mactavishes or Pendreighs, surged forward capturing new markets.

Hector Dunbar and Elliott Pendreigh were contemporaries. They had been born in the same year and gone to Fettes together; but Elliott had gone on to study textile technology at Edinburgh University, and then had travelled round the world studying the wool business which he loved. When he joined the family firm he was twenty-five and Hector had already been in it for nine years; but in no time at all Elliott knew as much as Hector and a lot more besides. Elliott was a wool man through and through, or rather a knitting man because his business was knitting garments from woollen yarns produced by other mills. But Elliott knew all about yarn spinning too. He knew everything there was to know about wool and knitting, its production and technology, the sources of raw material. He had seen the camels in Peru from which llama wool came, the Australian sheep which gave merino, and he had travelled in the high altitude mountainous areas of China and Mongolia where the hardy mountain goats had their bellies combed each year for the fine underhairs that were used in the manufacture of cashmere.

When Elliott Pendreigh had become chairman of the firm on the death of his father in 1910 he had one thing on his mind – expansion. He wanted the knitted Pendreigh goods to be the finest in the world, eclipsing anything produced by Murdoch Dunbar & Sons on the other side of the Drume.

The irony was that Elliott's father, Walter Pendreigh, had been very like Hector Dunbar, not really interested in the business, so that Elliott had had to work hard to build up his business while Hector just sat on all that his grandfather had achieved and let it go down.

But Malcolm Dunbar had resembled Elliott. He was twenty-six when he was killed and had been in the firm since he was seventeen, learning the business as his father had but loving every moment, using all his spare time for study, taking time off during the year for foreign travel. At the age of twenty-three he had gone to the war, unable to resist the challenge to his patriotism by the struggle in France. He had promised that when he came back Dunbars would be modernized, new ideas would be introduced and they would have nothing to fear from their rivals the Pendreighs.

No one dreamed that he would never come back or that, far from being content to be rivals, the Pendreighs would wish to take over the ancient firm of Dunbar altogether.

The row between the Pendreighs and the Dunbars raged all winter after the initial scandal in the summer when Margaret had raised her voice in the marquee to Elliott Pendreigh and everyone had stopped talking to listen.

Or rather there was no 'row', in the sense that the protagonists never met. It was a curious, typically Branswick phenomenon in that certain families refused to speak to each other without anything ever really having been done which could be said to have sparked it off. Elliott Pendreigh tried to arrange a meeting with Hector Dunbar, but Hector refused to meet him, to see or speak to him and if he met him in public he cut him dead. As the company was a private one and Hector the majority shareholder, there was little that Elliott Pendreigh could do except vow to fight Dunbars in the market place by making the quality of his merchandise that much better than anyone else's.

Pendreighs had done well in the war. They had made comforts for soldiers, woollen sweaters, knitted blankets and helmets. but they had also continued to supply London ladies with well made underwear, beautifully finished with silk bows and lace tops or frilly trimmings. They started making elegant jumpers that fashionable

61

women liked to be seen in, and when the men came home from the war they had ready for them, as well as the finest knitted socks and underwear, smart sweaters and Norfolk jackets which they wore to shooting parties accompanied by their ladies wearing Norfolk coats, the very latest thing in plain or cable stitch, with one of the new tubular knitted skirts and long embroidered jerseys underneath.

Hector had been proud of what his daughter Margaret had said to Elliott, though he still thought that women should have nothing to do with business. But she had put the Dunbar point of view, put it well and prevented any further incursions from the Pendreighs. He wanted to send her to a finishing school in Switzerland and finally Margaret agreed, anything to get away from the gloom of the house, the reproach of her brother Cullum and the torment of her broken affair with Ruthven Pendreigh – broken even before it had properly begun. That summer there had been no more meetings between the families, on tennis courts or anywhere else, and early in the autumn Margaret had left for the school near Gstaad a few weeks before Ruthven went back to Oxford and Cullum Dunbar started as an apprentice in the yarnstore like his father before him. And, like his father before him, Cullum hated it.

The suggestion that he should leave Oxford and enter the business had initially come from Susan, one night after dinner, about a week after the Victory Parade and the scene in the marquee. At first Hector had refused to consider the idea, but gradually his daughters persuaded him otherwise. It was true, he eventually conceded, he had not given Cullum a chance and the duplicity of the Pendreighs had made him feel very vulnerable. Finally Juliet and her solicitor husband were called upon for an opinion and the whole family, except Cullum, were unanimous: he should not return to Oxford, so he did not.

As his father before him, when he saw the weight of opinion was against him Cullum gave in. He had not really wanted to be a scholar any more than he wanted to be a Master Hosier; but the Oxford lifestyle had suited him. It was very different in Branswick, walking through the dark mornings down the hill, knowing that there was nothing to look forward to until he walked up the hill again at night and he could have some whisky in his bedroom and stretch out on his bed.

'Gi' it a minute more.' Willie Laing said, expertly kneading the sodden garment which Cullum had fished out of the tub for him to appraise. ''Tis still a wee bit bare. See, Maister Cullum, ye can feel how bare it is.' Willie passed the lambswool jumper to Cullum who ran it through his fingers as he had so many times watched Willie doing. However he still thought it felt like a mass of soggy wool as he always did. 'Feel it, Maister Cullum, *feel* it,' Willie urged, reaching for the garment as if to show him how.

'I can feel nothing,' Cullum said. 'Wet wool is all it is to me.'

Willie lifted his eyes to heaven in an attitude of patient exasperation. He had this conversation at least once a day with the man who one day would run the Dunbar business. Even Hector Dunbar could tell when a garment was perfectly milled and when it was not; and Willie, who knew him well, respected Hector's judgement. Every morning the Head Millman consulted with the owner about the batches being milled and what they decided then was one of the most important decisions made in the whole mill during the day. But Cullum didn't seem to want to learn. His attitude in the Milling House was of enduring something he intensely disliked, and the men knew it and despised him for it. Maybe he thought he didn't need to bother; but they knew that, for a business to be successful, he did.

'An undermilled garment is "bare", young man. It has no surface.' Willie rubbed the wool of the jumper in Cullum's hands with the fingers of his good hand. 'Ye can

63

tell at a touch. If it is milled too much it is duffy, like a blanket; "felted", they call it. All ye can do then is throw it away. That is why milling is so important. Without good milling ye would have no business. See how bare this is? Feel it again.'

His eyes seemed to implore Cullum to take an interest in what he was doing, to maintain the fine traditions of the Dunbar name, but Cullum abruptly threw the garment back in the milling tub and savagely pushed it under the others with his long poaching stick.

'I'll never make a millman,' he said, eyeing Willie, who wiped the sweat off his forehead with a long bony hand which had the first and second fingers missing, the sure sign of an expert millman. When he had been an apprentice Willie had trapped his hand in the revolving drums of the wringer through which the milled garments were passed before they were mounted on the boards used to shape them while they were drying.

'Ye don't *have* to make a millman, Maister Cullum,' Willie laughed, 'and I don't know whether I'm glad for ye or sorry.'

Cullum resentfully stirred the frothing mass with his stick, taking care not to catch it in the huge trampling feet, known as 'dollies', of the milling machine which stood ten foot high in the centre of the Milling House at the far end of the mill. The machine was driven by a belt stretched across the ceiling which activated the dollies whose spatula ends, nine inches thick, pummelled and buffeted the woollen garments against the oak sides of the mill.

Knitted and seamed but otherwise unfinished garments were sent in batches to the Milling House where they were first scoured, or thoroughly washed, in order to remove the oil which had been sprayed on the yarn when it was spun to make it more facile. But the really important process was the milling or pounding of the scoured garments to break up the fibres and produce what woolmen called a surface interest: that is, a garment which had a perfect handle and finish, was soft and pleasing to the touch. The moment of deciding exactly when this stage had been reached was of crucial importance, and an experienced person like Willie, who had been Head Millman for twenty years, could time it to within a second.

Willie, critically watching the mass seething in the tub, as though he could divine the exact moment of readiness, suddenly pointed with his maimed hand, and called above the roar of the machine, 'That'll be ready, Maister Cullum. Quick now.'

Unhesitatingly accepting Willie's word, Cullum set to with his stick, lifting the heavy, sodden bulk into the dry tub waiting to take it to the wringer. His wellington boots sloshed to and fro across the wet sud-covered stone floor and his rubber apron ran with the moisture from the garments which he passed swiftly from tub to tub. Willie took one, felt it, sniffed it for good measure, and threw it after its fellows.

'Perfect,' he said with satisfaction.

As Willie crossed the milling house to where the wrung garments from a previous batch were being transported to the boarding house next door, Cullum finished his task and started to drain the milling tub for the next load. He hated the Milling House. He thought he would retain its peculiar smell in his nostrils for the rest of his life; a damp, oily, all-pervasive smell that even seemed to cling to the clothes which he changed back into when he left work.

Like his father before him he was serving a long and hard apprenticeship. He had started in the yarnstore where the spun yarn waited on large cones to be knitted. Next he had gone to the hand knitting frame that could knit intricate stitches and patterns; then on to the larger power frames that could make fully fashioned knitted goods, and the smaller rib frames that knitted ribs. Now he was in the Milling House, after which he would follow all the processes of the milled garment until it was ready for distribution.

He started at eight in the morning, working with three other millmen who each had his appointed tasks. He had no breakfast at the house but at ten-twenty there was a ten-minute break when an apprentice went out to fetch hot pies from the pie shop. The mid morning pie was a hallowed tradition in the mill and there was even an official Pie Boy. Each pie cost twopence halfpenny, the pie boy making a halfpenny on each sale. On Saturday he charged threepence, thus making a whole penny profit. Pie Boy was a position much sought after because it enabled him to earn more in a week in profitable commission than in actual wages paid by the mill. The other workers ate their pies in the packing shed but Cullum, in view of his position, had his brought to him in the Milling House and this breaking of his fast with hot, succulent, crumbly meat pie was the one thing in the day he looked forward to. He thought he knew how prisoners, or others forcibly deprived of freedom, valued slight breaks in their routine like this. He would sit on a three-legged stool by the door and savour the hot aroma and fragrant taste of freshly baked pie mingling with the steamy, oily smell of the Milling House. All too soon it was over and, as the men came back, he got to his feet and resumed his work.

By six o'clock Cullum had cleaned out the milling and scouring tubs, sluiced the floor and changed with his fellows out of his working clothes and into his suit. He always did this more quickly than the others because they liked to chat and he wanted to get away. On this day he nodded to them briefly and went through into the boarding house where the wrung, freshly milled garments were stretched on boards which were loaded on wheeled bogies and pushed into the drying room to regain their shape. This led to the drying room where the boarded garments were dried and shrunk in the Hosiery Drying machine. The drying room was even hotter than the Milling House and Cullum hurried through it, into a passageway and up the back stairs to the binding room where the girls who operated the circular binding machines were also finishing for the day. They were known as 'greasy binders' because the knitted pieces were seamed before being milled. The 'clean binders' in another department did what other binding was necessary after the oil had been removed, such as attaching collars, special cuffs or other trimmings involving fine work.

Some of the girls looked up as Cullum passed by and one or two exchanged knowing smiles, but he proceeded swiftly through the checking department into the trimming department where all the completed garments were given a thorough inspection and minor or major faults dealt with. Cullum stopped at the looker's table where a pretty young girl was peering critically at a shetland sweater, one of a batch of several she had had that day.

'Not finished yet, Eileen?' Cullum looked at his watch.

A slow blush spread up Eileen's cheeks, but her eyes did not waver from her work. 'I promised I'd finish this batch Mr Cullum.'

'There's no need for "Mr", Eileen.' Cullum quickly looked around and, lowering his voice, bent over the table. 'Is there? After the other night?'

Eileen's blush deepened and she looked as though she wished she could have buried her face in the garment she was inspecting.

'I wondered what you were doing tonight Eileen? I've got my car. Would you fancy a bite in Selkirk?'

'I told Ma I'd be home, Mr . . . er, Cullum. She was verra angry with me the other night, bein' so late.'

'Did you tell her you were with me?'

'Of course not.' Eileen raised her eyes and looked at him. 'Whatever would she think o' that?'

Cullum perched on the edge of her table and attempted to stroke her hand. She quickly removed it and held the sweater close to her eyes as though searching for minute faults, oblivious of his presence. Cullum could see the rapid pulse in her neck and was not deceived. He knew that none of the girls told their parents because of his reputation. Well, it suited him. That way he didn't feel too responsible if something went wrong or one of the girls got carried away by strong emotion. He liked Eileen. She was sensible and very, very pretty. He had not seen her nude because the back of his car gave little room for anything but the basic activity he had them there at all for. He couldn't take them back to his house and he certainly couldn't go back to theirs. It was either the back of the car or a cleft in the moors in summer. When he had completed his apprenticeship he would have an office of his own. That more than anything made him look forward to being management.

'Come on Eileen,' he said. 'Tell your mother . . .'

'I canna, not tonight. I have tae wash mae hair.'

Cullum got off the table and gave an exclamation of annoyance. 'Whatever excuse will you think of next?'

Eileen had been a lot more difficult to get than some of the others. Some said 'no' at once and he knew by their expressions that was that. Some were too easy and he quickly lost interest; but Eileen had awakened his curiosity as well as his desires. He would play her game. He bent low over the table again until his face was almost touching hers.

'I could take a room at a hotel one night – oh, not near here. Peebles or somewhere like that. Would you like that? We could have a grand meal, a few drinks and . . .' He winked at her. 'You know, not like the car; more comfortable.'

'I'll have tae think about it,' Eileen said primly, laying the sweater on the table and smoothing it with her hands. There was just the slightest alteration in the tone of her voice; it was not as brisk and defensive as before.

'Well think soon,' Cullum said. 'I can't wait forever. Let me know tomorrow night if you can do it, and when.'

He turned away abruptly before Eileen could reply, but he knew from the expression in her eyes that the point had gone home. Either she made up her mind quickly, or he found someone else. He never had two girls at the same time, but he didn't mind one after the other, in rapid succession.

And what did they get out of it? He sometimes wondered. Usually a drink, occasionally a meal, a chance perhaps to be lifted out of the humdrum ways of everyday life by being dated by the future head of the business. Maybe some were ambitious and hoped that his attachment would become permanent; that their looks and their charm would succeed where so many others had failed.

But there was no chance of that. Long ago Cullum had decided not to let his emotions become involved with one of his father's employees. He knew the family would never stand for it.

CHAPTER FOUR

Margaret Dunbar returned to Branswick in the spring of 1920 just as the country was in the grips of a depression, the inevitable aftermath of war. It affected the hosiery business in Scotland as much as any other because of the high cost of raw materials, the industrial unrest brought about by unemployment and the fact that the returning war heroes had no jobs to go to.

'Things are not too good abroad, either,' Margaret told her father. 'The poverty in Germany is terrible and in France there are shortages of everything. Switzerland is all right though.' She yawned. 'That's why it's such a *ghastly* place to be. I couldn't stand it a moment longer, Daddy.'

She sat by him in her favourite position on the arm of his chair, her hand curled lovingly about his neck, while his arm encircled her waist. Looking at them, Susan thought she had not seen such an expression of contentment on Hector's face since Margaret had gone away, even when he was playing with his little grandson. Susan was glad to have Margaret back too; it had been a grim year with her father and Mary's moroseness, Cullum's discontent and the ever-present worry about the business. Now the whole family seemed to be looking to Margaret to change things; irrationally perhaps, her return, like the spring, introduced an element of hope that things would be better.

'We missed you, darling.' Hector pressed her hand. 'I'm glad you came back, though you're more of a lady than ever.'

'Tell me about the business.' Margaret kept her tone

inconsequential. 'And the Pendreighs. Is that all over? Are we speaking again?'

'No, *not* to the Pendreighs. I can never get over Elliott's deceitful behaviour,' Hector said firmly. 'They're not having an easy time either. We have many unemployed in the town and the Scottish Council of Textile Trade Unions is trying to get its clutches on all our workers. Well, I've told *our* people that if they want to join a union they must go elsewhere. There are plenty to take their places.'

'But we must talk to the Pendreighs sometime, Daddy.' Margaret said lightly, bending and kissing the top of his head. Truthfully, she had not thought of Ruthven for months, but now that she was home again the first thing she'd done was look out of the window at the Pendreigh house. 'Why don't I go down to see Netta? She was my best friend at school. That business was *such* a long time ago, Daddy. It had its effect and that's that.'

'Ruthven is coming home to join the business I hear.' Susan glanced at Margaret. 'Elliott hasn't been in good health and Dirk wants to be a vet. Maybe we should start speaking to them again – if they will speak to us.'

It was late afternoon. Margaret had come home on the morning train from Edinburgh, after travelling from London the previous day and spending the night with her sister Juliet. Taking tea in the lounge with her family, looking at the familiar sight of the town from the window, smoke rising from the Dunbar mill, Margaret knew that some things never changed. She was glad they didn't, and she was glad to be home again. She had felt in a vacuum in Switzerland, knowing that time was passing and that she did not know what she was going to do. A year ago she had been a schoolgirl; now she was, well, a lady as her father had said.

The school in Switzerland had paid little regard to scholarship, emphasizing the importance of manners, movement and deportment, how to be a gracious hostess,

71

and how to converse with men. How, in short, to prepare for marriage. Margaret no longer felt gauche or awkward in company; not that she ever had, very much. But she doubted now if she would have been so outspoken to Elliott Pendreigh. A certain naïveté had informed her behaviour then. Her natural dress sense was enhanced and she read the American magazine *Vogue*, now published in England, eagerly every month. It would, she thought, be rather nice if there were something for her to do now that she was at home, something other than hanging about waiting to get married as Susan and all the other girls she knew so obviously were.

'Yes I'll go down and see Netta Pendreigh tomorrow.' Margaret got up. 'She can only turn me away.'

'I really don't wish you to call on the Pendreighs Margaret.' Her father's tone changed. 'If anyone should make an overture it's them, not us.'

'But, Father, they did make overtures and you rejected them.' Susan began to move quietly around the room, gathering up the tea things before summoning the maid. 'Elliott wrote to you twice. Didn't he even apologize? Everyone says it's so silly, as we were life-long friends. I think Margaret's right.'

'Well I forbid it.' Hector, his mood changed, lumbered to his feet and went over to the whisky decanter. As he poured his drink his hand shook slightly. Margaret thought that her father had not only aged but looked worn. He brought his drink back to his chair, then changed his mind and, standing in front of the fire as though to emphasize his authority, put his glass to his lips. Margaret flopped from the arm of his chair to the seat he had vacated and stretched out her long legs clad in cream-coloured silk stockings.

'Daddy, a year ago you forbade us to go to the Victory ball. I intended to defy you but I didn't because I didn't get the chance. I tell you, in all honesty, I would have gone but for the fuss with the Pendreighs. Maybe I was

72

wrong then because I was still a schoolgirl; but now I'm a woman.'

'You're eighteen,' her father said testily.

'*Almost* a woman; anyway I haven't come home, Daddy, to be told what I may and may not do. I wish to make that clear because if I feel stifled at home I shall go away.'

'And where will you go, may I ask?' Hector raised his head, admiration in his eyes rather than anger. He applauded his youngest daughter's spirit even if it sometimes caused him anguish. He was very proud of the way she had spoken out to Elliott Pendreigh. He wished that Cullum possessed the spirit Margaret had, or that he himself had shown more of it when he was reluctantly pushed into the business at the age of sixteen and then married off to his family's choice when he was nineteen. It was true that he had grown to admire and depend on his wife if not actually to love her, and he'd missed her excessively when she died. But he had spent all his grown life not doing the things he wanted to do in order to please someone else, and it was clear his daughter was not going to be like him.

'I shall go to London,' Margaret said. 'I would rather like to model clothes.'

'A mannequin?' Her father's voice was incredulous.

'Yes, why not? I like clothes. People say I wear them well. All sorts of society girls are becoming mannequins. I thought I could be like Madeline Seymour and be a mannequin at Jays.' She looked at her father with a naughty glint in her eyes.

'She's an actress!'

'Yes but her family is genteel. Her father's a painter. They mix in society. All sorts of girls are doing all sorts of things you wouldn't have dreamed of before the war, Daddy. That's why women got the vote and why Lady Astor is now in the House of Commons. Women are working in offices and factories, here in the mills . . .'

73

'Yes,' her father expostulated, his fond expression vanishing completely. 'Women, but not *ladies*. Women have always worked, but ladies never have and I don't intend that my daughters should either. How would that reflect on me? I never heard of such a thing. A mannequin!' He tossed his whisky down and went over to the decanter to pour himself another.

'I'll go and change for dinner,' Margaret said, watching his shaking hand. 'I haven't seen Cullum yet. What time does he come home?'

Susan looked at the clock. Cullum often didn't come home until late, just before dinner. She knew too that he often went out again afterwards and no one knew at what time he eventually went to bed.

Cullum's private life was mysterious. He mixed with the younger set in town but seemed to have no special girlfriend. Who, then, did he see so late at night? It worried Susan, but she had no one to speak to about it, and she would never have dared mention it to her brother. She hoped that tonight because of Margaret he'd make an effort, or did he still resent her too?

Cullum was lying on his bed, his whisky glass on his chest, his eyes closed. He couldn't face Margaret until he'd had a drink; now he'd had two and he felt better. He wasn't aware of the knock on his door or of it being pushed ajar. He was half asleep because, although the mill no longer started work at six but at eight, he still got up early to be on time. At Oxford he'd hardly ever got up before noon. He'd never been known to attend a morning tutorial or lecture.

'You look all in,' Margaret said softly and sat on his bed.

Cullum opened his eyes wide, then half closed them again. Margaret took the whisky glass from his chest and put it beside the bottle on the table. She wondered when he'd started drinking alone in his room. She bent down and kissed him, noticing that he had more beard on his cheek. He looked older. She took a hand and shook him.

'Come on. Don't pretend. It's Margaret, your little sister come home from abroad.'

'Hello Margaret.' He raised his head and returned her kiss, then flopped back again. She noticed the tense white line round his mouth.

'Have you not forgiven me Cullum?'

'What was there to forgive?' He opened one eye and squinted at her.

'I know that you didn't want to leave Oxford.'

'Oh that!' He pretended he'd forgotten, leaned on one elbow and poured himself out two inches of neat Scotch. 'I'd have come to the same conclusion eventually if you hadn't. Now that Ruthven Pendreigh's going into the business I've got a head start on him. He's not finishing his degree either.' He laughed, but it was a bitter laugh. 'Why in God's name does everyone want to go into knitted goods? Believe me, if I never saw another vest or pair of woollen drawers I'd be a happier man.'

'Father says you're doing well. He says you've made great progress and people like and respect you.' Cullum snorted but Margaret continued quickly. 'Father says you've taken to the business more naturally than he did.'

'That's not saying much.' Cullum drained his glass and sat up, propping his head on his pillow. His sandy hair and blue-green eyes made him look appealing and still younger than his years. 'Do you realize, Maggie, that Dunbars are no longer interested in Dunbars? Neither Father nor I like what we are doing. Then why the hell are we doing it?'

'To make money.' Margaret's voice had a tone of finality and she spread her hands on her lap and stared at her long, tapering, well-manicured fingers. She was wearing a blue dress with a V-neck, the dropped waistline low over her hips. Her dark, wavy hair was shorter and she wore the latest pointed shoes with a strap. Cullum thought she looked about twenty-five, poised and with a beauty that was quite remarkable. She had taken to wearing make-up. He wondered what Father would think of that? Well, it wouldn't matter; with her looks she would soon be married. Margaret's eyes went from her fingers to her brother's face. 'Do you think most people do what they like? Do you think all bankers have a passion for banking, all steel manufacturers a passion for steel? People are in business to make money, Cullum, people of our sort. In a way we are just like the workers who toil where they do because they have to. They have no choice and neither do we. Do you think every Dunbar since great-great-great-grandfather Murdoch liked what they were doing?'

'They seem to have, and when they did Dunbars prospered. Under Father it hasn't and it's not going to under me either. I haven't the feel for it. I'm not interested in it. If I never saw another knitted loop I'd be a happy man.'

'I see.' Margaret lowered her head. 'It does sound pretty hopeless.'

'Oh we're not doing so badly. In fact business is picking up. I'll stick it, because I have to, but I can't pretend to like it. I think we're even doing better than the Mactavishes; but I tell you Margaret, why Father didn't want to sell to Pendreigh I will never know.'

'But you didn't want to sell either. None of us did.'

'I admit that was my reaction at first. It was a sort of family pride, I suppose. But knowing what I know now, I wonder he didn't accept the first offer he had. I tell that to you straight.' Cullum swung himself off the bed and started undoing his tie, glancing at the clock on his mantelpiece. 'We must get ready for dinner. The Macallisters are coming. I wouldn't be surprised if the Macallisters weren't interested in Dunbars too. And I tell you this Margaret,' he waved a finger at her, 'don't, please don't, try and interfere again. If we get a good offer we should take it. Take it and get out, because this business is

76

going to go down and down.' Cullum pointed his thumb towards the floor and with his other hand tilted the whisky bottle into his empty glass.

The Macallisters, driven out by one of the pogroms afflicting that unhappy country, had come from Poland at the beginning of the nineteenth century with the name Laskey and settled in Glasgow. Joseph Macallister's father had a Polish accent because he'd been born in Stetin. Joseph, however, had a soft Scotch brogue and his wife was a Cameron, descended from Cameron of Lochiel who supported Bonny Prince Charlie, and his brother Archibald who was the last Jacobite to be executed in England. The Camerons had money, but so did the Laskeys, who changed their name to Macallister in the 1880s. Their fortune came from trade, from linen and textiles, and at one time they had a mill on the Craigie that produced high quality knitted underwear.

The main Macallister business now was the spinning of yarn from all kinds of wool to be used by the knitting mills not only on the Scottish Borders but in the Midlands of England, wherever knitted goods were made. Macallisters had a large mill on the banks of the Tweed at Selkirk where the dyeing of the wool was done and some of the spinning, though it also had spinning mills in Galashiels and Peebles.

The Cameron money came from banking and investment, and Camerons had for centuries figured prominently in the arts, law and medicine in Edinburgh and Glasgow. It was thus a great cultural cachet when wealthy young Joe Macallister married a Cameron – Elizabeth – and he acquired a fine house six miles from Selkirk, also on the banks of the Tweed, which had formerly belonged to the Fyldes of Peebles, the last Lord Fylde having lost two sons in the Boer War.

Elizabeth Macallister entertained in some style at Fylde House, which was exquisitely furnished with great taste and lack of ostentation. Because the Camerons were not in trade it made their entry to the noble houses of the Border so much easier and several earls, barons, baronets and at one time a duke had made their appearances at the Macallister dinner table. Elizabeth Macallister was third cousin to Hector's wife Isobel, and this distant family connection was maintained by a meeting once or twice a year.

There were four Macallisters for dinner the night Margaret came home from Switzerland – Joseph and Elizabeth and two of their children: Bruno, the eldest and Isla the youngest. Elizabeth was a red-haired Cameron, but her children had inherited their father's dark Jewish good looks. Bruno was thirty and a war veteran. Isla, at twenty-three, had not the looks of the Dunbar girls, but nor was she plain, being an attractive, sensible girl with black hair and grey eyes, domesticated but artistic. Maybe in the back of her parents' minds was the idea that an alliance with her distant cousin, Cullum Dunbar, would not be a bad thing in this world where there was now a shortage of eligible men.

When Margaret came down for dinner the drawing room was empty. Hearing noises from outside, she found the party – with the exception of Susan who was supervising the preparation of dinner – assembled in the drive admiring a large blue Wolseley all-weather tourer which Bruno had driven up from London.

Cullum had his jacket off and was just closing the bonnet of the car while Mary sat in the driver's seat with her slim white hands on the large ebony wheel. As Margaret came slowly down the steps Bruno, who had been showing Cullum the engine, looked up, rubbing his hands on a piece of cloth. Margaret wore a dress of red chiffon over a red taffeta sheath which she had bought in Shoolbreds in London's Tottenham Court Road on her way home from Switzerland. It had a bodice and a sash all in one, tying loosely in a large bow at the back. Her stockings were red and she wore black leather shoes with a scalloped edge.

For a moment everyone's attention turned from the car to Margaret for, indeed, she seemed almost as out of place there as the huge shiny car, an intimation of new and disturbing things in an old and apparently changeless world. Margaret looked like a vital new force, powerful and disruptive; as capable, in her striking new dress, of displacing the old order as the motor car was a threat to the horse-drawn carriage.

Hector and Joseph Macallister were standing slightly apart from the rest, smoking cigars, and it was her father who broke the silence that had suddenly descended on the group with the arrival of Margaret. He extended a hand to greet her, exhaling smoke into the evening air, a look of pride on his face.

'You'd hardly recognize young Maggie, would you Joe?' he said, drawing her forward. 'She returned from Switzerland just today. She's quite the lady now, isn't she?'

He looked at his friend of many years' standing who went up to Margaret and kissed her on the cheek.

'She is indeed grown up, and very bonny if I may say so. How are you Margaret?'

'Well, thank you, Uncle Joe.'

'You'll not have seen Bruno and Isla for some time, have you?'

'No.' Margaret looked gravely at Bruno, who was hastily straightening his bow tie, eyeing her admiringly, and then she smiled and kissed Isla who stood on the outskirts of the group with her mother. 'Hello Isla, hello Aunt Elizabeth.'

'We haven't seen you since you left school.' Elizabeth returned her kiss, examining her critically, not sure whether she approved of what she saw or not. 'Yes, I must say you've changed. You'll feel out of place in Branswick.'

'No, I feel at home here Aunt.' Margaret looked at her

79

boldly, knowing what was going on in her mind. 'I shall always feel at home in Branswick.'

'Hello Margaret.' Bruno shook hands and then, leaning forward, kissed her on the cheek. 'May I?'

Everyone laughed because Bruno had already done what he'd asked permission to do and this broke the awkwardness.

Margaret's eyes sparkled mischievously. 'I don't think I've seen *you* since you came in your uniform sometime during the war. You were going to France and you came to say goodbye.'

'That was 1916,' Bruno said smiling at her.

'Well not since then. I was very impressed.'

'I hope you still are.'

'I'm impressed with the car,' Margaret said pointedly, running her fingers lightly along the polished chrome as though ignoring the nuances of his remark. 'Isn't she beautiful?'

'Try it.' Mary got out of the driving seat and Margaret was about to get in when Susan appeared on the steps and said that dinner was ready. Elizabeth suddenly shivered and Hector hurried her up the stairs, followed by the rest of the party.

Over dinner Margaret noticed that Bruno was looking at her a great deal, covertly from beneath lowered lashes and once or twice quite openly and admiringly when she said something which made them all laugh.

For, on the whole, it was an awkward evening. Everyone seemed to have grown apart and changed, maybe because of the war. Cullum hardly ever said anything to Isla and certainly never looked at her in the way Bruno looked at Margaret. Mary, who had gone to a lot of trouble to make herself look pretty in a simple dress of emerald green especially purchased from Branswick's one and only shop selling couture clothes, was shy and diffident; but Margaret guessed, from the glances she gave Bruno, that she would rather like to marry again.

Hector and Joe, who usually got on well, argued a good deal about trade and business conditions and whether the Coalition should stay or reform itself into the customary political parties of before the war. Susan talked sensibly to Elizabeth about matters to do with the house, and afterwards Hector suggested bridge which he, Joseph and Elizabeth enjoyed. Susan was asked to complete the foursome and the table was set up in a small parlour off the hall which Hector used as a study if he needed to work at home.

In the drawing room those who were left looked at each other while Margaret served the coffee and Cullum put a fresh log on the fire.

'Cold for April,' he said, to no one in particular.

'Anyone play the piano?' Bruno went over to it and started strumming, such a cacophony on the keys that Margaret had never heard before. She gave him coffee and put her hands over her ears.

'What a din! *Whatever* is that?'

'It's jazz.' Bruno continued banging away; it was difficult to know whether he was playing right notes or wrong ones. 'It's the rage in America. It came from the negro musicians who used to play in the brothels in New Orleans. Now they're closed and they've had to find somewhere else to earn a livelihood. The musicians I mean.' He glanced at her and she knew he was trying to impress her with his sophistication. Was he trying to embarrass her too?

'It sounds dreadful.' Nevertheless she found her feet were tapping.

'Played well it's wonderful. I heard Jelly Roll Morton in Chicago, and when you hear a true jazz player it's as good as anything you'll ever hear.'

'When were you in America?' Margaret leaned on the piano sipping her coffee, oblivious to the others in the room.

'I was there last year. I was still in the Royal Flying

Corps, as it was then, and we gave a display to impress the Yanks. I could have stayed there. It's a wonderful country. They've invented a box that can play music in one place that you can hear in another miles away. Imagine, music over the air!'

'It sounds incredible,' Margaret said.

Bruno got up and closed the lid of the piano. 'I know, let's go for a spin in my car.'

'Now?'

'Why not?'

'But it's dark.'

'You can drive in the dark. I've got lights. I'm going home in the dark. I'll be very careful.'

'It would be divine.' Margaret's eyes sparkled. 'Cullum, did you hear that?'

Bruno didn't look too pleased as she turned towards her brother. He hadn't reckoned on other people.

Cullum had started playing two-handed whist with Isla while Mary sat huddled once more by the fire, apparently having abandoned her efforts to attract Bruno.

'That would be a lot of fun,' Cullum said. 'Isla?'

Isla shook her head. 'It's *terribly* cold. Believe me, with that hood down you'll freeze.'

'Mary?'

Mary just shivered and shook her head.

'It appears it's not popular,' Margaret grimaced and went to refill her coffee.

'*We* can go,' Bruno said brightening. 'Cullum can entertain the ladies.'

'Oh Margaret, *should* you?' Mary looked up dejectedly.

'Yes,' Margaret said.

'You do get your own way don't you?'

Bruno was steering the car very carefully down the hill. It was a heavy vehicle and it made such a noise that they had to shout.

'I *what*?' She had on the fur coat she had worn all winter

82

in Switzerland and a woollen cap pulled down over her head.

'Get your own way. Do what you like.'

'I try. Why do you say that?'

'It's the first thing I noticed about you – apart from the way you look.'

'Oh.'

He'd placed a rug round her knees and she needed it. She put her hands underneath and even then she was shivering.

'It's a lot of fun this, isn't it?'

'I love it. I love engines and speed.'

To show what he meant he accelerated as the car reached the flat and went roaring along by the side of the river.

'Where to?' he shouted.

'Wherever you like!'

He looked at her, his eyes glinting through his driving goggles in the moonlight. 'I wish you meant that.'

He was, she decided, a very attractive man, but with the hint of something rather repellent about him. She felt he could be very pleasant but, conversely, very nasty, even cruel, if you gave him the chance. This slightly disagreeable aspect had little to do with his physical appearance; it was something intangible, something indefinable. He had been an air ace in the war and this undoubtedly gave him glamour. His right cheek bore a long scar where he had been involved in a near fatal crash and his right eye seemed slightly lower than the other. If this was what made him look slightly evil it wasn't his fault. He had rather heavy saturnine features, like his father, and black wavy hair heavily brilliantined and greying slightly at the sides. He was very old, about thirty, and he had been married. He was the only person she had ever known who had been divorced. His wife had left him during the war for another man who had a safer job than flying airplanes in France. It had been hinted that there was some other reason as well, something they didn't know about, that nobody talked about.

Margaret suddenly shivered. If he wasn't almost family she would feel very nervous alone with him like this in the night.

They drove along by the Drume through the forest, and then out into the valley that lay beyond Branswick.

There was a crescent moon and the stars were very bright in the sky, like diamonds on a velvet backdrop. It was difficult to speak as the car roared along and she sat back conscious of the speed, of the air rushing past and of this attractive experienced man, who had obviously wanted her all to himself, beside her encased in a thick leather coat with a collar that almost concealed his face. The fact that he was a distant cousin didn't make it any less exciting, or dangerous.

They roared through the valley, past the silent houses where everyone went to bed very early, past the sleeping cattle in the fields and then started to climb the lower reaches of the Branahae. When they came to the top an aspect of enchantment presented itself to them. The countryside lay below them like the phosphorescent crests of so many waves undulating in neverending folds towards the horizon. On each side of the road the burgeoning leaves slumbered heavily on the trees and the dark birds' nests, visible through those branches that were still sparse, were silent.

Bruno stopped the car and removed his goggles. He was panting slightly as though he had been in a race. He rested his gloved hands on the wheel and gave a deep sigh. 'It is magnificent country isn't it?'

'It is.' Margaret didn't know why she whispered.

'Is that why you stay?'

'Stay?' She looked at him and he moved closer towards her. 'I've been away. I only just came back.'

'But you're not going to go away again are you?'

'I don't know.' Margaret felt a heaviness in her heart. She didn't know; she couldn't decide whether to go away again or stay. 'I'm very glad that I'm home; but I don't know for how long I'll feel like that. I didn't like Switzerland much or being a young lady at a nice academy. I think all that sort of thing has passed. Don't you?'

'Passed? How do you mean?'

'Women are going to come out of their shells.'

'Oh they're going to do that all right!' Bruno's arm encircled her waist. 'And I must say I don't mind at all.' His mouth was very close to her ear. 'You're terribly beautiful in the moonlight Margaret.'

'*Only* in the moonlight?' Her attempt at levity made her voice shake.

'No, all the time. I've hardly been able to stop looking at you.'

'I think other people noticed too.'

'I don't care if they did.'

She was glad she had her thick coat on because his hand was cupping her breast. 'Don't you think we should get back?' she said and looked at him. She knew then he would kiss her and he did, very firmly and powerfully, taking her breath away, stopping any protest she might have made. He held the back of her head and kissed her hard and she thought how smooth and experienced his kiss was compared to Ruthven's who had that thick gamekeeper's moustache which somehow got in the way.

It occurred to her that she did, in general, find the most awkward places to be kissed in – against a wall and now the front seat of a car. The thought almost made her giggle.

'You come out of your shell very nicely Margaret,' he said breaking away with reluctance.

'I didn't mean like that!'

'Oh I think you did, really.'

He bent down again swiftly and she lifted her face, this

time returning the kiss, making it linger, aware of one of his hands trying to unfasten her coat, one trying to edge its way up her skirt.

Finally Margaret put a hand on his chest and thrust him away. 'Bruno, we are in the middle of the country on a cold night!' She felt very nervous.

'Are you cold?'

'Not really.'

'Well then.'

He lurched towards her and she moved swiftly along the seat.

'I don't want to have to get out and walk back, Bruno. But I will.' She put a hand on the door.

'I believe you.' He pulled himself up and sat straight in front of the wheel. 'You're a most extraordinarily determined young woman. You can see it in the way you look and move about. You *would* get out and walk, wouldn't you?'

Her eyes glinted. 'Yes I would, even if it took me until daybreak.' She felt nervous no longer.

'Well, I won't do it again, if you don't want to. Not here anyway. I don't promise not to try anywhere else.'

'There aren't many places you can try.'

'You could come to London.'

'To London! Just for a kiss?' Margaret threw back her head and gave her warm, enticing laugh.

'I thought you might go to London anyway if you were restless. I belong to an aerodrome in Croydon and I could take you flying. Altogether, we could have a wonderful time.'

The way he stressed the word 'altogether' left her in no doubt as to what he meant. After all he was an experienced man who had been married and been to bed with a woman, most probably with more than one.

'My father doesn't want me to go to London. I don't quite know what he does want, probably for me to get married, but certainly to stay at home.'

'Would you like that?'

'Not really. It's very dull and a bit dismal. I'd like to be a mannequin, if you want to know.'

'A mannequin!' Bruno started to laugh but the look on her face stopped him. 'You're perfectly serious, aren't you?'

'Of course. I like fashion and clothes. Some very respectable girls are mannequins.'

'Yes, you'd do it very well.' Bruno looked thoughtful and his hand moved to the ignition button which was a feature of this very modern car. 'Do you know anyone in London? Anyone you can ask?'

'I thought I'd write to Harrods or Shoolbreds; they employ mannequins.'

'I know Tristan Fleming.'

'Who's he?'

'Flemings? In Oxford Street.'

'Oh *that* Flemings.' Margaret suddenly felt excited. Flemings was a new, very chic store that had opened at the end of the war.

'I could speak to him if you like.'

'Could you really?'

'It wouldn't do any harm would it?' He looked at her, adjusting his goggles and the engine roared into life.

CHAPTER FIVE

Tristan Fleming was an angular young man who had lost a leg during the war flying with the same squadron as Bruno Macallister. This had put paid to any notion he had had of taking up flying as a career, and he had been quite receptive to the idea of joining his father's elegant new emporium in Oxford Street, just down the road from that of Gordon Selfridge. Flemings was smaller than Selfridges and was aimed particularly at the fashion-conscious woman. It did not sell furniture, carpets, household goods or anything of that nature, but concentrated exclusively on clothes, accessories, hats and the growing trade in cosmetics. Flemings had been opened in 1918, just as the war was in its closing phases and people were ready for some relief from the gloom of war-time life. Women flocked to it and some couturiers said that it had already begun to change the London fashion scene.

'You move beautifully,' Tristan Fleming said, puffing at a cigarette in a silver holder. He wore a double-breasted suit in a fine houndstooth check and his elegant brown shoes were partly concealed by a pair of camel-haired spats. 'Tell me, have you been a mannequin before?'

'No, but I went to a Swiss finishing school. They were keen on deportment there.' Margaret smiled at him, feeling relaxed for the first time since the ordeal of walking across the room for him had begun. She had selected her outfit with care: a matching coat and skirt in grey gabardine, the skirt made of four pieces and gathered at the waist, and a hip-length coat with soft pleats at the sides and back, the low waistline controlled by a loose half belt. The coat had long narrow revers and a flat collar, the sleeves were loose and bell-shaped. Underneath she wore a plain white shantung blouse with a V-shaped neckline, a low waistband, and a soft scarf knotted loosely at her neck.

Skirts were longer this year and hers, slightly barrel shaped, was about six inches above the ankle. She wore black stockings and black court shoes with laced fronts. Unusually for her Margaret also wore a grey gabardine hat with a stiff crown and a drooping brim, larger at the sides than at the front.

The room was unfurnished except for a few gilt chairs set around a raised platform in the middle. It was however a gracious room with heavy flocked wallpaper, a gold Wilton carpet and thick satin drapes at the windows secured by velvet bands. It was also well lit with a large chandelier made up of myriads of tiny crystal drops, and candle-shaped sconces on the walls. The windows looked onto Cavendish Square so that the natural lighting was good too, despite the heavy foliage of the waving oak trees. The room was where Flemings showed their fashions twice yearly, or privately from time to time to important customers.

Tristan perched on one of the gilt chairs, gazing at Margaret. He patted the empty chair beside him and watched her as she walked towards it.

'You're a friend of Bruno Macallister?' He raised an eyebrow. 'A *close* friend?'

'Good heavens no!' Despite her poise, Margaret blushed at the way he had emphasized the word. 'He's a very remote cousin. My mother and his mother were, I think, third cousins.'

'Oh I see – that sort of relationship. Very proper.'

'Very.' Margaret gazed at him rather severely.

'And you are . . . how old?' Tristan glanced at the letter she had sent him, which he held in his hand and in which she thought she had written all the details that would be necessary. 'Oh I see. Eighteen. *Only* eighteen.'

'I'm nineteen in October.'

Tristan lowered the paper to his lap and gazed at her again. 'And what does your father think of your becoming a mannequin?'

'He doesn't like it, of course.'

'Why the "of course"?'

He had adopted a rather needling tone and Margaret was determined not to be daunted by it.

'Because I don't need to work and Father thinks that no girl should work unless she needs to. He can't see that she should want to.'

'You have a private income?'

'I have shares in my family's firm.'

'Dunbars. Ah. Why *do* you want to work Miss Dunbar?' Tristan lit a fresh de Reszke and stuck it in his holder.

'Because I am bored at home. I have an unmarried sister, a widowed sister-in-law, a father and a brother who run the business. I spent three months there in the summer and I nearly went mad. Besides, I like clothes and fashion.'

'So I see.' Tristan nodded his head approvingly. 'And you wear them well. Can you start on Monday?'

'This Monday?' Margaret felt excited, then alarmed.

'Is this Monday not convenient?'

'It's so soon.'

'Your father doesn't know?'

Margaret glanced at her feet. 'Not yet. I didn't know if I could get a job.'

Tristan laughed and stood up. He took the stick that hung on the back of his chair. 'Long may your modesty continue! You will have no difficulty getting a job in the fashion world. Well, you must sort this out between you and your father. Four pounds a week.'

'*Four* pounds!'

'Maybe more if you do well, eventually.'

'Oh but it seems a lot! I'm not complaining.'

Margaret stood up and Tristan moved their chairs in line with the others.

'That's a change. Let me know when you can start.'

'This Monday.'

'What will your father say?'

'Leave that to me and my father,' Margaret said, drawing on her long grey gloves.

Margaret was an instant success at Flemings. They liked her style, her charm, her personality, above all her professionalism. She was punctual, she understood her instructions, she was always neat, well dressed and fastidiously clean and she had a friendly manner that the clients liked. Mannequins who were too remote or standoffish could discourage clients who wanted to identify with what a woman wore. A mannequin who was too aloof and too beautiful didn't sell any clothes at all, because no client felt she could compete with her and that the clothes she wore couldn't possibly suit her.

Margaret lived in Half Moon Street, in a house belonging to the father of a girl she had known at the Gstaad finishing school, Olga Pasalaris. Even by the cosmopolitan standards of the finishing school Olga had been extraordinary: spoilt and capricious, wayward and eccentric. She smoked, she drank and she stayed out at nights, supposedly with men. She had almost been expelled from the school, which had never contemplated such action with anyone since its foundation as an establishment for completing the education of the children of the rich.

Olga's father, a Greek merchant, was very wealthy. Her mother was a Hungarian countess, beautiful, volatile, extravagant and impulsive, but sadly lacking in the attributes of motherly care. Olga spent much of her childhood alone in a large house in the care of servants while her

91

mother lived with a series of lovers in Europe or America, and her father travelled the world amassing further wealth. Olga had grown up much faster than most young girls and was well ahead of Margaret when they met, but despite their disparate backgrounds they were immediately drawn to each other, perhaps recognizing a mutual talent for rebellion; a restless, adventurous disposition.

Yet, despite their friendship, the stifling confines of the academy for young ladies had proved too much and each had withdrawn without parental permission. Olga because it was either that or expulsion, and she preferred to go voluntarily, and Margaret because a term without Olga would seem unendurable. Olga left to seek out one or other of her wandering parents, now divorced, and Margaret went home to Branswick.

But her time at home that summer had not been a success. Whatever its drawbacks Switzerland had offered her a tantalizing glimpse of what the adult world was like; but it was very different from Branswick where she was still treated as a child, the youngest, the baby. She had travelled on her own through London and Paris on her journey to and from Gstaad, and she was aware of how men looked at her – men of the world, not the boys she had grown up with; attractive, older, cosmopolitan men whose glances hinted at a world that had immediately shut its doors to her when she came home.

Despite her feelings of rebellion as far as her father and his attitude to the Pendreighs was concerned, Margaret had bowed to his wishes and avoided them. She saw Netta and Ruthven at a party at the tennis club and once she was drawn against Netta at a tournament; but there was no social intercourse whatever, just the most fleeting of smiles and a nod of the head. Besides, between her intention to visit the Pendreighs and her decision to come to London, there had been Bruno. Her encounter with him, however unsatisfactory its nature, had reminded her of those glances the men gave her as she travelled by herself across the continent: it was a bold, rather frightening invitation to step out once more into the adult world.

So, when Margaret had received a letter from Olga Pasalaris saying she was coming to London and inviting her to stay, the way was immediately clear; the door opened again, leading – who knew? – to the sort of adventures she could never expect in Branswick. She had announced her plan to her father – announced, did not seek his permission – and despite his disapproval, his warnings about the future, she packed her bags and travelled south, ostensibly for a holiday with her friend. Her father, naturally, didn't approve of young women who were allowed by their parents to live alone in houses in Mayfair. Everyone knew what happened in Mayfair; it was a den of sin.

But Margaret had brushed her father's fears aside and, because he loved her, he let her go; maybe he also knew how futile it would be to try and stop her. What he would have said had he known her heart was also set on getting a job is another matter.

Margaret had not seen Bruno or the Macallister family again after that night in April, after that unexpected, rather exciting physical encounter with her cousin. However she thought about him a lot; he quite put thoughts of Ruthven Pendreigh, who was forbidden anyway, out of her mind. Perhaps her decision to stay with Olga was also influenced by the knowledge that Bruno was in London – that experienced man with his mysterious past, his almost frightening but powerful physical presence.

She didn't write to tell him she was coming; she didn't ask him to contact his friend who was the head of Flemings. She did it herself, thus setting a style that she would follow through her life – making her own way by her own endeavours. But the mention of Bruno's name had interested Fleming and he had immediately seen her and, after his invitation, Margaret lost no time immersing herself in her new life.

The fact that Margaret wanted to work amused Olga, whose prime aim in life was the reckless single-minded pursuit of a good time. She was out every evening and came home very late with men who were still there in the morning. Margaret guessed where they slept even though she had a room at the top of the house and never saw Olga at breakfast time, only the men who, after sheepishly introducing themselves, buried their faces in the morning paper.

Olga was fast. That much was obvious. Her lack of roots, her peripatetic way of life, the basic insecurity of family affections made her cling to ephemera and surround herself with acquaintances who shared her lifestyle. No one seemed to do any work; in this Margaret was unique and, Olga considered, rather quaint. She introduced Margaret to her friends as though she were pointing out some remarkable curiosity in this frenetic, demanding world in which she lived.

A mannequin! Few of them had ever known a woman who worked, let alone a mannequin. Was it quite respectable, even decent? Had her father lost his money? Did her parents approve? What sort of people were they, anyway, to let a daughter come to London by herself and get a job? Olga's friends were like herself: lazy, rich, nihilistic, content with superficial pleasures.

Because she worked and worked hard, because it was important that she always looked her best, that she was fresh and clear-eyed, Margaret liked a regular life, a routine that was circumscribed by the time she went to bed and the time she had to get up in the morning. She invariably rose at seven because it took an hour to bath, to dress carefully in the clothes she had pressed and laid out the night before, and to make up her face. It took twenty minutes to have her breakfast and a brisk ten-minute walk through Mayfair to get to work. She never arrived later than a quarter to nine in the morning, often coinciding with Tristan Fleming, whose chauffeur deposited him at the entrance to the store in a green Hispano-Suiza every bit as elegant and streamlined as its owner.

Tristan Fleming was polite and friendly towards Margaret but never familiar; she was an employee and rather a junior one in the strict hierarchy, above the sales staff but below the buyers, the merchandisers and well below the departmental heads and the management.

Besides herself there were three other mannequins and at half past nine each morning they gathered with the buyers, merchandisers and Tristan Fleming to discuss the work programme for the day. There were individual clients who, by appointment, had special shows to help them select their outfits for the season. There were visitors from abroad and designers, manufacturers and couturiers who came to show their designs, specially tailored to the Fleming image which was smart, elegant and streamlined, like the Hispano-Suiza, and catering mostly for the rich and very rich.

The girls were busy all day modelling gowns, dresses, sportswear, knitwear, night attire and underwear. With underwear no men were ever present, and the exquisite garments in silk or crêpe-de-Chine, hand made and hand embroidered by the finest seamstresses, were shown behind closed doors and drawn curtains to specially selected very wealthy clients who would not only order them in large numbers but tell their rich and titled friends about them too.

Margaret enjoyed her work. She loved clothes and she enjoyed showing them, knowing that she did it well. At the end of the day she was tired and she would go back to the Half Moon Street house. Sometimes Olga had only just got up and was preparing herself for the evening's entertainment with the help of her maid, choosing clothes from the large selection in her wardrobe and discarding them, selecting something else, holding it against herself and discarding that. The result, however, usually justified the fuss and was invariably spectacular.

Olga always knew exactly to the minute what the current fashion was; how low the waist, how high the skirt, what length the hair should be, what colours were in and what were out and what materials everyone was wearing. The latest thing was fulgurante, a mixture of silk, satin and crêpe, and Olga had an evening dress and a tea gown made up in it. She was not strictly beautiful; but she had allure. She had a long lean face, rather like a famished greyhound, and deeply recessed soulful eyes that seemed to mirror the sad Magyar past of her maternal ancestors. Her hair was very short at the back, almost shingled, and fell forward over her face, the ends tapering towards her long, full sensual mouth which always looked rather sulky as though she were about to burst into tears. She had large lustreless grey eyes and her whole aspect of the world seemed to be based on suspicion and mistrust.

For all that Olga was very attractive to men. She had a good body and she showed it well, she dressed it well. She moved easily and gracefully because she was tall and slim with the boyish hips which were becoming fashionable and hardly any bust. Above all she exuded sexuality, a quality that seemed like a permanent invitation to interested males, and they were not lacking. In days which had seen the beginnings of women's emancipation Olga was very emancipated indeed, free with herself, not choosy enough in Margaret's opinion, careless about who her companion for the night might be, as long as there was one, and that he had sufficient money and knowledge of the London night scene to entertain her.

One of the first nightclubs in London had been opened in 1913 by the beautiful ex-actress second wife of Norwegian dramatist August Strindberg. It was called the Cave of the Golden Calf and was patronized by artists, guardsmen and their companions, mostly from the *demi-monde*. Galician gypsies played accordions and Lillian Shelley sang 'Popsie-wopsie' and everyone had a very good time. During the war there had been a proliferation of similar clubs, but they were still not the sort of places to which nice girls were supposed to go.

Olga Pasalaris knew them all.

Margaret had been in London for a month when Olga suggested one evening that it was time she stopped taking life so seriously and learned to enjoy herself. Olga was doing her face and nails in front of her mirror, the nails scarlet to match her lipstick. Her long hand rested on the dressing table and she leaned over squinting as she painted each nail because she was short sighted and should really have worn glasses. She wore a silk dressing gown which fell to the floor, opening in the front and showing that all she had on was a pair of camiknickers in pure silk crêpe-de-Chine with a long-waisted bodice.

Margaret sat on Olga's bed watching her and wondering what it was that made her so attractive to men when, if you itemized feature by feature, she was really rather plain, even ugly. Margaret Dunbar, although she was nearly twenty and quite sophisticated, did not yet know the meaning, let alone realize the importance, of availability.

'You might as well be back in Branswick for all the fun you get darling. You don't know *anyone*. Do you?' Olga peered at Margaret through heavily mascaraed eyelashes. 'I wonder you are not bored to death.'

'I like my day at the store. It makes me tired.' Margaret yawned and took off her hat. She always wore a hat to work now because it was the thing to do. She shook her hair which was bobbed very short at the back, showing the tips of her ears. She lay back on Olga's double bed; her bedroom had once been her parents' before they were divorced. Margaret thought about the men who every night slept in this bed with Olga. Who was it last night and

97

who would it be tonight? She felt embarrassed even to be entertaining such thoughts, and sat upright again. Olga laughed as if she could read her mind.

'We're having rather an amusing party tonight at the Fury in Wardour Street. It is the very latest in daring, naughty nightclubs. Ricky Spender and Mark Arnold are picking me up at nine. I said I'd try and persuade you to come.'

'Oh I couldn't. I'd never be able to get up in the morning.'

'Just come for a short time. You'll be back by midnight if you wish, I promise. Come on darling, you want to enjoy yourself, don't you?' Olga looked up from her manicure and peered at her again. 'Well you do, don't you?'

It was true that Margaret had no social life. She thought this was where her upbringing showed. However daring, however extravagant her behaviour as far as her family were concerned, she was really a very quiet, rather prim country girl out of her depth in the town.

'If you're sure I'll be back by midnight?'

'Promise.' Olga jumped up, brandishing her lacquered nails in the air and kissed her on the cheek. 'Oh we'll have such fun! One thing with you, there will be no problem about what to wear.'

The Fury was in a basement; it was dark inside and the air was acrid with smoke. A small band was playing in one corner and couples were dancing to the new Gershwin tune, 'Swanee'. Candles glittered on the tables which were very close together and waiters wove skilfully in and out of the gyrating throng with trays crammed with bottles and glasses.

The party that Olga and her friends were joining had already arrived and loud war-like cries greeted them as they made their way towards a cluster of corner tables.

A few faces were familiar to Margaret; most of the men

she had met at some time or the other, over the breakfast table. She was greeted warmly and room was made for her. Olga promptly sat on some man's lap and as the waiter, peremptorily summoned, came over Ricky Spender ordered champagne.

Mark Arnold was a tall rather serious-looking man, an ex-flyer. Now he was a broker in the City and Margaret felt safe with him, which was more than she could have said if her partner had been the aptly named Ricky Spender, an ex-Guardsman with carroty hair and a scarred face, the result of war wounds. He had already been drunk when he arrived and had driven his pre-war six cylinder Pierce-Arrow at a hair-raising speed along Piccadilly.

'Dance?' Mark said, getting up and holding out his hand. Margaret preferred to dance than drink and got up with alacrity, taking his hand and allowing herself to be led onto the small pocket-handkerchief sized dance floor.

Margaret was a good dancer, having perfected a natural aptitude at the sedate *thé dansants* in Gstaad. The music of the small band was gay – '*Where do flies go in the wintertime? Do they go to gay Paree?*', a pantomime hit of 1919 – and the dancing fast. Mark Arnold twirled her expertly around the tiny floor and there were laughing couples colliding into one another and a good deal of cross-chat.

'I see you do this a lot,' Mark shouted, eyeing her admiringly, his face glistening with sweat.

'Do what a lot?' she shouted back.

'This. Dance!'

'Oh no. I'm a working girl.'

'A what?'

'I work.'

'Really? How frightfully amusing.'

'*I know where the flies go,*' the band's male singer warbled,

99

'Lay their eggs and fly away,
Come back on the first of May,
Hatch their eggs and oh! What joy!
First a girl and then a boy!'

Heads bobbed, feet shot up in the air, corks popped and couples whirled. Margaret flung back her head, closing her eyes, surrendering her body to the thumping, frenetic music.

'*First a girl and then a boy*!' boomed a voice in her ear and an arm encircled her waist from behind, squeezing her hand.

'I say . . .' Margaret turned, colliding with a dark, familiar curly head. 'Bruno!'

'Bruno!' Mark Arnold echoed. 'You old rogue, take your hand off my girl.'

'Sorry,' Bruno smiled, mopping his face with his handkerchief. 'Couldn't resist. Might I have the next dance?'

He stepped back and Mark and Margaret continued their frenzied romp until, with a roll of drums, the music stopped and all the hot excited couples started clapping and changing partners.

Mark took Margaret's arm and led her through the crowd back to the table where Olga was reclining across a large cheery-faced man who appeared half asleep.

'Know Bruno Macallister well, do you?' Mark enquired.

'He's a distant cousin.'

'Really? We were in the same squadron.'

'Darling, where did you learn to dance like that?' Olga waved her glass in the air, spilling most of the contents over the black jacket of the supine man.

'At school.'

'I wish I'd been to a school where they danced like that.'

'You did. St Étiennes.'

Margaret laughed and accepted a cigarette, blowing a long spiral into the air. She felt exhilarated. Mark poured her some champagne and refilled Olga's glass.

'St Étiennes! You danced like that at St Étiennes?'

'You should have gone to the *thé dansants*.'

'Darling, they were *so* boring.'

'She's a natural,' Mark said. 'She knows Bruno Macallister.'

Olga sat up and looked around. 'Bruno Macallister! Is he here?'

'He's a cousin of Margaret's.'

'Why didn't you say – he's divine. There he is. Bruno!' Olga threw out her free arm, spilling more champagne on her partner who grunted and moved.

Bruno pushed his way through the crowd and leaned over to kiss Olga, grimacing at the man underneath her.

'Is he alive?'

'Just about. I don't even know his name. Bruno darling, why haven't you been to visit your little cousin?' She pouted and some of her mascara began a wet trail down her cheek. 'She lives with me!'

'I didn't know she lived with you. I'm not sure her parents would approve.'

'Not approve of me?' Olga shrieked with laughter and the man beneath her stirred and began to try and heave her away.

'Oh he *is* alive! Goody. What's your name darling and where do you come from?' She looked at him curiously as though he had crawled out of a hole. He straightened up, put an arm round her neck and tried to kiss her. Olga shuddered and pushed him away.

'Isn't he horrible!' She stood up suddenly, shaking her startling silver fulgurante evening dress which was backless with draped hip panniers over a short skirt. Around her head, low on her forehead, was a silver band to which were attached ostrich feather tips. The man she had been sitting on abruptly fell lengthways, disappearing under the table. 'I think he's drunk.' Olga gazed at him, then down at her new, very expensive dress. 'Oh dear, and I'm very wet.'

'So is he.' Bruno glanced at the recumbent figure. 'And so are you. Drunk, I mean.'

'I am not drunk! What a nasty thing to say.' She draped her arms round his neck and tugged him towards the dance floor, wiggling her behind provocatively. 'Let's dance, Bruno.'

'I'm dancing with Maggie. If you can still stand up I'll dance with you next.' He reached for Margaret's hand and, not quite knowing what to do, she gave it to him and allowed him to lead her away.

'That was a bit brutal wasn't it?' she said as he took her in his arms, leading her into a slow foxtrot.

He looked surprised. 'Brutal? I don't understand.'

'The way you spoke to Olga.'

'Oh, she's too drunk to take it in.' He held her tighter, leaning his head against hers. 'How on earth did you come to be living with her?'

'I knew her at finishing school. My father sent me there to learn how to be a lady.'

'I see, and you met Olga!' Bruno threw back his head and laughed. 'If only he knew!'

'Is her reputation really as bad as that?'

Bruno nodded seriously. 'Very bad. Her mother had a reputation too. They run in families. Now, how long have you been in London and why didn't you tell me you were here?'

'I didn't want it to get around at home. Father thinks I'm on holiday. In fact I'm working. I wrote to your friend Tristan Fleming and he gave me a job. I hope you don't mind, Bruno.'

Bruno didn't reply at once, circling with her round the small patch of floor, holding her firmly. At length he said, 'I don't mind. I just wish you'd taken me into your confidence. I can keep a secret too, you know. Or was there something else?'

He paused and looked at her and several couples collided with them. Margaret was glad it was so hot because she knew she was blushing. He was thinking of the night in the car and so was she. She raised her head and smiled at him.

'Maybe there was something else.'

'You didn't want to see me? There was nothing to be ashamed of you know.'

'I am not ashamed. I'm just not . . .'

'No commitment, nothing. A kiss in the car.' He shrugged and resumed dancing. 'People do it all the time.'

'*I* don't do it all the time.'

'I'm glad. As long as you feel like that you won't take after Olga.'

'That's a rotten thing to say.'

She looked up at him, her eyes glinting. He gazed deliberately over her head, still pressing her close. She remembered he'd been married; he'd served in the war. He made her feel vulnerable and slightly silly, young and inexperienced. He pressed her tighter and leaned his cheek against hers.

'I'm not a rotter really. Will you have dinner with me tomorrow?'

'I can't be late. I'm working. In fact I must go home now.'

The clock on the wall said it was nearly midnight.

'I'll take you home.' He stopped dancing abruptly. 'Do you have anything to pick up from the table?'

'Only my purse. My coat's in the cloakroom.'

'I'll get your purse. You wait for me by the door.'

'Shouldn't I . . .'

'I'll explain.'

She watched him as he walked away through the crowd. He was in control, masterful. She didn't really know whether she wanted to be controlled or mastered, not by this cousin, this much older man.

He took her home in a cab, saying nothing until they stopped outside the door. In the half light from the street lamp he looked at her.

'You're really very determined, Margaret, aren't you?'

'Determined to do what?'

'I don't know. Get what you want in life. Taking this job without telling your father; doing it on your own. You'll have to tell him sometime. He'll get to hear about it. He's bound to.'

'I'll tell him soon. I just wanted to see how it would work out.'

'You are a mannequin?'

'Yes. I love it. I love fashion and life in the store. And now I have to go to bed early and get my beauty sleep.'

'I'll see you get your beauty sleep.' He leaned over and kissed her lightly on the cheek. 'I'll pick you up at about seven tomorrow. All right?'

'All right.'

He opened the door for her and she got out. He waited until she had unlocked the door and as she stood on the threshold he waved.

She waved back. She felt she was on the verge of a new important experience.

CHAPTER SIX

The boom of the immediate post-war year, 1919, was over. 1920 had been a year of disputes, industrial unrest and even talk of a general strike. At Paisley the Coalition government headed by Lloyd George had lost its eighth seat since the General Election in 1918. Atrocities continued on a daily basis in Ireland and the Lord Mayor of Cork died in Brixton Prison after a prolonged fast.

On the brighter side, attempts to conquer the air continued unabated and Colonel van Rynveld and Quintin Brand flew from England to Cape Town, for which they were being knighted by the King. A matrimonial clauses bill gave women the same rights in divorce as men, and women were admitted to full degrees by Oxford University for the first time. The Prince of Wales, eternally popular, returned from a glamorous tour of Australia and New Zealand. The first Court since 1914 was held at Buckingham Palace; Cambridge won the Boat Race and the butter ration was increased from an ounce to an ounce and a half a week.

However, there were still half a million unemployed, of whom 265,000 were ex-servicemen. Russia continued to worry the Western nations although in Lloyd George's opinion Bolshevism was a passing phase that would not survive. Europe was struggling hard to rebuild itself after the war, the Treaty of Versailles which ended it was ratified and the League of Nations was established in Geneva.

Very few of these world events, however, affected those who were determined to have a good time, come what may. It was a mood that prevailed among those who had

returned from a war during which they had never expected to enjoy the sweet life again. Hardly any who had
fought in the war remained untouched by it; it was an
experience that emphatically influenced the mood of the
twenties.

This mood also helped contribute to the emergence of
the new breed of women, very different from their
pre-war sisters. They had shown that they could work as
well as men; many had assisted in the war effort, in
factories and as nurses both at home and right in the heart
of the war zones. Now they tried to free themselves from
their legal and psychological bondage to men, while
continuing to acknowledge their emotional dependence
on them. They cut their hair, shortened their skirts,
smoked, drove cars, drank and wore cosmetics. For a time
no young girl who had not come out would have dreamt of
making up her face. Even by 1920 things were different,
although some went to more extremes than others.

Margaret Dunbar typified the reasonable, new kind of
woman; her friend Olga Pasalaris its extreme. Everything
Margaret did was daring but reasonable; if she did not
dare tell her father she worked, at least she was working in
a store and not in a nightclub, some of which were little
better than brothels. If she smoked and drank it was not in
excess; the make-up she wore was restrained, the clothes
in good taste. She might kiss a man but she would not go
to bed with him. Olga, on the other hand, did everything
to excess. She smoked too much, was frequently drunk,
her clothes though expensive were outrageous, her make-
up exaggerated, and her friendships with men left much to
be desired – though not on the part of the men. They got
exactly what they wanted and she had twice been to a little
clinic in the countryside of Hertfordshire to be relieved of
the consequences.

Margaret sometimes wondered what she was doing
sharing a house with a girl like Olga, yet she was fond of

her. She had seen Olga in despair too many times to envy her and she knew that fundamentally, if unadmittedly, her friend was unhappy. She was rootless and lost, whereas Margaret knew that if the worst should ever come to the worst for her there would always be home; always a place where she would be welcome, where the rivers met in the town on the Scottish Borders where she had been born.

But if Margaret developed during that autumn of 1920, if she deepened her knowledge and expanded her personality it was largely due to Bruno Macallister. He didn't seem to work; he was, he said, exploring a range of things to do and he was available whenever she needed him. Often when she came home the blue Wolseley was outside the door or, if it wasn't, there were sometimes flowers instead and a note. He was amusing, clever, light-hearted and knowledgeable. He knew where to eat and dance, which play to see and which book to read. He took her to Ciros, the Embassy Club and the Café de Paris, to the Grafton Galleries which had a negro band, and to Rectors in Tottenham Court Road which was suitably sleazy and debased. He took her to the Fifty-Fifty in Wardour Street which was well patronized by society and the arts, and to the Silver Slipper, Uncle, the Hambone and the Cave of Harmony, which were patronized by almost everybody. There were tea dances at the Savoy and the Piccadilly Hotel and sumptuous dinners at the Ritz.

He took her back to Half Moon Street and if he could, if they were alone, he kissed her, but he never attempted or suggested anything more. She felt that half of her was in love with him and half wasn't; there was still a peculiar chilling quality about him that prevented her from doing what all the other young girls were doing – falling in love.

It was that Bruno did everything almost too well. He was punctilious, courteous, he arrived on time; he looked right, dressed well for whatever occasion, dinner, *thé dansants*, a nightclub or the theatre.

107

They saw *The White-headed Boy* at the Ambassadors, *Lord Richard in the Pantry* at the Criterion, *Chu Chin Chow* at His Majesty's, *The Prude's Fall* at Wyndhams, *French Leave* at the Apollo and Fay Compton as Barrie's *Mary Rose* at the Haymarket. They saw almost everything. London was continually and frantically, in those post-war years, bent on having a good time and the productions at the theatres reflected this diversity.

September and October passed and Hector Dunbar wrote to ask Margaret when she was coming home. She never asked for more money and he wanted to know why. He threatened to come down and see for himself, so she wrote and told Susan about her job and asked her to tell her father. For some days she heard nothing.

One evening after a tiring day she put her key in the door and as she opened it she heard voices from the lounge – Olga laughing loudly and a deeper murmur that was familiar. She tossed her hat on the hallstand and rushed in.

'Cullum!'

Cullum got to his feet, smiling awkwardly; he put out his arms and embraced her, then held her away and looked at her.

'I'd hardly have recognized you.'

'Oh Cullum, she hasn't changed *that* much!' Olga, cigarette in her mouth, got up and took his empty glass. 'I'm mixing cocktails darling, will you have one?'

'Not too much gin.' Margaret collapsed into a chair and looked at her brother. 'You've come about the letter?'

'Father wants you to come home with me.'

'Well I'm not coming.' She took the glass Olga held out for her. 'Thanks.' She grimaced as she sipped it. 'Oh it *is* a bit strong on the gin.'

'I thought you'd need it darling, with the ominous note from the parent.'

'There's a note?'

108

Cullum handed her a letter. She opened the envelope, trying to still a feeling of agitation.

'Dear Margaret, (her father wrote)

It was with a heavy heart that I learned of your rashness in taking employment in London without asking my permission. May I remind you that you are still a minor and subject to my jurisdiction.

Cullum is coming to London to attend the burial of the Unknown Warrior as the representative of our family and I have asked him to bring you home.

If you do not come you will be hearing from my solicitor.

Your loving but sorrowful father,

Hector Dunbar.'

Margaret finished her cocktail and placed the letter on her knee. 'I see,' she said. 'It is rather final isn't it?'

'I'm afraid it is.' Cullum crossed his legs. 'He says he will have you made a ward of court.'

'Oh how preposterous!' Olga seized Margaret's glass and vigorously agitated the cocktail shaker. 'He really is a dragon. What will you do darling?'

'I'll go home and explain things to him. I'll tell him that if he insists on my staying at home I will not disobey him, but that as soon as I am twenty-one I will leave home for good and come to live in London.'

'She will too,' Cullum said, looking at Olga.

'Yes I will. Father is being absolutely absurd.'

'You should have told him, Maggie. He thinks you have been deceitful.'

'Do you?'

Cullum avoided her eyes. 'I was a bit shocked, I must say. So is Susan.'

'And Mary of course.'

'Of course. They think you haven't been straight with Father.'

109

'How could I be straight with him, knowing what he'd say?'

Cullum shrugged and drained his glass. 'I've got two tickets for the ceremony if you want to come with me. They came from Malcolm's old regiment.'

'I'm going with Bruno.'

'Bruno? Bruno Macallister?'

'Yes.'

Margaret took her fresh drink from Olga and then told Cullum how she and Bruno had met and how they were seeing quite a lot of each other.

'I see. Another thing Father doesn't know.' Cullum's voice was reproving.

'Cullum, I'm not going to spend my life telling Father everything. Or you, for that matter.'

'I can see that, Maggie. I don't think Bruno has behaved very honourably either, if he knew about your job. We only saw his parents last week.'

'Maybe he hasn't told them. We're not in love or anything like that! Don't be silly.'

Olga sat down nursing her third cocktail and stared frankly at Cullum. 'You know you are quite, quite delicious.' She sipped her drink, gazing at him over the rim of the glass. She had on a coat-frock, low-waisted and strapped with leather. They were popular in London but, as a fashion, had not reached the Scottish Borders, and Cullum was both shocked and rather intrigued at the display of leg encased in flesh-coloured stockings. She had several rows of beads round her neck and wore a small silk hat with drooping feathers that curled over her brow. It was difficult to tell whether she was going out or coming in. In fact she had been in all day, having only got up at four, and was waiting to receive callers who were invited in for cocktails between seven and nine. Then she always went out.

Cullum was quite unused to women dressed like Olga who called him 'delicious' and he blushed and inspected his stubby countryman hands, with their square fingers.

'Darling, you didn't tell me you had such a divine brother.' Olga looked soulfully at Margaret. 'Hiding him away in those Highlands of yours.'

'The Borders,' Margaret said smiling.'Don't embarrass him.'

'I could come to the Abbey with you.' Olga moved her chair closer to Cullum. 'Seeing that Margaret is going already. I would simply *adore* it.'

'The seats are not in the Abbey, but in Whitehall.'

'Oh. Aren't you going to the Abbey, Margaret?'

'Yes, Bruno had a friend who won two VCs and is going to be in the Abbey to represent his mother. They are his tickets. Outside is still very nice.'

'They're near the Cenotaph,' Cullum said. 'You'll get a good view of the King.'

'I suppose that will do,' Olga shrugged. 'Better than nothing.'

As the sun sank over Boulogne they had brought the body 'from the Ypres front' and put it aboard HMS *Verdun* lying in the harbour. The plain pine coffin had been placed in one made of oak, iron-bound and with a sword from the King's personal collection fastened to the lid bearing the inscription:

A British Warrior who fell in the Great War 1914/18.

This was the Unknown Soldier, whose body had been selected at random from the many anonymous dead, and whose burial in Westminster Abbey was to serve as a homage to the fallen, a reminder of the huge sacrifice in lives of those who had fought for liberty.

Now, two days later, in the golden haze of morning, a gentle autumnal mist obscuring both Westminster and Trafalgar Square, the multitude, the bereaved, the servicemen and ex-servicemen, the great and the humble led by the King himself waited in Whitehall to pay their last respects.

111

Covered with the Padre's Flag, the Union Jack which had been through the entire campaign on the Western Front, and borne on top of a gun carriage drawn by six black horses, the coffin trundled through the streets of London filled with silent, mourning crowds. There was no bunting, no gaily waving flags, no streamers or brightly coloured awnings such as had decked the route for the Victory Parade the year before. What few official flags there were hung limply at half mast, and the only flowers were arranged in formal wreaths or bound with ribbons of black, to be laid at the Cenotaph after the ceremony.

> Who is he that cometh, like an honoured guest,
> With banner and with music, with soldier and with priest,
> With a nation weeping . . .

Preceding the solitary coffin was a party of Life Guards making a rare and splendid splash of colour with their red coats, white plumes and shining cuirasses. Behind them were four mounted policemen with their prancing horses, and following them the bands of the four regiments of Foot Guards, the wailing pipes of the Scots Guards and the drummers banging with muffled sticks on drums encased in black. Just in front of the gun carriage marched the Firing Party and the Bearer Party, both drawn from the Third Battalion of the Coldstream Guards, and ranged on either side of the coffin were the distinguished pall-bearers, representatives of the Navy and Air Force on the right side, the Army on the left.

Behind the coffin wound the long ribbon of men, some in uniform and some not. The colours ranged from khaki, navy blue and slate blue to the more exotic colours of the Indian regiments and the sombre blacks, browns and blues of civilian dress. There were hats of all kinds: the reds and yellows of the Indian turbans mingling with the peaked and forage caps of service personnel; the top hats of black-coated gentlemen who had undoubtedly been of

112

the officer class, and the cloth caps of the brown or blue-suited Tommies and others who had served in the ranks. Some were limping and some walked with sticks; some were blind, led along by their comrades. And as this pathetic but heroic remnant passed, reminding many who had served in the war of guiding wounded, blinded and gassed comrades through the trenches and dugouts, those in the crowd whose eyes had hitherto remained dry now broke down and wept.

The gun carriage with its burden reached the massed ranks of the onlookers, who on a more cheerful occasion would be waving flags and shouting but who now stood humbly silent, while the Guardsmen lining the route slowly reversed arms in a majestic gesture and stood over them with hands clasped and heads bowed in memory of comrades who were no more.

In front of the veiled Cenotaph the gun carriage drew abreast of the King and the royal princes who saluted as it came to a halt. Then the King, stepping forward, reverently placed a wreath beside the trench helmet and the side-arms which were the coffin's sole adornments, as behind it the twelve distinguished pallbearers formed a single line across the road.

When the chimes of Westminster struck a quarter to eleven the long column of mourners representing the fighting services parted to right and left, coming into line three deep on each side of the Cenotaph. As the procession came to rest, the band played the opening notes of *O God our help in ages past*, which was taken up by the massed Abbey choir in white surplices and by those in the crowd whose emotions still enabled them to sing.

Olga, dressed in black, threw back her head and gave voice, her eyes on the sheet in front of her. But Cullum found himself so blinded by tears that he could not see, and his throat so choked he could not sing. They had seats on the stand just below the Home Office. Behind them in the windows banked with purple stood Queen Mary,

113

Queen Alexandra, the Queen of Spain and the royal princesses.

All during the singing the drums never stopped their awesome rolling, almost submerging the sound of brass and voices. When the hymn was finished the Archbishop of Canterbury, facing the coffin, intoned the Lord's Prayer which was taken up by the whole congregation. '. . . For ever and ever, Amen'. The echoing words were interrupted as Big Ben's chimes boomed out again: eleven o'clock. The King, touching a button, released the flags which hid the Cenotaph. They fell away, revealing Sir Edwin Lutyens' great monument to the dead carved in white stone.

As Big Ben ceased, the entire assemblage bowed their heads in a silence broken only by the quiet, heart-rending sobbing of many of the bereaved. Then, suddenly, the strident triumphant notes of the Last Post sounded and the King laid a large wreath on the north side of the base of the Cenotaph. He was followed by the Prince of Wales, the Prime Minister and representatives of the Colonies and the peoples of France.

Now the Archbishop of Canterbury and his assistant clergy took their place at the head of the procession. With great solemnity the gun carriage accompanied by its pallbearers moved past the Cenotaph, followed by the King, the princes, the members of the government and other dignitaries. The mourners from the fighting services marched in stately line, six abreast, and the vast concourse assembled in Whitehall, those in the streets and those in the stands, at the windows and on the surrounding balconies, watched in muted reverence as the cortège made its way towards the final resting place of the Unknown.

When the procession had moved away, four sentries from each of the services, leaning on reversed arms, took up their stations at the four corners of the Cenotaph, while from Scotland Yard emerged a line of policemen to lay their wreaths until the entire base was a mass of flowers.

Cullum, his eyes still misted with tears, gazing at the retreating coffin, felt a hand grasp his. He turned his head and looked at Olga's mournful face, infinitely compassionate.

'I understand,' she whispered. 'Many of my family perished in the war. Like your brother we do not know where some of them lie. Believe me I am with you, Cullum, and with Margaret.'

The smile was so beautiful, the eyes so understanding that he felt a surge of gratitude and, taking her hand, pressed it. So, hands linked, they descended with the rest of the bereaved towards the street.

The great vaulted interior of Westminster Abbey seemed to radiate with a rich, melancholy light. All eyes of the thousand-strong congregation, most of them women, rested almost hypnotically on the coffin-shaped aperture of the grave in the centre of the nave. It was surrounded by a broad low platform covered with a white-edged purple cloth, the whole dappled by the flecks of coloured sunlight that streamed through the ancient stained-glass windows.

Margaret and Bruno had been in their seats in the nave since nine o'clock. They had arrived at the Abbey just as, not far away in Victoria Station, the coffin of the Unknown Warrior was being loaded onto the gun carriage in preparation for its journey through the crowded, hushed London streets.

For a time they had sat in silence, occasionally smiling to greet a familiar face, watching the progress of the sun in its path through the windows, along the pillars of the nave until it rested on the grave. Margaret was thankful that it was a sunny day; somehow rain would have made what was scarcely bearable intolerable.

115

Now precisely at ten o'clock to the music of the band of the Grenadier Guards, the one hundred officers and other ranks who had been awarded the Victoria Cross, commanded by Colonel Freyburg V.C., took up their places as guard of honour on either side of the gangway from the screen to the grave. All the while the monotonous toll of the funeral bell rang out above London, accompanying, like the persistent melancholic beat of a metronome, the sounds of the music playing both within the Abbey and outside it.

The congregation consisted mainly of the bereaved, mostly, sadly, wives and mothers. Margaret felt she too had her place there, because among all the war dead was her brother Malcolm. Like thousands of others whose loved ones had no known grave, she wondered if the aperture in the ground were being prepared as the last resting place for him. Six bodies had been selected from the war areas in France and, lying in closed coffins, one had been chosen at random. No one knew who, whether he was an officer, or a man from the ranks, a lord or a commoner. All that was known was that he had died fighting for England.

Perhaps the decision to bury an unknown soldier in the Abbey was intended not only as a tribute but to allow each bereaved person to think that maybe their lover, their son or husband was the body in the coffin, and to take comfort from it. The Unknown represented, not the least for the Dunbar family, the faint hope that their own dead had a known resting place after all.

Bruno Macallister, who was still in the Royal Air Force reserve, was in uniform, the badges of rank on his sleeve; the DFC, the Air Force Cross and campaign medals on his chest. Around his neck was the ribbon of the Légion d'Honneur awarded by the French for heroic action over Arras when he had nursed his stricken plane home thus sustaining the wound to his face.

His presence comforted Margaret; the glances he gave

116

her, the occasional pressure of his hand brought consolation. For he had been there and he had survived. Margaret was dressed entirely in black, a long black coat almost to her ankles with a black fur collar and cuffs, a close-fitting hat with a circular band of black feathers. In her lap was a small, slightly wilting posy of flowers inscribed 'To Malcolm' which she hoped she would have the chance to lay on the grave.

Precisely at half-past ten, to the tune *O Valiant Hearts*, the Dean, wearing a black embroidered cope, headed a procession up the nave from the grave to the High Altar, its gleaming plate dimly lit by candles. When the clergy had assembled in the sanctuary the organist played the first chords of *O God our help in ages past* which was taken up as vigorously as possible by all those who were able, though many of the women broke down and one or two had to be escorted from their places. As the great strains of the hymn faded away the congregation knelt for prayers led by the Precentor.

> Lord have mercy
> Christ have mercy
> Lord have mercy
> Our Father which art in heaven . . .

The words of the Lord's Prayer were scarcely concluded when the great bell of the Abbey boomed the first stroke of the hour and, suddenly, unexpectedly overcome by emotion, tears gushed down Margaret's face and she covered it with her hands.

'Oh God,' she whispered silently, 'have mercy on Malcolm, and Ian Lyall, the Pendreigh brothers, Hamish Fairholme, Ian Macpherson and Hilda Mactavish who was torpedoed at sea.'

Even that small litany of names from one tiny part of the British Empire did not encompass all the people she knew who had died. How many more were there, magnified a million times, from all corners of the globe? How

117

many women would never sleep by their husbands again, perhaps never again know the love of a man? How many mothers would never again embrace the sons they had borne, and how many children never be enveloped or raised up in loving, fatherly arms? There were millions, millions – all colours and all creeds from the world over – Europe, the Near and Far East and the Americas. This had been a global war from which few had escaped, one way and another. And this was not to take count of those who had survived only to live lives of suffering: blinded, maimed, incurably brain-damaged or mentally ill.

'Oh God let there never be a war again . . .'

Lost in her grief, locked in her own thoughts – grief and thoughts which she shared with so many others – she could not have said how long the silence lasted as the great clock struck eleven times. Then an anguished sob from among the crowd brought them abruptly back from oblivion, breaking the tension, and the organ intervened gently, insidiously, with the opening strains of the exquisite hymn 'Contakion.'

More prayers followed and then singing *Brief life is here our portion* the choir processed to the North Porch and out of the Abbey to receive the body of the Unknown Soldier. From outside came the slow, melancholy strains of Chopin's Funeral March as the cortège reached its destination. Still the relentless tolling of the bell continued, until the words 'I am the resurrection and the life' echoed through the Abbey, and the Burial Service had begun.

Every eye in that vast church from whatever vantage point strained for a glimpse of the coffin borne on the shoulders of its bearers. Few noticed the King walking behind, the Prince of Wales or other princes of the blood, the Prime Minister and statesmen, the military leaders and high state dignitaries who followed. Very few noticed Queen Mary who, with three other queens, princesses and

118

their ladies, came in from a side door, quietly taking her place at a purple-covered dais near the grave.

The unaccompanied choir sang the opening sentences of the burial service and then *Man is born of a woman* to the music of Croft and Purcell, as the processional came into view beneath the screen and the coffin was reverently lowered onto the open bars of the grave. The King took his place at its head, facing west.

Margaret tried to recall Malcolm's face. Was it lying under that flag, scarred, maybe unrecognizable? Or was it still somewhere in the French earth, sinking deeper into the ground; or were his bones disintegrating in some grave marked 'unknown'? How had he died? Had he felt pain? Had he known fear? A bird seemed to flutter in the ceiling, maybe it had flown in through the great doors with the coffin and, glancing upwards, she imagined that she saw the soul of the dead, free at last, ascend to heaven.

The twenty-third Psalm was read by the Dean and, during the singing of the hymn *Lead Kindly Light*, the bearers came forward. They removed from the coffin the King's wreath, the steel helmet and side-arms and then, very gently, as though laying an infant in its cot, they lowered the coffin into its final resting place, on soil that had been there since the foundations of the Abbey had been built. The King was handed a silver shell of earth taken from France which he sprinkled on the coffin while the Dean committed the body with the words:

'Earth to earth, ashes to ashes, dust to dust.'

As Kipling's hymn *Recessional* concluded the service, a great wave of released emotion seemed to surge through the congregation, many of whom, men and women, openly at last gave way to tears.

The Dean spoke the blessing, after which there was a pause. Then, very softly at first like a surreptitious whisper, a roll of drums commenced, slowly gathering momentum

119

until it became a powerful, heart-throbbing roar deafening the ears of all who heard, and then gently diminishing again as an echo does, faint and fainter still, seeming to say: 'Did you hear me, did you hear me souls of the dead? For we shall all rise again and death shall be no more. Yes, we *shall* see God.'

Then scarcely had the last drum notes faded when, from high up in the arcades, the bugles called the Reveille, a startling, commanding strident summons to resurrection, to the glorious wakening from misery and heartbreak and death.

Margaret looked up as though she had heard the call and understood its message. Her eyes were dry.

'Good-bye Malcolm,' she whispered. 'Rest in peace.'

As she turned Bruno gently took her hand, entwining his fingers through hers, pressing them to his chest.

CHAPTER SEVEN

After the ceremony Bruno and Margaret joined the thousands who passed along by the side of the grave. Then they walked through Parliament Square to Whitehall, and took their places at the end of the long queue waiting to pass the newly erected Cenotaph, stretching from Downing Street to Trafalgar Square. They spoke a little, sometimes about the war, sometimes about mundane things, but above all they seemed to share a mutual sympathy, a likeness of mind which the tragedy and glory of this day had enhanced. The dead did not really slumber; if they lived at all it was in another dimension. But it was as though, that day, the heart-beat of the nation slept quietly in that awesome grave awaiting the sound of the last trumpet.

That day Margaret began to wonder seriously about her feelings for Bruno, about a possible future with him. Bonds she knew were not really forged by dancing, by dating in smart restaurants or stealing furtive kisses in darkened hallways or the front of the car. Attraction came from that and, perhaps, a kind of love, but the deep caring that, in Margaret's youthful view, made a lifetime's partnership, came from experiences like this, shared in common, almost divinely inspired; a meeting of twin souls, a thankfulness in being alive and enjoying life together.

Later they ate at a restaurant in St Christopher's Place, near where Bruno lived. It was full of like-minded couples, most of them dressed in mourning, many of the men in uniform. There was no excessive gaiety or laughter, but nor was there melancholy. It was the quiet sort of celebration that comes after a funeral, respect for the dead tinged with relief that one still lived.

When Bruno suggested afterwards that they walk across

121

the road to his flat, it never occurred to Margaret to do anything but accept. There was no hint in his invitation of anything other than a desire to extend the comradeliness and companionship, the intimacy engendered by the events of that tremendous day.

Margaret had never before been inside Bruno's flat. It was on the second floor of a tall red-brick nineteenth-century house in Wimpole Street, a few doors along from where – many years before – Elizabeth Barrett had lived waiting to be rescued from her reclusive life by Robert Browning. It was a furnished flat consisting of two intercepting rooms, a bathroom and a very small kitchen. There were a number of other apartments in the house occupied by well-to-do bachelors like Bruno, serviced by a couple who lived in the basement. The man cooked breakfasts, valeted clothes and cleaned cars which were kept in the mews behind. The woman cleaned, made beds and kept the house spotless with the help of a daily maid.

The furniture was heavy, functional but quite tasteful: a large leather sofa, leather armchairs, bookshelves in the alcoves on either side of the fireplace with heavy unread volumes bound in leather. There was a large mahogany sideboard, a couple of occasional tables, and a small folding table by the window, a good Wilton carpet on the floor and a Persian rug by the hearth. When they arrived a fire burned in the grate behind a wire-mesh guard and illumination came from a solitary standard lamp in one corner by the side of a small leather-topped desk which was clear except for a blotter, a pen holder and a bottle of ink.

Margaret, appreciating the relaxed, masculine atmosphere, removed her hat and outer coat and sank into one of the deep leather chairs in front of the fire. She wore a belted coat and skirt, also in black, with a white button-up blouse underneath. She was pale and there were dark rings round her eyes.

'Brandy?' Bruno put a glass in her hand without waiting

122

for an answer and at the same time switched on a small table lamp by the side of the chair. Margaret smiled at him and stretched her legs.

'It's very nice here. Very peaceful. It was a lovely meal, thank you. A lovely day – a tragic day, but lovely.' He bent impulsively and kissed her cheek, then took her hand and kissed that too. 'Did you ever think you would die Bruno? Not come back?'

Bruno straightened up and, taking his own brandy from the sideboard, sat opposite her unbuttoning the slate blue jacket of his uniform which fastened at the neck showing a white shirt and stiff collar underneath. He looked very distinguished and handsome.

'No, I never thought that. It never crossed my mind. I don't think any of us ever allowed it to cross our minds, because the only way to survive was to think you could not die. And yet all round us were the dead and dying; every day men who had flown with us did not come back. What was the point of thinking you would not survive?' He shrugged his shoulders and smiled.

It was then that Margaret imagined herself to be in love with him. That rather crooked smile on his face, because of the scar that divided his right cheek, now made him lovable in her eyes, not evil. Had she really ever thought he was evil? His dark brown eyes blazed at her and a lock of the carefully brilliantined hair fell over his forehead. Was what she had thought of as evil really the distillation of her own fear, a desire to find fault in someone she found almost frighteningly attractive?

She closed her eyes and when she opened them again the expression on his face had changed, as though he had known what she was thinking. The air around them seemed suddenly charged with the sort of static electricity that precedes thunder.

'I wish I hadn't come here tonight,' she said.

'Why?' He put down his glass and crouched by her on the floor, taking her hand.

123

'I don't know. It's just that . . .' She shook her head and felt tears in her eyes. 'I feel very emotional. It has been a very emotional day hasn't it? I thought so much about Malcolm and Ian and all those who didn't come back and . . . you.' She looked at him and the tears started to pour down her face. 'You might not have come back either. I couldn't bear to think of that.'

He took her hand and stroked it tenderly with the back of his thumb. 'But I did. I did come back. It's no use thinking about what might have been.'

'I think I'm in love with you,' Margaret blurted out. Then she continued hurriedly, 'But I don't really know what love is. I mean I haven't been in love before. Is that strange?'

He smiled at her and again his lips brushed her hand. 'Never? Not a little bit, with anyone?'

'Well, with Ruthven Pendreigh, perhaps. Perhaps just a little bit with him; but then our families fell out and that was the end of that.'

'But he's just a boy!' Bruno laughed, and getting up from the floor, removed his jacket. Then he sat on the arm of her chair and put his arm around her shoulder.

'He's not a boy! He's older than Cullum. Well, maybe compared to you he's a boy.'

She looked up at him and felt the need to be reassured by him; he was so much older than she was, so much stronger. Did he love her at all? Had he been courting her or what? How did he see her; how did he feel about her? She realized she knew nothing about his innermost feelings; simply that he was urbane, sophisticated, correct, exciting and good to be with. He obviously found her good to be with too; but what did he really feel about her? She felt confused and wanted to know.

Bruno bent down and kissed her firmly on the mouth and she leaned back and closed her eyes, aware of his hand unbuttoning her jacket, groping for her breasts. A pleasing, erotic sensation gripped her and she grasped him round the neck, pulling him so close that eventually she felt stifled.

When they drew away his eyes were dark and a large throbbing vein stood out on his forehead.

'It's very uncomfortable here Margaret.'

She saw his eyes travel to the half open door that led into the bedroom. He stood up abruptly, reaching for her hand, half pulling her out of her chair. She got to her feet and he embraced her again, gently removing her jacket, tossing it on the chair she had left.

'Come on,' he murmured.

'Come where?'

'It's much more comfortable lying down.'

She moved away from him and tried to tuck her blouse back into her skirt. 'I think I should go home.' She knew she sounded timid and uncertain and she felt it; she really didn't know what to do.

He began to unfasten his stiff clerical-like collar, then took a cigarette from a silver box on the mantelpiece and lit it, throwing the match impatiently into the fire.

'Margaret, I don't want to seduce you. We can just lie and hold each other. It's pleasant isn't it? Look, like this.'

He dropped to the floor and pulled her down so that they sat facing each other rather awkwardly, the light from the flames flickering in their faces. He looked very noble and strong with his livid scar and his bright, almost feverish eyes, his tousled, curly black hair falling now quite freely over his forehead. He leaned forward and kissed her again just on the lips and then, lying recumbent, made a cushion for her head with his arm and motioned for her to lie beside him.

She did as he bade, her back to the floor, her head propped uncomfortably on his extended arm.

'You look quite pale with fright,' he said, bending over her. 'Don't be a silly goose.'

She felt like a goose, waiting to be plucked, as his free hand quickly and expertly unbuttoned her blouse and he

125

scooped first one breast and then the other from the inadequate restriction of her silk petticoat and buried his face between them. The free hand roved swiftly over her body, tugged unsuccessfully at the waistband of her skirt and then caressed her stockinged knees, moving upwards across the inside of her thighs, past the rolled tops of her stockings, beneath her silk camiknickers until it rested on her bare groin. But somehow she didn't think it would stop there. The very fact he had got so far, and with such ease, such little resistance, terrified her and any languorous, teasing desire she had for him fled. She began to struggle, pushing the obscene intrusive hand away from where it had started to probe and desperately trying to pull down her skirt. She was aware that she had let him go much, much too far.

'Please don't, Bruno!'

She sat up, shamefully conscious of her bare breasts, the nipples strangely pink and moist from his kisses, the prickly burning flush that she felt spreading from her chest to her face. She hastily rearranged her petticoat to cover her nudity, aware of her flapping blouse, her crumpled skirt; aware, above all, of the shoddy indignity of the situation. She didn't know how people could call love a noble thing if it were like this.

Bruno was trembling too, looking very angry; and she wondered why she should feel humiliated if he did not. It was true that he didn't look quite as dishevelled as she; but then this was obviously something he was used to.

'You're leading me on, Margaret,' he snapped.

'I'm *not* leading you on,' she replied indignantly. 'You said we were just going to lie together.'

'Come on, you're not as naive as that. What about your friend Olga?'

'What *about* Olga?' she enquired hotly. 'I'm not like her.'

'No, at least Olga doesn't tease. Men don't like teasers.'

'I'm not teasing.'

'Then don't.' He put an arm around her, a lazy, amorous look again in his eyes. 'Come on, relax. You're making a great thing about this, you know. Anyone would think you'd never done it before.'

'I haven't.'

'I'd almost believe you, if I didn't know what a hot number you were.'

Suddenly, brutally, he pushed her down on the floor, tugging ferociously at the front of her petticoat. She felt a strap snap as it came away and a breast fell lewdly outside the shattered garment. Fumbling with the buttons on his trousers Bruno now lunged astride her, ruffling her skirt up over her waist, a hand rudely intruding again beneath her silk knickers.

Her distaste and fear now grew to an overwhelming panic. As his mouth bore harshly down on hers, she bit savagely into his lips, tearing at his hands, kneading him in the groin with her knee.

'God damn you, you bitch!'

As the blood started to spurt from his lip he rose with a roar, standing over her, a terrifying yet slightly comical figure in long underpants with his trousers round his knees. As though her last moments were upon her she scrambled to her feet, dodged past him and ran into his bedroom, closing the door sharply behind her. Quickly she turned the key, and then she stood gazing at the door, distraught and very afraid.

After a while she tottered over to his bed and sank upon it, gazing listlessly at herself in the oval mirror of his dressing table. Her chest was red with weals and one breast still hung naked on the side with the broken petticoat strap. Beneath her crumpled black gabardine skirt, so immaculate at the beginning of the day, one stocking was round her knee and the other had a gash in it as though she'd caught it on a nail. Her hair was disordered and her make-up spoiled, grotesque on her tear-stained face. She thought she looked ridiculous and absurd and she hated herself.

'Oh God,' she sighed and put her head in her hands.

No sound came from the other side of the door. Slowly she got up and combed her hair, her hand trembling, with the silver-backed comb on his dresser. She pulled up her stocking and tied a knot in the broken strap. She dabbed at her face with a handkerchief and then she went and stood facing the closed door, her pulse still throbbing in her neck.

Slowly she turned the key and, opening the door, peered into the room.

Bruno, now fully clothed, his tunic fastened to the neck, stood with his back to her puffing a cigarette. She stole into the room and picked up her blouse, quickly putting it on and fastening it, then her jacket which lay on the chair. She groped round for her black court shoes and found them under the desk. Finally she put on her hat with the band of black feathers, looking disconcertingly correct, and the long, elegant woollen coat.

'Could you take me home, Bruno?'

'You can take yourself home, you stupid bitch!' He turned round snarling and she saw now that he really could look very evil indeed. What had chilled her before was mild compared to the terrifying aspect he presented now. 'Did you think I was going to rape you or something? Everything that you got, you wanted.'

'I didn't . . .'

He held up a hand, the tip of his cigarette glowing. 'Don't come to me with your sobs and protests. You knew damn well what coming here meant. A woman who really has no intention of making love to a man doesn't go alone to his flat at the dead of night. I thought when you accepted my invitation you *knew* what you were doing. Oh I knew you were a virgin, don't look at me like that.

128

You've got virginity written all over you. I thought it was something you were anxious to get rid of, like Olga.'

'You keep on comparing me with Olga.' Margaret's voice was low and she looked into the fire knowing that her face was red with humiliation.

'In fact I like Olga better,' he continued airily. 'You know where you are with Olga. Look, Miss Dunbar, I've been in the war; I've faced death every day for four years. I thought I might never know a woman again, never sleep with one, never feel her body next to mine. I'm not a boy, you know. I'm a man, a fighter. I've no time for silly virgins who think they can go so far but no further. I thought you'd appreciate that by now. Why do you think I've been courting you for all these weeks? I'll tell you why. I wanted to go to bed with you, to make love to you. I desired you terribly – then. Now you make me sick! You're a washout. Go away.'

Margaret walked slowly to the door of his flat, thankful that her long coat prevented him seeing how much she was trembling. She drew on her black gloves as slowly as she could and tried to straighten her hat with what little shred of dignity and aplomb she felt he had left her. Then she stopped.

'Bruno!'

He gazed sharply back at her, his lip curled with contempt, a fleck of white cigarette paper on his lower lip.

She raised her head and her beautiful aquamarine eyes were like swirling whirlpools reflecting rage and humiliation, while there was a high colour on her cheeks.

'I want to say this to you Bruno. Tonight you have behaved as I never thought any man could behave, certainly not a cousin, someone I have known and who has known me all my life, someone who has known my family and my dead brother Malcolm. What makes it so awful, so contemptible is that it happened *today*, on this day of days. That *you* could have entertained the thoughts you did on a day like this! It was a sacred day, for me anyway and as I walked with you, particularly in St James's Park after it all, I experienced a rapport that I cannot express nor, now, imagine I could feel for you.

'Naive you might think me, and naive I certainly am. Yet I am also – old-fashioned word! – a lady. I trusted you. I would never have started anything like this that I felt would get so out of control. Maybe I should have gone as soon as it started (did I not try?); but never in my wildest dreams, Bruno Macallister, would I have expected anything remotely like this, anything so animal and degrading, from one whom I considered not only a warm friend and companion, not only a cousin, but also, and more importantly, an officer and a gentleman.

'I did not think gentlemen behaved like this.' She raised her head a little higher, feeling her dignity returning, and tilted her chin at him. 'I did not think they took advantage of inexperienced women. For I am inexperienced, I do not deny it, and I *am* a virgin which you seem to regard as some sort of disgrace. Well, I am not ashamed of it; I do not feel disgraced. I have only ever kissed one man in my life before you. Maybe you think Olga set the standard. Well what Olga does she does not do for money, but because she wants to do it. But I do not and what you have done is dirty and vile. It has dishonoured me, and it has dishonoured you. And never, never think I will forget it or expunge it from my memory.'

Now she found she was shaking so much that a terrible cold seemed to have enveloped her, as though she had a fever. She saw, to her satisfaction, the expression on his face change from contempt through anger to stupefaction, and she slammed the door in his face and ran down the stairs out of the front door and into Wimpole Street. It was very dark, a darkness that was only emphasized by the few flickering gas lamps. A fog was starting to form, swirling down from the park at the end of the road. There was no one about and she turned towards Wigmore Street hoping to find a cab. But what few cabs there were were private. Suddenly out of the shadows a man approached her, his smile grotesque in the immediate overhead light from the lamp.

She gave a little scream and fled across the street, down St James's Street, avoiding dark St Christopher's Place where they'd had that lovely romantic dinner only a few hours before, their fingers sometimes meeting across the table.

In Oxford Street there was more traffic but no free cabs. Cars crawled along by the kerb and one or two stopped as she approached. Her fear intensified and she crossed by Selfridges, running down North Audley Street into Grosvenor Square, where the eerie lights outlined couples intertwined beneath the trees despite the cold and the increasing fog. Shivering, she continued swiftly along South Audley Street into Curzon Street which ran alongside Shepherd's Market, where solitary women stood in the shadows or a light occasionally flared casting into silhouette two faces in earnest conversation, a man's and a woman's. Bargaining taking place. One or two women looked at her with hostility and a man started to follow her as she ran into Half Moon Street where, nearing collapse, she put her key into the door wrenching it until it swung open.

Inside the house was in total darkness. No hall light gleamed as it usually did. The clock from the Christian Science Church in Curzon Street chimed two. Margaret did not divest herself of her hat and coat but crept upstairs, still too horrified and ashamed – but above all *angered* – for coherent thought. Now that she was safe her legs appeared to give way and she clutched at the banister for support.

How much of what had happened was her fault? Of course she should never have gone back to his flat; it was all too clear now. But Bruno was a distant relation, someone she had known for years, a man to whom she

131

had come so close in recent weeks as to believe herself in love with. Maybe that night she had hoped he would declare his love for her, perhaps even propose. In the brutal light of what had happened she realized how much she had bound up her fortunes, her future, with Bruno Macallister, war hero, man of experience, protector. What a fool he must think her now; what a fool she thought herself.

She stopped outside Olga's bedroom door. If Olga were awake maybe she could comfort her, because Olga, experienced Olga, did not lack compassion. Was Bruno naturally base by nature or had she been at fault in trusting him?

There was no light from under the door and she was about to tiptoe past when she heard movement and low laughter, then a man's voice. Margaret leaned her head against the door, suddenly feeling nauseous.

The voices were scarcely more than whispers, but there was no doubt as to the identity of Olga's lover. The man in Olga's arms was her brother Cullum.

CHAPTER EIGHT

Margaret put down her book and gazed at her father. For some time now, she realized, she'd been reading to herself, her voice droning on without an audience. Her father was asleep. Or was he? She peered closer but it was difficult to tell. He sat with his chin slumped on his chest, his mouth slightly open, his eyes closed, his breathing regular. But then he often sat or lay like this when, it subsequently transpired, he was wide awake, because if people had been talking round him he would afterwards refer to what had been said.

She leaned forward and touched his shoulder. 'Father?'

But his chin sank lower on his breast and his lips suddenly puckered, releasing a faint snore. Margaret sighed and leaned back. They were in a corner of the terrace, sheltered from any breeze although it was a hot day. Her father wore an overcoat and had a blanket round his legs, well tucked into the corners of the deep armchair which was his favourite when he was downstairs, and was moved to the terrace or the drawing room or wherever he wanted to be. It was moved about like a hospital bed because it was, in fact, for him a kind of hospital: hospice, a shelter. He felt safe and comfortable in it.

Nearly two years had passed since Margaret had returned home with Cullum after the Burial of the Unknown Warrior. She had done what her father had asked her; she had accompanied her brother home. But she had not meant to stay, not for any length of time, certainly not for two years. On the other hand, neither had she wanted to go back to the Half Moon Street house and to life with Olga with all the mischief it had brought about; she had not wanted to return to a possible meeting with Bruno

Macallister, or to resume any of that old life again. All she had wanted to do was to continue with her work.

But this had been denied her. Soon after Christmas 1920, just as she was preparing to go back to London, her father had had a heart attack. Her bags were all packed; everything was ready. Tristan Fleming had acquired lodgings for her with another of his house mannequins in Bedford Square. He had kept her job open for her and was anxious to have her back again.

But how, everyone asked her, could she leave her father when she was partially responsible for what had happened in the first place? Everyone knew that the worry about Margaret on top of everything else had undermined her father's health. Guilty, anxious, Margaret agreed to stay, but just for a time until he got better. She wrote to Fleming resigning her job. His charming reply offered to keep it open for her or to find her another when the time came, whichever the case may be.

That was in January 1921. Now it was August 1922. Two years – well, seventeen months. Seventeen months of dullness, domesticity and a kind of quiet anguish because she felt her life had been cut off in its prime. Susan ran the house and Margaret nursed their father.

At the time Hector Dunbar's heart attack had not been considered a very bad one. In fact it was quite mild; any other man might have made a complete recovery very quickly, but not her father. It was as though he used this indisposition to establish a convenient state of invalidism. He became what he had, perhaps, wanted to be for many years: a professional invalid. Now that he was an invalid people had to stop making demands on him, expecting him to do things he didn't want to do because, he said, he could no longer do them. The doctors assured him that the scar on his heart had healed; that he was perfectly fit and could move and do all the things he had done before.

But, no, he was an invalid. He made that quite clear.

He felt he could have another attack at any moment and so, in order to prevent it, he must move about slowly or, preferably, hardly at all. Some days he didn't get out of bed and, of course, he never went down to the mill. Such an action could, he insinuated, possibly kill him. In fact he never went out of the house except on to the terrace and then very well wrapped up, whatever the weather.

Margaret rose and wandered across the terrace, perching on the low wall that surrounded it. Below her was a lawn encircled by trees and below that the other houses and gardens of the people who lived on the hill. Below them all was the town, misty now in the heat haze that rose from the rivers mingling with the smoke belching forth from the chimneys of the mills. On a day like today the Dunbar Mill could scarcely be seen except as a shadowy outline shimmering through the mist.

In the spring of 1921 Mary had taken Murdoch and returned to live with her parents. Hector, not strong enough to resist, had allowed her to go, though his grief at losing Murdoch didn't help his convalescence. They now hardly ever saw Mary or Murdoch, maybe twice a year. Mary no one missed but not seeing Murdoch, Malcolm's son, grow up was a terrible wrench. When he was really depressed Hector could talk of little else but his absent grandson. One would have thought they had moved to another continent, rather than fifty miles north to Edinburgh.

What a drab, miserable life it was, Margaret thought. From the Pendreigh house came the sound of tennis balls thumping back and forth between racquets. She saw the Pendreighs at social gatherings in the town, she sometimes played with them at the tennis club and Cullum played cricket with Ruthven and Dirk; but they never met privately. The effect of such a meeting on her father would be incalculable. He had traced, time after time, all the events that had led up to his heart attack, and among the two most prominent were the treachery of Elliott Pendreigh and the disobedience of his daughter Margaret in taking a job in London.

There was a step behind her, a hand laid lightly on her shoulder and Margaret half turned. Susan smiled down at her, a cup of tea in her hand.

'How long has he been asleep?'

Margaret took the cup and stirred the tea. 'I don't know. You know he looks like that most of the time. I'm reading Arnold Bennett largely to myself. Luckily I don't mind!'

Susan sat next to her on the parapet with her back to the town so that she could see the house and their father, their shoulders almost touching, one looking one way and the other another.

'Margaret, don't you think you should have a holiday?'

'Where should I go?'

'There are lots of places you can go. Even if you only went to Juliet in Edinburgh it would be a change. She would love to have you. Or you could go to Aunt Ella in Bournemouth, or to . . .'

'What makes you think Father would let me?' Margaret gazed at her, her mouth slightly twisted. 'It might bring on another heart attack.'

'If you took a break? Don't be so cynical.'

'I am being realistic. He doesn't trust me. I told him I was going for a holiday last time. I guarantee that if I said I was going away Father's condition would deteriorate. I'm sure he could just bring on a heart attack by thinking about it. You think I want that on my conscience? I have enough as it is.'

Susan touched the back of her hand. 'I'm sorry. You must feel trapped. I didn't realize it was so bad.'

'Of course I feel trapped! And guilty. Father was an ill man and I made it worse. We didn't realize how ill, but he is ill, was ill. He is mentally ill, but it's just as bad as being

136

physically ill. Well, he is my father and I am responsible for him. Unless he tells me to go away, I will not go.'

'Perhaps he would go too? To Aunt Ella's?'

'You think he would travel all that way?'

'Or Juliet's?'

'He hates Edinburgh. Besides, he's afraid. He wants to stay here and you know it.'

'Yes I do, but I'm worried about you. Quite a lot of people say you don't look well.'

Margaret ran her hands over her face. 'I look drab, but I'm quite well. Physically I'm perfectly well.' She looked at her sister, a little half smile on her lips. 'I tell you, I am quite resigned to my lot – a spinster destined to spend her life caring for her father. I suppose I deserve it.'

'But why should you *deserve* it? What nonsense!'

Margaret had never told Susan about Bruno Macallister, never mentioned his name; but Margaret felt she was paying now for what had happened then. The memory of that terrible débâcle on such a solemn day still haunted her. She felt she had mocked God and now she was being punished. She often thought of that night, especially when she could tell a man was becoming interested in her, when he sought her out as a tennis partner or wanted to take her on the river alone. Whenever this happened, and there were many occasions, she was evasive, even cold, until the message eventually got home and the attentions ceased.

Margaret began to get the reputation among the young men in the town of being an iceberg; some found it attractive and went on trying, but most of them gave up. They were looking for suitable, respectful wives who would not cause trouble, and they had all heard how Margaret had spoken to Elliott Pendreigh in public and how she had brought on her father's heart attack by running away to London and getting a job – as a mannequin! In Branswick, jobs in London and mannequins were

137

synonymous with sin. By her behaviour Margaret Dunbar, though beautiful, had shown that she was neither really suitable nor respectful enough to be a docile wife. Quite a few young men wanted to keep clear of Margaret Dunbar and those who were still attracted felt too scared to press further, knowing what their families would say if they started taking her out. Fast. Even after seventeen months of blameless living in Branswick Margaret had a reputation. She was considered fast. Who *knew* what she'd been up to in London? Why, her father had had to send Cullum to bring her home.

'Did you hear that Ruthven Pendreigh is engaged to Cathy Macdonald?' Susan's words suddenly broke into her thoughts.

'Yes, I heard last night.' The tone of her voice didn't change and she continued to gaze stonily over the town.

'And you don't mind?'

Margaret threw back her head and laughed; not a gay laugh, not a merry mirthful laugh, but a sardonic rather brittle laugh such as Susan only ever seemed to hear from her these days. Margaret scarcely ever laughed gaily or naturally as befitted a young attractive girl who was nearly twenty-one, and Susan knew why. The previous sparkle, the joy in life had seemed slowly to ebb from Margaret since she'd been at home and Susan, too wounded and hurt and brittle herself, felt there was little she could do about it.

'*I* mind about Ruthven?' Margaret looked at her incredulously. 'I haven't had anything to do with Ruthven Pendreigh for three years. Yes it was three years last month, wasn't it, that we had the Peace celebrations? Since that day I have never for a moment been alone with Ruthven Pendreigh.'

'He likes you though.'

'Like me he may! But he would never do anything to upset his parents and no more would I again do anything

138

to upset mine. No Susan, our love never got started. It began and ended on the same day.'

Margaret felt a choking sensation in her throat which surprised her. She really had thought she had ceased to care about Ruthven Pendreigh, as she had ceased to care about Bruno Macallister. Both men had wooed and then hurt her, one by his subservience to his parents, the other by his brutality. She did not find it at all hard to resist men now; she had closed her heart to affection because to open it was only to be hurt. Before she was twenty she had been very badly hurt by two men and that had been enough, quite enough, to make a girl careful about her emotions in future.

'They say Ruthven Pendreigh would have been chosen as Cornet next year; but if he's married he cannot be. Maybe they'll choose Cullum. Cullum will never get wed!'

'Do you think Cullum is well thought of enough?' Margaret looked at Susan with some surprise.

'I think he is *very* well thought of. People were impressed that he left Oxford to step in and help with the business, and I think they are more impressed with the way he has run it since Father has been ill. It is only *you* who do not think well of him, and I don't know why.'

Nor could I tell you, Margaret thought, how our brother got into bed with a harlot the very same day he had been paying homage to the memory of Malcolm. How could *he* forget that and do what he did? She, Margaret, had saved her honour on that same day; Cullum, ever weak, had lost his. Margaret had not forgotten it, nor let Cullum think that she had.

But at dinner that night Cullum did not look like a man in the grip of shame. Indeed, he seemed extraordinarily pleased with himself, happy and expansive, and sent for a bottle of wine even though it was a weekday.

Since their father's illness the Dunbar household had stopped dressing for dinner. Seeing that Hector seldom came down to eat with them he didn't know and when he did they dressed. All sorts of little things in the household had changed since Hector had decided to embrace the lifestyle of an invalid. One less pleasing thing was that Cullum now drank his whisky openly and not in his bedroom. This enabled his sisters to see the quantity he got through, several before dinner and several after; but they could do no more about it than they had with their father before. They just watched and wondered how long it would take the liquor to get him as it had Hector.

For Cullum was now the master of the house in a very subtle way that neither Susan nor Margaret could quite put their fingers on. He didn't give orders or bark commands; but he was no longer the diffident boyish Cullum. He ran the business and he was the head of the house. He had assumed their father's role.

'You look very happy tonight, Cullum,' Susan ventured over the soup. 'Happier than usual. Is business good?'

'Business?' Cullum gazed at her blankly as though wondering how the business could contribute to his happiness or lack of it. 'The business is as it always is, neither particularly good nor particularly bad.'

'Indifferent to the business as always,' Margaret murmured.

Cullum looked at her sharply. 'Could you explain that remark to me please Margaret?'

Margaret put down her soup spoon and gazed at him with her clear expression. 'I mean I do not think that the fate of Dunbars is close to your heart, is it, Cullum?'

'Of course it is close to my heart – without it we starve!' he snapped.

'Not close enough I think,' Margaret continued, still looking steadily at him, her fingers absently crumbling a bread roll on her plate. 'I hear that everyone is doing better than we are; that Pendreighs are going into outerwear on a very big scale, that Mactavish . . .'

140

Cullum waved his hands as though what she had to say was of no significance. 'Our business is based on underwear, and now that ladies' clothes are shorter than ever we are going heavily into the manufacture of silk stockings. Are we not called the silk house of Branswick because of our pure silk, and silk and wool underwear? Hendersons the silk-spinners gave Father exclusive rights to their silk, and although we don't have the monopoly of silk underwear any more we are still the leaders in the field.'

Margaret sat back, studying her plate of cold, congealing soup. 'I hope you'll forgive me Cullum if I say I think you are mistaken. Remember, I have had a little experience in the fashion business. If you ask me, the important thing to concentrate on in our business now is the manufacture of knitted *outerwear* cardigans, skirts, jumpers, coats for men and women.

'This is the age of the jumper, the sweaters and pullovers that are so popular in America. Pendreighs are already establishing a lead in fashionable outerwear; they are becoming known for their styles as well as their quality. They even employ a designer, I understand. Where is our design department?'

Cullum looked at her angrily, grasping the stem of his wine glass as though for support.

'*Designer* did you say? We have no need for any designers. Our business is based on good, solid garments that are well made from good yarn and that sell well. There's no need to *design* a vest or a chemise, a pullover or a skirt! We have machines that do that for us, foremen who understand what their frames can make. We were the first people, for instance, with lace top underwear; it brought us great profit and prestige. We have no need for designers!'

'But that was at the end of the last century Cullum, when great-grandfather was alive!' Margaret expostulated. 'The war has brought many many changes, not least to fashion. I tell you Dunbars are old-fashioned! Our merchandise is out of date. We shall soon be overtaken by more progressive firms! In fact we *are* being overtaken already. Mark my words!'

'I think Margaret is right,' Susan said slowly. 'Believe me we do not mean to defy you or Father, Cullum. But it is our business too, one in which we have a great interest. As you say, our livelihoods depend on it. Pendreighs are getting an increasing reputation for style as well as quality. Dunbars will be left behind.'

Cullum banged his fist on the table so that all the silver and plate shook. Margaret was reminded of how like their father he was. He was impatient; he drank too much and he had no real interest in the business. The family relied once again on an unstable male figure.

'I wish I could have some say in the business,' she said bitterly before her brother could reply. 'Oh yes Cullum, you may look at me, but is it so astonishing a suggestion? I'd love to have a job and something to do. I'm bored out of my mind here in this house, at Father's beck and call. It's no life for me, for anyone!'

'I'd have thought your first venture into independence did enough harm,' Cullum said darkly.

'And I am to pay for it ever more?' Margaret's eyes glistened and she felt close to tears. 'I wanted to work. Is that a sin? This is 1922; it is not 1822. Women are going to universities, taking careers, becoming doctors, lawyers. Why shouldn't I work in my family's business? I'd love it.'

'I believe she's serious.' Cullum looked with wonder at Susan. 'What sort of job would you do there, for instance? Would you be in the yarn store or in the trimming department? As a clean binder or a greasy binder? A bar-filler maybe?'

'Spare me your scorn, Cullum.' Margaret smiled at the

142

maid who came to remove her plate, nodding to indicate she had finished her soup. 'I could learn all those things, certainly, as you did; but I'd like to do something creative. I'd like to study the market and fashions and maybe introduce some new designs. I love fashion. I read all the magazines. Susan is absolutely right. If we don't change we won't survive.'

'Well you're not interfering with my business,' Cullum said with a note of finality. 'I left Oxford to run it, and having made that sacrifice, run it I shall. I want no petticoats interfering.' He banged his hand on the table again. 'There, you have taken all the pleasure I had out of the day. Did you know Ruthven Pendreigh was engaged?'

'Why should that give you pleasure?' Susan glanced at Margaret who remained impassive.

'Because I may be selected as the next Cornet. Everyone thought Ruthven would be chosen next year as the Cornet. I have ridden every year in the Cornet's procession. Now what is to prevent it being myself?'

'Maybe your drinking and the way you chase girls,' Margaret said contemptuously. 'Or do you think people don't know about it?'

'Margaret, hush, that's enough!' Susan urged, but Margaret shook her head.

'I wish you would settle down, Cullum.' Margaret's expression was hard. 'Has not our family enough on its plate? Do you think Malcolm would have got himself a reputation as the town rake? No, he would be in control of the business, introducing new ideas and new fashions and, with his family, he would be a model of respectability. I do not think you should even want to be Cornet. You are twenty-four, Cullum. You should be thinking of the future, of the business, and not just of yourself. You should be looking for a wife and a home of your own.'

'This would be my home if I had a wife,' Cullum said, 'and *then* where would you be?'

Margaret got up and put her chair under the table. 'I could quite well fend for myself. If your wife looked after Father, for presumably you don't mean to throw him out too, then I should be free. Quite honestly, I'd go back to London and forget that such a place as Branswick ever existed.'

'But Margaret you haven't finished your meal,' Susan cried as her sister made for the door.

'I'm not hungry,' Margaret said. 'Good night.'

For a while there was silence between the two left in the room. Cullum swirled the red liquid in his glass and eyed it.

'Margaret is right, Cullum,' Susan said, taking his plate and helping herself to sweet from the sideboard. 'A married man cannot be Cornet. Nor can you be Cornet for two years afterwards. If you're chosen you cannot contemplate marriage until you are twenty-eight. I agree with her. I think marriage will help to stabilize you, as well as make you happy. There are very many pretty girls in the town; the choice is wide. Why not select one? A suitable girl who will love you and make you happy?'

'And what about you?' Cullum snapped. 'Why don't you select a suitable young man and settle down too?'

Susan sighed and looked sadly at him. 'Where are the men?' she said. 'Where are they? They were all lost in the war.'

CHAPTER NINE

Whether it was his drinking or his reputation with women, no one knew, but Cullum was not selected as the Cornet the following May. The ancient ceremony known as the Common Riding went back to the Battle of Flodden in 1513 when the English army plundered the Borders and the Scottish King James IV was killed. In the following year a band of youths set out from Branswick to resist a new English Army camped nearby, captured its flag and returned in triumph to Branswick. The tradition of selecting a Cornet, who represented the brave youth of 1514, stemmed from that time and was combined with the ancient ceremony of Riding the Marches, by which the common land was defined and protected from unlawful encroachment by neighbouring landowners.

The Cornet with his followers carrying a replica of the famous flag rode the boundaries of the common land each year in June amid great ceremonial, and the office of Cornet was one much coveted by local men. A Mactavish was in fact selected for 1923 as Cornet. Angus Mactavish whose sister had been torpedoed carried the flag; Angus Mactavish who was at Edinburgh university, a popular good-looking local boy who played rugby for the town and had an unsullied reputation.

Cullum rode that year as usual in the Cornet's procession but he was bitterly disappointed, a fact that he took little trouble to conceal from his family.

Although the weather was bad it had never stopped the town from celebrating and nor did it now. On the Wednesday of the week in which the Common Riding was held, the town council held a reception at the Town Hall for those who had left Branswick and returned for this happy occasion. On the Thursday, the 'nicht afore the morn', the ceremony known as Colour Bussing took place, again in the Town Hall, one of the most colourful of all the ceremonies. The Cornet's Lass, surrounded by her own companions all gaily dressed, 'bussed' the flag by tying her ribbons of blue and gold to the head of its staff; it was a relic of olden days when men wore the colours of their ladies into battle. The lass then handed the banner blue to the Provost who, as Chief Magistrate, gave it to the Cornet, charging him to ride the marches of the Commonalty of Branswick and return the flag 'unstained and unsullied' at the end of the mission.

The Cornet then began his walk through the town accompanied by his supporters and drum and fife bands, halting at the 1914 memorial, which was erected just before the war, to pay tribute to his sixteenth-century predecessor.

On the day of the Common Riding itself, the Friday, the bands assembled at six o'clock in the morning and amid great ceremonial, in which the Provost, councillors and officials all took part, the Cornet with his mounted supporters rode to the outermost part of the common and turned a sod to mark the boundary as ancient custom demanded. The cavalcade then returned to the moor where horse-racing followed, accompanied by much jollity, picnicking and so on, until the Cornet and his men remounted to complete the riding of the boundaries. Finally the flag was dipped in the River Drume at a spot which once formed part of the old march of the town, and the whole exciting day finished with a dinner and a ball.

Despite Cullum's disappointment, all the Dunbar family with the exception of Hector took part in the festivities. Mary Dunbar came from Edinburgh with Murdoch, accompanied by Juliet, her husband Angus Monroe and their four children. Andrew Dunbar and his wife Lily came too but stayed in a hotel because there was no room for all of them at *Woodbrae*. Despite the cold and the intermittent rain they picnicked on the moor, attended the bussing, for which there was a lottery for tickets, and of course the final ball on the day of the Common Riding itself.

On the Wednesday the Monroes, and Andrew and Lily, went to the reception for 'exiles' to take as much advantage of the festivities as they could.

Margaret had looked forward to the ball throughout the long dreary winter, while she read to her father and looked after his creature comforts, or helped Susan round the house, or visited the houses of friends, other girls like her with not enough to do, many of them anxiously waiting for a husband, thinking that time was passing them by. She had designed and made her own dress, trying to avoid aggravating the situation between herself and Cullum and dreaming, always dreaming of what the future might bring.

The dress she had designed for 1923 was not quite as daring as the one for the ball she had missed in 1919, which still hung in the wardrobe, unworn but hopelessly out of fashion.

Earlier that year the opening of the tomb of Tutankhamun at Luxor in Egypt had inspired a rash of Egyptian fashions, particularly in evening gowns and head-dresses. Slave bangles, oriental ringed scarves became popular and so did 'barbaric' jewellery and long earrings. Knowing the conservative nature of Branswick society, Margaret eschewed the extremes of the Egyptian craze. Her black velvet dress had a square-fronted bodice attached to a short cape at the back by means of narrow shoulder straps. The skirt was straight to her ankles, and her one concession to prevailing fashion was an Egyptian girdle round her hips, the ends hanging nearly to the ground. Her hair, very short at the back, waved forward over her

147

face, touching her cheeks like a close fitting cap, and she was sparing with the make-up.

Margaret was enjoying the ball. There was no lack of partners and Angus Mactavish, the Cornet himself, danced with her twice before going off to the other hotel where a second Common Riding ball was being held because one hotel was not large enough to contain all who wanted to come.

It was a jolly party, even Mary was gay and danced a lot, and cordial words were exchanged with the huge Pendreigh family who sat at the next table, Ruthven eyeing Margaret out of the corner of his eye despite the presence of his young bride Cathy whom he had married at Christmas. But Margaret didn't look at Ruthven Pendreigh, didn't glance at him once, although she knew he was there. She felt animated in a way she had not felt since that heady spell in London three years before, when she and Bruno had danced night after night at all the well known clubs and she had been so full of excited anticipation about the future.

She had just finished dancing with her brother-in-law Angus Monroe, who was escorting her back to the table, when she looked straight into the eyes of Bruno Macallister. He had entered the room with his mother on one arm and his sister Isla on the other. She fancied he reddened as he met her gaze, but she could not be sure. She quickly turned away and sat in the chair Angus was holding out for her.

Angus Monroe was tall with grey hair, of which he had very little left, and the supercilious air and arrogance of a successful lawyer. He was fifteen years older than Juliet who was now thirty-three, but he looked even older. Margaret was fond of her sister but they did not meet often. Juliet had her own life, her own family and her own world bounded by the wider horizons of Edinburgh society. She was always very busy with her family and with a variety of good works that ensured she never had a moment to think. She never even considered whether the many good causes she surrounded herself with really achieved very much, or did what they were supposed to do, or helped those they were supposed to help. But no matter, the cause was the thing and a full diary was essential to one who liked to feel important as well as needed by her husband and children. Her eldest child, Tom, was now ten, her youngest five. She was a progressive-minded woman, a supporter of Marie Stopes who had shocked society the year before by her public lectures on birth control. Juliet Monroe thoroughly approved of controlling the population of the very poor, those who lived in the slums she visited in Glasgow and Edinburgh, and of people like herself who considered they had done their duty and did not want any more children.

Juliet was the least endowed of the Dunbar girls, as the eldest, for some peculiar genetic reason, often is. She had the same curly black hair as Margaret and Susan and the same good clear skin; but her eyes did not have that exceptional colour that Margaret's had, her nose was rather narrow and made her look sharp, her lips a trifle too thin. Her figure had filled out a little, making her look the responsible, matronly person she was. Her evening dress had a plain top with short shoulder puffs and a plain undraped skirt. It was blue, a colour that did not particularly become her because with her very white skin it made her seem pallid whereas Susan looked vivacious in green and Margaret alluring and stylish in black.

'Did you see Bruno Macallister?' Juliet reached over and touched Margaret's hand as she sat down after the dancing, leaning conspiratorily forward. 'I hear he's back living in Selkirk.'

'Really?'

'I thought he was married.'

149

'Maybe he is.'

Juliet frowned. 'Or maybe going to be married. Do you not see them at all?'

'Not at all, not since Father became so ill.'

'How odd – because they visited quite often did they not?'

'About once a year, maybe twice.' Margaret kept her voice noncommittal, her eyes on the dancers. She wanted to dance again and her feet tapped to the catchy tune of *Ain't we got fun?*

'I thought you were friendly . . .' Juliet began when a man approached Juliet, his hand outstretched.

'Juliet! Of course I might have known you would be here. And Angus. It's very good to see you.'

Angus stood up, smiled and shook hands and Juliet put up her face to be kissed then, glancing at the stranger, she turned to Margaret.

'I don't think you've met my sister Margaret, have you, Hamish? Margaret Dunbar, Hamish Ogilvy.'

'I knew your brother Malcolm.' Hamish bowed briefly to Margaret before shaking hands.

'In the war?'

'Yes.'

'Oh.'

For a moment they looked at each other, Margaret seeing a handsome man of about thirty to thirty-five with straight fair hair and a blond moustache. He had a rather jutting forehead and dark blue eyes and a narrow, aristocratic face. She wondered if he was related to the titled Ogilvys.

Hamish Ogilvy, in his turn, saw a very beautiful woman who bore a strong resemblance to her dead brother Malcolm. Dressed in black with her black hair tapering towards her cheeks and with those brilliant aquamarine eyes, he thought she was the most striking woman in the crowded room. In fact it was the sight of Margaret and a

150

desire to know who she was that had made him come up to the Monroes.

Angus fussed around getting another chair while Juliet introduced Hamish to Susan, Mary, Cullum and the two Macdonald brothers, cousins of the Dunbars, who made up their party. Margaret watched Hamish's elegant shoulders as he bowed to the ladies and then, as he took his seat, he turned attentively towards her.

'I was with the Highlanders of the 51st Division, the 4th Gordons. I was wounded at Courton about a week before Malcolm was killed, and invalided home shortly afterwards. Your brother was a very brave soldier.'

'I'm sure you were too.'

Margaret felt immediately attracted to Hamish Ogilvy. She had, in fact, noticed him before, when she was dancing with Angus Monroe. He had partnered a tall, pale woman who resembled him, and she'd seen him looking at her across his partner's shoulders. There was a curious feeling of inevitability about their meeting now as, abruptly, he stood up and extended a hand towards her.

'Are you free for this dance?'

'I believe so.' She didn't pretend to consult her dance card but held out her hand and he drew her up, his clasp very firm and reassuring. Despite the heat of the room his hand was quite cool and she felt this was indicative of a man who kept himself closely under control; who seldom lost his temper, or his nerve. He put the same cool hand under her elbow and silently they made their way to the dance floor where, with an instinctive symmetry, arms outstretched, they glided together into the broad steps of the tango.

When the music stopped he did not take her back to her table but led her to the bar where he ordered a whisky for himself and a gin and French for Margaret.

They both observed that it was very hot, and wandered through the double doors from the bar to a quieter lounge

151

with open French windows that led onto the balcony. There were a few other couples there too, leaning over and gazing at the moonlight on the Craigie which bubbled past the hotel towards its rendezvous with the more majestic Drume.

He lit her cigarette and then his own and watched her as she exhaled, noting the line of her throat, the curve of her bosom, the bare arms which were straddled at the top by the thinnest of straps.

'What do you do?' Margaret asked, aware of his admiration, excited by it.

'I'm in engineering.'

'Oh *that* Ogilvy! I thought you might be related to the Airlie Ogilvys.'

'I think we are, very distantly, but very very distantly.'

Margaret knew the big engineering firm of Ogilvy and Stewart on the outskirts of Galashiels. She saw that he was studying her face. 'I hope you're not disappointed?'

'About what?'

'That I'm only a distant relation to a noble family, if one at all.'

'Of course not,' Margaret laughed. 'That sort of thing doesn't impress me one bit.'

'I didn't think it would.' He had lowered his voice and was looking at her very intently. 'And you? What do you do?'

'The usual thing. Nothing.' She didn't try to conceal the bitterness in her voice.

'Is it usual, to do nothing?'

'It seems to be.'

'I understand your father has been ill.'

'*Is* ill. He's a permanent invalid.'

'That must be very trying.' Hamish moved closer to her; his voice was sympathetic.

Behind his head she could see the lights of the room they'd just left. A couple next to them were kissing, their

152

lips touching but their bodies apart. It was a gentle, affectionate kiss rather than a lovers' kiss. Margaret felt herself drawn towards Hamish and then she remembered where she was and who she was. She was Margaret Dunbar with that undeserved reputation for being rather fast. She didn't want to deserve it now by being seen kissing a total stranger on the balcony of the Craigmore Hotel. She stepped back and raised her glass unsteadily to her lips. It was quite ridiculous; she'd only known him for about half an hour.

'I had a career briefly in London as a mannequin, before Father was ill. I would like to work but the family are against it. My brother Cullum . . .'

'I know. I know quite a lot about you.' Hamish leaned his back to the balcony and lit another cigarette. 'Angus Monroe is my lawyer. *Not* that he has gossiped about you, I hasten to say.' He looked at her quickly. 'But I know that Cullum took over the business after Malcolm was killed and all that. Does he not want you to work?'

'No, he does not! One would never think the war had almost been won by women.'

'I know what a lot they did, in the munitions factories and in the field hospitals. I am all for women working if that's what they want.'

'I thought you would be that sort of man,' Margaret said gently. 'Don't you think we should get back now?'

He gazed at her and ground out his cigarette on the balcony floor. Lightly taking her arm he led her back to the dance floor and they resumed a tango as though they'd never left off.

This time when it finished he walked her slowly back to her table, and while she sat down next to Susan he remained chatting to Angus who had just partnered Mary in the dance. Lily and Andrew Dunbar came over to greet Hamish, Lily in a rather outrageous evening dress of yellow tulle over taffeta with a shaped pleated collar and

153

an all-pleated vandyke skirt, topped by an Egyptian head-dress such that Margaret coveted but would never have dared to wear. But on Margaret it might have looked attractive; on Lily it was almost grotesque. Although pretty, Lily was rather large, very jolly and, this evening, slightly drunk and the head-dress was tilted over her left eye. She draped her arm around Hamish's shoulders and kissed him on the cheek, nearly losing her balance as she did because he was so tall and she was rather short. Lily also had a cigarette in a long holder which seemed to be menacing one of Hamish's eyes.

'Careful with that, Lily! I don't want to lose an eye now having come through the war with both intact.'

'Oh Hamish!' Lily laughed, her face pink. 'You are such an attractive man. Were I ten years younger . . .'

'*Ten* . . .' Andrew Dunbar began indignantly, but Lily grasped his arm and swept him away, her feet tapping to the two-step. Andrew, by this time also rather drunk and feeling very merry, willingly complied, mopping his perspiring face. Hamish politely asked Mary to dance and she eagerly got up, her face quite animated.

'I think Mary would like to marry again,' Margaret murmured.

'Wouldn't she just?' Susan said, '*if* she had the chance. I hear she's all over the place in Edinburgh.'

'Well, Murdoch looks very well, we can't complain,' Margaret, who had her back to the dance floor, said philosophically when she saw Susan suddenly look up and smile and she heard a familiar voice say: 'And how are the beautiful Misses Dunbar tonight?'

Margaret did not turn her head but Susan half rose and stretched out her hand.

'I thought you were not going to talk to us, Bruno. You've been neglecting us.'

'Not at all,' Bruno said in his deep charming voice with its slight Scottish burr. 'You know that I am now in the business, so I've been very busy.'

154

'Yes, Father told us that you had decided to settle down.'

Bruno laughed, that well known deep-throated laugh the sound of which brought an unexpected lump to Margaret's throat. 'Did he indeed? Well maybe I have. Anyway, I am to learn all about yarn and so on, and . . .'

'Someone said you were engaged to be married,' Susan pursued, looking at him intently. This time Bruno did not laugh and Margaret could not resist half turning to watch his face.

'Did someone say that? No that part is wrong. Unfortunately. I am not such a lucky man. Susan, are you not dancing?' He reached for Susan's hand and she stood up and eagerly grasped his.

'I am if I'm asked, Bruno, thank you.'

'How are *you* Margaret?' Bruno, his tone casual, bent his head and looked into her eyes; but Margaret stared in front of her and as the music surged they disappeared from her view.

Well, it was inevitable; they had had to meet sometime, Margaret thought, watching the very correct way that Hamish and Mary danced. She was taken with Hamish, she could not deny it to herself, and even now she watched a little jealously in case he drew Mary towards him as he had drawn her.

Juliet appeared from somewhere with John Macdonald who held out his hand to Margaret, but she shook her head.

'I'm quite exhausted for a moment, John. Could we dance later?'

He smiled and looked at Juliet who also shook her head.

'I've danced every dance, John. Just look how vigorously Andrew and Lily are dancing! I don't know where they get the energy from. Maybe I'd be like that if I hadn't had four children.'

Margaret started to laugh as the music finished and

155

Hamish came back with Mary who immediately accepted John Macdonald's arm and went back to the dance floor.

'Would you like to dance again Margaret?' Hamish said.

'I've just said "no" to John.' Margaret smiled at him aware of the expression in his eyes. Could one fall so easily, so quickly in love? She felt almost overwhelmed, quite lightheaded. It was quite absurd, she knew; he was probably a practised ladykiller like Bruno, who did this sort of thing all the time, and who now obviously had her sister in thrall, his arms holding her tightly.

Juliet suddenly looked as though she remembered something and she touched Hamish's arm. 'How is Isobel, Hamish? It was rude of me not to enquire before. You must miss her on an occasion like this.'

Her voice was low and intimate, but Margaret heard every word.

'She's as well as she ever is,' Hamish murmured. 'I came with my sister Dierdre and Hugh and Alice Fogarty. Dierdre has her eye on some young man so I found myself free.'

Margaret stared at him, her body stiffening. Hamish had a wife. Who else could Isobel be? He had lowered his voice and he glanced at her before replying.

'In fact I must get back.' Hamish turned to Margaret and smiled wistfully, extending his hand. 'I'm so glad we met.'

'I am too,' she said automatically taking his hand, but she did not smile. How silly and girlish and foolish she'd been!

'I hope we meet again,' he said, and she felt the pressure of his fingers, but did not respond.

She continued to look at him, saying nothing, and after a moment he let her hand go and she watched that slim, elegant form move easily through the crowd to some table in the far corner, out of sight.

*

Despite the fact that the dancing continued until sunrise the Cornet had yet another hectic day ahead of him. While most of those who had been at the dances slumbered, the Cornet rode to the park to lay a wreath on the town's war memorial. Then later there was horse-racing on the moor.

The Dunbars and the Monroes had slept in, but they were all there now, up on the moor on a day that had started wet but was now dry with intermittent sunshine. All of Branswick seemed to be on the moor, gentry and commonalty alike. Even the aristocracy were there, the Duke and Duchess of Storrick who would present the prizes, with a party of family and friends and a larger number of retainers, picnicking beside a huge grey six-cylinder Rolls Royce Silver Ghost which stood majestically apart from the other cars.

Many people still had carriages and these stood on the side of the moor while the horses grazed on the short brown turf. But most of the Branswick gentry had by now purchased at least one car and, in imitation of the Storricks, they picnicked ostentatiously around their individual automobiles rather like votaries gathering around a deity.

For the motor car was still a rarity in 1923; only a very few people had the money to buy them, or the knowhow to drive them. But between them the Pendreigh family had quite a collection of cars, all on display on the moors today. There was a red four-cylinder Vauxhall, its elegant chrome flashes sparkling in the moments when the sun came out, reputed to do a hundred miles an hour. There was a brown six-cylinder Model 34 Marmon which Elliott Pendreigh had shipped back from the United States after a visit there in 1921, and there were several smaller cars, a new Austin Seven, two Morrises, a Cowley and an Oxford which belonged to the youngest members of the family.

If the Pendreigh collection of automobiles made something of a splash, so did the clothes that some of the

157

Pendreigh ladies were wearing. Ruthven's wife Cathy looked particularly pretty in a tailored pleated skirt with a plain white blouse and a long cardigan coat with hip pockets made at the Pendreigh mill; and Winifred Pendreigh had gone quite modish in a cloche hat trimmed with aigrettes, and a long Magyar coat with astrakhan cuffs. Moira Pendreigh who had married George Law in 1919, was also present with her husband and their three-year-old toddler and new baby, rocked in the arms of its nurse.

In another part were the Mactavishes, gathered round a huge black Studebaker with a fawn folding roof which Murray Mactavish, not to be outdone by Elliott Pendreigh, had brought with him following a recent visit to the land of the Motor Car. The Pattersons on the other hand, patronized the home market, with a blue six-cylinder Rolls Royce which was smaller than that of the Storricks but brand new, while the Hendersons, again in a large party, had a Redwinger Riley with a polished aluminium body and dashing red wings.

But perhaps merely thirty or forty automobiles could be counted on the moors that day, and perhaps another twenty carriages. The vast mass of people came up on foot, tossed down their picnic baskets, spread their rugs, got out their loaves of bread, their fresh haggis and pies and opened their bottles, while their children scampered about and their dogs got under people's feet and annoyed the horses.

For the prime purpose of the afternoon was the races that would mark the end of the Common Riding. Most young men who had ridden with the Cornet all week were there, and there were others besides, like Hamish Ogilvy from Galashiels and Bruno Macallister from Selkirk. Cullum Dunbar too was there, his mount rather apart from the rest, who had gathered in groups before being called to the starting post.

158

Cullum had been out of sorts all during the Common Riding. It was a mood that Margaret and Susan felt could not simply be attributed to jealousy. He had seemed preoccupied, morose and drank steadily in such a determined way that it was fortunate his horse-riding was not impaired.

But as she watched him that afternoon Margaret thought it was. She had not seen Cullum until this moment. He had not been to breakfast and she'd thought he'd left early to accompany the Cornet. She felt anxious about him and confided in Susan, just as the starter raised his megaphone to call the riders to gather at the start.

'See the way he rides the horse, *away* from the racers not towards them. I don't think he knows what he's doing.'

Susan looked to where Margaret was pointing; then Cullum seemed to sway from his horse and could only draw upright at the last moment. Bruno Macallister, on his way to the post, rode over to Cullum as though asking if he were all right. Margaret watched Susan's eyes follow Bruno. They had spent most of what was left of the ball dancing together and Margaret thought she had seen a light in her sister's eyes that had not been there since her engagement to Ian Lyall.

'You like him, don't you?' Margaret whispered as Bruno joined the racers.

Susan blushed. 'He was very charming last night; but I thought he liked *you*.' She looked enquiringly at Margaret. 'Did you not see him a lot in London?'

'Quite a lot,' Margaret said, watching Cullum.

'Did something happen?' Susan tried to hide the anxiety in her voice, but Margaret was not deceived.

'I came home.' She looked Susan straight in the eyes. 'I did not see him after that.'

'Oh.'

Susan pursed her mouth, but she looked reflective.

159

Suddenly there were cries from the onlookers as, just at the moment the starter of the race raised his gun, Cullum fell heavily from his horse. Margaret shouted and she and Susan ran forward while the riders and their disturbed horses gathered round the recumbent form on the moor, and the starter, looking perplexed, lowered his gun.

But before them was Hamish Ogilvy, who had been the first to jump from his horse and was now on his knees beside Cullum.

'Did he slip?' someone asked as Hamish took off his jacket and made a pillow for Cullum's head.

'I think his horse tripped,' Hamish replied briefly as Margaret knelt beside him. The smell of drink from Cullum's breath was overwhelming. Now a few other riders had dismounted, and gathered round, and Bruno joined those who were kneeling beside Cullum on the ground. He leaned forward, raised an eyelid, smelt his breath and straightened up.

'Let's get him back to the house,' he said briefly.

'Shouldn't we call a doctor?' someone asked, but Bruno shook his head. Ruthven Pendreigh, another of the riders, had also dismounted. and between them Hamish, Bruno and Ruthven Pendreigh carried Cullum to the large blue Wolseley tourer with which Margaret was so familiar.

'You come with me Susan,' Bruno said authoritatively as he got behind the wheel. 'Pendreigh will look after our horses.'

'I'll take you,' Hamish said quietly to Margaret pointing to his own black Austin 20 five-seater which was some way along the edge of the moor. Margaret looked around, but of the Monroes or her aunt and uncle there was no sign.

'All right,' she said walking silently with him towards the car, thinking that she had never expected to be with him again so soon. 'He was drunk wasn't he?'

'Dead drunk, I'm afraid. I don't think many people knew.'

160

Enough to talk.'

He opened the front side door for her and Margaret climbed in. She was wearing a tailored suit in wool loom knit stockinette with stripes in contrasting silk and a tight-fitting cloche hat, all the rage that year, with a rolled up brim. She looked very chic and very beautiful. Hamish wore grey jodhpurs and black riding boots with a well cut tweed jacket, a woollen shirt and tartan tie. He carried a soft green trilby in his hand which he flung into the back of the car.

In the distance the race had begun and they could hear the cheering crowd. All those who were picnicking on the moor had their heads turned in the same direction so that no one was looking at them.

Hamish put the car into gear and drove slowly off the moor onto the road.

'You think people will talk?' He glanced at Margaret.

'Cullum already has a reputation. Why did he have to do it, today of all days?'

'I'm terribly sorry.' A hand briefly brushed her knee to be replaced quickly on the steering wheel.

Margaret gazed ahead down the hill and into the valley where she could see, in the centre of the town, the rivers meeting just before the Dunbar Mill. Even from this height the town looked festive with flags and bunting on every building, and an almost complete absence of smoke to signify a holiday when all the mills were closed.

On a day like today Branswick did look beautiful, with the sun occasionally glimpsed through the thick white clouds moving slowly across the sky and the broad Drume meandering lazily out of sight towards the purple-domed Branahae mountains. The greenery was very young, that bright festive green of early summer, and the roses were coming out in the neatly tended gardens of the Vertig estate.

'Why didn't you tell me you were married?'

161

They were half way down the hill – they had scarcely got going – but Hamish stopped the car and turned and faced her.

'I thought you knew.'

'But I didn't *know* you!'

'You said *that* Ogilvy.'

'I meant the engineering Ogilvys of Ogilvy & Stewart.'

Hamish looked across to the hill where the Dunbars lived, separated now by the valley and the River Drume.

'I see. A misunderstanding. I thought you knew about Isobel.'

'Is there something wrong with her?'

Hamish gazed at her and she saw the suffering in his face, the involuntary twitching of a muscle in his jaw. 'My wife is an invalid. She had infantile paralysis three years ago, just after our youngest child was born.'

'I'm terribly, terribly sorry,' Margaret murmured; she felt that an invalid wife somehow ennobled her shattered feelings.

'She had it very badly and she's bedridden, though they don't rule out the possibility that she might recover some use of her limbs. She can move her arms and her head, but . . .' Hamish stared at the scene in front of him through blurred vision. 'The outlook is not good.'

'It must be very hard for you.'

Hamish straightened his head and turned towards her. 'It is. The trouble is also that we do not get on. Isobel was only eighteen when I married her in 1914, very quickly, because I felt I was going to be killed. I can't tell you why, but I did and I felt the same all during the war. I never expected to return.

'The thing was that when I was away Isobel had affairs, one very serious one. She was going to ask me for a divorce but the blighter joined the Navy and was killed in 1917. When I returned I found out everything but she promised to be faithful. I was shattered by the war and I didn't want my marriage to shatter too. I wanted to build,

162

not break; so I foolishly decided to give it a chance. But I don't think Isobel loved me any more. She felt sorry for me, wounded hero and that sort of rot. We had two more children (our first was born in 1915) which, in hindsight, was a mistake and then we decided we would part when . . . Well . . .' He looked up at the sky, then at her. 'I can't leave her now. She's dependent on me and my money, on the way we live. She has to have expert nursing care. She's also very afraid. In these circumstances it would be quite caddish to leave her for my own happiness.'

'Unthinkable,' Margaret agreed, meeting his gaze. She recalled their proximity on the balcony the previous night. She had the same feeling now as she had then, that she wanted to kiss him, and she felt the colour steal across her cheeks.

'I'm sorry,' he said softly. 'I'm sorry you felt deceived and I'm sorry for myself because I can offer nothing to any woman as long as Isobel is alive, and the prospect is that she will live for a very long time.'

'Why should I expect anything?' Margaret attempted her gay smile, but her voice trembled.

'Because I know that last night you felt something for me, as I did for you. Is it true?'

'Yes,' she whispered.

'I wanted to meet you as soon as I saw you. I have never felt such an instant attraction towards a woman, never, not even to Isobel; and when I saw you looking so lovely, dancing so animatedly with Angus I wanted to meet you. I *had* to know who you were. I know I did wrong. I should have stayed away; but I am a normal man and I . . .'

'It doesn't matter.' Margaret realized she was still whispering. 'I saw you too and I hoped you would come. It had to happen, I think.'

She smiled and he drew in his breath.

'You really are incredibly lovely. How wasted you are here! You should be some great hostess in Edinburgh or London. How I wish I had met you before.'

'I was only thirteen in 1914.'

'Yes, and you're very young now.'

'Twenty-two in October.'

'I'm thirty-five. It's a big gap isn't it?' He waited for her to reply but she said nothing. 'I wouldn't ask it anyway. You would be throwing your life away. I can offer you nothing. If you don't want to be unhappy, you must have nothing to do with me. After I've taken you home I will leave this valley and we need never meet again. It was chance that brought us together, but by our own choice we can avoid each other.'

Margaret knew that what he was saying was right. They should not see each other; they must not. She knew that he wanted to continue to see her, but he was warning her at the same time. She could see, reflected in his face, the conflict of his warring emotions: his desire and his fear.

She knew that she should agree; that they should part now, before anything could start that they would later be sure to regret. For how could anything but regret come of an affair between them? And 'affair' in the fullest sense she knew was in both their minds. She had had two unhappy romances, one that was humiliating as well as degrading, that had left a scar. Why court a third disaster?

But Margaret was bored with her life: reading to Father, going to the tennis club, bridge parties, endless ladies' teas for this or that; a little charity work, a trip or two to Edinburgh, the odd function at the mill. All meaningless, futile. Anything, anything that gave her existence a lift was surely preferable to the dreary routine she was accustomed to now? Although she was young and, she knew, beautiful, the men she met seldom attracted her. They were too near her own age, too inexperienced. The older ones were either bounders, like Bruno, or married, like Hamish. The ones in between had all been killed in the war. Yet, for the chance to experience passion, to feel excitement, to know love at last . . . His blue eyes gazed into hers and a sudden gust of wind ruffled his blond hair. He looked so sad, so lovable, so noble. Surely he could not hurt her as the others had?

Impulsively she reached out for his hand and, as he grasped hers, his face lit up with joy. Bringing her fingers up to his lips, he kissed them one by one.

PART II

Family Conflicts
1925–1936

CHAPTER TEN

Cullum Dunbar stirred in the large soft bed with its flock mattress, aware of the warm body next to him. There was no glimmer of light above the thick curtains so the house was still contained by the darkness of a Scottish winter.

'I ought to go,' he whispered, groping for his watch in the dark.

'I wish you'd stay,' Nan said turning to him. 'You don't have to answer to anybody.'

Cullum lay on his back, blinking, his eyes heavy with his post-coital sleep. 'I don't have to answer to anybody,' he repeated, finding the light switch and flicking it on. 'But I do have to think of appearances. Some people get up at dawn and if they see my car constantly going up the hill at that time they will talk.'

'Maybe they talk already.'

'Maybe they do.'

The soft yellowish light illuminated the room, the heavy sparse furniture, the homely pictures on the wall, the large double bed with its patchwork counterpane, the brown wallpaper peeling in the corner near the window where the damp was gradually penetrating the house.

'I wish I could get you out of here Nan.' One piece of hanging wallpaper showed the crumbling plaster underneath ulcerated by the damp. 'This place will soon not be fit to live in. Besides it's bad for William. Bad for your father too.'

Nan sat up and he saw that the purple nipples on her large pendulous breasts were erect with the cold. She reached for her woollen nightgown which lay on top of the bed and attempted to put it on.

'Don't,' Cullum said, cupping the palm of his left hand under her right breast.

169

'Och come on, Cullum,' Nan smiled sleepily. 'It's three o'clock in the morning. We canna start all that again.'

'I thought you liked "all that",' he said pulling her down by putting his strong right arm over her left shoulder. 'I thought you liked it very much.'

'I do,' Nan said snuggling down. 'But the cold is enough tae break the tail off a brass monkey.'

'All the more reason to stay here then.'

The embers of the fire still glowed in the grate, but they had left no warmth in the room. She lay with her face towards him, her breasts touching his chest. She smelled good, of warmth and love-making and her long hair lay unbraided on the pillow. Unlike all the fashionable ladies in the town Nan, good working-class Nan, still wore her hair braided about her head finishing in a soft bun at the nape of her neck. He ran his hands through her hair and then he caressed her smooth brown cheek, and the firm contours of her full sensuous mouth. Their groins touched and Cullum had a powerful urge to enter her again, to be enveloped by the warm, damp mysterious female part of her. It was like a tunnel in which he burrowed and felt safe. He felt very safe with Nan. Her body began to relax and he realized she was starting to slip away into sleep. If he did too the dawn would be upon them both before they knew it.

Cullum kissed her hard on the mouth, putting his hand between her legs. His touch told him she was ready for him and he climbed gently upon her without disturbing the bedclothes and loved her violently until she cried out, not in pain but in pleasure, the sound muffled by the pressure of his mouth against hers. She cried into his mouth and he swallowed the sound, gulping it into his lungs, like air.

'I love you Nan,' he said as he lay, gasping, on her inert replete body. 'You know I love you very much.' He was aware of her heart beating quickly beneath his own. The firm, rapid heartbeat was as vital as the life-force that had flowed from him to her; the force that bound them together and had produced a child.

'I know you love me, Cullum,' Nan said turning to ease his heavy body off hers. 'But now you must go or else you'll fall asleep again and not wake until daybreak.'

Cullum kissed her and then got out of bed, the cold suddenly striking him. He drew the bedclothes right over Nan, covering her to her chin, before going to the fireplace where his clothes lay neatly over an armchair. He dressed very quickly, then he stood in his overcoat and looked at her. But she was already asleep, her breathing heavy and regular, as one who has laboured well and has her reward. Well, she had laboured well and deserved to sleep. He didn't disturb her with a farewell kiss, but put the light off beside her bed and tiptoed out of the room, closing the door softly behind him.

Outside it was very dark and he walked quickly along the street by the side of the river, crossing the bridge which divided the town. A few hundred yards ahead of him was the Dunbar Mill and he came to the side street where he left his car, well away from the tale-telling gas lights overhead. He cranked it, climbed into it and coaxed its cold, protesting engine gently back along the way he had come, across the bridge to the other side of the river towards the hill and home.

Cullum shivered. It was cold and his breath misted the windscreen so that every few moments he had to wipe it. But he knew the way by instinct now; his car, like a trusted horse, could almost have found the way home by itself. How many times had he made this journey in the past two years, ever since he first became aware of the existence of a son by a casual affair with a mill girl he had hardly remembered?

It had been just before the Common Riding in 1923 that

171

one of his frameworkers, George Murray, had stepped out of the shadows of the mill as Cullum was preparing to walk home.

Diffidently, with cap in hand, George asked the favour of a few words and Cullum, ever friendly towards his workers, invited him for a pint at the Brewers' Arms on the corner nearby.

'It is about my Nan, sir,' George said, raising the frothing glass to his lips and looking nervously at his employer.

'Nan?' Cullum repeated, creasing his brow. 'Does she work at the mill?' Then, as the expression on George's face brought recollection, 'Oh your *daughter* Nan. How is she George?'

Of course he remembered Nan, a pretty buxom girl who worked in the trimming department and had suddenly left to look after her mother who was ill. He remembered Nan because, of all the mill girls he had taken to bed since he'd started work at the mill, she had been one of the prettiest; but also one of the most fleeting. Looking at George, he couldn't remember whether he'd been to bed with his daughter once or twice, certainly not more. Surely George wasn't going to bring that up now, nearly three years later?

'My daughter Nan has a bairn sir, called William.' George gravely finished his pint and set the glass firmly down on the counter. Cullum turned to the barman and asked for two more.

'I'm glad to hear that, George. I didn't know she was married.'

'She isn't, Mr Cullum.'

'Oh I'm sorry about that, George.'

'What I want tae say, sir, Mr Cullum – ' George was starting to sweat and tipped his cap onto the back of his head – 'is that the bairn is yours.'

'*Mine*?' Cullum nearly dropped his glass. He put it carefully back on the bar, aware of the drone of voices

172

round him as the millworkers slaked their thirst. 'How could it possibly be mine? I haven't seen Nan since, well,' Cullum scratched his head, 'I don't remember. You're not saying now . . .' Then he began to feel annoyed and called for a single malt whisky for himself to chase the beer.

'Nan never wanted it mentioned, sir. She didna want you tae know. She said what she had done was her fault and she must take the consequences. She didna want tae trouble you, and she doesn't know I'm speaking tae you now.'

'But how could she know the baby was mine?' Cullum expostulated.

'Because you were the only man she'd lain with sir. She swore that and I believed her because Nan was a good girl.'

'Well she wasn't very "good" with me.'

'She said it was difficult tae resist you, Mr Cullum, you were so persuasive; and I won't say Nan wasn't a hot-blooded lass, like her mother before we were wed. I didna know it then of course, not before she told me. But Nan was pretty and hot-blooded and the honour of you singling her out . . .'

'I see.' Cullum had singled out so many. Very few ever refused him, but he didn't realize they thought of it as an honour. 'Why are you telling me all this now?'

'Because Nan is in difficulties, sir, and I canna help no more. My wife died last month and her illness was a terrible expense.'

'You should have let me know, George.'

'I wanted tae before, but Nan begged me not tae. But we're in debt and Nan must work. She has nowhere tae put the bairn.'

'And how old is the, er, bairn?' Cullum's voice sank to a stupefied whisper.

'He is nearly three, sir. He was born in September 1920.'

'My God, this goes back nearly four years!'

'I'm afraid so, sir. And if you still have doubts, he even resembles you, Mr Cullum, with your red hair and large nose.'

'Does he?' Cullum paused, thoughtfully felt his nose and drank another whisky. 'You must realize this is a big shock for me, George.'

'I do, sir, and I'm sorry. If Nan knew I was telling you she'd kill me.'

'All you want is money then?'

For a moment he saw scorn flash over the frame-worker's face and that momentary expression, more than anything else, made him, Cullum Dunbar, feel diminished.

'Nan would like tae get away, sir, to Glasgow maybe where there is more work. She doesn't want tae work here where people talk. She has kept herself tae herself. I will miss her, but I canna keep her if she wants tae go.'

'Where will she live?'

'I have a sister in Glasgow, sir. She'll look after the bairn and Nan will work.'

Cullum finished his drink and started to fasten his coat, doing up the buttons as he gazed sternly at George. 'I'd like to see this child, George, before I decide whether to support him or not. I know you and I'm not saying you'd lie to me; but if he is my child I have a right to see him. You can take me there this instant.'

It was not very far away, the tenement that George Murray shared with Nan and his grandson, just across the bridge and along the road that ran by the Drume. It was a two-room tenement with a big front room in which there was a double bed in the corner and a back room in which there were two more beds, one for Nan and one for William. There was a lavatory on the stone stairs which they shared with the other inhabitants of the tenement, and an outside tap where they drew all the water they needed, heating it on the stove in the front room. It was poverty-stricken, but clean.

Nan was shocked to see Cullum, looking angrily at her father as she admitted them into the neat front room. In a corner was a toddler who did indeed bear a strong resemblance to the man his grandfather had brought to visit him. He was tall for a two-year-old with a sturdy body and Cullum's sandy hair and blue eyes. He didn't look at all like his dark-haired, dark-skinned mother.

She gathered William up protectively in her arms, hugging him to her, her eyes defying Cullum.

'I didna send Da tae see you, Mr Dunbar.'

'I know you didn't, Nan.' Cullum realized his voice was emotional and he reached out a hand to the boy in Nan's arms. Suddenly a pride and tenderness overwhelmed him, whose ferocity astonished him. This sturdy boy was his son; this quiet, brave girl its mother. He sat down and asked to take William in his arms . . .

So lost in reflection was Cullum that he missed the turning up the hill. He reversed his car and began the long slow climb as the dawn began to streak the sky and he noticed a few lights in the houses scattered on the hill.

He never knew if his household heard him come home. He supposed they did, but no one ever said a word. He knew Margaret came downstairs early but they never met because, after garaging the car, Cullum would go in by a side entrance through the hall and quietly upstairs to his room where he would throw off his clothes and climb into the cold bed to have a couple of hours' sleep before it was time to get up again.

Cullum liked his work no more than he had when he left Oxford and he knew this reflected in the business. Dunbars just jogged along making small profits, blaming everything on the economic climate, industrial depression and unrest. The Conservatives had won the election the previous October and Baldwin, that man who had risen so swiftly from nowhere, was again Prime Minister.

The Dunbars were Liberals and the election had signalled the virtual death of the Liberal Party brought about primarily by the struggle between Asquith and Lloyd George. The Liberals had emerged from the election with 40 seats but the Conservatives had a majority of 211 over all the other parties combined. Baldwin had promised ordered progress instead of stagnation, but six months later had little to show for it. The Conservatives said that the solution to the problem of unemployment was to encourage enterprise and be more competitive. That sounded very hollow to the ears of those faced with the import of cheap mass produced goods from a Europe still stricken by the effects of war.

Cullum wanted to sell the business. He wanted to leave Branswick and perhaps live in a small house in a faraway village with Nan and William; but he knew this was a dream. In the present economic circumstances, he could not afford to get her and his son away from the wretched conditions in which they lived in the tenement on the banks of the Drume.

The previous winter Hector Dunbar had suffered a second heart attack, much graver than the first, and died soon after. Cullum, who had expected an upheaval in their lives, was surprised to find that nothing had happened. Margaret remained where she was and did not talk about leaving home or returning to London. She had begun to come into the office to sort through the accounts and, indeed, spent an increasing amount of time there, but there was no more talk about full-time employment. Margaret was rather a mystery to Cullum; he felt he understood her less and less. Their father's death did not bring them closer together. They went their own ways and had little to say to each other.

When he got home one night in the spring the Macallisters' large new black Renault stood in the drive. It could do a maximum speed of ninety miles an hour and had servo-assisted four-wheel brakes and a four-speed gearbox.

With its 'coal scuttle' bonnet it had a distinctive foreign look; but it was imposing nevertheless, roomy inside and handsome to look at.

Cullum, who always walked home from work unless he was seeing Nan, was about to by pass the main door and go in through the side one that he used when he came home in the small hours, when Susan appeared on the steps of the porch and ran down to greet him.

'Cullum! You were sneaking away!'

'I was not.' He bent and kissed her, noticing the happy bloom on her face. 'I was going to . . .' He paused wondering what he could say, but Susan took his arm and pulled him up the steps. 'Come, we have a surprise for you.'

'The twins are here?'

'No, the twins are at home. Someone else.'

When he came into the drawing room Margaret was standing by the window pointing out something in the town to a woman by her side. From the back Cullum could not tell who it was. Bruno was pouring drinks and greeted Cullum with an extended hand holding out a glass of whisky.

'Have this, Cullum. Good day?'

Cullum shrugged and took his drink. 'I wish the Pendreighs would offer again. The trouble is they aren't doing too well either.'

'Here you are, darling.' Bruno gave Susan her drink and then put a proprietorial arm around her. They made a good-looking couple, Cullum thought, thankful that another sister was settled and happy. Bruno and Susan had married only three months after the Common Riding in 1923 and had soon become the parents of twins now ten months old, a boy and a girl, James and Hesther.

The Macallisters had bought a large house mid-way between Selkirk and Branswick so that they could see both lots of families regularly, and Bruno had become more and more involved with the family business,

177

frequently travelling abroad now to find new outlets for its yarn.

Hearing Cullum, Margaret turned and so did the woman next to her.

'Cullum, you remember Fleur Bulwer, don't you? She was one of my teachers at St Étiennes.'

'Of course I remember you, Mrs Bulwer.' Cullum went up and shook her hand. 'You were here a year or two ago, were you not?'

'I was here for Susan's wedding, Cullum, and twice last summer.'

'Of course. I'd forgotten. How time flies.' He felt awkward, noticing the quick flush on her face as she reminded him of his forgetfulness.

Fleur Bulwer was a handsome woman. She was not very tall but she had a good figure, her blonde hair in a shapely coiffure rolled tightly to the nape of her neck. She had brown eyes, well defined brows, a straight nose and a pleasantly shaped mouth. She wore good, fashionable clothes and was an amusing conversationalist. She had made an impression on Cullum at Susan's wedding, but that was shortly after his renewed affair with Nan and he was not interested in other women. When she stayed with the Macallisters they'd met again and he realized he liked her and found her attractive. Her husband had been killed on the Somme and she had a young daughter whom Cullum had never seen.

'How long are you here for, Mrs Bulwer?' Cullum politely offered her a chair, selecting one for himself nearby.

'I'm moving house, so as long as they can have me.'

'You are no longer in Switzerland?'

'Oh I left years ago.' Fleur Bulwer looked at him and gave a low musical laugh, but, once again, Cullum felt an unspoken reproach that he had apparently forgotten so much about her. 'I've lived in London since 1920 and now

178

I'm moving to Harrogate. I wish my daughter to go to school there.'

'Indeed.'

Cullum did not know what it was about Fleur Bulwer that appealed to him. She made him feel expansive, masculine and virile. She was a very feminine woman in a way that Nan was not. Nan was a sexual woman, a woman who enjoyed love for its own sake, for her sake, and not just to please a man. Nan was a strong independent woman who now worked as a bar-filler in the Mactavish mill while Cullum paid for a woman nearby to look after William. Nan would be up at six cleaning the house, preparing breakfast for herself, her son and her father, and then take William to the woman who lived two streets away before starting work at eight.

It was not, Cullum thought, that Mrs Bulwer looked as though she needed protection; far from it, but she had a sort of quiet elegance that seemed enhanced by male company. She started to tell Cullum about the house she had seen in Harrogate, and about the advantages of that attractive town on the edge of the Yorkshire Dales, and Cullum found himself thinking about her and listening intently to what she had to say, watching the way she moved her head and the intelligent light in her expressive, brown eyes.

Margaret had not taken kindly to her sister's marriage to Bruno Macallister; but it was so swift and so inevitable and now an accomplished fact, sealed by the birth of a son and daughter, that initial resentment had given place to acceptance. It seemed light years away and, consequently, unreal since she had wrestled with Bruno on the floor of his apartment, but the distaste for him was still there. He was very guarded in his attitude towards her, very polite and punctilious, never betraying by a glance or a word that they had ever enjoyed intimacy. He had certainly made Susan very happy and Margaret realized how crushed her sister had been during all those sad years since the death of Ian Lyall. Susan had been twenty-seven on her marriage and had immediately wanted to start a family. She felt that to have produced two first time was a bonus.

'Bruno has something he wants to talk about,' Susan whispered to Margaret, leaving his side and joining her sister by the window. 'I thought we could discuss it after dinner.'

'Is it a family matter?' Margaret looked at her speculatively.

'It is to do with us all. I think it's very exciting.'

'Then can he not talk about it now?'

Susan glanced at Cullum and Fleur deep in conversation and shook her head. 'Don't let's take Cullum away from her.'

Margaret tilted her head with surprise. 'You think he likes her?'

'Don't you? I always have.'

'But they've scarcely ever met. He hardly seemed to remember her.'

'I don't think that's true. When they have met there is always a little spark. Would you not like to see Cullum settled?'

'Of course; but I think he will remain a bachelor as I will remain a spinster.'

'What nonsense!'

'No it's true. We shall be the odd Dunbars living together at the big house on the hill until we are ninety, me looking after Cullum and Cullum not quite looking after the mill.'

Susan shook her head and smiled conspiratorily. 'What Bruno has to say will change all that.'

During dinner it was decided that the Macallisters and their guest would stay the night. A storm had blown up and as it grew dark the rain lashed against the windows. Fleur Bulwer was taken to see her room and she tactfully said she would stay there awhile and read as she knew Bruno wanted a family council.

Somehow it all seemed to have been prearranged, even the storm, as they settled in the drawing room round the fire, the curtains drawn to keep out the rain and the cold. Bruno stood in front of the fire, a glass of brandy in his hand, and Margaret and Susan sat together on the sofa while Cullum perched on a high chair, nursing the customary glass of whisky.

'I have discussed all this with Susan and my parents,' Bruno began rather nervously, his fingers clenched around his glass, his feet firmly apart on the rug as though to give him confidence. He had on a check suit, the trouser legs flared in the fashionable Oxford 'bags'. His curly hair was kept in control by brilliantine and he had grown a large moustache which made him look avuncular rather than sinister because it diverted attention from the scar on his cheek, grown less livid with time. Looking at him Margaret wondered how she ever found him either attractive or sinister. For a moment he glanced at her and, seeming to divine the meaning of the expression in her eyes, looked away. 'You know that for some years I have been studying the manufacture of yarn and I think I have come to have a very good grasp of the business. Unlike a lot of firms which have gone to the wall Macallisters is doing fairly well, and Father is very much still in control of the business which has now also been joined by my brother Jock.

'I must confess I have felt constrained and restless, and I thought that Susan and I and the children might move to Canada or South Africa and start a new life, reluctant as we are to leave Scotland. However, a new thought came to me and this I want to put to you tonight. It has Susan's full support.' Bruno looked at her for encouragement and, as she nodded, cleared his throat. 'I thought that something Cullum said to me earlier tonight might make my task easier.'

181

'And what was that?' Cullum began slightly aggressively, but Susan reached out and put a restraining hand on his arm.

'Listen to Bruno, Cullum. Don't speak until he has finished.'

'Well, Cullum said to me,' Bruno went on, 'that he wished the Pendreighs would offer again. He knows they won't and I know they won't. Branswick is in a recession and so is the knitting business. I hear the MacLeods might even be closing. There's a slump in demand, too many cheap European goods imported from abroad. Am I not right Cullum?'

'Right,' Cullum nodded. 'But I don't see where this is getting us.'

'You will.' Bruno swayed back on his legs and gazed for a moment at the ceiling as if seeking inspiration. 'I am suggesting that Macallisters buys into Dunbars; that we invest money for new plant and machinery; that we look to expansion and the future. Dunbars with our money and our help can start to think about its products and designs. I think we can do a lot more by using different types of yarn. For instance, as you know, last year I was in China and I could increase the importation of cashmere tenfold. Cashmere yarn makes a beautiful soft fabric, which I don't think is used enough. You could have a whole new line in knitted cashmere pullovers and cardigans made from yarn imported and spun by Macallisters in Selkirk. How about that?'

The crackling of the fire was the only sound that disturbed the silence. A log slipped onto the hearth and there was a sudden blaze. Cullum got up and poked the log back. Then he went to the table and replenished his empty glass. Margaret thought he had gone very white. When he turned he was nervously moistening his lips.

'And you? What part will you play?'

'Personally you mean?' Bruno said.

'Yes.'

'I would like to be joint managing director with you. I think I have a lot to offer. I'm well placed to come into the knitting side of the business. I've travelled a lot and know the market. If Macallisters supply most of your yarn we will all benefit.'

'*Macallisters* particularly.' Cullum did not trouble to keep the bitterness out of his voice. 'With the slump in knitted goods in this country and the cheap ones made on the Continent, Macallisters are without doubt experiencing difficulties in disposing of all their yarn.'

'Difficulties yes, but the situation is nowhere near as bad as yours is,' Bruno riposted smoothly. 'We have capital, ample supplies, good sources and – we have Cameron money to spare for investment. My uncle, Michael Cameron, is very anxious to take some money out of less profitable businesses, coal for example, and put it elsewhere.'

'Why is coal not profitable?'

'Because the coalmines are overmanned and the workers too well paid. They may not think so, but in economic terms of supply and demand they are. We've been having trouble all year with the miners and Michael thinks there will be greater trouble yet because the owners are as intransigent and as pig-headed as the unions and the men. He would like to pull the Cameron money right out of coal and steel and invest in textiles. He's thinking of quite a large sum.'

'How much?' Cullum gazed at him.

'What would you say to half a million?'

'As much as that?'

'Maybe more. Half a million invested in new plant, modernization. My ideas and . . .' Bruno looked at his feet and then at Margaret. 'And Margaret's ideas too. For she has them, has she not?'

'Margaret's ideas in the business!' Cullum expostulated.

Bruno quickly continued. 'I hear Margaret has done wonders in the accounts department. She has a very neat

183

analytical mind. I know, because of what she has said to Susan over the years and occasionally to me, that she is very interested in the running of Dunbars. She would love to have some part in it, an important part. Well, I for one think that she should, and so does Susan.'

'I have always thought so,' Susan said, looking defiantly at her brother. 'We talked about it years ago, Cullum. Well, now that Father is no more and Margaret is free . . .'

'This is blackmail,' Cullum interrupted.

'No, it is not. It's common sense.' Susan put her hand over her sister's as Margaret tried to speak. 'Don't say anything yet, Margaret. You have no interests now except Cullum and the house. You're free to do as you like and yet you don't go back to London as you said you would. Maybe you wonder what you could do there? Maybe you feel that you've been here too long to change; yet you're only twenty-three Maggie, and life is ahead of you, not behind. I know you already go to the mill occasionally and, as Bruno said, we've heard how well you have reorganized accounts. According to people we know they were in a shambles . . .'

'*What* people . . .' Cullum began aggressively but Susan continued calmly.

'People in the business; people whose accounts were never paid. Ours for one. Our head cashier had a terrible time getting Dunbars to pay their bills; now he says everything is much better. Oh we hear these things. We've been concerned about Dunbars for much longer than you think but we didn't know what to do.'

'It was why she married me.' Bruno tried to take the heat out of the situation by jocularity, but Margaret knew that was not why Susan married him. She had married him for love, and because she was desperate for a husband. Which came first, love or desperation, Margaret could not say. But Bruno had wooed her and won her; there had been no resistance, and yet it was a curiously unromantic

184

courtship where the lovers had never seemed to want to be alone. But Susan had a good practical business head too. If only she and Susan had been men. It was ironical now, Margaret reflected, her thoughts racing rapidly ahead, that their saviour should come in the form of Bruno Macallister.

'Well, you've obviously got all this tied up between you,' Cullum said bitterly. 'I shouldn't wonder if Margaret was in on it too.'

'I was not,' Margaret said quietly; but sad he should so mistrust her. 'It is no plot. Can't you see, Cullum, what good sense it makes? Macallisters are family – we are related to them through our mothers and by Susan's marriage to Bruno. It's much better than being bought out by people we don't know, or who don't care about us, and it is coming to that, Cullum, is it not? Without fresh capital, without new ideas, it may be sooner than we think. I may have helped tidy up the accounts, but I certainly know what financial trouble Dunbars are in and why people have to wait for their money.'

Margaret got up and walked over to her brother, standing beside his chair, looking placatingly into his stricken face. How she wished she understood him better. Had she tried enough? Had they not been too ensnared by the memory of Malcolm?

'You haven't failed, Cullum. You've kept the pot boiling; but you have never pretended to be in love with the business. Now, maybe, with fresh hope you will find that you are interested, after all. You've steadied down considerably in the past few years.'

'You're being patronizing Maggie,' Cullum said ungraciously.

Margaret flushed and raised her head. 'No, I'm not. But I want you to see what a *chance* this is. I swear I heard not a word of it before tonight. I swear that on my oath. But I do see very clearly what it could mean for us as a business and a family.' She went back to her seat. 'Moreover, I would like to be part of it. It's handsome of Bruno to suggest it, no doubt egged on by Susan.'

'Not at all,' Bruno said urbanely, selecting a cigarette from his silver case. 'In fact I thought of it. I thought you could be in charge of design and development. You could go to London and abroad to study new ideas. You would be a roving ambassador. We would set the business in order and start planning for the future. You have no idea what a difference it will make.'

'I have though, I have,' Margaret said, her eyes shining. 'Oh, do I *not* know what a difference it will make – to us all!'

CHAPTER ELEVEN

In the course of the summer and autumn of 1925 the Dunbar and Macallister families did, indeed, feel the effects of the changes promised in April. The formalities by which Macallisters purchased a share of the Dunbar business were speedily completed, though at one time they threatened to break down altogether. Margaret insisted that the Dunbar family should retain overall control of the business and that the Macallisters should have the minority share. Bruno opposed this and so did his father, supported by Susan on the grounds that the Macallisters and Dunbars were related twice over. Cullum did not particularly care either way, but Margaret was adamant. The rest of the family could have outvoted her; but in the end Cullum supported her and so did Juliet and Mary, the latter thinking no doubt about her son's future in the business.

Margaret thus demonstrated, very early on, a flair for business that was not just confined to putting the accounting house in order. She was tough and she was unbending even though, if the Macallisters had pulled out, the Dunbar business would have been in ruins. She was prepared to stand her ground and to gamble on winning. The Macallisters settled for forty percent of the business, leaving sixty percent shared among the Dunbars. Andrew Dunbar parted with his shares, for a price, so that the business now rested firmly in the hands of Hector's four surviving children and his grandson.

Susan and Margaret had seats on the reorganized board, and so did Mary, because the part she had played was quite crucial. Once the matter was settled there was no rancour on the part of the Macallisters, and Bruno moved into the office next to Cullum as joint managing director. Margaret was given a title of Director of Design and Development, a very new concept for those days and one which provoked much talk in local business circles. For no woman before had ever had a seat on a board, that anyone could recall, let alone been given an executive position.

Margaret Dunbar had become a figure of some mystery in Branswick. She had gradually withdrawn from social events, ladies' meetings and outings, parties, charity fairs and the like. She could no longer be relied upon for bridge afternoons, whist evenings or mixed tennis fours in the summer. She was considered something of a recluse. She had purchased a car, one of the little baby Austin Sevens, the first 'people's car' brought out in 1922 by Sir Herbert Austin, knighted for the guns and aircraft he had manufactured during the war. It was a four-seater costing £165, £20 cheaper than the Model T Ford. There was an official speed limit of twenty miles an hour all over the country but it was broken by everybody, Margaret included, and she was frequently to be seen speeding through the valley outside Branswick going no one knew where.

Now she was a director of the family firm and those who claimed to know about these things prophesied only gloom and disaster for one who had been so headstrong in her youth and who had so steadfastly refused to conform.

The young men who had once wished to court Margaret gradually married girls who fitted into the expected mould. They purchased solid, well built houses and proceeded to produce families: two or three children apiece was the norm. Their wives played tennis and croquet, and gave lunches and teas for other young marrieds like themselves. The beautiful, headstrong Margaret had got‘ her deserts; she had inherited the family eccentricity and would be a spinster, a category for which there was no place in that constricted society. Cathy Pendreigh had two children, and Moira Law four. Susan Macallister had two and there were scarcely any girls of Margaret's age still unwed. One rumour said that she did not like men; that some shameful experience in London had soured her. Another, contrarily, that she had borne a child who was cared for deep in the countryside where she went on her mysterious visits. A lot of damaging and untrue remarks were made about one whose beauty and style were still envied, but who had put herself outside the social pale by her inability to be like everyone else.

In the country as a whole there was little change. Winston Churchill, who had deserted the Liberal Party for the Conservatives in 1924, was made Chancellor of the Exchequer in the new Baldwin Government. In May 1925 he returned England to the Gold Standard at pre-war parity, a move which was opposed by Maynard Keynes among others. The troubles of the poor continued. Labour criticized the budget on the grounds that it was aimed at relieving taxation on the rich and adding to the taxation of the poor. Churchill loftily declared that it was in the interests of trade unions as well as employers to ensure that there was not growing up a general habit of learning how to qualify for unemployment insurance. He later said he intended no offence to the mass of the working people.

In May a move to introduce a 48-hour working week was rejected. The 50-hour working week continued but some saw a return to a 54-hour week. A Widows' and Orphans' and Old Age Contributory Pensions' Bill provided that widows of working men should receive ten shillings a week until they remarried. It was admitted that ten shillings a week was insufficient to keep a grown person in the necessities of life, but it was claimed that this would encourage people to help themselves. Obviously it was framed by people who had no conception of what it was like to be a widow with four children, say, and who was unable for practical reasons to do any more to help herself, or them.

In June there was a great demonstration by the unemployed in Trafalgar Square, followed by a debate in Parliament on unemployment. Lloyd George generously said that the Government could not be blamed for the Depression which mainly affected heavy industry – coal and heavy metals – but that it was not grappling with the crisis.

Yet all these events, the political bickering, the industrial unrest, did little to influence the lives of the people both rich and poor. The well off remained well off and the poor remained poor. The Dunbars, the Macallisters, the Laws, the Pendreighs, the Mactavishes and their friends continued much as they had ever done. If anything, they felt better off because life was more stable and, for women, freer. They had their nice homes, their servants, their parties and their motor cars. Some of them even had crystal wireless sets with which they could tune into the new British Broadcasting Company formed in 1922.

In Branswick, for those who did not live on the hill or near it, or who, with the advent of the motor car, had moved to large houses in small villages near Branswick, life continued much as before. Wages were low, there was some unemployment in the town, and many were too proud to ask for poor relief. They did not have cars or wirelesses and sometimes not enough to eat; but very few of them starved or went without medical help when they needed it.

Nan Murray continued with her job at Mactavishes' Mill and her son William was cared for by Mrs Anderson, who looked after five other children whose mothers had to work. Nan had few friends because her situation made her prefer to keep herself to herself. She was proud and independent and did not wish for pity, or the sufferance of others who had made respectable if humble marriages and whose children were legitimate. Even if they lived in tenements like hers and had more children than they could cope with and husbands who were out of work or who drank too much, they still looked down on her because of the shame she had brought on herself and her parents. Non-conformity among the lower classes in Branswick was as much a sin as it was among their betters.

Men tried to be familiar with her and some women often showed their contempt by being rude to her or ignoring her. She led a lonely life and, since the death of her mother, she felt she had no friend in the world. She looked forward to Cullum's visits more than she cared to admit, but during the summer they grew less frequent and Nan found her stoicism gradually eroded because she did not know why.

The answer lay in Selkirk, where Mrs Bulwer had unexpectedly purchased a house which had taken her fancy just when she was on the point of completing her acquisition of the house in Harrogate. She decided that she had more friends in Scotland – she had, after all, known no one in Harrogate – and her daughter Patricia could board there instead. It all happened very suddenly and no one could say whether the proximity of Cullum Dunbar influenced her decision or not.

Cullum Dunbar resented the invasion of the Macallisters. In his own way he had probably wanted the company to grind quietly to a halt, though how he would have lived if it had, he had not really taken the trouble to work out. He did not want a Macallister as a joint managing director, nor his sisters on the board, especially his sister Margaret coming in every day and sitting in an office near to his. His liaison with Nan had given him a kind of emotional peace and stability even though it had its unsatisfactory side.

He had never thought of marrying her – the social boundaries were much too strict and he would never at that time have dreamed of breaking them – but he had thought of going away and living with her, or of renting a little cottage outside the town where she could live and he could spend more time with her. He loved her and he loved bonny William. He was faithful to Nan; he no longer slept with any girl who came his way, nor did he lose himself so much in drink.

Cullum was set in his ways, ways that could have gone on forever for all he was concerned, had it not been for the advent of the Macallisters on that day in April 1925 which did, indeed, change things completely. Drink, always his weakness, his solace, claimed him again and he was frequently brought home in an inebriated condition after visiting a succession of public houses in the area, or was too ill to rise from his bed in the morning and unable to work.

Watching his rapid deterioration and knowing the reason for it, Margaret worried about it more than anything else that summer. It was a cloud on the horizon of her new-found happiness which had gradually come about because at last she felt secure about the future of the family firm, she had a part to play in its progress, and she was in love.

When Margaret drove out of the town in her little green Austin Seven it was not to see the unlawful fruits of a liaison, but her lover Hamish Ogilvy. For they had done what Cullum had only dreamed of doing: soon after the start of their affair in 1923 they had purchased a small cottage in a valley ten miles from Branswick, where they met whenever they could. They could hardly ever stay the night there or spend a lot of time together, but what time they did have was precious. They met and they made love and then they went their respective ways again, Hamish north to Galashiels and Margaret south to Branswick. The cottage, set in the hills, was a crofter's cottage and it had no neighbours or people who could spy on it and discover their secret. It was up a winding unmade road, past a small loch, right at the end of the valley. It had two rooms, no electric light and no running water. It was cold in winter and delightful on the few warm days which could form a

Scottish summer. All it had in one room was a large bed and a chair; in the other was a table, two wooden chairs and a sofa, and a gas stove on which Margaret made what meals they were able to eat together.

Margaret felt that she was married to Hamish Ogilvy and that what she was doing was not sinful. She was faithful to him and he to her, and she did not feel guilty. No sexual relations with his wife were possible even if he had wanted them, and so she did not have the agony of knowing that she shared the body of a man she loved with someone else.

Now on this day in September she waited for Hamish by the fire, which she had lit as soon as she came in, having brought logs in the boot of her car together with food and a bottle of wine. It was a wintry day and the cottage was bitterly cold because it had been unused for a month. Margaret had been in London and Paris and Hamish had taken his children to his mother's in Aberdeen for a holiday.

From time to time, after the fire was lit and stone hot water bottles placed in the bed, Margaret went to the window, longing for a glimpse of his car making its way slowly up the rough winding track from the loch. He was late. She looked anxiously at her watch because she had to get back before nightfall. She was bending to stoke the fire when she heard the familiar whine of the car. She ran to the door and flung it open, her face shining with anticipation.

Hamish waved when he saw her and, as the car stopped, she tugged open the door and he took her in his arms and kissed her.

'Why are you so late? I was worried.' She took his hat off, tossing it into the back of the car, and stroked his brow.

'I had a call to make in Moffat. It took me longer than I thought it would.'

'Never mind. You're here now.' She climbed off his lap and they got out of the car and walked into the cottage hand in hand. Hamish went immediately to the fire to warm himself.

'My goodness it's cold. It's like winter already.' He looked at her. 'Margaret, you've changed.'

'Changed?' Margaret put her arms round his waist and leaned her head against his chest.

'I think you're even more beautiful. More . . . special.' He kissed the top of her head. 'You do know that you are everything in the world to me, Margaret, don't you?' Margaret nodded but didn't speak. 'Don't change too much,' he finished in a whisper.

The happiness, the lightness, the joy suddenly left Margaret's heart and she looked anxiously up at him. 'How have I *changed* Hamish? If I'm more beautiful you should be happy, yet you sound sad.'

Hamish gently pushed her away from him and got out his cigarettes, offering her one. Margaret shook her head and perched on the edge of the small table by the window, her arms crossed.

'I think you've changed since, well, everything started to happen. I know you're very busy and preoccupied, but somehow it's different. I don't know how.'

'Different?' Margaret had to still a feeling of panic. 'What is different? Us?'

'No, no.' Hamish came over to her and put one hand on her shoulder. The smoke from the cigarette in his other hand spiralled between them, transparent but symbolic, like a barrier. 'Darling, I think you're very beautiful. More vivacious, more alive, more . . .' He threw his cigarette into the fire and took her arm. 'Let's go to bed.'

Hamish was Margaret's first lover, but she felt by now that she had learned from him all there was to know about the human experience of love. She couldn't imagine finding more satisfaction with any other man. He was

194

gentle, kind, vigorous, appreciative, imaginative and fun. They laughed a lot when they were in bed. It was frequently intense and passionate, but not a grim, serious business. Afterwards their rapport was always better than before, especially if they had not seen each other for some time. At first they sometimes felt constrained, or had a little quarrel, without meaning to or knowing why. Today had been a typical occasion, with Hamish introducing an odd little note which worried Margaret until he revealed to her again the fullness of his love and she felt secure and happy in his arms.

They hugged each other in the bed because it was so cold. Their breath billowed in front of them like vaporous clouds when they spoke.

'We should get a fire in this room,' Hamish said. 'I could have a fireplace made.'

'Do you imagine people slept here before?'

'Must have.'

'Imagine them making love, like us.'

'Not like us.' Hamish glanced at her. 'No one could ever do that. Margaret, are you happy with me?'

Margaret squeezed him, and then the little spasm of fear returned. She lay on her stomach and looked at him, tracing the contours of his face with a finger. His face, still noble and beautiful to her, was not quite so handsome or so carefree as when she had first known him. He was thirty-seven now and there were furrows on his brow brought about by business and domestic cares, possibly too by guilt at his affair with Margaret. For he had always thought of himself as an upright, honourable man who had fought in the war and subsequently been prepared to forgive his wife for quite blatant infidelities. Now she was a hopeless invalid, confined permanently to her bed and he enjoyed pleasure with another woman.

Even though she had no qualms about their relationship, Margaret knew that Hamish did and that it had aged him. His blue eyes were not quite so blue and his cheeks were slightly cavernous, as with a man whose conscience was slowly being gnawed by hidden anguish. In fact he was much thinner than he had been and was frequently plagued by bronchitis and a host of other ills whose origins were not necessarily organic.

But Margaret loved him. If he did not excite her physically as much as he once did, she loved him in a much deeper way because of what he was: a noble, loving, tortured soul stricken by conflicts that she had helped to create. She lightly kissed his lips and put her arm about him, gazing at him.

'Of course I'm happy, happy, my beloved. Hamish, what is the matter with you today? There is something, but I don't know what; something more than the usual worries and cares.'

'How do you mean "something"?'

'First you said I'd changed and would not say how, then you ask if I'm happy with you. It makes me afraid.'

'There's no need for you to be afraid, my darling. I am afraid. I'm afraid of losing you.'

'But that's impossible!' She leaned her cheek against his chest and laughed. 'Quite, quite impossible.'

'Why should you stay with someone like me? A married man who can give you nothing – no home, children, all the things women want.'

'But this is our home.' Margaret implanted kisses on each of his flat pink nipples and then kissed his chest, his neck and finally his lips, stifling his reply.

When they were dressed and eating at the table placed close to the fire he returned to the theme.

'Did you never want children, Margaret?'

Margaret tossed her head and smiled into his eyes. She wore no make-up and her skin was fair and unblemished, but there was a high colour on her cheeks, the aftermath of love. Her full lips were naturally red as though still

196

engorged with passion. Her shingled hair with its formal waves fell over her face, the fine arcs of her brows making her look statuesque and thoughtful.

'I never thought about children,' she replied after a moment, not altogether truthfully. She had certainly thought about avoiding children a good deal when her affair with Hamish had first begun. Being Margaret she had wanted to do the thing thoroughly and properly without shame, and had visited an Edinburgh gynaecologist who had fitted her with the diaphragm, invented by Dr Wilhelm Mensinga in the 1870s and known after him as the Dutch cap. It was still one of the most effective and convenient forms of contraception known. 'I mean, I've never positively wanted a child.'

'They say a woman always wants a child by the man she loves,' Hamish said rather wistfully. 'I would like you to have my child, Margaret.'

Margaret put down her knife and fork and clasped his hand across the table. 'Darling, that is hopelessly impractical,' she said softly. 'If I wanted a child I would certainly want yours; but the scandal it would cause at home would be unthinkable. Besides, you know, we took care. You *wanted* me to take care . . .'.

'Yes, I know, but . . . ' Hamish withdrew his hand from beneath hers still feeling, unreasonably he knew, a little hurt.

Margaret by now knew him so well that she could almost read his mind and, getting up, she went round to him and pressed her cheek against his. 'I think of you as my husband, Hamish. If it were possible, I would like your child. It would please you and, of course, it would give me immense joy. But I never think about it because of its utter impossibility. Instead I think about you, and Dunbars. Dunbars is my child and you are my husband and this – ' she gestured round the cottage, 'this, as I said, is our home.'

'Yes, Dunbars *is* your child. That's why you've changed. I know it now. You've given birth. You've had a child.'

Returning to her seat Margaret lit a cigarette. She blew smoke towards the ceiling and looked at her lover on the other side of the table, her eyes narrowed. 'Now I *know* what's the matter with you, Hamish. You're jealous.'

Hamish stared at her, moving his chair away from the table. 'Jealous? What a ridiculous thing to say!'

'For two years,' Margaret went on, 'two years last month, I have been your mistress. That is the word is it not? Mistress?' He shook his head but she did not pause. 'No, don't frown – I *like* the word mistress. It's very carnal; it implies some sort of possession. I am your mistress and you are my lover. Not master. Note the male equivalent of mistress in this context is not master.'

'Nor it is,' Hamish said softly.

'But then in April this year Bruno Macallister made the startling suggestion that his family should buy into my family firm and that I should be given a job in it. Through my sister, for I don't suppose he cared at all himself, he knew I wanted to work. I always have wanted to work. After Father died they all expected me to dash off to London or distant parts. But I did not. I stayed at home because of you, Hamish.'

'I know that.' He reached for her hand and pressed it.

'I love you, Hamish; you are the first thing in my life, as you say I am in yours – and I believe you – but you have your work, as well as your home and family. You are the busy head of an engineering firm. Your life is absolutely full to overflowing. When you creep away and meet me it is a little interlude. When I used to come and meet you it was the high point of my week, my life . . .'

'Mine too, I swear . . .'

'Yes, I know it was important; but it was only *one* of a number of things that were important. For me it was the one and only important thing that happened: to drive up

198

here once or twice a week to be with you. You were my whole world, Hamish.'

'Were?' His face looked solemn, anxious.

'Yes. It was not fair on you. Oh, all this has nothing to do with my love for you.' She rose and, coming round to him again, bent over him, putting her arms round his neck, leaning her cheek against his. 'You are still my whole emotional world. My love for you is unchanging. But you are no longer my whole world.' She kissed him and went and stood in front of the fire, hugging herself, looking at the floor. 'You know, Hamish, I have never been like other women, or most of the women I know. I have always yearned for something other than being a man's wife, the mother of his children, the mistress of a house. Oh I was an obedient dutiful daughter once Father had me back at Branswick. I accepted my lot and nursed him devotedly until he died. But I've always felt apart, somehow an outcast. Someone different.' She looked up and ran her hands through her short hair. 'I suppose I've always been ambitious. How fired I was with the idea of a career when I went to London! I loved the life of the store, the smart world, beautiful clothes. I wanted to be a top mannequin, travelling to shows in Paris and Vienna once things got back to normal after the war. All that was cut short because I had to be what Father wanted me to be. I *had* to. But all the time I was aware of the fact that Dunbars – over a hundred years old, one of the oldest companies in Branswick, which had been very successful and could be again – was going to the wall, and yet Cullum forbade me to have anything to do with it! Gradually I edged my way in as a clerk, helping out when people were ill, going through the accounts, trying to make some sort of order in a place where Cullum's defeatism was all-pervasive. The staff were demoralized; the workers only worked because they had to. There was no spirit, no sense of achievement. I felt despair but I could do nothing about it until Bruno came along and changed everything. Now I feel that Dunbars is going to climb. And I'm going to climb with it!' She ended on a triumphant note.

Hamish marvelled at the verve and energy that emanated from her. He knew then that one day he would lose her; perhaps he had always known the inevitability of it. For, as she said, Margaret was no ordinary woman and what he could give her was not enough.

He got slowly to his feet and turned his back on her, gazing out of the window at the Scottish hills dressed in autumnal browns, purples and reds. The very cold made the sky glow and he was reminded of the curious intensity of the light in Margaret's eyes.

'I know you aren't like other women,' he said quietly, his hands in his pockets. 'But I didn't know what it was you wanted. With your beauty I knew you could not lack admirers, and yet you have never married. Now I know what it is you want and that is why you have changed. You are on the way to realizing a great ambition, and who can blame you?' He turned to her and the sadness of his expression astonished her. 'But I will lose you, Margaret; one day I will lose you.'

Margaret ran over to him and clasped him again in her arms. 'Never, darling, never! What you can give me is everything that I need emotionally. Our life will be better now that I am no longer so dependent on you. In time I would have become a drone and a bore. We will still meet here; we will still love and enjoy each other, and it will be even better than it is!'

Hamish stroked her back and hugged her. She was very very precious to him, this exciting, vital, lovely woman. He often felt unable to believe his good fortune that he had her. But he would lose her. One day, as sure as night followed day, she would realize that what he could give was not enough, and she would go. He had to make use of the precious little time he had left.

He looked at his watch. 'It's five o'clock. We have to

go. When can we meet again?' He tried to sound brave and inconsequential, though it mattered so much to him. One day she would say 'never' and the light of love would be absent from those blue-green eyes. Or she might just not turn up, or send him a note instead.

Margaret freed herself from his arms and went to her bag, producing a small red leather-bound diary which she consulted, flicking through the pages, her brows knitted in a frown. 'I'm here for the next two weeks. Monday?'

She looked up at him and he nodded, making a note in his own book, a little circle round the date in case anyone looked at it. What they would make of all the little circles he didn't know.

'Where do you go after that?'

'I'm going to London to look for offices. We should have a London office if we're to meet all the important buyers and designers who come to England. They don't always want to make the journey to Branswick. Then I'm going to visit all the stores and find out what they would like in the way of fashions. Imagine, we're asking them! No one has ever thought of it before, and yet it is so important. We've just put our goods on the market hoping they'd sell! It seems absurd, doesn't it? Quite absurd! Women, you see, are becoming feminine again. Bosoms and waists are returning – ' Margaret laughed at the expression on his face. 'I want to develop a line of elegant clothes to be worn out of doors. I'm going to look for a designer and we'll be exploring all sorts of new yarns and mixtures. Bruno is going to China again to try and arrange for a bigger supply of cashmere which his firm will spin, and we're going to buy more merino and llama wool and make them up into all sorts of exciting things. We're buying more powerful machinery, some of the big frames made by Cotton, and we're going to enlarge the Dunbar mill so that we can employ more people. It's all very exciting.'

'You will need a man by your side, whatever you say,' Hamish said quietly. 'You'll want to get married and have children, sooner or later. You'll want your children to carry on the Dunbar tradition. Have you ever thought of that?'

'Nothing is further from my mind, I assure you,' Margaret said, looking at him tenderly. 'I think Cullum is going to marry Fleur Bulwer, and *his* children will be the natural heirs to Murdoch Dunbar & Sons, not mine, were I ever to have any.'

'Cullum to marry?' Hamish looked at her in surprise and helped to dry the plates she was rinsing.

'He's known this woman for a few years. Surely I mentioned her to you? She's two years older than him, but it doesn't matter. She is very clever and smart. I knew that she was interested in him but she was very skilful. If she'd made a false move she would have lost him. He has a woman, you know. It must be someone he's ashamed of, because he's very secretive about her – doubtless one of the mill girls. Maybe he has more than one, I don't know, but about twice a week he doesn't come home until dawn. His car creeping through the gates always wakes me because my bedroom is at the front.'

'And you never ask him?'

'Never.' Margaret finished washing the plates and, going to the door, opened it and threw the water outside. They brought the water in a pail from the loch and kept it topped up on each visit. 'Cullum and I have never been close. In a sense I despise him, I suppose. I can't help it. He's so unlike Malcolm that it's almost impossible to believe they were brothers.'

'Unlike you, too,' Hamish said gently.

'Yes.' Margaret closed the door behind her and leaned against it, the bowl in her hands. 'Very unlike me.'

'But you can't blame Cullum for not being like his brother.'

Margaret wiped the bowl and put it on the floor. 'I wouldn't object if he simply had a different personality. But he is so weak, and he drinks, drinks. That's the part I can't stand. In any crisis he always goes to the bottle. He'd been much better while things were calm, but as soon as the business with Macallisters blew up, especially the row about control, he started drinking. He really contributed nothing at all. I had to bully and cajole him, Mary, Juliet and Susan into saving the family honour, but especially *him*! I hope he does marry Fleur, because she might help him with this terrible curse of drinking. It runs in our family; but for me it is a sign of weakness in a man and I can't stand it. There, I've said it. I'm horrible, aren't I, darling?'

She blew him a kiss and then went over and started scrubbing the plain deal table. When they left the cottage everything would be spotless, the bed made, the floors swept, the crockery clean and put away. She was so capable, Hamish thought, not only in this but everything else.

'No, you're not horrible. Drinking is a weakness but it's also an illness. We don't really understand much about it.'

'I do.' Margaret wiped the table with a wet cloth. 'I understand if you drink too much you suffer, and so does everyone else. I had it with my father too and we've had several members of the family in the past who were drunks. No one admired them. Yet we had an aunt who had TB and everyone admired her because of the quiet, brave way she suffered. That was an illness too.'

She gazed at him and he lowered his eyes. In the face of her fierce pitiless logic he felt he had so little to say. Drinking was weak and Cullum was weak and that was all there was to it.

'Anyway, if he marries Fleur I shall have to find somewhere else to live. Still, I hope he does. I like her and I think she will be good for him. She's sharp and ambitious and will keep him hard at work. Oh, and I think she loves him too!'

Margaret went over to the chair where she'd left her coat and Hamish got up and stood behind her, helping her into it. It was a heavy coat of a purple mixture Harris tweed with large astrakhan fur collar and cuffs, and when she had it on it made her seem fragile and vulnerable, her face almost lost in the tight little grey curls of the baby lamb. He bent over and kissed her cheek, holding her in his arms for a long sad moment.

'I love you,' he whispered. 'Oh, I love you.'

Margaret sighed and stroked his face with the palm of her hand. Then she turned and kissed him. The partings were always sad.

They put out the fire, locked the cottage and hid the key under a stone so that whoever was first there next time would be able to get in. Then they made their way to her car and Hamish saw her into it, leaning his head through the window before she drove off. He felt such a melancholy today that it almost crushed him, and his face through the window looked so tragic that Margaret felt her heart turn over.

'I love you,' she said fervently, gazing into his deep blue eyes. 'Don't look like that. Until next time, my darling.'

He watched her car go down the hill and then, with foreboding in his heart, got into his new 'Bullnose' Morris Oxford and drove slowly along the track after her, unaware of the dust that he left in his wake.

CHAPTER TWELVE

'It appears all women over twenty-one will have the vote.' Tristan Fleming sighed and put down the *Daily Mail*. 'Rothermere calls it "votes for flappers".'

'So?' Margaret Dunbar raised her head from the documents she was studying and smiled. 'Is that so objectionable?'

'I suppose it's inevitable. Would you like to be Prime Minister, Margaret?'

'One day maybe,' she murmured, lowering her eyes to the documents about the sale of new merchandise to Flemings. 'Not just yet. However, I don't see why I shouldn't vote. I regard myself and my sex as equal to any man.'

'Oh I know that, darling. But if you aren't careful you may have to enter politics. They say the woollen industry will be finished if there is no protection.'

Margaret signed the paper she had inspected, and pushed her chair back from Tristan's desk.

'I'm not in favour of protection. Our family has always been Liberal and we are for free trade. Dunbars are for free trade too, even if it does cause temporary setbacks. What can any nation hope to gain with a barrier of tariffs round it? That's what is happening, will happen. It's happening to Europe and it'll happen to us. It's true we haven't had an easy time, but then who has? I see better times ahead.'

Tristan picked up a cup from the table at his elbow and tilted it elegantly to his mouth, crooking his little finger. He looked immaculate in his well cut grey suit, the jacket double-breasted, the trousers narrow and not favouring the wide 'Oxford bag' style which he deplored as 'vulgar'. His greying hair was very short and he had grown a small moustache to go with the monocle which, he said, he needed to improve the sight of his left eye. Margaret had doubts about the truth of this; she thought he wore it because it made him look like a dandy. Fleming was lost in this post-war world. He would have fitted in beautifully with the extravagances of the Regency.

'I think you must be unique,' Tristan said. 'The incurable optimist.'

'Better times ahead for *us*, I mean.' Margaret poured herself more tea. 'You have been very good to us, Tristan, trying our new styles, giving us displays.'

'And you give us very nice terms.' Tristan glanced at the bills of sale on his desk and smiled, stirring his tea. 'But I think you are winning. I think you're getting the edge over Pendreigh and Mactavish.'

'I'm going to concentrate on women's fashions.' Margaret lit a cigarette and exhaled. 'I may say I've had a lot of opposition from my board who want to stick to the same old things – underwear, stockings, men's pullovers. I think Bruno is on my side, but only just.'

'Do you ever wonder if the battle is worth fighting?' Tristan screwed up his eyes and looked at her through the spiral of cigarette smoke.

'Of course it's worth fighting! Winning would be no fun without a battle. We've nearly completed our new extensions to the mill. Next week we shall be installing the new wide frames. Jumper suits like mine will soon be the thing. They're so practical for the modern working woman; they're easy to wear and warm, especially in this freezing weather.' Margaret shivered and looked out of the window. The country was experiencing a spell of intense cold and frosts. Through the skeletal trees of Cavendish Square the roofs of the buildings opposite were so thickly iced it looked like snow, and conditions on the roads were hazardous. She had walked from the new office in Devonshire Place, taking great care in her pointed high-heeled shoes.

'Jumper suits *are* very popular,' Tristan agreed. 'Especially ones that are well designed.'

Margaret stood up and went to the window, gravely regarding the November scene. She had let her hair grow so that it curled close to her head at the nape of her neck and a large flat wave, the 'swirl', partly covered her forehead. The softer style suited her, Tristan thought regarding her profile, because she had beautiful hair and the Eton crop which she'd briefly patronized the previous year had made her look too hard and masculine, perhaps the image she was trying to put forward as a tough woman of business. He wondered whether she had ever thought about marriage. It was difficult to think of such a beautiful, passionate woman on her own. Or *was* she on her own? He knew nothing about her private life. If there were anything to tell, it remained a closely guarded secret.

'I want to employ a designer,' Margaret said at last. 'I've been beating my head against a brick wall for too long. Now this suit is smart, but it's plain. I know Chanel favours plainness, and the line is essentially the thing. But a little adornment or embellishment . . . What do you think, Tristan?' She held out the lapels of her plain blue Dunbar Shetland jumper that, with its straight matching skirt, had been made specially for her as a sample on the new wider frame. 'I could favour stripes, vertical or horizontal, maybe in another wool, or silk with contrasting colours. What do you think?'

Tristan nodded. 'Mmm . . . yes. I like what you have on, but I see your point. Some people are already making them you know, not with your quality, but with more style.'

'I know. You cannot beat our quality, but you can easily beat our styles. We're old-fashioned. In the old days Dunbars revolutionized ladies' underwear with its lace tops, its mixtures of silk and wool. We haven't done anything new for years except to copy what everyone else is doing. Well, I'm in London this time to look for a designer, and a house.'

'A house?'

'I'm tired of living in hotels. Durrants is very comfortable and convenient, but I'm spending longer in London now. I thought of St John's Wood, just across the park from the office. What do you say?'

'You'll live there permanently?'

'Oh no!' Margaret laughed and went back to her seat, crossing her slim elegant legs encased in the pure silk stockings made by Dunbars. 'I could not *dare* leave Branswick permanently. I need to keep an eye on things, though I daresay Bruno and Cullum would be quite pleased if I went.'

'Really?'

'They both resent me, even Bruno who was in favour of my appointment. They think I'm too bossy. Maybe I am, but with the two years we've had, the effects of the General Strike and so on, we have to be very aggressive now in our manufacturing and merchandising. I just wish my fellow directors would be bossy too.'

'But Bruno is a first-class salesman.'

Margaret looked thoughtfully at the man who first had employed her, then become a customer and now was a very good friend. In fact she treasured their relationship, and she confided in him almost as much as in Hamish Ogilvy.

'He's a *very* good salesman, very good; but Cullum is no good at all, at anything, so Bruno and I have to shoulder all the work. I am a good salesman too, am I not?'

'Excellent.'

'Well, we are too lopsided. We need a good production man and a good designer. The production man I think I have got. We are stealing him from the Pendreighs.' Margaret smiled briefly. 'Which gives me some satisfaction. I want a good designer. Then Bruno can travel the

208

world, concentrate on the market. I can concentrate on England, the Continent and the London office, and Cullum . . .' She shook her head. Words sometimes failed her where Cullum was concerned.

'Can go to hell?' Tristan whispered and got up and placed a kiss on her cheek. 'Come, Margaret, let me take you to the theatre tonight to relax.' He looked at his watch. 'If I hurry I can ask my secretary to get tickets for – what would you like? *The Constant Wife*? *On Approval*? *The Blue Comet* I've seen but . . .'

Margaret shook her head, taking his hand and pressing it. 'No. I'm seeing a house again at seven. I know, come and see it with me! I like it very much. If you like it too I'll buy it, then you can take me to dinner. How's that?'

'That's fine,' Tristan said, resuming his seat. 'Anything you say.'

The house was in Cavendish Avenue, near Lord's Cricket Ground. It was an imposing mansion, double-fronted, with seven bedrooms, two bathrooms, reception rooms and servants' quarters, the whole surrounded by a high wall. Because of the Depression it was regarded as a snip on the market. By eight o'clock Margaret had agreed to purchase it, and by nine o'clock she and Tristan were sitting in the Café Royal celebrating. A band was playing but she did not feel like dancing. She felt like eating and having an early night.

'Pleased?'

'Very.' Margaret finished her oysters and sipped the Chablis that Tristan, who was something of a wine connoisseur, had selected. 'It had a nice homey feel, don't you think?'

'As far as one can tell without any furniture. You'll have a lot of work to do on that.'

'I thought you could do it for me.'

'Me?' Pretending consternation, Tristan pointed at his breast.

'Yes, you. You can design and furnish it. You have such wonderful taste, Tristan. Besides, I know you like that kind of thing. Didn't you design all the décor for Flemings?'

'True.' He bowed his head. 'I don't know that I've the time.'

'Try and find it,' Margaret said, smiling at him. She knew that a certain smile could melt anybody, even Tristan.

'I will try,' he said, swallowing.

'Mon cher Tristan!' cried a voice.

'Yves!' Tristan jumped up and embraced the newcomer. 'How long have you been in London?'

'Two days. I was going to call you tomorrow.' The man called Yves was looking at Margaret, who still wore the smile she had used to charm Tristan. 'Who, may I ask, is your very beautiful companion?'

'You should know Margaret Dunbar,' Tristan said laughing. 'If you don't now, you soon will. She's going to storm London with her stylish fashions.'

'Really?'

'You're in the same business.' Tristan indicated a chair and asked a passing waiter for another glass. 'In fact, Margaret, here – if you can persuade him – is your designer. Yves Lamotte.'

Yves Lamotte shook hands with Margaret and sat down, accepting the glass of Chablis that Tristan gave him. He held it up and toasted first Margaret then his host. Margaret felt her interest quicken. He was the most classically good-looking man she had ever seen; simply that and no more. He had thick dark hair with a single deep wave in it which sprang naturally from his high forehead. His hair was longer than was customary and gave him an artistic look which was accentuated by his dark grey eyes, his long thin nose and a rather wide full mouth. He was very tall and had on black tails and a white tie as though he were going to a ball. His hands were long, tapering at the tips of the fingers, yet strong and masculine.

'But I am not looking for a job, alas. Dunbar . . . Is this the Scottish manufacturer of knitwear Dunbar?'

'The same,' Tristan said. 'Miss Dunbar is a director of the family business. She's very keen to introduce *haute couture* into their merchandise.'

'I am very glad to hear it,' Yves said, his strong mellifluent French accent enhancing his charm. 'It is not before time.'

Margaret felt momentarily tongue-tied, quite bowled over, like a young girl at her first grown up function. The main course had arrived and she had not noticed it. No, mesmerized rather than tongue-tied; mesmerized was the word. She thought he was a very assured, fascinating man.

'I have been in the fashion business all my life, Miss Dunbar, except naturally for the war which was when I met Tristan. I am also a painter and I design sets and costumes for the theatre; but I am interested in any design so to that extent, yes, I am a designer.'

Margaret laughed and threw up her hands. 'Alas then not for us, a relatively small hosiery manufacturer in Branswick.'

'Maybe you know of someone, Yves,' Tristan enquired smoothly, dissecting his *carré d'agneau*, prising the meat away from the bones with the delicate skill of a surgeon.

'I shall certainly give it some thought.' Yves got to his feet, finishing the wine in his glass and bowing. 'Delighted to meet you, Miss Dunbar. I am off to Grosvenor House, Tristan. The Perrys have a ball there. May I give you a call?'

'Please do.' Tristan smiled and waved a hand, then lowered his eyes to his plate as though the brief visit was already forgotten.

'What a charming man,' Margaret said, watching Yves move languidly through the crowd.

'Oh he's a charmer,' Tristan said drily. 'Very capable,

211

too, though I would take with a pinch of salt this business about how important he is and how busy. I happen to know he's had a very bad time.'

'Oh?'

'He invested a lot of money in a Paris production, a play, which failed horribly. He flits about too much doing this and that. He's tremendously talented but lacks application. His father is a Count.'

'Really?'

'So I suppose he's a Viscount!' Tristan laughed and put a hand over Margaret's. 'Don't be smitten by him, my dear. He can be a very dangerous man.'

'How intriguing,' Margaret said, her eyes still searching the room for a sight of him.

By Christmas time the purchase of Margaret's new house was completed. In January a team of decorators and designers moved in to implement the plans sketched by Tristan, who was in fact thrilled by his honorary commission. As his store ran so smoothly he found that he had time on his hands and he spent part of each day in Cavendish Avenue.

Margaret on the other hand spent January in Branswick, testing runs on the big new knitting frames, cajoling Bruno and Cullum, sketching her own designs for different styles and patterns, sometimes working on into the small hours of the morning. She would often stay at the mill until nearly midnight, the one single light burning on the second floor of the new extension that ran nearly to the bridge crossing the main street.

One night towards the end of January she made her way home in the dark, walking alone by the river and up the hill. It was still the custom among millowners in Branswick to walk to work and back, whether because they always had or because the exercise was good for them no one knew; very likely no one ever thought about it. It was not unusual for a woman to be seen out alone late at night in Branswick, although it was probably unusual for a *lady*. The women who lived on the hill or in the large houses on the edge of the town invariably moved around after dark escorted by their husbands or, if still unmarried, by their fathers or brothers.

But Margaret Dunbar, who never had done anything expected of her by Branswick society, had no qualms about walking home through the night by herself, enjoying the air, the brightness of the stars against the jet black sky, the almost uncanny stillness because the river had frozen over and no longer rushed by to its perpetual tryst with the Tweed. Earlier that month the Thames had overflowed its banks, causing widespread damage and some loss of life, and as she walked Margaret reflected on the uncertainties of fate that made one river burst its banks and another trap, under the ice formed on top, a party of small children.

Earlier that day an ambulance had raced through the town as several children attempting to play on the ice during their school lunch break had nearly perished. Apparently all had been saved. Margaret had heard about the near-tragedy, but no details.

When Margaret got home, Fleur was alone in the drawing room sitting close to the fire sewing. She was expecting her second baby in the spring and was already large, as she had been with the first. She looked up as Margaret came in and put down her sewing, straightening up and rubbing her back.

'Late again, Margaret? Have you eaten?'

'No, I'll get something.'

'Nonsense.' Fleur got ponderously to her feet and pressed the bell. 'I've asked Sandra to save your dinner and told her I'd let her know when you were in.'

'You're very sweet, Fleur.' Margaret smiled at her gratefully and tossed aside her hat, riffling through her

213

hair. 'My, I think I shall be glad to get back to London! It's so *cold* here.' She rubbed her hands and leaned towards the fire.

'I'll go and help Sandra,' Fleur said. 'You must be starving.'

Margaret had grown very fond of Fleur whom Cullum had married in the winter of 1926, to everyone's delight and, to most, surprise. For he had not seemed to pay any particular attention to Mrs Bulwer, even when she returned to live in Selkirk in the house she had just bought. But Cullum, used to stealth and secretive by nature, had been courting her since the previous summer. She supported him, she sympathized with him and she loved him. Nan had loved him too, but she could never give him the active support he needed against his family, particularly Margaret, and the Macallisters who had virtually taken over his business.

Fleur was firm and decisive. After they were married she supervised his drinking as strictly as she could, although she could do nothing about his inability to run his family business. If anything, after his marriage Cullum grew less interested in Dunbars than ever; he started instead to develop his passion for cars and took part in rallies, when he was sober enough, throughout England and Scotland.

A daughter, Morag, was born to Fleur and Cullum ten months after their marriage and now a second child was on the way. Margaret often wondered how happy Fleur really was with Cullum. Because she was away so much she saw very little of what went on, but she had her doubts. They did not seem a close, loving couple. She wondered if any woman could make Cullum happy, for as soon as he got what he wanted he lost interest in it and went on to something else. It was part of his inherent instability. As soon as he bought a coveted motor car, for instance, maybe already a collector's piece, he immediately wanted another.

But the main thing was that Cullum was now married to a good and sensible woman. He had a beautiful baby daughter and with any luck the next child would be a son. That was just about all one could hope for from Cullum, that and that it didn't take after him.

Fleur came in followed by Sandra carrying a tray which she placed on a table Fleur set out before the fire. There was a plate of succulent hot-pot and two dishes of vegetables.

'Oh thank you! That looks marvellous.'

Suddenly ravenous Margaret drew up her chair and Fleur sat opposite her.

'Is Cullum back?' Margaret enquired, glancing up after a few moments' eating.

'Back and gone out again.'

'Oh? On a night like this? Where?'

'I don't know. He didn't say. He's in one of his moods.'

'What sort of day did he have in Edinburgh?'

'He didn't tell me. He came in, had dinner and was reading the paper in front of the fire when he got up and suddenly went out of the door. A few minutes later he popped his head round to say he was going out, and out he went.'

Margaret grimaced. 'Strange. You'd think *he* was having the baby.'

'He seemed upset.'

'Oh.' Margaret looked round and picked up the evening paper which had been neatly folded and put on a small table near her chair. She glanced at the headlines about the dreadful weather and then at some items of national news which didn't seem to amount to anything much. She was about to put the paper down when a small item at the bottom of the front page caught her attention.

FIVE BOYS SAVED FROM DEATH IN THE DRUME

At lunchtime today five boys from Branswick Primary School were saved from a terrible death beneath the ice on the River

Drume. They had left the school unknown to their teachers. Ignoring warnings about the dangerous conditions, the truants ventured onto the frozen surface of the river at Traquair Park. The ice immediately broke beneath them and three of the five disappeared underneath. The two boys who by fortunate chance had remained on the bank ran to the lodge where the park-keeper was having his lunch. It was the timely intervention of Mr Jamie Musgrave and his teenage son Robert that saved these young Branswick lads from certain death. They were taken to hospital but two of them were later sent home. A third, William Murray, whose grandfather is a frameworker at the Dunbar Mill, has been detained for further investigation.

'Oh dear,' Margaret said, and read the paragraph to Fleur. 'I didn't realize one of the boys had something to do with us. I wonder if it was this that upset Cullum?'

'Would it upset him enough to go out at night?'

'No, I suppose not. The boy appears to be all right. I'll make enquiries tomorrow.'

Fleur stifled a yawn and looked at the clock on the mantelpiece. 'I know it's not very late, Margaret, but would you mind if I left you and went to bed? I've been terribly tired all day.'

'Of course dear.' Margaret held out her hand and, drawing Fleur towards her, kissed her. 'Take care of yourself. Is everything all right?'

'Oh yes, fine.' Fleur rubbed her back. 'I just get a pain in the small of my back. The doctor says it's normal. I think I had it with Morag too. I'll be glad when it's all over though.'

'I'm sure you will. Fleur, you know I'm going to London next week? The house is nearly ready.'

Fleur clapped her hands. 'Oh how lovely! You will be thrilled Maggie.'

'Yes, I am pleased. Tristan says it looks lovely. I shall be able to spend more time there now.'

Fleur sat down again and gazed at her sister-in-law. 'Maggie, I haven't liked to say this, but has it got anything to do with us? With you being unhappy here, you know, that you've bought a house.'

'Oh Fleur.' Margaret leaned over and clasped her hand again. 'What a silly thing to say, but how kind! You know that I've wanted a place of my own for years. When you and Cullum married I thought that was my chance, but neither of you, very sweetly, wanted me to go. In fact you forbade it.'

'Of course! It was such a large house; much too big for the two of us or even three. Even too big for four. There's plenty of room.' Fleur didn't add that she rather wanted the company of her gay, attractive sister-in-law to lessen the tension between herself and her new husband who, much as she thought she loved him, was given to strange moods and long silences. It was a case when three was better company than two.

'Well, it made a lot of sense. As you say it is a very big house and we have never got under one another's feet, have we? I've been careful to give you and Cullum all the privacy you wanted; but . . .' Margaret pushed the table with the tray away and spread her legs in front of the fire. 'Well, a girl does want a place of her own, not in Branswick maybe, but in London certainly. It gives me independence.'

'I understand. If that's all it is.'

'All, I assure you.'

Fleur got up again and walked slowly past the fire, hobbling like a cripple. Margaret felt sorry for her and also resentful that women had to suffer so much in order to give birth. She was thankful when she saw Fleur that she had no maternal feelings herself and that the curse of childbirth would probably never be visited upon her. Fleur turned at the door and smiled.

'Good-night, Margaret.'

'Good-night.'

As the door closed, Margaret leaned forward and picked up *The Branswick Evening Echo* once again, studying the same small paragraph, her brow furrowed in a frown.

Nan stood back as Cullum came into the room without greeting him. There was only one light on in the room and the usual miserable fire burned in the grate. Compared to outside it was warm, but not as warm as *Woodbrae* which had fires in all the rooms, whether occupied or not, and large modern heaters in the halls; there was even talk of having central heating installed before the following winter. Cullum took his hat off but not his coat; his face was pale and his breath smelled strongly of whisky. He had stopped at the pub on the corner to fortify himself before his visit. He stood with his back to the fire, looking at Nan, who had not moved since she'd closed the door.

'How is he, Nan?'

'He'll live, if that's what you mean, Mr Dunbar.'

'Oh Nan . . .' Cullum made a move towards her, but the expression on her face stopped him. It was not hostile; it was apathetic, but the expression in her fine eyes reflected the deep anxiety caused by the day's events. 'Nan, I'm terribly sorry. I only read about it in the paper. I came at once. How did it happen?'

'It was as it said in the *Echo*.'

'Yes I know, but, Nan, he *is* my son!' Cullum felt angry at the way she just stood there, looking accusingly at him, as if wanting him to go.

'For all the attention you've paid him these past eighteen months I think you've got a cheek to say that!'

'I can't undo what's done, Nan. I am his natural father.'

'Unnatural, I'd say. Only tae make an appearance when something bad happens.'

'I couldn't just sit at home, not knowing. Nan . . .' Cullum slumped into a chair, removing a hard cushion from behind his back and throwing it on the floor. 'Nan, I *have* wanted to see you, and him. I have, but . . .' He passed a hand across his face, closing his eyes. 'It's all very difficult. I did explain.'

He remembered well the explanation; the night he'd told Nan about Fleur after making love to her passionately here in this room almost exactly two years ago, a few days before his wedding. He'd made love to Nan because he had known it would be the last time and also because it would make the telling easier, or so he had hoped.

Nan, lying breathless and hot from love, had heard him out in silence and then she'd uttered a wail like the sad, lost cry of a night bird, her body shaking with sobs. He'd tried to comfort her, to tell her he loved her, but that the pressures of his family, the events of recent months . . . He hadn't told her how he needed Fleur in a way that he couldn't need Nan. How Fleur could help him in a way that Nan could not.

He never knew if Nan had heard anything of what he'd said. He couldn't explain to her how he could never contemplate anything more with her than a liaison, how even the eccentric Dunbars had to conform to a certain extent. How he could never take her as a wife or acknowledge William as his son, much as he might have wished it, except that he didn't, because it would never occur to a Dunbar to marry a girl from the mill. But she might not have heard that either.

After a while she'd got out of bed, dressed and asked him to go. It was as though she had wanted to make herself respectable before he left; that she could not permit him to go while she lay naked in bed, vulnerable and open to his love. She wanted him, belatedly, to have a very different last memory of her; that of someone respectable, who did not give herself freely, or abandon herself with such passion. But it was much too late for that, there could be no going back on the past.

While he dressed she had turned her back on him, because nudity betrayed intimacy, and then he had made one last attempt to explain. He would visit her and William, he would support them, he would always care for her . . . She had opened the door for him, staring at him with the contempt that had replaced heartbreak, and he had known then that he would not see her again; that everything between them was over.

Every week since that day in January 1926 an envelope had slid through Nan's door. The amount of cash it contained would vary but was always generous. Cullum saw George Murray at work but no words of a personal nature ever passed between them, no gesture which betrayed the closeness of their relationship: grandfather and father of William. From that day to this, Cullum had not seen either Nan or his son and now, looking at her, he was struck by guilt at what he had done and he wept.

Nan let him weep, perhaps realizing that it was partly brought on by alcoholic remorse, or perhaps because she was glad to see him cry. Finally he rose, dried his eyes and blew his nose.

'I would like to make amends, Nan.'

'How?' The word came out almost before she was aware of it, as though her control too had snapped.

'By seeing you, and him, as I once promised. But you did not make it easy for me that last time.'

'You didna make it easy for *me*, telling me on the eve of your wedding day.'

'I . . . lacked courage, I admit it. I always have lacked courage, Nan, unless I had a few drinks inside me. I lacked courage to oppose my father or my sisters, or the Macallisters or Fleur . . .'

'Fleur? Is she not your wife?'

'Yes.' Cullum sat down again, linking his hands in front of him in an attitude of dejection. 'Fleur set her cap at me, you know. She wanted me. I was quite happy with you, didn't want to wed. Fleur was all set to buy a house in Harrogate when she met me that time; then she changed her mind and came to Selkirk instead.'

220

Nan tossed her head back in scorn. 'You must've done something tae encourage her. She wouldn't have acted so alone.'

'Maybe I did.' Cullum shook his head. 'But I didn't mean to. She was sympathetic, you see. She was a sort of bulwark, a strong woman. I felt that with her beside me I could stand up to Margaret and Susan and Bruno; but of course I couldn't – can't. Fleur wanted marriage, a home and a baby. She'd been married before and had one child already, but she wanted it all again – home, respectability, husband. She soon got what she wanted, but she didn't make me stronger.'

'But you're having *another* bairn I hear.'

Cullum looked up. 'Oh, you know that?'

'There's not much I don't hear, Mr Dunbar. This is a verra small community. I hear about your drinking; I know you crashed your car last September through inebriation. I hear your sister is a big noise in the mill and that she and Mr Macallister make all the decisions. There's not much I don't know.'

'And despise me for.'

Cullum hung his head and Nan went to the stove in the corner and put on the kettle. Cullum looked at the wide bed where they used to make love. If only they could do so again he was sure she would give him strength. It would flow from her to him as it had before. He watched her as she made the tea, moving quietly about in an unfashionable green dress that looked as though it had been handed on from some ageing relation, her long hair tied back with a bit of thin ribbon. In her he saw Ageless Woman, the eternal mother figure, unswayed by fashions or the vagaries of current events. Nan was changeless, unchanging. Why had he not defied convention, sold his share of the business and gone to live with her? But stubbornly and foolishly he had clung on, wanting to show them that he was the boss. Now he was apparently a figure of fun in the community, always being hauled out of pubs and crashing

221

his car through drink. Nan put a cup before him and sat opposite him. She had more colour in her face now and her eyes were tranquil.

'Get that inside you, Mr Dunbar. 'Twill do more good than the Scotch.'

Obediently Cullum put the cup to his lips, wincing, shocked by the heat of the dark liquid.

'It's good. Now Nan, what shall we do?'

'What shall *we* do? I don't know what *we* shall do. I know what *I* shall do. I shall go on as I am, with mae faither and mae bairn.'

'I'd love to see him, Nan, I really would.' Cullum looked at her earnestly and felt a surge of hope. Her expression was not unkind.

'He wondered why you stopped visiting. I told him you had other important things to do. Of course he doesn't know who you were or what; but he was only five then. He's a clever boy as well as bonny and if you came into our lives now he would ask questions; he'd be sure tae, and he'd tell his friends that we were visited by the head of the Dunbar Mill and then they would ask why.'

'Yes.' Cullum sipped his tea thoughtfully. 'Yes, I can see that; but can we not meet, Nan? You and I?'

'Ah, *that* is what you're after is it?' Nan said, as though she'd caught him out. 'You're after resuming our relationship?'

'I've missed you, Nan. Very, very much.'

'With your wife and the bairn, and another on the way . . . I don't believe you, Mr Dunbar.'

'Please don't call me Mr Dunbar, Nan. Call me Cullum, like you used to. You know marriage is a political thing, a social thing, an economic thing. People marry for all sorts of reasons. I had such pressure on me to marry and Fleur seemed right. I wanted it to work. Can't you see that, Nan?' He looked at her pleadingly.'Please try and see it.'

'Aye, I see it all right.' Nan got up and brought over the large brown pot, tilting it towards his cup. 'I see I was never guid enough for you tae marry, only guid enough for bed. This other lady was guid enough for marrying, but not guid enough in bed. Is that not it?'

'It's a very crude way of putting it, Nan.'

She jerked up the pot and smiled at him as though she were suddenly secure in her own strength. 'I understand you verra well Mr Dunbar – Cullum. Verra well indeed. You do not lie with a man for as long as I lay with you without understanding something about him. I know about your weakness and your love of drink, about your need for a woman's body. But I'm not sharing you with your wife. Oh no.'

'But Nan, you won't be sharing me. Look, we have to have children, you know. For the sake of the business and the family I would like a son . . .' Cullum stopped, bit his lip. 'That is, a legitimate son. I hate the word but there it is. I would like a son who is a Dunbar. It is expected of me; it is the least I can do. Fleur and I have nothing in common in bed. She is not very keen on it. She wanted to marry the place and the institution, not the man. If this next baby is a son I promise you we will never have sexual relations again. I will not need it and she will not miss it. She's not like you, not like you at all, Nan.' He smiled as if in some memory and Nan suddenly lowered her head, feeling a blush stealing up her cheeks. 'We liked it a lot didn't we, Nan. Didn't we?'

'Aye.' Her reply was grudging. 'But a man can treat a woman awfu' bad. That's what I canna understand.'

Cullum got off the chair and knelt on the floor in front of her. If he looked foolish he did not care; he felt like a supplicant in front of a generous female deity, tall and proud and fertile. She had borne him a child from her loins and treasured him there countless times besides.

'I did treat you badly, Nan, and I can never do enough to make up for it. But if you give me the chance I will try. Look, Nan, what do you say if I buy or rent a cottage for you in a village some way from Branswick, and come and visit you there? Maybe stay some nights? What do you say to that? You can leave this place. After all, it *is* badly in need of repair, and it's damp, and I see the wallpaper is still hanging from the ceiling.'

'The Toon Cooncil nevva do anything they say they will.'

'Well, they have no money. That is one thing; but I have more money now. My sister is buying a house in London if you please! I can certainly buy a small cottage, or maybe rent one to start, and I can pay you more to make up for the loss in your wages.'

'I will leave Mactavish?' Nan's eyes lit up.

'Of course; no more bar-filling. William can go to the village school and if he is bright I'll pay for him to go away, maybe to Fettes or Loreto or the Edinburgh Academy. What do you say, Nan? What do you say?'

Cullum seized her hands and kissed them as Nan raised her head to the ceiling, her eyes still bright as though she had seen a vision.

CHAPTER THIRTEEN

George Murray stood watching his powerful new knitting frame at work. The repetitive clicking gave him a pleasant sense of security, of familiarity; though to those who stood on the threshold of the floor housing so many of these large machines, the noise was deafening. He stood in the centre, by his controls, and every now and then he would examine the individual pieces of knitting all being done on the one frame, up to eight pieces at a time. They slipped through the frame towards the floor and when each piece was finished he would gather it up, ready for binding on the floor above. Before this happened he would tip a bar, which fresh ribs had been threaded onto stitch by stitch on hundreds of tiny steel needles, over his frame so that when the new piece was ready to start being knitted the rib was incorporated into it. The basic process, though much more sophisticated and complicated now, had hardly altered since the Reverend Lee invented his knitting machine in the sixteenth century.

George had done this work since he was a boy and he was now nearing retirement. He was an expert frame-worker, as many in his family had been before him, and he liked the new machines. Apart from being more efficient they enabled him to earn more money.

Margaret Dunbar looked critically at the knitting which was sliding onto the floor from the frame, picked it up and felt it in her hands.

'It's nice, George, isn't it?'

'Aye, verra guid Miss Dunbar.'

Margaret held the wool to her face and sniffed it. It was

225

quite harsh and smelt of oil, yet when it had been milled and dried it would be soft and sensuous to the touch. 'This is the new cashmere yarn that Mr Macallister bought in China,' she told the approving George. 'We're going to use it more and more. Cashmere skirts and jumpers.'

'They will be verra expensive.'

'But people will buy them, George.' Margaret let the knitting fall back to the floor and gazed at him. 'I was very sorry to hear about your grandson. Is he all right now?'

'Och aye.' George scratched his head as though in embarrassment. 'He's out of hospital. He broke a leg.'

'Oh I am sorry.'

'The main thing was he didna lose his life.'

'Of course. Your daughter must have been very worried. It is your daughter's son, is it not, George, not your son's?'

'Aye.' He pressed a lever, thus releasing the knitting which fell on the floor to be gathered up for binding. Then he inserted a fresh bar with a rib attached and touched a button which set the knitting process in motion again.

'Did your daughter not once work here, George?'

'Aye,' he said shortly as he moved along the frame, adjusting work as he did so.

Margaret guessed that he was trying to avoid the subject. Memories of Cullum's adventures with the mill girls had revolved in her brain ever since she'd read of the schoolboy truants' misadventure beneath the ice, events connected by the hasty departure of Cullum who had not returned by the time she went to bed. But she had been so wakeful that she heard his car come creeping through the gate, and, looking at the clock on her bedside, had seen that it was nearly dawn. Millgirls . . . Cullum . . . William Murray . . . George Murray . . . When she got to the office the next day she had gone through the records of ex-employees and discovered that a Nan Murray left in 1920, no reason given. Eight years. Was it possible? She knew

226

then that she had to find out, one way or another. But now, several days later, she saw she would get nothing more out of George except that his demeanour seemed to confirm her suspicions.

She waved to George and walked along the shop inspecting the other frames as they throbbed away producing her first individual designs for matching jumpers and skirts.

But supposing she was right. What then?

Margaret knocked at the door of the tenement but there was no reply. Timidly she turned the handle and opened the door, putting her head round. Sitting by the fire, his foot on a stool, was an engaging youngster with carroty hair and blue eyes.

'William?' she said brightly, venturing in.

'Aye.'

'I heard about your accident. I've come to see you.'

'Are you from the Board?' William crouched back in his chair, looking frightened.

'No, I'm Miss Dunbar.'

'Oh.'

'You know who Dunbars are, don't you?'

'Aye. My grandfather works there.'

'Where is your mother, William?'

'She works at Mactavishes; but she's taken the day off tae look after me. I came out of the hospital yesterday.'

'Yes, your grandfather told me. You were very lucky, weren't you William?'

'Och aye.'

Watching him blush and bow his head, Margaret saw what an attractive boy he was . . . and how like Cullum. She could not remember Cullum as a young boy but she had seen pictures. But not only was there the resemblance; there was also the colour. Cullum's hair was not so carroty now, but his eyes were still that very deep

227

blue-green, eyes like hers. Dunbar eyes. Margaret knew then without any doubt that she was looking at her nephew. Unsure of her emotions she awkwardly held out a box of soldiers she had bought, together with a tin of sweets.

'Do you play soldiers, William?'

'Och aye.' He reached for the box and Margaret placed it in his hands, together with the tin of sweets. Then she heard the door open and she turned round. She saw a woman of about her own age and height, plainly dressed but not plain, without make-up and with her hair braided round her head. She wore a long dark green dress over which there was a black shawl, and in her arms was a selection of groceries – a packet of tea, a bag of biscuits, some bacon, a lump of butter, as though she'd been shopping very hastily and just gathered them up in her arms. The woman put the goods down on the table and wiped her hands on her skirt, looking startled.

'Nan?'

'Yes.'

'I'm Margaret Dunbar.'

'I know who you are, Miss.'

'I just came to see how William was.'

'Verra kind of you I'm sure.'

Nan turned her back to Margaret as though embarrassed by her presence. She slipped off her shawl, looked at her face in a mirror on the wall and then went over to William.

'Well? I've not been gone five minutes and you have a visitor.'

'I couldna help it, Ma, she just came in.'

Nan smiled at him and Margaret, watching her keenly, saw that she could have been a beauty; maybe was a beauty when not careworn and cold. She had high cheekbones and a brown skin and her coiled black hair was thick and luxurious, making her look like a figure in a Renais-

228

sance painting. But the room was bitterly cold. William had on a jersey and a topcoat as well as mittens on his hands, and the fire consisted of a few embers far back in the grate.

The meanness of the room appalled Margaret; the large bed in the corner; the threadbare furniture; the tattered rug on the floor. It was not dirty; it was very clean, but it was poverty-stricken. Yet Nan worked, George worked . . . Where did the money go? Frameworkers were quite well paid, by other standards.

'Oh you don't need to worry, William' his mother said reassuringly. 'This is Miss Dunbar from the mill.'

'I know Ma.'

'Verra kind of you to call, miss.' Nan turned, her bland expression inviting her to leave.

'I bought him some soldiers.'

'Verra generous.'

'Is there anything else I can do? I understand you work. Who will look after William while he needs care?'

'A neighbour will come in, miss; besides, he is almost old enough tae take care of himself. He'll come tae no harm.'

Margaret wondered what would happen if a coal fell onto the rug and the crippled boy tried to get to the door. She was filled with sudden pain. Her brother had left his son to live in squalor. She looked around her, noticing the peeling wallpaper, the patches of damp in the ceiling.

'It really is too bad the way the council keep these buildings!'

'We keep on at them, miss, but they say they have no money.'

'Well, it's disgraceful. I shall go and see the Provost personally about it.'

'Wull something be done *then*, Miss Dunbar?'

Nan looked at her coolly and Margaret returned her gaze, well aware of the difference between them. She,

Miss Dunbar, had only to see the Provost and make a fuss. Whereas Nan Murray could plead and plead for years and the pleas would fall on deaf ears because she was no one, nothing in the town, just a girl who worked in a mill, an unmarried girl with a son. Than that, socially, you could hardly get lower in the hierarchy of Branswick society.

'I hope so, Nan,' Margaret said quietly, then added hesitantly, 'I know it's very cold outside but could you slip a coat on and walk a little way with me?' She glanced at William who was still gazing at this very smart lady, dressed in furs with a small close-fitting hat, her high shiny leather boots trimmed with fur. Nan also appeared to hesitate. Then she nodded, taking a coat off the peg and putting it on. Then she went and poked the fire, placing another log on it.

'I won't be gone five munutes, William. You behave yourself now.'

'Yes, Ma.' He looked trustingly up at her and a lump came into Margaret's throat.

'Good-bye William, for now.' She quickly stooped and kissed his cheek, ruffling his thick tousled hair. 'There, I've embarrassed you haven't I?' She laughed as William shied away, putting a hand over his face. ' I know, you're a big boy now. Get better soon. I'll try and come and see you again.'

William didn't reply but peered at her through his fingers. A delicious smell came from the lady and the room was filled with a fragrance that reminded him of the sweet shop on the High Street, only much nicer. He nestled back in his chair and gazed at her as his mother opened the door and they disappeared from view.

A thin layer of snow had fallen that morning, lightly covering the street like a sprinkling of icing sugar on a cake, and the Drume beside which they walked was still hard with ice.

'I admire enormously what you have done, Nan.'

Margaret looked at the silent woman beside her, pulling her coat closely around her. 'He is Cullum's son, isn't he?' Nan nodded but did not reply. 'I only knew today for sure. My brother has never said anything to us.'

'He wouldna.'

'Do you see him, Nan?' Nan shook her head again, plodding sturdily beside Margaret. 'He read about the accident in the paper? That's how I found out. Fleur, his wife, said he had put the paper down and gone out. I put two and two together.'

'What are you going tae do about it, Miss Dunbar?'

The dark beautiful eyes looked both fearful and yet trusting, as though she were frightened as to what might happen but confident that it would not be too bad. Certainly things would change, now that the secret was known to the powerful Dunbar family.

'Why nothing. Nothing bad that is. I want to help. Does Cullum help, financially I mean?'

'Yes. After he told me he was getting married I didna see him again until the other night, but he always left money. Every week.'

'What did you do with the money, Nan?' Margaret was curious to know because of the penurious state of the house, the meanness of Nan's clothes at a time when even the poorest young woman liked to try and look pretty, and with the influx of cheap imported clothes, it was not difficult.

'I put it by. It's in the post office against a rainy day. For William, I mean. I never touched a penny o' it.'

'You thought it might stop?'

Nan shrugged.

'Nan, I *would* like to help.' Margaret stopped walking and Nan stopped too. The two women looked at each other, each seeming to search for some message in the other's face. 'I gather that Cullum and you had a relationship that went on until his marriage, but not after?'

231

'Aye.'

'But maybe he would like to start it again?' Margaret remembered the car coming through the gate at dawn the other day, just as it used to in years past. Nan did not reply and looked beyond Margaret at the passing traffic in the street. 'Nan, I don't want you to resume your relationship with my brother. Even if you already have, I do not wish it to continue; for both your sakes. For William's sake. Maybe you don't think I have the right to say this, but I think I do. I am intimately involved. Cullum has a wife and a daughter; his wife is shortly to have another child. She is a very nice person of whom I am very fond. I do not want her to be hurt, and I think it will hurt you too. It cannot be very satisfactory only seeing a little of a man, loving him but not having him.'

A bitterness crept into Margaret's voice for which Nan was at a loss to account. She could not know that Margaret was speaking from her own experience, from the five years of secret meetings, brief encounters with Hamish Ogilvy at the cottage in the valley. No, it was not an enviable state and Margaret sometimes wished it had never started, regardless of the happiness she had got from it. It left a woman with no real, recognized place in a man's life. She became a sort of moral outcast, unacknowledged by society. This great secret inside her was like a huge living lie, whatever other advantages it might have seemed at one time to bestow. Stolen moments did not constitute even half a life, only a fragment of it.

'I know that Cullum, for all his faults, is an attractive man; but he hasn't been good to you. He hasn't treated you properly. Don't give him a place in your life again, Nan. Look, I'm ready to pay for you to move away, right away to Glasgow or Edinburgh or a place of your choice, preferably where you have relations or friends. I will buy you a house and see you are supported and that William goes to a good school. It'll be a new life for you, Nan, and him.'

Nan threw back her head and started to laugh, a wild mirthless laugh, her eyes without merriment. Then she abruptly turned back the way she had come and ran up the street towards her home.

'Cullum has a woman.' Margaret turned over in bed and, reaching out, switched on the table lamp to look at her watch. 'He has a child by her; a boy aged seven, called William.'

'Oh, is that why you don't want to make love?' Hamish had his arm round her bare waist, the only intimate contact she had allowed except for a kiss. Her slim, usually compliant eager body had remained stiff and somehow angular as though, instead of being rounded and curved, he had suddenly discovered sharp corners and cold unfriendly surfaces as with a piece of strange furniture. He had never known her so unresponsive and unwilling in bed before.

'It was certainly a shock,' she lay back on her pillow, leaving the light on, 'but I don't know that it's the only reason.'

'When did you find out?' Hamish leaned on one elbow and looked at her.

'A few days ago. I met the woman – she used to work at the mill – and her son. I've got to have it out with Cullum. I mean, it's not right, is it?'

Hamish grimaced and moved his hand away from her waist. 'Well, who are we to talk about "right"?'

'Ours is something completely different. You can't compare us with Cullum and that . . . woman.'

'Because she's a mill girl?'

'After all Cullum is the *head* of Dunbars. If he had a reputation once it's a different thing now that he's the boss. Besides, he's married and I'm not. You can't compare the situation at all.'

'But I'm married . . .' Hamish interposed.

'I tell you the situation is completely different,'

233

Margaret said angrily. 'Why must you continually argue with me?'

'I'm not arguing, merely pointing out similarities. Anyway if the child is seven . . .' Hamish looked at her interrogatively.

'It was over years ago, but he started up again recently. *That's* what I disapprove of, not what happened in the past, though I can't say I'm pleased about that either.'

'You should have told me at dinner. It might have helped relax you. You've been strange all evening. Even over dinner you were strange. Why didn't you tell me then about Cullum? You could have got it out of your mind.'

'I didn't really want to talk about it.'

It was very cold in the hotel room which was unheated except for a gas fire, now unlit. Margaret pulled the bedclothes up to her chin. If she snuggled against Hamish she would get warmer, but she didn't want to excite his passion more than she could help.

'I think what you don't want to talk about is us, Margaret. I have never known you so unresponsive in bed.'

'I'm sorry.' Margaret paused for a moment and glanced at him. His face was a pale silhouette against the darkness of the rest of the room. 'But one doesn't always feel like it, you know.'

'That never happened before.'

'It's been five years Hamish. Five years of sordid little hotel rooms and meetings in the cottage.'

'You never said that before either. The cottage, surely, isn't sordid?'

'I didn't say it was.'

'You implied it.'

'Well this is sordid. The whole thing is getting on my nerves.' Margaret waved her arm in the general direction of the rest of the room and then quickly tucked it back under the bedclothes.

234

'You are my life, Margaret.'

'I don't think I am. Otherwise you would have done something about it before.'

'You know I can't. I made that quite clear at the beginning.'

'Trading on the needs of a passionate, frustrated virgin.'

'That's very unfair. To you as well as me.' Hamish took his arm from beneath her body and moved away from her. 'I didn't trade on anything. I desired you but I made it quite clear I would never persuade you against your will.'

'I knew very little about my "will" in those days. I was hungry for love. What's so wrong about that?' She looked at him, but he didn't meet her eyes.

'Nothing. I couldn't ask for anything more than you've given me. I've failed you. You're right.'

'Oh you *are* trying to make a martyr of yourself, Hamish,' she cried in exasperation. 'Am I expected to throw myself in your arms?' He didn't reply but she could sense his distress. Hamish hated scenes; but tonight it made her want to hurt him more. 'You're too nice, Hamish, that's the trouble. You want to be nice to everyone and in the end you're nice to no one. You're not a husband to your wife or a true lover to me, or even a good father to your children for all I know.'

'That's *very* unfair.' Hamish threw back the bedclothes and sat on the edge of the bed, his back to her. 'I try and think of everybody and I do what I can. I try and be as honourable as is possible in these circumstances. You're the one who's changed.'

He got off the bed and walked to the far side of the room where he had left his clothes. She looked at his body critically and it suddenly seemed to her rather comical, very white and thin with protruding ribs and a hairless chest. His legs, on the other hand, were covered with thick blond hairs and his knees resembled large whorls on the branches of a very spindly tree. She had never looked

235

at Hamish in this detached way before; never before had the sight of her lover made her want to laugh.

Suddenly she felt ashamed and looked away. 'Yes, I have changed. I'm sorry. It makes me mean. I think the situation frustrates me. It's not normal, Hamish. It's unnatural to go on meeting like this. I want a continuing relationship and we haven't got one.'

'That's because *you* are away such a lot. We used to see each other much more before you decided to go away, up and down to London all the time. I'm available; you're not.'

'I had to go away. I had to involve myself in the business, can't you see that? Can't you understand at all? What sort of life was it for me otherwise?'

'I always knew you'd leave me one day, Margaret. I've been very lucky.' Hamish moved over to her. He had his trousers on now and was fastening his shirt.

'I didn't say I was leaving you.'

He looked better with clothes on, and his handsome face with his sleeked back blond hair bore a noble if rueful expression. Five years. They'd been lovers five years. Was she now being fair to him? Cruel? Impulsively she reached out a hand and he took it and sat down beside her.

'I do love you so very much, Margaret. I love you and I desire you and I always will. Moreover, I admire you. You're a clever, ambitious woman and I've seen you develop so much over the years. I'm proud of you. Don't you think I'd love to have you recognized as my lawful wife? But would it make you happy? Is it really what you want, even if it were possible?'

Margaret squeezed his hand, her eyes slowly filling with tears. She felt so confused about Hamish; how, one moment, she could despise him, the next seem suffused with love.

'I don't know.'

'You must know.' He leaned closer to her, seeing the

brightness in her eyes. 'You *must* know – when you are honest with yourself, in the small hours of the morning, maybe, like now. You must know what you want.'

'I want Dunbars to be successful.'

'Yes, but apart from that. Oh the business, the business; always the business! Is it all you really think of? I sometimes wonder. What, I'm asking, about your *personal* life? Children? You're twenty-six.'

'One of my aunts had a child at forty.' Margaret managed a tremulous smile. 'Not that I want to emulate her. Nor am I conscious of time passing particularly. But I *am* tired of the furtiveness, Hamish; the way we have to arrange meetings, the way we can never go anywhere in public together; have to choose seedy little hotels like this when it's too cold for the cottage. Aren't you tired of it too, in all honesty?'

'I am never tired of being with you, however that is,' Hamish replied, 'but I know that you have changed towards me, particularly this last year. This is the first time tonight that you didn't want to make love.'

'It becomes so mechanical. We just have to "do" it because we're here whether we feel like it or not. Well often I don't, to be perfectly frank, and particularly I don't when it's freezing as it is tonight and I have to get up at dawn and go back to Branswick to be sure that everything is ready and packed before I leave for London. I have a thousand things on my mind, you know, apart from us. I don't always feel like making love which, quite honestly, is why we meet isn't it? This is why we meet: to make love, not to talk. Besides, when we talk we have so many rows, lately. Have you noticed how often we quarrel?'

'Oh yes, I've noticed.' Hamish sighed and examined the fingers of the hand he held in his. 'I've been aware for a long time that the sands were running from under me. I wonder each time if it will be the last.'

237

Margaret suddenly raised herself in bed and threw herself towards him, tears now freely coursing down her face, her throat choked with sobs.

'Oh Hamish, don't say that! Don't say that Hamish, please, please don't! Darling, please don't speak like that!'

For a moment Hamish held her in his arms, stroking her head and making comforting sounds, his lips brushing her thick black hair. Then he gently laid her back in the bed and quickly got undressed again before joining her.

Margaret had everything packed and was to catch the morning train to London the following day. A Dunbar car full of samples would collect her and take her to the station, and the samples of new merchandise neatly packed into hampers would be put in the guard's van. Margaret intended a prolonged visit to put her house in order and to extend the business as much as she could.

Her previous night with Hamish – full of tears, quarrels, reproaches and, as usual, finally passion – had really settled nothing. Half the time she felt resentful and critical of him; the rest of the time she felt she loved him as much as ever and could never envisage parting from him. He was always so patient, so good and so thoughtful that he invariably made her feel a heel. She knew he led a miserable personal life and that he lived for his meetings with her; like her he took refuge in his business, yet unlike her he could not look forward to an improvement in his private life unless his wife died. She was free; Hamish wasn't. She had no other person in mind, but if she ever did meet someone else she was free to do as she liked.

Hamish was a noble, dutiful man racked with guilt and the dread that he would lose her. When out of frustration she treated him badly, she was always full of remorse and vowed never to do it again, until the next time came around and the next furtive meeting was arranged. Somehow it was realizing how similar her life was to Cullum's that had made her sick with self-disgust; they were both indulging in different worlds but each one was built on the same fabric of deception and lies. In her heart she felt that her love for Hamish was noble, not to be compared with Cullum's for Nan. Yet how did she know? How could she be sure, and what would people say if they knew about her? Why, they would think it a sordid affair with a married man and despise her for it, as she despised others. Somehow one could never see oneself in a despicable role. That was left to other people.

It was well over a week since her conversation with Nan and she was still mystified by the way it had ended; but she felt there was nothing more she could do for the moment, as far as Nan was concerned anyway. It was not surprising that Nan resented her; but when she had thought about it, compared Margaret's offer to her own poor way of life, maybe she could change her mind. When she got to London Margaret intended to write and tell Nan that the offer would always be open.

But now she had to talk to Cullum, an inevitability that she had postponed until the last minute.

She spent her last day going round the mill, inspecting the newly completed additions, checking the samples that were to come with her.

'It will be our spring offensive,' she said to Bruno over coffee. 'Flemings are taking most of our new line. I want to have a crack at Harrods and Harvey Nichols, Shoolbreds and . . .'

'I don't know if I can get enough cashmere yet.' Bruno was looking at some papers that had arrived that morning from China. 'So go easy.'

'When I return I will bring a designer Bruno. I'm determined to find one; maybe two. He'll have an assistant and . . .'

'Margaret, I think our plain simple styles are the best, as I have told you before,' Bruno began patiently but Margaret waved a hand at him.

'Yes, you have told me before and I don't agree with you. You should see the things some people in the Midlands are doing! We're going to be left behind.'

'But there *is* a limit to our money. If we invest in good safe merchandise . . .'

'We will never progress beyond what we are, a medium-sized manufacturer of knitted garments. The expenditure on all this new plant will be wasted because we are doing the same as all our competitors. No Bruno, you have to trust in me and my judgement.'

Margaret paused and smiled at him. She now never thought of him as anything other than her co-director and brother-in-law. They never talked intimately, never spent any time together. That awful episode eight years before was as though it had never been. She could see it, now that she knew more about men, as perhaps an aberration on his part, an aftermath of war. She, too, had been young, completely inexperienced, easily shocked in a way she would not be now.

Bruno was now family, part of the business. He was also a good businessman; not inspired, but sound. She, Margaret, would provide the inspiration.

Susan had just had a miscarriage, her third, and was advised to have no more children. If she was upset she hid it, saying that she was content with the ones she had, the darling twins. But Margaret knew that in her heart Susan was disappointed. In her lovely house in the Branahae foothills, ten miles out of Branswick, she had hoped to become the mother of a large family, giving substance to the image she liked to project of herself and her husband. But Bruno seemed quite happy with two and as he was away a lot perhaps it was just as well, because Susan had enough to do on her own with a large house and young, agile twins, even though she had plenty of domestic help.

That night there was a small family dinner party at *Woodbrae*, a black tie affair such as they used to have before Hector Dunbar became ill. It seemed so many years ago now, another age. The best plate and silver had been put out, the best food prepared, scotch salmon, sirloin of beef, and there was champagne. At the end everyone toasted Margaret and her new venture.

'To success!'

'To success!' Margaret echoed, her eyes shining.

'And every happiness in your new home.' Susan got up and kissed her.

'*Our* home, Susan. It's the Dunbar family's London home. It's big enough and you are all invited to stay there when you are in London.'

'I'm dying to see it,' Susan said. 'When Bruno goes to South America in May I shall come and stay. You say it's our home but you have paid for it, Maggie.'

'Yes, but I'm giving it to you all. *All* my family.'

Margaret smiled at Fleur who sat awkwardly at the table, obviously longing for the time when she could stretch her bulk on the sofa and put her feet up. She had not had an easy time in this pregnancy and would also probably not have more children. Well, two were enough there too, Margaret thought gazing at Cullum, who sat slumped at the table, mesmerized by the liquid in his glass. Was he thinking of Nan, or what? It was very difficult to know what went on in Cullum's secretive mind.

After they had seen the Macallisters off and Fleur had announced she was going to bed, Margaret and Cullum went back to the drawing room as though by a tacit agreement that they should speak. Cullum immediately poured whisky for himself.

'Brandy?' He turned to Margaret who sat back in the low armchair, gazing at the fire leaping up the chimney and comparing it with the meagre embers she had seen in the tenement in Dumbarton Street by the side of the Drume.

'A very tiny one, Cullum. I had quite a lot to drink.' And so did you, she wanted to add; but Cullum's drinking, like his life, was never referred to by her. Whether Fleur said anything or not she didn't know; Cullum was so aggressive if inroads were made on his privacy that those near to him thought such matters should be skirted altogether in the interest of family harmony.

Cullum gave her her drink and sat down heavily, passing a hand across his face. His eyes were slightly bloodshot and he looked tired.

'I'll be glad when Fleur has the baby, won't you Cullum? I think it's proving a trial to her.'

'She wanted it,' Cullum said shortly putting his glass to his lips.

'But surely so did you, Cullum?' Margaret said rather sharply. 'Do you not wish for a son?' She meant no irony, she thought to herself, saying this.

'It may not be a son,' Cullum said glumly. 'All that trouble for nothing.'

'Trouble for Fleur, not you, I would have thought,' Margaret murmured. 'Well, women do have their place in the world, although I suppose they will always be second-class citizens.'

'Well, *you're* certainly not.' Cullum glanced ferociously at her. 'I wouldn't call you a second-class citizen, not by a long chalk.'

'No, I am decidedly a first-class citizen.' Margaret tried to choose her words carefully, aware of Cullum's danger-ous mood. 'But then I'm possibly exceptional. I also have to think of the position of my fellow sisters.'

Cullum emitted a bellow of laughter. 'Oh I *like* to think of you thinking of others Margaret! Oh that is rich! Surely, the only person you ever think about is yourself?'

Margaret, conscious of the need to keep control of herself, reached for her evening bag and drew out a slim silver cigarette case, a present from Hamish. She stared for a moment at her initials on the case, beautifully engraved by the best jewellers in Edinburgh. She lit the cigarette with an exquisite enamelled lighter, this time a gift from Tristan, and then she sat with the case on her lap, her thumb going over and over the initials, a compulsive gesture that betrayed her nervousness.

'I'm sorry you think that, Cullum.' She exhaled smoke into the air. 'I would have thought that, if you were honest, you would realize it was far from the truth. I don't think I have ever thought of myself enough; but maybe I'm deceiving myself. They say we seldom see ourselves as we really are. I have thought of the family and of the business constantly since I reached maturity, and for many years, while I led a dissatisfied stilted life here, I scarcely considered myself at all. You would not let me work and nor would Father. No one thought of me then, or if they did they kept it well hidden. Two and a half years ago things changed. I had done my duty and I felt able to accept the changes, pleasant ones, and to go with them for my own advantage; mine and the family's, and the business. I am proud of Dunbars and ambitious for it. If it was left to you . . .'

'Oh I know, we would have no mill and no home. We would all be in the poor house.'

'Or in a tenement on Dumbarton Street,' Margaret interrupted, the timbre of her carefully controlled voice steely, threatening.

Cullum jerked his glass, spilling the contents on his dress trousers. As there was little left it was only a small stain and he brushed at it with his hand and then completed the rubbing with his handkerchief. He put down his glass on the table by his elbow and, sitting back, joined his hands and closed his eyes.

'Oh I see. I'm to be ticked off. This is what it's all been leading up to, is it?'

'It is certainly not something of which you should be proud.'

'Or ashamed,' Cullum said, his eyes still closed. 'When

243

I knew the child was mine I supported it. I could have denied it.'

'Hardly with his looks!'

Margaret's laugh was sarcastic and Cullum opened his eyes, those blue-green eyes that William had, and stared at her.

'You've *seen* William?'

'Yes, and his mother.'

'And what clever detective work brought you there? Or did she come to you?'

'Of course not. One would think you knew her better. She's a very proud, independent girl. I found out by a simple logical process when Fleur told me you had got up suddenly and left the house after reading the evening paper.'

'Oh that.' Cullum sounded dejected and he closed his eyes again. 'Does Fleur know too?'

'You sound very calm about it all.' Margaret began to feel annoyed and shifted in her chair, putting her cigarette case away and snapping shut the catch on her bag. 'No, she doesn't know as far as I can tell; but that is not to say she won't find out. I should think all the town knows.'

'Scots are canny people. They don't gossip.'

'Lucky for you.'

'And what would Fleur do if she did know?' Cullum glanced sideways at her. 'Would she leave me and take my children? I doubt it. She's very happy and comfortable here and I think she has few illusions about me.'

'How *fortunate* for you, Cullum,' Margaret said scathingly, but keeping her voice low. It would not be unusual if Fleur found some reason to come downstairs again. Her condition made her restless. 'But I'm not thinking of Fleur. Though she has the misfortune to be married to you, she is, as you say, comfortable and well provided for. She even has her own not inconsiderable income I understand. I'm much more worried about Nan and your son William.'

'Why are you worried about them?'

'Because of the poverty they live in.'

'And what are you going to do about it? Why do you not take them to your lavish London home?'

'Oh Cullum!' Margaret got up and walked swiftly to the window gazing unseeingly at the darkness beyond, for the curtains had not been drawn. 'I find you quite impossible. When you neglect yourself I don't mind, but others . . . it is too bad.'

'I pay her an allowance.'

'Which she puts in a post office account. She never touches it.'

'She is thrifty.'

'No thanks to you! Did you never think you should do anything else?'

'What? Marry her?'

'Oh I don't mean that! That would, of course, have been out of the question.' Margaret impatiently drew the curtains and shivered against a small icy blast that had come in through a badly fitting join in the window-frame. 'You might have consulted me or Susan, or Bruno, and provided some money for her to move to better accommodation.'

'*Consult* you! What a reception I would have had! Besides, we didn't have any money until recently, and then you've blown it all . . .'

Margaret stamped a foot in rage. 'I have *not* blown it as you say, Cullum! The money I spent on the London house is my own; the legacy that Father left me. The offices in Devonshire Place were a necessity, and anyway they were not expensive. I have never squandered family money. Whereas you squander all yours in drink and cars!'

Cullum turned right round in his chair and eyed her solemnly. 'I have offered to buy Nan a small cottage outside Branswick and send William to a good school.'

Suddenly Margaret remembered the bitter laugh, the expression on Nan's face. Now she understood. She

245

wandered over to the sofa and sat down on its arm, crossing her legs.

'And what did she say?'

'She's thinking about it.'

'I suppose there are strings?'

'What strings?' Cullum put his hands behind his head and gazed at the ceiling.

'That she should be your mistress again.'

'She *is* my mistress again. She wants me as much as I want her.'

Margaret got up and, walking to the door, quietly opened it and peered out. The only sound in the hall came from the ticking of the ancient grandfather clock that some said had stood in the original Dunbar Mill in the 1840s. She firmly shut the door again and turned the key in the lock.

'I see.' Slowly she walked back and resumed her seat on the sofa. 'So it is all a *fait accompli*?'

'It happened the night I went to see her. Her father was at the hospital and she was alone. I love her. She's a good woman.'

'So is Fleur.'

'But not in the same way. Nan is very . . . how shall I say . . .' Cullum scratched his head.

'Sexual, perhaps?'

'Yes, sexual. Fleur on the other hand is not sexual at all. Between them I get the best of both worlds.'

'You're contemptible, Cullum.'

'Maybe you're prejudiced, Margaret.' Cullum lumbered to his feet and half filled his tumbler with neat whisky. 'You've never liked me. You always despised me after Malcolm – don't think I didn't know it. You made me feel very inadequate. Well, Nan and Fleur make me feel very good. They both love me and want me. I need their affection and I am not going to give it up. I'm fond of William and I want to be a father to him. You know,

246

Margaret – ' As though the sound of his own voice had given him courage, Cullum leaned forward and selected a cigar from a box on the table. He carefully snipped off the end and slowly lit it. 'You know, you're very sanctimonious about human relationships; yet what do you know about them?' He blew smoke at her, a gesture which she did not think he meant to be insulting, except perhaps unconsciously. 'Nothing as far as I know. You've never had an important relationship with a man; you've spurned them all. You don't even seem to like women very much. Are you still a virgin, Margaret? I doubt it, but I don't know. I think you're cold and that you know nothing, nothing at all about these human emotions that make men and women love one another.

'You may be a wizard at figures, a genius in the knitting business, and I admit you've taken to it like a duck to water; but as a human being you're a failure. There, I've said it. That's all I have to say.' Cullum studied the glowing tip of his cigar with satisfaction, as though he had done a good day's work, and took another sip of whisky.

'Thank you for that, Cullum,' Margaret said after a while, her voice unsteady. 'It's not a very flattering picture of me. Need I say it is quite untrue? But I don't want to go into that. That is how you see me and I don't propose to elaborate on why I think you're wrong. But believe me, my dear brother, I have as much human blood flowing through my veins as you have, and more compassion in my heart; for I would not have fathered a child and then left it to grow up with its mother in a slum with inadequate heating and the damp peeling the paper off the walls. Nor would I have ceased to see this child, as you did, and then enter its life again without regard for his happiness or the happiness of the mother.

'Swayed by your selfishness, your own carnality, you now resume a relationship that can only end in heartbreak for everyone, and I hope *you*, Cullum Dunbar, get the

247

biggest share of it. Good-night, and good-bye brother. I shall not be back until the spring.'

'Thank God for that,' Cullum said, but Margaret did not hear him as she unlocked the door, closed it behind her and ran quickly up the stairs to her room, her eyes blinded by tears.

CHAPTER FOURTEEN

The Dunbar offices in Devonshire Place were on the first and second floors of an elegant Regency house that had once been the gracious home of a well heeled minor branch of the English aristocracy. A scion of the family, who still owned the building, had turned the top two floors into a flat and let the rest. The ground floor was occupied by a firm of yarn importers who supplied yarn to the Dunbar mill, which was how Margaret had come to hear that two floors were to let.

Margaret hoped that one day Dunbars would occupy the entire building, as the owner was hardly ever in town, keeping his flat as a *pied à terre*. But for the time being two floors were more than adequate, with the offices on the first floor and show and storerooms on the second. Her office was a large front room with the original oak panelling intact, which she had furnished rather like the lounge of a private house, with Louis Quinze chairs bought at a sale at Sothebys, an Empire sofa in the Récamier style and a rosewood desk with a leather top, gilded round the edges. There were cream coloured satin drapes at the window, a heavy crystal chandelier and a large Aubusson rug on the polished oak floor. The paintwork was white and so was the ceiling, except for the intricately carved rose around the chandelier which was picked out in gold leaf.

Given the depressed times, the room had not been too expensive to furnish because antiques from the estates of impoverished Continental aristocrats were flooding the London market. The pickings of penurious or dispossessed German, Austrian, Hungarian and Polish nobility streamed over the Channel from their huge, empty, derelict castles and vast country houses. What before the war, in the heyday of Edwardian prosperity, would have cost a fortune in the saleroom could now be picked up for a few hundred pounds. It was a boom time for antique dealers and bargain hunters with money to spare.

The same was happening with the furniture that Tristan, knowing her taste, was acquiring for her house. Margaret was amassing a small fortune for the future in antiques and works of art. She usually worked sitting on the Récamier sofa, her papers spread around her and on a small marble-topped occasional table. All she ever did at her desk was make notes or take telephone calls.

When the phone rang on this particular day in February Margaret could not at first identify the caller.

'I beg your pardon. Who did you say?'

'Yves Lamotte, Miss Dunbar. We met at the Café Royal in November or thereabouts. Tristan Fleming introduced us.'

'Oh of course!' Margaret felt embarrassed at her apparent lapse of memory and consequent discourtesy. She had been so immersed in her work that even the deliciously accented voice had failed to identify the caller. 'How are you, Mr Lamotte?'

'I'm very well. I have some news for you which is why I am calling. I think I have a designer for you.'

'Oh really?'

'A very talented young man; but to meet him you will have to travel to Paris. Would that be possible?'

'Anything is possible,' Margaret replied. 'But if he is in Paris is he free to work for us?'

'I think it could be arranged, provided the inducements were right. He is English and wants to come home. His name is Peter Cartwright and at present he works for the house of Fumel.'

'Oh Fumel! They produce some exquisite things.'

'I thought you'd say that. Well, he has designed for them for five years. I told him about you and he is interested; but as he is working on the autumn collection he cannot travel at the moment.'

'When would he be free?'

'I should think when this collection is finished, in three or four months' time. How would that suit you?'

'It would suit,' Margaret said after a moment's thought. Fumel. Fumel provided the cream of the imported fashions from the Continent which rivalled her own merchandise for its style and chic. 'When can I see him?'

'Whenever you like. I am leaving for Paris tomorrow night on the Golden Arrow. Is it possible that you could join me?'

'As I said,' Margaret smiled into the mouthpiece, 'anything is possible. Give me the details.'

She pulled her pad towards her and made some quick jottings with a slim gold Cartier pencil.

It was very strange to be sitting opposite the man she had only briefly met once, whose name she had almost forgotten, and to speculate that she might have fallen in love with him. Margaret had spent the past twenty-four hours in an untypical state of intense excitement, not about the designer so much as at the prospect of seeing Yves Lamotte again. The memory of the meeting at the Café Royal very quickly reawakened her interest in someone she had not expected to meet so soon, rather than the undertaking they were engaged upon.

She had packed, dressed with care and was at Victoria Station early, going as planned to the bookstall on Platform 5. But even then he was there before her, looking tall and almost unnaturally handsome in an astrakhan fur coat with a matching cap set stylishly upon his head. Yves

251

kissed her hand as he greeted her, took her case and moved towards the train.

He showed her the couchette that he had booked for her, some distance down the coach from his, and then took her to the restaurant car where smoked salmon sandwiches and champagne were waiting for them.

'This is such a surprise,' Margaret said, gazing at him across the table, still mildly astonished to find herself where she was.

'I thought you might not have had much time to eat.'

'You were quite right. I had lots to do at the office, a late hair appointment and then scarcely time to go home, change and pick up my case.'

'I should have called for you, but I had a late appointment, too, in Belgravia.'

'Oh that was not necessary.' Margaret sipped her champagne. Suddenly overwhelmed by a feeling of happiness and ease, she closed her eyes, aware of the fragrant bubbles tickling her nostrils.

'You're tired?'

Margaret opened her eyes. Yves had an elbow on the table and was gazing at her with a half smile on his lips, his head slightly tilted as if in appraisal. It was quite clear that he liked what he saw.

'I've had quite a hectic time in London. New house, new office, new everything and I have hardly any help. I haven't even engaged a secretary; but there is a capable woman who opens the post and does odd jobs and she will hold the reins while I'm away. Also Bruno, our joint managing director, will be there from tomorrow until next week when he goes to Italy.'

'So you could spend a few days in France?' Yves nonchalantly tilted his glass.

'Would that be necessary?' Margaret looked at him with surprise. 'I thought a day or so . . .'

'I wondered if you would like to spend the weekend at

252

my parents' home on the Loire? They have a little château at Amboise.'

'Oh but I . . .'

'Hardly know me?' Yves laughed and refilled her glass.

'No, I didn't mean that.' Margaret watched the hundreds of tiny bubbles bouncing off the top of the freshly poured champagne. 'I mean that . . . it's too kind.'

'But is it possible?'

'Anything is possible,' Margaret murmured and it was at that moment, as their eyes met across the table in the Pullman dining car with its rose-coloured lamps, its air of quiet opulence, that she felt she had fallen in love.

Later, lying in bed in her couchette, with the lights of dimly lit stations fleetingly reflected on the ceiling as the train rushed past them through the night, she wondered when she had fallen out of love with Hamish. Because to fall in love with someone, surely you had to be emotionally free? Was she emotionally free? She thought back to the last meeting with Hamish and felt that she had been free then. Maybe she had been free for a year or more, but no fresh love had come to awaken her. Now one had. Or had he? Maybe he was as charming as this to everyone.

Yves seemed just the sort of man that any woman in her right senses would fall immediately in love with. Everything about him was enticing: his beautifully cut dark blue suit, surely made in Savile Row and sitting so perfectly on his shoulders; the cut of his shirt, a very pale blue with a stiff white collar, and his pale pink tie with a pale blue stripe. His whole demeanour was distinguished, immaculate and somehow very wholesome. You knew instinctively that he was a particular man, that everything he wore was freshly laundered and clean. You knew he did not eat or drink too much or have any excesses to offend the susceptibilities of one as fastidious as Margaret. She

253

wondered what he would be like in bed, and she sensed that would be good too; he would know exactly how to please a woman, his own satisfaction would not be paramount to hers.

Soon after the train rolled onto the boat, she closed her eyes and fell asleep, lulled by the gentle waves of the English Channel, and did not wake up until the train was in the Gare du Nord and the light was breaking through the blind of her window.

'Sleep well?'

'Marvellous.'

'I thought we'd breakfast in my flat?'

'That would be heavenly.'

Margaret had been already dressed when he put his head round the door, freshly groomed as though she'd woken in her own home. She was wearing a black woollen two piece made by Dunbars, a skirt and a long cardigan, with a white cashmere jumper underneath. Very soon they were through passport control and then in a taxi, Yves giving instructions in rapid French to the driver, who set off at a cracking pace through the tortuous streets of Paris.

'Have you been here before?'

'I went to finishing school in Switzerland, so I passed through Paris on my way there and back. I think I stayed the night but I can't remember.' She looked at him. 'It was quite a long time ago. The war had only just ended and everywhere was very chaotic.'

'You are as young as that?' He put a cigarette in a holder and lit it, blowing smoke through the partly opened window.

'Do I not *look* young?' Margaret laughed, not sure whether to feel annoyed or flattered.

'You look *very* young, but so poised and accomplished that I thought your looks possibly belied your age. You are a director of fashion, a business woman with your own

254

home. I thought – ' he studied the roof of the cab, 'maybe thirty-two or three.'

'No. I'm twenty-seven this year.'

'That's remarkable.'

'But why is it remarkable?'

'Because you are so beautiful too. I don't think I ever met a woman quite like you.'

'Oh.' Margaret grasped the strap above her seat as the cab swung into a broad tree-lined avenue and screeched to a stop before an imposing mansion block.

'This is the Avenue Foch,' Yves said as he opened the door for her after paying the driver. 'Named after our great war-time hero.'

'Did you live here all during the war?' Margaret gazed up at the block and then at the buildings around her.

'I was *in* the war, my dear. We closed the apartment and my parents stayed in their château.'

He took her elbow and shepherded her into the hall of the apartment block. It was vast with marble pillars and a shiny, patterned marble floor. A concierge rushed out to take their cases and escorted them to a large cage lift with black lattice work and a spacious interior.

'I'm on the fourth floor. We have a marvellous view.' He smiled at her as the lift creaked to a halt and the deferential concierge preceded them to a rather imposing door half way along the marble corridor.

'*Voilà, monsieur le vicomte!*' The concierge opened the door with a flourish, deposited the bags in the hall and bowed as Yves gave him a few coins. '*Merci monsieur. Au revoir monsieur, madame . . .*' He bowed again and closed the door.

'So you *are* a viscount!'

'Why? Did I say I was?'

'No, but Tristan said your father was a count.'

'Yes, he is a count.' Yves, sounding offhand, took her coat and hung it on an ornate hallstand. 'But I never use

255

my title. This is, of course, a family apartment, so the porter is always very particular to use my title and that of my parents. They like to keep in touch with the old order, you know, though I must say that as far as we French are concerned that all finished a long time ago. We have not had a king since . . .' He was ushering her into a large drawing room, exquisitely furnished and with four large windows which, as he had said, offered a panoramic view of Paris. 'I can't remember. We had so many in the nineteenth century, always being overthrown, restored and overthrown.'

'Was it not Napoleon III, the one who died in England?'

'That was it.' Yves looked at her with admiration, then turned as a diminutive woman, clad in a white apron over a blue frock, came into the room, and dropped a small curtsey. 'Ah Marie . . .' Yves broke into more rapid French, the woman looked at Margaret, smiled, bobbed and disappeared.

'That is the invaluable Marie. She will bring us coffee and ask us what we would like for breakfast. Now, my dear Margaret, would you like to bathe?'

'I would love to.'

'You look so perfect I can't believe it, but you are the kind of woman who would look right at any time. I can't imagine that you have slept in a train and washed in a tiny basin in those terrible cramped conditions of the couchette. But then I know you have. We have two bathrooms in this place and Marie will prepare one for you and another for me. Shall we meet here in say – ' he glanced at the slim watch on his wrist, 'an hour and then plan the day?'

'Perfect,' Margaret said. Somehow it was all too perfect. She felt she had been translated from reality into a modern Gallic version of Fairyland.

*

Peter Cartwright was an ethereally good-looking young man of about Margaret's age. He was tall and slim, with blond hair and a pale, rather feminine face. He looked about nineteen but Yves had told her he was twenty-six or seven.

They talked at length over lunch and made plans to see his latest designs that night at Yves' flat. Over lunch they settled all the details except the finer points that would appear on the contract. Salary was agreed (Margaret having first consulted Bruno over the telephone before she left London), terms and conditions of work.

Margaret said she was surprised he was prepared to live in Branswick and here came the first discordant note. He had thought the job was to be in London. He had looked at Yves, and Yves at Margaret, who said that, no, the design department was to be set up in Branswick.

This appeared to disconcert Peter Cartwright. Margaret thought for a moment that the mission had failed, because she could not possibly have her design department so far from the mill. Peter decided to think about it. That night at dinner, after she had inspected his clever, fashionable designs which were all and more than she could wish for, making her all the more determined to have him, he asked if it would be possible to spend part of the year in London and part in Branswick.

'After all, I agree I must be near the source of inspiration,' Peter said smiling charmingly at her. 'The Scottish hills and valleys, you understand, Miss Dunbar; but on the other hand I can get inspiration in London too and meet fellow designers. Would it not be possible?'

Margaret had already decided. Cartwright's designs would turn her house into one manufacturing *haute couture* garments. Yes, she said; it would be possible, because she hoped to have more of the house containing the office than they had at present. Now would be a good time to try and negotiate for the ground floor.

257

'That's quite large enough to start,' she said, 'because you would not be alone for long. I want a large design department with you at its head.'

'Admirable,' Peter Cartwright murmured, looking at Yves, and they toasted the deal in more champagne.

Margaret, of course, did not stay with Yves but at the Hotel Georges Cinq where he had booked her a room. This again was typical of the way the man operated, no *louche* suggestions, no hint of promiscuity. Despite his fascination she thought his tastes were ascetic and cerebral. He did not put a foot out of place the whole time they were together. They spent the morning making plans, lunch and the evening with Peter Cartwright, and in the afternoon he took her to a small exhibition of French Impressionists at a private gallery on the Champs Élysées and purchased an exquisite painting of lilies by Claude Monet. A present for his mother, he explained.

The following day was Friday and in the afternoon he was to pick her up and drive her down to his parents' château in Amboise.

It was all so incredible that Margaret could hardly believe it. It was as though the whole thing had been planned well in advance, but that would have been to strain incredulity too. How could Yves have known that Peter Cartwright would be free, or that she would be able to spend the weekend on the Loire, or even that the weather would improve and be almost like spring so that the drive down was as enchanting as anything else about the visit?

The journey was made in some style, Yves having acquired a brand new olive green Hispano-Suiza convertible, one of the most expensive cars on the market. Everything about the car was luxurious, from its upholstery in suede and leather to the solid silver Flying Stork mascot on its gleaming bonnet.

'I've never driven in such a car,' Margaret said, as they

bowled along at fifty miles an hour on the long straight road beteen Paris and Chartres.

'I only took delivery the other day.' Yves caressed the wheel. 'She's a beauty, isn't she?'

'Beautiful. I never knew, why Hispano-Suiza?'

'Spanish-Swiss,' Yves said, his eyes on the road. 'The car was the creation of a Swiss designer, Mark Birgit, and at the beginning he produced it only in Spain. Now a lot of them are made in France. Hispano made the engines for the Spad fighters during the war, and the flying stork was the mascot of Georges Guynemer's Stork Squadron which flew the Spads. I flew one myself. Wonderful planes.'

'So you were a flyer too? That's how you knew Tristan?'

'Yes, I flew British aeroplanes too and was seconded to a British squadron for a time.'

'Did you know Bruno Macallister?'

Yves wrinkled his handsome face and shook his head. 'Don't think so. Why?'

'He is my brother-in-law, joint managing director of the firm.'

Yves suddenly pointed to irregular twin spires on the horizon. 'Look, Chartres Cathedral.'

'Oh I'd love to see it!'

'Maybe on the way back. I told my parents we'd be there for dinner.'

He smiled at her and pressed his foot on the accelerator and Margaret settled back, wrapped in her fur, seeped in an all-pervasive feeling of utter peace and contentment.

It was almost dark when they arrived at the ancient town of Amboise on the banks of the Loire. Starkly outlined against the dusky sky was its famous château, the home of French Kings, also a some-time home of Leonardo da Vinci who had died in Amboise and was buried there. The château dominated the town, whose quaint

259

houses clustered against its walls reminiscent of a time when all citizens had been dependent upon the King. Yves drove straight under the walls along the banks of the river until he turned off up a narrow lane and then through large wrought iron gates which stood open, as if in welcome.

The château was a low, mainly eighteenth-century structure built of soft red brick. It had a pleasing harmony characteristic of the age with white-framed windows and a colonnaded portico over the front door. As they stopped, the door opened and a footman came running down the steps accompanied by two large barking dogs. In the wake of this welcoming party came a couple who slowly descended the steps, a tall white-haired man and a diminutive white-haired lady who walked with the help of a stick.

Yves, shouting instructions, was out of the car before the footman had reached it. He opened the door for Margaret and led her over to his parents.

'Maman, may I present Miss Dunbar? Margaret, my mother, the Countess de Lamotte.'

'I'm very pleased to meet you.' Margaret shook her hand, greeting her in French, not sure whether or not she spoke English.

Madame Lamotte looked very old. Margaret saw that she appeared so small because she stooped as though in pain, leaning heavily on her stick. Her hair was snow white and her face very lined. Yet her handclasp was firm and she pulled Margaret towards her and kissed her on the cheek, saying: 'I hope you don't mind, my dear. I want you to feel very welcome here.'

Margaret, just a little embarrassed, returned the embrace, pressing her face against the soft withered cheek. 'Of course I don't mind, madame! You are so kind to invite me.'

'And my father.' Yves had linked arms with the Count,

who looked much younger than his wife. He was still a handsome man, maybe in his late sixties, and his son bore him a strong resemblance.

'How do you do, monsieur?'

Margaret extended a hand but the Count, instead of shaking it, gallantly impressed a kiss upon it.

'We are so glad you could come, Miss Dunbar. Yves has told us a lot about you.'

'Really?' Margaret looked into Yves' face and laughed, an infectious happy laugh that few who knew her in the lonely years she'd spent as her father's companion in Branswick would have recognized.

They entered the house accompanied by the excited dogs, who bounced around a hall so full of precious objects that Margaret looked anxiously at the boisterous animals.

'Oh don't mind them! They have never broken anything yet though you might consider it a miracle.' Yves, lightly touching her arm, led her into a salon which seemed to run the length of the château. Along its walls were gilded mirrors which reflected the antique furniture, the many priceless objects of art, the thousands of tiny winking pearls of light that made up the four giant chandeliers. Fires burned at each end of the room and in front of one of them another couple awaited them.

'Margaret, this is my sister Dominique and her husband the Baron Guy de Crispigny-Lafranc.'

Margaret shook hands, already feeling rather daunted by her surroundings, the distinguished company in which she found herself.

The Baron and the Baronne were a couple in their forties, the man rather nondescript, the woman decidedly plain. Everything about her seemed disproportionate for a woman – she had big feet, and hands which hung rather awkwardly at her side, as though she did not know quite what to do with them, and a long thin neck that made her head look like a ball precariously perched on a pole. She had a very large nose and a wide mouth, and her hair was unfashionably scraped back, giving her a gawkish air. She had on a dark practical dress which made no pretensions to fashion, black stockings and flat black shoes. She looked like a solid, dependable member of the French bourgeoisie, and was about as far removed from her handsome aristocratic-looking brother as it was possible to imagine.

Yet, withal, she had an expression of such warmth and charm as she greeted the new arrival that Margaret momentarily imagined her to be beautiful; what the French call *jolie laide*. She had very good even teeth which sparkled as she smiled, the smile transforming her dark brown eyes into a vibrant, friendly glow. Margaret liked her immediately.

The Baron was of medium height, balding with little wings of hair sprouting out behind each ear, making him look rather like a comical cartoon of winged Hercules. His face, pleasantly cherubic, could have been that of a doctor or an amiable absent-minded professor. The homeliness of the Baron and Baronne allayed what nervousness Margaret still had, a process further aided by the glass of champagne put into her hand as she warmed herself before the fire.

Dinner followed soon after, the Countess saying that they would not change because it was already so late and Yves apologizing for not leaving Paris earlier. The meal was simple, almost frugal, consisting of three courses, fish, meat and cheese, and the light, dry white wine made by the Count himself, Château Lamotte, from vines grown on the banks of the Loire which bordered his estate.

Margaret felt that she was under inspection, especially by Yves' mother, whose eyes glittered kindly but speculatively as they rested upon her, which they frequently did during the course of the meal. She had the feeling that she was being shown off and wondered if she were here to be assessed by Yves' family. Was it really possible?

'My parents think you're very charming,' Yves said on the landing in front of her bedroom door, to which he had escorted her after saying good-night downstairs. 'I think my father is a little in love with you too.'

'Too?' Margaret's voice faltered as she looked at him.

'Well, it must be obvious . . .' Yves paused, as if searching for the right word. Then he bent forward and kissed her cheek, whispering in her ear: 'It must be obvious that I love you.'

Margaret started back, her heart beating rapidly, but he pressed a finger over her lips and smiled into her eyes.

'Don't say anything. Please. Not yet. I just want you to think about it. Good-night.' His lips lightly touched her cheek again and he opened the door for her, bowing very slightly.

She brushed past him, grateful for the solitude of her room in which to recover her emotions.

Margaret slept very little that night; as she tossed and turned in bed her mind seemed to spin, diving and gyrating like a whirligig. Ever since Yves had phoned her in London four days before, her life had assumed a new dimension, isolating her from her former existence.

Nothing about the last few days had been ordinary; the journey, the flat in the Avenue Foch, as large as a house with its many rooms and long corridors, the meeting with Peter Cartwright when everything went so easily, and then the glorious drive down to this jewel of a château nestling in the heart of some of the loveliest countryside in France. And now here she was, in a warm bed that could easily have contained three more people, in a room twice as large as her own bedroom and furnished with antiques made by some of the greatest French cabinet-makers.

By the time she felt her eyes beginning to close, her brain running down through sheer exhaustion, the first birds were already breaking into song in the park. When she woke the light flooded in behind the drawn curtains and she sat up, rather startled, wondering at first where she was, the surroundings utterly unfamiliar.

A knock on the door had awoken her and a maid entered with a tray, a bright smile on her face.

'*Bonjour madame, est-ce que vous avez bien dormi?*'

'*Oui, merci.*'

Margaret spoke good French, one abiding advantage of having finished her education in Switzerland. The maid was delighted to have a response in her own language and she chatted brightly, setting the tray on a table which she pulled up to Margaret's bed, drawing the curtains with a running commentary on the beauty of the day. Clearly she seemed to enjoy life. .

'Monsieur Yves wished me to bid you good morning, madame, and to say that he and his father and brother-in-law are going shooting. He wonders if you would care to join them.'

'Oh yes! But I can't shoot.'

The maid smiled. 'That is of no consequence, madame! The Baronne shoots with the men, but Monsieur Yves suggests that you and the Countess could join them for luncheon.'

'What a nice idea.'

'It is nine-thirty, madame. May I draw your bath?'

'Please.' Margaret felt immediately wide awake, despite the few hours' sleep; she quickly ate her hot croissants, spreading them thinly with apricot jam, and drank her fragrant coffee from a French breakfast cup as large as a bowl.

In half an hour she was ready, bathed, dressed and made up. She only had her woollen two-piece, not having been prepared for a weekend in such a grand country house, but she tied a gay scarf round her neck and combed her hair loose so that she felt more informal.

Yves was waiting for her in the hall, sitting on a chair reading the morning paper. He wore a brown suit with plus-fours and a polo-necked jersey. As he heard her footsteps on the stairs he jumped up, throwing down the paper and going forward to greet her. She raised her face and he bent and kissed her cheek.

'Did you sleep well, Margaret?'

'At first no, but eventually.'

'Why did you not sleep well?' he murmured.

'I think I was a little overwhelmed by . . . everything.'

He pressed her hand and took her out onto the porch. Three cars were standing in the circular drive, their doors open and various servants packing guns and hampers into the boots. 'Would it amuse you to join a shooting party?'

'Very much so!'

'I thought it might. There're only rabbits and that kind of thing because, of course, it isn't the proper shooting season; but as it was a fine day we thought . , .'

'You must have decided very early.'

'Oh we always breakfast at seven, my father and I. My mother is not yet up and will join us for lunch. If you like you can walk with us now.'

'Is your mother an invalid, Yves?'

'She is arthritic, very badly so, as you can see. She has taken all the cures and perhaps they have helped to prolong her life, I don't know; but she is nearly always in pain.'

'You seem to love her very much.'

'I do.' He looked at her. 'Is it so obvious?'

'Oh yes! How you hovered over her at dinner and afterwards, making sure she had everything she wanted, taking her up to bed. It must be very gratifying to have such a thoughtful son.'

'She has done a lot for me. Taught me to love art and beautiful things. I have always been my mother's

265

favourite. My sister is more like my father. Very practical.'

'Has she any children?'

'Two, a boy and a girl. They are grown up of course. My sister is older than I am. No one thought my mother would have any more children and then I came along!' He made a typically Gallic gesture with his arms. 'A present from the fairies!'

He looked so attractive, so vital and full of life that Margaret felt she wanted to hug him and she almost put out her arms as though inviting him to take her in his. She saw a spasm pass over his face as though he could divine her thoughts; then, lowering his gaze, he ran lightly down the steps to the cars, leaving her on the porch.

That day was as good as the one before, a day spent strolling in the woods, the wintry sunshine penetrating a thin mist which swirled about the trees, making the shooting of rabbits a chancy business. In the end the party bagged a round dozen which were to be taken to the market in Amboise during the week. Then they drove back to the house for an excellent dinner followed by a game of bridge.

Sunday was equally leisurely; church in the morning, the family sitting in their pew at the local church, followed by a large lunch. After lunch Yves suggested a walk, but no one seemed keen except Margaret who wanted to walk off the effects of the food she had eaten. The Baron and the Baronne were leaving after lunch, so before Margaret and Yves set out for their walk they saw them off, the Baron loading a Renault '45' which he said could do ninety miles an hour.

'Only he daren't,' said his wife, 'with me in it!'

'Are you going back to Paris?'

'Oh we do not live in Paris, would that we did! We are from Bordeaux. I thought Yves had told you?' She looked smilingly at Yves, as though chiding him for his neglect. 'That is why we have to start now, though we shall stay with friends in Perigord on the way and reach home tomorrow morning. It is a long journey. Good-bye, Margaret, I do hope we shall meet again. We so hope that Yves . . .' She paused, seemed to think better of what she was saying and awkwardly reached for Margaret's hand.

They did not kiss but shook hands, and Margaret noticed the look in her eyes, the expression that so resembled her mother's whenever she looked at her. The Count and Countess joined them to wave good-bye as the car began its journey home, then the Countess said she was going to rest and the Count that he would read the papers and have a nap too. Yves saw his mother to her room and then, well wrapped up, he and Margaret walked around the back of the house to the woods that ran right down to the water's edge.

Now that she was alone with him, completely alone for the first time that weekend, Margaret felt constrained in his company and wished he had not whispered those words to her on the Friday night. When he had taken her to her room after dinner the previous night he had merely planted a kiss on her forehead; but that night she slept well, as though the chaste fraternal kiss were more like a benediction than a declaration of love.

For a while Yves too seemed held back by some diffidence, and then, as he slipped his arm through hers, an extraordinary feeling of apprehension overcame her, a mixture of fear and desire. She felt that the vibration passed from herself to him, for he suddenly stopped and looked at her, taking his arm away and standing back a little as though he were admiring a painting or sculpture.

'If you could see yourself now . . .' He held up a hand and gestured towards the treetops. 'You would die of self love!'

Margaret took off her hat and shook it, laughing, letting her hair tumble over her face. He looked surprised, rather rebuffed.

'Why do you laugh?'

'Because it is such a Gallic thing to say. I can't imagine an Englishman, let alone a Scotsman, saying that!'

'How many men have said something similar to you, Margaret? You must have been loved by so many!' He looked angry, as though the very thought were too much to contemplate.

'Only one.' Margaret cast her eyes towards the leaf-strewn ground. 'I have only had one lover.'

'*Had*? It is past?'

'I think so.' She spoke slowly, reflectively, and he shivered and linked his arm through hers.

'Let us walk. It's cold.' He nestled up to her again. 'You know I have loved you since I first saw you, Margaret, that night in the Café Royal? I have been unable to get you out of my mind.'

'It seems incredible,' Margaret replied, 'but I think I do believe you. All this . . . seemed so planned. Was it planned?'

'In a way.' He walked with big strides so that she had to increase pace in order to keep up with him, tugged along by his arm through hers. 'I did not know how to see you again, what excuse I could make.'

'Did you bludgeon Peter Cartwright into wanting to leave Fumel?' There was a teasing note in her voice.

'Not at all! When he told me that he was bored it seemed the answer to my problem as well as yours. Yes, then I told my parents that I had found a woman who obsessed me, and of course they wanted to meet you. I think they hoped to encourage you . . .'

'I don't need encouragement,' Margaret said, looking at him gravely. 'I am in love with you too, Yves.'

'Ah, then it is true!' Yves stopped and turned towards her. 'My sister said she saw it in your eyes.'

'I think all the world saw it in my eyes. I felt it was written there like sign writing.'

'Oh Margaret, my darling!'

268

He enfolded her in his arms, pressing his cheek against hers. She turned her lips towards him, hungry for the feel of his mouth on hers, but he did not kiss her; he just continued to hug her as though he had something very precious in his arms. She touched his lips and flicked out her tongue and she felt him tremble, but when they did kiss it was rather chaste as though he was not practised in what to do. Their lips merely met and Margaret, thinking her own display of passion was somehow repulsive to him, drew away, feeling slightly abashed.

When eventually she looked into his eyes she saw to her surprise a kind of suffering, rather than the happiness she had anticipated, and she burst out:

'Yves, what is it?'

'What is what, my darling?'

'You look unhappy.'

'How can I be unhappy with you in my arms?'

Then she leaned her head against his breast and closed her eyes. Of course he was French, and very formal and aristocratic. Maybe aristocratic French ladies did not expect sexually exciting kisses at their first encounter. Maybe he thought she would be shocked if he went further. He was surely a man of such experience that he did not want to offend her susceptibilities.

'Tell me about the man you loved.'

'There's not much to tell. He is married, a Scotsman.'

'Oh. Good.'

'Good what?'

'Good that he is married; because he cannot marry you and I want to. Will you marry me, Margaret?'

She did not lift her head but lay against his breast, her eyes travelling along the ground, looking past the trunks of the bare trees in that beautiful ancient forest where French kings had hunted for centuries, maybe accompanied by the ancestors of the Lamottes, for there had been Lamottes in Amboise since the time of Henry II of France. The sun filtered through the ageless trees, a great

269

orange ball slowly sinking on the horizon in the thickly gathering mist.

'Do you not think we should get to know each other better?' Margaret looked at him anxiously, but his eyes were closed and his chin rested on his chest as though he were deep in thought. He shook his head.

'We know each other very well already. We can only get to know each other better, together.'

'Your sister said "We hope that Yves . . ." Did she mean that you would marry?'

'I suppose so. They have all wished it for a long time as I am the last Lamotte.'

Margaret started. She had not thought of children, but of course she would want Yves' children as, at times, she had wanted Hamish's. At times a woman, whatever she said or pretended to herself, wanted children by the man she loved. It seemed an inevitable part of love, cunningly ordained by capricious nature.

'Why did you never marry, Yves?'

He shrugged and his arms tightened around her. 'I never met anyone I wanted to marry. As I am nearly forty that seems extraordinary doesn't it? Yet it is true. Then I saw you and I knew: that is the woman for me. The most beautiful, ethereal creature I have ever seen. I idolize you, Margaret.'

He opened his eyes and bent his lips towards her and this time he kissed her fully, not passionately, not as Hamish had kissed her, but a prolonged, satisfying kiss that justified her longing.

'We should get back,' she said unsteadily, raising her head. 'It is getting dark.'

'Say you will marry me, otherwise I will keep you here all night.'

'But that's blackmail . . .' She began to laugh.

He shook her by the neck, his eyes hard, almost frightening. 'Say it!'

Margaret's teeth chattered, she did not know whether

through cold or fear, but still the overpowering sense of joy bubbled in her heart.

'I will marry you. But only because I want to get in from the cold.'

'Vixen,' he said and buried his face in her hair.

CHAPTER FIFTEEN

The wedding between Margaret Dunbar and Yves Lamotte was planned for June, in London, not Branswick or France. It was a kind of compromise because Yves and Margaret wanted a quiet wedding, his parents a large one, and Cullum and the Macallisters none at all.

Her family without exception had been shocked by Margaret's abrupt announcement that she was to marry a man thirteen years older than herself whom she had known only a few days. It seemed to them rather uncharacteristic, because though she was adventurous and ambitious, she was not impulsive. Margaret was undeterred, thinking that when they met Yves they would fall for him as she had. Besides, she was too in love to care; too happy at the thought of having a companion who shared her own interests by her side. Yves was artistic, cultured and urbane. He left the Ruthven Pendreighs and Hamish Ogilvys of her old world far behind. Hamish Ogilvy – was that fair? She realized she had scarcely thought about him since she'd met Yves for the second time. The hardest part was writing to him announcing her marriage:

Dearest Hamish,

You said it would happen and it has. I have met someone else and we are to be married quite soon. I hope this isn't too great a shock to you, my dear, because I feel you've had an inkling for some time that all was not as it should be between us. I met him briefly before Christmas in the company of Tristan Fleming, but it was not until February after you and I had that talk in the hotel in Edinburgh, that I realized how I felt about him.

From then on things moved very quickly, so I don't feel I was ever unfaithful to you. Dear Hamish, thank you for the good times we had together and forgive me for the bad bits. I don't think it could have gone on much longer, whatever happened. His name is Yves.'

She merely signed it 'Margaret'. It was difficult to know how to finish a letter that had seen so many drafts.

When Hamish's reply came it was very stilted and correct, as though he'd made a good many attempts too. He said he thought what was happening had been inevitable and wished her every happiness. He enclosed an antique gold brooch as a memento of their years together. She did not show it to Yves but put it in a drawer, still wrapped in the tissue paper in which it had arrived.

In April Fleur gave birth to a son who only lived a few hours and Margaret travelled alone to Branswick to see her. After a long and painful labour, Fleur was dispirited and depressed, unsupported by Cullum who took refuge in his usual method of assuaging grief: the bottle.

There was also a crisis in the business. The latest figures, even taking account of the money that had been spent on new building and machinery, were very discouraging. Dunbars were still not pulling their way and Cullum blamed Margaret and Bruno for spending so much time away from the mill. Margaret had said that what they were doing would ultimately be to the benefit of Dunbars: new designs and new orders both at home and from abroad for the planned new range of merchandise. They had stopped making silk stockings, which were now being replaced by rayon and artificial silk made much more economically in the Midlands, and they had begun to cut down on the manufacture of underwear. Cullum said it was all a big gamble, but his grumbles were ignored. Margaret had a very clear idea about the future for Dunbars as well as herself.

273

It was an unhappy visit for Margaret not only on account of Fleur, but also because of her family's opposition to her marriage and the state of the business. Branswick seemed no longer to possess the charm of her old, familiar home and she was anxious to be away. She avoided Cullum as much as she could, knowing that any words from her would only make him worse.

One day she arrived at the mill to receive a request to go straight to Bruno's office. To her surprise she found him smoking a large cigar and chatting to Ruthven Pendreigh. Both men rose to their feet as she came in and Ruthven warmly shook her hand.

'I hear I am to wish you much happiness, Margaret.'

'Thank you, Ruthven.'

'Sit down, Margaret.' Bruno pointed to a chair. 'Ruthven and I have been having talks and I think you should know their substance.'

'Oh? Is he still annoyed about Jimmy Macfarlane joining us?' Jimmy Macfarlane was the production manager who had been wooed from the Pendreigh mill. 'I'm afraid that's business, Ruthven.'

'I know it is, Margaret.' Ruthven did not smile. 'But I don't think he has improved your fortunes any more than he did ours. I hear your latest figures are very disappointing.'

'Strange you should know them, seeing that we do not publish them.'

She stared hard at Bruno who studied the blotter on his desk.

'The fact is, Margaret, that Ruthven and I have been having informal chats for some time – you know, in the club and various interests we have in common when we meet outside.'

They both liked salmon fishing in the Tweed, Margaret knew, and Cathy Pendreigh and Susan were very friendly.

'Business is bad for both of us, Margaret,' Ruthven

274

interrupted. 'Let's face it, the depression is hitting textiles as well as the ability of people to buy our goods.'

'Silk stockings – we have so much stock in the storeroom.' Bruno ruefully gazed out of the window as though he could see a trail of unbought silk stockings disappearing into the sky like the tail of a balloon.

Margaret carefully crossed one leg over the other and studied the large diamond on her left hand that Yves had given her to mark their engagement. 'What are you both getting at?'

'We thought of a merger,' Bruno said abruptly. 'A combination of Pendreighs and Dunbar. My father is all in favour of it.'

'And yours too doubtless.' Margaret gazed at Ruthven, suddenly seeing very clearly that day nearly ten years before when she had given Elliott Pendreigh a piece of her mind. She seemed to see, too, the slim dark eager girl she had been, freshly returned from Switzerland to conquer a new and exciting post-war world. Well, that had been a disappointment for everyone, not least herself; but now nine years later she found the world an even more exciting place offering just as many chances, both personally and for the business.

'Yes, Father approves,' Ruthven said nervously clearing his throat as though he, too, could recall the day of the Victory parade, 'although of course he has retired and I'm the one who makes all the decisions.'

Margaret got up and wandered slowly to the window, gazing at the broad Drume passing on its tireless way just beneath her. On the other side was the hill where they lived, its large houses, some pink-faced, some white, most made of grey stone, visible through the tiny spring leaves on the trees. Branswick was a cold place, she thought, remembering the château on the banks of the Loire, the huge apartment on the Avenue Foch, her own London house. Had she outgrown Branswick? Was it too small

275

and provincial for the sophisticated woman she had become?

'We've just invested nearly a million pounds in new machinery,' she said, 'the extension to the mill. We're starting a design department and I've engaged a very expensive and talented designer who has helped to put the French knitware house of Fumel very firmly on the post-war market.'

'Fumel was known before the war . . .'

'But not as much a household word, even in England, as now.' She turned and looked at Ruthven. '*Pendreighs* certainly have much to gain from a merger with us. I daresay their business is undercapitalized and their machinery old-fashioned.'

'But Pendreighs' name is much better known than yours,' Ruthven expostulated. 'We got going on outer wear as soon as the war was over, long before you did. We're top suppliers to all the main London stores. We've employed a designer for years.'

'I know that, but only one. I am going to have a team, working here in Branswick and in London. We shall soon catch up, don't worry.'

'But I would have thought with our name and outlets and your – admittedly very useful – advanced modern machinery, we could be an irresistible combination.'

'Our name is just as good as yours,' Margaret said firmly. 'It's not quite as well known but it will be. We're well known for quality. We shall soon be even better known. I see no reason at all for us to take you along in our wake.'

'I like that!' Ruthven reddened with anger and looked at his fishing companion for support.

'I'm sorry but it's true, Ruthven,' Margaret continued. 'And I will fight you every inch to get my own way.'

'You'll have a battle,' Bruno said quietly. 'Susan agrees with me and so does Cullum. Juliet . . .'

'When they have heard my side of it none of them will

276

agree with you!' Margaret snapped. 'If they have any sense. I'm surprised at you, Bruno, throwing all this away.' She threw up her arms in a gesture that embraced all their plans, all the new development, the whole future of Dunbars. 'Have you no guts? You've invested a lot of time and money in this business, your family's money, your time, and now you want to go over to the other side just when we're beginning to make a turn along the right road.'

'I see no evidence that it *is* the right road.' Bruno picked up a balance sheet whose contents Margaret knew only too well. 'Even allowing for recapitalization our figures are well down on last year, and that was quite a good year compared to the one before.'

'Why don't you just settle down with your future husband, Margaret?' Ruthven lowered his voice; smiling at her in an avuncular manner. 'I hear he's a French count with vast estates on the Loire.'

'*An* estate on the Loire, not too large and not too small, and don't be patronizing, Ruthven. You know I was never suited just for domesticity. If I stayed at home to look after my father it was because I had no choice.'

'But surely the count will want an heir?'

Ruthven looked at her suggestively, and Margaret felt she would rather like to hit him. Even now, over the years she recalled their former intimacy, their first and last, embrace.

'My future husband is *not* a count. His father is a count and he is entitled to call himself a viscount; but he does not. He's a working man, a clever designer, and we have agreed that our marriage will be a partnership and that I will continue to work even in the event that I do have a child, which we both hope for, certainly.'

'You're a very modern woman, aren't you Margaret?'

'Wasn't I always?' Margaret returned his gaze and was gratified to see that he averted his eyes first. 'Did you imagine I only began to work because I thought I was on

277

the shelf, Ruthven Pendreigh? That I turned to it as an alternative to marriage? Did you think that now I have "captured" a husband I will down everything I've worked for these past three years and be content to breed, yearly perhaps, in my husband's home on the banks of the Loire? You should know me better.'

'*I* know you better.' Bruno got slowly to his feet and faced her. 'I didn't think that for a minute; but I thought you might let something go. You will have to, Margaret. You can't have a family and be a full-time business woman.'

'Oh yes I can. I believe having a child does not take more than twenty-four hours or so, hopefully much less, and during that time it is true I shall not be able to come into the office. But before and after . . .' She smiled. 'Have you gentlemen not heard of modern maternity care? Or nursemaids? I assure you I shall have the best doctors and the best help I can find. Anyway, we are anticipating. I'm not even married yet.'

'But it *is* a thought, Margaret,' Bruno insisted, leaning beside her on the windowsill. 'This time next year you might be a mother. The actual bearing of a child is one thing, but a woman is not always well when she is pregnant. Have you considered that? If you were not to be married I don't think I would have entertained Ruthven's suggestion so strongly. You have been a tower of strength; but with a husband, children, a new home in Paris . . .'

'Oh no, I will not let go, I assure you Bruno.' Margaret's smile was icy. 'I do not intend to be a housewife – and Yves knows this – nor a full-time mother. The flat in Paris will run as it does now without me doing the daily accounts and my London house already has a house-keeper, two maids and a gardener. Apart from being married I will not be any different. I assure you that, with my good health, I do not anticipate a difficult time during pregnancy. I will not give a minute less to the business than I do now. Also we will have Yves. I want to propose that he joins the board, eventually . . .'

This bombshell she had wished to reserve until after the wedding; but as things were now she felt they might as well know it. Not only was she determined to stay, but to expand their activities and include her husband too.

'Oh I don't mean as an ornament, but as a working director. I think Yves has great skills as a businessman. He's very artistic, a designer himself. It's true that Peter Cartwright will be in overall charge of design, but at board level . . . So you see, Bruno, I have great plans. They do not include merging with the House of Pendreigh. If you want a fight, it's up to you; but I assure you I shall win. Juliet and Mary will never disagree with me and I shall win over Cullum too, as I always do. You will simply be outvoted and made to look silly. We Dunbars have always been very stubborn. You may control forty percent of the business but we have sixty percent and that's precisely why I insisted on it, having this sort of contingency in mind. I doubt if your wife would even side with you to take control of the business out of the hands of her family. If she did I don't think I would ever speak to her again. Now, excuse me.' Margaret looked at her watch. 'I have an appointment with a young artist who would like to join our design department. Good-day, Ruthven,' she smiled. 'Do give my kindest regards to your wife, and your father . . .'

She left the room without glancing over her shoulder.

When he had heard the story some time later, Tristan Fleming laughed.

'And of course you won.'

'Of course I won! We had a full-scale family row, but I won. Bruno and Susan didn't speak to each other for a week, but then we heard that Pendreighs were really doing very badly indeed, worse than us, and that clinched

279

my argument. After that they all congratulated me, and said what a wizard I was.' Margaret slipped on a new cardigan and walked in it to the end of the room, turning as she had in her modelling days so that the customer could see it both back and front, and then walking slowly back to him. 'It's lovely isn't it?'

'Lovely.' Tristan fingered the fine cashmere. 'It is separated here?'

'In the Macallister mill. They have new, very secret plant that separates the thick black hairs from the soft hair of the goat's underbelly. I tell you, we shall be able to produce in time as many garments made of this cashmere as you want. I will give you an exclusive contract and design specially for you. "A Cartwright Design produced exclusively for Flemings". How about that?'

'Nice,' Tristan nodded. 'And Cartwright will design in cashmere?'

'And other yarns too, of course. But I want to make cashmere the basis of our trade.'

'But isn't it *terribly* expensive, darling?' Tristan winced and sat down.

'That's just why I do want to concentrate on cashmere, because it *is* so expensive. I want to appeal to the very top end of the market. To become snobbish. Tristan, there are always people who will pay for something good, whatever the economic climate. Don't you think?'

'Oh I agree.' Tristan carefully put a fresh cigarette in his amber holder. 'But is this the time to do it?'

'It's *just* the time. We are approaching the thirties. A new era is opening up; the war is behind us and the economy will soon pick up. Everyone says so. I am appealing to top market clients who can pay. Our exports will go mainly to wealthy Americans. I am relying on it. Yves and I talked well into the early hours of this morning planning it all. How do you like: "DUNBAR DESIGN: A NEW FASHION FOR A NEW ERA"?' Margaret sat down beside him, folding her hands over her crossed legs and leaning forward, exuding enthusiasm and excitement.

By 1928 fashions had, as one fashion writer put it, 'taken another step in the same direction'. The hemline was just below the knee – it had gone up and down by varying amounts since the war – and hair was short, but not bobbed or shingled. Only subtle changes in women's clothing were thus noted, but also the fact that 'a woman who is subtle was a most attractive creature, a bit dangerous perhaps, but well worth knowing.'

Margaret Dunbar might well have been the model for the writer. She was the very personification of the young, emancipated women of the late nineteen-twenties. In March the vote was finally given to all women over the age of twenty-one, so the long campaign for women's suffrage was over. But it made as little real difference to Margaret as it did to most women. True they had a right which they should have had years before, but in themselves they felt free. They had their own money and spent it as they liked, saw who they liked and wore what they liked. That is, if they were unmarried. For the married woman things were slightly different because, although legislation was moving ponderously forward to give married women the same rights as their husbands, especially in the matter of divorce, it still had a long way to go.

The film stars of the twenties influenced many of the fashions of the bright young things, in particular the way they made up. Lopsided clothes were worn with a nonchalant slouch, a careless air, especially when it came to evening dresses where bits of material, loose scarves and accessories seemed so essential an adjunct to that popular dance that had arrived with a bang in 1925, the Charleston.

Yes, looking at Margaret, Tristan could see Dunbar Design becoming the rage, because it sprang from her. It was her: chic, elegant, rather casual, independent – above all, good style. Margaret's sense of style was equal to her beauty. She was never over-dressed, never vulgar or mannered. She was stylish, and would impart her style to Dunbar Design whether Peter Cartwright were there or not. It would be right for the age because she had been born with the century and, as the century moved, so did she. She and the spirit of the age were one.

'Dunbar Design? It's a sort of slogan?'

'Yes, for our new range. "Dunbar Design exclusively for women of quality", that sort of thing.'

'You think it will work?' Tristan smoked in silence for a while, almost afraid to look at those blazing confident eyes. 'I don't know. Frankly I don't know. It means standing on your head. Gone are all the knitted vests and woolly pants . . .'

'Gone, gone!' Margaret cried. 'And in their place will come beautifully made, *expensive* knitted jumpers, matching coats and skirts with clever patterns intricately woven on our hand-knitting machines. Lovely twin-sets in angora, mohair or cashmere in subtle colours produced by Macallisters. Dresses, coats, all made of wool knitted on our new large Cotton frames. Eventually I'd like to do the same for men – transform our image there too; but first I want to concentrate on the ladies. I'm going to approach duchesses, titled women, people of quality to model for us.'

Tristan stretched out his legs, threw back his arms and laughed. 'Oh now, that is ridiculous!'

'It is not ridiculous! Lady Louis Mountbatten, Lady Diana Cooper, the Duchess of Storrick – people like that. They will all appear in the pages of *Vogue, Harpers* or the *Ladies Journal*, photographed in their country homes in our superbly made, beautifully designed cashmere.'

'But they won't do it for money. They don't need money.'

'All women need money, though I agree the first is very

282

wealthy in her own right. I don't know about Lady Diana and the Duchess. It will just be the thing to do; titled ladies will be queueing up, you'll see. "The Countess of So-and-So pictured at Cedarwood, her country home in the Cotswolds, in a jumper and skirt designed by Peter Cartwright for Dunbar".' Margaret waved her hand in front of her, as though completing an imaginary piece of writing. 'I have it all planned. And this is where Yves will be so useful. He *knows* people like this, intimately. We can use French women too, the Duchesse de this or the Comtesse de that . . .'

Margaret's eyes shone and she got up and started pacing about, looking at the floor, her hands on her hips as though she could see the whole plan written there, and all that had to happen was to realize it.

'Is this the main reason you're marrying Yves?'

Margaret suddenly stopped her pacing, closing her eyes as though she had had a shock. Then she opened them and, raising her head slowly, stared at Tristan.

'I beg your pardon?'

'I'm sorry, darling. It must sound frightfully brutal.' Tristan dusted a fictitious speck of dust from the smooth barathea surface of his coat.

'It sounds frightfully *rude*,' Margaret said. She picked up her handbag from the table and riffled through it, producing the silver cigarette case, and the enamelled lighter Tristan had given her. He could see how red her cheeks had gone as she abruptly flicked open the lighter and applied the flame to her cigarette.

'I can't understand why you're marrying Yves. I thought just, maybe, in the light of what you've said, this might be the reason. It can't be for his money.'

'Did you ever think of love?' Margaret's expression, as she confronted him, was far from lovelorn.

'Oh you're *in love* with him! Genuinely?'

'I find this very insulting, Tristan; quite untypical if I

283

may say so. It makes me wonder if you're ill. Do you have a chill? Does your head ache? Of *course* I love Yves. I'm besotted.'

'Oh I see.' Completely unabashed, Tristan repeated the word to himself as if he didn't believe it. 'Besotted. Well.' He shrugged.

'What makes you think I should not love Yves?'

'I can see why you should love him, or think you do, but not marry him. For one thing you hardly know him. You're always in London or Branswick and he's always in Paris or Milan or Vienna. How can you marry a man you don't see?'

'Have you ever heard of love at first sight?'

'*Heard* of it darling, but never *met* it. Isn't it the sort of thing you only meet in novels? Certainly I never expected to hear it from that sensible, rational, *clever* lady, Margaret Dunbar, who is going to set all London alight with her new bold fashions in cashmere.'

'Where the heart is concerned, Tristan,' some of the anger had left Margaret's voice, 'business plans or acumen hardly come into it. I know that now. Yves said he fell in love with me that night we met in the Café Royal. I knew I loved him when I sat opposite him in the Pullman as it was pulling out of Victoria on its way to Paris.'

'Too, too romantic.'

'Please let me speak Tristan.' Margaret, looking strained, held out her hand appealingly to him. 'I've known you too long and liked you too much for me to let this affect our friendship; but you do appear to be labouring under a misapprehension. I have fallen in love, and so has he. I'm nearly twenty-seven and he's nearly forty. Yet we are both blind to any faults in the other. It's the most glorious feeling I have ever had. Even the sound of his footsteps thrills me, and if he were to come in through that door . . .' She looked towards it as though expecting it to happen.

'You would faint?'

'No I would not faint!' Margaret banged her heel angrily on the Wilton carpet. 'Now you're being facetious and I don't know why. Are you jealous?'

'Oh not at all *jealous*, darling.' Tristan tipped his cigarette from its holder into an ashtray. 'You know that sort of thing has no interest for me. I'm just worried, frankly. Love is all very well; blind passion, yes, has its place they say. But you're going to take on for life a man you know nothing about. I agree he's *divine*, with a face like a god; he has all the polish and charm you could ever want; but . . . what do you actually *know*?'

'I know he's from a good family. I've met his parents, his sister, all delightful people. His brother-in-law is a baron. I've seen both his homes and met many of his friends. He's hidden absolutely nothing from me. He's gone out of his way to introduce his family, and yet he hasn't met mine. So he's hardly hiding anything, is he? I know he loves painting, is a connoisseur of food and wine, adores the theatre . . .'

'But what does he do for a *living*? I must say I have never been able to find that out. Have you?'

'Well, I suppose he . . . You said yourself he was a designer.'

'Yes, but I also said I thought he didn't do very well. I don't know how he gets his money or where it comes from.'

'But his family . . .'

'Are not wealthy. That I do know.'

'But their homes . . . they have furniture and *objets d'art* worth a fortune.'

'But they're *assets*, darling, not *cash*. Anyway, they want to hang onto those, not sell them; besides, the market is very depressed, as you know because of all the bargains you have snapped up.'

'He just bought a Hispano-Suiza, a *very* expensive car.'

'Are you sure it was his?'

'But why should it not be his? Oh really Tristan, now

you're being not only rude but absurd! Should I have asked to see the deeds of ownership? What exactly is this leading up to?' She put her hands on her hips again, staring down at him. He waited a moment before replying.

'I can, if you like, admit that I see what *you* see in him; he is very handsome and can charm birds off trees. He must make any previous men you knew seem like clodhoppers. I know you are not all that impressed by his title, because you're a sensible Scots lass from the banks of the Drume, but maybe it titillates you a little.' Tristan flickered his fingers in front of her face. 'You know, it helps. Maybe it gave you this idea for designing only for the rich which, I must say, may work, because even the not-so-rich will want to own what the very rich can afford. It's quite a good idea, but I want to think some more about it.'

'The difference between Selfridges and Flemings, that's what it is.'

'Yes I know, and that worked, although we offered a very extensive range of merchandise. And, of course, we cashed in on the post-war feeling when people yearned for luxury after years of austerity. I'm not sure that is so applicable now. But to get back to Lamotte. Why does he want to marry you? You're beautiful and I do not know why in God's name you haven't been snapped up before. You cannot have lacked admirers. You have poise, elegance . . . also, perhaps, money?'

'*I* have money? You think Yves is marrying *me* for money?' Margaret's beautiful eyes grew as wide as saucers. 'That's even more insulting than what you said before. I have no money, no fortune.'

'You have a good business, a lovely London house, but above all you have *prospects*. Yves believes in Dunbars and you, particularly you, and I must say I agree with him. I suppose you plan to take him on the board . . .' He looked at her, askance.

'Eventually, but . . .'

'There you are then. He will have a job, with prospects, a perfectly lovely, charming wife and a beautiful home designed and furnished by me in a very good part of London.'

'I think you're despicable,' Margaret said, grabbing her coat from the chair and shrugging herself into it. 'And I'm not going to invite you to the wedding. Furthermore, I don't care if you buy our new merchandise or not. I will have an exclusive contract with Harrods or Debenhams or someone else.'

'Oh don't let it interfere with business, darling, *please*,' Tristan wailed as she made for the door. 'Never, never let your private life interfere with business.'

'I thought this would be our room, darling.' Margaret opened the door of the room that Cullum usually had when he stayed at the house. 'It's bigger than mine, and the view's nicer.' It faced the back garden and from the double window could be seen the pavilion of Lord's Cricket Ground.

Yves strolled into the room, looking around, his fingers in the pockets of his grey alpaca suit. Margaret walked to the door in the middle of the left hand wall and opened it.

'And we could make this into a dressing room for you.'

Yves raised his eyebrows as he walked through the door into the next room. 'Why, it's enormous, darling! Do I need such a big dressing room?'

'Well, you do need a dressing room, Yves, don't you? I mean, I've never been married before, but I thought all men of substance required a dressing room.'

Her expression gave no indication as to whether she was serious or not. Yves studied her smiling face for a moment, then shrugged and walked back into the first bedroom, sitting on the single bed which was rather dwarfed by the large room.

'Does Cullum never come with Fleur?'

287

'Yes, why?'

'This is a single bed.'

'They have separate rooms. You don't need me to tell you why. Now, darling, how about green silk on the walls, and I thought the carpet . . .' Excitedly Margaret gestured into the air as though she could already visualize the bridal suite.

Yves leaned back watching her for a moment. Then he extracted his cigarette case from his breast pocket and carefully, fastidiously, fitted a cigarette into his silver and ebony holder, without lighting it.

'I think separate rooms is an awfully good idea, my darling. Don't you?' He interrupted her.

Margaret looked at him, startled, as though he'd broken a dream. 'You mean for *us*?'

'Why not? There's plenty of room. It's a huge house. It's only this modern trend towards small houses that insists on thrusting spouses together. It was never so in olden times. My parents always had separate rooms.'

'But Yves . . .' Margaret sat on the bed beside him, clasping her right knee between her hands. She didn't look at him but ahead at the wall, as though still covering it in her imagination with apple green silk.

Yves slipped an arm around her shoulder and drew her close to him, kissing her on the cheek. 'I've upset you darling haven't I? I didn't mean . . .'

'Yves.' Margaret turned to him and her arm tightly encircled his waist. 'Let's go to bed – here, now. Please, I want to.' Yves' eyes widened and he carefully put the unlit cigarette in its holder on the bedside table. 'I'm shocking you Yves; do you think I'm disgusting?' She looked earnestly into his eyes because she wanted to know. She felt there was so much about this man she was completely in ignorance of, and they were to be married in less than six weeks' time.

What worried her more than anything was his apparent

lack of passion. He was so beautiful, he had such masculine elegance and charm that she was still half in awe of him; regarding him, subconsciously perhaps, as a precious, much-coveted object rather than the man of flesh and blood who would father her children. Of course they had had very little time actually together. She had rushed home to Scotland to break the news to her family and he had stayed in France. They had met together in Paris at Easter, but his parents had been there too with his sister and brother-in-law for a great family celebration.

They seemed to be surrounded by people all the time and even when they were alone they were perpetually on the go; reorganizing the house which Yves would share with Margaret, planning to expand the firm, deciding where and how to honeymoon. She was so in love with Yves, so mesmerized by him, so proud of being seen with him, that she had scarcely had time to realize, until Tristan spoke to her, how little she actually knew him as a person.

But the sexual side worried her a lot because she was a very physical person. Her passion, her sexual need for Hamish had kept their affair going for five years; there had been very little else. Yet Hamish wasn't earthy; in many ways he was a cold, aloof man, but the proximity of Margaret never failed to arouse him whatever the circumstances. Yves seldom kissed Margaret full on the lips; he had never once lost control of himself and he had never suggested bed. Yet they had discussed once, laughingly, how many children they might have and what they should be called. It had all seemed slightly unreal.

Looking at him now, in this room where she hoped to share a bed with him permanently, she felt a need to know; to have the answer to so many unspoken questions. Tristan had annoyed her so much, she realized in retrospect, because there was a suspicion of truth in what he said. It was as though he had forced open some chasm in the dark recesses of her mind that she would have preferred to keep tightly shut. Once open, it never completely closed again. Was she afraid of letting in too much light?

She didn't know Yves, or much about him. But she knew enough about him to want to marry him and the rest would surely follow. But did Tristan know something about Yves that she should know: something disreputable, something to his disadvantage? And if she knew it, would it affect the way she felt about him?

No, nothing could affect the way she felt about him. She had never lost her head like this before. Besides, Yves wasn't bad; Tristan was jealous of a marriage between two of his friends. Sometimes people were; they liked to compartmentalize their friends so that they never met, keeping them selfishly to themselves. She had met his family; she knew where he lived. It was true that she had only ever been introduced to family friends, people mostly the age of his parents. She had met no contemporaries, male or female. They never discussed money or sex, as though they were both delicate, grey areas best avoided. Although this might be like Yves, it was not at all like Margaret. She was forthright, she was definite. Was she turning into some timid, diffident person because of him?

Maybe her thoughts showed on her face because he leaned forward as though to reassure her, his eyes warm and loving, and he brought her hand to his lips, stroking her face and brushing the hair off her forehead with a tender, intimate gesture.

'Margaret, my darling, have you any *idea* how beautiful you are? How could you possibly disgust me? Do you know that I love you very, very much?'

His hands moved to untie the bow of her grey shantung blouse and then, still looking into her eyes, he very carefully undid the small pearl buttons until she sat in her slip. He eased the straps off her shoulders and sat back, looking at her exposed breasts as though surveying some wonderful, precious work of art. She wanted him to touch her, to feel the contact of his flesh against hers and she took one of his hands and brought it to her breast.

'Feel me,' she said urgently, 'love me.'

Almost hesitantly he traced the outline of her breast with one finger, then tenderly, deftly, he circled it round and round the aureola of her nipple, before finally leaning forward to kiss it with his lips.

'Exquisite,' he murmured and he seized her in his arms, half closing his eyes in rapture as he buried his face in her neck. 'Oh my darling, can it be possible that you want me as much as I want you?'

In answer Margaret lay back on the bed, pulling him down with her until she cradled his head in the crook of her arm. Then she slipped off her skirt and wriggled free of the rest of her underthings until she lay completely naked beside him, her legs slightly bent. Yves sat up, his face suffused with colour and again, as though she were too fragile to touch, he gazed for a long time at her body, running his hands along it with the same timidity, the same air of wonder as when he had first drawn her slip off her shoulders.

Margaret wanted him so badly that she moved towards him, insinuating a hand inside his silk shirt. 'Please, darling,' she said. 'Please.'

Yves momentarily looked uncertain as to what to do next; then he got up and swiftly removed his clothes, putting them neatly on the chair in front of the dressing table. As he came over to her she raised her knees, her legs slightly parted, and reached up with both arms to draw him down beside her.

It was a full, complete experience but not an entirely satisfactory one. His lovemaking was perfunctory and, she felt, lacking in ardour. Yet the pleasure he gave her was out of all proportion to his expertise. She felt she had nailed the suspicion and doubt that had hovered in her mind; here was truly a man who was capable of satisfying her, of giving her children, and she was sure that, in time, their mutual technique would improve. After all, when she had first gone to bed with Hamish that hadn't been very satisfactory either, and she had put that down to her inexperience and his shyness. Most people developed technique by being together and making love often.

'No single beds for us,' Margaret murmured in his ear.

'Sorry, darling, was I a bit clumsy? It is a bit cramped.'

He still lay on top of her, the fast beating of his heart like a tattoo against her naked breast. She felt they adhered together, united as man and wife at last by the mystical process of sex: the Biblical term 'knowing' that only came from a carnal relationship. She realized at this moment that she had not even thought of her Dutch cap, but she didn't care. They were to be married anyway, and certainly taking precautions hadn't occurred to him. Her legs were entwined over his and her hands linked together behind his back, trapping him. She felt he was hers in the same way as she had become his, and she pressed him tightly to her and kissed him.

'I love you,' she said.

He sank his head into the pillow beside her and closed his eyes.

When they were dressing it was nearly twilight and he said that he thought green silk on the wall would do very well, and the bed should be a large one. He was in a jolly mood.

'Tristan will do it all for us,' she said without thinking, straightening her skirt as she looked critically at herself in the mirror. 'Oh. No he won't.'

'Why should Tristan do it anyway?' Yves stood behind her knotting his tie in the same mirror.

'He did the rest of the place. He likes that kind of thing and is marvellous at it.'

'Then why shouldn't he do this room?' Yves shrugged

on his jacket, then went back and took the unlit cigarette from the bedside table and lit it.

'We had a row.'

'A row with Tristan? Impossible!' Yves took a comb from his pocket and started to comb his hair, sitting back on the unmade bed, his long elegant legs crossed in front of him.

'No, it is possible. He felt I shouldn't marry you.'

Yves put his comb back in his breast pocket and took up his cigarette which lay smoking in the ash tray. His eyes half closed as he inhaled. 'Did he say why?'

'He said I didn't know anything about you.'

'That's not true.'

'That's what I said.' Margaret came and sat beside him, feeling very different from an hour before. The tangled bedclothes seemed to seal their intimacy and she felt proud of him, sensuous and possessive.

'Is that why you wanted to go to bed with me?' He slid his eyes around without turning his head, as though he wanted to observe her reaction surreptitiously. 'To make sure?'

'Make sure of what?' Margaret, blushing, was glad of the twilight. They had not put on the lights while they dressed.

'Well, Tristan . . . I suppose you must have wondered about him.'

'But I wouldn't wonder about *you*. You're not a bit like Tristan.'

'I was clumsy, though. Inexpert. I haven't slept with a woman for a long time. I'm sorry, darling, if I hurt you.'

Margaret seized his hand in both of hers and brought it to her chest. 'You didn't hurt me at all. I was inexpert too. After all, we didn't know each other in that way; but we do now and it will get better and better.'

'I can see you've had a lot of experience, Margaret.' Yves spoke quietly, almost shyly.

'Only with Hamish. You're only the second man I've ever been to bed with.'

'And what about the man with the funny name?'

She looked surprised. 'Ruthven? What's funny about it?'

'It looks like one thing and yet is pronounced another.'

'It's spelt R-u-t-h-v-e-n and pronounced R-i-v-i-n. We're very used to it in Scotland. No, I never went to bed with Ruthven. Only Hamish.'

'But he was a good lover?'

'Well, I didn't know any different. I don't really know now whether he was good or bad.' Margaret paused and kissed the back of the hand she still clasped between hers. 'You never talk of any of your affairs, Yves.'

'Darling, what *is* the point?' Yves gently withdrew his hand and got to his feet, straightening his jacket, his air immediately bored, as though he wanted to change the subject. 'I'm much older than you. I've had many affairs. I have not had any for some time. Maybe I'm undersexed, I don't know. But if this is some sort of test . . .'

His face darkened and she suddenly felt frightened. She stood up and flung her arms around him. 'Oh darling, it is no such thing! How can you say that?'

'You brought up Tristan, I didn't. Maybe we should postpone our wedding so that you can be quite, quite sure.' His tone quivered with sarcasm. He gently disengaged himself again and, leaning down, angrily stubbed out his cigarette in the onyx ashtray by the bed.

Margaret felt panic rising in her breast and bitterly regretted what she had said. In an effort to regain her composure, she walked slowly over to the window and stood looking at the silhouette of the old man with the scythe on the tower at Lord's. Then she turned towards him.

'Yves, please forgive me. I love you and I know you love me. I was worried, I'll admit it, that you didn't appear to want to go to bed with me, but I never for a *moment* suspected you were anything but a completely normal man.'

Yves looked at her in that detached, sophisticated way he had that seemed to age him and make her feel like a juvenile. It was an expression compounded of mirth and disdain, as though the matter hardly merited discussion. He leaned against the wall by the side of the bed, his legs crossed, his fingers playing with his empty cigarette holder.

'Margaret, my dear, it's not at all the done thing, in most circles I know anyway. Most women I know who get married are still virgins, strange as it might seem to you. I knew you weren't a virgin because you told me about Hamish. I'm sure my mother and father, and yours too probably, would never have considered a conversation like this before marriage or, indeed, after it. I would never have discussed sex with you had you not brought it up. In the circles where I moved in France it is simply not done, my dear, and on the whole I approve of that. Men and women should retain some mystery for each other. I know things have changed since the war, but I am pre-war vintage. I was nearly thirty when the war ended and I was born in the old century when men and women respected the conventions. I'm sorry, Margaret, if I've disappointed you; not done as you expected. Unless a man pushes you into bed as soon as he sets eyes on you, I suppose you think he must have unnatural inclinations . . .'

Margaret covered her face with her hands. 'Not at all. I . . .' She turned her back on him.

'It's very alarming if that is the case. Clearly I sensed your unease because it is quite obvious you are a woman of strong passions – in everything. Yet I could not contravene my own natural instincts, which were to behave as a fiancé and not a seducer. You might have misunderstood my motives had I been too pressing about getting you into bed. After all Hamish did not actually behave very honourably, did he?'

Yves raised his eyes and without looking, keeping his eyes on her, put a fresh cigarette in his holder, lit it and exhaled the smoke. It seemed a rather indolent, contemptuous gesture. 'I am a man of honour and I thought I was behaving like one, and that my wedding night was the proper time for seduction, not before. Yet you challenged me today to prove myself and I had to accept. All I can say now is that, if you think we are incompatible . . . ' He looked at the ash on his cigarette and neatly tipped it into the tray by the bed.

Now Margaret felt engulfed by the fear that, by her bold, crass behaviour, she would lose what she most wanted in the world. How dignified he'd been, how proper. He was a Continental aristocrat and she was a raw filly from the Borders, a primitive if ever there was one. How must she look in his eyes? Could he still possibly love her? She started to tremble. The sky above Lord's was blood-red as the sun sank behind the pavilion. She turned and held out her hands to him, the tears coursing down her face.

'Please, Yves . . .'

He strode quickly across to her and enfolded her in his arms, kissing the tears from her face, smoothing her brow with his long artistic hands.

'My silly little girl. My silly, silly little girl,' he murmured. 'Whatever shall I do with you?'

CHAPTER SIXTEEN

The house, though small, was double-fronted, two floors high and with a blue door in the middle which opened onto a tiny hallway. To the left of the hall was the sitting room and to the right a large kitchen, with a black range in which a fire always glowed, winter and summer, particularly this summer of 1931 which had seen very little sun. There was a plentiful supply of logs stacked in the grate to one side of the range; there was never a shortage now of logs or coal. A flight of stairs ran up from the hall to the first floor where there were two bedrooms. A bathroom had recently been installed in what used to be a third tiny bedroom facing onto the back garden, at the end of which a stream flowed under the stone wall into the valley. This stretched as far as the eye could see, with no houses intervening, before it sloped into the foothills of the mountains, now, in high summer, clad with bracken and purple heather, and usually a perpetual mist because of the weather.

But today was an exception. It had dawned warm and sunny, growing increasingly hot as the day advanced. Now, in mid afternoon, as the sun began its descent, the air was very still, the only sound being birdsong and the persistent hum of bees as they dipped from one pollen-filled blossom to the next.

Cullum felt very peaceful. He stretched in his deckchair which Nan had placed under a sycamore tree and put his hands behind his head, leaning back and closing his eyes. He was in his shirtsleeves and a fleck of sun, glancing through the leaves, picked up the colour of his sandy hair, grizzled a little at the sides now and lacking the burnished lustre of his son William's hair.

Nan quietly laid the tea tray on a white table beside him on which he had put his pipe and the morning edition of *The Scotsman*. He opened his eyes and encircled her waist with his arm.

'Is there any news?' she said, glancing at the paper.

'The King is returning from Balmoral. There's no doubt something is afoot. Some people say there will be a change of government. For my part I wish Lloyd George would return and save the country, as he saved us during the war.'

'But there is no chance of that?' Nan poured the tea into heavy porcelain cups and looked at him anxiously.

'No, Lloyd George is in the wilderness. The next Prime Minister will be Baldwin, again, you mark my words.'

As she reached down to hand him his tea Cullum tried to kiss her and she nearly dropped the cup.

'Oh Cullum! Let me put my cup down first.'

'Put it down, then.'

She emptied the spilt tea from the saucer onto the grass and refilled the cup, this time successfully placing it by his side. Then she fell into his lap and put her arms round his neck.

'Happy?' she asked.

'Ecstatic.'

'I wish it could be like this forever.'

'So do I. One day maybe.'

She looked at him, noting the creases round his eyes, the furrows on his forehead, how much older he had grown in recent years so that he looked more like a man in his middle forties than one who had just had his thirty-second birthday.

Cullum had spent most of the previous year in a nursing home to cure him of the alcoholism that had seemingly taken a firm grip on him after the death of his infant son. While Dunbars struggled to remain afloat and the country to keep its head in increasing economic depression following the collapse of the American stock market in 1929,

Cullum had spent most of his time in a pleasant room in a large house in spacious grounds outside Edinburgh. Twice he had come home and twice he had gone back again. But by the previous autumn he had not had a drink for six months and he and his doctors had felt that he had recovered sufficiently to go home for good.

The first thing Cullum did was to rent for Nan the house he had promised her, and now he contrived to spend as much time there as he could while William was at school in Edinburgh.

Nothing worried Cullum very much now, neither the business nor the fortunes or misfortunes of the country. Having reached the depths of mania induced by alcohol, he felt that he had climbed to the other side; the serenity that had come with it could not be disturbed by anything, only enhanced by the presence of Nan.

'I'm going to tell Fleur about us,' he went on staring into the valley. 'I have made up my mind.'

'Oh Cullum, please don't! Wait until you are quite better.'

'I am better. I can face up to it now. You know I don't go in much for this psychiatry, but the fellow I had at the hospital helped me a lot. He says all this drinking and mental collapse was because I was trying to live up to what was expected of me rather than what I wanted to do. I never wanted to go into the business and I never really wanted to marry Fleur.'

'But you drank before that.'

Nan's direct gaze momentarily disconcerted him but he hugged her and smiled. He thought how difficult it was to deceive her and this honesty of hers also seemed a proof of her love.

'Even that I have an answer for, my dear. That was because of the competition to keep up with Malcolm. I was nineteen when Malcolm was killed and I knew how badly the family wished it had been me not him. Then I started drinking. You see,' he hugged her closer, 'I'm very

299

weak, Nan. I was born weak, like my father. The Dunbars have either been weak or strong, no in-betweens, and I am one of the weak ones. I had a weak father but a strong mother and brother, and three strong sisters. I had no chance at all. Without you, my darling, I think I would still be in the bin.'

Every week Nan had visited him, having had the connivance of the hospital authorities in ensuring that her visits did not clash with Fleur's.

'I think if you tell your wife, Cullum,' she said cautiously, 'the family feeling will be such that you will soon be back in hospital again. What will your sister Margaret say, for instance?'

'Oh, the countess! Who cares what she says? She has enough on her plate with seeing that Dunbars survives.'

'And will it survive?'

Cullum screwed up his eyes as Nan clambered off his lap and sat on the grass at his feet, drinking her tea.

'Yes it will. Peter Cartwright is undoubtedly a genius and the decision to go into cashmere in a big way was the right one. It was a terrific gamble, but it came off. We spent a fortune on advertising, building a new image. "The Duchess of Storrick pictured at her country home near Branswick in a cashmere twin-set by Dunbar Design". It was terrific. All due to Margaret, and that husband of hers.' Cullum lowered his voice derisively.

'Why do you not like him, Cullum?'

'Well, for one thing, he doesn't like me! He's only been here once since their marriage and he told Margaret that he thought we were all very provincial.'

'And she told *you* that?'

'We had a row the last time she was at home, and out it all came. "You are all so provincial, just as Yves says," she blurted out before she knew what she was saying. We of course were against building up this new idea that Dunbar just designs for the aristocracy; but Margaret was adamant and, as usual, Margaret was right.'

'I must say, she is a verra clever woman,' Nan murmured. 'And very kind tae William and me, even though she dinna approve of my relationship with you. She sends money tae him and presents and always visits when she comes up. He likes her verra much.'

'She thought I behaved badly. I did. I want to make up for it, Nan.'

He bent forwards and she raised her lips. Nan closed her eyes, feeling so happy that she wished, just then, she could die and never know pain or remorse again or the long lonely days when she did not see Cullum. She did not read and she did not listen to the wireless, but she spent her time in making the little house even prettier and more cosy for when he would come again. She was good with her fingers and had made all the covers for the beds, the chairs and the cushions, as well as the curtains and some small rugs that lay on the floor of the kitchen and the living room.

The house in the valley was such a contrast to the tenement by the river, where her father still lived, that she sometimes wondered what she had done to deserve such good fortune. So many women like her had husbands who were out of work, too many children, and lived in overcrowded conditions where there was not enough room and insufficient to eat.

Here in Homerton no one knew her. She did not fraternize with the local people and shopped only once a week in the village shop-cum-post office, where she was known as Mrs Murray, a widow with a son at school in Edinburgh. This latter fact enhanced her status a little; it was thought that, even if she were not a lady, her husband must have been someone because the sons of working women did not usually go to boarding school in Edinburgh.

Cullum lay down on the ground beside her and started to unbutton her dress.

'Not here!' she said laughing, tugging at his hand.

'Why not?'

'Someone might come.'

'No one ever comes.'

'A farmer may pass in the field and see us. Let's go inside.'

She made to get up but he pinioned her beneath him. 'I'd like it here under the tree in the shade. Doesn't the thought excite you?'

Yes, it excited her. The grass was quite high where they lay and it was, indeed, a very solitary spot with only the house behind them and the valley beyond the high garden wall. He eased off her dress and her light cotton drawers and she lay naked on the grass, voluptuous as some nymph in a Nordic saga with her thick black hair and her dark brown skin, her face darker than the rest of her body after so much time spent out of doors. Nan also loved to garden and the fruits of her labours were apparent everywhere.

Cullum gazed at her for a long time, savouring her, not touching her but looking. She implored him with her eyes, not speaking and, raising her arms, fastened them about his neck, drawing him down so that he lay again beside her. Then she unbuttoned his shirt, as he had her dress, and drew down his trousers and they embraced each other under the overhanging branches of the sycamore tree, with only the birds to observe them and the bees that danced busily from flower to flower.

The entire third floor of the Dunbar London office was a showroom with a space in front for the mannequins and gilt chairs ranged around three sides of the room. Selected buyers were invited and given champagne and afterwards they were entertained to lunch by the directors in the dining room on the ground floor.

The autumn was a busy time for London fashion houses and Dunbars was no exception. Peter Cartwright had been at work all year with his team and the result more than justified everyone's expectations.

Dunbar Design had been launched eighteen months before, in the spring of 1930, to coincide with the flight of Amy Johnson from England to Australia and the twentieth anniversary of the accession of George V to the throne. The twin themes were royalty and sports and the 'Airgirl' separates – jumpers, pullovers and cardigans – were launched against a blown up picture of Miss Johnson who had been delighted to cooperate with Dunbars in her pioneering adventure. She was the most famous woman in the world:

> Amy, wonderful Amy!
> How can you blame me
> For loving you?

went the popular song, released on the successful completion of her flight. People were informed that she had travelled all the way to Australia clad in cashmere, for it kept out the cold better than any other fibre, and the impact was tremendous. 'Airgirl' cashmere – long-waisted, high-necked cashmere sweaters – sold like wild-fire to the wealthy and the not-so-wealthy alike, to the sporty as well as the sedentary.

It was more difficult to persuade the monarchy to endorse cashmere, although naturally Margaret tried, but the note was one of respect for that ancient institution and the implication that the aristocracy to a man – and particularly to a woman – were clad in cashmere designed by Peter Cartwright of Dunbar.

But the previous October the market had crashed in America, and Dunbars' potential customers there were trying to persuade their servants to stay on without wages as an alternative to joining the queues for free food and work, both of which were in very short supply. The plan to open a Dunbar office in New York had crashed with the rest of the market, and that year for the first time Dunbars made a considerable loss, which led to new talks with bankers and a promise by Macallisters to bale them out for one more year only.

At the time of this crisis Margaret had been expecting a baby. Despite all the care that she had promised herself she would and did have, no one could have the baby for her and her confinement was painful and protracted. Her obstetrician said she had worked too hard for too long, not rested enough before the birth, and he cautioned her, as her newly born daughter lay snugly in her arms, that if she were to have more children she would have to take more rest.

Margaret, stitched and suffering from the effects of all the drugs she had been given to assuage the pain, had assured him that nothing was further from her mind than to have another child. That was November 1929.

Now, nearly two years later, she sat in the front row with Bruno, Cullum, Susan, Juliet, Yves and all the most influential buyers of knitwear in London, and critically watched this vital show they had worked so hard for so long to put on. Margaret was not wearing the cashmere being shown by the mannequins, but a day dress, made of georgette, with a motif of large blue and black flowers. It had a tucked bertha, a draped lingerie collar and inset 'godets' in the skirt to give fullness, the hem twelve inches from the ground. Her short jet-black hair was elaborately waved and her scarlet nail varnish matched the deep red of her lips. She wore two rows of pearls round her neck and a gardenia corsage, and the hand she held to her cheek showed a richly bejewelled wedding finger. She sat between Bruno and Yves, her head tilted sideways, her mouth pursed in concentration, and from time to time they exchanged notes, ticking off an item on the list with their pencils and smiling when the audience greeted a girl with a round of applause.

Dunbar Design had already arrived. With this second

show they hoped to establish it as one of the foremost *haute couture* knitwear houses with an astonishing range, both in cashmere and other yarns, of outerwear for all occasions: for evening, for day and on the sports field, mostly as spectators, because elegant women were expected to observe rather than participate.

The exceptions of course were people like Amy Johnson and Helen Jacobs, who typified the new age of modern womanhood. Dunbar Design's 'Sportsgirl' look of white pullovers and cardigans, some with coloured ribs and embroidered motifs on the front, became indispensable to the young go-ahead girl. Her mother, on the other hand, bought the cashmere twin-sets or skirts which she wore with pearls, brogues and, seemingly, a dog – an airedale of course or a wire-haired terrier – perpetually held in the crook of her arm.

It was a long way from the remote, almost inaccessible reaches of Inner Mongolia to the elegant showroom of Dunbars, where a sophisticated concourse of discriminating fashion journalists and buyers now sat watching the parade of beautifully designed, elegant garments worn by London fashion models. Cashmere, one of the world's rarest natural fibres, was painstakingly combed once a year in the spring by goat-herders from the soft underbelly of the hardy mountain goat. Some said that the Romans wore garments made of cashmere, but its modern use could be traced back to the fifteenth century when, in the Kashmir city of Srinagar, it was realized that the underfleece of the domestic goat could be woven into beautiful shawls that were both uniquely soft and warm. News of this skill reached Western Europe in the eighteenth century, but the amount of cashmere available was small, mostly due to the difficulty and complexity of separating the soft underbelly hairs from the tough black outer hairs of the goat which could not be used. Transport added to the difficulty.

The matted oily cashmere thus obtained from the goats

by their herders was transported on the backs of various pack animals – yaks, camels, horses – across China to Tientsin, a journey sometimes taking the best part of a year. Some separation of the coarse outer hairs from the fine ones (de-hairing) took place in China but it was not an easy process. A firm that had successfully developed a method of producing the fine soft cashmere fleece was started near Glasgow in the early nineteenth century and purchased by Bruno Macallister's grandfather in the 1880s. Thus, for many years, Macallisters had had something of a monopoly of supplying the cashmere to knitters like Dunbars and their competitors. At first it was mainly used for underwear. Dunbars' catalogue of 1902 listed vests made of merino and cashmere, shirts and pants of Indian and ribbed cashmere, and ladies' vests and combinations (euphemistically called 'dresses') made of the same material. In addition cashmere hose for men, women and children were also listed.

It was really thanks to Bruno Macallister and his father that the show they were currently watching was possible. By dint of journeys made to the Chinese mainland they had secured almost a monopoly, importing the raw fibre to Scotland and separating it on their highly secret machines. The fleece of one goat produced only a scarf, three were needed for a man's pullover and seven for a lady's dress. Twenty-four goats produced a man's overcoat.

Bruno had facilitated the method by which the supplies reached the ports by going to Mongolia himself and helping to speed up cross country transportation. The goat fibres were shipped directly across the world and down the Clyde to Glasgow where the coarse hairs were removed, resulting in the very soft downy produce of fine, raw cashmere. It was then sent in bales to the mill at Galashiels, where it was dyed and then teased on a teasing machine so that the fibres were lying roughly in the same direction. At the same time oil was sprayed on to give the soft cashmere the resilience needed in spinning.

The next stage was carding and spinning, in other words combing and stretching. The Macallister mill's huge mechanical rollers with thousands of small teeth gradually combed the bulk yarns into a continuous thread, which was transferred onto cones ready for spinning. This was done in Selkirk where the soft thread was spun on huge machines, the principle of which had varied little, only becoming more sophisticated, since a poor weaver from Blackburn, James Hargreaves, had invented a spinning machine in the eighteenth century and named it after his wife Jenny.

But it is doubtful if those in the Dunbar showroom that day in September 1931 thought much about the labour that went into producing the fine yarn that had originated in mountainous regions thousands of miles away. Their immediate concern was with the finished product, in particular the new single-ply cashmere which Macallisters had perfected and which enabled a garment of exceptionally fine quality to be produced. No one else in Branswick had single-ply cashmere, and Pendreighs, moreover, had said they did not intend to use it but would stick to two-ply which gave a much bulkier and, in their view, warmer garment. They saw cashmere as essentially a warm fabric to be used in underwear or for out-of-door sweaters and cardigans.

But Dunbars, busily experimenting over the past few years, had discovered that, without losing its heating properties, cashmere could be made into all sorts of more elegant garments suitable for ladies of leisure to wear during the day or in the evening. They had produced jumpers and twin-sets that went well with skirts for country or town wear. There were cardigans that could be worn in drawing rooms or on the golf course according to their style or how they were finished: large horn buttons for out of doors and tiny gold or silver ones for indoors worn on a cold day over a cashmere dress. This too was simple but elegant, with a contrasting stitch or colour, a pattern hand-knitted into the fabric, or with a motif – a leaf, a fern, a diamond – embroidered onto the breast or pocket.

There were black cashmere tops, sleeveless or with long sleeves, the necks rounded or scalloped, their plain elegance emphasized by a row of diamantes, to be worn with long cashmere skirts for evening. There were white cashmere jumpers with pale blue or pink stripes to be worn with matching skirts and a long plain white cashmere cardigan. There were cashmere scarves to be tied casually round the neck, the berets made of cashmere worn at a rakish angle to give 'the thirties' look. Finally there were long, belted, hip-length cashmere jackets, just the thing to be seen in at point-to-point races or for a round of golf at Gleneagles.

No one had ever seen such a display of cashmere, soft, luxurious, cunningly designed to pamper and flatter, something which the well dressed, well heeled woman could hardly afford to be without – whether she could afford the price or not.

The show, which went on from eleven to twelve-thirty, moved without a hitch. It had been carefully rehearsed a dozen times, even though many of the garments had only just been finished and rushed down from Branswick overnight.

Dora Rowntree, Margaret's right-hand woman in charge of running the London office, stood at the door with a watch in her hand, timing each presentation like a stage director, giving the cues to come on and walk off. Peter Cartwright and two of his assistants, shirt-sleeved and perspiring, helped the mannequins in and out of their garments; and two hired maids detached them from their hangers or hung them up on rails that were carefully labelled to show in what order each should be shown. Below the rails were shoes, boots, hats, handbags and accessories to go with each ensemble.

It was a scene of tireless confusion, yet of order and showmanship because everything at the front must be seen to be perfect. Every girl must look right, with the correct accessories and make-up but, above all, with a composed, calm, cheerful manner embodying the style and graciousness, the comfort and practicality of the clothes she wore.

The climax of the show was a series of evening ensembles in black and white; then, at the very end, the leading model Clare Amory appeared alone, wrapped in a beautiful, brilliantly coloured cashmere shawl over a plain cashmere skirt and jumper, and the enthralled audience rose to its feet and applauded as Clare Amory sank to the floor in a deep curtsy.

Margaret, exultant but exhausted, felt drained by the time Clare walked out of the room and a buzz of conversation broke out as everyone started comparing notes with their neighbours.

'I could do with another glass of champagne,' she said to Yves, immaculate as ever in a grey suit, grey shirt and mauve tie.

'Certainly, darling.' He got up with alacrity and Margaret turned to Bruno who was still making notes on his programme.

'Very successful?'

'Very. They loved the evening ensembles with the long skirts and sleeveless tops.'

'My dear, perfectly amazing!' Bruno's chair was grabbed by a large lady in a fur coat and a cloche hat with a feather. 'I want an exclusive on the "Christabel" day dress. Is it named after the suffragette leader?'

Margaret enigmatically studied her scarlet nails. 'I'm not *quite* sure she gave it her approval; but, certainly, we had that idea of the emancipated woman in the wake of achieving the suffrage.'

'It will appeal enormously, I know, to our younger

women with its bold revers and classic style. It is contemporary, yet timeless. I love the colours. Are they Peter Cartwright's too?'

'Peter thinks of everything,' Yves murmured, sidling up with a tray on which there were several glasses and a bottle of Taittinger champagne. 'Yes, Peter designs the colours which are dyed to his specification, after endless hours of experimentation, in our Galashiels mill. When he designs a garment he has everything in mind, from the very inception to the finished product. For instance, he even designed the buttons for our "Godiva" twin-set.'

Helen Somerset-Brown, the doyenne of London knit-wear buyers, a formidable and powerful lady, graciously accepted a glass of champagne and smiled. She had been instrumental in making everyone sit up and look at the new Dunbar Design style when it was first launched, because she had been one of the very few important buyers to attend the show.

After Helen's report on the show which introduced Dunbar Design, there was a stampede the following season for tickets and some less important buyers had to be asked for a second show. Helen was in her seventies, wrinkled, rouged, over made-up, and very fat, due to the frequent indulging of her craving for chocolate and cream cakes at Appenrodts' on the corner of the Haymarket and Piccadilly Circus. But she had spent most of her working life in low menial positions, until the post-war boom of the big store began to transform ladies' fashions and she came into her own as its Queen. Everyone went out of their way to flatter Helen Somerset-Brown because if she did not like something she said it, very loudly, and her influence was enormous.

'I love the name. Rather naughty because, of course, the very *opposite* is true of the "Godiva" set, with buttons up to the neck. Who thought of the names? You, Yves?'

'Margaret and I on the whole thought of the names, Helen. Margaret certainly thought of "Airgirl" because

310

she knew Amy and I thought of "Godiva". Who thought of "Christabel", darling?'

But Margaret was looking at Bruno who was talking earnestly in a corner to Clare Amory, and did not hear him. 'Sorry? I was thinking of something else.'

'"Christabel". Whose idea was it?'

'I *think* it was mine.' Margaret got up and put a hand on his arm. 'Yves, darling, will you look after Helen, and Sonia who is descending on us.' She put her cheek out to be kissed. 'Sonia, darling, how *heavenly* of you to come! I hear you only arrived back from Paris this morning.'

'I *flew*, my dear!' Sonia Haspach, swathed in mink and exuding personality as powerful as the fragrance she was wearing, clasped her hands and pretended to tremble. 'All the way by airplane! I must be quite, quite mad!'

'You will, they say, soon be able to fly to Australia as a matter of course.' Yves laughed and handed her a glass, as Margaret smiled and moved away.

'To Australia! Are you mad, darling? Only for Dunbar would I fly the Channel! But seriously, my dear Yves, the show is a triumph. Is it not a *triumph*, Helen?' She bent and kissed the older, smaller woman. 'Who would ever have imagined knitwear being *haute couture*? Were those real pearls on the amber evening jersey?'

'Of course! We could only make one though and that is already marked for . . . well, I'm afraid I can't say who.' Yves rolled his eyes as though to signify someone Very Important Indeed.

'I bet I know! Princess Mary!'

'I can't say I'm afraid.' Yves attempted to look modest. 'But you might not be a thousand miles out if you concentrated on and around the Palace.'

'The Duchess of York!'

'I really can't say. *Please* don't ask me, Sonia.'

'Oh alright, you naughty boy. When are we going to meet Peter? Sometimes I wonder if he exists.'

'Oh he exists. I think he will show himself today. Last

year he was too nervous; but that was his first big show. With the single-ply cashmere . . . isn't it divine?'

'Too divine!' Sonia squeezed her hands together and gazed raptly at the ceiling as though hearing sounds of a heavenly choir. 'So *versatile*! I can't wait to call on you with my order book. In fact I have it now.' She groped in her bag, but Yves deprecatingly shrugged his shoulders.

'*Darling* Sonia, we can't possibly today. All these people . . .' He gestured around, putting a cigarette in his mouth, and lighting it with an expression of amazement. 'I don't know who half of them are.'

'Maybe spies for another house.' Helen Somerset-Brown leaned over and replaced her empty glass with a full one. She was ready for lunch.

'Oh dear no! All our invitations were strictly vetted. Even Ruthven Pendreigh was refused one and I hear he is *most* annoyed.'

'You will leave Pendreighs far behind now. They made a mistake not to go into single-ply cashmere. Their show in July was just the same as the one last year – plain, sensible, good taste, but . . .' Helen shrugged her heavy but still expressive shoulders and tilted the glass to her lips. 'They rely too much on tradition.'

Sonia Haspach too reached for more champagne. Buying was thirsty work. She was a clever Austrian buyer who did not like what was going on in her country where rioting earlier in the year by the *Heimwehr*, the Fascist party, and imitators of Hitler's National Socialists in Germany had been followed by the collapse of the Credit Anstalt, the largest Austrian bank. In April Sonia had packed her bags and left Vienna and by the summer, due to her international reputation, she had a job with Gloria Varney, a shop in Knightsbridge which catered almost exclusively for the aristocracy and had an influence that its relatively modest size belied.

'Which is what people once said of Dunbars,' she said in her thick, guttural accent, 'but no longer. Your reputation

312

even reached me in grim Vienna; but Yves, why did you not have your show in July when everyone else has theirs?'

'We shall next year, but this year and last we couldn't make it because of the amount of work involved. Besides, everyone is here in September. I'm amazed.'

'And if they're not here they come. It is all due to the genius of Margaret, Yves, and you.'

'No, Margaret primarily.' Yves looked vaguely around the room for her. 'She is quite unrelenting. She hasn't taken a holiday since our honeymoon. But this year I'm taking her to St Moritz for Christmas. I am insisting.'

'And Yvonne too?'

'Oh no. Yvonne is too small to ski! She will stay with her nanny and Margaret will have a perfect rest.'

'Ah, there Margaret is, talking to Bruno and . . . what is that girl's name?' Sonia took out a pair of elaborate tortoiseshell spectacles from her bag and peered across the room. 'I must say she is most remarkable.'

'Clare Amory,' Yves nodded appreciatively. 'She is intriguing, isn't she? Not beautiful, but striking. And she is so natural and uncomplicated. No temperament at all.'

'Does she work for your house?'

'She will from now on. She was with Isobel and then Baroc. Now she will work for us. And here *is* Peter. Oh Peter!' Yves broke off, waved and half the people around him turned and began clapping as Peter Cartwright modestly, almost hesitantly, made his way into the room. Yves went over to greet him, draping an arm round his shoulder and leading him to the group he had left in the middle of the floor, which was now enlarged by the addition of many other buyers, all jostling to see the genius who had transferred Dunbars from a mere knitwear house into *haute couture*.

Peter looked tired and drawn and Yves gave him champagne as, with his free hand, he shook hands with all those held out to him.

'Congratulations.'

'Thank you.'

'Marvellous show.'

'Thank you. Thank you.'

'You have made Dunbars into the first knitwear house in England.'

'In the world,' Yves said. 'Oh Nancy, how *kind* of you to come! Yes, lovely show. Do you know Peter?'

No one knew Peter, few had ever met him; but now, a slight very handsome but rather ungainly figure in the middle of the floor, too tall and with a pronounced stoop, looking rather myopic and decidedly bewildered, he was the centre of attraction, the star of the show.

'Peter is all in.' Bruno emerged from the corner where he was still chatting to Clare Amory, Margaret Dunbar and the buyers from Dickins & Jones and Jays.

'He lives on his nerves.' Clare too felt all in, but as a professional mannequin, she was never allowed to show it. She was an extremely tall elegant girl with a figure that adapted itself to almost anything. She could be hipless and bustless for sports garments, voluptuous and seductive for the evening tops and the long clinging skirts which few women with hips larger than 34″ could wear. She was a classic brunette with waved hair, a white face and deepset eyes that were almost black, but she was not beautiful. She had a broad nose, a wide mouth and a rather prominent chin. Hers was a striking, expressive face and men found her bedworthy while women found her interesting. She could be passive and vivacious, virginal and seductive. Like all good mannequins she was an exhibitionist; she enjoyed displaying herself, making the best of her face and her figure, both of which were rather extraordinary and not in the usual mould. Off duty her clothes were flamboyant rather than elegant, favouring large hats, long skirts and hand-made shoes. She was possibly one of the most famous mannequins in London and Dunbars had paid a great price to get her from Baroc,

314

the well known, rather expensive wholesale house in Marlborough Street. But they needed her as they'd needed Peter Cartwright. She was a gamble and in this, her first show for them, she had paid off.

Now as many people would come to see Clare Amory as the clothes by Dunbar Design she modelled. Her personality gave sex appeal to Peter Cartwright's well made, well designed clothes so that the leisured upper-class lady who was supposed to feel good in them could feel rather naughty as well – a combination that was to prove irresistible.

'Are you lunching with us, Clare?'

'Oh Margaret, I'm only the paid help!'

'Don't be nonsensical. We want you to. Don't we, Bruno?'

'We insist,' Bruno said warmly. 'We've got oysters, duck in aspic, and . . .'

'I've never met your wife, Bruno,' Clare murmured. 'Is that her in the emerald dress?'

'Yes, you recognize her, of course.'

'She and Margaret are alike. I must say the colouring . . .'

'Let me introduce you to her.'

Bruno took Clare by the arm and steered her through the throng. Margaret turned to talk to the Pontings' buyer and to the representatives from Paris houses who had just joined them. Out of the corner of her eye she could see Yves and Peter Cartwright revolving slowly in the middle of an admiring crowd and Bruno with an arm round Clare Amory's waist, which he quickly removed as soon as Susan saw them. Cullum was drinking orange juice soberly in a corner and Fleur was somewhere at the far end of the room with Juliet and Lily Dunbar.

The family had made it an occasion. It *was* an occasion. Margaret, alone for a moment and knowing it would not be for long, leaned against the wall wishing she could ease off her very high-heeled shoes and have a cigarette. But she would not be able to do that for many hours; it would be impossible to relax at all for days, maybe weeks, as the rush of orders were telephoned in or taken personally at more lunches, over more drinks or at individual visits to the more important stores.

But it didn't matter. Nothing like that mattered. Exhaustion must, and would, be overcome. Dunbars had arrived on the international scene and she, Margaret Dunbar Lamotte, knew more than anyone else how much of this success was due entirely to her.

CHAPTER SEVENTEEN

That night the talk at the family dinner party was initially about politics and the state of the nation, which now had a National government for the first time since 1922. The very fact that the parties had agreed to merge their differences for the common good, above all that Conservatives had agreed to serve under a Labour Prime Minister, was almost a cause for concern rather than reassurance. For matters to have come to this pass, things must be very bad indeed.

Margaret, presiding at one end of the table, opposite Yves, was content to listen and observe, to luxuriate in the elegance of the scene. The lights from the tall tallow candles in their silver candlesticks were reflected in the highly polished surface of the inlaid mahogany Sheraton dining table. At each place there was a full setting of Queen Anne silver fish knives and forks, ordinary knives and forks and spoons and three glasses for champagne, claret and the sweet white Sauternes with which they would finish off the meal.

The long dining room, with its French windows which opened on to the garden in summer time, was illuminated solely by candles. In addition to those on the table, there were three pairs on the sideboard – also Sheraton but not matching the table – from which the two maids served the meal. Besides Margaret and her two sisters there were Cullum, Fleur and Bruno, and Aunt Lily who, like Juliet, had come without her husband. Aunt Lily was thrilled by the upturn in the Dunbar fortunes because, apart from anything else, it gave her a chance to come alone to London on these exciting trips and stay in Margaret's elegant home.

317

The men wore black ties and the women long dinner dresses, mostly in the classical style moulding the figure except for Aunt Lily who, being rather plump, did not find the new clinging 'silhouette' line very suitable and opted instead for a wide-skirted 'crinoline' dress favoured mainly by the young. It suited her to be young, anyway. She greatly feared the rigours of old age.

Gazing at the scene, Margaret reflected that on the whole she had always been used to gracious living, but this must be its epitome – a table beautifully set with polished glass and silver, the finest food freshly sent that morning from the shops in St John's Wood High Street and prepared by the cook whose artistry was the envy of many of her friends.

Cocooned in her elegant house, buoyed up by success, it was difficult to imagine how bad things were outside, especially in South Wales and the industrial North. But whenever Margaret thought of poverty she remembered Nan Murray in the tenement in Branswick, the little boy huddled in his chair, his leg encased in plaster, his hands in a pair of warm mittens. Because it had touched her family, because the little boy *was* her family, the memory haunted her. So, although she was used to this manner of living, the awareness of another side of life was always with her, and she was continually grateful for being able to live as she did.

'There is no doubt that the individual parties cannot govern,' Bruno said, looking up from his soup. 'You need a broader spectrum in times of crisis. We are scarcely ever without a crisis now. I think we shall have a National government for good.'

'If we'd have had Lloyd George . . .' Cullum began.

'Oh Cullum, Lloyd George is an old man!'

'Ramsay Macdonald is not in the first flush of youth,' Cullum replied irritably, glaring at Bruno. 'And Lloyd George's principles are always so sound. Look at his stand on free trade. He said he would fight for it to the end, and now we have a National government pressing for tariffs. I ask you! The King should have sent for Lloyd George.'

'I have always liked Ramsay Macdonald.' Aunt Lily looked nervously round the table. 'He is so charming, besides being Scottish. My father knew him when he was a boy. He says . . .'

'Scottish or no,' Juliet pursed her mouth severely, 'Ramsay Macdonald has saved this country. Consider his achievement: a Labour politician who has united all parties under his premiership when the country was on the brink of ruin. I think it is remarkable.'

'But he has not united *all* parties, my dear,' Bruno said patiently. 'The only united party is the Conservatives. Both Liberal and Labour are in disarray. Ramsay Macdonald has been ostracized by his own side. They will have nothing to do with him. That's why he has become a Tory. Imagine a Labour leader saying he thought the unemployed would be only too pleased to contribute to the national emergency by taking a cut of ten percent in their benefit! I thought that was rich.' Leaning back, he began to choke, his napkin up to his mouth, until his face was red with laughter.

Fleur looked at him disapprovingly. 'I don't see how something like that can amuse you, Bruno. Do you know there are two and a half million people unemployed? Many of them are in pitiful conditions. I think it's a disgrace. There's great unrest in Glasgow, and rightly so in my opinion.'

'I agree with Fleur.' Juliet continued to look severe. 'You have only to see how the unemployed live, the conditions of their homes, the pitiful state of their ragged children, to be moved with indignation. I wonder that Ramsay Macdonald, who is a great Scotsman, cannot do better for his own people.'

'Well, the King set an example by taking a cut in the Civil List.' Margaret looked towards Yves. 'Yves, might we have more wine? And the Prince of Wales has offered ten thousand pounds from the revenues of the Duchy of Cornwall.'

'Ten thousand pounds wouldn't *begin* to make a dint in the poverty in Glasgow.' Juliet held up her glass as Yves went round the table. 'I wonder I am not ashamed to be here drinking wine and eating food like this.'

'You cannot help others by starving yourself, my dear Juliet,' Yves smiled at her. 'And life is to be enjoyed, you know. If you can.'

'I am much more worried about the five shilling Income Tax. Imagine Income Tax five shillings in the pound! And it will never go back, you can be sure of that. I can tell you, we shall all be feeling the pinch if things go on like this.'

Bruno also accepted wine, but Cullum, as usual since his cure, shook his head despite the craving he had for alcohol brought on by the stress of what he knew he had to tell Fleur. If only he had a glass of whisky, a full glass. His eyes widened hopelessly as he ruminated on the impossible.

Margaret was proud of Cullum. He had fallen to the bottom and climbed up again. Sensing the strain behind the climb she had begun, for the first time in her life, to respect him. One could despise an alcoholic, but not a man who strove so hard to overcome it. This was more like the stuff that the Dunbars were made of; the stuff that had made Malcolm give his life.

'I must say we're not too badly off,' she said, nodding her thanks to Yves as he sat opposite her at the head of the long table after dispensing the wine. 'I never thought two years ago we would be toasting success in champagne.'

'And what success!' Lily lifted her glass. 'When I reflect that in 1919 Andrew advised you to sell out!'

'1919 was a long time ago, Aunt Lily. That was the year when I told Elliott Pendreigh what he could do with

320

himself. I was not yet eighteen, as I recall. I don't know if I would have the courage to do the same thing now.'

'We've frequently thought of selling since then,' said Cullum staring into his orange juice. 'Why we did not I cannot say.'

'I know.' Susan also lifted her glass. 'Because of Margaret. At one stage I was quite ready to listen to Bruno and Cullum and go in with Ruthven Pendreigh.'

'It seemed the best thing at the time.' Bruno took care to avoid Margaret's eyes. 'How could we see into the future?'

'*Margaret* saw into the future,' Susan insisted. 'You know that quite well, Bruno. Margaret was the only one who had any vision, any guts. I toast Margaret – Margaret, a true Dunbar!'

To Margaret's embarrassment everyone rose to their feet, glasses raised, all eyes on her. She sat back in her chair and momentarily closed her eyes, overcome with emotion. It was at times like this that she knew how weak she inherently was, how she was driven on by . . . she didn't know quite what: ambition, frustration, the desire to make a mark in the world. But of this weakness her family knew nothing. She thought that, maybe, Susan guessed it; but only Susan.

'To Margaret, to Margaret,' they said in unison. Then there was silence while they toasted her. When they sat down Bruno remained on his feet. He gave a little cough and raised his hand for attention.

'Ladies and gentlemen, family should I say, I think it is up to me as a Dunbar only by marriage to make a speech.'

'Hear, hear.' Cullum thumped the table.

'You all know the subject of this speech. We have just toasted her. Margaret. Margaret Dunbar Lamotte who has made the company what it is today. And what a day! How appropriate that we should toast Margaret on this day of all days. Was our show not the most successful that

321

we could ever hope for? Was there one significant knit-wear buyer, both in this country and Europe, who was not there? And who have we to thank for this?'

'Peter Cartwright,' Margaret murmured.

'No, Margaret.' Bruno gave an oratorical flourish. 'You. You are responsible for Peter Cartwright, but before that you were responsible for insisting that we went on, that we did not sell or merge. We thought at times, I'll confess it now, that you were a bully, a bit of a tyrant. We thought you were misguided and wrong, but some instinct made us trust you. Thank God for that. We thought the thirties would be better than the twenties. We did not know that the American market would crash in '29 and there would be thirteen million people in that unhappy country out of work. We thought a vast export trade would bring us riches from America, and we were on the point of opening an office there in Fifth Avenue.

'We did not know when we entered the thirties that there would be more unemployed in this country than ever before except for the strike in 1926, and that the cost of financing the unemployed would prevent our recovery. And we did not know last New Year's Eve as we toasted the New Year that things would get worse not better, that we should be nearly driven from the gold standard and forced to have a National government as an emergency.

'So the slogan we coined two years ago when we introduced Dunbar Design to a sceptical audience, "A new fashion for a new age", could have been very optimistic indeed; but it was not. It was a success. And why?' Bruno pointed across the table. 'Because of Margaret, who not only bullied us into experimenting with single-ply cashmere, but planned and then executed a sales and publicity campaign that was daunting by its sheer cheek. She approached ladies of fame, title and wealth to promote our products. What a nerve! When she saw the Duchess of Storrick, Her Grace thought she was being asked to add to her list of charities by supporting the local industry. Her Grace did not know what she was letting herself in for when she graciously consented but, I understand, when she saw a full page in *The Tatler* she was not displeased!

'Now, dear family, I have said enough. We all know the debt we owe to Margaret, and might I add a final word in praise of someone else?' Bruno gestured towards the other end of the table. 'To Yves, Margaret's husband, who has made her so happy, who has supported and encouraged her, who has given her a lovely daughter and everything to live for. May all three of them, Margaret, Yves and Yvonne live happily ever after.'

As all the family stood up again Margaret bent her head, blinking back the tears that welled behind her closed lids, not trusting herself to reply.

Fleur lay nervously in bed, waiting for Cullum to emerge from the bathroom where he had gone to undress. It was so long since they had shared a bedroom, never mind a bed, that she felt almost as apprehensive as she had on her first wedding night, though she had felt equally ill at ease on the second.

Fleur had never enjoyed the marital act, considering it a duty rather than a pleasure, something that a woman was expected to do in order to perpetuate the race and to please men, in that order. Having done her bit to perpetuate the race, three times over, she would quite cheerfully have forgone the latter duty had not Cullum so desperately wanted a son. The death of baby Duncan, whom they had only had time to christen before they buried him, had thrown her into a deep depression and Cullum back on to the bottle, the beginning of a breakdown from which he had only just recovered.

At home they had separate rooms and Cullum never came to hers. She thought it was part of his illness and, as it suited her, she had been content to bide her time before attempting to fulfil her duty to provide an heir again.

As Cullum emerged from the bathroom attired in his silk pyjamas, his silk dressing gown tied firmly around him, she smiled timidly. She wore a new crêpe-de-Chine nightdress she had bought the day before in Harrods, and had prepared herself very carefully for that strange and unwelcome act that assured the continuation of the species. After all, she was thirty-four now and they did not have much time.

But Cullum seemed in no hurry to join her. He had a cigarette in his mouth and he walked to the window, slightly parting the curtains and peering out. Fleur said nothing, aware of the increasing rate of her heartbeat.

'Have you noticed that Yves and Margaret have separate rooms?' He closed the curtain and went over to the chair by the bed, dropping into it and stretching his legs.

'Well? So do we.'

'Yes, but I wonder if it is for the same reason?'

'What reason is that?'

'That Margaret doesn't enjoy it either. I think it's strange for a relatively newly married couple, don't you?'

'No, not particularly. As Margaret works so hard she probably likes to sleep well. Besides, is that the only reason *we* have separate rooms?'

'What do you mean?' Cullum ground out his cigarette in an ashtray on a table by the bed.

'I thought you didn't want to sleep with me either.'

'Don't be silly! I've been ill.'

'But has it impaired . . .?' She looked at him, her narrow plucked eyebrows raised.

'No it has not impaired my capability, if that's what you want to know.'

'I didn't know. I'm glad. Come to bed, Cullum. Don't let's spoil a happy day by argument.' She moved over and patted the place by her side. She smiled at him but she felt very frightened; his attitude was so strange.

Cullum got up and slowly undid his dressing gown, placing it neatly over the chair in which he had been

324

sitting. He was only thirty-two but his hair was already greying at the sides. How much his illness had aged him. Her heart went out to him in pity, but she couldn't call it love. She had never really loved him, and his behaviour since their marriage, however much it was due to illness, had not helped. She had married him for security and status, but she had also expected to be a good wife; to be able to feel, eventually, some strong emotion for her partner in life, but she never had. Yet she did not feel she had failed him. On the contrary, he had failed her; because whatever one said about alcoholism being an illness, it was also a sign in her eyes of weakness too. It was contemptible.

After all, she reasoned, alcoholics brought about their own downfall by drinking too much in the first place. No one became an alcoholic in one go; it took time. That time was when they should learn about their weakness and how to control it. It wasn't as though they had an organic illness that they couldn't help, like cancer or heart disease. They could help it. In this way Fleur refused to think of an alcoholic as an invalid, and withdrew her compassion.

Alcoholics made life so miserable for everyone else; their wives, their business partners and, not least, their children. His daughter Morag, small though she was, despised her father and she was ashamed of him. She had seen too often the commotion that he caused when he was brought home insensible in the small hours of the morning and put to bed. She had heard his alcoholic ravings when no one could quieten him, and suffered his moroseness for days on end after one of his spells of noisy mania. The whole household had revolved around Cullum and his drinking and the whole town knew about it.

Fleur on the other hand, though resenting it as much, bore it with a certain detached stoicism in which she managed to combine both contempt and distance. If her husband drank, she seemed to say, it was nothing to do with her and if anyone felt sorry for her she didn't need

325

their pity. She could quite cheerfully have lived without Cullum, as she'd had to several times when he was in hospital, were it not for her feeling of social obligation and the status it gave her. She seemed to think a husbandless woman was more an object of compassion than the wife of an alcoholic; and now that he had definitely given it up, as far as anyone could tell, the overall situation had improved. Still she had to endure intercourse with this man resulting, maybe, in nine uncomfortable months of pregnancy in order to provide him with an heir. And people talked about the status of women! It was demeaning and, to her way of thinking, always had been and always would be.

She looked at the table where, under a clean handkerchief, she had concealed a lubricant which the doctor had advised her to use because she had never been able to respond naturally to her husband herself. Tonight she would do her best.

Cullum sat on the edge of the bed, as if in thought, and then gingerly climbed in beside her. It was not the action of an eager lover. Nor did he nestle up to her, but rather kept strictly to his own side. Then he put a fresh du Maurier in his mouth.

'You're smoking a lot.'

'Well?' He blew a thin stream ahead of him.

'I suppose it's better than drinking.'

'I thought you'd say that.'

'Oh Cullum, I'm sorry. It was beastly!' Unexpectedly moved by the tone of his voice, she impulsively turned to him. 'I didn't mean it.'

'But you did. It's always in your mind isn't it? When is he going to start drinking again? It's just a matter of time.'

'I don't think that at all. Look, tonight . . . you were wonderful. All that drink flowing. In fact, there has been plenty of it about all day, and never once . . .'

'But you were watching me, weren't you?'

'No of course not. I can't help noticing . . .'

'Always watching,' Cullum ruminated, staring in front of him. 'Is it going to be today, or tomorrow when he starts again? An alcoholic is never cured. It's a weakness; a sign of a weak man. Give him a push and he'll go over again. He can't take anything really hard. Is it still the orange juice, or has he tipped some gin into it?'

'Cullum, that is not true. Now don't be silly; don't torment yourself.'

She moved nearer to him so that she could feel his body; between them were only thin layers of silk and crêpe-de-Chine. She raised her hand from the bedclothes and touched his bare chest where his bright ginger hairs protruded just above the top button of his pyjamas. She put her lips to his cheek and kissed it, rubbing his bare flesh with a finger, trying to stimulate her own desire as well as his.

'Don't you want to make love? We haven't for a long time. You can if you like.'

'Oh thank you!' Cullum's smile was heavily sarcastic, and Fleur felt offended.

'I *am* your wife Cullum. I know you want a son. I am prepared to try and give you that son.'

'And hope it lives longer than the last one.'

Fleur withdrew her hand and moved away as though he had hit her, her eyes smarting with tears. 'Oh that is very cruel!'

'Well, I'm sorry.'

'You would think I couldn't produce healthy children, but I can. I have two lovely daughters. What you say is bitterly hurtful. I'm only trying to make up, Cullum, to be closer to you. I want to. I really do. I know you've been ill and have tried very hard to recover and I want to help you.'

'You can help me by not forcing yourself to make love to me when you don't want to,' Cullum said. 'Your body is trembling and I know it is not with desire.'

'But I want to give you a son, don't you understand? I

327

know how much you want a son.' Fleur groped under the pillows for the handkerchief she had expected to use for something else, and vigorously wiped her nose.

Cullum got out of bed and slowly put on his gown, tying it very tightly at the waist.

'Cullum,' Fleur said sharply, 'what are you doing? Are we to have no sleep tonight? At least let us sleep. Forget about the other thing.' Feeling, despite herself, hurt and rebuffed she tried to settle down again, convinced now that her husband's alcoholism had damaged his virility.

Cullum lit another cigarette, then sat down again on his side of the bed, his body slightly turned towards her. 'I needed a drink very badly tonight, Fleur, but I didn't have one. Maybe if I had I might have felt better because I know I have handled this badly.'

'What badly? What are you talking about?' Startled she looked at him, feeling very nervous again.

Cullum turned right round and gazed at her, his blue-green eyes sad and wistful. He did not want to hurt her but he knew now that there was nothing else he could do, and that hurt she had to be; someone had to be in this mess.

'Fleur, I've been wanting to talk to you for some time, but I've lacked the courage. I don't know why I'm doing it now unless I thought that having the family here will help, because they have to know.'

'Know? Know what? What *are* you trying to say?' Her voice was fluttery, alarmed. She felt not only apprehension now but panic. She had never seen such an expression on his face, so grim and unsmiling and, yes, determined in a rather frightening kind of way.

'I have a son, Fleur. He is just twelve years old. His name is William and his mother has been my mistress on and off for that many years. There, now I've told you.' Cullum got up and went again to the window, plucking at the curtain to peer out as he had before, a futile gesture to try and calm his nerves. 'Her name is Nan Murray. She once worked at the mill in the trimming department. She was very pretty, very

328

young and I took her to bed at a time when I went to bed with a lot of girls, just after I had to leave Oxford and assume the burden of the business with Father. I don't excuse myself, but it happened. I had a reputation.'

Cullum then told her all about Nan; how he had found out about his son when William was two; how he had started to see her, the conditions in the tenement in Dumbarton Street. How she had never been demanding, being content to have him as he was. How she had only taken money for William and put it in the post office, never touching a penny for herself.

Then he told her how he had given Nan up to try and make his marriage work; how cruel he had been, not seeing her or William, and then how William had nearly drowned and he had resumed his relationship with Nan again.

As he spoke Fleur was remembering the night Cullum had come home from Edinburgh and then gone out after flinging down the paper. That had been the year things had got worse and the business had nearly failed. And Margaret . . . Margaret had picked up the paper and read it twice over. Margaret had known all the time!

Fleur heard him out, surprised by her own calm, almost the feeling of peace as she lay propped on her pillows and listened to this long tale of deceit. He had deceived two women; herself and Nan; but she did not feel any pity for Nan Murray. Women who behaved like that got what they deserved.

Cullum came to the end, telling her of the house at Homerton and how happy he and Nan were together. He omitted nothing, the visits to the hospital, William's school, everything. When he had finished he too looked at peace, and he pulled himself upright in the chair into which he had slumped during the course of his tale.

'So that's it. I'm sorry.'

'I see. I don't suppose you're sorry at all.'

The tears that had threatened at one time to ruin her

composure had gone; instead she felt steely, calm and resolute – a woman fighting for her man. A man she had to have, because marriage and respectability were fundamental to her life.

'Yes I *am* sorry,' Cullum insisted, looking at her earnestly. 'I haven't been a good husband to you. I've caused you misery and suffering and I'm sorry.'

'Have? You mean you *are* causing me misery and suffering.'

'Fleur, I want to end it all.' Cullum got up and began to pace the room, cracking his fingers one by one. 'I want a divorce. I want to marry Nan and give William my name. I don't want to turn you out of the house; you can have that, for life of course. One day I would like William to have it. I'll live with Nan at Homerton and you . . .'

'Oh no,' Fleur burst out, her only emotion one of profound indignation. 'Oh no you won't, Cullum Dunbar. You have reckoned without your family and me. I will never divorce you; never, never, whatever grounds you give and you have given me plenty. I will never release you to give that bastard your name. You can be sure of that. Also you can be sure that your family, your Margaret who can influence you so much, will make certain that you never leave *Woodbrae* either. That, whether you continue to visit that woman or not, you will go on just as you have up to now – living at *Woodbrae*, going daily to the mill. Nothing will change. I promise that. Nothing.'

At the family meeting the next day Fleur did lose control, whether calculatedly or not it was difficult to say; maybe she did not know herself, or maybe the sympathetic, indignant audience helped. She wept and she stormed; she even tore her handkerchief and, watching her, Margaret could only feel pity, anger and contempt for Cullum who had reduced a good woman to this.

Cullum had gone to Margaret's room that morning and told her before the rest of the household was awake.

Margaret, lying in bed drinking her early morning tea, had heard him out. Then she told him what he must do; said what Fleur had said she would say. She said it again now, once Fleur's tears had subsided.

'You cannot possibly marry Nan. You must know that, Cullum. You always knew it. We discussed it a long time ago.'

'You knew all about her of course! And I thought you were my friend.' Fleur, her cheeks tearstained, looked at her reproachfully.

'I was your friend. I *am* your friend,' Margaret insisted gently. 'Years ago when I first found out I told Cullum he could never marry her, and he said he knew that. He agreed. I asked her to give him up, too. I did all I could.'

'I did not know her as well then, or love her as much as I love her now.' Cullum raised his chin, trying to pretend he was in control of the situation.

'That's beside the point, Cullum. You can thank yourself for all that has happened. I am sorry for Nan and for nice William as well as for Fleur. But you have your duty as a Dunbar whatever other duties you may think you have. That is the first one. A scandal at this moment could well rock our business . . .'

'Nonsense!'

'Shatter confidence. People do not get divorced willy-nilly, whatever you may think. It's a social disgrace. Nor do they go off and live with mill girls in cottages however good and nice they are, and I know Nan is both. I like her; but she is a mill girl, a working-class girl. You could never be seen in public with her, take her, as you could Fleur yesterday, to our London show.'

'*Why not?*' Cullum almost shouted, thinking of his lovely, nubile Nan.

Margaret looked astonished. 'Because she would not *know* how to behave, what to do, what to say. I wonder you ask. She is very sweet and pretty . . . but no.'

'Margaret, you're wasting your breath,' Fleur said, her

331

tears subsiding. 'I am not divorcing Cullum, whatever happens.'

'Then I will live with her!' Cullum shouted out loud; and Margaret and Susan looked nervously towards the door in case the servants could hear.

'Lower your voice, Cullum,' Juliet said sharply with the peremptory authority of the elder sister, or as though she were speaking to one of her deserving cases in need of restraint and correction. Indeed she had managed to combine with this family visit to London several others in connection with her charitable duties, and was late for one now. She glanced at her watch. 'It is quite out of the question for you to marry this Murray girl or to live with her. You would be ostracized and so would we. Is it fair to Margaret after all she has done? I can't *think* of the shame, or of what Angus would say were he here.'

'Oh I know what Angus would say alright,' Cullum laughed bitterly. 'What a mine of understanding and compassion that man is!'

'Well, he's nearly always right,' Juliet said defensively. 'He may be stubborn and opinionated, but he has not been a lawyer for all these years without knowing what's what.'

Looking at them then, his three sisters, Cullum knew he was defeated. It was as though a militant, threatening, gang of women had been set against him – his three sisters and his wife. He could see that, once again, he would give in and obey them, however much he wanted not to. They had always ordered his life and they would now. They emasculated him, rendered him powerless. If he did not obey they would ostracize him, harry him and make him turn to drink again. And this he did not want. He had seen the snakes in the bottom of the pit and his delirium had been terrible. He never wanted to live through that and the fear of madness again.

He would still have Nan; he would see her, things would be as they were now. They could not stop him doing that.

But he could not marry her or live with her or give William his name. Better that he had never spoken, that he had kept his precious other life to himself. He put his head in his hands, while Margaret placed an arm round him trying, wordlessly, to comfort him.

CHAPTER EIGHTEEN

When the family had returned north it was some time before Margaret and Yves could speak about personal matters. They were busy all day and entertaining or being entertained every night.

They were stirring times for the country too. Just after the family had left for home, a fresh financial crisis made Britain go off the Gold Standard to which it had returned in 1925. Sir Stafford Cripps, for the Opposition, denounced the government's economy moves as 'panic measures concerned to avert the inevitable consequences of the capitalist system' in a speech which Mr Boothby, MP, dismissed as 'sentimental claptrap'. The pound dropped to a gold value of sixteen shillings, but internal prices remained the same while a fillip was given to exports.

Little of all this touched the Lamottes, or indeed the mass of the people, except the two and a half million unemployed and those on the fringes. Although many productions failed because of the adverse economic climate there were some successes on the London stage, including *Autumn Crocus* by a new woman writer using the pseudonym of C. L. Anthony in which Fay Compton scored a notable hit. At the Playhouse Somerset Maugham's new play *The Painted Veil* gave an important emotional part to Gladys Cooper, and Geoffrey Tearle was impressive as Hamlet at the Haymarket.

But the hit of the season was Noel Coward's *Cavalcade*, which had its opening night at Drury Lane a few days before the General Election called by the National Government to confirm it was in power.

The glittering first-night audience – the ladies beautifully gowned by Molyneux, Lachasse or Peter Russell, the men all in white ties – would have made a visitor from another planet rub his eyes. Impossible, seeing this lavish display of wealth, to imagine the country was in the middle of a depression. There was an air of opulence and leisure. Champagne was drunk in the intervals and a line of chauffeur-driven cars blocked the streets of Covent Garden to collect people at the end.

But this was the thirties, more cynical and less hopeful than the twenties, and those who had no money went to great pains to conceal the fact. They would entertain lavishly, go to a first night or to dinner at Quaglino's and then starve the rest of the week. It was the age of deception, of pretending that things were not as bad as they seemed. After all, the war had been over fourteen years and for ten of these the English economy had been depressed. Now there were more storm clouds on the horizon. It was too ridiculous: one just lived for today, taking what one could and paying for it later.

Noel Coward's play, jingoistic and determinedly middle-class, nevertheless struck just the right note for a country which had recently left the Gold Standard and had a general election looming:

'Let's drink to the hope that one day this country of ours, which we love so much, will find dignity and greatness and peace again.'

Cavalcade was a call, if not to arms, at least to hope, to patriotism. It said goodbye to the decadence of the twenties, symbolized by the couples who mechanically danced the Blues as the lights went down. Slowly a softly illuminated Union Jack appeared on the darkened stage and the entire cast turned to the auditorium and sang 'God Save the King', thus administering a *coup de grâce* to the already weakened emotions of the audience. There was hardly a dry eye at the end, and then Noel Coward himself, spectacularly handsome and graceful, standing in front of the curtain: 'After all, it is a pretty exciting thing these days to be English.' No wonder the entire Royal Family was to attend two weeks later.

It was magnificent theatre, an emotional moment, and Margaret and Yves were as much under its influence as any of the people they met and talked to subsequently in the foyer.

'Darlings, do come to the Embassy! We're throwing a party!' Helen Overton, Lady Overton who spent a fortune at Gloria Varney on Dunbar clothes, swept up on the arm of her boyfriend Captain Nigel Curtis of the Coldstream Guards. (Her husband would have been out with his girlfriend somewhere else – the couples taking care not to clash.) 'Everyone will be there!'

'We can't. We're already invited to Ciros. Thanks, Helen.'

Yves smiled, bowed, kissed her on the cheek. So many women eyed him, splendid in white tie and tails, his black hair just slightly greying, a coif in the front carefully drawn back from his forehead. Margaret's dress was by Madame Schiaparelli, one of the Paris couturiers she favoured, the others being Lanvin and Chanel. In black, her preference for important occasions, it was of peau de soie, the bodice cut to enhance her waistline, swathed into a large bow at the back. The skirt was full with a draped panel below the bow. She wore long black gloves and a diamond necklace, a wedding present from Yves, a family heirloom.

They made a magnificent couple. Everyone stared openly as they passed by. They could have been Royalty for all the attention they got. Margaret was the embodiment of elegance and chic with her beautiful clothes, her very white skin, blue-green eyes and black hair fashionably coiffured. People asked who they were. Surely they were one of the most graceful and glamorous, successful and talented couples in London?

The foyer of the theatre was crowded as Yves, nodding to people he knew – and he seemed to know them all – carefully steered Margaret towards the door.

'I'll go and get the car,' he said.

'No, I'll come with you. It will be terribly crowded trying to park outside. Grace, darling, how *lovely* to see you!' Cheeks touched, hands met. Grace Rounhill was going to the same party as the Lamottes. 'Can we give you a lift?'

'No thanks, darling. Henry has gone to get the car.'

'I told Yves . . .' Margaret began and then stopped, her eyes on a couple at the far end of the foyer just making, like themselves, for the door. The man had his arm through the woman's and as they talked animatedly their heads almost touched. 'I told Yves I'd come with him.' Margaret waved and caught up with Yves who was just going down the steps of the theatre, putting a hand on his arm. 'Yves! Stop!'

He looked behind, catching her hand. 'What is it?'

'Look, to your right. Look there, just crossing the road.'

Yves squinted in the direction she was pointing. 'It's Bruno. Who's the girl with him?'

'Don't you recognize her?'

'It's Clare!'

'Yes, Clare Amory.'

'But what are they doing together?'

Margaret didn't reply, watching them cross the road then disappear towards Covent Garden on the other side. 'I didn't know Bruno was in town,' she mused aloud.

'Well, it's none of our business.' Yves took her arm and together they found the Buick parked in Kemble Street at the side of the theatre. It was a 1929 Model 55 tourer which Margaret had bought from an American manufacturer who had been in England at the time of the Wall Street crash. He had had to sell his car in order to raise the

337

money to get home. It was a beautiful car in two shades of brown, and for Margaret it was an important acquisition, almost a talisman, because, apart from its elegance, David Dunbar Buick had been born in Scotland before going to Detroit to manufacture plumbing fixtures where he had made his first car in 1903.

As Yves eased the Buick into the mainstream of the traffic, the lights of the Strand almost dazzled Margaret, and yet all she could see was the couple very close together with eyes only for each other – Bruno and Clare. Were they having an affair?

'Don't brood about them, Margaret.' Yves put a hand on hers. 'It's none of our business.'

'It is very much our business. She is our employee and he, as well as being a co-director, is my sister's husband.'

'But it doesn't affect us.'

'It doesn't affect *us*; but it could affect the family.'

'Well, don't say anything, I beg of you.'

'Yves, do you mind if we don't go to Ciros? I'm terribly tired.'

'You don't want to go to the party?'

'No. Do you?'

'Not really.'

'We had a very hectic day today and tomorrow is as bad. Graham Parkes is coming sharp at nine . . .'

'You don't need to explain. We'll go home and have an early night. I'll ring Angela first thing in the morning to apologize.'

'Thank you Yves.'

She settled back in her furs, watching the familiar lights of London go by as Yves turned the car and drove along the Strand, up Regent Street, through the Park to St John's Wood. He really was a very accomplished man: thoughtful, correct. They seldom argued or even disagreed. He was the perfect partner, business partner. As a marriage partner, well, that was something else.

338

One of their maids, Christine, was still up when they got in and Yves asked for sandwiches and a bottle of champagne.

'Champagne?' Margaret raised her eyebrows as Yves solicitously took her fur wrap, and then stopped to poke the fire as Christine drew the curtains before leaving the room.

'I thought it would cheer you up. Besides, we were supposed to be going to a party. Let's have one here.'

'You're very sweet, Yves.' She reached out and he gave her his hand, then he bent and lightly kissed hers. She put up her face inviting him to kiss her lips, but that familiar veiled look came into his eyes and he rose, still clasping her hand; but his touch was impersonal. That she was used to too. He made sure she was comfortable and then sat opposite her, crossing his legs and lighting a cigarette, blowing smoke into the air. Everything he did was neat and elegant.

'Really a very fine performance. Just what we need at times like this; the country on the brink of catastrophe. Herr Hitler causing trouble in Germany.'

'Do you think we really are in for bad times, Yves?'

He flicked his ash into the fire. 'Yes I do, but not for us. Not for Dunbars. I think we will go from strength to strength because we have a good product and people will always buy good things. I don't care what anyone says: there is plenty of money about. You only had to look at the audience tonight!' He gazed at her fondly. 'You're not listening, are you, Margaret? You're thinking about Bruno.'

'I'm thinking about my family. I've never stopped worrying about Cullum and Fleur since they left. And now I have this! Why do men have to have affairs all the time? Why can't they be happy with what they've got? Both Fleur and Susan are handsome women, good wives and mothers. I can't understand it.'

'Maybe he isn't having an affair. Bruno, I mean.'

339

'What else? Why the secrecy? I think they saw us and slipped out as quickly as they could. I knew he liked her, you know. He was very keen to employ her and then at our show he practically monopolized her for the rest of the day. Even Susan noticed and asked me about her. Of course I told her Clare was married and there was absolutely nothing for her to worry about.'

'Have you met her husband?'

'No. He's a semi-invalid, you know, something from the war. But she never talks about it. I've never heard her mention his name.'

'Mmm. Don't worry about it, darling.'

Yves got up as Christine came in with a tray and helped her to put it on a small table. He took the champagne which she had put in a bucket of ice.

'Beautiful! Thanks Christine. You're doing very nicely. By the way, did Miss Yvonne settle down? She was very restless when we came in to say goodnight.'

'Oh yes, sir,' Christine smiled. 'Went down as good as gold. Nanny said it was the excitement of seeing you and madam all dressed up.'

'That's good. Thank you, Christine. You may go.'

'Thanks ever so much sir.' Christine, neat in her black and white maid's uniform, gave a little bob.

Yves uncorked the champagne and poured it, handing Margaret her glass and lifting his own. 'Cheers darling.'

'Chin-chin.' Margaret raised her glass and smiled at him. If only you would love me Yves, she thought, I would be very happy. But you don't love me at all and I don't think you ever have.

'What are you thinking of my sweet? Not of Bruno and Clare again?'

'No.' Margaret took a sip of the wine. 'I was thinking about us.'

'Us?' He looked surprised.

'Yes, us.'

340

'But there's nothing wrong with us, is there, darling?'

'Isn't there?'

'Not that I'm aware.' He handed the plate of daintily cut chicken sandwiches to Margaret. 'This girl really does these things frightfully well. She was a great find.'

'Yes, wasn't she?' Yves would avoid anything personal. He always did.

'Darling what are you saying about us? I thought we were very happy with each other.' He sat down balancing his plate on his knee.

'I love you.'

'I know you do, my darling, and I love you.'

'You don't love me.'

'Oh Margaret!' He put down his glass and wiped his lips on a napkin. 'Please don't start that again. What more can I do to show you that I love you?'

'Make love to me.' The words, thus uttered, were very stark; a command rather than a question, even a reprimand. She didn't look at him, but gazed into the fire as though afraid of the expression she would see in his eyes. Her own were very sad. 'You do everything but make love to me, Yves. You are attentive, kind, charming, thoughtful, everything a woman could want. I am envied, I know. People think we must be the happiest couple in the world. You remember what Bruno said on the night of our show?' Yves nodded but said nothing. He turned to the table and refilled his glass, taking another sandwich as though he were enjoying himself. 'I had the greatest difficulty not weeping, not because I was happy but because I was unhappy. It is true, I thought, I have so much; but the most important thing to me I have not got; and I think for that I would throw up Dunbars and all that we have done. Just to have your love, Yves.'

Yves munched his sandwich thoughtfully, finished it and wiped his lips again; then he took a fresh draught of champagne.

341

'That is nonsense, Margaret. I do love you. I love you as much as I can. Maybe I do not have very deep emotions. I don't know. I am a controlled person, as you know, and do not show my feelings.'

'Most men show them in bed.'

'Well.' Yves shrugged. 'There I must be deficient too. I don't know why. I'm happy as I am. Why don't you take a lover if you feel frustrated?'

Margaret wondered if she had heard correctly. The fire crackled, the Fabergé clock on the mantelpiece ticked, there was the occasional sound of a car passing in the quiet street outside. Could she possibly have heard that he, her husband, had suggested she should take a *lover*?

'I beg your pardon?'

Yves selected another sandwich. 'You're not eating, darling. Yes, you heard me. What you're saying is that I am a good husband, but not a good sexual partner. I admit you're right. I'm not easily roused. I never have been, and you knew that from the beginning when you lured me into bed before our marriage to find out if I could perform satisfactorily or not.'

'That's terribly crude, Yves.'

Yves threw back his head and laughed. 'Well, darling girl, if I may say it now, though I didn't dare then, you were rather crude yourself. A man is a little put off if he isn't allowed to take the initiative, you know, and you did rather throw yourself at me. You make your needs too apparent, my sweet. It's not – what's the word – aesthetic.'

'I would have thought "aesthetic" was a very funny word to use for sex.'

'No it's the right one. Men like a little more circumspection in women. Some might call it, old-fashioned word I know, modesty. I'm too fastidious I think. Anyway, I'm not easily roused, and I'm not ashamed of it.'

'You've not been roused at all for months, almost a

342

year! Don't you call that overdoing the fastidiousness?'
Margaret suddenly felt like weeping, her emotional grip
on herself threatening to give way. To be seen to do the
right thing was very important to them both, even in
private. Again Yves nodded.

'Is it as long as that? Well, as I said, find some rude
mechanical who will give you physical pleasure. I assure
you I should not object.'

'I think that is the most horrible thing I have ever, *could*
ever, imagine one human being saying to another, let
alone a husband to a wife: "Get someone else".'

'But darling, I am not saying "marry someone else" for
Christ's sake! I love you and I love being married to you. I
love our home and our baby daughter and the sight of you
is always a pleasure to me. Tonight, for example, you look
superb. You are so beautiful, you dress so well, you are a
priceless joy. I assure you of that.'

'An adornment.'

'Not an adornment, Margaret; don't be girlish! That's a
stupid thing to say.'

'Tristan once accused me of marrying you for what you
were – a French aristocrat. Now I am saying you want me
for what I can do for you, embellish you like a possession.'

Yves shook his head and picked his teeth with a silver
tooth pick he carried in a case in his pocket. He looked at
her abstractedly. 'Did Tristan say that also? Tut tut. I'm
very surprised. He did interfere a lot didn't he? Why do
we never see Tristan by the way? Is it still because of
that?'

'Yes.'

'Very silly. I must ask him round. Now to return to the
point, what do you think most marriages are, Margaret?
Have you ever thought? They are for convenience, because people are accepted in couples rather than as
individuals. Why did Fleur marry Cullum, or Cullum
Fleur? Just for that. Why did Bruno marry Susan and

Susan Bruno? To be respectable. People don't like to be alone, even though in their hearts they might prefer it.'

'That is very cynical and also untrue. I happen to know Susan is very much in love with Bruno, which is why I was so unhappy tonight seeing him with Clare.'

'And that is why you are speaking like you are now, my darling. If you had given the matter some thought you would have realized many things are best left unsaid. I thought you had more discretion.'

'I am to pretend about my marriage, is that it?'

Yves appeared to consider the question carefully, then shook his head. 'No, not at all; but you say you love me and I believe you do. I love you just as much, but I cannot always show it physically. Therefore you want something I am unwilling to give; but it is not big or important enough to destroy our marriage. I think we have built a fine relationship. We get on well. We like the same things. *I* am very happy. You don't love anyone else, do you?'

Margaret shook her head mutely.

'Well, then. I would never object if, very discreetly, you took a lover in order to satisfy those cravings of the flesh which are perfectly natural.'

'You're suggesting I have an affair?'

'If you like. There are dozens of men always ogling you. I wonder you have not had one before, if you feel as you say you do.'

'I have been very tempted Yves; but infidelity is not in my nature. I want to be faithful to you.'

'It's not being unfaithful darling. I'm making you free; free to love, but not to fall in love, if you understand the difference. I would not like that at all.'

'But supposing I can't help it?'

'You must choose someone who has what you want, but whose other qualities you do not particularly admire. When I said "some rude mechanical" I meant just that.'

'A servant?'

344

'Not necessarily a servant but, you know . . . I believe the book by D. H. Lawrence which has caused such a storm in Paris is about the relations of a Lady Chatterley with her gamekeeper because her husband is impotent.'

'But you aren't impotent, Yves.'

'No, I'm not impotent.' Yves got up and selected a cigar from a box on a side table. He sniffed it, inspected it, removed the band and clipped it. Then he applied a spill to it, which he lit from the fire. Finally he blew out the spill and threw it into the flames. 'Margaret, I am beginning to find this conversation mildly distasteful. I'm surprised at you. I thought you had more sense, more control. You are very different privately to the persona you present in public.'

'I am not ashamed of my feelings. Why should I be ashamed to show them to you?'

'No reason, and, I must say, you certainly have very warm feelings.'

'And they disgust you?'

'Not at all.'

'Do you realize that to have my husband not wanting to make love to me, not even wanting to talk about it, makes me feel rejected? I think I *must* have done something to disgust you.'

'My darling, I do vaguely find the sexual act disgusting but that is not your fault; it is mine. I certainly do not find *you* disgusting, and never did. Maybe it was something my nursemaid did to me when I was a little boy, but I don't know. That is how I feel and I can't help it.'

The complacent expression had left his eyes; now, indeed, they began to show pain. Margaret wondered how much further she dared probe. They had certainly never talked so intimately before, even when his behaviour had begun to puzzle then to wound her.

'When we made love I thought it was wonderful, not disgusting. Love between men and women is beautiful, or should be.'

345

'Well, there you are. I'm sure you are normal and I am not.'

'But how can something I find beautiful not be beautiful for you, too? I can't understand it.'

'I have no idea my love. And now I do beg you . . .'

Margaret sat forward on the edge of her chair. She knew she was beginning to nag, but she couldn't help herself. She felt a sort of desperation at Yves' insouciance that made her untypically reckless.

'Of course, in the light of what you're telling me now, I understand why I had to seduce you rather than the other way round before we were married. The sexual act must always have disgusted you?'

Yves grimaced and brushed the tip of his nose with a beautifully manicured finger. 'In a way yes. I mean there are times when it is necessary, for procreation and so on; but I do think it was a singularly charmless way of the Almighty to go about his work. I suppose he had his reasons; maybe to shame us into an awareness of our mortality.'

'I don't find it at all shameful. I think if you'd been honest with me before our marriage, Yves, it would have made a lot of difference.'

'Would it?' Yves shaded his eyes from the bright central candelabra and looked at her. He was aware of how sad his wife had grown; no longer a splendid, vibrant, beautiful woman; but crushed. He suddenly felt very guilty about what he'd done to her and, going over to her, knelt on the floor in front of her. 'I abase myself, darling. Would you not have married me if I'd been honest?'

Margaret smiled despite herself, yet she was close to tears. He put out a hand and she took it, feeling its texture; the hand of an aesthete not a workman. His body had a silky texture, too, as though he were lacking an extra skin. She closed her eyes at the memory of his body, trying not to feel betrayed.

'I don't know, Yves. Yes I do. I *would* have married you. I loved you beyond reason; so I would have been irrational.'

'And do you regret it now?' His voice was very low and he used her hand to lever himself to his feet. She flung back her head and met his gaze.

'No. I loved you then and I love you now. I would love to go to bed with you at this moment and feel your bare skin against mine.'

Yves turned away and got a cigarette out of a jade box he had bought on one of his trips to China. His half smoked cigar lay forgotten beside the chair he had vacated. 'Why are you like this tonight? It has been so long since you even . . . why, I thought you had gone off it too.'

Margaret lowered her head and twined her fingers through one another, making and unmaking a steeple. 'Well, there was your attitude and there was Yvonne. I didn't feel like it after she was born. I thought you were being considerate and leaving me alone. But now . . . it has been too long.'

Yves reached for her hand; he was very given to touching, to the fond familiar gesture even if the full sexual act repulsed him. 'I'm sorry, darling. I really am.'

Margaret half rose in her chair as though she intended to embrace him, but the look in his eyes made her sit down again. She felt so desperate for love, for passion, that her other emotion was to hit him, to try and bring home to him what a frantic state he had reduced her to. But she neither embraced him nor struck him; she sat tight in her chair with her legs closely together and her shoulders hunched up. She realized she was cold, and a very faint shudder seemed to travel up from her feet to her heart, striking it with icy darts.

There was a discreet tap on the door, which opened.

'Could I take the things now sir?'

'Of course, Christine.'

Margaret remained immobile in her chair, frightened by her lack of control, the strength of her emotions.

Yves went over to the table and put the plates back on the tray. 'Mrs Lamotte is not hungry, but we'll keep the champagne. Go to bed now, Christine.'

'Yes, thank you, sir. Good-night sir, good-night madam.'

'Good-night Christine.'

They waited until she had shut the door.

'Do you think she was listening?'

Yves shrugged. 'I don't think she's that sort of girl; but servants do hear things. So . . . Come on my darling, you said you were tired.'

'Tired but not sleepy. Too restless. I came home tonight because I hoped to seduce you.'

'Ah, was that it?' Yves smiled as though he found the idea amusing.

'Is there *no* chance Yves, no chance at all? I'm afraid I just don't understand.' Margaret passed her hand across her brow, running her fingers through her hair.

'No chance of my making love to you? Well, not tonight anyway. Like you, I'm tired.'

'Not ever?' She felt desperate; she felt ashamed of herself too for revealing such desire even to her husband. But she couldn't control it. This asexual, uninvolved life of theirs she suddenly realized she found insupportable. It was like acting on the stage; as glittering and as empty as *Cavalcade*. A marriage devoid of real meaning.

'Well, I can't say about *ever*.' He began to turn out the table lights.

'Would it not be a good idea to see a doctor?'

'No it would not!' For the first time he sounded angry. 'I am quite capable. I just don't want to.'

'To be disgusted by something natural is not normal.'

348

'I hear it disgusts a lot of women, who regularly refuse their husbands.'

'A pity it doesn't disgust me.'

'Yes, it is a bit.'

He took her arm and led her out of the dark room, across the hall and up the stairs. She felt they moved like beautifully dressed automata, the metaphor of the stage remaining in her mind. The house was completely silent and then the clock struck one.

'Good Lord, I didn't realize it was so late.'

They stood outside her room, the room she had slept in by herself, since Yvonne had been born, Yves still with his arm through hers. Her desire for him was quite overwhelming, irrational. It threatened, she felt, to disturb her emotional balance. She faced him and tried to kiss him, but he moved his head away. Then she threw her arms violently around his neck and drew his body towards hers. With equal violence he broke her grasp, his strong hands seizing her wrists.

'Margaret, this is ridiculous! Control yourself, please.'

'But Yves, can't you *understand*? I want it, I want you. I need . . .'

'Margaret, if the servants heard you, think how awful you would feel.'

'Yves, *please*.' She gazed at him, she tried to press her lips against his, but the cold icy response told her that, unlike a man, there was nothing she could do. She had not the strength or the power. Husbands could rape their wives – indeed it was not called rape in marriage; it was a duty, part of the marriage vows. But a woman could not force a man to whom she was married to perform an act to which she also had a right. There was no fairness in the world; no equality in sex. She felt herself engulfed in her misery, her grief and humiliation.

Sensing her defeat he drew away from her, smiling down at her with only a mild expression of reproof.

349

'Please don't do that again, Margaret. You will regret all this tomorrow.'

'I regret it now,' Margaret said, her heart suddenly filled with hate at the distant expression on his face. She drew back her hand and struck him with all the force she could muster, and he staggered, momentarily losing his balance. Then very slowly he righted himself, one hand rubbing the cheek she had hit.

He looked at her for a moment, his expression fathomless. She had committed the unforgivable sin: lost control, made a fool of herself. She felt then that she would never restore in his eyes the image he told her he had of her. She would never again be beautiful, aloof and sophisticated; to him her arm would always be poised in the act of striking him, her face contorted like a shrew, a vixen.

His behaviour said more to her then than if he had turned on her and beaten her to pulp, which she wished he had. It would have shown that something moved him, that part of him was as human as she was.

Instead he turned and, without a word, walked along the corridor to his room, pausing for a moment at the threshold, nursing his cheek and gazing at her, before he went in and shut the door quietly behind him.

The tears streamed down her face, over the diamonds he had given her, onto her bosom, prominent and beautiful above the bodice of her gown, a bosom that men, she knew, admired and coveted. But not Yves. She could see herself as he saw her – pathetic, frustrated, a physical woman needing sex, like a woman of the street. She wanted then to raise her voice, to scream, to tear her hair, like the harpy she was, to call to the heavens to witness her humiliation.

And then the rage suddenly left her, as unexpectedly and swiftly as it had come, to be replaced by a feeling of such desolation that she sank to the floor. Careless of the effect on her beautiful dress, she lay there, pressing her face into the soft thick pile of the carpet, kneading it with her fingers as though it were the soft, comforting breast of her long dead mother.

CHAPTER NINETEEN

Margaret opened her eyes, blinking them rapidly, aware at first of a feeling of disorientation. The room was in darkness though she knew it was daylight because the closed shutters had an aura of sunlight. Yet it was not morning; her wakening did not have the fresh sensation of morning. Margaret always woke early and enjoyed the feeling of a fresh, new day. Then she knew. She put out a hand and touched the body of her slumbering lover, who gave a little snore and turned over, his back to her. She leaned on her elbow and rubbed the sleep from her eyes; then she glanced at her watch on the bedside table. It was nearly five.

She was in the bedroom of a hotel in Rue Jacob, on the left bank of the Seine in Paris. It was a rather small room on the third floor, typically French, with a large bed, a huge wardrobe, a basin in one corner and a bidet. She reflected, rather wryly, that a good part of her extramarital sex life had been spent in small hotels where the light was poor, the beds either too hard or too soft and the sanitation sometimes questionable. Still, this time she felt she couldn't really blame herself; she would have been quite happy, loyally and faithfully, to share Yves' bed had he wanted to love her as a husband should.

She shook a cigarette from the packet which belonged to Bob and lit it with his lighter, a large explosive French affair from which a blue light billowed like a blowlamp. Then she propped herself on her pillows and smoked her cigarette, not really thinking, relaxed and at peace.

'What time is it?' Bob muttered.

'Five o'clock. Time to go.'

'Where is Yves arriving?'

'At Gare du Nord. He's coming over on the boat from Dover.'

Bob stirred, shook himself like a dog and sat up, also rubbing sleep from his eyes. On the table by the window were the remains of their lunch: sausage, cold ham, a long French loaf and an empty bottle of Chablis.

'It's rather sordid, isn't it?' Margaret gazed at him.

'What is?'

'This.' She gestured around the room.

'I don't think it's sordid at all. This is rather an expensive hotel.'

'Well, it looks sordid. I feel sordid. I rather like it.'

'Oh Margaret!' Bob heaved himself off the bed and disappeared through the door that led to the small bathroom and toilet. She could hear him loudly relieving himself, then the splashing of water in the basin after the chain was pulled. When he came back he was drying his genitals on a large white towel and, still with the towel in his hand, he lifted the empty wine bottle and frowned.

'I'm thirsty,' he said.

'There is some Perrier by the basin.'

Bob took the bottle from the floor, poured some water into the glass from which he had drunk his wine and came and sat on the bed by her side. He offered her the glass.

'Thanks.' Margaret raised her head, took a drink and leaned back. 'Making love is thirsty work.'

'Making love with you is thirsty work.'

'Oh? Am I not like the others?' She raised an eyebrow.

'You know there aren't any others.'

'I only have your word for it.'

'Then you must trust my word.'

Margaret yawned and closed her eyes. What did it matter anyway? She was not in love with Bob and he was not in love with her, whatever he said. They used each other for mutual convenience. That was what she meant by being sordid. They made love at odd hours in peculiar places, and it was not at all like the polished, sophisticated

353

married woman she felt herself to be. Or perhaps it was, now that she realized that so much on the surface of herself was a veneer. Perhaps this was what she was really like, which was why she enjoyed it so much.

Bob leaned over and kissed her, then drew the sheet back and looked at her breasts, pulling it right down until she was exposed altogether. He ran a hand across her breasts, down over her stomach and around her thighs, caressing them. Then he inserted his hand between her legs.

'Please don't start that again, Bob, or I'll be late.'

'You rouse me terribly you know.' He bent and kissed the place between her legs that was the source of such pleasure, but she pushed his face away.

'I tell you I haven't time.'

'You hardly ever have.'

'Well, nor do you.'

She got up and sat beside him, looking at him. Bob Morgan was a very hairy man, his torso almost covered with hair which then ran from the thick bush at his groin down his legs. He was rather short, dark, thickset and powerful, like a navvy, and she was reminded again of Yves' suggestion that she should get a 'rude mechanical'. Well, Bob was not a mechanical but he was as good as, as far as bed was concerned. He was a very physical man and he awoke a passionate, physical reponse in her, something she had never experienced before, not with Hamish and not with Yves. But once they had made love she felt little affection for him, just repletion. She didn't want to know him any better than she knew him now. She was sure that, had he known about Bob, Yves would have approved; but he didn't know and she wouldn't tell him.

Bob kissed her again and held her breasts but she knew she had to resist, so she jumped off the bed and ran over to the washbasin, pressing down the stopper and drawing hot and cold water. Then she sat on the bidet, turning on the tap and swilling herself between her legs. She stood up in front of the basin, and sluiced her body with water, around her breasts and across her stomach. She was aware that Bob was watching her and, as she raised her arms to rinse her armpits, she could see from the mirror in front of the basin that he was looking at her. She saw him rising and coming over to her, standing behind her and pressing his naked body against hers, cupping her breasts in his big navvy's hands, biting her shoulder with his strong teeth.

Then he got a towel from the wooden rail and wrapped it round her, turning her towards him so that he could kiss her again, rubbing her wet body at the same time. She felt herself drowning in erotic sensation, as was his intention, and she knew that if this went on she would surrender and get back into the bed with him. She pushed him away.

'Bob, *please*! You'll have to run me to the station. The train gets in at seven.'

'I'll meet him, if you like, with you.'

'Don't be silly. Even I am not as shameless as that, coming from a hot bed where I've been making passionate love with my lover to meet my husband. Anyway, we'll see you tonight at dinner. Heinrich Schultz will be there. He has fled from Germany.'

'I know. You've closed the Berlin office?'

'We had to. Almost all our staff were Jewish and after that awful business with the Reichstag fire the Jews are in more danger than ever.'

'But they say it was the Communists.'

'And the Jews. Yves says it was the Nazis themselves. Anyway Heinrich cabled us and we told him to leave at once. Yves is going to try and go to Berlin to see if he can salvage anything; but I doubt that he can. No one wants to be in Germany at the moment.'

Margaret sat on the bed pulling on her stockings and Bob reluctantly started to dress too. When they were ready he drew back the shutters and opened the window, leaving it open to air the room. They took the lift to the ground floor and Bob gave his key to the concierge before escorting her to his hired Citroën in the street outside the hotel.

Margaret had known Bob Morgan for a year. He worked for Quintock & Barnes, the firm which handled the publicity for Dunbar Design, although he wasn't very high up in the hierarchy, and their attraction had been immediate. He was five years younger than she was and unmarried. She had been aware of his interest from the beginning and he knew that she was not averse to him. But he was not on the creative side of the agency and there were few opportunities for them to meet. But gradually Bob made them. Meeting her had served as a spur to his ambition and, from being just a junior account executive handling unimportant clients, he tried to edge his way into the very important new account that had come from the emerging firm of Dunbar. Because he was able and knew what he was doing, Margaret helped him. She enjoyed the game they were playing and the power she had over someone she wanted to sleep with. In the end she suggested he should handle their account and, as a reward, he offered her his body which, as a dog sniffs a bitch on heat, he had known all the time she wanted.

Their affair started in his little flat in Maida Vale, not too far from the Dunbar home. It was convenient to call in there on her way home from work if she were not with Yves, and she was frequently not with Yves after the painful scene when she had practically crawled to him to make love to her, the humiliation of which never left her. From then on she had withdrawn herself, if only to try and salvage a small degree of pride. If he was aware of it he did not show it. Nothing in his manner altered at all; or did it? Was it simply that she no longer gave him the opportunity for any intimacy because, more and more, their life was lived in semi-public as the momentum behind Dunbar Design increased. The days were spent hard at work, and every night was a business or social occasion. Even weekends were geared with an eye to furthering Dunbar and Yves, who knew everybody of importance socially, never refused an invitation which he felt would show some return.

For in the course of that year, 1932/33, Dunbar Design had finally arrived. Ladies of title expressed their eagerness, in the subtlest of ways, to be photographed wearing the exquisite cashmere.

'Anonymous but noble' was one of the slogans accompanying a photograph of a member of the aristocracy in an elegant cashmere dress or twin-set. But most of them did not want to be anonymous. There was a certain cachet in being photographed by the famous photographers, Baron, Vivienne or Oliver Messel for example, with the single word DUNBAR underneath. Sales soared and even the American market was penetrated, despite the depression; the advent of Roosevelt with his promise of a new order now gave fresh hope to all those who had begun to despair. But even in America, as in England, there were always people with money. There were ladies from the American Social Register who were equally anxious to be seen between the covers of *Vogue*, *Harper's* or *Vanity Fair* clothed in cashmere by Dunbar, and many many more anxious to buy them and, above all, to wear them where other rich ladies congregated.

Peter Cartwright's design team expanded. The lease of the entire house in Devonshire Place had been purchased for Dunbar, and the top two floors were devoted to design. New wools were constantly being experimented with, new colours and styles tried; but nothing disturbed the supremacy of cashmere and the Macallister mills in Galashiels and Selkirk had continuous shifts producing the precious yarn. Events in the Far East worried the Dunbars because of the threat of a war between China and Japan; but so far the supply from those remote mountain ranges was uninterrupted.

Now it was the turn of Paris. Here the word 'Design' had a different connotation; it meant to draw, and so a

357

new slogan was found after much thought: '*Dunbar d'Écosse*', Dunbar from Scotland; as though nothing else needed to be said. Through the connections of Yves, members of the French aristocracy had to be held back, so anxious were they to endorse the soft, beautiful cashmere products from Scotland. All the main stores clamoured for the merchandise and Printemps, Galeries Lafayette and Bon Marché had window displays draped in tartan to coincide with the opening of the Paris office and show-room in the Boulevard des Capucins, which was why Margaret and Bob were here, shortly to be joined by Yves and Cullum.

Yet, in the middle of all this, Margaret found time for a lover, needed a lover. Bob Morgan was the reason she felt so fulfilled and relaxed. She looked at him in the driving seat, his blunt sturdy hand that knew all the intricacies of her body on the wheel of the Citroën, his eyes gazing in front of him in that rather dogged way he had. He was not a handsome man, with a rather square face, nondescript thinning hair, an aggressive mouth and a pugilistic chin; but he was attractive; he was sensual. He was essentially a stubborn, unsubtle man; a trier. He worked hard for success, and many in the agency wondered that he'd got as far as he had, for on merit he scarcely deserved it.

They seldom went out to dinner alone or met in private other than to make love. Margaret thought that one day it would not be enough and he would want to leave her, maybe to marry; but she would find someone else. He had given her confidence and she knew that there would always be men who wanted to go to bed with her, and that she had a husband who did not care if she did so long as she was discreet. She was not promiscuous; one lover at a time was all she wanted, and she felt no need to replace Bob provided he toed the line and did not become too possessive or start talking about love.

Bob stopped the car outside the Gare du Nord and looked at his watch.

'You have a quarter of an hour. You look lovely.'

'Thank you, darling.'

She held out her hand, took his and pressed it. She wore a green tailored coat and skirt styled by Chanel and a small close-fitting straw hat with a large orange bow by the side of her left ear. Her hair was hidden under the brim of her hat and she looked as though she wore a mask with her plucked eyebrows, her orange lips and those curiously coloured bewitching eyes.

Bob wanted then to say 'I love you Margaret', but he knew she would laugh. He knew she never thought of love between them, but only sex. They never discussed her husband and he did not know what their relations were. In a way he was a little afraid of Margaret, more than a little in awe; but when he was in bed with her his fear vanished. He felt there that he was masterful and powerful and that she craved him. Making love with her was like a match between two fighters, with neither quite knowing which one was the winner; but it was exciting and stimulating, and he always wanted more.

Margaret, in her direct way, had told him at the beginning she would never be anything more than his mistress, that she loved her husband and wanted to stay married to him; that their life together, their daughter and the business were too important for her ever to want to make a change. He had wanted her so much he scarcely listened to her, unable to believe his good fortune that such a woman wanted him. Even then he was not sure how long it would last and when she got dressed he always watched her closely in case it was for the last time. But surely, just to have a mistress like this was a privilege; more than a privilege for a man who had never been to public school or university, whose father was a clerk in a warehouse and whose family lived in Surbiton.

He could still smell her fragrance as he watched her walk into the Gare du Nord, a tall, slim figure drawing glances from every man she passed; yet two hours before she had lain in his arms.

Wasn't that enough?

Some of the streets in Kentish Town had been built at the time of the Crimean War. They were full of tiny terraced cottages and had such names as Cathcart Street, Raglan Street and Alma Street. Clare Amory lived with her husband Douglas in a street such as this, in a cottage that Douglas had bought after the war when he was invalided home from the front.

When Douglas was well there was no better companion; he was amusing, talkative, inventive, enterprising and thoughtful. He was, moreover, a good lover. But when his depression came on he was like a stranger, and his nature became the reverse of all these things. Sometimes he had to go into hospital and have shock treatment which he feared so much that he would beg Clare not to let them do it. He became like a child again. But she had no choice; she had to let the doctors do what they thought best.

Clare had met Douglas in 1925. He was a photographer and she met him at the Lucie Clayton Model Agency for which she then worked. She was just eighteen and he was thirty-three. He was going through one of his good phases and she had no difficulty falling in love with him because no one was gayer or better company or, in her eyes, better looking than Douglas Amory when he was well.

He didn't tell her about his illness, or the fact that he had been married once already and his wife had left him after the war and taken their child, until after they were married. Like so many victims of neurasthenia, he always hoped for a cure. Every time his depression lifted, he thought that he was better for good. He didn't tell her, in fact, about his past until after his first depression when he was so bad that she thought he had gone out of his mind and he had to be hospitalized.

When her parents found out they said that she had grounds for divorce because she had been so grossly deceived. They were angry that their beautiful talented daughter was married to a mental cripple. But she said she didn't want a divorce. Shell-shock and a head injury had made him ill, and because she loved him so much she would look after him, like any sick person. They had married for better or for worse; now that she knew the worst the only difference it made to Clare, when she knew the truth and the poor prognosis, was that she decided not to have any children. She saw how incapacitated Douglas was when he was ill and she knew that, with him, she had enough to look after and she would also have to be the main breadwinner for the rest of her life.

Since 1930 Douglas had not had work; the depression affected photographers like anyone else and because he was not especially brilliant and not always available he was judged to be expendable. He had been twice in hospital since 1930, directly as a consequence of the depression which seemed to reflect so strongly the state of his own still shell-shocked mind.

Clare on the other hand had done well; she was never short of work and could command the highest fees, sometimes as much as £10 a week while the average wage for a good mannequin was £5 or £6. She got more, too, for photographic work. But out of this she had to buy her own clothes and accessories, had to visit the hairdresser at least twice a week and always had to look smart and well turned out. However, even for a top freelance mannequin work was not always regular. There were seasonal fluctuations and trade was sometimes poor. So when Dunbars made their offer of a fixed post with a large salary she knew she could not refuse; she needed the money too badly because of her many expenses and because of the fact that she had to keep Douglas and their home.

Bruno Macallister had first seen her when she modelled for Isobel, the couturier in Regent Street. He was immediately captivated by her and asked her out. She refused. He knew then what sort of woman she was and he bided his time. When Dunbar Design was created he suggested to Margaret that she should see her and Margaret knew, like him, that the versatile looks of Clare Amory were just right for the Dunbar style: sensual and intimate, or healthy and out of doors. She could adapt herself to whatever the occasion demanded.

Clare told Bruno at the very beginning that she knew what he was after and there was nothing doing. She had a husband and she loved him and she did not believe in mixing work with pleasure. Bruno found her fascinating and planned his strategy accordingly.

Soon after she had started working for Dunbars a call came from the hospital which, to Douglas, was like a second home. Douglas had had a prolonged fit during his shock treatment and was very ill. As it happened Bruno was alone in the office when the call came and he broke the news to Clare himself, offering to drive her there. It was then that he learned for the first time about Douglas and the life Clare led away from the glamour world of fashion.

Douglas recovered, but he was in hospital for three months and, at one time, there was a chance he might never come out. Clare turned to Bruno because of his kindness, his concern and the fact that she felt he understood her. He never asked her to go to bed with him because he was sure that one day she would. If he behaved properly he knew that, inevitably, she would want to. It became to him the most serious love of his life, far surpassing anything he had known before because it was based not on greed or desire or ambition, his foremost emotions before he had known Clare, but on compassion. To him she was the ideal of unselfish, sacrificial womanhood and he loved her for her own sake and not just the prospect of one day having her beautiful body.

Then, inevitably as he had hoped, one day his wish was granted.

When Margaret had seen them at the first night of *Cavalcade* they were already lovers. They had seen her

362

too and they realized how careful they must be, because to have met by chance like that was courting disaster. But there were few opportunities for them to be together. Bruno spent more time in Branswick and abroad and Clare could hardly ever leave Douglas at night when he was home. He knew she never worked at nights.

Thus the absence abroad of Margaret and Yves in the spring of 1933 was an opportunity the lovers could not miss. Yvonne was in France too, staying at Amboise with her grandparents, and the house in Cavendish Avenue was empty except for one of the maids, because Christine and the cook had been given a holiday.

All Margaret's family used the house when they came to London; she had made it clear when she first bought it that it was to be considered the London family home. For one thing it was very large with a number of bedrooms of all sizes running off the different corridors, and it was also very convenient, being only a short taxi ride from Devonshire Place and thus the heart of London. On a fine morning if exercise were called for one could even walk down past Lord's and through Regent's Park to Marylebone Road.

No member of the family was even expected to give notice of his or her arrival. A full staff was kept, the rooms were always clean and the beds aired and the place had the convenience of a hotel with the intimacy and comfort of a private house.

Bruno used it a lot during his frequent trips to London or *en passant* for the Continent or America. He even had his own room with attached bathroom, and he kept spare suits, shoes and underclothes there so that it really was like a second home.

The only thing that bothered him about taking Clare to Cavendish Avenue was the presence of the staff, but that was taken care of by the fact that two were on holiday.

Clare told Douglas that she had to be in Paris for the opening, something he could never check on, and Clare and Bruno spent the kind of week that lovers dream about – alone; attempting to make something normal out of an abnormal situation.

'Will the maid talk?' Clare said on their last night together as they prepared for bed.

'I've given her twenty pounds and told her it's nothing to do with anyone else. Jobs are scarce enough so she doesn't want to get the sack.'

'Twenty pounds! My goodness; that's a small fortune. Supposing she starts blackmailing you?'

'Then she'll be out on the street!' Bruno took off his waistcoat and began unfastening his tie. They had been to see *The Green Bay Tree* at the St Martin's and then dined at Quaglino's. They had agreed that the next day Clare must go because the Lamottes were due back the day after.

Clare had not started undressing but moved restlessly round the room, smoking, managing to look both mysterious and desirable in a long evening dress of rose-coloured chiffon which fell over a straight sheath to the knee, breaking out into a fishtail of frills.

'What are you thinking of, darling?'

'Oh, the play, the food, the Germans, the . . .'

'Us?'

She paused and looked at him. 'Us? I always think of us.'

Bruno put an arm round her shoulder, drawing her down onto the bed. 'What do you think about us?'

'How nice it is to be together.' She rested her head on his shoulder.

'Is that all?'

'Yes.'

'I can't believe it.'

She smiled up at him and his heart turned over as it always did when he was close to her, saw her large black eyes gazing at him. She touched the scar on his cheek and tenderly ran her finger along it from the beginning by his chin to his eye.

'Ours is a "doomed love", as they say,' she declaimed

364

with deliberate theatricality. 'We know it can never be any different. We should be thankful for what we have.'

'You're very philosophical, my darling.'

'I have to be. I've lived with an invalid for eight years. You've a wife you love very much and two children.'

'I *like*; but not love. I have never loved Susan.'

'Then why did you marry her?' Clare looked at him in surprise, her finger still on his cheek.

'Oh darling,' Bruno laughed. 'That's a very naive question. Not everyone is like you; not everyone marries for love. I was almost told to marry Susan.'

'*Told*? By whom?'

'By my father. He wanted an alliance with Dunbar. It was a sort of dynastic thing.'

'But how ridiculous!'

Bruno felt affronted and, gently pushing her away, got off the bed. 'There's nothing ridiculous about it. My father could see a recession coming. He was, and is, a very astute businessman. He knew that with a recession we might not have a market for our yarn, because all the yarn of spinners like us would be competing in a shrinking market. So he thought it would be nice to buy Dunbar, but he knew how the family felt about it. They never spoke again to their lifelong friends the Pendreighs after Pendreigh made an offer for the firm. Besides, he thought it was time I settled down and we knew that Susan, whose fiancé had been killed in the war, was pretty desperate that she might be left on the shelf.'

'Why Susan? Why not Margaret? Surely Margaret was much more beautiful?'

Bruno frowned. He still felt uncomfortable when he thought about that night with Margaret. 'You know what Margaret's like. I didn't fancy sharing my life with that temperament.'

'In fact you didn't love either?'

'No. Margaret was more beautiful, but Susan had a nicer disposition. It was quite easy to hook her. No trouble at all.'

'It sounds very cynical, Bruno.'

He sat on the bed again and drew her into his arms. 'Clare, don't think of it like that. I liked Susan enough to quite fancy the idea of marriage to her. She was goodlooking, sensible, and would make an excellent wife. She has. The pity of it is I hadn't met you. I told you before and I repeat it: I have never ever loved a woman as I love you. I had never been in love until I met you. I grant that I like women and I've had many affairs – before my marriage and after. But I never ever fell in love, truly in love, until I met you. Please believe me.'

Clare didn't need to look into his eyes. She believed him. He had wooed her so constantly, looked after her so tenderly, shown such compassion and, above all, friendship that she knew what he was saying was true. She kissed him. 'Darling Bruno! Of course I believe you; but I feel sorry for Susan. It seems that you haven't behaved at all well there.'

'On the contrary.' He took out his cigarette case and lit two cigarettes, passing one to her. 'On the contrary, I have behaved very well. I think I have made Susan happy; happier than she would have been without a husband. I don't think she would ever have married if I hadn't asked her. There were a lot of single girls around then, and there still are a lot of single women of Susan's age around now. It was a tragedy, but all the men were killed in the war. I'm not boasting, but there were very few of us left.'

'But couldn't you have married for *love*? I find it so distasteful, darling.'

'But I did love Susan, after a fashion. My father said I would love her more after we were married and it was true. I did. But I've never been *in* love with her as I am *in* love with you. I've never ever felt passionately about Susan. You torment me, I can't get you out of my mind. That's being *in* love.'

'Darling, I don't know what you call it.' Clare draped one arm round his neck and gazed into his eyes. 'I'm terribly sleepy and if we don't go to bed now we may not be able . . .'

Bruno, seized by desire for her, almost maddened by grief at the thought of losing her, threw her roughly down beside him on the bed and tenderly, clumsily, frantically began to undo the complicated fastenings of her couturier dress.

'I love you wild, like this,' Clare murmured, closing her eyes in ecstasy. 'Forget about the buttons.' Then, arching herself, she pulled her dress high up over her waist, tearing it asunder at the knee and, grasping him firmly by the arms, pulled him down on top of her.

CHAPTER TWENTY

Margaret went straight from the station to her house, taking a cab from Victoria. Yves had gone to Berlin because of the troubles in Germany and they had left Bob Morgan, Cullum and Dora Rowntree to tie up the threads of the opening week. Margaret had had a cold and wanted to get home.

The maid Peggy was surprised to see her as she opened the door.

'Oh madam,' she said bobbing, 'you wasn't expected back until tomorrow or the day after.'

'I know Peggy; but I have an awful cold. Or rather I had, the sea air seems to have cleared it.'

The cab driver came up the steps with Margaret's bags and she tipped him and thanked him.

'Run me a bath, Peggy, will you? The train makes one feel so filthy. How is everything?'

'Alright, madam.'

'Good.'

Margaret swept into the hall and riffled through the post on the hallstand. There was a pile of letters and there would be more at the office.

Peggy ran upstairs and Margaret followed her, going straight towards her bedroom at the far end of the house, the one she used to share with Yves when they were first married. She was surprised to find sheets outside the door of one of the spare rooms, and she paused in the act of taking off her hat. The door was half open and there were cases on the floor, articles on the dressing table. Above all, there was a strong fragrance of a vaguely familiar perfume.

With her hat in her hand Margaret walked slowly to the

dressing table, looking at the contents, and then at the half-packed open suitcases on the floor. A long rose-coloured chiffon dinner dress, badly torn at the knee, hung on the wardrobe. Margaret turned round and saw Peggy standing at the door, her face pink with confusion.

'What is this Peggy? Visitors?'

'Mr Macallister has been here, madam.'

'And *Mrs* Macallister?'

Margaret went swiftly out of the room, motioning Peggy to follow her. Once in her bedroom she removed her coat and skirt, giving them to Peggy who put them on a hanger. Then she sat in front of her dressing table, taking her make-up off with cotton wool soaked in Ardena.

'Did you start the bath, Peggy?'

'Yes'm.'

'Thank you. That's all then.'

'Would you like breakfast, madam?'

'Just coffee please. In about a quarter of an hour.'

'Yes madam.' Peggy hovered.

Margaret looked round. 'Is there something else Peggy?'

'About Mr Macallister, madam . . .'

'Peggy, I'm asking no questions. After all, it's hardly my business, is it? Or yours?'

'No, madam.'

Peggy withdrew backward, her hand over her face, suppressing a nervous giggle.

'I suppose you bribed the girl,' Margaret said. 'Anyway I wouldn't demean myself, or you, by asking her questions. I just wish you had found somewhere else to do it.'

Like a hotel, Margaret thought. She would never have taken Bob to the flat in the Avenue Foch if empty. This was what disgusted her; the blatancy of it all.

'I'm sorry, Margaret, what more can I say?' Bruno felt like a small boy, sitting there in front of her. She was

369

standing, leaning against the side of his desk, her arms folded.

'Bruno, I warned you some time ago that you couldn't have an affair with a member of our staff. Did I not say that after I saw you both at *Cavalcade*?'

'We had already begun our affair then.'

'So I thought, and I hoped you would have taken it as a warning.'

'Why should *you* warn me, Margaret? What business is it of yours?' He glared at her, hostility overtaking his previous embarrassment.

'It is every bit my business,' Margaret said, 'as I told Yves. You are my brother-in-law and Clare is not only our employee but a married woman. The scandal if this got out would be terrible.'

'That's all you care about, scandal, isn't it Margaret?'

'No.' Margaret unfolded her arms and sat opposite him, stiffly erect in a high wooden-backed chair. 'I care about Dunbars, passionately. And I care about my family and the happiness of its members.'

'Happiness!' Bruno laughed. 'By pushing Cullum and Fleur back together do you consider you made them happy?'

Margaret's eyes flashed. 'We all agreed.'

'*You* agreed, Susan and Juliet and *you* agreed. I had nothing to do with it.' Bruno got up so that he stood over her. 'I kept right out of it.'

'Because you felt vulnerable. You had affairs with other women. Oh, don't think I didn't know! The sight of you tearing round after the mannequins after each fashion show was pathetic. Moreover, knowing you Bruno Macallister, I never thought you capable of fidelity; that was why I was so sorry you married my sister.'

'What do you mean, *knowing* me?'

Margaret flushed. 1920 was a long time ago; but she still remembered that humiliating night after the ceremony at the Cenotaph. 'I knew what a base sort of person you

370

were, incapable of fine feelings. You once tried to seduce me on Armistice Day and don't think I ever forgot it.'

'You brooded on it until *now*?' Bruno looked incredulous. 'You let it . . . all these years!'

'Oh don't be silly.' Margaret crossed and uncrossed her legs impatiently. 'I scarcely ever think about it; but it was quite a traumatic thing for me, so how could I ever forget it? I was young but you weren't. You should have known better. Then, as I grew older and knew more about the world, I realized that quite a lot of men are like you; but I was still sorry you'd married Susan. I've always found it difficult to like you.'

'And I you.'

'I know.' Margaret nodded. 'There has always been that constraint between us, has there not? But we've managed very well.' She got up and began to walk round his desk, her hands on her hips. 'We've never referred to the past and we've built a good business together. Dunbars is as much your creation as mine, and you have been generous to me in your tributes. I am grateful to you, Bruno. Please don't spoil it now.'

'I am very serious about Clare.'

'I thought you might be. Clare is no ordinary person. But has she not an invalid husband?'

'Oh there is no chance of marriage; she will never consider it. I just wanted you to know that this was no light flirtation. It's something big and important for both of us.'

'What a pity, then, you made it so sordid by fornicating in my house.'

'Oh Margaret, don't use that word!'

'Fornication, I said,' Margaret spoke very slowly, 'and fornication I meant.'

When Bruno hit her he realized he was returning the blow she had administered to him thirteen years before wounding both his pride and his *amour propre*. She staggered, catching her heel in the rug by his desk, and fell

371

headlong on the floor. As she fell she struck her temple on one corner of the desk; whether or not she passed out for a moment or two she did not know, except that she was then aware of two people on the floor kneeling by her. One of them was Clare Amory, who had her hand at the back of Margaret's head trying to raise her head.

'Bruno, what *have* you done?' Margaret heard her say. 'She's bleeding.'

'Oh Christ, call a doctor.'

Margaret struggled to sit up. She felt nauseous and she was aware of the sensation of something wet on her cheeks. She touched it and saw that her fingers were covered with blood.

'Don't call a doctor,' she said shakily. 'It's just a flesh wound.' She tried to smile and, getting her handkerchief from her pocket, dabbed at her cheek. Then, Bruno taking one arm and Clare another, they gently helped her up into Bruno's chair. Bruno was so white-faced that Margaret thought he, not she, would be the ambulance case.

'I don't know how I can begin to apologize . . . ' Bruno said, but Margaret waved a hand.

'Oh don't try. It was partly my fault. Fornication is a very emotive word. I provoked you.'

'Fornication . . .?' Clare stood upright.

'We were talking about you, Clare.' Margaret looked at her. 'I'm afraid that the conversation got out of control.'

'*You* were talking about fornication, Mrs Lamotte?'

'Yes.' Margaret's gaze faltered. 'It's an ugly word, isn't it? Very biblical. There, I'm alright now. Perhaps one of you would fetch some warm water in a bowl and I'll deal with the damage to my face?' As they both made for the door, she said, 'You go, Bruno. I'll explain to Clare.'

Bruno looked reluctant, but turned obediently on his heel and closed the door. Margaret pointed to a chair. 'Do sit down Clare and let's try and be civilized about this. I happened, completely by chance, to find out that you have spent the last week in my house. I returned two days early and the maid was turning out Bruno's room. Of course I at once recognized your clothes and your make-up. You must realize Clare, that much as I like and admire you I cannot tolerate something like this. Bruno is not only my sister's husband, but the joint managing director of our business.'

'But how can a private relationship concern *you*, Mrs Lamotte?'

'Please call me Margaret as you usually do.' Margaret offered her a cigarette. 'As I said, I'm trying to be as civilized about this as I can.'

'But it's none of your business.'

'Yes, it *is* my business. I told Bruno it was my business; the business of us all. We cannot tolerate relations like this with employees and I am afraid I'll have to ask for your resignation. I'm sure you'll have no difficulty in finding another job.'

The door opened quietly and Bruno closed it again carrying a bowl of water carefully in one hand.

'There,' he smiled as though some magic might have transformed the situation he had left.

'I've told Clare she must resign, Bruno.'

'Clare resign? Are you crazy?'

'I think *you're* crazy, Bruno, you and Clare.' Margaret took her compact from her handbag and carefully inspected her face in the mirror. 'It's not too bad, just a little cut by the hair-line. Thank goodness for that. Now, what were we saying? Oh yes. About Clare; she will have to go.'

'Supposing *I* go?'

'Don't be silly.' Margaret looked at him with contempt. 'You have well over a million pounds of Macallister money tied up in the business and you are its managing director. Whether or not you want to pursue your affair after Clare leaves *is* none of my business; but while she is an employee it is. I hope you will think of Susan and your

373

family and give her up completely. In fact, I think you should spend some more time in Branswick, especially if we introduce the men's line.'

There was some controversy about whether Dunbars should go as heavily into men's fashions as it had into women's. For once, Margaret had no very fixed views about it. If they did, more plant would have to be acquired and Bruno's presence in Branswick would become even more necessary.

'All in all I think everything is working out for the best. You've had your fling and now it's over.'

'It is by no means over,' Bruno said. 'I have not the slightest intention of giving up Clare.'

'I see.' Margaret sat back and studied her face, cleansed and now with fresh powder, rouge and lipstick on it. The results seemed to satisfy her. She snapped her compact shut and put it back in her bag. She wore a beige coat and skirt with a dark brown tie blouse; her very high heeled shoes were made of lizard skin, a present from Yves from the Rue de Rivoli to celebrate the French opening, together with a matching lizard skin handbag. She joined her fingertips together and studied her carefully varnished nails. 'Clare, have you considered the scandal it might cause? Have you considered what would happen if Susan were to divorce Bruno, and then your husband divorced you? "Famous London Mannequin in Divorce Scandal." How would it look in the papers, with a view to your getting another job? Employers are *very* particular about the respectability of their mannequins.'

'Are you threatening us, Margaret?' Bruno took a few steps towards her as though he wanted to strike her again.

'No I am not. I would never dream of telling Susan. But what about the girl Peggy? Susan comes here quite a lot; what about all the people who must know? Susan is bound to find out, if she doesn't have suspicions already.'

'But Susan would never divorce me!'

'Can you be so sure?' Margaret again looked contemp-

374

tuously at him. 'Susan has her pride too. She is, after all, a Dunbar. I think Susan would be very disgusted to hear how long Clare has been your mistress.'

'I don't want Bruno to be divorced,' Clare said quietly. 'It may surprise you to know this, Margaret, because I can see how much you despise me, but I love my husband very much. A divorce might hospitalize him for good. I certainly don't want to be cited as co-respondent in a court of divorce.'

The expression on Margaret's face softened and she put out a hand to touch Clare's arm. 'I'm sorry Clare. Believe me, I don't mean to be cruel. I'm thinking of the happiness of everyone concerned.'

'I find that hard to believe, Margaret,' Clare said bitterly. 'All you think of is appearances. How much do people know, what do they see? Never mind what goes on underneath, eh?' A crimson flush slowly spread up Clare's cheeks and Margaret looked at her in surprise.

'What do you mean "goes on underneath"? I'm not trying to hide anything.'

'Aren't you?'

Suddenly Margaret thought of Bob and her hand started to shake so much that she clutched the seat of her chair. Did people know about her and Bob? She closed her eyes and opened them again, aware of a sharp pain at her temple where the desk had struck her. She shook her head, but avoided Clare's eyes.

'Not that I know of.'

There was a shadow over her and Clare stood about six inches away from her, her finger pointing menacingly.

'What is it the Bible says about the whited sepulchre? Or the beam in one's own eye? You mean to say that all these years you haven't known about your husband? That you can condemn Bruno and me for mere adultery, when your husband . . . At least ours is a *normal* relationship.' Clare abruptly collapsed into a chair, the accusing hand limp by her side.

Bruno went over to her and knelt by her, rubbing her hand between his. 'Clare, darling, what on earth . . .?'

'I want to hear what she means,' Margaret said quietly. 'Let her speak, Bruno.'

'I'm sorry.' Clare shook her head. 'If you don't know, it's not fair.'

'But I want to know.' Margaret, feeling suddenly more composed, stood up and went to pour a cup of coffee from the pot that stood on the central table. It was cold, but it was black and strong. She raised the cup to her mouth and looked at Clare. 'I do want to know. Yves is having an affair? With whom?'

'I thought you must know.'

'Well, I don't. Pray enlighten me.' Margaret finished the bitter dregs and grimaced.

'Peter Cartwright.'

Outside there was the sound of a horn in the street, and angry voices. With the slow, mechanical movements of an automaton, Margaret went to the window and looked out. A man had got out of a taxi and another was getting out of a car into which the taxi had nearly collided. They were shaking their fists at each other. People got worked up about such silly things, she thought.

'Peter Cartwright? I don't really understand. What has Peter Cartwright got to do with all this?'

Clare, her anger gone, looked incapable of speech. Her hand flapped in front of her.

'Peter Cartwright and Yves . . . Oh I see.' Margaret sat down again and fumbled for a cigarette from the box on Bruno's desk. 'You mean Peter Cartwright and Yves . . . have a relationship?'

'I thought you *must* know.' Clare looked desperate.

'How could I know?' She looked wonderingly at Bruno, who avoided her eyes. 'I never thought Yves . . . I didn't know. I never imagined.'

'I'll send for more coffee,' Bruno said, but Margaret held up her hand.

'Please don't. I can see now why Clare is very angry. She thought I knew, and Peter Cartwright is an employee.'

'I feel very ashamed,' Clare said hanging her head. 'It must be a terrible shock.'

Margaret nodded slowly. 'It is a terrible shock, as you say. On the other hand it explains so much. No, I never for a moment suspected . . .'

'Forget about it,' Bruno said looking anxiously at Clare. 'Let's forget all of this.'

'Oh Bruno don't be so absurd!' Margaret lit the cigarette she held in her hand and blew out the flame. 'We can't forget any of this. What's been said in this room today has transformed all our lives. You must think me very naive, but I never suspected. Did *you* know, Bruno?' She looked at him almost as a suppliant.

'No, I didn't, I swear. I'd have knocked the fellow down if I'd have known. What a disgusting carry on! Are you *sure*, Clare?'

'Peter Cartwright told me himself, because he often wondered if Margaret knew. He was very jealous of her. He said he thought she must have realized because Yves is quite open about it at times.'

Yes, now she could recall the number of occasions she had seen them together, Yves with his arm round Peter's shoulders or chatting intimately, heads almost touching, in the corner of some room. But Margaret had never in her life come directly across homosexuality; she was hardly aware of its existence. The only person who had ever talked about it quite openly was Olga Pasalaris and, remembering some of her friends, Margaret thought now that she knew why. None of them were at all like Yves; so how could she suspect her husband, of all people, to whom the sexual act was so disgusting? But only with women apparently. Why had Yves never told her? Never tried to explain? She had given him plenty of opportunity.

Margaret rose, extinguishing her half smoked cigarette

in an ashtray. There was so much to do: buyers to see, people to meet, a business to run, but, above all, appearances to keep up.

'I'll have to think about all this,' she said. 'We really can't take up any more time discussing it. Bruno, do you think two-ply for the men's cashmere? And should we adopt the same style of advertising or go for the sporty image?'

Clare looked at Bruno, and then at Margaret. Margaret impatiently stubbing out her cigarette, her mind turned to matters of business.

She had never known a woman like her.

CHAPTER TWENTY ONE

Margaret sat in the Buick as Yves came out of the station, suave and elegant in a grey cashmere coat, made in Savile Row using cloth woven in Scotland from yarn supplied by Macallisters. On his head he wore a black Homburg made for him by Locks, the hatters in St James's Street. He looked so handsome, so in control, that Margaret felt a consuming sense of despair about what she had to say. If only they could be like any other husband and wife, any normal, loving husband and wife . . .

She hooted the horn and waved, and his face broke into a smile; he indicated to the porter that he should take his cases to the large brown car parked outside the station. He walked leisurely over to Margaret, a cigarette between his lips. Before he got into the car he threw it on the pavement, stood on it, and then removed his hat before leaning over and kissing her.

'Darling, how sweet of you to come!'

'I've only just arrived, I thought I'd miss you. The traffic is terrible.'

'Something will have to be done about it. They say there is now automatic traffic control in Trafalgar Square.'

Yves, always up to date with the news, disappeared behind the car giving instructions to the porter. Then he climbed in beside her, tossed his hat in the back seat, leaned back and sighed.

'Oh God, what a journey! There are thousands of Jews trying to leave Germany. They're actually smuggling them on the train. Jews all over Paris; I can't tell you how pathetic the poor souls are with their hopeless faces and remnants of luggage.'

'It's perfectly dreadful. And the Berlin office?' Margaret put the car into gear and eased it out of Victoria station towards Grosvenor Place.

'No possibility of reopening. Germany is in a furore. You know that Hitler polled forty-four percent of the poll in the German elections? There's now a decree ousting all Jews who hold official positions.'

'I know, I read about it. Anyway, thank God, Heinrich and his family are all safe. He'll be invaluable in the Paris office.'

'Vienna is in a turmoil, just as bad as Berlin. No chance of opening there. In fact I think the German and Austrian markets are finished for the moment. Maybe Hitler will do something about the economic situation; there are still about four million people unemployed. And people have to carry their marks around in cases just to pay for a cup of coffee.'

'You think that will justify what he is doing to the Jews?' Margaret shot him a glance as she crossed Grosvenor Place.

'Of course I don't, darling! But what's happening in Germany has been brought about directly by the consequences of the war . . .'

'Which they started, don't forget.'

'I don't, but the reparations demanded of them were punitive. We never let them recover their economy. They were desperate. Hitler is supported by the professional and middle classes ruined by the war, as well as the unemployed. He has a very wide spectrum of support, that's the most surprising thing. I don't excuse Hitler, please don't think that; but . . .'

'Oh don't let's talk about it, Yves. It's too sickening. Is everything alright in Paris?'

'Everything is fine. Bob Morgan came back yesterday and Cullum, I believe, comes back tomorrow. He seems rather to enjoy Paris; a change from all his domestic worries at home.'

'Cullum is not the only one with domestic worries at home.'

'Oh!' Yves, startled, looked at her as she turned into

Hyde Park. 'Do other people have domestic worries? Not you, I hope, darling. Are the servants all right?'

Margaret didn't reply. She drove along the carriage road which ran parallel to Knightsbridge, and then turned right towards the Serpentine. It was a lovely spring day and she had the hood down, her face flushed by the breeze. She was aware of Yves gazing at her.

'You look extraordinarily beautiful today, darling.' His expression turned to one of surprise as she parked by the lake. 'Why are we stopping?'

Margaret put on the brake and turned to look at him. She wore a leather driving coat and had on a matching check beret and scarf. She put an arm languidly across the back of his seat, cultivating an air of apparent calm to hide her nerves. 'I thought we should talk.'

'Here?' He looked around.

'It's as good as anywhere. The servants can't hear.'

'Is it as personal as that?'

'Yes.'

'Oh.' Yves leaned back and groped for his cigarette case. Behind him the trees in the park were almost in full leaf and a few couples strolled about arm in arm. Children played near the lake watched over by solicitous mothers or nannies. It was a very calm, familiar, English scene. It was so difficult to think that in Germany Jews were being stoned in the street and opponents of Hitler herded into concentration camps. Yves offered her a cigarette but she shook her head. He blew smoke into the sky and then smiled at her. 'You're being *very* mysterious. I hope it's not something unpleasant?'

'It depends which way you look at it. I personally think it's disgusting.'

'Oh?' His eyes rounded.

Now that the time had come Margaret found herself in difficulties and knew that, despite her attempts at control, the tone of her voice bordered on the hysterical. 'I know about Peter Cartwright . . .' The lump in her throat made her feel she was choking and she could not go on.

Yves said nothing for a moment. He sat there smoking, looking past her, apparently regarding the calm sunny waters of the Serpentine. 'Who told you?' he said at length.

'Never mind who told me. Why didn't *you* tell me?'

'Did Peter tell you?'

'No.'

'Ah. I'm glad of that. He made me a promise . . .'

'He made you a promise! What about the promise *you* made to *me* at our wedding: to love and to cherish, to be faithful unto death?'

Yves glanced at her and smiled. 'Well, darling, you made promises too.'

'But that has nothing to do with it! I can't understand how you can be so calm, Yves. As far as I understand it, and I must say I find it difficult to believe, you had a relationship with Peter Cartwright *before* we were married.'

'Yes.' Yves leaned his head back on the leather seat and closed his eyes. His face looked very peaceful.

'Do you realize, Yves, you have blatantly and consistently lied to me from the day we met? Your lack of passion always worried me; yet I accepted your explanation that your sexual drive wasn't very strong. You asked me once if it would have made a difference, if I'd known that, to our marriage and I said it wouldn't. Now I can tell you this: had you told me you were homosexual I would never have married you.'

'Are you sure?' He had opened his eyes wide and looked at her ingenuously.

'Of course I'm sure!'

'I'm not. You wanted to change me, as it was. I was a challenge. You found out I wasn't much good in bed the very first time, at the house. Remember?'

'Oh I remember.' Margaret leaned back and studied her hands on the driving wheel. 'I remember very well.'

'You thought I would change and become more passionate, didn't you?'

'It was the first time. I imagined you were nervous; I was.

382

I thought our *mutual* technique would improve. I loved you enough to hope it would. The funny thing is that it did, to a certain extent. When one had the opportunity, that is.'

'If I had told you I was bisexual, which I am, liking both men and women, you would have hoped to tip the scales permanently onto the side of women. I know you, Margaret. You wanted me and you were determined to have me.'

'To some extent that's true,' Margaret concurred. 'But I don't know that I'd have gone all the way had I known the truth. Most normal people are disgusted by the thought of relations with members of one's own sex. Besides, I can't understand.' She looked at him rather helplessly. 'I simply can't understand it at all.'

'What can't you understand? That I loved you? Can't you understand that?'

'How can you love me when you love a . . . *man*!'

'Dear Margaret,' Yves' voice had the patient tone of one explaining something quite simple to a backward child, 'you are *so* conventional and I expected differently of you. Some people can love men *and* women. I tried to tell you that.'

'Not before we were married.'

'No, possibly not.' Yves looked thoughtful. 'Well, it was hardly the time, was it? But I did love you. I was besotted by you and I wanted to marry you.'

'I was like a beautiful *thing*; not flesh and blood.'

'Well, put it how you like.' Yves shrugged. 'It does depend on how you see beauty. I can always admire it, whether in a man or a woman. Can't you?'

'Please don't talk to me like that. I think it's horrible.'

'Well, you shouldn't . . .'

'Yves, it destroyed our marriage.' Margaret felt close to tears, struggling in the void of his lack of comprehension. 'I wanted a man to love me, to love me in bed. All I got from you . . .'

383

'I know, that was not very successful. I thought it would be better because you were so lovely, in many ways like a beautiful boy, when I first met you with your short hair and mannish clothes.' Yves made as if to touch her, but she moved towards the door. There was a nostalgic look in his eyes. 'What funny days they were, weren't they, with women trying to look like men? Well, I must say, they succeeded. I found you very fascinating; but you were, as you say, a woman and I found I could not love you as you wanted. I did in fact have affairs with women, quite a number, when I was young – older married women, on the whole – but I found increasingly that I was attracted to men. The war brought it about mainly. Comrades in arms spend a lot of time together.'

'Were you ever Tristan's lover?'

'Oh no!' He put a hand placatingly on her arm. 'But of course Tristan knew about me liking men. That's why I suppose he tried to warn you off marrying me. He did try and warn you, didn't he?'

'Yes, I suppose he did; but he put it in a very roundabout way. He merely said I didn't *know* you; if anything, the hint was that you were marrying me for my money.'

'Outrageous!' Yves leaned back censoriously, folding his arms, his mouth pursed in disapproval. He sighed deeply. 'What a little pervert that man is! Oh well, I suppose it's his nature. I forgive him. No, Margaret, you must believe me that I wanted to marry you because I was attracted to you, I loved you and, as the years have gone by, that love and admiration have increased. I think we are a very harmonious pair; we work well together and I like to think I have made my contribution to the success of Dunbars.'

'Oh you have.'

'Well then? Why break something that works so well?'

'I don't want to break it. I want you to break with Peter.'

Yves loosened the cashmere scarf at his neck as though

384

he were hot, although the longer they sat in the open car the colder it had become. 'Darling, that's ridiculous! I don't have a *physical* relationship with Peter and I have not for many years. What I told you about my physical distaste for sex goes for men too. I love Peter in a very spiritual way, as I love you.'

'I don't like being loved spiritually.'

'A lot of people would think it was better than the other thing. It's truer and deeper. If you grew old or lost your looks I would still love you. I can't imagine someone like Bruno being able to say that. Can you?'

Margaret grimaced and avoided meeting his eyes. She knew that in his way he was being sincere, but that he simply couldn't comprehend how she felt.

'Seriously I can't,' Yves continued. 'I am not Peter's lover but I am deeply fond of him. It would be ridiculous to try and change that. For one thing we scarcely ever see each other, as you know. It's not as though we go holing off to bed every time we meet like some people I can think of. Peter was very upset when I married you because he was jealous; but his feeling for you now has quite transcended that and he understands.'

'How kind.'

'Don't be such a cynic, darling; it doesn't suit you. We are all older and wiser than we were in 1928, and happier too, I like to think. Bisexual people are never very happy, you know; they're always trying to conform and never succeeding. But I am much happier than I was and I owe that to you. I don't have sordid little affairs with men and I want you to believe that. I'm happy with our marriage and I adore our daughter, as you know. I would have liked a son but I respected your wishes not to have more children.'

'That was said impulsively after Yvonne's birth. I would do anything now to resume my love life with you.'

She looked him full in the face and he averted his eyes, staring fixedly at the gleaming walnut dashboard.

'Darling, we might have six daughters! Think of that. What a bore. Please try and understand, Margaret; try and have a little pity for me in that large, generous heart of yours.'

'My heart feels cold,' Margaret said, looking straight ahead. Her cheeks glowed and the tip of her nose was slightly pink with the cold. 'And bitter. All these years I have not been happily married and at last I know why.'

'You're being very silly, Margaret.' A note of impatience entered Yves' voice. 'You have a lot to be grateful for. Our marriage is good and enduring in a way that many other marriages are not. Besides, I believe you do not altogether lack that which you value. You told me once how important passion is to you and I suggested, you may remember, that in that case you should take a lover.' Yves flicked one of the little curls that surrounded her beret and gently touched the top of her head with his palm. 'And you did. *I* am not jealous, so why should you be? What on earth have you to complain about – a lover, I hope a good one, and a fond, caring husband? Isn't it more than most women could wish for?'

Margaret jerked her head out of reach of his hand. Her face had gone scarlet, her eyes very bright now as she stared at him.

'How do you know I took a lover?'

'Because everyone knows.'

'Everyone knows?' Her voice was scarcely audible.

'Of course, darling! This is a very gossipy business. You think that that suburban little stud, Bob Morgan, could keep something like that to himself? Getting the elegant, beautiful, *detached* Margaret Dunbar Lamotte between the sheets? I must say I was a bit disappointed in you, darling. I did not mean *such* a "rude mechanical". He is very, very vulgar; but perhaps he's good in bed and that, as far as you are concerned, is the main thing.'

Margaret visualized suddenly Bob's thick, hirsute, naked body and she felt she wanted to retch over the side of the car. Then she had a vision of him as she had seen him the last day in Paris when he took her to the station, standing waving in his double-breasted blue striped suit, which seemed a shade too large, and wide American-style trilby, smoking a cigarette. Yes, vulgar was the word; very vulgar indeed. '*Everyone* knew?' she whispered again.

'Well, most people. Clare Amory knew. I don't think Bruno knew unless she told him. I'm sure Dora Rowntree knew, and lots of people in the business knew. Or guessed. Lots.' He looked at her and smiled. 'But don't be so ashamed, darling. Only, if you do choose another lover, pick one with a little more style; one not quite so common. I mean a real labourer, if you like, with sweaty hands and smelly feet and armpits, or a man with a little more class, more style. I don't think I've ever heard Bob say one intelligent, interesting thing; on the other hand you didn't pick him for that did you?'

'You make it sound so disgusting,' Margaret said.

'But then you made me and Peter sound so disgusting, and it isn't, or wasn't. Who knows what beauties you found in the body of little Bob Morgan . . . '

'Please don't, Yves. Stop.'

'Alright I'll stop. I'm glad we talked because I was getting sick of him. Peter is beautiful and a genius. Bob is not at all attractive, I don't think anyway, and not even very good at his job. He's clumsy. Everyone knew why you wanted him to take our account, but I never thought it was wise. But with you at the helm, controlling everything, it was never really all that important. He was just another functionary, like that nice new chap we have to open the door in Devonshire Place. I hope Quintock & Barnes will sack him and send him elsewhere. That's if you don't mind.'

'I never want to see him again.'

'Good. I thought you might feel like that once you knew the secret was public knowledge. Oh *quite* public, I assure you. Try and be a little more circumspect next time around sweetie.'

'I hate you, Yves.'

'No you don't. You feel humiliated. You'll get over it in time, as you always do. Now . . .' Yves reached in the back of the car for his hat and put it on his head. 'I'm a bit chilly, darling, aren't you? Shall we find somewhere nice for a spot of lunch?' He put a hand on her shoulder and patted it. 'Come on, old thing, cheer up! We've all still got a lot to learn, haven't we? Now, where shall we go? If only there were an R in the month we could have oysters.'

CHAPTER TWENTY TWO

In August in Scotland the sun, when there was sun, could be very hot. This was such a day; in the early morning the valley had been covered in a heat haze and when she got up early, as she always did, Margaret couldn't see the loch at the bottom of the hill. But now at eleven the mist had cleared, the sun shone out of that almost violet Scottish sky and Margaret wanted to be out of doors. She had made the twin beds that had replaced the large double bed in the bedroom; she had washed up the breakfast dishes and tidied the kitchen, and now she had finished sweeping through with the thick broom while the sun beckoned through the open door. She took a large mug of freshly brewed coffee, put on a big straw hat and flopped into the comfortable cane chair outside the door where, early in the morning, she had sat drinking her first cup of tea of the day, inhaling the sweet, fresh smells that came from the dew-drenched grass.

Yvonne, playing nearby, came running over to her, the little Scottish terrier Jock, a present from Fleur, at her heels.

'Mummy, Mummy are you going to play?'

'Oh darling, let me sit for a while. Auntie Fleur will soon be here with Morag and we'll have a lovely picnic for lunch.'

Yvonne reached up trustingly for a kiss and then scampered away again, Jock running before her. She was a lovely child, her pale complexion tanned by the sun, her black curly hair tousled like a gypsy's. How Margaret loved her; how, now that she had got to know her, she missed those years of infancy when she had scarcely seen her. Certainly she had not known her. Margaret felt she had only been a proper mother to her daughter during the past year, and she wondered if she regretted all those years when she had been so busy building up Dunbars that Yvonne had been a peripheral part of her life, a small appendage seen only twice a day like some Victorian child, brought in for a kiss and a cuddle before being taken up to her nursery again, and tucked safely out of sight.

Did she regret it? Margaret lay back in the chair and shielded her eyes from the glare, tipping the brim of the straw hat over her face. Certainly she regretted not knowing Yvonne, scarcely being aware of her progress from babyhood to being a toddler. When did Yvonne take her first steps? She didn't know. When exactly did she say her first words? She couldn't remember. But, for the rest, it was difficult to say whether one regretted the past or not, because the past was the past, it was over and done. If she had one abiding regret it was the way that part of her life had ended; the dreadful humiliation of Yves' revelation that her affair with Bob was public knowledge, the realization that people maybe pitied and despised her, knowing that despite her glamour she was a woman as mortal as everyone else, prey to the same elemental passions and prone to the same mistakes. Had she got to know herself then; to see herself as seen by others? Had she liked what she saw?

No she hadn't; emphatically she had not. In retrospect those moments of passion seemed coarse not beautiful, her liaison with Bob Morgan shabby not noble. It was not one of the great love affairs of that or any age – no Antony and Cleopatra, no Abélard and Héloïse, about Margaret Dunbar Lamotte and Bob Morgan. How people must have sniggered, imagining her furtive couplings with common, rather shaggy, hairy little Bob.

The chagrin she experienced then had changed her life, sending her north to Branswick, to her home where the rivers met: where she had always known the truth lay, and where she would find her real self.

At first, she had wanted to resign and abandon Dunbar altogether, perhaps go abroad, to Italy or the South of France. But Europe was a restless place then as it was now and Yves, although anxious to comply with her desire to get away, courteous and charming as always, had been unhappy about her going too far from home and taking their daughter with her. He had suggested she stay with his parents, but she couldn't bear that: couldn't bear for them to know what a mockery her marriage had become. Besides, had they not deceived her too? Had they not known all those years that their son was not like other men, or at least suspected it? No wonder they were all relieved when he married; no wonder they had made such a fuss of his intended bride! They were just as culpable in this deception as he had been.

Were they disappointed that he only had a daughter? Or did they still hope for an heir to the Château of Lamotte? The thought was ironic. She had never really known the truth about Yves and she felt now that she never would. Why *had* he married her? How wealthy had he *really* been? Perhaps the Hispano-Suiza had not after all belonged to him, because she never saw it again, and when he came to London everything to do with the house came from her. Unmercenary then as she was now, she had been too emancipated to talk about marriage settlements, and his financial affairs were, and remained, a mystery to her. He had worked hard, it was true, he had earned his director's fees; but he had traded on his name and his flair, rather than any real business ability, to advance the advertising campaign that had established Dunbar in the first rank of knitted goods.

She saw Fleur's car coming round the loch, a baby Austin that Fleur preferred to the large dangerous affairs that Cullum liked to drive. Fleur would have a basket of good things to eat and maybe a bottle of wine for them to share over lunch. She got up to welcome her sister-in-law, who had become her closest friend during her year of exile at Branswick.

Yvonne saw the car too and started to run down the dirt track with Jock barking frantically, maybe anticipating a canine friend to play with too. But he would be disappointed. Fleur didn't really like animals and only tolerated Jock for Yvonne's sake, because Yvonne had so few friends and had missed her nanny who had been left behind in London. The nanny had become like a mother to Yvonne, a mother that Margaret, the real mother, then wished to replace. Had she succeeded? She had tried hard, but to establish a rapport with a daughter whom she had so neglected was at first not easy. Yvonne was very self-contained and assured, a little madam, by nature not unlike Yves. She never wept, never had tantrums; but always got her own way by dint of being controlled, combined with a stubbornness, certain of what she wanted in life and how to get it. Yves had been like that too; he got what he wanted and he had never thought about the consequences – like damaging the life of the woman he had married or even, apparently, realizing that he had damaged it.

Fleur waved from the car and Morag, her blonde hair gleaming in the sun, leaned excitedly out of the window half opening the door before the car had stopped. Margaret rushed up to the door laughing, hanging on to her straw hat.

'Be careful, Morag! There are enough car accidents as it is without one here.'

'Oh we never exceed the speed limit, don't worry.' Fleur turned reprovingly to her daughter. 'In fact I don't think I even *dare* do thirty miles an hour.' A speed limit had just been introduced in March, but very few people took any notice of it except Fleur Dunbar. Margaret certainly didn't and went racing about the countryside in her distinctive brown Buick as though she were taking part in a Grand Prix race.

The women kissed and the girls joined hands and raced back down the hill towards the loch, Jock out of his mind with joy at the prospect of two companions.

'Be very careful girls! Don't fall in the water.'

'Oh *Mummy*, always fussing!' Seven-year-old Morag turned round and put out her tongue and Fleur lifted her fist and shook it at her, but when she turned to Margaret her expression was soft and relaxed.

'She's such a bad example, that daughter of mine.'

'She is not. She's a treasure. I don't know where Yvonne would be without her. I'm so grateful to you Fleur.'

'Nonsense.' Fleur put an arm around her waist and lightly squeezed it, and then she began unloading baskets from the boot of the car.

'Ham, bread, cheese. I've never got used to haggis, but there's a fresh one for you. Oh and this . . .' She held up a bottle of hock. 'I got this from the cellar. We should have asked the girls to put it in the water.'

'I'll put it in a bucket in the kitchen. It's just as cool. Have you had coffee?'

'No, I'd love some.'

'Sit in my chair and I'll get you a cup.'

'But you . . .'

'No, I'll squat on the grass. I want to get the sun on my bare legs, see.' Margaret held out a shapely leg and Fleur smiled.

'You're brown already. You're a lovely colour.'

'It won't last much longer. This weather never does.' Margaret put the wine in a bucket of fresh spring water and heated up the coffee in a saucepan for Fleur, pouring it into a large earthenware mug. 'It's all very primitive out here,' she said. 'You'll have to excuse it. No saucers.'

'I love it.' Fleur flung her head back and closed her eyes to the sun. 'I wish we could stay here with you, but there simply isn't room.'

'No. I sometimes feel like building an extension, but it's hardly worth it for the time we spend here.'

Margaret crouched on the ground at Fleur's feet, spreading her legs, and sipped her coffee. She wore a simple cotton dress, bare at the neck, and sandals. She had let her hair grow so that it was almost to her shoulders and she wore no make-up. Fleur thought that Margaret was still one of the loveliest women she had ever seen; perhaps better without make-up and simply dressed, because her natural beauty shone through. Make-up detracted from the colour of her eyes, focusing the gaze of the onlooker on her lips which had usually been bright scarlet or magenta or orange. Her clear skin, pale rather full lips and luminous blue-green eyes were, quite simply, not in need of any adornment. Like this she looked wholesome and earthy, as though vibrant with life from some inner source.

'Happy, Margaret?' Fleur's tone altered as she looked at her.

'Very happy. At last. I think the simple life suits me. I really could live here all year round and tend sheep!'

'Oh Maggie!' Fleur burst out laughing. Fleur was one of the few people who called her by the familiar and diminutive, Maggie.

'No really, I could, except for the weather.'

'And Yvonne.'

'Yes, and Yvonne.' Margaret peered down the valley. 'I hope they're alright. They're monkeys those two. They should have been boys.'

'They get on so well. What a blessing.' Fleur lightly touched Margaret's shoulder. 'And you're a blessing to me. You've made such a difference to my life.'

. Margaret reached for Fleur's hand without looking at her. She knew that Fleur was not happy with Cullum. They had no married life and went their separate ways, sharing only a roof over their heads. Nan's name was never mentioned. It was assumed that he saw her, but no one knew. And Margaret, since she'd been north, had been too scared of the truth to try and find out. When she came to the cottage she drove straight through Homerton without stopping. She was not even sure which Nan's house was, but she continued to write and send money to William at his school.

'And what would I have done without you? When I came home I was practically an emotional cripple. You helped restore my senses.'

'Nonsense! You would have recovered. You always do.'

'That's what people think.' Margaret pressed her hand. 'But all my strength had evaporated. I had put so much into . . . everything and then I found I had nothing – only shame.'

'How can you be ashamed of falling in love?'

'I wasn't "in love"; that's what made me ashamed. I just used that crude creature for sex, and everyone knew that I needed a stud and laughed at me.'

'If they knew about Yves they wouldn't laugh at you.'

'But did they know about Yves?' Margaret looked at her again. 'Yves is very skilled at camouflage. I don't think that, to this day, most people know about Yves. I mean, he's not "obvious", is he?'

'No, not at all.' Fleur put both hands round her mug, drinking deeply from it, then raised her head. 'There are certain things that, knowing what I do, I could pinpoint – his elegance, his charm, the way he walks; but that is also very Gallic and aristocratic. But you know, Maggie, I think you place too much importance on that. All people really knew was that Dunbars were reorganizing. Bruno was taking over the London office and you were coming home to supervise the new men's range. Yves comes up here every so often and you go to London. I should think most people have hardly noticed it.'

'Oh they have. In the trade they have. I saw Tristan Fleming last time I was in London and he knew all about it. But then, he knew about Yves. This time Yves cut him dead, but I felt grateful for what he'd tried to do. I spoke to Tristan for the first time in years, and he was just as sweet and gentle as ever. The point was that I loved Yves so much when I first knew him that I honestly think I would never have believed anything about him that destroyed my image. Even that. I was head over heels in love.'

'And are you still?' Fleur spoke gently.

'No. No, that's all gone. Quite gone.' Margaret stretched on the grass, resting on her hands spread out behind her. 'Funnily enough, I like him better now. I mean I'm quite fond of him. I know I can't have him for a lover, so I have him for a friend. That's what he wanted. We're good friends. He understands women well. Besides, it's very hard to hate Yves. He can be cruel but not callous. He was so mocking about Bob; but then he was kind afterwards. And, of course, he was right about Bob: when I saw him as Yves saw him I felt sick. He knew too that I had to get away and he really devised this plan. It works quite well, doesn't it?'

'I never feel you're as involved in Dunbars as you were.'

'Don't you?' Margaret squinted at the sun and put on her hat again which had fallen on the grass. 'Well, it's not so exciting now that it runs itself. We're doing extremely well; we're building another extension to the factory. We have money in the bank. The men's range will be launched in the autumn; that will be a success too. "Now Gentlemen have the privilege of Ladies . . .Cashmere for men by Dunbar Design." Besides, I like my leisure. I love my daughter. I like my golf, the cottage here.' She gestured round.

'Has it taken the place of . . . everything else, Margaret?'

Margaret rose to her feet and shook bits of grass off herself. 'If by "everything else" you mean love – yes. I'm not in love with anyone and I never want to be again. Men have always made a fool of me. Now love is something I can do without. Shall we walk down and see the girls?'

'Yes, let's have some exercise.' Fleur was aware that Margaret wanted to change the conversation. Since the outpourings of her wounded heart when she'd come home the previous June to Branswick they seldom dwelt on intimacies. Margaret was a private person, and did not like to talk about herself.

She got up and the sisters-in-law linked arms and began a leisurely stroll down the hill. The varied smells of summer came up to greet them; the bees swarmed around them in the heather and a little cloud, the size of a powder puff, appeared in the sky. It was a perfect day.

'By the way,' Fleur said casually, 'someone enquired after you today.'

'Oh. Who?'

'Hamish Ogilvy. Do you remember him?'

Margaret felt her heart lurch, but she did not stop walking. As far as she knew, Fleur had never been aware of her relationship with Hamish.

'Of course I remember him; but I haven't seen him for years. Why did he call?'

'He said he'd like to come for dinner. He wants to talk to Cullum.'

'Oh does he? What about?'

'He didn't say. I think it's something to do with machinery. He's coming on Wednesday. Will you be there?'

'I expect so,' Margaret said. 'If I have nothing better to do.'

He hadn't changed much. He'd put on a bit of weight, which seemed to suit him; he was broader, his hair was thinner and not as fair, and he'd shaved off his moustache. She couldn't decide if she still found him attractive or not. His blue eyes were just as blue, his gaze over the dinner table just as penetrating. Certainly she felt uneasy in his presence, as if he'd exposed a nerve she'd kept carefully controlled. It was six years since she'd been to bed with him.

'I hear you still keep the cottage,' he said after dinner as they sat on the terrace waiting for coffee.

'How do you know that?' She looked at him without smiling.

'When I rang, Fleur said you went there for weekends.'

'With my daughter.'

'I know. What a sweet child she is! Did you know my eldest son is now up at Oxford?'

'Really? And how's your wife?'

'She doesn't vary much, except that she's now in a nursing home. I travel such a lot there was sometimes no one to look after her at home, and the various nurses would never stay long.'

Margaret looked down on Branswick, the lights beginning to come on in the houses opposite on the Vertig hill. The lights of the Dunbar mill blazed continually, as they did all night because the machines now never stopped knitting. A Dunbar living on the hill could look upon the mill at any time, day or night, and know that with every second several miles of knitting were being produced.

'You really have been terribly successful.' Hamish followed her gaze. 'I knew you would be. You haven't changed a bit.'

His voice fell to a whisper as he looked at her, his blue eyes enigmatic. If she wanted him she could have him, they seemed to be saying; he was not going to plead with her, but he was there. She wished he hadn't come, or that she had not been there when he had. But although a small inner voice told her to stay away, a more clamorous, insistent one told her not to.

'I hear you've been very successful too.'

'Yes. We had a few bad years in the depression; but now with this speed-up for armaments we're doing very well.'

'But you don't make guns!'

'No, but we make bits for them, and for tanks, aeroplanes and all the nasty instruments of war.'

'Do you think there'll be a war, Hamish?'

Cullum had heard the word 'war' and came over to

them. Fleur was pouring coffee from a table by the French windows.

'I wouldn't be surprised, I'm sorry to say. Even Baldwin who was formerly dead against aerial warfare says now that Britain will be made as strong as any country "within distance by air". You know what that means. Bombs.'

'How ghastly.' Fleur joined them, putting down a tray of delicate Minton coffee cups on the parapet round the terrace.

'Churchill's the warmonger,' Cullum said. 'Always was. He says we can't expect France to disarm when she's so frightened of Hitler.'

'Then he's right,' Margaret said. 'The French are *very* frightened of Hitler. And Yves has some personal experience of what life is like in Germany. He was in Berlin just after Hitler became Chancellor.'

'Now he's President.' Cullum sipped his coffee. 'God knows where it will all end.'

Hamish looked at his watch and the dusk settling over Branswick. 'I should be getting home,' he said. 'My car was playing up on the way here.'

'Why don't you stay the night in that case? We've plenty of room. More coffee?' Fleur looked over her shoulder, but her eyes were on Margaret, not Hamish.

She was expecting the tap on her door and when it came she put on her light and got out of bed, reaching for her gown. He stood at the door fully dressed. It was a hot night but even then the beads of perspiration on his brow were excessive.

'May I come in?' he whispered.

She opened the door and stood aside to let him pass. He stepped into the room, standing in the middle looking around. She went to the bedside table and took a cigarette, fastening the sash of her dressing gown firmly before she lit it.

'I expected you,' she said.

399

'I thought you might. Could I have a fag too?'

She gave him one and lit it for him, looking into his eyes. 'There's nothing doing, Hamish. It was all over in 1928. I gave you five years of my life and that was enough.'

'It was very precious.' His voice broke with emotion and she felt surprised. He had looked so controlled, almost insouciant. 'I've never forgotten you, Margaret. I've always missed you.'

'I'm married now, Hamish.'

'Yes but not very happily, I hear.'

She sat down and exhaled smoke across the room. 'Bruno told you I suppose?'

'Yes.'

'Did he tell you all about Yves?'

'He told me he was a poof and that he'd treated you very badly. What a rotten cad the man must be.'

'He isn't a cad and he didn't treat me badly. He treated me quite well. I've only been treated badly by men who liked sex.'

'I didn't treat you badly!'

'You were selfish. I think we should still have been having our affair if I hadn't met Yves.'

Hamish sat on the bed beside her, his hands loosely joined in front of him, the cigarette smoke staining his fingers. 'Well, that was as much your fault as mine, Margaret darling. You were free any time.'

'I was not free. I was in love with you.'

'There were *thousands* of men after you. You were the prettiest girl, woman, this side of the Border. Still are.'

He touched her hand but she jerked it away angrily, stubbing out her cigarette in the ash tray.

'Did Bruno also tell you about Bob?'

'No. Who's Bob?'

'A fellow I went to bed with.'

'Was there something wrong with him?'

'No, he was just very, very common. I made a perfect

fool of myself. When I finished with him he tried to demand money.'

'How ghastly!'

'Bruno sent him to America after having had him fired from his job here. He was absolutely no good at it anyway. Advertising wasn't his thing, exactly. Bruno was quite ruthless, however, and said he'd make sure he never got another job here if he stayed. He said if he ever saw his face or heard from him again he'd meet with a nasty accident on a dark night!' Margaret started to laugh. 'You know how *ugly* Bruno can look with that livid scar when he makes a threat. Bob believed him.'

Hamish stared hard at her. 'You've laughed. How I *love* to see laughter on your face. You must have had a terrible time, darling. Very decent of Bruno.'

'Please stop saying "darling", Hamish. All that's in the past, you know.'

'Sorry, dar . . . Margaret. I can't help feeling so intimate with you.'

'You'd better go if that's the case.'

'No, I won't move a muscle.' His boyish expression couldn't conceal his rapture, his delight at being near her.

'Anyway, from hating Bruno I suddenly began to like him. He was very, very decent about all that. We're all part of suffering humanity, aren't we, Hamish?'

She leaned back, joining her hands around her knees. Part of her gown fell away revealing a long brown leg. Hamish swallowed.

'I'm afraid so,' he said, hoping she wouldn't realize he could see her bare leg. 'No man is an island unto himself sort of thing.'

'I thought I was such an island.' Margaret gazed at the ceiling, leaning even further back on the bed and showing even more leg. 'Impassive, impregnable, unswayable. During the early years of my marriage to Yves, the years when we built up the business, I became someone that I can hardly recognize now. I think I was deceived by my own image. I hardly knew my daughter, for instance; wasn't that wicked for a mother?' She looked at him and saw where his eyes were resting. She hastily uncrossed her legs and smoothed her gown over her lap.

'Don't punish yourself too much, Margaret.' Hamish looked at the floor. 'There's no cause to hate yourself. To me you were always a lovely, lovable person, never hard.' His hand moved towards her.

'Ah, but that was before I was really successful, before Dunbar and I became synonymous. Nothing was done without my say-so. I ruled the roost from north to south, east to west, glorying in my power.'

'And now?'

'Now I'm based in Branswick, merely a director. Bruno is the big boss in London and Cullum divides his time between there and Branswick, happier than he was but still not happy. Bruno has all the power I used to have. Bruno runs it now, as far as I'm concerned.

'Do you mind?'

'Of course not – I gave it to him! Yves is a director too, mainly in charge of continental sales and advertising. His boyfriend Peter flits to and from London where our main design office is, so he's happy. I go to London for board meetings four times a year. Yves comes up here to see Yvonne. I work from nine to five. I never go abroad and I seldom bring work home. I spend weekends and some odd days when we're not too busy in the cottage. I'm devoted to my daughter, my life here in Branswick and the business, in that order. What a change from Madame la Directrice.'

'Do you miss it at all, the "Madame la Directrice" bit?'

'Sometimes I miss the excitement. Every day there was a challenge. But I was too hurt by what happened; too shocked about Yves, humiliated over Bob. I wanted to disappear into a hole in the ground. Can you understand that?'

'I can,' Hamish moved imperceptibly closer, 'because I understand you.'

'Yves and I are not going to divorce, Hamish.' She looked at him, aware of his proximity. 'We have agreed, for Yvonne's sake. Besides, neither of us particularly wants to be free.'

'I understand,' Hamish said. 'I'm not free either; but I still want you.'

'It's quite out of the question.' Margaret moved up towards the head of the bed, as though to emphasize the distance between them. 'I'm sorry I let you in; but, well, you are an old flame.'

'I'm very interested in you, Margaret, and all that happens to you, regardless of how I feel about you. I was so sorry to hear about your troubles from Bruno.'

'Yes, he was very good, especially as he had troubles of his own. But I can't tell you about them I'm afraid.'

'I think I know,' Hamish said, reaching past her for another cigarette and accidentally brushing against her bosom. 'He was very drunk at the time he told me all this; he unburdened his soul.'

'He told you about Clare Amory?' Margaret had been aware of his nearness, of his hand against her breast; it stimulated erotic images in her mind, and the desire that she thought had gone, or maybe that she had fought, began slowly to flow back again. She had not slept with a man for eighteen months, as though she were paying for the sin of knowing someone as gross and venial as Bob.

'Yes. He said she finished the affair because she was too ashamed.'

'We were all very ashamed then, I remember. Clare resigned from the firm and took a job with an agency. She thought she'd behaved badly to me. I believe they never meet now, and poor Bruno has settled down to a life of domesticity and fidelity with Susan.'

Hamish, his cigarette unlit, put his hand on her breast, this time not accidentally. Their eyes met. Suddenly she realized her desire for him was overpowering. Was it just for him or was it merely for any man? He slowly unfastened her gown and gazed at her figure moulded in the folds of her pale green voile nightdress: her deep cleavage and the contours of her breasts. The pulse at her neck beat very quickly and her lips were parted as he remembered them so many times before.

He reached for the hem of her nightdress and pulled it gently up over her thighs. 'Just once? Couldn't we?' he said, bending forward to kiss her and, as she lay back, he drew the pale green voile, so light and diaphanous, right up to her neck.

CHAPTER TWENTY THREE

As a contrast to the elegance and leisure projected by the ladies' styles in cashmere, the image adopted for men was rugged and sporty, the countryman approach. A new range of sweaters, pullovers, cardigans and jackets was designed: 'Countryman Cashmere – by Dunbar'. Eminent golfers, cricketers, and tennis players were persuaded, again without difficulty, to model the new line shown to the trade in a week of fashion shows at the Dunbar office in Devonshire Place. One show was no longer enough for buyers who now came from all over the world.

Margaret went up to London for the launch, bringing Yvonne with her. She had been so busy supervising the production of the final models for the show that she had not seen Yves since early in the autumn, when he came to Branswick for a board meeting. The new extension to the mill was nearing completion, so that it now ran almost the complete length of the riverside between the two bridges which crossed the Drume, one by the Craigie and the other bisecting the main street and Dumbarton Street where the tenements were. The extension was a gamble because its financial viability depended on the success of the men's range. Dunbars had an overdraft again and Cullum had been very doubtful about the wisdom of installing new and expensive machinery. In fact, he'd voted against it, once again isolating himself from the rest of the family.

Cullum stayed away from the trade shows as well, but he was scarcely missed. Bruno was such a prominent figure now, known to all the foreign buyers, that for most of them he typified Dunbars even though he was a

405

Macallister. The week of shows was a hectic time and Margaret attended each one, flattered at the warmth with which old customers greeted her presence in London again.

Yves was usually by her side, smiling, attentive, some might even have said loving. The new range was not designed by Peter Cartwright but by his assistant Roderick Macpherson, and Peter stayed away so as not to steal the limelight from Roderick, a robust young Scotsman with a wife and three children who lived near Branswick. People in the know thought that the reason Yves was able to pay so much attention to Margaret was because Peter wasn't there. It was curious how the Lamottes could still appear very much a couple, even though everyone knew they lived apart.

The shows were, of course, a success. Although the motif was sporty there was also a line of very luxurious, very expensive, single-ply cashmere sweaters for men, called 'Jubilee' in honour of the King's Silver Jubilee, the celebrations for which were to be held in May when the garments would be available in the shops. The decorations in the showroom and on the buffet lunch table were in purple and silver. An elaborate brochure in colour, illustrating both men's and women's styles, had been prepared on which the Royal Arms were cleverly interwoven with the Dunbar shield, managing to convey the impression that royalty was somehow connected with the house of Dunbar yet without provoking the wrath of the Lord Chamberlain's office which supervised these things very strictly.

Tristan Fleming had attended the show in person for the first time for many years. Afterwards he came over to Margaret, stooping to kiss her cheek as though there had never been a breach between them.

'A fabulous show darling.' He gazed across at Yves, who was talking to a group of American buyers who had come over specially on the *Normandie* from New York.

There was now great rivalry between transatlantic liners to see which could cross the ocean first and be awarded the Blue Riband. The previous September Queen Mary had launched a great new liner named after her, but it would not be commissioned for another year. 'And you both seem very happy. *Quite* the loving couple, I would say.'

'You must come and have dinner with us.'

'I'd love to, darling. How long are you here?'

'Oh, quite a while,' Margaret said, smiling mysteriously.

'We must do some shows if Yves will release you. Have you seen *Lady Precious Stream*?'

'No.'

'It's absolutely divine, you'd love it. I've seen it five times.'

'Then make it a sixth with me.'

Tristan squeezed her arm tightly and kissed her again, exuding that special fragrance she always associated with him, a rather delicate, subtle fragrance that was neither masculine nor feminine but something in between.

Bruno Macallister detached himself from the throng that invariably surrounded him and made his way slowly over to Tristan and Margaret, shaking hands, grasping shoulders in his passage, moving with almost regal, confident ease.

Everyone admired the way Macallister ran Murdoch Dunbar & Sons Ltd. A reputation that he had been building up since 1925 had cemented itself in the past two years. He was thought to have flair, drive and very good business sense. He was innovative and encouraged young designers, and different combinations of yarns. Although Dunbars had made their reputation in the way they presented and marketed cashmere, they used many other wools too – shetland, merino, llama, alpaca and, of course, beautiful soft lambswool from the Scottish hills. They imported yarn from all over the world and Bruno had been among the first businessmen to make use of passenger flights so that he could get everywhere more quickly and snap up deals faster.

Bruno lived for his work since he and Clare had parted. His relationship with Susan was amicable rather than loving, while he and Margaret were friendly but wary of each other, though he had not been sorry to see Margaret go north. Although he admired what she'd done he also resented it. He was a confirmed believer in the superiority of the male, and any woman who tried to challenge that view he regarded as something of a freak, be she a cabinet minister like Margaret Bondfield or a businesswoman like Margaret Dunbar. Lady athletes and lady pilots were acceptable. Lady athletes could not perform as well as men – everyone knew that – and lady pilots, especially, seemed only to emphasize male superiority by making a joke of what they did, like Amy Johnson mending her aeroplane with sticking plaster on the way to Australia. What man would have done that? No it was an amusing, frivolous, womanish thing to do.

Now forty-four, a little heavier due to his love of good food and wine, his lack of exercise, Bruno was nevertheless a presentable, handsome, capable man, the kind that women loved to be seen with and men considered a good sort. His hair was still thick and curly, but almost uniformly grey and over the years the scar on his cheek had become part of his skin, rather than something superimposed on it. Some people never noticed it, and the droop in his right eye, for some reason, seemed only to make him more attractive to women. He dressed expensively, in the best possible taste – quiet, subdued colours for his shirts and ties; the finest cloth for his suits, flannels, jackets and blazers. He belonged to all the right clubs and his house in Knightsbridge was the scene of frequent entertaining for people of all kinds from the arts, business and the professions, many of whom he had never met before.

He made a bee-line for Tristan because Flemings was

the only real rival to Harrods, apart from the fact that he had known him in the war. He grasped his hand.

'Ages since I saw you, Tristan. How very good of you to come.'

'I always came in the old days.' Tristan screwed his monocle in his eye and regarded Bruno appraisingly. 'You look astonishingly well yourself, old man. I would have taken you for a captain of industry or a very distinguished Harley Street quack.'

Bruno laughed, showing a sprinkling of gold teeth amid all the firm white molars. 'Hardly flattering old boy.'

'I call them all quacks.' Tristan waved a hand dismissively.

'But what makes you visit us personally this time?'

'To see Margaret of course. I love Margaret, you know. I never forget how lovely she was that day she walked into my salon – when was it now? 1918? 1919? What light years away those days do seem now! She was like a nymph, yes a wood nymph, tall and straight as a tree, beautiful as . . .'

'Oh Tristan *stop*!' Margaret caught his arm and pretended to shake him. 'I feel like something out of *A Midsummer Night's Dream*.'

'You *were* a dream,' Tristan said gravely, taking the hand on his arm and kissing it. 'You still are, and that is why I am here. But also to acclaim . . .' He struck a pose and looked around the crowded room, 'to acclaim the realization of a dream. Because Margaret became something much bigger than I ever thought possible. For me Margaret *is* Dunbars.'

If Bruno was not too happy with this speech he was careful to hide it. He beamed at Margaret and put an arm through hers, hugging her to him in a gesture which could have been an acknowledgement of her genius and the fact that she was his sister-in-law, or vaguely patronizing. 'Of course Margaret is Dunbar. And doesn't she look well, Tristan?'

'Very well.' Tristan ran his eyes over her appraisingly. 'I love the dress, darling, and the little weight you've put on suits you.'

Bruno stood back frowning and looked at Margaret's figure. Women, that year, were trying to be truly feminine, and bosoms were back in fashion. The 'romantic' image was appealed for but, with the high taxation and growing fear of war, not easy to attain. Business women like Margaret tried to combine seriousness with a certain romanticism, and so she had selected a calf-length dress of floral printed crêpe-de-Chine with a collar, and over it she wore a sleeveless coat of the same material which floated behind her as she walked. On her head was a broad hat of pedal straw with a band of artificial flowers. Many women had their hair piled on their heads exposing the neck, as Susan now did, but Margaret still wore her hair fairly long, cut to make the most of its natural curl and parted at the side.

'Margaret put on weight?' Bruno finished his inspection. 'Never.'

'Oh she has,' Tristan said rather archly, taking his monocle out of his eyes and letting it dangle on its velvet ribbon round his neck. 'Just a teeny bit; but it's *very* becoming.'

'Are you lunching with us, Tristan?' Margaret waved to Heinrich Schultz who had come over from Paris.

'Certainly, darling, as long as there's salmon and plenty of champagne, which, of course, there always is.'

'I haven't seen Tristan Fleming for ages,' Yves said later that night as they sat over a nightcap before going to bed. The Macallisters had been there for dinner, also Heinrich Schultz and his wife and two of the most important buyers from America. As well as the shows and business lunches, they had entertained or been entertained every night that week and Margaret felt exhausted. She eased her shoes off her feet and wriggled her aching toes in their pure silk stockings.

'He looks just the same,' she said, sipping her whisky.

'Has he forgiven me for marrying you?' Yves allowed himself a half smile.

'Apparently. He said we seemed a very loving couple.'

'I do my best, in public, darling, not to let you down.' Yves abruptly got up and came over to her, and she held up her hand which he bent down and kissed. Then he sat on the arm of her chair and put his other hand protectively round her shoulders. 'You look very beautiful today, blooming in fact. I do love you so much, you know that, Margaret, don't you?'

'In your way, I suppose you do.' Margaret took his hand and squeezed it. 'Peter will be so pleased about the show. After all, Roderick was his discovery.'

'Oh he'll be thrilled. I had a card from him today from Switzerland. Of course it was all about work though he is supposed to be on holiday.'

He planted a kiss on the nape of her neck and got up, but Margaret kept hold of his hand, and he looked surprised.

'Yves?'

'Yes, darling, what is it?' His tone of voice was slightly apprehensive and Margaret smiled.

'Oh don't worry, I'm not going to try and seduce you. I need your help.'

'Is anything the matter, my sweet?' He perched on the arm of her chair again, and she turned round so that she could look at him while still holding his hand.

'I'm pregnant, Yves. I think Tristan noticed it today, so it must be beginning to show.'

'But my darling . . .' Yves stood up rapidly and went to pour more whisky in his glass. He turned and stared at her, his face aghast. 'But my darling, how . . .'

'Well, the usual way. I don't know of any other.'

'When? How long?'

'I'm four months pregnant. I saw a gynaecologist in Edinburgh just before Christmas.'

'He must think it's the immaculate conception seeing that we haven't slept together for donkey's years.'

411

'I didn't tell him that. He just said, "You are in excellent physical shape, Mrs Lamotte, and your husband must be delighted. Congratulations."'

'Charming.' Yves sank onto the sofa opposite her, looking suddenly worn. 'Have you thought of getting rid of it, Margaret?'

'Yes I have. That's the first thing I thought of when I suspected. And then . . . Well, you want a son, don't you, Yves?'

'Margaret, are you serious? I couldn't possibly . . .'

'Why not?' Margaret rose and, wandering over to the table, poured herself a drink. Her sapphire-blue taffeta evening dress had a full skirt and a bodice with a detachable cape. Her face was very pale and her eyes large and luminous. Yves thought she looked rather frightened, not as calm as she was trying to appear. She came back and sat with calculated casualness by his side on the sofa, and placed a hand on his knee. 'Why not?'

'Because it wouldn't be . . . my son!' Margaret could never recall hearing Yves splutter. This was the first time she had seen him actually groping for words.

'But no one will know that. We don't want to get divorced, do we, Yves? I thought it would be nice to have another baby, before I'm too old.' She shuddered. 'Or there's a war. I may not have another chance. If it is a boy I'd be delighted. Besides, even if I wanted to marry the father I couldn't.'

'He's married too?'

'He's my old lover Hamish Ogilvy. You might as well know everything. We only met once which is the irony. He came round for dinner, ostensibly to discuss machinery for the new extension with Cullum, but in reality to try to get me to go to bed with him.'

'Which was successful.' Yves sounded censorious.

'Yes. I didn't mean to; but you know I've had no one since well – ' She lowered her eyes. 'I can't bear to mention that ghastly man's name. There isn't a soul in

Branswick one could possibly have an affair with. I'm a woman after all, and Hamish was very persuasive. We just fell into bed and of course neither of us had any precautions to hand. One never thinks of that kind of thing at moments like that.'

'One should, Margaret,' Yves remonstrated, his eyes reproachful.

'Oh I know one *should*; but one doesn't. Anyway, it was a very remote chance, wasn't it? There are only a very few days in the month when a woman can get pregnant. Well, that was one of them.'

'But does he know?'

'No. I told him then I didn't want to start an affair again and that night was for old times' sake. I haven't heard from him since, so he must have accepted it. Maybe he was just curious, or maybe I've lost my appeal. I don't care anyway. It's over.'

Yves got up and poked the fire, glancing at his watch. Then he stood with his back to the newly kindled flames, looking very aloof and handsome, rather daunting.

'Please, Yves . . .'

'But I don't see why *I* should acknowledge a . . . a bastard,' he finished.

'Because of what I did for you, that's why,' Margaret said firmly. 'I left you with Peter didn't I? I didn't make a scandal that would have upset your family. I could have taken you through the divorce court, you know.'

Yves' laugh was ironic. 'You never would, my love, because of your own precious family's name. I would have divorced you if you really wanted it, but you didn't. Now . . .'

'Oh, you're going to divorce *me* now, are you?'

'I don't know . . .' Yves turned his back to her and examined his face in the oval mirror above the mantelpiece, running his hand across his closely shaved chin. 'I'll have to think about it. A lot of things are involved . . .'

413

'Such as?'

'My name, and money . . .' Yves looked at her through the mirror. 'This child will have my name . . .'

'But you haven't got any money! At least you never seem to have, apart from what you earn as a director. I've kept you for all these years, a fact for which you'd think you'd be grateful.'

'That's not *quite* true, my darling. I feel I've earned my keep, as I always intended. It was mainly through me that Dunbars became so well known. Think of all those greedy aristocrats I knew, all hungry for a few pounds and a comfy sweater or two because their estates were heavily mortgaged on account of the depression. But I'm not talking about *family* money anyway. It *is* true the Lamottes. are not well endowed as far as actual cash is concerned, but that's another thing we never discussed before we were married. You accepted me as I was. What funny, secretive days they were.'

'I loved you too much to worry about money anyway.' Margaret folded her arms and leaned back, half closing her eyes. 'You know now that I'm very vulnerable. A pregnant woman always is, whether she likes it or not. Frankly, I don't, but I am going to get bigger and it will soon be obvious, as it is to some now, that I'm going to have a baby. How much do you want, Yves, to acknowledge paternity?'

'Ah, now we're being practical. Good!' Yves rubbed his hands and sat opposite her. 'I would like a settlement; a hundred thousand now, and five thousand a year for life.'

'Impossible.' Margaret stood up and walked agitatedly to the window, then back again to the middle of the hearthrug. 'You know that I haven't got that kind of money, anything like it. Besides, with our heavy investment on plant I can't even raise it.'

'Ask Macallister to find the money. He's got plenty. Or your sister Juliet and her rapacious husband.'

'Yves, I *promise* you that, if and when . . .'

Yves solemnly shook his head, spreading his legs before him with an air of apparent satisfaction. 'Sorry, Margaret. No promises. Alright, on payment of *fifty* thousand and a promise of fifty more, say in a year's time, plus so much a year – I won't be too specific at the moment, but I think I could take a drop of a thousand or so – then I will sign the register as papa. If you don't have the money to hand by . . . when?' He looked enquiringly at her stomach as though expecting it to answer.

'June.'

'By June, I will then accept from you in writing that the terms will be honoured and that will be enough. It will all have to be drawn up by lawyers, though. If ever I want to disown your child I shall, unless it is properly done. It may cause one hell of a stink, but I shan't care.'

Margaret stood by the fire, feeling more alone and isolated than she ever had in her life. She would have to ask Bruno and all her family to chip in with the money, so they would all have to know. She thought how little one knew a person until they humiliated one – Yves had now done it twice. The calm, imperturbable, unflappable Yves, who called himself an aristocrat, was just as crude as Bob Morgan when it came to the crunch. All that men seemed to want out of a woman was money or sex; they were interchangeable.

She clasped her hands and unclasped them, the diamond and sapphire rings he had given her sparkling on her fingers. Then she threw back her head and gazed at herself in the mirror. She was very pale, with dark shadows under her eyes. She did not look her best, and she still had another five months to go, when she would get heavier and more tired, less able to fend for herself, no matter how much her family protected her. They would have to know now, whatever happened. First Bob, now this.

'You'll get the money, Yves,' she said, 'if I have to sell the rings you gave me. I suppose they're not on loan?'

Yves looked pained. 'On *trust*, Margaret. I'd hoped you

would want Yvonne to have them one day. One was a gift to one of my ancestors, supposedly anyway, from Marie Antoinette.'

'Oh I forgot about Marie Antoinette – ' Margaret looked sceptically at the large diamond surrounded by smaller ones. 'I thought she was broke too. The lawyers will draw everything up this week. Angus Monroe will see to it. I'll have to spend more time here with you too, just for appearances.'

'But darling, that will be *delightful*. . .'

Relaxed now, gratified that he had his own way, he smiled expansively at her. There was no crook like an amoral, aristocratic crook. Now, as when she had learned about Peter, Margaret felt that she hated him. But that negative emotion, like so many others, was one that she would have to learn to overcome.

London was *en fête* for the week of the Silver Jubilee in May of that year, 1935. Thousands poured into the capital and throughout the land every town and village had its own celebrations. There were bonfires in Hyde Park and two thousand beacon fires throughout the country, including one in the hills above Branswick where Margaret was awaiting the birth of her baby. It was thought that London would be too noisy and tiring for her in May and Yves, ever the thoughtful father-to-be, had promised to travel to Branswick for the birth.

The extension to the Dunbar mill had been opened by the Duke and Duchess of Storrick in March and the men's range was in full production by the beginning of May.

Once the legal formalities had been completed, Margaret and Yves shook hands, had a drink and decided that the matter of the birth should be treated like a business arrangement, as with two directors in a company who didn't particularly get on, but worked together for the good of the whole. Each should make every effort to please the other. They were seen about a lot together and

Yves even gave a party in February to celebrate the prospect of the birth of a possible heir. The fifty thousand pounds had been lodged in a bank in France, and he felt he could afford to be expansive, even paying for the party himself.

He took Margaret frequently to the theatre – to *Viceroy Sarah* at the Whitehall in February, and to see Beatrix Lehmann and Ralph Richardson in the new Priestley play *Eden End* at the Duchess. They also enjoyed the cinema and saw Elizabeth Bergner and Douglas Fairbanks Junior in *Catherine the Great*, Leslie Howard as the Scarlet Pimpernel, Anna Neagle as Nell Gwynn, and Norma Shearer as Elizabeth Barrett, with Charles Laughton as her wicked father. They saw Greta Garbo as Queen Christina twice.

Apart from the theatre and the cinema, millions of people now had wireless sets, and some were talking about the possibility of moving pictures being seen on a small screen in the comfort of one's home. Pirandello's *The Man with the Flowers in his Mouth* had actually been shown to the thirty people in the country who had these television sets, as they were called.

At the beginning of the year there was talk of 72-year-old Lloyd George entering the government. Cullum said he would save the country and get rid of Hitler, but his views were not shared by many. Most people were beginning to think that sooner or later there would be another war, and a Royal Commission was announced to enquire into arms traffic and manufacture. Hitler reintroduced conscription into Germany, thus interrupting the disarmament talks yet again. Anthony Eden found Stalin's views, when he visited him in Moscow, more to his liking than those of Hitler. The House of Lords had a purely academic debate about the virtues of capitalism versus socialism. Hardly anyone took any notice.

But Margaret, awaiting a new life, dreaded the thought of war and avoided reading the newspapers. Yves cosseted her and protected her and gave her what affection he could – affection that now had a price tag of fifty thousand pounds, with more to come.

If Margaret felt bitterness in those months she kept it to herself. She didn't show it to her family, who were the people who knew, and she certainly didn't show it to the rest who did not. She remained calm, equable, busy but inwardly rather frightened. How could anyone possibly envisage another war who was old enough to remember the last one? She was now thirty-four and she had been seventeen when her brother Malcolm had been killed. Yet she could remember that, the peace celebrations, and the burial of the Unknown Warrior as though they were quite recent events.

She thought of her nephew, Malcolm's son young Murdoch, now at Cambridge; of Cullum's son, William, who would be fifteen this year; of Susan's twins, Hesther and James, now ten, and Juliet's two sons, Tom and Paul, who would be just the right age if there were another war. Were all the young men of today to be sacrificed, as Malcolm's generation had with him? Could it be possible that after years and years of disarmament talks, there was now a race to re-arm? And what if her own child were a boy? It is true he would be too young to fight, but people now lived in fear of war from the air because the attempts to halt the building of military aircraft had been as futile as preventing the race for conventional weapons. Baldwin, who had done more to stop it than most statesmen, had spelled out the danger to ordinary, defenceless citizens from air attacks. When Margaret went home to Branswick at the beginning of May it was also because its remoteness made it as safe a place as one could find, and if war broke out she could have her baby there without fear of death falling out of the skies.

Margaret was not alone in worrying about the threat of war, the menacing noises being made by the Nazis in

418

Germany and the Fascists in Austria. The nation as a whole was worried and welcomed the Jubilee all the more because, as the Archbishop of Canterbury said, the Throne was steadfast and strong. They threw themselves into the festivities, celebrating an institution that had gone on in England uninterrupted, except for a brief time in the seventeenth century, for nearly a thousand years. As governments crumbled in Europe, as monarchies had tottered and vanished in the last war, to the British people the Throne remained a symbol of hope and endurance.

If Bruno Macallister had a fantasy about the role of women, Clare Amory did not really fit into it. She was neither docile and submissive nor strictly beautiful: she was vibrant, impulsive and alluring. She was not a partner like Susan, or a plaything like some of the girls he went to bed with, picking them up at a party or a show and using them for a good time. Clare had thrown him over, but she continued to haunt him. She was an obsession, constantly at the back of his mind, and though he had not seen her he sometimes called her on the phone to ask how she was and he frequently thought about her.

The Jubilee provided the occasion he had been looking for. He had phoned her to say he needed a partner for a party at the Ritz, and Susan had gone north with Margaret to spend a few days at home. Would she not come, just for old times' sake? Just because they might all be at war soon and who knew what would happen then?

Clare, lonely and unhappy, missing Bruno as much as he missed her, did not need much persuasion. She accepted, telling Douglas that it was something to do with her work. After all, who *did* know what the future would bring?

They danced and they drank, they ate and they talked. They had a wonderful evening, and he drove her home slowly through the streets, crowded with revellers, because he did not want to lose her again. He had not asked her to come back to him; not yet. He wanted to establish

419

in her mind what a good person he was to be with, not dangerous, but loving and comforting. He had the impression now that he had a chance.

'You'd better drop me off at the end of the street,' she said, as they left the Kentish Town Road.

'Is he at home?'

'He may have gone to bed, or there may still be a party going on at the pub; but you couldn't come in anyway.'

Bruno stopped the car two blocks away from her street. Groups of happy, drunken revellers, arms linked, danced past them singing, waving Union Jacks and Jubilee flags with portraits of King George and Queen Mary. Bruno put off the car lights and took her hand; how cool it was and soft, lying in her lap.

'Clare, I have never ceased missing you. Please . . .'

'Don't ask, Bruno.'

'But you're not happy. You can't be happy. You don't look happy.'

Clare smiled bitterly in the dark. He could see the profile of her face, outlined against the orange glow of the street lamp. Her large nose looked rather Jewish, her heavy-lidded eyes were elusive and haunted.

'That's not surprising is it? Douglas has added drink to his troubles. He occasionally beats me up.'

'My darling, can't you *leave* him?' Bruno leaned over her hand and kissed it; then he warmed it by pressing it against his chest.

'For you, do you mean?' He saw her eyes gleam and when he didn't reply her voice was low and accusatory. 'You'd never leave Susan, would you, Bruno?'

'I can't,' Bruno whispered. 'I have no reason to leave her. It would hurt her too much. She's never done anything to hurt me. But I hate to think of you being so unhappy. I can help to support you, Clare, find you a place. If he beats you, you *must* leave him.'

'We'd start our affair again wouldn't we?'

'We might.' He gazed at her hopefully in the dark.

420

'I could never do that.'

'It wouldn't make any difference. If you didn't want to, I wouldn't force you. I just want you to be happy. I would still support you and help you. I would never ask you to do anything you didn't want to do; but the thought of him beating you . . .' He banged the wheel of the car in his rage and frustration.

'You're very sweet, Bruno, and I believe you. But I must go now.'

'Think about it, please, Clare. Give me a ring.'

'I will. Maybe I will.'

Clare stepped quickly out of the door, closed it and leaned over towards Bruno, giving him her hand. He took it and kissed it, feeling suddenly hopeless, and, at that moment, a crowd came surging up the street nearly sweeping her away with them. The crowd, though happy and good-humoured, reeked of drink and Bruno grew alarmed at the thought of Clare walking alone by herself up the street. He swiftly got out of the car, locked the doors and came round to her.

'I'll walk you home.'

'Oh no. You can't.'

'Of course I can. I can't leave you like this. You could be hurt.'

'But if he sees you . . .'

'He won't see me. I'll leave you at the gate.' Bruno took her arm and steered her along the pavement, holding her close, until they came to Alma Street.

When they reached the gate they found the front door wide open but there were no lights inside. There was something sinister about that gaping black hole.

'My goodness,' Clare said. 'What could have happened?'

'I'll go and see . . .' Bruno started for the door but she held him back.

'No, he may be waiting for me.'

'With the lights off? What is he, drunk and waiting to beat you up? If you ask me he's not there.'

421

'Please Bruno, don't . . . I'll go in and you wait here.'

'Alright.'

Bruno reluctantly opened the gate for her and slowly, apprehensively, Clare went up the short path to the door, standing for a moment on the threshold, looking in. She turned to him and waved and at that instance Bruno heard her give a gasp and saw a white hand reach out and drag her through the door.

He ran up the path and into the hall, groping for the light switch because it was pitch dark. In the front room off the hall he heard sounds of scuffling and suddenly Clare screamed. Bruno found the light switch, and rushed into the front room as Clare cried: 'Run away!' and screamed again.

The scene was macabre, the pale yellow light from the tiny hallway affording little illumination. All he could see was Clare and, clasping her round the waist, a man with wide staring eyes, his mouth open in an ugly rictus. There was a strong smell of drink in the room. He crouched forward and it was then that Bruno saw the gun in his hand, a large, clumsy pistol of the type that had been regulation issue in the war. It was a heavy gun and it shook in the man's hand. Bruno decided he was completely drunk and he advanced warily, his hand out as if asking for the gun, one eye on Clare.

'Give me the gun,' he said softly.

'Bruno, please run,' Clare gasped as if the man were hurting her. 'I don't want you to be hurt. Go, *please*.'

'I won't be hurt,' Bruno said calmly, taking another cautious pace forward. The man crouched lower, his left hand, which grasped Clare, digging obscenely into the pit of her stomach.

The sight immediately outraged Bruno and he lurched towards him, one hand outstretched. Outside in the street the crowd were boisterously singing *There'll Always be an England*.

Douglas just managed to steady his gun when Bruno

was within about two feet of him and, with an accuracy that in his state was remarkable, shot a neat hole through his forehead. Then, as Bruno fell, he pointed the gun at Clare.

CHAPTER TWENTY FOUR

Branswick mourned Bruno in a muted way the day he was buried in the cemetery just outside the town where the line of council houses ended on the Vertig hill. The Dunbar mill closed for the day and its solitary flag with the Dunbar shield flew at half mast. As the funeral procession passed through the streets, there were faces at many windows, curious rather than sorrowful.

The town had not really known what to make of the murder of Bruno Macallister. The details had not been quite so lurid in the local press as they had in the London papers and the nationals. There had been an air of Scottish reticence about the whole thing. At first it was made out that Bruno had been trying to save an employee from a deranged husband; but when the truth emerged at the inquest a less noble version was presented and the national banner headlines read:

DERANGED HUSBAND KILLS WIFE'S LOVER.

The *Branswick Chronicle* merely said that he had been killed in tragic circumstances, though most people had read the *Daily Mail* and the *Daily Express* reports as well.

It was perhaps a tribute to the Dunbar family that so many people turned out for the funeral. Maybe it was more as a gesture of support for Susan than to honour the man himself.

For an hour before the funeral a solitary bell tolled as it had the day Margaret and Bruno attended the burial of the Unknown Warrior at Westminster Abbey. Riding immediately behind the coffin with Susan and her daughter Hettie, Margaret remembered that day; and all the years since that had involved Bruno seemed to pass before her eyes like a cinematographic record, vividly realized scenes presented in swift succession. Loving him, hating him, accepting him, liking him. Now she was mourning him. She knew that much of her attitude to men came from Bruno – the terrible sense of betrayal after she respected him so much had seemed to be the pattern of her life ever since. No man ever quite matched up to what she expected of them – and Yves was the last in a line of betrayers. Hamish had not betrayed her; but Hamish had been selfish. She felt a certain satisfaction in the fact that the child she was carrying was his and that he would never know it. It seemed an appropriate kind of justice.

All the women mourners drove behind the cortège while the men, in top hats and dark coats, walked as custom dictated, headed by Bruno's old father, his brother and his son. Then came the male members of the Dunbar family – Cullum, Andrew Dunbar, Angus Monroe and his sons, Murdoch Dunbar, and then the Macallister and Cameron relations who had come from all over Scotland. After them came the Pendreighs, the Mactavishes, the Laws, the Hendersons, the Turnballs, the Laidlaws, the Scotts and all the people who lived on the hill overlooking the huge mill by the Drume that Macallister money had helped to build. Also there were the Ogilvys of Peebles, Hamish and his two sons Christopher and Rory. Behind the gentry came a stream of millworkers, dressed in their best with cloth caps on their heads, men who owed their jobs to Bruno and the prosperity of Dunbar.

After the ceremony in the church the procession re-formed and climbed slowly up the hill to where the grave had been prepared. As the coffin was lowered into it a solitary bagpiper played *The Warrior's Lament* and then Susan, who throughout had shown a stoic and resigned calm, stepped forward and threw a handful of earth on her husband's remains.

There was a reception at *Woodbrae* and Hamish solemnly shook hands with Margaret and introduced her to his sons, tall, good-looking boys with blue eyes and blond hair like their father. Hamish congratulated Margaret on her condition and she introduced him to her husband who stood protectively by her side.

Two weeks later she gave birth to an eight pound eight ounce son after a labour which was a tribute to the progress made in obstetrics since Yvonne was born. Yves, as proud and apprehensive as any father, waited anxiously in the house for the telephone to ring. He then drove with Susan and Fleur to the nursing home with an enormous bunch of roses wrapped in cellophane and a bottle of champagne to toast his heir. No one smiled at the pretence; in fact the few who knew could have forgotten it in their happiness at Margaret's safe delivery and the birth of a son.

Three weeks later the baby was christened Charles Malcolm Dunbar Lamotte and all the workers at the Dunbar mill were given a day's holiday and a week's bonus in their pay packets. Everyone said that little Charles looked just like his father; indeed, there was a fortunate resemblance because, had he been fair and blue-eyed instead of dark and blue-eyed, Margaret would have had some explaining to do outside the immediate family circle.

Margaret engaged a nursemaid, Yves went back to London, the family discussed a stone for Bruno and then everyone tried to forget the whole tragic business. Although doubtless Susan, iron-willed as she was, dwelt privately on the tragedy in many lonely, bitter moments.

Another person who could not forget was Clare. She had been shot in the spine as, tearing herself away from Douglas, she had tried to escape from the room. She had fallen upon Bruno's body and, just before she lost consciousness, she heard the sound of another shot and thought it was the end for her. But this one Douglas had kept for himself.

Clare had wanted to die, yet she lived. She was taken to a hospital for spinal injuries and eventually told that she would never walk again. Her career as a mannequin was finished for good. Douglas had no money and her parents said they hadn't any either, implying that people who lived as she had eventually got what they deserved. The citizens of Clare's family's small town in Sussex took a far less charitable view than the Scots; but then, they were talking about a woman.

As soon as she was better Yves went to see her and promised her the support of the Dunbar family. They felt it would have been Bruno's wish that she should be provided for, whether in a nursing home or in a place by herself.

Margaret wrote to Clare, but she didn't go to see her. She spent the whole of the summer in Branswick, going to her cottage with Yvonne and the baby whenever she could, rather as though the past year had not happened, sometimes wishing it had not, yet loving her baby son.

One night late in September, Margaret was awakened by what she thought was a flicker of morning sunlight playing on the walls of her room at *Woodbrae*. But the sun didn't flicker like that. She jumped out of bed, flinging aside the curtains at the window.

A sheet of flame about fifty yards high was leaping from the new extension of the Dunbar Mill and, even as she looked at it, the telephone rang and she could hear bells ringing all over the town, as engines converged from different parts on the mill.

Everyone in the house was immediately wide awake. She and Cullum dressed; Fleur tried to pacify Yvonne while the nanny soothed baby Charles. Both children, as though alerted to disaster, had simultaneously burst out

427

crying. The maids ran around falling over each other and one or two of them broke down in tears as well. Margaret and Cullum raced down the hill just as all the lights in the houses started flickering on. Margaret had on a warm jumper and trousers, a heavy coat on top. She had never known she could run as she did, nor what she would do when she arrived at the scene, for about three fire engines were there before them and steady sprays of water jetted forth from half a dozen hoses which had been directly put into the Drume.

There was smoke everywhere and the noise seemed to make it all worse, but no disorder, as though the fire brigade had been preparing all their lives for such a terrible emergency as this. First it was ascertained the new extension was empty, then the hoses were applied from six different positions. But it was hopeless. The flames had already got a hold. In the rest of the mill, it was subsequently discovered, none of the frames ever stopped their mechanical knitting as long as the emergency lasted. The fire brigade managed to contain the blaze to the new building, which had been empty because an all-night shift was not yet in operation there. But despite all their efforts, it was gutted.

How had it happened? No one knew. By dawn the fire was out and only a few sparks occasionally flashed from what was now a blackened shell, the walls still intact, the windows glassless, like gouged eyes, and the beams of the roof exposed like the skeleton of a giant dinosaur that had been discovered after the passing of thousands of years.

Margaret worked all night to make sure that everything that could be done was being done, that everyone was safe, and that the operators on the working frames were ready to stop them and evacuate themselves at a moment's notice. Those who lived in houses nearby came out to offer tea to the workers; two ambulances and three police cars stood by, and blankets and stretchers were ready in case they were necessary.

Slowly dawn broke, but there was no sun, just a heavy overcast sky and a few drops of rain. Margaret leaned dejectedly against the bridge, watching the firemen go in and out of the wrecked building ensuring that nothing ignitable remained. She rubbed her eyes and found that they smarted. She felt heavy and lifeless as though something inside her too had been burned out.

'Cup of tea, Miss Dunbar?'

'Thank you.' Margaret mechanically reached out her hand and smiled. A familiar gaze met hers.

'Oh Nan . . .' She didn't know what to say. 'Thank you, Nan. How did you come to be here?'

'I was with my Da. He hasn't been well.'

'I'm sorry to hear that.' Margaret stirred the thick, strong tea with a spoon Nan had given her.

'I'm sorry about the fire, Miss Dunbar.'

'It's a terrible tragedy Nan. How . . . how are you? And William?'

'Me and William are fine, Miss, thank you. I hear you've a bonny new bairn yourself.'

'Yes. He's nearly three months.'

'I see you sometimes going past our house tae your cottage in your big brown car.'

Was it a reproach? Margaret couldn't tell. It could be that, or a simple statement of fact. She looked into Nan's eyes, but they were fathomless. She sighed and shook her head. 'I'm sorry Nan. There's so much to say, but not now. Not now, do you mind?'

'I understand, Miss; but stop by at the cottage one day if you like. William is a real bonny boy; just like his faither. You'd be welcome.'

Margaret passed the empty cup to Nan, who accepted it wordlessly then turned and walked away.

Margaret sat down on the steps by the bridge and felt

429

like weeping. Whether it was because of Nan or the fire she couldn't tell. A fireman called to her and she was glad to get up and see what he wanted. Cullum emerged from the new building and there were people, people everywhere. She was now superfluous and felt she could go home and have a bath. Then she saw Cullum joined by a familiar figure in a sheepskin coat and, as she looked at him, he saw her and waved. Cullum beckoned her over.

'Hello, Ruthven.'

'Margaret, I'm *very* sorry.'

'It's terrible, isn't it? I can't take it in.'

'Cullum was saying no one is hurt.'

'No, there was no one in the building, thank God; and it was very well designed. It had fire doors between it and the old building, just like a ship. Well, we shall just have to rebuild . . .'

'Rebuild?' Cullum, eyes bloodshot, the stubble of beard on his chin blackened with smoke, looked appalled at the idea. 'How can we rebuild?'

'It can be done in six months,' Margaret said with an optimism she was far from feeling. 'We can have production going within a year.'

With one accord the three of them stepped back and gazed at the smoking ruin. Ruthven slowly shook his head.

'You're an optimist, Margaret, but then you always were.'

The chief fire officer called over to Cullum, the night foreman also came up to see him and he went off with his arm round one, talking to another, while a reporter hovered with his notebook and pencil poised, wanting a word.

'I don't think there's anything more I can do here.' Margaret looked after Cullum. 'Have you got your car, Ruthven?'

'Yes, let me run you home.'

'How did you hear of the fire?'

'Father rang. He said the sky was lit up. He thought the *whole* place was on fire.'

'I haven't seen your father for years.'

'He's still quite agile. I say, do you remember when

'Oh I remember. Don't remind me.' They rounded building and walked up a narrow road to the High St where Ruthven had left his car. He lived with his wife in a village near Homerton. The streets were thronged with people, some apparently feeling the need to get out into the street, even if there was nothing they could do. Some were on their way to work at the mill or other mills, and some were stocking their shops prior to opening. Early morning buses trundled past and one or two fire engines were slowly clambering up the narrow lanes that led from the mill.

Margaret climbed into the front seat and Ruthven got in next to her, looking at her to see if she was alright.

'Need a rug?'

'No thanks. I was quite cold but now I'm warm. It's very kind of you to run me up, Ruthven. I'm taking you out of your way.'

'Isn't it the *least* I could do? Besides, I was going to see Father and Mother. The children are staying with them.'

'Oh?' Margaret looked at him. 'Is your wife not well?'

'Cathy is very ill.' She realized now that Ruthven's grey drawn face, his subdued air was not just because of the fire. 'She has TB. I thought you might have heard.'

'No, I hadn't heard.'

'She's been at a sanatorium in the Trossachs, but the doctors would like her to go abroad. Of course, with the situation in Europe as it is, I don't know what to do.'

'How long have you known this?'

'Only a few months. Cathy was never strong; she always had a weak chest. I've seen her go down in the past year.'

431

'It must be a terrible worry for you.'

'It is a worry, and business is a worry. But you've had your troubles too. That business with Macallister was shocking. Now this. What will you do?'

'I daresay we'll survive. We always have.'

Ruthven grimaced. 'Cullum is no survivor. By the look on his face tonight . . .'

'Of course he's upset by what has happened.' Margaret's tone was sharp, defensive. 'But he has never given in. He conquered his alcoholism by willpower, you know. He hasn't had a drink for years, and we haven't had a smooth passage even before the terrible thing that happened to Bruno. Cullum is much stronger than you think.'

'But is he strong enough to see this through and carry the business?'

'The family will rally round him.'

'And there's you.' Ruthven glanced at her.

'Of course there's me; but I have my own small family now, my young daughter, my new baby son. I don't mean I'm just going to settle down to be a mother, that's not in my nature, but I don't want to take a front seat. We'll all help, but then there is a new generation coming on. Malcolm's son Murdoch is seventeen now and we're hoping that he'll want to come into the business after he goes to Oxford.'

They had crossed the bridge and were driving along the far side of the Drume from where the damage to the mill looked truly horrific. Margaret shuddered and her gloom was reinforced by what Ruthven had said about Cullum. She had defended him, but did he really have the will to survive, the power?

'Then there's Juliet's son, Tom,' she continued cheerfully. 'He's in his last year at Edinburgh. Then he's going to read for the Bar. He is a very nice boy and very capable, a bit like Malcolm was. The sort of settled, steady boy we'd like in the business. Tom will probably become a lawyer like his father, but he may want to join Dunbars. It's just a question of waiting a year or two and biding our time. You see it's all very dynastic still, Ruthven. No room for Pendreighs I'm afraid.'

'That's the last thing in my mind.' Ruthven smiled. 'Although I often think that, if it wasn't for what happened that day, you and I might have married.'

'Do you really *often* think about it?' Margaret's tone was bantering.

'Well, not often; that's an exaggeration. And I've been very happy with Cathy, as I expect you have with Yves. I expect he's delighted about his son.'

'Yes, delighted,' Margaret said, as they turned into the drive of *Woodbrae* and Fleur came running out to meet them.

Despite Margaret's optimism the rebuilding was slow; it was a bad winter and for several weeks of it Branswick, along with the rest of the Scottish Border country, lay below feet of snow and no building was possible. There was also the question of insurance and all sorts of legal matters to be sorted out, although it was soon established that the fire had been started by a faulty electrical connection, and not deliberately.

However, all production in the mill was badly affected. The January trade show had to be cancelled because smoke from the fire had penetrated the yarn store and thousands of cones were unfit to be used; so the ladies' wear suffered and the manufacture of the men's range came to a complete standstill.

By the end of April the new building was well advanced, but so was the size of the Dunbar overdraft.

The nation at large felt that prosperity was just around the corner. Unemployment was the lowest since 1930. Baldwin's popularity as leader of the Coalition (following the resignation of Ramsay MacDonald) had been confirmed by elections in November, and in January 1936 the country had a new and popular King. The old King, the grandson of Queen Victoria, had been loved; but Edward VIII was felt to be more a man of the people and great things were expected of his reign. His accession typified the enduring quality of the monarchy which had been such a prominent feature of the Jubilee the previous year. Everyone hoped that he would soon marry and have a family of his own.

On the other hand the international situation showed no signs of settling down. Hitler had occupied the demili-tarized Rhineland, thus contravening the Locarno Treaty, and France, who felt threatened, clamoured for action against its former adversary. Mussolini had invaded Abys-sinia and there were rumblings of unrest in Spain.

In the six months since the fire Margaret had constantly, and against her inclination, travelled back and forth to London cajoling, pleading, intervening, postponing, tak-ing action wherever it was necessary. How they missed Bruno in this crisis! Cullum had been confirmed as sole managing director at a board meeting in the autumn and now Susan tried to take a more active role as a director; but the burden fell on Margaret. Yves began to travel more abroad and Cullum hardly ever left Branswick, saying that the rebuilding programme needed his constant attention. It was an unhappy, dispiriting and rather alarm-ing time. No one could be sure that the predominance of Dunbar in the knitwear field would last.

In April a board meeting was held in Branswick to review progress and make plans. Present were Margaret, Susan, Juliet, Yves and Joe Macallister. Bruno's death had brought Joe and Susan very close together and he had picked her up in his Bentley and brought her to the mill.

Susan had never thought Bruno was entirely faithful. The way he used to eye women in public was an indication of a sexual restlessness that he showed at home; she didn't

434

think it was just confined to looking. But when the blow had fallen the extent of his deception was almost too much to believe. Unlike many women who clung to their faithless husbands whatever the provocation, Susan rejected Bruno and any thought of honouring his memory except in public. What he had done was despicable, she felt, a disgrace to him and his family.

Although she grieved, few people recalled her shedding a tear. To those, like her immediate family, who had known her for a long time her behaviour reminded them of the young woman who, nearly twenty years before, had learned of the death of her fiancé in the war and had not shown much emotion then.

It was perhaps this lack of emotion in Susan that had made her husband wander in the first place. She did not show her feelings easily. She was a controlled and rather cautious woman who could feel love very strongly, but not show it. She also disapproved of displays of affection on the part of others. Her relationship with her two children was equally restrained, although she loved them very deeply. They were growing up as independent and fair-minded as she, and the opinions that others held about them were never of overriding importance. Some people said the Macallisters were cold; but when Bruno was murdered they said the control shown by his widow and his children was heroic, an example to those who broke down under grief.

Susan soon went about her business in her own quiet way. By his ignominious death Bruno had shown the world, in a particularly blatant way, that his wife could not keep him. She thus had to hold her head higher and show even less feeling in order to recover her self-respect.

Margaret's emotional life was something she could never understand. She could not conceive how a woman as fastidious as her sister could sleep with the sort of man the family had known Bob Morgan to be, or how she could have a child by someone she refused to name and then foist it on her husband.

But beneath this criticism of her sister, which she kept to herself, Susan loved her as much as she could love anyone. The two embraced warmly when they met in the boardroom before the meeting and then hugged Juliet who came in after them, having driven from Edinburgh just for the day, regarding the necessity of attending the board meeting as just one more event in a busy life. Looking at them together few would have said they had changed much over the years, except that Juliet was just a little plump now, and Susan had some grey hairs, maybe due to her bereavement. The three of them had the same glorious thick curly hair, although differently styled, and the often rapturously quoted blue-green Dunbar eyes. But Margaret had kept her looks the best; she was still tall and slim, conspicuously graceful, and her make-up enhanced her looks, being neither too much nor too little. She wore a tailored dress in fawn shantung with a fur stole round her shoulders, and a wide-brimmed straw hat with a band made of the same material as her dress. Susan wore a grey check suit and Juliet, functional rather than smart, a skirt and a Dunbar twin-set with a row of pearls. What the sisters chose to wear that day seemed an exact expression of what they were: Margaret fashion-conscious and chic as ever, a woman to whom her clothes and appearance were important, whatever the circumstances; Susan painstaking, but sensible, and Juliet too busy to take any interest in clothes; but all of them clever, alert and markedly sophisticated in their different ways.

They chatted for a while with Joe Macallister and Yves until Cullum arrived late and looking rather harassed, asking that the meeting should start without delay. He had a sheaf of papers in his hand and had been talking to his secretary as he came in.

'Is Mary here?' he barked, looking round after greeting Joe and his two sisters.

'No, she sent her apologies.' Juliet took a letter from her bag. 'She's visiting Oxford with Murdoch. She will agree with any decision taken by the majority.'

She handed the letter to Cullum. Glancing at it, he gave it to his secretary, who sat quietly by his side taking the minutes all during the meeting. Then he drank from a glass of water, cleared his throat and launched into a pessimistic account of the business, the financial situation and the general outlook. The building was behind schedule; sales had been poor because of diminished stock; the overdraft at the bank was the highest it had ever been and the outlook was far from encouraging. Bruno Macallister's death, in his opinion, had dealt them a mortal blow in more senses than one. Gloomily he finished and looked around at a very subdued group of fellow directors, groping for some other papers by his side and whispering again to his secretary.

Yves passed a neatly folded handkerchief across his brow, adjusting his pince-nez as he studied his copy of the report which had been circulated in advance.

'Well, the outlook is very gloomy, Mr Chairman; but are you not being a *trifle* pessimistic? Cashmere is as strong a sales line as ever. I was in Rome only last week and . . .'

Cullum raised his hand and shuffled the papers before him. 'If you don't mind Yves, I have a statement of a personal nature to add to my report which will, I'm afraid, alter the situation even further. I had meant to keep it until later, but I'm convinced the moment to make it is now.' He whispered to his secretary who, looking rather nervous, rapidly turned over the pages of her notepad until she had found a clean sheet.

'As you know,' Cullum said, 'when the fire happened I felt that it was the end of all we had tried to do for

437

Dunbar. I couldn't see how we could survive and rebuild, because although the last years had been good we depended very much on keeping ahead of the fashion; our cash flow was constantly stretched. This year we were not able to hold our usual trade show in January and the July one will be very small.

'It's almost as though there has been some intervention on the part of the Almighty to stop us succeeding. I cannot explain it.' Cullum paused and for a moment his head sank on his chest. Margaret was reminded of their father; it was a well known attitude of defeat adopted by the Dunbar men when they felt they were losing. She felt a tremor of apprehension. Then he looked up and his eyes seemed momentarily to seek comfort from Margaret. He cleared his throat and leaned over what was obviously a prepared statement.

'It may be the wrong time to say this to my family and fellow directors but I have made a decision which is of enormous personal importance to me and us all. I informed my wife this morning.'

Cullum briefly gazed out of the window as though reliving that painful scene in the house on the hill.

'I am leaving Fleur to live with Nan Murray, who has been my companion for many years; whose devotion saved me from alcoholism, as you all know. I would like to marry Nan if Fleur would divorce me; but she still says, as she has said before, that she won't. No matter. My mind is made up. I feel I cannot live without Nan or I will begin to drink again. I nearly started when we had the fire and it was only her influence that dissuaded me. It is, sadly, a compulsion that never entirely leaves me and it was solely due to her that I did not return to the hospital.

'I want to resign from Dunbars as chairman. In order to make it easier for you to release me, I have disposed of my entire shareholding. I propose to invest the

438

money, and to be able to live on it with Nan and my son William in the countryside. That is all.'

Cullum sat back and Margaret could see that the hand which held his papers trembled. No wonder he had sought comfort from her. She saw that everyone around the table was staring at him as though doubting the evidence of their ears. Quickly she spoke.

'May I ask to whom you have sold your shares, Cullum?'

'To Elliott Pendreigh.'

A buzz broke out but Margaret reached for the chairman's gavel and banged the table. 'Do you not realize, Cullum, that you had an obligation to offer them to your family first? It is written in the articles.'

Cullum closed his eyes briefly before opening them again. He looked very tired, as though he had not slept. 'If I'd done that, as you well know Margaret, we would have had another family scene, a family brawl and I would have ended up bowing to you as I always have. Whenever there's been a crisis, something with which I disagreed, I've always given in. I'm no match for you and Susan and Juliet, and I never have been. I feel at last that I am free and my own man. That *I* have made a decision and no one is going to alter it. The articles were made up, I believe, in order to prevent Macallisters gaining control of the firm. Well, Bruno is dead and his shares, as you know, were divided between his father and Susan. So the Dunbar family remains in control even with Elliott Pendreigh and Joe having a substantial share. I took legal advice and that is what I was told. Bruno's death had the effect of negativing the articles, which we should have rewritten.'

'I notice you didn't consult any family lawyers, or my husband,' Juliet said bitterly. 'Because you know the advice would have been very different. And why, of *all* people, Elliott Pendreigh?'

'Because he has always wanted a part in Dunbars. I

know you think they're enemies; but I consider them as friends, old friends. I could sell my shares to whom I pleased. I also wanted speed and secrecy, and I knew that in Elliott I had a ready and willing buyer.'

'Did Ruthven know of this?' Margaret felt she was still unable to assimilate the news.

'I don't know, nor did I ask. The shares were bought personally by Elliott. Ruthven, as we all know, has been abroad with his wife Cathy in Switzerland where she has gone for her health. The old man is in control again, for the time being. Now I think I am going to leave you to discuss this. I move that Joe Macallister temporarily takes the chair until a new chairman is appointed.'

'Seconded,' Juliet said, watching her brother as he rose slowly from his chair like an old man. He gave an awkward bow and then went very swiftly to the door in case anyone should try and prevent him leaving.

Joe Macallister, took the chair and gravely regarded those around him. 'I am speaking as the only one here who is not related to the Dunbars except remotely by marriage. I realize what a grave and unhappy day this is for all of you, how wrong you must think Cullum was to do what he has done. Yet is he wrong? You know that Cullum has devoted nearly twenty years to a business that he has had no interest in, and he hasn't done too badly. He kept you all together, and he helped towards the prosperity of the firm. For that, I think, he needs thanks, not reproach.'

'I reproach him for not consulting us,' Susan said. 'He has not been straight; nor honest.' She looked as though another blow was almost too much to bear and her lips trembled.

Joe sat back and rapped the baize-covered table with a short stubby finger. 'I am an old man, and I lost my dearest son in circumstances that grieve every waking moment of my day. But I do not want to see Dunbar go

440

down, a proud business that was founded a hundred and forty years ago. I know none of you wish it; yet what is to be done? Talk with Elliott Pendreigh?'

'Never,' Margaret said, her eyes blazing with scorn. 'Never, never, never.'

'Then it is up to *you*, Margaret.' Joe, leaning forward, beamed at her kindly. 'I know how you feel, and in time this is how you will make your family feel. They will not want to merge with Pendreighs for stubborn reasons of their own. Well, then, there's only one thing to do.' He pointed a finger at her as though he were peering along the barrel of a gun. '*You* Margaret, must assume the chairmanship of the family business you love so much. I feel, and I am sure the board will agree with me, that you and only you can save it now. There is no one else!'

Joe sat back and relit his pipe which had smouldered in an ashtray in front of him.

Yves gazed at Margaret and put his long fingers firmly over her hand. 'You must answer, Margaret. I think Joe has the answer. It is for a Dunbar to save Dunbars.'

'I must have time,' Margaret said, but Joe shook his head.

'There is no time. Once the news of Cullum's resignation gets out you will be bombarded with offers and bids. None of you will know what to do for the best and the confidence of the bank and of our customers will be eroded further. Already Bruno's death has done us a lot of damage, because people do not like personal scandal in business. It saddens me to say it, but I know it is true. There were too many whispers. Then, almost on top of that, came the fire.

'Now we are faced with yet another scandal, when the news gets round that Cullum intends to leave his wife and set up house with his mistress, an ex-employee of the mill. What sort of impression will that create, coming not a year after Bruno's death? People will wonder if the Dunbar and Macallister families are fit to run a business at all.

441

'No, today we must emerge from here a board united behind its chairman. The only one I think people will have any confidence in is you, Margaret, and I do not mean disrespect to Yves or your sisters.'

'You must do it.' Susan leaned forward, the grief in her eyes replaced by a light of hope. 'You *must* do it – not only for us, but for our children.'

The children. Margaret's eyes gazed out of the window towards the hill where the large houses were, overlooked by the largest of all, *Woodbrae*, home of the Dunbars, built by another strong Dunbar chairman, her great-uncle James.

For the children? She had two nephews who were nearly ready, others growing up. In *Woodbrae* was her own little son, Charles, who might join Dunbars in the fifties. There was Yvonne who might emulate her mother and decide that simply marriage and home were not for her. Was it not her duty to preserve the business for the new generation?

She looked round the table at the board, every one of them related to her. She thought of the widows, Susan and Mary, and the woman who was not a widow but would be like one, Fleur. And herself, not a widow but not a wife. She had to think of herself too.

It was quite true that, if she refused, the days of the firm as a family concern would be over. They might even have to go into liquidation or sell at any price. *Woodbrae* might have to go and the London house. She really had no choice.

She joined her hands on the table and looked at the rings on her fingers. Maybe she would have to sell the Marie Antoinette diamond, after all, if she did nothing now. And Yves, would he renege on his promise if he were not paid? The thought caused her lips to flicker briefly with amusement. Her gaze rested on him and the look in his eyes, more than anything else, decided her.

'I'll do it,' she said at last, and the sigh round the table seemed to issue not from many mouths, but one; as though it were a spontaneous expression on the part of those present of unanimous, heartfelt relief. 'I may not succeed, but I'll have a jolly good try. I do it not so much for the present generation, for us; but for our children.'

She looked at Yves and he smiled, nodding his head sagely, because he knew what precisely she meant.

PART III

War and Resolution
1943–1951

CHAPTER TWENTY FIVE

Already it was hard, looking at the emaciated figure of her brother, to remember that he was a man of only forty-four – a man who a few months before had been tall, vigorous and strong. Now the aseptic white hospital bedclothes outlined his skeletal frame, and his cheeks were sunken like those of a very old man. Most of the day he slept while the tubes and apparatus that emerged grotesquely from under the sheets went on with the mechanical job of keeping him alive. Gazing at him, Margaret was reminded of how quickly their father went once he had decided to go.

Had Cullum decided to go? It was true he had a melancholic, fatalistic streak; but he had seemed very happy with his desk job in Edinburgh, having joined Malcolm's old regiment the Scots Borderers soon after the outbreak of war in 1939. Nan had moved up to be with him, and it was not until a year ago that the first intimations of the disease that had reduced him to such straits became apparent. Cullum had never had a very good digestion and in the third full year of the war he had started to complain of stomach pain. Gradually he lost weight and then he had an operation in Edinburgh Infirmary for an intestinal obstruction. Something much more serious was found; he had been removed to London to be under the care of a leading abdominal surgeon, but it was difficult to believe that he would see out the spring.

'What's happening to the war, Margaret?' Cullum said in a faint voice. 'No one tells me anything.' His eyes remained closed as though the effort of speech were already too much for him. His eyelids were transparent

447

and thinly veined, sunken into their sockets. His voice seemed to issue from a cadaver.

'The Eighth Army has withdrawn from the Mareth Line. The Prime Minister has spoken of his visit to Washington. The Russians . . .'

'But are we *winning*?' Cullum's voice assumed a note of urgency, and his eyes suddenly opened, searching hers anxiously.

Were we winning? The tide had certainly turned after the dark years of '40 '41 and '42. Now, in the spring of 1943, the pursuit of Rommel in North Africa, following the victory at El Alamein, had given hope to everyone. The Germans had been defeated in Stalingrad and were being routed on the Russian front, and RAF and American planes were nightly inflicting a terrible toll on German cities with their bombs. Death from the skies had come at last. How everyone had dreaded the concept in the thirties; how impossible it had all seemed. But so had a war like this, a war that was in its fourth year, involving almost the whole globe.

'We shall win, Cullum,' Margaret said firmly. 'We cannot lose with Churchill.'

'You say that in the same voice you used to announce some plan we all disapproved of.' Cullum gave a weak laugh. 'It's the "Maggie will have her own way" tone.'

'Well, if Maggie has her own way we shall certainly win the war.'

Margaret smiled and leaning over him looked into his eyes, trying to instil into him her own optimism and determination as she always had. But what she saw only increased the private terror she invariably felt whenever she visited Cullum: that his time on this earth was nearly over.

'It's ironical, isn't it Maggie, that I was too young for the last war and too old for this? They didn't want to take me at all you know. And now I'm dying.'

448

Margaret had often wondered if he knew how serious his illness was. The sick had a habit either of self-deception or of wanting to be deceived; or maybe it was their attempt at self-preservation. This had been his fourth operation and now he was fed purely by intravenous injection, unable to take any nourishment by mouth, not even water. He scarcely had any stomach left; but still the doctors had held out some sort of hope which enabled her, now, to say still in a voice resonant with conviction: 'You are *not* dying, Cullum, and we *are* winning the war.'

'Have you seen all these gadgets?' Cullum tried to look down at his body but lacked the strength even for that. 'I'm hardly a man at all.'

'It doesn't mean you are dying; you are very ill, but not dying. And we have been very sick in the war but now we are getting better. Both you and the country will pull through.'

'I still wish . . .' Cullum began but the door opened and a nurse came in carrying a tray.

'Time for our injections, Mr Dunbar. Then we have another visitor.' She looked at Margaret who got up and gathered her things together. She always sewed or knitted when she was with Cullum; the rhythmic click of the needles helped her to maintain her composure.

'I'll go, Nurse. Who is the visitor?'

'Lieutenant-Commander Murray. A very handsome young man, if I may say so.'

'You *may* say so, Nurse.' Cullum smiled weakly. 'He's my son and he takes after his father.'

'Well, then, your son is waiting to see you, Mr Dunbar. Isn't that a nice surprise?'

'It's a lovely surprise,' Cullum said, his voice stronger. 'He was missing, believed killed, on the North Atlantic run last winter. He was sixteen hours in the water after his ship was sunk by a U-boat. It was a miracle he survived.'

Tears started to trickle from his eyes, looking like drops of rain on his yellow, withered cheeks, and the nurse bent and stroked his brow in a gesture that Margaret found infinitely moving. Yes, Cullum was dying. Nurses usually only became so tender with terminal patients.

'I'll go and see William,' Margaret said briskly, 'and tell him you won't be long.'

'Maggie . . .' Cullum raised his voice as she turned to go, turning his head painfully so that he could look at her. 'Do you think he should see me . . . like this?'

'Of course he should see you! You imagine you look much worse than you do.'

'Don't go, Maggie. Come back.'

Margaret smiled at him and then at the nurse, glad that neither saw her tears as she walked slowly along the corridor, past half-open doors containing other sufferers, to the waiting room.

'You look as though you've been crying, Margaret,' William got up as she came in and awkwardly advanced towards her, one hand outstretched, as though he did not quite know what to do. 'Is Father worse?'

Margaret sat down and wiped her eyes with her handkerchief. 'I'm afraid so, William. You must prepare yourself for a shock. I don't think he has long.'

'They didn't tell me it was as bad as that.'

William sat next to her and crossed his legs. He wore his naval uniform with a polo-necked navy sweater instead of a shirt and tie. On his left breast was the ribbon of the Distinguished Service Cross which he had been awarded for heroism at sea. Nan and Cullum had attended the ceremony at Buckingham Palace just before Cullum's illness began. Nan had changed her name to Dunbar by deed poll, but William declined to do the same. Perhaps he felt that his father had been too long in recognizing him; or perhaps it was to show that he was proud of the independence of his mother.

William had turned into a fine young man, one of whom any mother or father could be proud. He had won distinctions in two of the three subjects he took for his Higher School Certificate and had gone into the Navy before the outbreak of war. His full ginger beard made him look even more handsome, Margaret thought, as she wondered what more she could say.

There was something very strong about William; he was the sort of man you trusted and told things to. Yet he was also very aloof. She knew that he included her in the same bracket of reserve that he maintained towards all his father's family; a politeness, but a definite desire to keep his distance. In this category he put his aunts and cousins and all those who had, at some time or other, ostracized or wounded his mother. He was an unfathomable young man, someone who revealed little of himself. It did not surprise her that he was proving a hero in the war. He had that calibre.

'He looks dreadful today,' Margaret said at last. 'It's difficult to know what keeps him alive. I think it's the thought of seeing you. Will you go in alone when the nurse comes? I'll wait for you out here. I don't . . .' Margaret dabbed at her eyes again. 'I don't trust my emotions in front of him.'

They sat in silence for a while and then the nurse came in and said, 'Your father would like to see you, Lieutenant-Commander Murray. Will you come in too, Mrs Lamotte?'

'I'm going to stay here.' Margaret gave a reassuring smile to William as he looked at her. 'I'll get on with my knitting.'

William, who had been on convoy duty and had not seen his father for several months, did not recognize him. The shock was so violent that he looked towards the door as though wondering if he could run out before he gave himself away. Cullum's eyes remained closed, but slowly he raised his thin grey hand and it groped the air, searching for his. William put his own strong young brown hand in that of his father. It was like being grasped by the claw of a bird. Cullum opened his eyes, as though the very act gave him pain, and drew him down.

'Do I look so very terrible, William?'

'No, Father. No.' William knelt on the floor and grasped his father's hand, looking at him, smiling bravely. His fear had gone as it had when he saw the hull of his ship sink beneath the waves, and he knew he was alone except for a few comrades like himself. The dead bodies of others floated about like corks bobbing on the water while the U-boats glided beneath him like sinister sharks, ready to surface at any moment and strike again. Then his fear had gone because he was face to face with a desperate reality; and to be one step ahead, retaining all his faculties of ingenuity and cunning, was to remain alive. When the U-boat finally surfaced he pretended to bob about with the other corpses, and when it submerged he clung to one of them through the long night, until the dawn and rescue came.

'I'm very proud of you William, very sorry for my misdeeds, very ashamed of them. For many years I wasn't a good father to you.' Cullum wrinkled his brow as if trying to recall some distant unpleasant event, the memory of which still caused him pain. 'It wasn't easy in those days you know. But still, I was weak; I confess I was weak.'

'Don't torment yourself, Father. What's past is past. It did me no harm.'

'No, it didn't.' Cullum seemed to gain strength from his son's young hand and he squeezed it. 'You're like your mother and my brother Malcolm, a strong man, a strong Dunbar. If I die, William, and I know I am going to but not when, I want you to take my name. You can hyphenate it if you like; Murray-Dunbar. Will you promise me?'

'I cannot promise it, Father. I'll have to think about it.'
The sweat on William's face was evidence of his dilemma.

'I would like it more than anything.' Cullum sighed and
closed his eyes again, his hand slackening so that he let
William's fall. 'I wanted to marry your mother; but Fleur
would never let me. I asked her before this last operation
to give me a divorce so that I could at least repay the
wrong I did you and your mother and legitimize you. I
begged her. But she would not. Now it's too late. I shall
die soon; but I want you to know how I felt. How much I
love your mother, and you.'

'I know that, Father.' Tears came into William's eyes
and he buried his face in the bedclothes.

'Ah, good, you're crying,' Cullum whispered, trying to
kiss his son's carroty head. 'Now I know that you really
love me.'

Margaret did not see Cullum again that day, and William
went back to the hotel in Baker Street where he was
staying with his mother, after promising to come to
dinner. Nan had refused to stay with Margaret since
Cullum had been transferred to London because she did
not feel she was 'family', despite Margaret's protestations,
and also because she wanted to be alone. She had spent
most of her life alone, cut off from the Dunbars and now it
was too late to change. Cullum's illness had made Nan go
into herself and, except for William when he was on leave,
she saw few people.

Margaret went to the office where she telephoned the
house to give instructions about dinner. She still had her
two maids, but the gardener had joined up. Dora Rowntree was the only person left at the London office because
those of the design staff who remained had all been
transferred to Branswick. Margaret tried to put the constant nagging ache about Cullum from her mind and
settled in her chair to study a sheaf of notes and figures,

453

but it was hard to concentrate. The air-raid warnings had gone the previous night, and, although she had remained in her bed, she had not slept, remembering those frightening days of 1941 when the fighters repulsing the waves of German bombers had screamed all day over London. Since then the raids had been spasmodic and not very damaging and most people, like her, took little note of the sirens and did not trouble to get out of bed.

The war had made surprisingly little difference to the house of Dunbar. Indeed, in many ways it consolidated what had become a highly successful business with a world-wide reputation. Yarn had been rationed by the Limitation of Supplies Order; the war in the Far East had cut short the supply of wool from Australia, and cashmere was almost impossible to come by. Yet the garments produced by Dunbars and others like them who had remained in production (some factories had been requisitioned by the government for the manufacture of armaments) were of such superior quality that order books were full; and what 'non-utility' garments they were able to make went to the United States and countries in South America. Many people in England for the first time were able to wear knitted Dunbar garments that, during the twenties and thirties, only the rich were able to afford. The 'utility' Dunbar sweaters, jerseys, cardigans and pullovers were popular because they were warm and durable, easy to launder, fashionable over slacks and indispensable on cold nights for ARP wardens, or under siren suits or over nightclothes when the wearers had hurried to the shelters. Whatever Dunbars could make they sold and, in addition, they had big government contracts for underwear and woollen garments for men and women in the Services.

In 1941, Yves despite his age, and because of his persistence, had been dropped into France to serve with the Maquis and since then Margaret had only seen him once. Occasionally she received a letter from an unknown part of France, but she had not heard from him now in months. Yvonne and Morag were at the boarding school in Harrogate to which the Dunbar girls had gone; Charles was at prep school in Edinburgh, and Murdoch Dunbar was with the Third Tank Battalion of the Scots Guards, which formed part of the Sixth Guards' Tank Brigade. Juliet's two sons Tom and Paul were in the Army while Susan's son James, now nineteen, was training as a pilot with the RAF.

Yes, despite the war, Dunbars were doing well. The turnover in 1941 had been the highest ever, and its period of greatest prosperity had coincided with the time in 1936 when Margaret had assumed the mantle of Chairman and Managing Director.

Which was just as well, she thought, riffling through the papers in her hand. Many firms had suffered because their senior personnel had left to join the war. Mactavishes had gone over entirely to munitions when Angus, who had been Cornet in 1923, and his two brothers had joined the Army, and 73-year-old Elliott Pendreigh was once again at the helm of his family firm after Ruthven and his brother Dirk went to the war. Hamish Ogilvy, whose daughter Fiona was married to Tom Monroe, was in a reserved occupation as an engineer. His firm was one of the largest manufacturers of munitions' parts in Scotland. Margaret hadn't seen him since Tom's wedding in 1939. Because Dunbars had a woman at the top it remained stable, and had prospered more than its competitors.

The phone rang and Margaret got up to answer it as Dora Rowntree put her head round the door. Margaret lifted the receiver and said 'One moment please,' then to Dora, 'Yes?'

'There's a man downstairs wants to talk to you personally, Mrs Lamotte.'

'Who is he, do you know?'

'He has a foreign accent. I think he's French. He says you know him, but he won't give his name.'

455

Dora Rowntree sniffed rather disapprovingly at this lapse of good manners.

'You'd better ask him to come up.' Margaret frowned as she put her mouth to the receiver. 'Hello?'

'Aunt Margaret?' Murdoch Dunbar's voice seemed very far away. 'I'm in London. I wondered if we could meet?'

'Of course we can meet. When?'

'Could we have dinner?'

'Dinner? Oh wait a moment. Nan and William are coming to dinner. Why don't you come too?'

There was a silence as Murdoch appeared to think about the situation. 'Well, it's a family thing I want to talk to you about.'

'We'll talk before.' She looked at her watch. 'If you pick me up here we can have a drink and then talk. Come early.'

'I'm going to see Uncle Cullum now. I'll come straight from the hospital.'

'Alright, I'll expect you.'

Puzzled by the urgency of his tone, an urgency mingled with excitement, Margaret put down the receiver and returned to her chair, forgetting all about her caller. There was a cough and she looked up, startled.

'Jacques!'

She rose quickly again and went to the door, grasping the hand of the man, still clad in his raincoat, who stood looking at her gravely. He kissed her hand and held on to it, pressing it. Jacques Lichine was on the staff of the secret organization housed in Dorset Square which had sent Yves to France.

'Jacques, come and sit down. Have you had tea?'

Jacques shook his head and suddenly something about his demeanour made Margaret's heart beat faster.

'Have you got news for me, Jacques . . . news of Yves?'

Jacques nodded and looked around him. 'If you have any brandy Margaret . . .'

'Brandy? You want brandy at this hour? I've got whisky.

456

We Scots are never without it you know. Oh *brandy*. You mean for *me*?' Margaret sat down abruptly, the rhythm of her heart making a deafening noise in her ears. 'There's something *bad* about Yves, Jacques?'

'He's dead, Margaret. I'm sorry to be the one to tell you; they wanted to send you a telegram but I preferred to tell you myself.'

Margaret was never to forget that day, in April 1943, when she learned that she was a widow; that the man she had been so strangely married to for fifteen years was dead. She seemed to look down upon the tableau of herself and Jacques Lichinc, the one standing, the other sitting, in the timeless elegance of the office that she had made and kept as like a private drawing room as possible, with its period furniture, its French carpet and its white and gold décor. She seemed to see the gravity of their faces, the statuesque, almost stylized repose of their bodies, and she was aware that it was very still with no sound of traffic coming from the street outside or the Marylebone Road a few hundred yards away.

Strangely. Why had she used that word? Because it had been a strange marriage; no marriage really, but a partnership beginning with love and ending with friendship; with hatred, distaste and a kind of loathing playing their parts somewhere in the middle. She had long ceased to feel really married to Yves; but then she didn't feel she was not married to him either. Perhaps a lot of marriages were like this: partnerships, a convenient way of living while each party went about their own separate business.

'Thank you for telling me, Jacques.' Margaret gave him her hand and he pressed it again. 'You'll find the bottle of Scotch in the cupboard; there are glasses there too.'

She watched Jacques's swift neat movements, but when he put the glass in her hand she did not drink from it immediately. She did not want to look as though she needed the support of strong liquor. Jacques took off his

457

raincoat and sat opposite her. He was in the uniform of a French Army officer and he looked very military with his hair cut *en brosse* and his pencil-thin moustache.

'Yves died very bravely. He was captured by the Germans and tortured, but he said nothing to betray his comrades. He died under interrogation so we know that he suffered; but we also know he said nothing, we know that for sure.'

'I'm glad.' Margaret took a sip of her drink, realizing what an inadequate, seemingly heartless thing it was to say. Yet the thought of Yves under torture was almost too much to contemplate. 'I'm glad, I mean, that he died bravely; because the memory is important, is it not? For him and you as well as for us?'

'Yes, his children and friends will honour him. We of the Free French will honour him. General de Gaulle has sent a personal message through me to you, expressing his sorrow and admiration. He wrote it in his own hand.'

Margaret took the envelope that Jacques held out to her and mechanically opened it after reaching for a paper knife. The General sent his condolences. The Vicomte de Lamotte would always be remembered etc. etc. She put aside the letter and linked her hands loosely in her lap.

'How kind of the General. How *very* kind. I will answer it, of course.'

'I believe it is his wish to honour Yves with a decoration; but that will be announced later. Yves was betrayed.' Jacques got up and refilled his glass, noticing that Margaret had hardly touched hers. 'He belonged to a cell in Paris that had networks as far as the Spanish border. Somewhere along the line there was a traitor; but he managed to warn his comrades who escaped capture, at the expense of his own life. He was really very brave indeed.' Jacques held up his glass as if in a silent toast, and then reached for his raincoat. 'I must go, Margaret. I wish there were something more I could do. But : . .' He

458

shrugged. 'Alas, I have to do this painful duty too often. We have many enemies from the Vichy government who can infiltrate our work. Frenchmen betraying Frenchmen. At least you do not have this in your country.'

'We have our spies too, I expect.' Margaret got up and helped him with his coat. 'But your people who are brave are very very brave, and that makes up for a lot.'

She knew it was curious that she, a very emotional person, had felt no need for tears, no desire to break down or comfort herself with drink. Not yet anyway. It was difficult, at this moment, to analyse exactly how she felt. Maybe Jacques thought she was too calm, but Jacques Lichine was a very brave man, a soldier, and Yves had died a hero's death. She, Margaret, his widow, would behave as the widows of heroes should behave, and show no emotion in public.

'By the way – ' Jacques put a cigarette in his mouth and glanced at her. 'Would you tell Peter Cartwright?'

Margaret nodded her head, her expression impassive, her face briefly lit by a sad smile. 'I will tell Peter myself,' she said. 'You and I know how much he and Yves meant to each other.'

Jacques puffed hard at his cigarette and then stubbed it out in the ashtray. 'You're a remarkable woman, Margaret. How lucky Yves was to have you.'

'And I was lucky to have Yves.' Margaret swallowed. If he was to have honour as a patriot, she did not want that honour to be demeaned as a husband. 'Don't think he didn't support me, because he did and it was he more than anyone else who helped to put Dunbars on the map. He was a brilliant salesman and publicist.'

'And a true Frenchman. He had no need to do what he did. He could so easily have stayed out of the war on account of his age.'

Jacques momentarily bowed his head, then he brusquely took Margaret's hand, kissed it and left the room.

Margaret was standing by the window when Dora brought in Murdoch Dunbar a few moments later. He had on his khaki greatcoat over his uniform and carried his peaked cap with the check band and badge of the Scots Guards in his hand. He kissed Margaret, putting his arm round her shoulder.

'Dora told me. Need I say more? I am terribly, terribly sorry.'

Margaret shook her head but said nothing, aware of his manly hand on her shoulder. In the years since Murdoch had grown up she had become very close to him. Both in his appearance and manner he resembled his father, Malcolm, and she hoped that he would enter the business after the war. He was just approaching his twenty-fifth birthday and was everything the sisters, who had seen so little of him when he was growing up, hoped he would be. She turned to face him and put her hand over his.

'He was very brave. The General himself sent me a letter.'

Margaret gestured to the piece of paper lying on the sofa and then she leaned her head against Murdoch's chest and, to her intense surprise and humiliation, she wept.

'Oh Murdo, I'm so sorry.' She raised her head at last and looked at him. 'I didn't think I'd do that.'

Murdoch took out a large white handkerchief and smiled. 'You're always so brave, so controlled Aunt Margaret. Let yourself go a little. People don't mind, you know.'

'I wish you'd call me Margaret. "Aunt" makes me feel so old.'

'I try to remember. It's difficult to get rid of a lifetime's habit. There.' He finished wiping the tears from her cheeks and put his handkerchief away. Margaret sat down and joined her hands in front of her, twisting and untwisting her fingers.

'It isn't as though we were . . . close. You know about

460

our marriage, Murdo; but in the end I became fond of him, as people can become fond of each other after they've been through a lot together. Yves gave me a lot of unhappiness, but . . .' Margaret shrugged. She never knew how much the family knew about Yves, outside her brother and sisters. She assumed that their Scottish reticence had prevented gossip, but she could never be sure what Cullum might say to Nan, or Juliet to Tom or Susan to James and Hettie. What *was* known was the fact that, for whatever reason, they led pretty separate lives.

She had not thought she would cry; she had not even thought she would hear herself say she was still fond of Yves. Could she still really be fond of someone who had driven such a hard, ruthless bargain; who had sold his name for money? But that was seven years ago and he had kept his word. He had even seemed to become genuinely very fond of Charles who, correspondingly, adored and admired him. Yvonne loved him too. What now would she say to them? Somehow the possibility that she would lose Yves, that his work was dangerous had never occurred to her. She had expected that some people she knew would be killed in the war, but not Yves. There had been something about Yves that had made one feel he would always be able to take care of himself; that, if anyone could, he would survive.

'Now Murdo –' Margaret looked up and gave her customary bright cheerful smile. 'Why are you here, darling? You sounded so frightfully mysterious on the phone.'

Murdoch, seeing the whisky bottle, poured himself some in the glass Jacques had drunk from, and put it to his lips. Although he had the dark hair of his mother he had Malcolm's features and the blue-green Dunbar eyes. He was taller than Malcolm had been and was a very striking, not strictly handsome but well built young man who liked all forms of sport. Now, as he gazed solemnly at Margaret, his eyes lit up.

461

'I am in love Aunt . . . Margaret, I mean.'

'Oh Murdo, that's wonderful news!' Margaret, getting up, ran over to him and threw her arms around his neck. 'I wondered if it was something like that. You sounded so excited. And who is the very lucky girl? Do we know her?'

Murdoch gazed at her and put his hands loosely round her waist. 'Hettie. Hesther Macallister.'

Margaret for the second time that day had a feeling of shock and closed her eyes; but it was not an unpleasant shock as the first one had been. It was just that it was unexpected.

'Hesther *Macallister*?' She stressed the surname as though she wanted to be sure she had heard right. Murdoch nodded.

'My cousin, Hettie. I have always liked her you know.'

'Yes, I know that. But love . . .'

Murdoch had spent more time with the Macallisters, as he was growing up, than with the Dunbars. James enjoyed sport and outdoor activities as much as Murdoch and the two boys had been close despite the difference in their ages. James had always seemed to regard Murdoch as an older brother, and his twin sister Hesther was a bit of a tomboy and liked sports too. Margaret had always thought that when Murdoch fell in love it would be with someone very beautiful, very feminine. Hesther, though a lovely natured girl, was neither. She was in her second year at Oxford studying medicine.

'Hettie is so *young*,' Margaret heard herself saying.

'She's nineteen,' Murdoch protested, colouring. 'My mother was not much older when Father courted her.'

'True, but there is not the same sense of . . .' Margaret put her hands to her face. 'Oh I don't know how to say it. Doom I suppose. Why, we are winning the war aren't we Murdo?'

'Yes, but we haven't won it yet, Margaret.' Murdoch looked solemnly at her. 'There is a lot of fighting yet to do. There are all sorts of rumours about the second front. We're training hard. I know what you mean about Father's generation; but some of us may have to go too. I mean, not come back. I'm not saying I believe that will happen to me, in fact I feel pretty sure it won't, but Hettie and I would rather marry now and not wait until the war ends.'

'*Marry*.' Margaret felt as though she had lost her breath. 'You're talking about *marriage*?'

'What else?' Murdoch smiled. 'That's why I want your help.'

'Oh God she's not . . . ' Margaret looked up at him helplessly.

Murdoch frowned and shook his head. 'No, nothing like that. In fact we want to wait . . . until we're married. I think it's right, don't you? Besides Hettie's not that sort of girl. We want a proper Church wedding and all that sort of rot. But we are very much in love and we want it soon.'

How like Murdoch, and Hettie too; upright and god-fearing, not wishing to presume the marriage act until they were man and wife. One heard a lot about the immorality of the present generation, Margaret thought, but some age-old principles still adhered. She was glad. There were all sorts of rushed marriages because the girls were pregnant. How stupid of her to think that such would be the case with Murdoch and Hettie. Though she had never thought about it, they would make a very fine couple indeed. They had the same ideas; the same principles and interests.

'Susan won't object,' she said. 'Have you asked her?'

'No. But Hettie thinks she will. She says her mother will want her to finish her studies and we thought we'd talk to you first. Hettie will still go on to qualify, of course, if she wants to. I would never stand in her way.'

'Is Hettie in London too?'

'No, she's in Oxford. I've spent the last few evenings

with her though; we decided we wanted to marry at Easter when I came home on leave. James was away and Aunt Susan was busy with her war work and Hettie and I had a lot of time together. We realized then that we wanted to marry, and yesterday we decided we didn't want to wait. There is also the business of being first cousins. We think both Mother and Aunt Susan mightn't like that.'

'Oh that's very old-fashioned. I should think they would both be *delighted* you love each other. I am.'

'Oh Aunt . . . Margaret!' Murdoch threw his arms round her again. 'You'll help?'

'Of course I'll help,' Margaret said smiling at him. 'I'll *insist*! You can't think how pleased your father would have been.'

Murdoch kissed her on the cheek and held her to him for a moment. She was aware of his strong male body, and thought how lucky Hettie was.

'You've always been my favourite aunt. Do you mind if I don't go back with you for dinner? I'd like to sprint down to Oxford and tell Hettie you approve. Then I think we'll try and go to Scotland for the weekend and breast the family. Can you come up too?'

'No I can't,' Margaret said. 'I think Cullum is dying. You'll have seen how ill he is. In fact Susan may already be on the way down. I spoke to her this morning. Why not wait until she comes?'

'I thought Uncle Cullum looked dreadful,' Murdoch agreed. 'But is he really going to die? The nurse said the operation was successful.'

'It was; but I think he's too weak. I don't think he will outlive the spring.'

'How awful,' Murdoch said grimly. 'Combining a wedding and a funeral. It almost seems like bad luck doesn't it?'

'Whatever do you mean?' Margaret said, feigning surprise. She caught him by the arm. 'Oh don't be so

464

ridiculous,' she cried, squeezing him. 'I have the strongest conviction that one day you are going to run this company. Don't you know I'm grooming you as my heir? We must have a Murdoch Dunbar at the helm again.'

'But Margaret, I haven't decided yet,' Murdoch laughed.

'My support for your marriage depends on it.'

'Then YES!' Murdoch caught her round the waist again.

Such happiness was so infectious that, despite her very real joy, she almost felt jealous. Here was a young life in the ascendant. What would happen to her? No husband, no lover; just her children, her nephews and nieces to live in and through. That and, of course, the business. The business was her lifeline, an antidote to loneliness, an excuse, a fulfilment. Yet when she had agreed to take over, her first thought was of the younger generation who would inherit the family firm.

'As my heir you *automatically* enjoy protection,' Margaret said kissing his cheek. 'With that nothing can *possibly* happen to you in the war.'

CHAPTER TWENTY SIX

Margaret had never been to Peter Cartwright's house and it took her some time to find it. He lived right on the Border near Coldstream, where Scotland and England merged, and he spent a large part of the week there working quietly on his designs in his studio.

Margaret had travelled up overnight to inform the family about Yves' death and she asked them not to tell anybody else until she had told Peter.

'I can't think why you make such a fuss about a man who brought you so much unhappiness,' Susan had said testily. 'I'd just send him a note.'

'I feel differently now.' Margaret had shown to her sister a face of unusual serenity. 'What's the point? It happened such a very long time ago. I owe it to Yves to break it to Peter myself; that much I can do for his memory.'

The house was a large stone building that looked as though it had been built with the twin purposes of keeping out both the cold and the enemy, even though it was a late nineteenth-century construction and there was no possible threat to the Scots then from their old foes the English. It stood on the side of a hill overlooking the Tweed, and a long tree-lined drive led from the wrought iron gates to a rather imposing front door with a grey stone pillared portico. She had not realized Peter lived in such style, and accordingly was not surprised when the door was opened by a maid in a black and white uniform with a frilled apron and cap.

'Would you say it's Mrs Lamotte?'

The maid bobbed and disappeared through a green

baize door that opened off the hall. There were several watercolours on the walls and she recognized Peter's signature on most of them. She knew he was a gifted artist and two of his oils hung on the walls in the Cavendish Avenue house. But looking around her she realized how little she knew about the man who had been her husband's lover for so many years; whom Yves had certainly loved better than her, whatever he said.

Peter was not the sort of person who was easy to know. Despite his beauty he had always been intensely shy; he was withdrawn, nervous and something of a hypochondriac. He took good care of himself and had carefully arranged the sort of lifestyle that suited him. Because he was such a brilliant artist this was comparatively easy; people made things easy for him. He was allowed to choose his own hours and to work wherever he wished.

Consequently, over the years Margaret had seen comparatively little of the man whose name was synonymous with the success of the house of Dunbar. Since she had learned about his relationship with her husband that had suited her very well. Peter was too valuable to lose; she had to tolerate him, whatever rancour she felt towards him for destroying her marriage. Yves always used to say it was ridiculous to blame Peter and maybe, in a way, Yves was right. There was something very blameless about Peter, with his air of innocence and the way he had of blinking at the world through the gold-rimmed spectacles that he seemed to use to shield him from too much admiration.

As he came through the door now, his hand extended, he looked more bewildered than ever and when he saw her face and the black outfit she wore he stopped and said: 'You've got bad news.'

Margaret looked enquiringly towards the open door of the drawing room. 'May we?'

'You'll have to tell me now,' Peter said.

'Yves is dead, yes. I'm sorry. He was killed by the Nazis. He died very bravely.'

Peter put one hand on his cheek and with the other pointed towards the door. Then he followed Margaret in and shut it. It was a light and pretty room with some recognizably good pieces of antique furniture and a golden cashmere carpet that had been a present from the firm after the success of Dunbar Design. From the mullioned windows there was a view of the Tweed and the Border hills that eventually led to Branswick.

'I've asked Mary to bring us coffee,' Peter said distractedly, standing with his back to the fire. 'Please sit down.'

Margaret took a seat and extracted her cigarette case from her handbag. 'Do you mind if I smoke?'

'Of course not.' Peter looked round and picked up a heavy ashtray made of Venetian glass, placing it on the table by her side. Then he straightened up and looked down at her. 'I knew he would be killed. I told him so. Every day I waited to hear and when I saw you in black . . .' Peter removed his glasses and covered his face with his hands. She remembered, when she had first seen him in 1928 that, despite his beauty, he looked prematurely aged with very fair hair that was almost white and a stoop because he was so tall. He had always been myopic but he wore glasses only at the drawing board; now he wore them all the time. He had the face of an aesthete and the build of an invalid, being almost skeletal he was so tall, and his stoop was more pronounced. He was still attractive, but not in the same way he had been when he was twenty-six. He had aged much more than Yves, who had always retained his bold, striking good looks.

Margaret wondered what to do now as she sat smoking quietly, watching a man she hardly knew. Should she get up and try and comfort him, or invite him to sit next to

468

her? She wished she hadn't come and had written instead; the sensible thing to do, as Susan had said.

Peter produced a handkerchief from his trousers' pocket and rubbed his face with it. It was an awkward gesture, rather clumsy and unlike him. Margaret always associated Peter with delicacy and fragility. He was meticulous, methodical and very, very neat. Now he rubbed the large handkerchief all over his face as though he were polishing a wide pane of glass and then sniffed, put it back in his pocket and resumed his spectacles. Behind them his eyes were red and very bright.

'I'm terribly sorry Margaret. It was very good of you to come.'

'I felt I had to tell you myself. I don't know why.'

Then the maid came in with the coffee and they watched her in silence as she put down the tray and set the cups, coffee pot and jug on a small table.

'Shall I pour, sir?'

'I'll pour, thank you, Mary.'

Peter managed a wintry smile, and the maid looked uncertainly at Margaret and swiftly left the room. Peter's hand trembled as he lifted the coffee pot and he spilt some of the black liquid on the table.

'Black or white, Margaret?'

'White please.'

The cup wobbled in its saucer as he brought it towards her and he said he was sorry he'd spilt some more and went back to the tray for a paper napkin until Margaret said it was quite alright he shouldn't bother, and she neatly tipped the spilt liquid back in her cup, and drank from it.

'Do sit down, Peter. I realize you're terribly upset.'

'Terribly, terribly . . . but I knew.' Peter, his eyes wide with shock, stared out of the window.

'You really had a premonition?'

'Oh yes.'

He looked as though he wondered that she hadn't too, and she knew that he thought she lacked any feeling for Yves.

'I was very fond of Yves, Peter. I do want you to know his death shocked me too.'

'Oh I'm sure it did. I'm sure.' Peter tried to hide his confusion by drinking noisily from his cup. Margaret thought that everything he was doing was clumsy and awkward, as though he were being torn apart by grief. He was the very antithesis of his usual neat, fastidious self.

'You must hate me,' he suddenly blurted out, again uncharacteristically.

'No. No, I don't. It was all over a long time ago with me and Yves. I think if it hadn't been you it would have been someone else. People seemed to find him irresistible.'

'He had magical charm,' Peter whispered, his eyes glistening as though he could somehow look back into the past. 'I must say you were always very good about it, Margaret. Always very nice to me.'

'We had to be, didn't we, Peter?' Margaret's smile was ironic and she lit another cigarette exhaling the smoke and looking at him through half closed eyes. 'We needed you for Dunbars.'

Peter gave a nervous little smile. 'That sounds horribly mercenary, Margaret – but I suppose it's true.'

'Of course it's true. You were a genius and we needed you then as we do now. The fact that you were my husband's lover was a *fait accompli*. He explained it all to me. I had to throw you out or leave myself, but Dunbar needed both of us. It was pointless throwing Yves out; we needed him too. Besides, I was a fool and Yves knew about my foolishness. So we settled on a compromise.' Margaret abruptly rose and walked slowly to the window. The brow of a neighbouring hill was dotted with sheep and bushy trees that, from the distance, looked like tiny porcelain figurines. 'I think compromise is best. It worked didn't it?'

'Yes it did. You were marvellous, Margaret.'

'On the contrary,' Margaret smiled bitterly at the memory. 'I was enraged and very jealous. I was only saved from the consequences of my jealousy by my own folly. You know what happened. Yves and I separated and I came up here. I was just surviving; there was nothing marvellous about it.'

She went to the mirror on the far side of the room and, stooping, rearranged her little black pill-box hat with the veil that just covered her eyes. She had applied a lot of make-up to hide her pallor, and she thought she could see little channels of powder in the tiny wrinkles of her skin. She was past forty. She was ageing. Her cheeks were almost orange with rouge and the pencil black was very marked over her eyes. She thought she looked a sight. She straightened up and pulled at the short jacket of her classical pre-war Chanel suit.

'I must go, Peter. I practically stole the petrol to get here and I must hurry back. We have so few cars now with the rationing.'

'I know. I work at home most of the time.'

'Well, you don't lack inspiration,' Margaret said appreciatively. 'Your new collection is excellent, utility or no.'

'Thank you, Margaret.' Peter stood up and gave her his hand. 'Thank you for that compliment, and for . . . coming yourself. It can't have been easy '

'It wasn't. We've never talked, have we, Peter? Always business, never anything personal. Maybe now we can be friends. Now that we no longer have Yves between us.'

She could see Peter's Adam's apple rapidly moving up and down as he strove to control his voice.

'I'd like that a lot. Please come and see me again. Yves loved this house.'

He took her arm and steered her to the door. She stopped on the threshold and looked about; but no picture of Yves was to be seen. Maybe it was by his bedside.

As they went into the hall she put her hand over Peter's. For the first time he smiled and she saw the light behind his vivid blue eyes and was reminded of the beautiful young man she had first met in Paris in 1928. She should have known then.

'I don't like to think of you alone in your grief, Peter,' she said. 'Would you like to come back to Branswick and stay with us?'

Peter's eyes suddenly filled with tears and the lenses of his spectacles misted over. He took them off and wiped them vigorously with his handkerchief, then stuffed it into his eyes again and rubbed them.

'You're far too kind Margaret, far, far too kind. But he is here, you know. He said he would never leave me and he won't. I can feel him everywhere.'

His face was lit again by the same seraphic smile, but Margaret suddenly shivered and looked uneasily around as though aware of some vital presence that she couldn't see.

'Good-bye, Peter,' she said, glad to step outside into the light, her duty done.

All the windows in the row of cottages were criss-crossed with tape to protect them against the perils of flying glass when the bombs fell. Kentish Town, being near two main London railway stations, Kings Cross and Euston, had been fairly heavily hit and, as Margaret drove through looking for the street she sought there were gaps and piles of rubble where a house, a shop or a factory had once stood.

Margaret had not announced her visit and did not know what she would find. She had not seen Clare Amory since 1934, nearly ten years before. In a way she wished she didn't have to do what she had to do now and could let the past lie buried.

The little cottage was covered with late flowering pink

clematis, and the tiny patch of front garden was pretty and well cared for, with dahlias, scabious and chrysanthemums mixed with coniferous shrubs and one or two floribunda rose bushes. Margaret looked at it appreciatively as she knocked on the door, her head bent, listening for sounds from within. She was about to decide that either Clare no longer lived there or was out, when she heard the bolts being drawn back and the door slowly swung open. Clare sat in a wheelchair staring at Margaret, no sign of welcome on her face, and then she spun it slowly round so that Margaret could get past her into the hall.

Remembering the terrible events of 1935 that had happened in this very cottage Margaret felt apprehensive and uneasy and she stepped cautiously inside.

'There's no need to be afraid,' Clare said in the low melodious voice that Margaret remembered so well. 'The ghosts have all been exorcized. Do go in.' She pointed to the room off the hall and Margaret walked in, again with caution, as a soldier might approach a minefield. Clare slowly followed her, skilfully manoeuvring the chair in which she had lived for so many years.

'I didn't know whether to come . . .' Margaret began.

'I didn't know whether to let you in,' Clare replied, indicating a chair. 'Please sit down. I saw you from the window. I sit here all day, you know, looking out; so I miss very little that goes on. I saw you arrive, park your car, look at the house, look at the houses next door, wonder whether to come in or to go away again. Was it such a painful decision?'

'Yes.' Margaret looked at her, also without smiling. 'Yes, it was; but I had to come.' She sat gingerly on the chintz-covered chair Clare had pointed to and peeled off her gloves. 'Yves is dead, Clare. He died in the spring, or rather he was murdered by the Nazis. He died a hero's death and General de Gaulle has invested him post-

473

humously with the Croix de Guerre. As far as I know Yves left no will; he did not expect to die; but a week ago I received a letter he had written just before his capture – it had been given to a friend who hadn't been able to get it to me for obvious reasons. In it he asked me to go and see you if anything should happen to him, and to make sure you were alright. It was almost as though he had had a premonition. I didn't realize he came to see you so often before he left for France.'

'Yves was very, very good to me,' Clare said quietly. 'I thought of him as my greatest friend. I think he understood about suffering.'

As she spoke the tears welled up in her eyes and ran down the cheeks of her still arresting face. In fact her looks were remarkable, as though all the pain and anguish she had endured for so many years had somehow refined her peculiar kind of beauty and given it depth. Her hair was drawn straight back from her head without a parting. Her wide mouth and broad nose, the lips slightly parted, the nostrils slightly flared, gave her features an almost Arabic cast which the intensity of her expression, her blazing brown eyes, did much to enhance. Her appeal was definitely oriental, slightly primitive, and it was difficult to believe that here was a woman deprived by fate of all sensation below the waist. She seemed so vibrant, passionate and alive.

She had on a jumper and cardigan and a rug loosely wrapped around her knees. As she continued to gaze in front of her with the tears pouring down her face Margaret was stricken by a terrible remorse that she had neglected this beautiful, sad and apparently noble woman for so long.

'I'm sorry,' she whispered, but she let Clare cry because she too knew the cathartic, healing quality of tears. Clare turned her wheelchair round, away from Margaret, as though to try and recover her composure, and looked out of the window to the little garden which she tended with such love. Then she wiped her eyes and blew her nose and turned to face Margaret again.

'Can I make you some tea?'

'That would be lovely,' Margaret replied. 'May I help in any way Clare?'

'Oh no I can manage. Everything has been made easy for me, you see. I shan't be a minute.'

While she was gone Margaret studied the room. There was a low bed in the corner and only one armchair, and she realized that Clare slept here, that all her life was lived in and around this small room. Yet it was charming and very personal with lots of books, some knitting and a utility wireless set in the corner. It was also very clean as though the covers had been freshly washed and the carpet recently hoovered. There were little brass and porcelain objects that gleamed and shone. Not a trace of dust anywhere.

When Clare came back, bearing a tray on her lap, Margaret got to her feet and, taking the tray, placed it on a small table.

'Can you not walk at all, Clare?'

'I can hobble about a bit with two sticks; but I hardly ever do. It's so painful it's not worth the effort. They said I might have another operation when the war is over. There is a unit at Stoke Mandeville Hospital which is doing marvellous things for Servicemen with spinal injuries; but of course they must come first. I live in hope.'

'Shall I pour?' Margaret looked enquiringly at her.

'Please do.' Clare returned her scrutiny. 'You're just as lovely Margaret, just as elegant.'

'Thank you.' Margaret passed her her cup. 'And you're just as beautiful too, Clare.'

'I was never strictly beautiful.' Clare passed a hand across her face tucking back a stray wisp of hair into the thick smooth expanse that swept back from her brow.

'Well you are now. Do you do any work at all?'

Clare laughed, throwing back her head and showing her beautiful even teeth. At that moment she looked like a woman who spent a lot of time out of doors, and not an invalid at all. One imagined her playing golf or riding horses, or swimming in the sea.

'Who would employ *me*?'

'Then how do you live?'

'I have a small disability pension and the War Office gives me something in recognition of Douglas's injuries in the last war. There is, in addition, the stipend that Dunbars were good enough to arrange for me, which is paid monthly into my bank account. I don't need very much. This house was paid for before . . . it happened, and I need very few clothes. I love reading and I have my wireless. I follow the war day by day.'

'Do you have many friends?'

'Well, friends . . .' Clare appeared to give the matter some thought, then shook her head. 'No, not really. I was in hospital for eighteen months, you know, and by the time I came out I think most people imagined I was dead. There have been one or two. Local people very kindly shop for me, though I can go to the end of the street in my wheelchair, and one of them cleans for me every day. That's sufficient. I have a telephone in case of emergency; but I've never had to use it for that, so far. Frances Golding, who was a model with me at Lucie Clayton's, always keeps in touch, though she is married now and lives in the country. Then there was Yves . . . I have missed him more than I can say since he went away. I never thought he would be killed. Did you?'

'No. It never crossed my mind.'

'Did you tell . . .' Clare stirred her tea. 'Did you tell Peter?'

'I went to his home and told him personally. It was the first time I'd ever visited his house, the first time I'd ever

476

spoken to him about anything other than business.'

'That was brave of you,' Clare murmured.

'How much we torture ourselves unnecessarily when we won't face the truth.' Margaret looked up, aware of Clare's eyes gazing earnestly at her. 'I thought I faced the truth about Yves and Peter but I didn't. I always pretended it wasn't happening. I suppose that's easy to say now that Yves is dead. I think Peter and I realized there was both good in Yves and bad, evil really; but he exercised such fascination over us both that, posthumously, we've forgiven him. And we're free of him, because he tortured us both; of that I have no doubt.

'But I also know that Peter loved Yves more than I did, or ever could, and I found out how the kind of love I thought repulsive – I mean homosexual love – could perhaps transcend what I called love but was, I suppose, primarily passion, sex, call it what you will.'

Margaret lowered her head, unexpectedly close to tears. She was being terribly emotional but she felt, in a way, that she had missed out on knowing what real love was. She knew all about passion and desire, but love? How much had she loved Hamish, apart from the passion they'd shared? When that had cooled, because he wasn't free, she grew tired of him and fell in love instead with a man who had the looks and physique of a god. Then when Yves denied her access to his bed she'd taunted and humiliated him. Maybe if she had *really* loved Hamish or Yves she would have been more understanding about the predicament in which each found himself – the one tied to an invalid wife, and the other drawn to the same sex.

But it was too late to reproach herself for this now. Perhaps she was asking too much nobility of soul from a young passionate woman to whom quite normal creature comforts were being denied. She felt her emotions were very basic, human ones and the sort of love she was talking about was given to a very few. Maybe Yves had shown it to her at last in choosing to die for his country; because he had voluntarily given away a life that he loved to the full.

Clare was watching her sympathetically, as though aware of the thoughts rushing through her head. 'Don't reproach yourself, Margaret. Think what a burden I have on my mind about Bruno, even poor Douglas.' She propelled her chair across the floor and reaching for Margaret's hand, clenched it.

'Cullum died in June.' Margaret put back her head and sniffed, grateful for the pressure of Clare's strong hand. 'He had stomach cancer. He died quite peacefully and wasn't in pain; but I miss him more than I can say.'

'I'm so sorry, Margaret. You've had a terrible time, and the burden of the business to shoulder as well.'

'That's no burden really. It runs itself. Cullum had had nothing to do with it for years; but I became very close to him in his last years, particularly his last months. You know he left his wife and went to live with Nan who'd been his mistress for years? They have a son William who's now twenty-three. I think that in his last weeks William also became very close to his father and forgave him many things. No, it has been a very sad time for us all.'

'And what happened to Nan after Cullum died?'

'She went back to live in the cottage they shared outside Branswick. William has returned to the Navy. He serves mostly in convoy ships.'

'And Cullum's wife?'

'Ah.' Margaret's eyes clouded. 'Cullum never wanted to see her again. She refused to give him a divorce to allow him to marry Nan. He said that unless she changed her mind he didn't want to see her, and he never did. She waited outside the room when he was dying; but he never wanted to see her, never forgave her. He completely cut her out of his will too, which was no hardship because she

478

had money of her own and he had very little; but he left *Woodbrae* to William instead of his daughter Morag. She feels the sort of bitterness towards her father that you might have expected William to feel. William, however, has refused to accept the house as long as Fleur wants to live there, which shows, I think, what sort of person he is. He says he doesn't want to drive Fleur and Morag out of their home. Or me either, because of course when I'm in Branswick that is my home. You can imagine how this has impressed our family. Clare, to change the conversation, I wonder . . .'

Margaret got up and walked to the fireplace. On the mantelpiece was a picture of Bruno, the cheek with the scar turned away from the camera. It must have been taken when he was about thirty, for he looked as he did when Margaret first knew him, handsome, virile, slightly devilish. She gazed at it for a moment then she turned to Clare.

'Clare, please don't misinterpret what I am going to say; but I do need help in the office. Dora Rowntree who has been my treasure for so many years is leaving to be married. Of course I'm delighted for her because she is in her fifties! But she has met a retired colonel who came to live in her village and they are to be married. Which shows that romance can flourish at any age, a comfort for us all. What I'm saying, Clare, is that I'd like you to take Dora Rowntree's place.'

'Are you serious?' Clare nervously slid the palms of her hands around and around the shining rims of her wheels.

'Perfectly serious. You could confine yourself to the ground floor, man the switchboard, that kind of thing. I need a sort of super receptionist to take Dora's place.'

Clare bowed her head. 'It's terribly kind of you, Margaret, but no. I'm almost totally immobile. I would be no use to you.'

'But you *would* and I'd like to have you. I'm not doing it for charity, Clare, really.'

'You are. You're sorry for me.' Clare gazed at her, not troubling to conceal the hostility and suspicion in her eyes.

'I *am* sorry for you. Of course I am. To deny that would be hypocritical. Who wouldn't be sorry for a beautiful woman, formerly one of London's most successful mannequins, confined to a wheelchair? I think you're very brave and I admire you. However, I do *not* pity you; I think this plan is what Yves would have wished, and Bruno. And I wish it too. Please, Clare. You've no idea how invaluable Dora has been to me and to have to teach a beginner would be awful. You know the ropes. You know the business. That is half the battle.'

Margaret saw the distrust vanish from Clare's eyes to be replaced, as she had hoped it would be, by a gleam of excitement.

'You really *do* mean it?'

'I really do mean it.'

'I'll think about it,' Clare said evasively.

'Say "yes" now.'

'But what about transport, all that kind of thing? I can't take the tube to work you know.'

'All that can be sorted out. Say "yes".'

'What about Susan?'

'Ah, Susan.' Margaret paused for thought. 'Well, Susan hardly ever comes to London. And her daughter is married and expecting a baby and living with her.'

'Hesther is married? My goodness, she was a little girl when I last heard of her! Bruno was so proud of his twins.'

'Well, she's still only nineteen, but she and my nephew Murdoch fell passionately in love and decided they couldn't wait. They got married by special licence in May. They didn't waste any time and now Hettie is pregnant and has left Oxford, of course. She says she'll resume her studies when her children are older; but I have my doubts. Anyway, Susan will not make problems. She has a life of her own. After all, what happened, Clare, is a long time ago.'

'Some people never forget,' Clare said.

CHAPTER TWENTY SEVEN

In the autumn of 1943 the tide of the war definitely seemed to be turning for the better and people were agitating for the invasion of occupied Europe. In September Allied troops landed at Salerno following the fall of Mussolini in July. In July too the first bombs were dropped by the Allies on Rome, an action that produced an outcry in England because of the historical treasures in that city. But Anthony Eden said that Rome would be razed to the ground if it would help the war effort. It was a long way, morally, from the ideals of the thirties when the thought of bombing innocent people had been so abhorrent. Now nothing seemed abhorrent in this long and terrible war, and the tales that were coming out of Germany about the fate of the Jews provoked more horror still.

Tom Monroe, the eldest son of Margaret's sister Juliet, had served with the Eighth Army in its African campaign and been wounded at El Alamein, where he had almost lost a leg. He had been sent home on convalescent leave and then he was given an administrative job and transferred to another unit in preparation, it was said, for the invasion of Europe. His wife was Hamish Ogilvy's daughter Fiona, and she stayed at home in Edinburgh with her two young children because she was nervous about the bombs in London.

Fiona was a very nervous girl altogether, bombs or no bombs. She had not had a happy childhood, with her mother an invalid and her father constantly away, and of the three Ogilvy children she seemed to be the most affected, although all were blighted in some way. The eldest, Christopher, a rebellious unhappy boy, had become a Communist at Cambridge and gone to Spain where he'd been killed at the Battle of the Ebro; and Rory, the middle one, had supported Mosley and been faced with internment, like him. He had been rejected from the Army and now drifted about Scotland doing odd jobs, mending roads or looking after sheep in the hills.

Fiona was timorous and shy, as well as of a nervous disposition. But she had a sort of fey Scottish beauty, masses of fair curly hair the colour of her father's, and an elfin, heart-shaped face. The combination had aroused the passions of Tom Monroe who was very different to her in every way: strong, resolute and rather stubborn. He was going to follow his father into the law and had been called to the Scottish Bar when he and Fiona were married, six months before war began when she was a very youthful twenty and he was a sturdy, robust twenty-six.

By 1943 Tom was a major in the Royal Artillery. He had enjoyed his war, and was twice mentioned in dispatches. The leg which had been shattered at El Alamein made him fear at one time that he would be invalided out of the Army; but now he had a desk job at Aldershot, though he walked with a permanent limp. It made him look rather interesting, because he was very tall and well built, like his father, and, although nearly bald and by no means conventionally handsome, he had an arresting face, full of character, and had inherited much of the natural Dunbar charm from his mother.

Tom often came to London for a night out with the boys after he was posted to Aldershot and he stayed either at his Club, the Army and Navy in Pall Mall, or if it was full, as it frequently was – nights out with the boys being popular in those war-torn days – at the house of his Aunt Margaret in St John's Wood.

It was there he met Clare Amory. And, having met her,

he knew instantly that she, not his wife, was the woman he had been looking for all his life.

Margaret was not slow in noticing the attraction between Clare and Tom. The meeting was completely fortuitous. She and Clare had been working late at the office because they had a rush of government orders to complete, and Margaret had suggested that Clare stay the night with her so that they could get to work early the next day. Usually Clare was collected and taken home by taxi but this night she was driven home in Margaret's Sunbeam, a pre-war model which she liked to use (in preference to the treasured Buick which she kept in the garage) because it was good on petrol.

'There's Tom,' Margaret said with surprise, parking her car in front of his, outside the house. 'Have you ever met my nephew Tom, my eldest sister's son?'

'I don't think I have,' Clare said.

And that was how she met Tom.

After the first meeting Tom came much more frequently to London. Margaret had never been particularly close to her nephew Tom, who was nearest to her in age being only twelve years her junior. There was a spirit of rivalry rather than friendship between them, almost a suggestion of flirtatiousness. So Margaret was surprised when he started to call regularly at Devonshire Place until she realized how much time he spent downstairs chatting to Clare.

'I think you come to see Clare rather than me,' Margaret chaffed one day.

'That's a lot of rot,' Tom said gruffly, but she saw his colour heighten nevertheless.

By January 1944 Margaret was rather sorry she had asked Clare to work at the office, not because she was not a success, which she was; in fact she was so good at her job that one hardly noticed her disability. She sat behind her desk exuding charm and confidence; she was capable, efficient and adaptable and soon Margaret forgot she had ever employed Dora Rowntree or that she had ever thought she would miss her. Clare, like Dora, rapidly became indispensable. But Margaret was worried about Tom. She knew that Tom had not gone home for Christmas where his young family had been eagerly awaiting him, and she suspected that he spent it with Clare Amory in London, although he had told Fiona it was something secret to do with the war.

It was not only in Tom that Margaret noticed the difference, but also in Clare. Clare took on a bloom that some women have when they are in love, a softening of the features, an almost supernatural glow. And, more than that, she seemed almost continually happy; in a permanent state of euphoria.

One day Margaret asked Tom if he and Clare were having an affair and, being a Scotsman given to brusqueness and honesty, he said that, yes, they were.

By this time it was March. The war in Italy had received setbacks with the German offensive at Anzio, and the futile bombing of the ancient Abbey of Monte Cassino by the Allies. Britain had begun daylight raids on Berlin and there were persistent rumours about the Second Front. General Eisenhower had been given supreme command in Europe, much to the disgust of General Montgomery who was made his deputy. Some way had had to be found to say 'thank you' to the Americans for keeping the war effort going on so many fronts; and what was more painless than promoting an amiable American general who had proved his prowess in North Africa?

Margaret and Tom, this day in March, were dining at Margaret's house on chicken and home-grown vegetables that Margaret had just brought down from a visit to Scotland. She had arrived to find Tom staying in the house, and this very circumstance reminded her of the time she had returned unexpectedly to find that Bruno had been staying there with Clare. Only this time there was no trace of Clare; but the suspicion she had been there remained in her mind and so she had asked him bluntly.

'Yes,' Tom said. 'How did you know?'

'It's pretty obvious. Was she here last night?'

'No. I go to her place.'

Margaret pushed back her chair and threw her napkin on the table. She hated to leave food when it was so scarce; but she was suddenly overcome by a disgust that was almost physical. She groped for her bag on the floor, extracted a cigarette from her case and lit it. 'I would have thought that woman had caused enough trouble in our family.'

'What trouble?'

'Oh Tom. You know about Bruno . . .'

'That was years ago.'

'Not to those who remember it. To me it seems like yesterday. Bruno, your uncle, was *murdered* because of her.'

'That's terribly exaggerated. She was merely an innocent party – the affair with Bruno long over. Her husband was crazy. Besides, if you thought that, then why did you employ her?' Tom angrily pushed back his plate and groped in the side pocket of his uniform jacket for his pipe.

'I was sorry for her. I like her. I admire her; but really . . . this! This is too much!'

'She didn't want to, Margaret.'

'I should just think she didn't!'

'But like any other woman, or man, she needed love. She needed it so much.'

'Then why did it have to be *you*? You have a young wife and two small children.'

'I understood Clare. I think having a leg injury myself made me appreciate what it was like to be crippled. My leg nearly had to come off you know. It would have if there hadn't been a very good sawbones in Alexandria who saved it for me. I'd have been on crutches but for him.'

Margaret blew smoke impatiently into the air, exhaling from her mouth and nostrils at the same time. 'Tom. I appreciate all that. I know Clare needs love. But there are some things we must learn to do without and, in my experience, another woman's husband is one of them.'

Suddenly Margaret felt a twinge of guilt. She was talking to Hamish's son-in-law. Was it remotely possible that he knew about her and Hamish? Was she really one to start preaching about stealing another woman's husband?

But that was all such a very long time ago, and Isobel, who was now dead, had been an invalid. Why, it was over twenty years since she and Hamish had started their affair. How dead that all seemed too; dead as the dodo. She felt she and Hamish had been destined once more to come together to produce Charles; but after that there was not a spark left. Even the fact that Charles was Hamish's son was something she hardly ever remembered. He looked like her son and Yves'; he thought he was and she had come to accept he was too. There were only a few people left now who knew differently. But if she could trust anyone to keep her mouth shut that person was her sister Juliet, and Angus she felt was the same. She stubbed out her cigarette in a glass ashtray and got up, straightening her non-utility Dunbar skirt and jumper, a modest affair made of lambswool that was selling well in America. She stood warming herself in front of the fire.

'I want to marry Clare,' Tom said. 'I want to look after her for the rest of my life. This isn't just a little thing, Margaret, a mere affair.'

'Oh God,' Margaret cried, 'Bruno said that too! What *has* this woman got that makes men so mad about her — even if she's paralysed?'

'Something very special,' Tom said quietly. 'Even if she

487

is paralysed. I still love her and I want her. I've had a lot of light affairs in the past few years, Margaret. Affairs in Tunisia, in Algeria. Affairs here. Why do you think I came up to London? To get women. Oh, perfectly nice, clean, *respectable* women who are the wives or sweethearts of men overseas, all of whom are having affairs too. We all want love, Margaret. At least most of us do. My wife Fiona doesn't seem to need love at all. Why do you think she doesn't come to London?'

'To be away from the bombs. I'd have thought that was quite understandable with two young children.'

'Yes that, and because she doesn't want to sleep with me. She could leave the kids with mother or Philippa.'

Philippa was Tom's eldest sister. Her husband was the captain of a minesweeper and she liked to surround herself with children – hers and those of other people – to take her mind off the danger her husband was constantly in.

'I didn't know that.' Margaret folded her arms and moved away from the fire to resume her seat.

'Our sex life has never been any good. I'm sorry, Margaret. I know this sort of thing is distasteful, but because of the disapproval in your eyes I feel I have to explain. There's something wrong with Fiona; she's afraid of it or something. She won't see a doctor and she won't take advice. It's like raping your own wife, making love to her, and what decent man wants to do that?'

He relit his pipe which had gone out in the passion of his oratory. Hearing Tom speak like this was so untypical that Margaret felt moved despite herself. Steady, phlegmatic, reliable Tom, the most unimaginative person one could think of, had a problem that she had never even suspected. Maybe that was why. Could he be too un-imaginative to help Fiona with her problem? Yet he was imaginative enough to know how Clare felt living in a wheelchair.

488

But that was because he was in love. Love gave certain insights that not being in love lacked. He loved Clare and he did not love Fiona. It was as simple as that.

'I'm sorry,' she said at last. 'Terribly, terribly sorry, Tom. Sorry I was critical. I'm fond of Fiona, you know. It's awful when two people don't click. I know that, to my cost, with Yves. You know that we had no sex life together, or scarcely any?'

'Enough to produce two children.' Tom smiled and Margaret, apprehensive again, wondered if there was any meaning in his smile.

'Yes, enough for that. Yves wanted an heir for his family.'

Tom got up and took his turn in front of the electric fire. Coal was rationed, scarce, and Margaret saved it for the evenings she was at home and liked a nice fire in the drawing room. When she was at Branswick the fires were kept going by a plentiful supply of logs. Sometimes she had wondered if she should shut the London house and office for the duration of the war; but now everyone said it would be over very soon anyway. The Second Front was round the corner. Tom carefully packed tobacco into the bowl of his pipe and applied his lighter to it, squinting through the flickering flame at Margaret. Then he extinguished it, put it in his breast pocket and pulled at the pipe until it was drawing well.

'I know about Charles, Margaret. About his parentage I mean.'

'Oh.' Margaret suddenly felt cold despite the glow radiating from the fire.

'Of course it is a secret with me forever. I want you to know that; but I felt it might make you more sympathetic to me in my dilemma if I said I knew.'

'Yes, it does. I was just thinking about it. Age makes one forget the follies of the past; just another of its drawbacks.' Margaret smiled ruefully.

'I thought you were thinking about it because of the way you looked at me.'

'I'm surprised I must say,' Margaret tried to measure her words carefully, 'that your mother told you. I was thinking, then, she wouldn't have done.'

'She didn't. As you know, Dad drew up the settlement. Well, I found it when I was looking through some family papers. It was a legal matter and only Dad has the key to the box and he gave it to me, forgetting I didn't know about Charles and Hamish.'

'Hamish doesn't know either. I hope you didn't tell Fiona?'

'Good heavens no! That sort of thing is a sacred trust. Being a lawyer is like being a doctor or a priest. I told Dad I knew and he was very upset, but I gave him my word that the secret was safe with me.'

'I'm glad of that. Yes, Hamish and I had an affair in the twenties. He was my first lover. He was always an honourable man and would never leave Isobel. Then I married Yves, not knowing that he was basically homosexual.'

'He really was a swine!' Tom wrinkled his nose in disgust.

'In a way he was; but in another way he wasn't.'

'But he was an extortionist. That settlement . . .'

'Yes, we had a price to pay. I had to have a second mortgage on this house; but, you see, it has all come back to me now; isn't that ironic? Yves died intestate and I have inherited everything. I think dear Yves thought he had a charmed life and would never die, or at any rate certainly not be killed in the war. Or maybe he preferred to leave it all to fate, because of the way he'd come by the money. I believe he did a lot with it. I suspect he helped Peter Cartwright to buy his lovely house at Coldstream. But although there isn't much actual cash left, one day Charles will inherit the Paris apartment and the lovely château at Amboise, if either are standing by the time this dreadful war is over. Legally, you see, Charles is the son of Yves and it must never be known otherwise. That was the bargain we made.'

'I'm sure a lot of similar bargains have been made,' Tom said. 'We'll destroy that document if you like. I'll do it myself, shall I?'

'Thanks Tom. It would be a weight off my mind.'

Tom went over to her and put a hand awkwardly on her shoulder. 'You've had a rough time, Margaret, haven't you? You always seem so serene, so full of equanimity. I can't explain it. When I knew, I admired you more than I can say.'

'There was no need to admire me. The whole thing was quite unplanned. Hamish and I met again after a number of years and . . . Charles was the result. But he must never know.'

'He will never know from me. Anyway, he's very happy with his new young wife.'

Margaret laughed. 'So I hear! I was a bit hurt that he didn't ask *me* after Isobel died. No, I'm joking. We had grown too far apart by then. I imagine what's-her-name was convenient and could comfort him.'

'Moira. Moira Armstrong.'

Margaret had only recently heard of Hamish's marriage to a woman twenty years his junior who had been in the ATS.

'Let's talk about you again, Tom.' Margaret looked at the clock and got up. 'Shall we have coffee in the lounge? You know Sarah my maid is leaving? She wants to join the WAAF! I think she thinks it might be a good place to find a husband. Maybe I should join too. Anyway Christine is staying on. I sometimes think, Tom, that after the war servants will be very hard to come by. Women who formerly went into domestic service are already finding there are other, more pleasant things to do.'

'I don't know about more pleasant, making munitions and so on, but maybe better paid. Yes, after the war a whole lot of things will change. They always do.'

They went to the lounge where Margaret served the coffee and put a match to the coal fire. Then they sat on either side of it, watching as the flames caught the paper and sticks, curled round the treasured pieces of coal and leapt up the chimney.

'Clare is quite a bit older than you, Tom.'

'Six years. It makes no difference. I've thought of that.'

'What about your children?'

'I'll see them.'

'Do you think Fiona will give you a divorce? Fleur would never divorce Cullum.'

'I know. I don't know what Fiona will say. She's bound to be hurt. Anyway I'm leaving that until the war is over, because Clare agrees that there is no point in changing things now. I hardly ever see Fiona and if I can I'm going to try and go to France with the invasion troops. They'll still need pen-pushers there as well, you know. But one thing I want you to promise me, Margaret, if you will . . . This talk has brought us closer together, hasn't it?'

'In a strange way it has,' Margaret replied. 'I started by feeling so angry, and now I feel I understand, a little better anyway. Now, what is it you want me to promise?' She replaced her cup in its saucer and looked at him gravely.

'I want you to look after Clare if I go. I haven't got much money to leave, and what there is is rightly Fiona's and the children's. Clare knows this.'

Margaret sighed and closed her eyes. 'Oh Tom, please don't talk about "going". I have this conversation every time I see Murdo or James or William or your brother.'

'We *have* to have it on our minds. Everyone involved in this war has. Civilians as well as those directly engaged.

492

What was unthinkable in 1914 is happening now; people are being deliberately killed, whether soldiers or not. I think there's less chance of me going than most people because I'll never be fit enough for active service; but there's always the odd bomb or shell. It could happen to anyone. It could happen to you.'

CHAPTER TWENTY EIGHT

One of the great joys given to the Dunbar family in the year 1943/44 was the marriage of Murdoch and his cousin Hesther, or Hettie as they called her. In a life that was full of storm and fear of the unknown, of war and memories of family troubles in the past, it seemed like a precious oasis of peace, happiness and fulfilment in which the family, to a certain extent, were all able to share. Susan soon overcame her initial doubts when she saw how satisfactory their union was and she realized that, at the back of her mind, there had always lurked a suspicion that they were very well suited. Only she had been inclined to think that the marriage of near relations was not a good thing and best avoided. The happiness of Murdoch and her daughter dispersed that fear. They had so many common interests that, once the knot was tied, it seemed the obvious thing all along.

Their honeymoon was spent youth hostelling in the Highlands; they were keen on walking and outdoor life, little given to intellectual or cultural pursuits. There was a vigour and spontaneity about them that was appealing because it was so natural and healthy. Some people who were fanatically keen on the out-of-doors managed to make it seem repellent; but Hettie and Murdo did not. One thought that, because people like them enjoyed it so much, it must be good. They liked to rise early and go to bed early; they liked gardening and bird-watching, camping, fishing and riding. Susan planned that, after the war, she would make her home over to them and she would find a cottage nearby. After all, hers had been intended to house a large family and now she anticipated that she would see this happiness realized in the marriage of Hettie and Murdo, as all the family called him. Murdoch always seemed rather a pretentious name, and their Murdoch was far from that.

Everyone hoped that Murdo would go into the business, though he sometimes talked about making the Army his career. Susan thought that, if she gave them her home, it would tip the scales on the side of Dunbars, for the rural pursuits they so enjoyed together, the delight in country and family life would be practically incompatible with a service career.

Murdo remained in England for most of that year, engaged in secret manoeuvres in the South of England, where he was stationed. As soon as they knew of Hettie's pregnancy he begged her to stay in Scotland and, when he could, he hitch-hiked up to spend a weekend with her. At Easter they were able to spend a few days alone together in a cottage by the side of beautiful Loch Leven in Fife, lent to them by a friend of Angus Monroe. Every day they fished in the loch and went on long walks despite Hettie's size. At night they sat by the log fire and read or listened to the wireless while Murdo carved a toy boat which he said would be his first gift to his son.

'How do you know it'll be a boy?' Hettie enquired one night laughing.

'I have that feeling. Besides you're such a size.'

He came over to her and caressed her rounded belly, his eyes full of love. She leaned back in her chair, luxuriating in her fecundity, in her youth and strength, and his warm masculinity.

'The doctor says it has nothing to do with the sex. We could have a big, bonny girl.'

'I don't mind what we'll have this time, because there'll be many more. Won't there, Het?'

'I hope so,' Hettie said looking into the fire. 'I think six is a nice round number; though what will happen to my medical career then?'

Murdo got up and reached for his pipe from the mantelpiece. 'I think motherhood will suit you best, Het. It suits you now. With six children and me to look after . . .'

'I hope I'm not trailing after you with six children from camp to camp.' She raised an eyebrow and looked threateningly at him, putting a hand in the plaid of her maternity smock.

'You'd rather I left the Army after the war, wouldn't you Het?'

'If it's left to me, yes; but it's your decision. I've always said that. Aunt Margaret is very keen for you to go into the business.'

Murdo put his pipe in his mouth and left it there unlit, moving it from one side to the other. In his polo sweater and corduroys he looked the personification of the healthy, satisfied male. He hadn't shaved that day and his dark stubble made him look so rugged and attractive that Hettie wanted to take him in her arms and make love to him in the gentle and caressing way they did now that she was so heavily pregnant. She sank further into the chair looking forward to the time, very soon, when they would be in bed together, their arms around each other.

'I wonder why Aunt Margaret is so keen?' he said. 'She loves that business. She has many years ahead of her yet.'

'Maybe she doesn't love it as much as she pretends. Maybe she's tired. She's had it all to bear during the war you know. And planning for afterwards. I think she would like you with her, Murdo.'

'Hmm.' Murdo lit his pipe, sending clouds of smoke into the air which made her want to cough. Like most men he was not especially thoughtful about the effects of pregnancy on a woman. 'I'll be second fiddle for a long time with Aunt Maggie.'

'You've the business yet to learn! It'll take years and years, and then when you're ready I'm sure Maggie will be glad to step down. She's always said she wants a Murdoch Dunbar to run the business again.'

'By the way,' Murdoch said as though in an afterthought. 'If I'm away when our son is born I'd like him to be called after my father – if that's alright with you.'

'It is alright with me,' Hettie said, her eyes again turned to the fire, as though the glowing embers enabled her to see visions. Or maybe it was to conceal sad thoughts; for the memory of her own father and what he had done to a mother she loved still hurt her too much for her to wish to call any child after him. Sometimes she envied Murdo for having a father he had never known and could therefore venerate and love.

Young Malcolm Dunbar was born on 6 June 1944 – D-Day, by happy chance. While his father was forging across the Normandy beaches with his armoured regiment, Malcolm, weighing nearly nine pounds, made his way lustily into the world in a nursing home in North London. Susan had begged Hettie to stay in Scotland for the birth; but her daughter had had an intimation that the landings would be soon and she hoped that Murdo would be near her when the baby was born, near enough to visit and see his son. She had not seen him since the blissful days they had spent together at Loch Leven at Easter. Although he did not know it, and nor did she, that was his embarkation leave before the assault on Europe.

The birth was an uncomplicated one and ten days later Hettie took her new son back to her aunt's home in St John's Wood, still declining to go north in case Murdo should be able to get brief leave to see her and the baby. Her decision worried her mother and her aunt because, almost a week to the day after the Normandy landing, the first flying bombs had fallen on London, 'doodlebugs' as they soon came to be known, terrifying weapons that dropped from the skies like huge beetles, bringing undiscriminating death.

'Even Margaret is thinking of closing the house and the office,' her mother told her one day. 'This is the worst threat we've had; worse than 1941. They can land anywhere. They're not aimed merely at stations or military installations, but at *us*.'

'Darling Mummy,' Hettie said her eyes shining, relishing the sensation of her contented baby suckling at her breast. 'You know nothing can happen to us. Murdo and I have planned the future. It is all written. Up there.' She looked at the ceiling and Susan felt a terrible misgiving in her heart, combined with an envy that the young could be so certain of things. 'Besides,' Hettie went on, 'Murdo could come home on short leave at any time. He promised me he would try when the baby was born, and I know he will.'

Margaret and Susan, worried but unwilling to worry her, agreed to stay in London during that warm summer when the Allied troops charged through Belgium and France and death fell from the skies of London.

Besides, Margaret had to admit to herself that she liked having the family around her. Young Malcolm was a joy and freckled, commonsensical Hettie, whom motherhood had made beautiful, gave one some hope for the future. She was so practical and good-natured, so sure about everything. They all agreed, nevertheless, that whatever happened they would go north in August and spend that month together with Charles, Morag and Yvonne who would all be home from school. James had been sent to the Far East with the RAF and William was with the fleet in the Mediterranean, helping to give support to the forces in Italy and prepare for the invasion of France by the Allies from the south.

* * *

Tom Monroe had never, to his bitter chagrin, again left England. He had been seconded to the War Ministry in Whitehall and, although his family didn't know it, he was living with Clare Amory in her little cottage in Kentish Town while keeping a small flat in Islington as a 'front'. Margaret's attitude to Clare after her talk with Tom the previous March was to behave as though nothing had happened. Clare knew that she knew, but they had only once talked about it, one day in Margaret's office studying samples of a new synthetic yarn.

'Blended with wool you wash it and it scarcely needs ironing,' Margaret said running the soft yarn through her fingers. 'It's nylon, you know.'

'Wool and *nylon*!' Clare exclaimed, laughing.

'Why not? We had wool and silk for the remarkable ladies' vests that made Dunbars' fortune at the turn of the century. I've got to think so hard about the future, Clare. The war could be over any day. Then what?'

'Tom says it will take a long time to get back to normal,' Clare began slowly. Then she stopped. It was the first time she had mentioned his name, and she did it almost hesitantly, perhaps with deliberation, as though she were testing the ground.

'Tom is perfectly right,' Margaret said matter-of-factly. 'Tom . . . Well . . .' She looked at Clare and then sank onto the sofa, the yarn forgotten in her fingers. 'He did tell me everything, as you must know. I started by feeling hostile, but . . .'

'That woman again,' Clare said, plucking at the rug which she always wore round her knees so that people could not see how spindly and wasted her once beautiful legs had become.

'Well, yes, in a way "that woman again". I suppose I should envy you the appeal you have for men. I only wish it wasn't always for married men of my family!'

'You have appeal for men too, Margaret.' Clare

wheeled her chair nearer to her. 'I see the way they look at you; they want to ask you out, but they don't dare.'

'I have grown forbidding,' Margaret said. 'Haven't I?'

'In a way.'

'I don't want married men too, you see, and, let's face it, that's all there are around for women of my age. I'm nearly forty-three, you know.'

'You look ten years younger.'

'Whether I look it or not,' Margaret said as she lit a cigarette, 'that's the age I am. Forty-three in October. As for you and Tom, Clare – ' Margaret joined her hands and stretched her arms. 'There's nothing I can say. I suppose fate brought you together and that's it. I only hope that when the family come to be told, and it must be soon now, the mess won't be too awful.'

'I am quite happy to continue like this as Tom's mistress, without upsetting his family. After all, I'm quite used to it. I did it for years with Bruno.'

'But it would never work. There's nothing Tom could do down here. He's a member of the Scottish Bar. They have a very different system from England.'

'I could live in Edinburgh. I'm prepared to.'

'Are you?' Margaret looked at her quizzically. 'Well, I must say you've got guts, and courage; but you always had. The only thing you didn't have was sense.'

Clare gazed out of the window, her face immobile with sadness. Slowly she propelled her wheelchair in the same direction. 'That isn't a nice thing to say, Margaret. Don't you think women are often at the mercy of fortune?'

'Yes. Yes, I do.' Margaret moved behind her and rested one hand on her shoulder. 'And forgive me. I'm sorry. I'm a fine one to talk about sense, who spent the best years of my youth having a liaison with a married man, then got married to a homosexual and ended up sleeping with one of the commonest creatures on God's earth. I wonder what happened to Bob Morgan, by the way?'

'Didn't Bruno send him abroad?'

'Oh yes that's it. Bruno packed him off – to America I think. Maybe he's a GI!'

They had looked at each other and spontaneously, happily they both burst out laughing.

Despite the bombs, the worry about their men who were fighting, the shortages and the general weariness of war, Margaret, Susan and Hettie had a very happy month watching baby Malcolm put on weight, revelling in his comeliness and beauty. Hettie was full of milk, which was a good thing because cow's milk was in short supply, though mothers with babies had priority. She also had extra rations which Margaret ensured went to her. There was always a little meat, chicken or fish for Hettie while she and Susan experimented with peculiar mixtures consisting largely of vegetables done in all sorts of interesting ways. The population of Britain remained fairly well nourished throughout the war, and when it was over they were found to be statistically healthier than when it had begun. Coarse brown bread and margarine were subsequently found to be more nutritious than the white domestic loaf and farm butter, better for health. And people avoided obesity because they couldn't eat more than was necessary.

In the evening the women played cards, listened to the wireless or wound up the gramophone. Then they went early to bed, trying not to listen for the awful sound of the buzz bombs with their motors which suddenly cut out to be followed, hopefully at a distance, by an explosion. Hettie said she never missed a wink of sleep, except for the baby, and Susan took sleeping pills. But Margaret found she developed a habit of cat-napping all through the night, and it was with some relief that she finally saw daylight appear round the curtains and she could get up and make herself an early morning cup of tea. Usually when she came down she found Hettie already up, nursing Malcolm in the sitting room before the open door that led into the garden.

One Sunday in July Margaret was up especially early because the sun had streamed through the windows and she thought she would do an hour in the garden before everyone was up. The whole of the garden had been given up to the growing of vegetables and she was particularly proud of her beds of lettuce, peas, carrots and large plump cabbages. This day Hettie was in the sitting room as usual but looking somewhat more tired than Margaret had seen her. Malcolm was at her breast but her head lolled over the sucking baby as though she were fast asleep.

'Hettie, didn't you sleep well?'

'I had terrible dreams.' Hettie jerked her head up and attempted to smile. 'I hope Murdo is alright.'

'Oh darling, they always say dreams are the opposite.' Margaret put a hand on her shoulder. 'I have a feeling that Murdo is *quite* alright, but I still think we should go to Scotland soon. I'm not happy in London with these wretched doodlebugs. Maybe next week? I'll talk to your mother.'

'But what if Murdo . . .'

'Hettie.' Margaret sat opposite her niece, pulling her gown tightly around her. 'You can't wait here all summer for Murdo. He said in his last letter he didn't think he could get leave. As soon as he does, and even if we're in Scotland, I personally will make sure that you two and the baby are together in the shortest possible time. Now, I must make some tea and then water my lettuces. Have you seen them? They're absolutely huge.' She made a balloon shape with her hands and then went to the french windows, stretching her arms and taking deep lungfuls of air. 'It *is* a beautiful day. Who would ever think the world was at war?'

'I thought I'd go to church today, Margaret. There's a service at the Guards' Chapel at eleven.'

'Oh good, we'll all go. I haven't been to church for months and I'm sure your mother would like to go.'

'What about Malcolm?'

'Christine can look after him.'

'It's Christine's day off. She's already gone.'

'Oh.' Margaret looked thoughtfully at the garden, itching to get out and water the dry earth. Water was scarce too and watering was only permitted now and again. 'Well, look, we'll take the baby with us. Lots of people do.'

The thought seemed to cheer Hettie up and she smiled, moving Malcolm from one breast to the other. 'That's a nice idea. Then in the afternoon I can have a long sleep, having done my Christian duty.'

By ten the garden was watered, breakfast eaten and the dishes washed; and the three women in their utility best climbed into the Sunbeam, Margaret and Hettie in front and Susan in the back seat with her grandson wrapped in a shawl.

Margaret drove down Baker Street towards the Guards' Chapel in Wellington Barracks in Victoria. The air was balmy, the sky blue; it was mellow and hot. To the south of London the sky was full of barrage balloons but from the centre of the city they were invisible. It was good to know that they were there, all two thousand of them, high up in the sky stretching from Cobham to Limpsfield, intent on the duty of keeping the deadly invaders from penetrating the capital.

'It's an awful pity to take the baby indoors on a day like this,' Susan said gazing at his sleeping form. 'Why don't I wait for you in St James's Park?'

'What a good idea,' Margaret said. 'It will be heavenly by the lake and we'll join you afterwards. Maybe the kiosk is open for coffee.'

There were very few cars about and few people in the streets. London seemed to be slumbering on this hot, peaceful morning. It was more difficult than ever to think

503

that, over the Channel, the Allied Forces were engaged in desperate fighting against the enemy. Margaret drove through Mayfair, along Piccadilly to the Haymarket, through Trafalgar Square, under Admiralty Arch and up the Mall. There were a few cars parked by the side of the park and she reversed into a space half way along the Mall. At one end Buckingham Palace, shuttered and deserted, seemed to indicate that the Royal Family were in Windsor and a few khaki-clad sentries paraded before the black wrought-iron palings.

'We can leave the car here, see your mother and son safely settled and then walk to the chapel,' Margaret said, glancing at her watch. For some reason, though she had heard nothing, she looked nervously up at the sky but it was quite clear.

Despite the war and wartime conditions the park was an oasis of peace and beauty, full of flowers, colour and the exotic birds, who seemed to have little idea whether it was war or peace, nor to care either. Several people had had the same idea as Margaret and her family and the park was quite full, the benches crammed with people enjoying the beautiful summer day. One was entirely occupied by a slumbering soldier stretched full-length, his forage cap over his face. No one disturbed him, as if sensing that his need for sleep, whatever the reason, was greater than their desire to sit down.

There were now no deckchairs in the park and Susan selected a spot on the grass under a tree, by the green iron bridge that crossed the lake.

'I wish we'd brought a rug,' she said, putting Malcolm tenderly on her lap. 'Although, of course, we were all going to the service weren't we?'

'Hettie!' A voice joyfully interrupted their concentration and they turned to see a young woman running over to them. She clasped Hettie by the arm. 'I haven't *seen* your baby! Oh, isn't he a treasure!'

504

The woman bent down and Susan obligingly dislodged part of the shawl so that the full beauty of Malcolm's slumbering face could be revealed.

'Who's he like? You or Murdoch?'

'We can't decide. He's like us both. Of course we're first cousins, not that Murdo's seen him yet.'

'He's adorable,' the young, pretty woman enthused, and Hettie introduced her as Jill Courtney, the wife of one of Murdoch's brother officers.

'Are you going to the service?' Jill said.

'Yes.'

'Then let's go together; but we must hurry. We're late.'

'Look, if you two don't mind,' Margaret said suddenly, 'I think I'll stay with Susan and my nephew after all. I didn't sleep too well and I might fall asleep during the sermon and disgrace you. It's so *heavenly* here. Do you mind, Hettie?'

'Of course I don't mind. I'll say a prayer for you.'

'Please do, darling. A big one; and hurry back. I've been hoarding food coupons and I've got the tiniest piece of roast beef you ever saw for lunch; but best roast beef it is. *Also* a nice bottle of Burgundy, pre-war of course.'

'What fun!' Hettie clasped her hands together, her eyes shining. She looked so much the embodiment of health and happiness that Margaret realized her eyes had momentarily been riveted on her niece. With her dark curly hair and brown freckled face, slightly Jewish-looking, like Bruno's, she resembled a Sephardic gypsy, a woman of the earth and the sun, close to the heart of natural things. She did not have the Dunbar eyes, but deep brown irises, tawny-flecked near the pupils, and they enabled her to seem serious yet, at the same time, full of laughter as a warm spring bubbles underneath the earth. Margaret, who had always been fond of Hettie, had never thought her beautiful; but since her baby was born she had been transformed and today she looked almost extraordinarily lovely.

'Jill, would you care to have luncheon with us?' Margaret said, aware that Hettie had begun to look at her curiously. 'I'm sure we could stretch the roast.'

'Thanks but I'm meeting friends at the chapel, Mrs Lamotte, and I'm going back to eat with them.'

Margaret watched the two young women in their wedge-soled shoes, their bright utility cotton frocks, as they linked arms and made their way across the bridge towards Wellington Barracks which could just be glimpsed through the trees. As they walked Hettie took a scarf from her black shoulder bag and began tying it round her head. Jill had on a wide straw hat with a velvet bow and carried a pochette.

'What a nice girl,' Margaret said slumping down beside Susan. 'Did you know her before?'

'No. Most of these young army wives are doing some sort of war work or they live in the country. I wish Hettie did have a few more friends, though. It must be a bit dull with us.'

'I think she's very happy.' Margaret's lingering eyes saw Hettie's green-spotted dress merge with the trees and then she vanished out of sight. 'She's utterly wrapped up in the baby and Murdo; other people don't matter. I hope to God he does come back.'

'Whatever makes you think he won't?' Susan looked at her sister in alarm and drew her grandson protectively to her breast. He opened his mouth, gave a yawn, looked at them with his brown eyes and then went to sleep again.

'I don't think he won't. I just hope he does. Do you realize that Hettie has made a most perfect marriage, as far as one can see? Better than either of us?'

'As far as one can see,' Susan said quietly, leaning against the trunk of the tree under which they were sitting. 'Both you and I were very happy at the beginning of our marriages. Who can see into the future?'

'Yes, you're right; but somehow one has no fears about

those two. I wish I'd thought to bring a thermos of coffee, but, as you said, we were both supposed to be going to the service. This is God's way of punishing us for being irreligious. I'm terribly thirsty. Shall I see if the kiosk is open?'

'I don't think it is.'

'I'll just go and see.'

Margaret got up and, at that instance, the dreaded chug of the buzz bomb sounded, as yet only a sound in the distance, and shading her eyes she looked up at the sky.

'Curses! This was all we needed to spoil the day.'

'I've become used to them, I must say,' Susan said nonchalantly. 'Anyway, they never seem to fall anywhere near us.'

Margaret started to walk towards the round kiosk by the lake; but the sound grew louder and she stopped, looked up again and then ran back to Susan.

'It's getting nearer, Sue. Perhaps we should take cover?'

'Oh darling, wherever could we go?' Susan, utterly unperturbed, looked round and smiled. 'Buckingham Palace, or that terribly secret place they're supposed to be running the war from?' She jerked her head in the direction of the vast concrete bunker on Horse Guards' Parade which was alleged to contain a whole underground complex for carrying on the war.

Suddenly Margaret saw the bomb, a black, horizontal object like a very large bug – hence the word, she supposed, 'doodlebug'. As it came nearer she felt herself suddenly start to tremble. How idiotic they'd been to come to the heart of London, near the Palace, Westminster and Downing Street. Surely all the bombs would be aimed in that direction if they could be aimed at all, which no one was sure about? Having survived so much in the war had made them too blasé.

'Oh Susan, I think it's going to drop on the *Palace*!'

She stared, her eyes fixated on the awful monster moving towards them. Then, suddenly, as they watched, the engine cut off and a fat black stick dived past her eyes, disappearing above the trees in the direction of the Palace and Wellington Barracks by its side. There was a crunch as though the earth were caving in, the trees seemed to sway, all the ducks and birds shrieked and flew in all directions, and the people on the benches dived to the ground, hiding their faces in their arms. Margaret threw herself against Susan and Malcolm, protectively putting her arm over his head. Then there was an eerie silence and, as they looked up, they saw a thick spiral of smoke rise slowly above the trees like a funeral pyre. She looked at Susan with horror and then closed her eyes.

'It *can't* be,' she murmured.

Susan's voice was very calm. She hugged her grandson, cradling him in her arms. 'You'll have to go and see,' she said. 'We must know, mustn't we?'

Margaret got up and, with others in the park, started to run towards the Barracks while around her was the sound of sirens, bells and the roar of fire engines and ambulances converging on the spot behind the trees.

When she saw the chapel at first she thought that it was alright, because it was standing in the centre of the Barracks. Then she saw that the smoke came exactly from its centre and at the same time she realized the roof was missing. Already it had been cordoned off; all sorts of official-looking personnel, ambulance men and black-uniformed firemen were rushing towards it as soldiers streamed out of the Barracks on either side. A crowd had gathered and, as she joined them, people began to stumble from the door of the chapel, their hands over their faces, some assisted and some bent double either in pain or grief. Some seemed to stagger as though they couldn't see, and some fell as soon as they emerged from the door; but Hettie in her bright green spotted dress wasn't among any of them.

Margaret knew she could not get near the chapel and she did not try. Other people, obviously friends or relatives, were trying to claw their way through the crowds and were being politely but firmly held back by the police. One woman screamed continuously and a uniformed nurse tried gently to lead her away. Margaret thought that probably quite a few people had stayed in the park as she and Susan had while their more religious loved ones went to the service.

Why was it that always the good had to be punished?

She went back and told Susan, who had remained sitting by the tree, her grandson safe in her arms, but with her face pointed towards the Barracks. With the stoicism that she had learned about Ian Lyall, her brother Malcolm and her husband, Susan now heard Margaret tell her that the chapel containing her daughter had had a direct hit and that people were stumbling from the wreckage.

'If anyone will survive Hettie will,' Margaret said firmly.

Susan looked at her, her face lit by a sad resigned smile. 'Why do you say that, Maggie?'

'Because I *always* say things like that. I'm always optimistic.' She paused and a hand instinctively reached out to touch Malcolm as though he were a talisman. 'Well, we have to keep our spirits up, don't we?' She gazed at Susan, trying to smile; but her heart was frozen with fear and dread.

Together they walked to the chapel, but the crowd and the confusion had grown. Ambulances raced away, their sirens ringing and on the ground were many, too many, still bodies covered with sheets.

A policeman told them they could do absolutely nothing. The chapel had been full; and in the interest of the injured, of those lives who could be saved, they must stay away. But he also said that there were many dead.

'She might come back to where we were,' Susan said helplessly and Margaret nodded.

'She would do that. I saw some *walk* out. If she was a bit late, and I think they were, they would be at the back. That's very sensible, Sue. Let's go back and wait; because there is nothing else on God's earth that we can do except wait.'

They waited a while longer, but little Malcolm was fretting and undoubtedly getting hungry. They now had to face the problem of what to do with a baby who hitherto had only been fed from the breast.

'There's a bottle in Hettie's cupboard,' Susan said when Margaret posed the problem to her. 'She got it from the hospital just in case. We'll boil the milk.'

'In that case we must go.'

They both looked towards the smoking chapel and Margaret gently turned her sister away. 'As soon as we've fed Malcolm I'll come back.'

'Can't you stay and let me take the car?' Susan's expression was agonized.

'Darling, you couldn't drive with the baby lolling in the back. He's much too young. No, we'll be very quick and I'll come straight back. I promise. Things may have sorted themselves out a bit. I'll go straight to the chapel and I'll insist on finding out what's happened.'

'She may be home by then . . .'

Even Margaret knew it sounded hopeless.

Once home they found the bottle, as Susan had said, in Hettie's cupboard where she kept all her baby things; they sterilized it and boiled the milk. While it cooled and Susan then fed her grandson, Margaret rang the Barracks, the police, the local hospitals, but when she could get through there was no news and usually the lines were continually engaged.

After she'd fed him Susan put Malcolm into his pram in the garden and came to the door with Margaret.

'I wish you'd eat.'

'I can't. There may be something we can do. But we do have to know, don't we?'

Susan nodded and put her arm round her sister's shoulder, partly for comfort and partly anxiously, urgently propelling her out of the open door. 'I wish I could come with you, but . . .'

They both stopped and stared as a dun-coloured army vehicle drew up and stopped by the door. A young Guards Officer emerged from it and in his hand he carried a black war-time shoulder bag, covered with dust and torn at one end as though it had been wrenched from under a heavy object. He held out the bag, as if it spoke volumes.

'I'm terribly sorry,' he said to them as they dumbly stood aside to let him in. 'I know Murdoch Dunbar very well, and Hettie of course . . .'

'You were at the wedding,' Susan said. 'Please do come in. I know your face but I'm afraid I can't remember your name.'

'Barnes. Jim Barnes. I'm due to go to France with the Infantry next week.'

'Did you see . . .?'

Now that the dreaded thing had happened Margaret marvelled at her calm, her own and that of Susan. Malcolm lay contentedly in his pram in the garden and, on that beautiful summer afternoon, a blackbird sang in the laburnum tree. Afterwards she and Susan would give way to grief; but not now, not in front of Captain Barnes.

'Yes. She must have died at once.' Captain Barnes bowed his head. 'The roof caved in completely.'

'We'd . . . hoped she might be at the back. She was late.'

Jim Barnes shook his head. 'She was at the very front. You know people usually sit at the back and latecomers have to make their way to the front. Ridiculous, isn't it? Like concerts and lectures.'

They both nodded solemnly, as though the stupidity of people who would sit at the back when they should be

511

taking places at the front were a matter of the gravest consideration.

'Where is she?' Margaret asked.

'In the mortuary. As I knew her and Murdoch I said I would tell you. I came as quickly as I could,' he said after an awkward pause. 'I knew you'd be frantic.'

'We were in the park when it happened. Originally we were all to have gone to the Service.' Margaret gestured wordlessly. The thought that but for this quirk of fate they might all be dead, including the baby, seemed too unreal, too grotesque to dwell on. 'We had to get back to feed Malcolm and I was just going back when . . .' She removed her hat and put it on the hallstand.

'It's terribly kind of you.' Susan led him into the lounge; then abruptly sat down and clasped her hands in front of her. 'Won't you have a drink?'

'I must get back,' Captain Barnes said. 'It's a terrible mess there. But there are hundreds of helpers and my C.O. said I could come. I wanted to bring this . . .'

He gave them the bag and Margaret took it, hugging it to her as though it were part of Hettie. In it would be her lipstick, her powder, her purse, her identity card, maybe the most recent letter from Murdo. All the precious things she had in the world would be in that bag; that tatty, dusty, precious little black war-time utility shoulder bag.

'I do appreciate it, Captain Barnes,' Susan said, staring at the bag in Margaret's hand as though she couldn't believe that this was all that was left to them of Hettie. 'It was such a *nice* day, such a happy . . . Well, it's futile isn't it? It's futile now to say she should never have gone. We were all going to go, even the baby . . .' Her voice trailed away as if in wonderment at the mysterious ways of God.

'They were singing a hymn when the bomb fell.' Captain Barnes swallowed. 'I don't know if you believe in that sort of thing, but if you have to go and you do believe,

512

then . . . it was a good time to go. Full of grace and all that . . .' He got up and straightened his jacket. 'I'm sorry I had to bring you the news. Believe me . . .'

Margaret had a sudden thought and rose with him.

'Did you know Jill . . . Jill Courtney? She was there too. She would have been next to Hettie. They went together. If they hadn't met I should have gone.'

Jim Barnes shook his head. 'Hettie was beside an enormous piece of stone. In fact I think she was just struck by it and that killed her instantly because she was practically unmarked. Her face looked so peaceful, as if she'd fallen asleep. When I saw her I thought . . .' He stopped and looked at the two women who were listening to him with almost exaggerated concentration. 'I'm sorry, this must be very distressing for you. I know Jill Courtney, but I didn't see her. Maybe she was under the stone. Oh God, if she was there too we shall have to get the news to her husband. You know, you expect it of men fighting, but with women and children . . . Yes, there were children there too.'

He passed a hand wearily over his face and Susan rising said quickly: 'Captain, maybe if you go to France and you see Murdo . . . you'd tell him yourself. I mean, tell him what you told us, about the singing, how she looked . . . peaceful, you know I don't know why it helps to know how someone died, but it does. Believe me, it does. Murdo's very religious as Hettie is . . . as Hettie was.' Susan swallowed and her voice faltered. 'They believe in God and his mercy. Maybe their faith will help him to understand. For myself I cannot . . .' She turned and flung herself on Margaret's breast.

'Weep, weep,' she said softly, stroking her back. 'Captain Barnes won't mind. Will you, Captain Barnes?'

'Of course not,' the Guardsman said gruffly, then he looked towards the open windows to where, just beyond them, stood the pram in the middle of the vegetables that

513

were being grown to win the war. 'Is that the baby? Do you think I could?'

Margaret nodded and Jim Barnes tiptoed outside and gazed at Malcolm Dunbar, that day made motherless by enemy action, sleeping peacefully in his pram.

CHAPTER TWENTY NINE

Morag Dunbar had never seemed a very happy girl. She was a lifeless sort of creature, locked in resentment about the way her father had treated her mother and, consequently, full of mistrust of everyone. She managed, while at school, to create a world of make-believe for herself in which she always had the starring role; a world that was neat and uncomplicated and full of happy families, lawful offspring, dutiful women and handsome men of the Prince Charming type.

She had never enjoyed the slightest rapport with her father Cullum when he was alive, and when he died she dismissed him without difficulty from her mind. She left school the same year and immediately set about looking for a husband, the only means by which she considered she could quickly escape the boredom, tedium and humiliation of Branswick which, to her, was synonymous with prison.

She had to her advantage a rather dull brain and considerable looks – she was blonde and blue-eyed and, to all appearances, very vivacious. She also, very early on, exuded a quality of sexuality that attracted the men. Consequently no one was very surprised when, six months after she left school, she married an American Air Force captain she had met at the home of a friend with whom she was staying outside Manchester.

What did surprise everyone, however, was the fact that her mother not only approved of the marriage but announced her intention of going to America with her daughter to help her to set up her new home and perhaps to settle there herself. Fleur's eldest daughter Patricia had

515

for some years been married to a doctor with an extensive practice in the Midlands, so there was no need to worry about her.

Like her daughter, Fleur could not be said to have had a happy life, though how much of it was Fleur's fault and how much that of Cullum or people around her was almost impossible to judge. Fleur had lost her first husband through circumstances not of her making, and she had striven for a time to do her best for the second. Even when she found he had a mistress and a son by her, she had still tried to keep her marriage afloat; but when Cullum deserted her for Nan Murray she grew more and more bitter and her last years in Branswick were so unhappy that she suffered from an almost permanent form of melancholy that needed medical aid from time to time.

In all her vicissitudes, however, Fleur had nourished an affection for Margaret. She felt that, like her, Margaret was no stranger to suffering; that Margaret understood and sympathized because she had been let down by men as much as Fleur had. Men were really the cause of all women's sufferings, in Fleur's jaundiced opinion. Like Fleur, Margaret had been let down by Cullum, had had to shoulder the burden of running the firm in wartime and then, with the cruel death of Hettie, had been struck the unkindest blow of all.

After Hettie's death, Margaret had blamed herself for not doing something she had thought so often of doing before; she closed the London office and house and came north with Susan and the motherless baby Malcolm. Clare Amory was left to look after Devonshire Place in the role of caretaker, to forward mail and, if it was hit by a buzz bomb, to see that Margaret got to know about it.

Murdoch Dunbar was officially informed of his wife's death, and was given forty-eight hours' leave from France to attend her funeral and see his infant son. He was in such a state of shock that his commanding officer pro-

516

posed he should have extended compassionate leave; but Murdoch refused. The funeral was in Branswick and no one could recall seeing him smile at all, even when he held gurgling Malcolm in his arms during the baby's baptism, arranged on the same day as his mother's funeral. Very few afterwards could even remember him saying anything.

It was as though life had been extinguished not only in Hettie but in Murdoch too and nothing, not the words of his mother nor of Susan, or Margaret, not the sight of his new-born son, not the comfort of his cousins and friends, not the consolations of religion nor the strength of his faith could give him solace. He went back to France as embittered as he had left it, to find the only release from his grief that he could – in action and the sounds of war.

Morag was married in January 1945, not in Branswick because she hated the place, but from the home of the friend where she had met her American captain so that all his friends from the nearby US Army base could attend. Yvonne was her bridesmaid and, from the way the US personnel looked at her, Margaret was afraid that her daughter would be next to cross the waters; but Yvonne seemed rather inured to masculine glances and anyway she said she did not like Americans. No one asked her why.

Some days after the wedding, Fleur told Margaret of her plans as they were sitting in the lounge at *Woodbrae* after tea. Although it was dusk the lights had not been turned on and the glow of the fire was all that illuminated their tired, thoughtful faces.

'I really like him *quite* well,' Fleur said unconvincingly. 'I mean I don't *know* him . . .' She looked at Margaret as though inviting reassurance that her son-in-law was everything a mother could want for her daughter.

'He certainly *seems* very nice,' Margaret said, unable to put much enthusiasm into her voice. 'But then one doesn't know with Americans, does one?'

'Of course, we know *nothing* about his family.'

'What does his father do?' Margaret sipped at her tea which had gone cold in her cup.

'He's a farmer in – is it Dakota the place is called? Yes, Dakota. He *looked* awfully nice in his picture. His mother is dead, Gene's mother I mean, and I thought . . . I don't know what you'll think about this Maggie, but I thought I'd go to America and make my home with Morag. She'd like that. She'd like me to go with her. Gene is going to be sent to Europe and we know she doesn't want to stay here. Morag always felt that everyone in the town pointed at her because of Cullum . . .'

'Which was ridiculous,' Margaret snapped.

'Well, she *is* a sensitive girl and that's the way she felt. I can't say I blame her, though I personally felt people more or less accepted it; never gave it a thought really. The thing is, Margaret – ' Fleur got up and walked restlessly to the window. 'I'm not very happy here either. I'm not a native of Branswick, am I? I don't really fit in. You have to be Scots to be accepted by the Scots, I always say.'

'I don't think that's true, Fleur. The townspeople have always liked and admired you. They didn't admire Cullum when he left you, anyway, and it showed in the sparse attendance at his funeral.'

'Oh that was horrid.' Fleur shuddered. 'When I think of Bruno and . . . poor Hettie.' (People hardly ever mentioned Hettie without pausing before saying her name and preceding it by the adjective 'poor'). 'Why, the cemetery was filled to overflowing for *her*. I think people thought Nan would go to Cullum's funeral so they kept away.'

'William was very brave, I thought, and noble,' Margaret said. 'He didn't draw attention to himself and yet he didn't hide himself. He was very dignified.'

Fleur thought for a moment then drew the curtains against the dusk and put on a small table lamp. 'Yes, he was. I didn't talk to him, of course, and I was glad he

518

decided not to come to the reception. *That* was courteous of him. I suppose he must have thought I should make way for his mother to attend; but I couldn't. I was Cullum's legal wife.'

'I don't think William thought that at all. He realized it was a very sensitive situation. In fact, he's a remarkably sensitive young man; the more I know him the more I like him. One can't help liking him. He has made the best out of a very unhappy situation and come well out of it. It might have crushed a lesser boy.'

'I suppose he hates me for not divorcing Cullum. It would be unnatural if he did not.'

'That I don't know.' Margaret leaned forward and poked the fire. 'We aren't that intimate and I don't see him all that often. I expect, after the war, we shall see less and less of him as he makes his own life in whatever he intends to do.'

'What does he intend to do?' Fleur looked at her sharply.

'I think he's going to University. He joined up straight from school. He said something about science or engineering.'

'Margaret, about the house . . .' Fleur sat down next to her, her hands tucked under her arms, her head bent. 'You know it is left to William after my death?' Well, I'm not going to die yet, I hope, but I may never live here again. If I like America I shall certainly stay there. They say if there is ever another war after this, America will be the only safe place . . .'

'Oh Fleur,' Margaret cried impatiently. 'Please don't start talking about another war. This one hasn't ended yet and let's hope that when it does it is the last.'

'I'd like you to live in the house in my place,' Fleur went on. 'Yvonne likes Branswick much better than Morag did. I want you to know that it's your home and always will be.'

Margaret slowly got a cigarette from her bag and lit it. 'Thank you, Fleur but . . . I'm not sure. I mean the house is *not* left to you until you die, is it? It is for you to live in as long as you want. If you were to live elsewhere I'm not sure that William wouldn't have a right . . .'

'Oh *he'll* know all about his rights,' Fleur said, bitterly. 'I'm sure of that. If you ask me, that young man with his nice manners hoodwinks you. What is he, after all, but the illegitimate son of a mill girl . . .'

'Oh Fleur please!' Margaret looked up at her in disgust. 'That's unworthy of you! You may hate William and you may hate Nan and you may have every right; but I think William has behaved *very* well . . .'

'He put pressure on Cullum to leave the house to him!'

'He did no such thing! Of that I'm sure. He was very embarrassed at being left the house . . .'

'Oh yes . . . ?'

'Yes.'

The two women stared at each other and Margaret wondered if this was the end of a long friendship. She liked Fleur, but she did not love her. Fleur protected herself too much by an invisible, impenetrable circle of reserve really to engender love. Margaret sometimes thought that this was what had repelled Cullum, who had needed warmth and love more than anything else. Perhaps if Fleur had shown more passion, more animation, even possessiveness, she would not have lost him as irrevocably as she had. In the same way, although she respected and admired Fleur, she thought her a victim of her own resentment, of the bitterness that had eaten into her soul.

'Yes, he was,' Margaret repeated firmly, anxious to have the last word on the subject. 'Very embarrassed indeed.'

'Then *why* did he not give it up?'

'I don't know.' Margaret got up and threw her cigarette

520

into the fire. 'Maybe that did have something to do with his mother. I mean, Cullum left very little money. Maybe William thought the house was security for her. I'm sure he was not thinking of himself.'

'I think he's pulled the wool over your eyes,' Fleur said. 'Anyway, if that's the case I shan't say I've left. I'll say I'm going on a holiday. *That's* alright I suppose?'

'I think that's fine,' Margaret said, sorry about the row; sorry they'd had words they might not so easily forget.

The Battle of the Reichswald Forest was the opening phase of Campaign Veritable, the object of which was the ultimate conquest of Germany. According to the original plan, it should have started at the end of September 1944, following the operation at Arnhem when the chances of outflanking the comparatively light defences of the northern end of the Siegfried Line and slicing into the Ruhr would have been better. There were many reasons for this delay. One of them was the failure of the Allies to capture a bridgehead over the Neder Rijn at Arnhem, and another was the fact that Allied intelligence had underestimated the German recovery after the collapse of France and Belgium.

By February 1945 the build-up for this, the largest Allied offensive since the Normandy landings, was of colossal proportions involving the surreptitious movement of thousands of troops and supplies over ruined roads, railways and bridges which had to be repaired before they could be used. Nearly a hundred new bridges had to be built, some 35,000 road vehicles strictly controlled and enough fuel laid on to keep the British XXX Corps, responsible for the attack, supplied for at least 150 miles. By the evening of 7 February some 200,000 men, backed up by a full complement of tanks, guns and other weapons and air support 'on the maximum scale', were waiting behind the Canadian troops manning the forward positions between Nijmegen and the dark Reichswald Forest. The plan was for a series of blows, first by bombs, then by massed artillery and finally by forces on the ground designed to shatter the end of the Siegfried Line and erupt on to the Rhineland plain.

The directive from the Canadian General Crerar was clear enough: 'To clear the Reichswald and secure the line Gennep-Asperden-Cleve.'

Murdoch Dunbar had been in action continually since the Normandy landings, in command of a squadron of tanks attached to 6th Guards' Tank Brigade. He had fought in France and in Belgium and now here he was on the Dutch-German border waiting to go into action in one of the most important offensives of the war. The men had sensed the scale and importance of the attack because of all the preparations. The weather, though, had been atrocious and was becoming worse every day. The German defenders had 160 million cubic metres of water held by dams behind the left flank, and their right flank was protected by a flood which extended all the way to a river running across the entire front. Men, guns and huge tanks were swallowed in the mud, which led many to compare the conditions with those at Passchendaele in the First World War.

At five o'clock on the morning of 8 February, the heaviest barrage employed by the British in the Second World War opened against the German troops defending the Reichswald. At H-Hour, ten thirty, yellow smoke signalled the first 300 yard lift and the infantry started to creep forward.

The Fifteenth Scottish Division had orders to break the Siegfried Line and take Cleve – tasks that sounded very simple but, in fact, were not. They had been given substantial support including the whole of the 6th Guards' Tank Brigade consisting of 178 Churchill tanks. From the 8th to the 10th of February Murdoch Dunbar had only six hours' sleep, and that taken at odd intervals usually in the turret of his tank watching carefully over those under his command. The hazards of the mud were almost as grave as the danger from bullets and shells and at one stage during the capture of Elsenhof the whole of his Corps was bogged down in the mud and had to be dug out, many of the men using their bare hands. To add to the terrible conditions of the roads was the steadily rising flood water from days of continuous rain and the breaching of nearby rivers. The battle which was supposed to have been over in two or three days was settling down into something that would prove to be long, protracted, and bloody.

On 11 February the Scottish Division launched a two-prong attack on the historic Rhineland town of Cleve from whence had come, in the sixteenth century, the fourth of Henry VIII's wives, Anne, whose ill looks were to save her head. The 227th Highland Brigade and the Scots Guards' tanks were on the left, the 44th Lowland Brigade and the tanks of the Grenadiers on the right. The Gordon Highlanders and the Scots Guards' tanks led the way, reaching the crossroads at the eastern edge of the woods at dusk.

No living soul was to be found in Cleve, which had been the object of saturation bombing before the Allied attack. Huge craters made the roads impassable and, as he rumbled through in his tank, Murdoch could not make out one entire house standing. However, many cellars had been reinforced by the populace in a vain attempt to withstand attack and, when the troops alighted from the cramped conditions to straighten their legs, they found the cellars full of food: smoked hams, dried fish, sausages, cheeses and black bread. The men joyfully launched themselves onto the food having existed on sparse compo rations for days.

Murdoch sat with his sergeant in a corner of a deserted ruin, eating his food and regretting only the absence of wine or whisky to go with it. He smiled at his sergeant whose face was blackened by mud, smoke and fatigue.

'I think this is the best meal I ever had, Sarge.'

'I agree with ye sir.' The grimy Scotsman wiped his mouth on the arm of his sleeve and smiled. 'Though they do say the best meal is always the last.'

Murdoch leaned back against the crumbling wall. 'I wonder who lived here. Where they are now? Don't you often think, Sarge, that the real victims of this war have been the innocent? The women, the children and the old men?'

'I dinna think of it, sir,' the sergeant replied. 'Though I ken ye have a personal reason for saying that.'

'I think I would say it anyway. As we went through France and Belgium I was more sickened by the pathetic sight of the refugees fleeing from the war that they had been powerless to prevent. The innocent always suffer.'

Sergeant Black, who had been with Murdoch during the entire campaign, tipped his tin hat forward and scratched behind his ear. 'Ye'll be thinking of the wife, sir, that bonny lady so cruelly killed by the V-bomb.'

Murdoch was silent for a moment and he tried to visualize what Hettie had looked like but found he could not, as though war had wiped her image from his mind. Then he reached into an inner pocket for the photo he always carried of her, very dog-eared now and torn, and stared at it. As some people said their prayers night and morning Murdoch took out her photo from his pocket like a religious ritual and studied it. Then he put it carefully away and when he tried to summon up her face again he always found that her features evaded him, like a chimera.

The events of the previous summer had left a deep imprint on Murdoch Dunbar. It had turned a happy man of cheerful and sanguine disposition into a savage one, bereft of hope. After Hettie's funeral he went back to the war with gusto, and he found in the ceaseless advance against the enemy not only a way of revenge but a way of expiating her death. For it was he who had wanted the baby and, because of the baby, Hettie had been in London and the bomb had fallen on her. After the wedding she had said that she wanted to continue her studies because no one knew how long the war would last and, one day, as a doctor, she might be useful. But, as his father had before him, Murdoch wanted to feel that he had engendered life because, if anyone were killed, it could not possibly be Hettie, but him.

He didn't keep a picture of the baby in his pocket and he hadn't loved the baby when he held it in his arms. He knew it was unreasonable, and he hoped one day he would feel differently and be able to give to his motherless son the love his mother had given to him. But just now, in his mind, the baby was synonymous with Hettie's death and even though he knew he was wrong, he nevertheless blamed the poor creature for it.

Murdoch enjoyed the war, the ceaseless activity and the company of men. He had been offered leave but had declined it, choosing instead the odd extended weekend in Paris or Brussels where he ate and drank well but never went with a woman. His life was dedicated to the memory of a twenty-year-old girl who had briefly been his wife, and to pursuing the war to avenge her death.

Murdoch no longer said his prayers night and morning, nor did his once strong religious faith sustain him; he felt unable to equate the destruction of the Guards' Chapel in the middle of Divine Service with his previously held notions of a just and merciful God. What he had seen in Europe since had diminished his faith even further; but in its place it had given him a kind of peace.

He put the photo carefully in his wallet, fastened it in his pocket, leaned back again and closed his eyes. Yes, he had found peace; not in trusting God, not in humanity, not in the memory of Hettie, but in himself. He realized that the centre of one's being was the source of peace, not the presence or the actions of others. He thus became a very independent man and a dedicated soldier admired by his colleagues.

'When I go home I'm going to study philosophy, Sarge,' he said, getting to his feet.

Whatever for, Sergeant Black wondered as he trudged behind Murdoch out of the damp dark ruin.

During the night of the 11th, forward companies of the Gordons pushed through the ruins of Cleve succeeding in capturing a damaged road bridge over the Spoy Canal. Just after three thirty the brigade reserve, the 10th Highland Light Infantry with a squadron of Scots Guards' tanks and some Crocodiles from the 79th Armoured, moved across the canal, over the bridge that the sappers had repaired, to clear the north-east part of Cleve before dawn on 12 February.

On the 13th Murdoch and his squadron were able to have some rest because the terrible ground conditions, caused by the floods, both man-made and the result of the exceptionally heavy rain, made tank movement almost impossible and the assault was continued by the 15th Scottish moving out of Cleve. Murdoch managed to write a letter to his mother, which he put in the pocket where he kept his wallet and the torn picture of his wife. The small Bible that his mother had given him he had discarded when he decided that his religious faith was dead.

On 14 February the sun unexpectedly shone from a clear sky. XXX Corps rested while the Allied aeroplanes made over 9,000 sorties, pounding the enemy lines along the front and deep into Germany. However the next day, 15 February, the weather was bad again and the Germans were able to start moving their armour. By the 16th Murdoch with his squadron had moved well away from Cleve, sent to support the Royal Winnipeg Rifles in clearing high ground in the Louisendorf area. Cleve Forest was behind them and ahead was Calcar, with the Moyland wood to the north.

Murdoch had managed to have more sleep during the night than he had for weeks, and he felt in good form as his squadron moved out in support of the Royal Winnipeg Rifles mounted in their unarmed 'Kangaroos', tanks whose turrets had been removed and were used for carrying infantry under small-arms fire or shelling. As they approached the high ground they were met by a hail of shell fire and multiple rockets from the Germans hidden above the ridge. The Kangaroos slowed down, but the tanks pushed on, reaching Louisendorf alone. The tank guns began to fire on the village but Murdoch saw that they would have to retreat unless the infantry dismounted from their vehicles to take over the assault.

'We'll have to get these buggers onto the ground!' he shouted to Sergeant Black. 'I'm going to get out and try and guide them to their positions.'

'It's a terrible risky thing tae do, sir,' Black called back. 'We'll have tae retreat.'

'Retreat? Balls!' Murdoch roared in true soldier fashion. 'We'll lose the village.'

He jumped down from his tank and, dodging among the shells, went up to each Kangaroo, motioning for the men to come down and follow him, showing them where they could take up their positions with the maximum of stealth. The Canadians looked at each other and then at the fearless Scotsman who had left the protection of his tank to walk among them. They clearly thought he was crazy, but reluctantly they began to climb out of their carriers and assume the positions indicated by Murdoch.

Murdoch was approaching the last carrier when he slipped in the mud, fell on his face and had difficulty getting back on his feet. He suddenly thought that to drown in the mud would be the worst fate of all and, making a superhuman effort, he righted himself, cheerily waving to Black, who was watching him anxiously from the gun turret. Just as Murdoch raised his arm to the sky in a gesture of victory, a shell burst at the foot of the carrier he was approaching, killing all the men in it, and Murdoch Dunbar, instantly.

'Happy are the dead which die in the faith of Christ,' the padre said, looking anxiously at some flak exploding in the air, high over the bodies as they were lowered into quickly dug graves outside the village of Louisendorf which, partly thanks to Murdoch Dunbar, had been successfully captured two hours after his death. Sergeant Black who had recovered the body of his Captain, had extracted from his pocket the wallet which contained some official documents, an identity pass, the picture of his wife and the last letter he had written to his mother. In due course these would be returned to her along with his other effects, his officer's cap and the insignia of the Scots Guards.

No one wrote that he and his men would lie forever among the hedgerows of Germany; but his courage, which was witnessed by many, and for which he was post-humously decorated, remained in the minds of those who had watched him dismount from his tank and run among the Canadians spurring them to action. To some it had looked like a mission of suicide, but that might be said of many brave actions where the participant survives to tell the tale. Most thought it was in the finest traditions of the British Army for which Murdoch had given his life, as had his father before him.

Sergeant Black, who had been with Murdoch since the invasion, threw earth on his coffin, as did other officers and men who had served in Murdoch's squadron. No one spoke; all eyes were dry. This unhappy task had been done too often in the course of the war to provoke emotion in fighting men. It merely served as a lesson, a reminder of their own mortality. In the distance came the sound of gunfire, and the rain poured relentlessly down. As earth was shovelled into the grave, Dougal Black thought of the last proper meal he and Murdoch had shared in the ruins of Cleve, and was glad it had been a good one. Then he turned his back upon the grave and went to rejoin his squadron, which now had a new commander.

CHAPTER THIRTY

William Murray stood at the window of the house on the hill and looked at the great Dunbar Mill which occupied a central stretch along the bank by the swift-flowing Drume. The smoke from it, and from so many others, billowed upwards, merging with the overhanging clouds. A steady stream of rain obscured the Vertig hill and the surrounding mountains from sight, as well as the tenement along the river where he had been born and spent most of his boyhood.

It was extraordinary how often he had thought nostalgically of this picture, though not from the vantage point he occupied now, when standing on a windswept, rain-lashed deck at sea. The peace, the normality of Branswick. How he'd longed for it. And now the Peace was here. It was eighteen months since the war had ended and a year since he'd been demobilized and begun his course at university.

'I love Branswick,' William said, 'but I don't know that I want to spend the rest of my life here, which is what it will mean if I accept your offer. Strange even to hear myself say that! I was just remembering how often I thought of this scene when I was at sea. The town with the rivers meeting in the middle and our tenement by the side of the Drume. I used to stand at our window and watch the river for hours on end because it seemed to me to lead to an exciting, fairytale world which I didn't think I'd ever see. And now I have and what a different, dangerous place it was to the one I imagined.'

He turned to Margaret, who put down her tapestry work and came to stand beside him.

'Yes, the Peace. The second Peace for me. The consequences of the first one were enormous to me and all our family, as well as to the world. I wonder what this one will bring?'

William looked at her incredulously. 'You remember 1918 all that well?'

'I remember every minute of it. I was seventeen and still at school. My brother had been killed in the war and also my brother-in-law to be. This time I lost a dearly loved niece and nephew, the children of my brother and sister. How cruel, how ironic. Both wars have affected our family terribly, as they have countless other families in the land. I hope and pray there will never be another one.'

'Amen to that,' William said gravely. 'The atomic bomb has cast a shadow over mankind which could alter the course of history. Compared to the next war the past two may turn out to have been skirmishes.'

Margaret clasped his arm and drew in her breath. 'Oh please don't say that! Please don't even *think* it. When I consider the younger generation growing up I can't bear it. Let's think instead of the future; it could be a good one for us all. I'd like you here in Branswick, William.' She linked an arm through his. 'Your future in the business would be assured. You say you love it, so . . . ' She looked at his stern profile but he continued to gaze in front of him.

'It is where I belong,' he said. 'The place I shall always come back to, as you have, but do I want to live here, work here all my life?'

'What do you think you would prefer to do, William?'

'I thought some career in science, industry or the Civil Service.'

'But knitting is in your blood, your mother's blood and in your father's.'

'You mean my mother would think it some kind of triumph to have her son in an important position in a mill

531

where she was once a humble worker, my grandfather and his father before him frameworkers all their lives?'

'I can't see Nan thinking of that as a triumph. She's much too sensible. This is the post-war world, William. The war has made everyone equal. We're desperate for women to work in the mill where the pay and conditions are good. Our order books are full and we make and export as many non-utility sets as the government will let us. We recently had our licence raised from £50,000 worth of goods to £75,000. When I was in the States I found that the Americans were crying out for our merchandise. Even though their own knitwear industry has expanded the quality is not a patch on ours. I thought you might like to go to America and see our operation there. It would give you the chance to travel.'

'I've done plenty of that!'

'Oh not in a battleship! It's different, isn't it? The river you watched so often could, after all, lead to a new and exciting world. The fact is,' Margaret continued, sighing and folding her arms, 'that I need you, William. There is no one else who will take over from me, no one from my family.'

'What about James?'

'James definitely doesn't want to come into the business. He's staying in the RAF after his successful wartime career. My sister Juliet's children have never been interested, besides Tom . . .' She frowned. Tom had found himself reluctant, now that the war was over, to confess to the truth about Clare; besides, he was not yet demobilized and when he was he would resume his legal practice at the Scottish Bar.

'Murdoch's death was a terrible blow. Somehow we had all set our sights on the fact that one day he would run it.'

'And I'm second best, I suppose.' William's voice was without rancour. In fact nothing he ever said or did disturbed the impression of an amiable, good-tempered, well balanced young man, sure of himself and his place in the world.

'I confess I don't know whether we should have had this conversation if Murdoch had been alive.' Margaret walked back to the sofa where she had left her embroidery and sat down. 'But second best? No. The war has changed many things. Isn't it ironic? Here I am asking Cullum's son to come into the business. After Malcolm's death Cullum had to come into the business, and after his son's death I am asking you.'

William turned his back to the window and began gently pacing up and down. He had retained his sailor's beard and the oval of ginger facial hair framed his wide generous mouth. He was so like Cullum that no one could have mistaken the relationship, and yet he did not have that suggestion of weakness about his face that had been Cullum's disadvantage. Cullum had always a placatory smile on his lips, an expression in his eyes that said he wanted to please. When he grew aggressive, through drink or stubbornness, the hostility in his eyes conflicted with his weak features and made people despise him rather than respect or fear him. William had no such signs of weakness. His demeanour was confident, his expression determined though courteous, as one who weighs matters up before making a decision, a thing clearly he was doing now.

'What makes you think I would be more successful than my father?' he said after a while and Margaret, waiting for his reply, had resumed her embroidery.

'Because you are a different person. Cullum lived his life in Malcolm's shadow; you had no such disadvantage. Oh I'm not saying you did not have disadvantages, and how well you've overcome them; but you didn't have the presence of an overpowering brother whom everyone loved and admired. Cullum once said to me that we wished he had died and not Malcolm, and in a way that was true. We were all to blame for what Cullum was and yet he did some good things. He was faithful in his fashion to your mother; he invited public scorn by leaving Fleur to live with her. He gave up drink in quite a heroic manner, because alcoholism is a sickness you know. As far as I know he never drank again after his cure. He was tender and considerate towards people, and in a way deserved to be better loved. I loved him much more in his last years, and reproached myself for the way I had behaved towards him before. I know he thought me domineering and interfering, and that he always resented me.'

'But what would people say if I joined the firm? That I was going to be like him? That I had no right there? You could see he was unpopular from the few who attended his funeral. They never forgave him for living openly with my mother, and I am the son of that mother.'

'They never forgave him for leaving *Dunbars*,' Margaret said gently, snipping off a piece of coloured silk. 'Dunbars *is* Branswick and more was expected of him on that account. To let down Dunbars was considered a graver crime than letting down his family. Anyway, William, I have put the seeds in your mind, I hope. I know you want to complete your university course, and I have many years left in me yet, I trust. Think about it.'

William was about to reply when the door opened and a tall dark girl, very much like Margaret, came swiftly into the room, rubbing her hands together and shivering despite the fur coat and hat, the high suede boots she was wearing.

'Oh golly it's cold! They say this is the coldest winter since records began.' Yvonne Dunbar-Lamotte ignored the young man standing by the window and addressed her mother. 'Mummy, I tobogganed all down the hill this morning, right to the bottom!'

'You must be careful of traffic, darling.'

'Traffic! There is none. I saw no cars out on the streets all day. They say . . .'

534

'Yvonne, do you remember your cousin William Murray? Won't you say hello?'

Whether or not Yvonne had seen William when she came into the room was difficult to say. Some women attracted the attention of men by pretending to ignore them. Now she looked at William, slowly beginning to unfasten her coat.

'Did we ever meet? I don't think so.'

'We met in London, Yvonne,' William said matter-of-factly. 'It was just after my father died. You came home from school.'

'Oh, I remember.' Margaret could not be sure whether the colour in Yvonne's cheeks was from the cold or something else. 'Yes, I remember the beard and your naval uniform.' She took off her coat, revealing a long red Dunbar Shetland sweater and slacks tucked into her boots, and then she went over to William, her hand outstretched. 'How do you do – again!'

'How do you do, Yvonne,' William smiled, aware that she was no longer a schoolgirl but a remarkably handsome young woman, almost as tall as he was, with a well developed bust and nicely curved hips accentuated by her green twill slacks. 'You're very like your mother.'

'*And* my father,' Yvonne protested. 'Aren't I like Daddy too, Mummy?'

'Yes, a bit.'

'You had very handsome parents, Yvonne,' William said generously. 'Hence your own beauty.'

'Oh what a charmer,' Yvonne glided away from him. 'Do you speak like that to all the girls?'

'I don't know many girls,' William said truthfully. 'I was in the Navy all during the war and now I'm in the science faculty at Edinburgh, which is almost exclusively male.'

'I can introduce you to lots of girls,' Yvonne said, 'if you like. Are you staying here?'

'I'm staying with my mother just for the holiday. I have digs in Edinburgh.'

535

'I don't know that you'll be able to get back tonight, William,' Margaret looked out of the window. 'It's not yet four o'clock and it is already dark. Couldn't you phone your mother and say you'll stay here? After all it is your house.'

'Oh do,' Yvonne said. 'I want to hear all about the war.'

Yvonne Lamotte at seventeen was mature for her years, so that many people mistook her for someone in her early twenties. She had the aristocratic elegance and poise of her father and the rich Scottish beauty of her mother, with Margaret's thick curly black hair, white skin and chiselled features. But she had Yves' dark grey eyes which, besides their luminous quality, had a particularly fascinating way of fastening on people who interested her, making them feel flattered by her attention. Already she had many male admirers and as she apparently had no ambition, unlike her mother, everyone thought it would not be long before she followed the example of her cousin Morag and got married.

Yvonne had left school that Christmas, despite her mother's wish that she should stay until she was eighteen and take her Higher School Certificate. But School Certificate was enough for Yvonne and, remembering her own schooldays, Margaret had yielded to her wish to join the adult world. Young girls, she thought, were so much more adult now than she and her contemporaries had been; or was that a delusion every succeeding generation had?

Unlike her cousin Morag Yvonne loved the small-town life of Branswick and felt happy and at home there. After all it was not very different from Harrogate where she had been educated, though Harrogate, with its lack of industry, did not have the extremes of social nuances that existed in Branswick. Yvonne enjoyed being a member of one of the best known families in the town, someone who lived on the hill, whose father was a war hero and whose

536

mother was that unusual phenomenon, a successful business woman. She liked tennis and golf, dinner parties and coffee mornings and supporting the local rugby team; standing on the touchline cheering on her favourite beau, or supporting him at a suitable distance from the confines of the cricket pavilion.

For Yvonne liked the sort of athletic young men who played rugby, who admired women but felt they had their place – whether it was on the touchline or in the home. Many women liked being treated thus by men. They did not feel they were inferior to men, but different. They enjoyed the small, supportive things women were supposed to do because they emphasized the female role as a counterpart of the masculine one.

Yvonne subscribed to, and upheld, this acceptable view of femininity, even if she did so subconsciously. Maybe it was a way of rejecting the example set by her mother, who all her life had been surrounded by ledgers, samples, order books and figures; who had frequently been away on business or at meetings; who had come home late at night or not at all and for whose sake, Yvonne was quite sure, she had been packed off at an early age to boarding school instead of being allowed to enjoy the delights of a conventional home. Holidays, especially in wartime, were often spent with relatives because her mother was so seldom at home. Thus she came to resent this remote parent who was acting as a kind of mun, whereas the absence of her father was perfectly acceptable because he was doing what men were traditionally supposed to do – go away to war, even to be killed.

At quite an early age Yvonne had set out to compete with her mother, but on very different terms. At seventeen she knew that she wanted soon to marry one of the eligible young men who had been at Fettes or the Edinburgh Academy, or maybe in the war, and who were now at university before taking jobs with the family firm. Just the very thing that Margaret had resisted twenty-seven years before, after the previous war, her daughter was hoping would happen to her.

Yvonne was very friendly with Russell Pendreigh, the eldest son of Ruthven. He was twenty-two, at Cambridge, a keen rugby player and cricketer, destined to go without argument into the family firm. She was also on good terms with scions of the Mactavish, the Law and the Turnball families – all regular young men in the conventional mould. It was possible to tell, even at this age, that Yvonne would never court disaster with married men, or have liaisons with the ambitious, unscrupulous or simply vulgar, or ever marry a homosexual, though of course she had no idea that her beloved father was in this unmentionable category.

Although William Murray could not be said to be in the conventional mould of acceptable young men – he was rather old for one thing and the illegitimate son of her wayward uncle for another – Yvonne was instantly attracted to him that dark January day in 1947 during one of the worst winters since 1880/81.

If it was because he did not know many girls or was too shy to approach them, or because he did not feel it necessary to look further, William reciprocated Yvonne's interest. They met as often as they could. Yvonne went up to stay with her Aunt Juliet in Edinburgh at the slightest pretext and William was always making some excuse or other to come to *Woodbrae*.

Margaret was aware of the interest but not of its seriousness. She couldn't imagine any girl of Yvonne's age wanting to settle down and marry and, although she grieved that Yvonne had no intellectual or business interests, she was really too busy and preoccupied to do much about it.

For the post-war years, though they brought prosperity for Dunbar, also brought problems. Clothes were still rationed and the supply of yarn was greatly restricted. Cashmere was in short supply and Margaret was thankful for their close relationship with Macallisters because Dunbars were given priority. The Americans were crazy about cashmere and even before the war was over Peter Cartwright, exempted from war service because of a weak chest, had prepared a range of stunning designs with which to capture the American market.

Margaret had made three visits to the US in 1946 and planned two more in 1947. Yet, by the spring of that year, she had to admit to herself that she was exhausted. She never took a holiday and she worked until late at night, every night. It was thus not surprising that she remained ignorant of the state of affairs between her daughter and her nephew until a visit that Ruthven Pendreigh made to her home one night in April, following a board meeting at the mill earlier that day, Ruthven having joined the Dunbar board in place of his father. He said he had wanted to talk to her and she invited him to come to the house for a drink.

Ruthven had had a very successful war. Despite his age he had served with distinction in the Royal Scots Regiment, achieving the rank of Colonel and the award of the Distinguished Service Order and Bar. He had been on various war-time and post-war commissions and it was not until the autumn of 1946 that he was demobilized and came home to Branswick just in time for the death of his father Elliott from pneumonia. Ruthven's wife had died in Switzerland in 1942 and he had moved once again into the house below the Dunbar home. At the age of forty-nine he was an attractive, distinguished-looking man, his hair rather sparse and grey, but still with a good figure and the healthy, handsome face of a man who had had much from life and expected more.

Margaret realized, as she gave him his whisky, that she had scarcely had time to look at a man or think in sexual terms for many years. In fact now, at her age, she thought she was rather past it; and that the rest of her life was destined to be spent in dignified widowhood, her still considerable energies directed towards her business and her family.

'You're looking very well, Margaret, but rather tired,' Ruthven said accepting his drink. 'Do you ever take a holiday?'

'When do I have time for a holiday?' She poured a small measure of whisky in her own glass, filled it with cubes of ice, squirted in some soda water and sat in the chair by the fire, facing her one-time suitor and current business partner. 'I had a few lovely days in Virginia with Fleur in the autumn but always it is business, business.'

'Has Fleur settled?'

'I think so. She seems very happy.'

'And Morag?'

'Yes, she's fine. She's having a baby. Fleur is very excited. Now, what was the point of this visit Ruthven? Is it to talk about family or business or a bit of everything?'

'Still the same Margaret. So direct.' Ruthven stretched his legs comfortably before him. 'A bit of everything I think. But mainly about Russell.'

'What about Russell?'

'I think you know he is very interested in Yvonne. I mean, they've been friends for years, that sort of thing . . . rather as we were.' He looked at her, but she sipped her drink carefully and deliberately, avoiding eye contact. 'Things are very different now of course than they were when we were young. I mean I wouldn't oppose Russell if he wanted to marry a Dunbar. There is no rivalry between us now, is there?'

'Of course not.' Margaret looked at him in surprise. 'But are they thinking of *marrying*? It's news to me. Yvonne is terribly young; she's not yet eighteen!'

'Is it news to you that she is seeing a lot of her cousin William?'

'William?' Margaret paused. 'Yes, that is news to me; but then I hardly ever see Yvonne. I've been away almost every week, commuting, and I went to Italy in March. Yvonne is perfectly happy to look after herself; seems to enjoy it. I still have my old housekeeper here. She stays a lot with Juliet in Edinburgh or with Susan and Malcolm, whom she adores. Although she's young, she's very grown up, you know.' Margaret frowned. 'I suppose I don't really supervise her enough. But to think of marriage is ridiculous! I mean . . .'

'But does she not talk about William when you do see her?'

'No.' Margaret sat back nursing her glass. 'She never talks about boys, men. Yvonne and I do not confide a lot, you know, Ruthven. Perhaps it's my fault, I don't know. I would say that Yvonne and I had a good but not a close relationship. She's a very independent young woman.'

'As you were.'

She looked at him, but she did not smile. 'If you like; but she has no ambitions as far as I know. I wanted her to go to university or at least take a secretarial course; but all she wants to do is to enjoy herself, not like me at her age at all. But then I think the young have been more involved in this war than the last. The bombing brutally brought it into our homes, and the wireless too, of course, which we didn't have. I think Yvonne just wants to enjoy herself for a while and I have no objection as long as she keeps out of trouble. Which I sincerely hope she does.' She looked startled for a moment. 'What is this about William? Are you serious?'

'Perfectly serious. Russell is twenty-three in June, and I think he hoped to become engaged to Yvonne this summer. Maybe marry a year later.'

'Well I certainly had no idea of *that*!'

'To be perfectly truthful, I don't think she has either and, of course, neither did I because I was away such a lot too. Since Cathy died the children have become very close to my mother. Mother told me about Russell's hopes about Yvonne and how upset he was that she no longer saw him. It was very abrupt, just after Christmas apparently, when she met William again. Russell thinks his age and maturity appeal to her.'

'Maybe they do,' Margaret said slowly. 'Yes, he stayed here in January when we were snowed up. They did get on well, and I like William very much. But as for marriage . . . I don't even know if it's a good thing. I share Susan's unease about the marriage of first cousins.'

'Especially, perhaps, cousins so oddly related.'

'How do you mean "oddly"?' Margaret looked at him sharply.

'Well, William – you know, being illegitimate . . .'

'I don't think that has anything to do with it! Not in this day and age, surely, Ruthven? Cullum would have married Nan if he'd had the chance, and William is a particularly nice young man of whom we were very proud in the war.'

'But would you *like* them to marry?'

'I don't know that I would have much choice if they wanted to. As far as I know it has never come up. It may interest you to know that I have suggested William comes into the business when he graduates. I *am* tired, you know, Ruthven. You noticed it. I badly need people around me I can trust and delegate to. There is no one. Joe is very old, you have your own business, my sisters and sister-in-law are not really interested, nor are my nephews. Murdo's death was an irreparable loss.'

'How about Russell? He graduates this year.'

'Russell in *my* business?'

'Yes, that's the other thing I wanted to talk about. He is keen to go into hosiery. I propose to take a very active part in rebuilding Pendreighs. Dad managed wonderfully during the war, and Dirk is keen too. We have plenty of good, up and coming young executives. We've had to delegate, which you seem reluctant to do, Margaret. There wouldn't be much scope for Russell for some years in Pendreighs. We have shares in Dunbar. I think it would be ideal.'

'But how would he and William get on?'

'Is William definitely coming in?'

Margaret got up and put a log on the fire. She felt suddenly agitated and ill at ease. She sat down again abruptly in her chair, smoothing down her woollen dress over her knees. 'Well, no. He didn't seem awfully keen, to tell you the truth. He says he wants to be a research scientist.'

'Then think about Russell. Also if Yvonne saw more of him it might rekindle her interest. You wouldn't object if there were a marriage between a Pendreigh and a Dunbar now Margaret, would you?'

'I'd have to give it careful thought, Ruthven,' Margaret said with pretended gravity. 'Also take my daughter's wishes into account. It seems I don't know her very well. I haven't been a very good mother, have I?'

'Oh I don't know. ' Ruthven got up and refilled his glass helping himself to two lumps of ice. 'Drink, Margaret?'

'No, I still have some thanks.'

He came back and stood in front of the fire, very much at ease, and, looking at him, Margaret thought that the years had been very good to Ruthven Pendreigh. No doubt one day he would find a new young wife, like Hamish, several years his junior.

'I think you've been an excellent mother. Yvonne is a lovely girl, beautiful, sparkling, witty and very well mannered my mother says, and things like that are important to her. Charles, from the little I've seen of him, is a very good-looking, polite boy. Both your children are a credit to you. And, *and* do not forget, for the past ten years you have run Dunbars practically single-handed. It's the most

543

eminent firm in its field, the most successful. Thanks to you.'

'Ah, is *that* why Pendreighs want to penetrate us again? I detect a dark plot!'

Margaret smiled and Ruthven thought how beautiful she was, her blue-green eyes as alluring as ever, her dark hair braided about her head and piled up at the back. He could imagine it loose, flowing over her shoulders, shoulders that, in his somewhat heightened imagination, were naked like the rest of her. He quickly cleared his throat as though she might be able to read his thoughts, his erotic, disturbing thoughts that had nothing to do with her soft woollen dress and its long fashionable skirt. The 'new look' that Christian Dior had just introduced in a Paris trying rapidly to recover from the war.

'There is no plot, Margaret. No attempt to take over. I have a job to do rebuilding Pendreighs and you are very successful, a turnover of half a million pounds! But, I must warn you, there could be trying times ahead. Firms are short of capital and starved of good labour, yarn is in short supply. Joe told me today that Macallisters are not having an easy time and this confirms what I've heard.'

'I've heard it too,' Margaret said looking anxiously into the fire. 'Just how serious is it?'

'Quite serious. Joe wants to retire and his younger son Jock never had the flair that Bruno had; besides, he's not a well man. Joe tells me that Gouldhursts are interested in buying them and he is considering it.'

'That would be dreadful.' Margaret stared at Ruthven aghast. Gouldhursts were a giant conglomeration embracing all sorts of industries other than the manufacture of textiles.

'If Gouldhursts bought them it would, of course, curtail the supply of yarn, particularly cashmere, to you. I know you can't buy Macallisters because they are too big; but they would fit very nicely into the Gouldhurst pattern for the future.'

'I'm not sure we couldn't buy Macallisters if we put our minds to it. The bank might help.'

'Oh Margaret, you'd be taking on too much. It would kill you.'

'That's what you think.' Margaret smiled and the years seemed to drop away from her so that Ruthven could recall how lovely she had looked at the age of seventeen when he held her in his arms, the one and only time, in the narrow passage that led up from the Drume to the High Street.

'Well, in that case you'd need to extend your management. You'd need Russell. You know, in the old days the nobility used to apprentice their sons to a fellow noble; the child would grow up in the household and sometimes marry into the family. That's all I'm proposing. As I failed in my attempt to marry you, I would like my son to marry your daughter. I'll be honest about it.'

'You didn't try very hard, Ruthven,' Margaret said quietly, very aware of his tall elegant form in its well cut grey suit, army tie and white shirt. Was she, after so many years of celibacy, beginning to find a man attractive again? She hoped not. She must banish such thoughts from her mind because she was fated to be disappointed by men; if she fell in love again with Ruthven after such a long passage of time he would be sure to announce his engagement to some young woman, one of the many young women who were looking for husbands after this war just as they had been after the last.

Ruthven bent down and gazed into her eyes. 'Didn't I? I loved you, Margaret, you know. Maybe I was too in awe of my father, or maybe I was frightened, just a little bit, of you. But you haunted me. I married Cathy on the rebound. I like to think I made her happy, and we were happy, very happy; but I always carried a torch for you. I still do.'

Margaret's heart leapt; and something inside her breast

seemed to give, like an ice flow melting under the spring sun. Outside it was dark, but it had been a lovely day making up for the rigours of the winter, a harbinger maybe of the summer that was to come. She put up her hand and touched his.

'Let's think about the younger generation, shall we, first?'

Ruthven looked at her, smiled and straightened up. 'There's something else that might make you change your mind about Russell and the business. I've been asked to sit on the Scottish Committee to consider a Festival of Britain in 1951. It will be a great affair to promote industry and national achievement, rather as the Exhibition of 1851 ushered in a new era. They very much want a woman member, someone prominent in industry or the professions. Someone has suggested Dame Esther Macfarlane who is a professor at Edinburgh, but I would like to propose you. Do I have your permission? It'll mean a lot of hard work; but, well, it'll be a very important, prestigious position. The King and Queen are to be patrons of the Festival. To be associated with its planning will enhance you and your firm.'

'For my own fame I'm indifferent.' Margaret put her glass on a nearby table and, joining her hands behind her head, leaned back in the soft comfort of her chair. 'But I would do anything to increase the fame of Dunbars. If you would like to, please put my name forward. Now, Ruthven, I'm alone in the house and I'm having some cold chicken and salad for dinner. Would you like to join me?'

'Nothing I'd like better Margaret.'

Despite the post-war gloom, Ruthven thought, things for him personally were taking a decidedly roseate glow. He had survived the war with honour, he was about to assume the directorship of his family firm; his own family were flourishing and he intended to recommence his courtship of the woman who, twenty-eight years before, he had passionately wanted to marry.

CHAPTER THIRTY ONE

Fiona Monroe was twenty-eight years old, but just now she looked about fifty, or more. Her straight hair, which she usually wore in a fashionable bob with a side parting and a large wave in front, was bedraggled and uncurled and her face was unmade-up. She was normally of slim build but now she looked emaciated and her large, usually mild blue eyes had a quite untypical, frenzied gleam. Margaret was appalled.

Juliet had rung her from Edinburgh during the day to ask her to come over as soon as she could. She then told her briefly that Tom had baldly announced to Fiona that he was leaving her and wanted a divorce.

'He did it very badly,' Juliet said, almost hoarse on the phone with distress. 'I don't know what got into him.'

'I'll come at once,' Margaret said and got into her car, driving over to Edinburgh where she reached Juliet's house before dark. Angus was hovering around looking distraught, and Juliet's normally calm face bore the quiet look of anguish that spoke of divided loyalties. Margaret found as she entered the room that she had gone straight into the battle. Apparently the blame was being laid at her door because, knowing about Tom and Clare, she had offered the latter a job.

'That was *before* I knew about Tom,' she insisted. 'Tom hadn't even met her.'

'Then you should have sacked her!' Fiona screamed. 'You connived in his adultery.'

'I did what I could,' Margaret spoke as quietly as she could, 'but it was not my business. Tom and Clare were of age and would have resented my interference. Sacking her would have been interfering. Anyway, I was sorry for her.'

'Sorry for her! The conniving scheming bitch! She, who'd already taken Uncle Bruno away from Aunt Susan and then murdered him.'

'She didn't murder him and she was nearly killed herself.'

'Margaret – ' Susan was reluctant to enter the drama, but she had been called to the family conference too. 'You don't need to make yourself sound so sympathetic towards that awful woman.'

Margaret knew she was putting herself out on a limb by what she intended to say, but she had to be honest. She actually preferred Clare to Fiona and, moreover, she knew Tom's point of view. Juliet and Susan had never been very fond of Fiona, because she was a difficult person of whom to be fond. This was the first time Margaret had really ever seen her display any sort of animation. She was a pretty, listless, anaemic-looking woman who normally seemed fully to justify Tom's description of her as lacking warmth and passion. However, she was the mother of Tom's children. She was also the deceived wife and, as Susan had little love for Clare, the women of the Dunbar family instinctively felt they should take her side whether they wanted to or not. All in all it was a wretched situation.

'She's *not* an awful woman, that's the point. She's actually a very nice, brave woman who has suffered a great deal, physically and mentally. She was a very successful mannequin and her career was ruined.'

'It was her own fault.' Susan interrupted on Fiona's side. 'She could always have said "no".'

'Don't you think it would be better to have had experience of that kind of situation yourself, Susan, before you judge others? Who knows what sort of pressures she was under?'

548

'Oh Margaret,' Susan said impatiently. 'You really are bending over backwards to defend her.'

'Because she's like her, Aunt Susan, that's why,' Fiona cried, her voice shaking with spite. Then she raised her hand and pointed her finger at Margaret. 'You're as bad as she is! She's a slut and so are you. Like attracts like, you know.'

A silence fell in the room, a silence as sudden and profound as all the raised voices and screaming that had gone before. Susan started towards Margaret and then decided to stay where she was. Juliet also looked acutely uncomfortable. Angus's face went very red. He was in his sixties and suffered from high blood pressure. Juliet looked at him anxiously and told him to sit down. He sat next to her and she took his hand.

'You should explain that,' Angus said after a great effort. 'It's slanderous as far as I know.'

'Oh no it isn't,' Fiona spat at him. 'You know quite well the reputation Margaret had before the war. Everyone knew. She left her husband and went with other men; she always had. She was a slut. Everyone knew she went with other men, including my father. My mother knew. She hated you, Margaret. If you knew the extent of her hatred you wouldn't sleep at nights. I think it must reach you from the grave.'

'Oh for goodness sake, Fiona, control yourself,' Juliet said in her clipped Edinburgh accent. 'You're talking absolute nonsense. If I thought this was going to turn into an attack on Margaret I would never have asked for her help. I asked both my sisters here so that we could all decide what to do for the best.'

'Well, *did* you sleep with my father or didn't you?' Fiona glared at Margaret as though she hadn't heard a word of what her mother-in-law had said.

Margaret, who had felt herself turning pale from shock, concentrated on the rapid beating of her heart to try and slow it down. 'Well, as you apparently know all about it, yes, I did – long ago. I was much younger than you are now. I can't excuse myself, but you can't blame me entirely you know. He did the asking.'

'Led on by you, I don't doubt. It's always the woman. If this siren hadn't set her sights on Tom he'd be here now where he belongs, with me and the children. Tom was affected by his wound in the war and she took advantage of it. Do you realize our children will grow up without a father? Do you realize that?'

'Not *completely* without a father,' Susan intervened. 'Tom has promised to see them a lot. He loves them. He says so.'

'That "siren" happens to be a cripple,' Margaret said, at which Fiona made a gesture as though she were going to strike her.

'There you go, defending her again! What sort of man falls in love with a hopeless cripple anyway? What sort of perversion is that, I ask you?'

'I can't say,' Margaret said faintly. 'Your mother was a cripple too, don't forget.'

'I'm not likely to forget. My father never went near her. He went to you instead and then others like you, all whores who gave their bodies for gain.'

'I never got anything from your father, I assure you. In fact, altogether he had a most distorting effect on my life. Why talk of something that was over twenty years ago anyway? Why torment yourself?'

There was another pause and now Margaret thought she would find out if Fiona knew the truth about Charles. Despite what he'd said Tom might have told her. If she knew, Fiona would certainly not miss the chance of taunting her with it now; but apparently Fiona didn't know for she hesitated, her chin trembled and she collapsed in tears across the sofa putting her head in Susan's lap. Susan tenderly put a hand on her long blonde hair and stroked it as though she were a baby.

550

'There, there,' she said. 'There, there. Don't upset yourself so much. We must decide how to build, not destroy.'

'*He* has destroyed!'

'At least your children have a mother and father. Poor little Malcolm has neither.'

As though the thought of this deprivation only added to her misery, Fiona wept anew and the sisters gazed at one another in despair.

'B-bb-e-tter to have n-no f-father than one who l-le-left you,' Fiona sobbed, kneading the skirt of Susan's dress in her hands.

'I'm not sure about that. Besides, Tom might come back.'

Fiona sat upright and looked at her aunt. 'Why do you say that?'

'He might. He might tire of Clare. Men do.'

'I'd *never* take him back. Not after this; not after he's deceived me. I hate him too much, and *her*.'

The way she said it, slightly lifting her head and looking at her, Margaret was unsure whether she was referring to herself or Clare.

'I swear she didn't know about Charles,' Tom said. 'All she learned about you she learned from her mother and that was years ago. Hamish had affairs after you and she put a detective on him. Despite her infirmity she was jealous. He found out he was being followed and owned up. I don't know why he had to mention your name.'

'He was always a bit afraid of Isobel, even though she was bedridden. I think she was his conscience. Well, that's over anyway. It was mighty unpleasant I can tell you. She seemed to think I was behind the whole thing.'

'It was unpleasant for me to tell her,' Tom put his face in her hands, 'and the kids. Anyway, she said she won't divorce me which is what I thought she would say. I can't

551

go back to the Bar, you know. My legal career in Scotland is finished.'

'Can't you read for the English Bar?'

'I can't afford to, Margaret.' Tom looked at her in despair. 'I have to keep Fiona and the kids, and Clare. I'm very hard up.'

'Then how about working for Dunbars?'

'You know that never appealed to me.'

'On the legal side; just a temporary appointment if you like.' Margaret leaned back to get the full force of the sun on her face. After the coldest winter for decades, it was now the hottest summer since 1865. Whenever she could she came home, bathed and changed and sat in the garden, where they were sitting now before dinner. The vegetable patch had been turned back into a lawn and there were two deck chairs under the laburnum tree. 'I want to expand, Tom. You've got a good brain. You'll have to go into business of some sort. We can't stay as we are and Gouldhursts are going to bid for Macallisters. I want to make a counterbid.'

'But it will cost the earth.'

'I know that; but the bank will back me. I saw them in Edinburgh. I said if we're deprived of our chief source of yarn, particularly cashmere, we will be finished. Gouldhurst want Macallisters because they are the main spinners of cashmere; this yarn will then go to knitters which they own, not us. Already I'm having to go into other kinds of knitwear; now everyone can afford to dress by Dunbar. The potential is enormous; but only if we buy Macallisters.'

'What does Joe Macallister say?'

'He's delighted, but only so long as we outbid Gouldhursts. He wants as much money as he can to retire; no family favours.'

'Can you outbid Gouldhursts?'

'Yes. If Dunbars go public and get a stock exchange

552

quotation, we can raise the capital like that. The bank will do the rest. You see why I need a keen legal brain.'

'I do indeed,' Tom said beginning to look excited. 'Supposing I just accept a consultancy and see how it goes?'

'Working for me full time,' Margaret said firmly. 'Say, for two years?'

'Done.' Tom got up and shook her by the hand. 'I hope you know what you're doing Margaret.'

'I do,' Margaret said watching the blackbird flit from branch to branch in the laburnum tree. 'I always have.'

The next six months were the busiest of Margaret's life. 1947 had seen the collapse of the immediate post-war optimism. Not only England but the whole of Europe had been on the brink of ruin, and had been saved by the Americans in the form of the Marshall Plan. Ernest Bevin, the Foreign Secretary, after declaring that it was an 'ignoble thing to be dependent on anyone', decided that to accept fresh American aid was better than to go to the wall. The fact was that the dollar gap was no less a threat to the British standard of living than the U-boats during the war.

In Europe Dunbars met competition from Italy's rapidly developing knitwear industry, where garments from houses like Dazza and Metalloni were in a class of their own. Dunbar now exported sixty percent of its production and the threat to the supply of yarn from the Gouldhurst bid for Macallisters was a very real one.

The beginning of 1948 saw the growth of Russian hostility in the international sphere and the atmosphere was compared to that of August and September 1939. The Communist coup in Czechoslovakia in February made Churchill declare that 'the menace of a third world war rolls towards us in this island'. Lord Pakenham on the other hand thought that 'something rather splendid has been happening in England', due to the increased productivity the previous winter.

And indeed there was much to praise about post-war England. There was less distinction between the classes, and more state aid had been ushered in with the Welfare State proudly proclaimed by Labour. The poor were much better off. On the other hand the middle classes thought themselves worse off because of the increased cost of living, persistent shortages and scarcity of domestic labour. Servants, so prolific in the thirties, were becoming a rarity. A house which in 1938 had cost £380 to build now cost £1,242 and there was a housing shortage. Food, clothes and petrol were still rationed. The meat ration had actually been reduced to one and twopence worth a week.

Margaret left the mechanics of launching Dunbars on the Stock Market to Tom while she concentrated on the hundred and one other things she had to do. There were new designs for the following winter, the tracking of scarce supplies of yarn because order books were full; and there was the problem of fulfilling them and getting them to purchasers in time. The mill was working to capacity and already she was having to think of trying to acquire more space. Buying Macallisters would suit them very well because one of their mills had room for expansion, and there was now no longer any more space by the side of the River Drume.

Then there was a new image to create for Dunbars; a more popular, glamorous image suitable for the post-war world. Ladies of quality and duchesses did not appeal so much to the modern women, many more of whom were working. Instead the advertising agency drafted an ambitious new programme for attracting young actresses and sportswomen to model the exciting new range of Dunbar woollens for women, which had to supplant the classic cashmere which was solely for export.

'Naturally, from Dunbar' supplanted the snobbish

appeal of 'Dunbar Design', though this tag continued to be used successfully in the USA where duchesses still had a pull. The emphasis was, as always, on quality; on the fact that Dunbar garments were made from real wool rather than the increasingly used man-made fibres. 'Naturally, from Dunbar' was applied to a whole range of *haute couture* and sporty designs which were advertised by British ballerinas, British actresses and British sportswomen. 'British is best' was the idea a war-weary nation tried hard to believe in.

The creation of the new image, the full order books, the mill working to capacity were all good augurles that, when the public was invited to buy shares in the firm, they would be eager to do so.

In addition, there was the work Margaret did with her usual diligence and energy on the Committee for the Festival of Britain, intended to show all that the nation could offer in terms of past achievement and current progress, particularly industrial progress. The Festival was all the more necessary because British pride was at a low ebb. There were shortages and difficulties at home, trouble abroad and increasing dependence on American goodwill, aid and the power of the mighty dollar.

Margaret's only relaxation was an occasional night out at the theatre or a concert with Ruthven Pendreigh, whom she saw regularly because of their work on the Festival Committee. She began to look forward to their outings because she enjoyed being with him. The fact rather worried her.

One night he said as he drove her home after seeing *The Happiest Days of your Life* at the Apollo, 'Did you think any more about Russell, Margaret? You said you'd let me have an answer soon. It's all the more important now because – ' He switched off the engine as they arrived outside her house and turned towards her. 'I've had an offer from Gouldhursts. It's a very attractive offer and I

555

think I'm going to accept. There will be no room in the reorganized firm for Russell at all.'

'Oh don't say *you're* succumbing to Gouldhursts?' Margaret found it hard to suppress her irritation at the news, coming after a relaxing and pleasant evening.

'It's not a question of succumbing. It's a question of necessity. I hadn't realized how badly we had gone down. When I took over after Father's death, I found we were rather as Dunbars were in the twenties in relation to us – old-fashioned, in need of fresh capital and new machinery. Gouldhursts will give us all that and let me remain Managing Director.'

'If you wait a few years we'll buy you,' Margaret said humorously, not unaware of the irony of the situation.

'I can't wait Margaret. It's bad. It's either that or bust.'

Margaret gazed at him, his handsome silvery head outlined by the light of the street lamp. He looked elegant and sure of himself in his dark evening clothes; one hand lay lightly on the wheel of his car and the gold bracelet of his wrist watch gleamed beneath two inches of stiff white shirt cuff. 'I'm sorry,' she said, stifling an impulse to put her hand on his arm. 'Will you come in for a nightcap?'

'Not tonight, Margaret. I have to catch the early train to Scotland. I'd love to another time.'

'Another time then.'

He leaned forward suddenly and kissed her very lightly on the lips, his right hand still holding the wheel, his left gently encircling her waist. She stayed very still, not moving, not wanting to give herself away; reluctant to betray her own need.

'You're a very lovely woman, Margaret. You always were. Why isn't there a man in your life?'

'Too busy,' Margaret said disengaging herself, trying to keep her tone light. 'Too busy for men.'

'Men can be complementary you know.'

'Not in my experience. They take over. Besides, I'm too old.'

'Rubbish!'

He straightened himself up and put both hands on the wheel, and she thought how nice it would be to throw over her inhibitions and do what he wanted her to do, invite him in again for a drink and go on from there. But no. She was too uncertain. In a way she was afraid, afraid of herself and of what renewed romantic involvement with Ruthven Pendreigh might do to them both, the consequences it might have.

'Thank you for a lovely evening.' She pulled her evening cloak round her shoulders and he got swiftly out of the car and went round to open the door for her, leaning his head towards her.

'Let's do it again, very soon?'

'I'd love to.'

She smiled because she knew his question had a double meaning: 'Let's go out', or 'let's kiss again'. It could be either. 'About Russell,' she said turning her head as she walked towards the gate. 'It's alright. Tell him to give me a ring. Oh, and I talked to Yvonne about William. She likes him, but it's nothing serious. Maybe Russell's in with a chance.' She blew a kiss at him and closed the gate behind her; but he remained standing there for some time after she'd gone in.

Yvonne disentangled herself from William, breathing very hard, her face red and rather angry.

'I said no!'

They were lying on the bed of his room in his student digs because she liked to kiss, but when he started to put his hand up her skirt or feel her breasts she didn't like that at all. She felt frightened of herself and of him. The situation, which happened often, got them both into a very excited, agitated state and invariably ended in a row.

The attempts at lovemaking between them were disastrous because he was a young man of twenty-eight with

557

very little experience, and she was a girl of eighteen with none at all.

William had quite normal feelings about the opposite sex, but he was inhibited by shyness. His war service had been spent almost exclusively in male company and the few women he'd slept with were casual war-time affairs. He once got very keen on the sister of a brother officer, but by the time he came round to declaring an interest she was engaged to someone else. Since he'd known Yvonne his only interest had been in her; but he was rather frightened of her mother, and of what his own mother would say if she knew how much he cared.

His own emotions were very involved and he wished the person he was in love with were not a close relation. William had little love for the Dunbars as such; he didn't hate them, but he resented them. He resented their arrogance and the instinctive superiority they seemed to have towards everyone who was not a member of the family. Yvonne was arrogant, and his father had been arrogant. The three aunts were, he thought, very arrogant indeed, especially Yvonne's mother. They were, he supposed, largely unaware of this and would have been very hurt if anyone had told them; but to him it was very obvious and always had been.

He didn't feel he was a Dunbar nor that he had any of their arrogance. He was a Murray and a Murray he would remain; the working-class son of a working-class mother, despite his father or his war record as an officer in the British Navy, or his public school, or his place at university. Nothing would ever change his ideas about class and this, loving Yvonne as he did, troubled him a great deal.

Yvonne lay on her back and pulled her jumper agitatedly right down over her skirt. Her prominent breasts rose and fell rapidly because of the excited state she was in, a state compounded of thwarted sexuality and ruptured dignity. William watched her, feeling frustrated and angry too. He had once got as far as feeling one of her nipples and he'd wanted to crush her breast in his palm and strip all her clothes off and take her there and then. The violence of his desires frightened him, and he felt ashamed when he remembered them until he saw her again and she lay down, wanting to kiss.

'We can't go on like this,' he said tetchily. 'We can't mess about like this all the time. It's bad for a man you know. You lead me on, and then . . .'

'I do *not* lead you on.' She turned to face him, pretending to be prim yet smiling enticingly, her warm eyes taunting him.

'You're a cockteaser.'

'What a disgusting thing to say!'

'Well, it's true. You like to lie down and kiss. You always fling yourself on the bed in that provocative manner. You've no idea what it does to me.' He nervously touched his crotch as though in pain. He was quite sure that such repression would ultimately damage his reproductive powers. People said that it did.

'Why don't you make up your mind about me, William?' Yvonne sat up and folded her arms around her legs. 'You can't decide, can you?'

'About what?' He felt himself blushing under his beard.

'You know.'

'I want to sleep with you, if that's what you mean.'

'Yes, but it's not what *I* mean. I don't want a baby. Imagine what my mother would say.'

They both closed their eyes involuntarily, as though in mutual horror at the thought of what her mother would say if such a dreadful thing were to happen.

'We needn't have a baby,' William said hopefully. 'I can use . . . well I've got "things".'

Yvonne screwed up her eyes in distaste. 'You mean those rubbers?'

'Yes.'

559

'How horrible.' She shuddered.

Suddenly he saw the sheath as a repulsive object and shuddered too. Imagine obtruding a nasty rubber sheath between his body and that of his beloved. Out of the question, especially the first time. What, then?

'It's better than nothing,' he said dejectedly, and then his hope faded as Yvonne got off the bed. She wore a fawn Dunbar cashmere sweater (exclusively for export) and a skirt of MacLeish tartan which she had a right to wear through her grandmother. She had very long legs and she moved with such grace that men frequently stopped to look at her in the street while she, well aware of her impact and their attraction, swept on as if she hadn't noticed. Now she stared at herself in the mirror over the mantelpiece.

'Am I *so* bad looking?'

'You know perfectly well you're not.' He lay with his hands folded behind his head. She came back and sat beside him on the bed, her eyes running provocatively along his body, dwelling, he thought, on the place that was still throbbing.

'William, we've known each other for over a year. Can't you decide?'

'What do you mean "decide"?'

'Oh *William*! What do you *think* I mean?'

'You know I love you.'

'Yes I know. You've told me thousands and thousands of times.' Her face was flushed and the thick tendrils of black hair were moist on her brow. She exuded desirability and sexuality and, as if to torment him further, she hung over him slightly so that her breasts brushed his chest. He groaned and closed his eyes, putting one arm loosely round her back.

'Now don't start kissing again, William! I'm talking seriously.'

'About?' He opened one eye.

'The man is supposed to ask. Not the woman.' She sat up and pursed her mouth decorously.

His hand fell by his side and he raised himself on one arm. 'Are you talking about marriage?'

'I thought you'd never ask.'

'Marriage!' He flopped back on the bed and gazed at the ceiling with its solitary yellow light. It was not a pleasant room and now it was quite hot with frustrated passion, the windows misted over, and the counterpane beneath him was crumpled as it usually was after a visit from Yvonne. His landlady often asked what he did on it, a question she accompanied with a knowing look. He said he studied in bed to save putting shillings in the gas.

'Don't make it sound so dreadful. Didn't you ever think of asking me to marry you?'

'Of course I thought about it.' He put his arm over his eyes to shield them from the bare light. 'But what will your mother think about it?'

'You've always got my mother on your mind haven't you?'

He thought for a while and nodded. He propped himself on his elbow again and his eyes had a faraway look. His shirt hung out of his trousers and she thought he looked beautiful; he didn't know what a job she had resisting him. 'Yes. She's the most awesome woman I've ever met. You know, when I was a little boy I fell in the river and went to hospital. I'd broken my leg. One day your mother came to visit me at home and I thought I'd never seen anybody like her, she was so tall and elegant, and lovely. She wore high boots and a fur coat and hat and she gave me some soldiers. She smelt of toffee. I never forgot it. I still remember it every time I meet her and I see the same tall, aloof, elegant woman looking kindly down at the little boy in the tenement in Dumbarton Street.'

'Oh darling!' Yvonne threw herself next to him and

561

hugged him, both hands on his cheeks. 'You don't know how lovely that makes you look. What a sad story; but it has a happy ending.' She raised her head and stared into his blue-green eyes. 'You can marry the princess's daughter, and get what all little frogs desire. You can turn into a Prince Charming too.'

'But won't the princess mind?'

'No. I think she likes you very much.'

'Won't she mind that I'm a bastard and working-class and all that kind of thing?'

Yvonne gazed at him, her grey, passionate eyes round with indignation. 'If you say anything like that again I'll hit you! It's a word I don't like, and I never want to hear it repeated. You were a *love* child. Your father, my uncle, loved your mother and it's a very, very romantic story. Ours is a most unusual, interesting family, don't you think? I like to think you and I are related by blood as well as everything else. My father was awarded the Croix de Guerre and our cousin Murdoch, the Military Cross. They said he should have got the V.C., but they had only recently given a lot away at Arnhem to make up for it being such a disaster.' She raised a hand and stroked his hair. 'Mummy loved Uncle Cullum and she likes you. I know she'll approve of the whole thing. When Murdo married poor Hettie, no one objected at all. We Dunbars really only like one another. Only a Dunbar is good enough for another.'

'What a ridiculous, impossible, *arrogant* thing to say! How can I love you? I must be crazy?'

He tapped his forefinger at his temple, and crossed his eyes in imitation of an idiot, but she dug her fingers into his red curls and shook his head vigorously.

'It's *true*. Everything I say is true. I'm a very positive person, like Mummy.'

'You can say that again. Tell me, did you ever talk to her about us?'

Yvonne appeared to consider the matter carefully. 'You know Mummy and I don't find it easy to talk about important or intimate things. I don't think we really know each other well enough. It may seem an odd thing to say, but I've been at boarding school since I was nine and we haven't spent much time together. I don't think I could sit down and have a heart to heart with Mummy as I could, say, with Aunt Susan. Maybe it'll change when I get older. She has asked me about you because she knows we meet; she heard it from somebody though she won't say who. I was very evasive and said it was nothing important; then we dropped the subject, which I think relieved her as well as me. Besides, what could I say? I'll be glad when I can tell her the truth. I don't think she'll mind; lots of people in our family have married young, and I know she likes you and hopes you'll join the firm.'

'I don't really want to join the firm, Yvonne. I want a scientific career. I told your mother as much.'

'I see.' Yvonne let his head go and sat back on her heels, remaining on the bed. 'That's that then.' She got off the bed and went and sat in the chair by the gas fire.

'That's what?' He sat up and looked at her, suddenly overcome by a feeling of remorse coupled with anxiety.

'That's it!' She dusted her hands together. 'I don't want to marry a scientist travelling here, there and everywhere. I want to live in Branswick and do all the things I do now. I want to live in *Woodbrae* overlooking the mill as my mother, uncle and aunts did when they were young, and I want to participate in all the things that happen in the town – the tennis, the cricket, the rugby and the Common Riding. That's the sort of person I am.'

'But if you wanted to marry me, wouldn't you want to do what I did?'

'No, not if it was that.'

'You mean you wouldn't want to marry me at all?'

'No, not if you didn't want to live in Branswick. I'm quite certain about that.'

563

'Then you can't love me.'

'I do, and I want to marry you; but I want *you* to live in *Woodbrae* and walk down the hill every morning to the mill and come home at night and have a drink before dinner and see me and our children, and . . .' She joined her hands, stretching them up to the ceiling as though she were praying. 'That's what I want. I want it passionately. It would be the best life for us. I want you to be part of Dunbars and . . . part of me.'

She looked at him with the utmost candour from under lowered lids. It was a calculated look, conveying such rampant, uninhibited sexuality that William's febrile heart nearly doubled its beat with excitement. But it was not only overtly passionate; it was compounded, too, of a rapturously innocent but devouring love that promised an ultimate realization of all the dreams and fantasies that had developed into his permanently unfulfilled state of longing for her. 'Part of her' meant, at last, his right to her body; a right to make proper, real love to her, fully naked, fully exposed, both of them unashamed and unpretending. 'Part of her' meant sharing her bed, having children by her, growing old with her.

Part of Yvonne meant, also, being part of Dunbars.

'I'll have to think about it,' he said, rather unsteadily. 'I'm not sure it's what I want.'

'But *I* am what you want?'

'Yes.'

She leaned over him again and placed her hand on his bare chest just inside his open shirt, just over his heart. She had, instinctively, all the female wiles without the experience. He thought that once she had the experience she would be something very sensational indeed.

'Then you can have me.' She kissed his lips and he encircled her with his arms, drawing her down.

'Now?' he murmured hoarsely, his mind somersaulting, scarcely able to believe his luck.

564

'No, silly! *If* you agree to join Dunbars. Then you can marry me . . . *then* you can have me. In that order. Besides,' Yvonne continued after a pause, 'Mummy is going to take Russell Pendreigh into the business. You know Russell always liked me and . . .'

'*Russell Pendreigh* into the business?' William shot up and Yvonne nearly fell off the bed.

'Yes. Don't you like him?'

'I certainly don't. I don't want *him* in the business, if I'm going to be. Nowhere near it, or you!'

He looked so angry, so possessive and proud that her heart melted with joy. 'Well, you'd better hurry up then and tell Mummy you've changed your mind.'

CHAPTER THIRTY TWO

The boardroom at the Dunbar Mill had looked more or less the same since Charles Dunbar had run the firm, Margaret's great-grandfather. It was in the oldest part of the mill on the top floor, and he had had the mill boardroom panelled in fine polished walnut, in keeping with the aspirations of a man who had brought his firm to prosperity. At the same time he had purchased the large round boardroom table, also in polished walnut. For nearly seventy years the members of the board had deliberated round it, the chairman sitting in the middle, opposite the window with its view of the hill where the Dunbar house stood as though keeping sentinel watch over the town as a whole, but particularly the mill by the river. The position of the mill to the house and the house to the town was somehow of central importance in the lives of the family which had been so integrated with both.

This day in August 1948 the current chairman, Margaret Dunbar Lamotte, took up her place in the centre of the table, smiling at the members of the board who grouped themselves around her, straightening her notepad and her pencils, the blotting pad in front of her, having a word with the secretary who sat, as she always did, on the chairman's left. It was ten o'clock in the morning and the heat mist, which had risen from the river, so that when she woke up it obscured the mill, had cleared. The sun flooded the boardroom, making the polished wood of the panelling and the table round which they sat gleam.

When everyone was in their seats Margaret glanced at her watch which she had taken from her wrist and put on the blotter in front of her, took a sip of water from the glass by her side and began.

'Good morning, ladies and gentlemen. Thank you for all being so punctual. This meeting, as you know, is an extraordinary one called to consider the acquisition of the Macallister enterprise, now that we ourselves are a public concern. First I would like to read the minutes of the last meeting and if you agree they are a proper record I will sign them.'

'Taken as read Madam Chairman.' Joe Macallister glanced up from the documents he had been studying.

'Seconded,' said Ruthven Pendreigh, raising his hand.

'Is it the wish of you all that I sign the minutes?' Everyone nodded their assent, and Margaret signed her copy of the minutes and gave it to her secretary who inserted it neatly between the pages of the minutes' ledger.

'There are one or two items before we begin the business of this meeting.' Margaret glanced at her notes. 'In the first place I would like to announce that my future son-in-law William Murray will join the firm next month.' She leaned back and looked at them all, smiling and relaxed. 'As you know, it gave me great pleasure to learn of the intention of William and my daughter Yvonne to marry. William graduated this summer with a Bachelor of Science degree and I think he is in every way a suitable person to join our growing management team. He will of course learn the business from the bottom, as my brother and father, his grandfather, did before them. It's a source of great happiness to me to know that my late beloved brother Cullum's son will soon be a member of the family firm.'

'Hear, hear.' Everyone nodded again, signifying their approval, except Ruthven Pendreigh who remained silent and unsmiling, his face impassive, his eyes fixed at some spot on the table midway between himself and Margaret.

'Now, the other extra item is that, providing we agree to

go ahead with the purchase of Macallisters and our offer is accepted, I propose to reconstitute the board so that our major shareholders are represented, now that we're a public company. I would also like to give places to people who have served us so long and so well, like Peter Cartwright in overall charge of design and Jamie Paterson who has achieved such miracles in the production department. However, these proposals I will be putting before you in due course.

'Now, ladies and gentlemen, as you know the share issue which we put on the market was oversubscribed and we are now a million pound company. It is very gratifying to know how much confidence the public have in Dunbars and its products. I feel that, in this year 1948, we are on the brink of expansion undreamed of in the days of my great-grandfather Charles who, more than anyone else, brought Dunbars into a position of prominence. I feel that he would approve of these changes.'

Margaret then went on to sketch a history of the firm to date and outlined some of her plans for the future. Underwear would be phased out altogether, and the emphasis placed on men's and women's outer wear, particularly the production of goods made in cashmere once the restrictions were eased. She told of the success of the new advertising campaign 'Naturally enough, Dunbar . . .' and the enthusiasm of young actresses and sportsmen and sportswomen to model for the firm. She praised, in particular, the skill of the advertising agency and she had some harsh words to say about government restrictions and the plight of the pound in relation to the dollar, so that the only way out that many people could see was the devaluation of the pound to make exports cheaper. This in the long run she thought would benefit Dunbars; but they would have to sell more to make the same amount of profit, and production would have to be increased. Everyone would have to work harder.

She then went on to the proposal for the acquisition of Macallisters, a private company in which Joe Macallister, who was on the Dunbar board, held the majority interest. A price had been agreed which was more than Gouldhursts had offered, and she now invited everyone to consider the proposals before them and then proceed to a vote.

As they studied the documents, which had been circulated in advance, Margaret closely examined the faces to either side of her. Susan and Juliet sat side by side, Susan wearing new spectacles and looking rather solemn as she pretended to study papers she did not in the least understand. Juliet knew that, as the whole thing had been drawn up by Tom, it must be all right and didn't even glance at hers. She started whispering to Mary who sat on her other side and who hadn't looked at her papers either because she knew exactly what she had to do. Mary, although only in her early fifties, was white-haired and looked very frail. The death of Murdoch, to whom she had devoted her life, had been a terrible shock to her. She and Susan, drawn together in mutual grief, lavished all their starved affection on their five-year-old grandson whom they took turns to look after, though he spent most of his time with Susan.

In the reconstituted board it was proposed that Susan, Juliet and Mary would stand down in favour of Tom and Margaret, though retaining their shares in the firm without having the power to vote. Joe Macallister, still alert despite his age, was also going to retire, and so this was the final meeting, before the reconstitution that would follow the acquisition of Macallisters.

When Margaret considered they had had enough time she put the motion on the table that the acquisition of Macallisters should go ahead and all hands were raised in agreement.

'That's very satisfactory,' she said. 'Thank you, ladies

and gentlemen. In due course you will receive papers containing my proposals for the reconstruction of our two companies, to be known as Dunbar-Macallister, and our plans for the future which will involve building an extension at Selkirk and the possible acquisition of an entirely new mill at Peebles which once belonged to the Mactavishes.'

'Madam Chairman – ' Ruthven, who had not said a word during the entire meeting, raised a hand, his pencil stuck high in the air.

'Mr Pendreigh?' Margaret leaned over the table and smiled at him. Whenever she was in the same room with him she was conscious of their mutual reawakening of interest. Whenever he was there she knew she was conscious of herself as a woman rather than as that asexual, dignified functionary: the Chairman of the Board.

'Madam Chairman, Mrs Lamotte, it's with some hesitation that I introduce to this meeting what you may consider a note of discord; but I feel it my duty to do so.'

'Feel free to speak Ruthven,' Margaret said, a slight feeling of apprehension impinging on her euphoria.

Ruthven gravely raised his eyes to the ceiling and joined his hands before him in an attitude of prayerfulness as though silently summoning the assistance of the Almighty. 'As you know, my company has been acquired by Gouldhurst Limited, the large conglomerate which has interests in shipping and hotels as well as textiles. My seat on the board of Dunbars comes from my individual holding of shares purchased by my father many years ago. I must tell you, Madam Chairman, that I have disposed of these shares to Gouldhursts and it is my understanding that, now that Dunbars is a public company, they will be making an offer for the purchase of the entire, newly restructured company.'

As an indignant buzz broke round the table Margaret seized the chairman's gavel and banged it hard on her blotting pad.

'Please, ladies and gentlement! *What* do I understand you to be saying Mr Pendreigh? This is quite monstrous!'

'It's perfectly good business, Margaret,' Ruthven said mildly, changing his tone. 'I knew for a long time they wanted to get their hands on Dunbars and so did you. But as long as it was a private company they hadn't a chance. They also wanted to buy Macallisters, but then they saw that it would make better business sense to let you complete the purchase and *then* come into the open market with a bid for the two. I believe you will be handed a letter to that effect after this meeting. I'm only giving you advance warning of what I know.'

'We shall resist it, Ruthven.'

'I was sure you'd say that, Margaret, which is why I wanted to bring it up here before the entire board. I knew if I told you privately exactly what you'd do, and how you'd react. I hope Joe and I and your family will help you think differently. Look – ' he leaned over the table and started doodling with his pencil on his blotter. 'Gould-hursts are a fine organization; they have years of expertise in this kind of thing, a first-class financial basis from which to operate. They buy a firm, give it what it needs, then leave it to get on with it. I am *very* satisfied with their purchase of Pendreighs and you will soon see what a difference this will make. They leave us alone; but we are free from worry as long as we make profits. I can see that, with Dunbar-Macallister under the same umbrella, there is nothing we could not achieve together. A plentiful supply of yarn, fine mills, good designers, world markets . . .'

'Which is what you and your family have wanted for the last thirty years, Ruthven Pendreigh!' Margaret tapped her pen on the bare boardroom table, emphasizing every word as she spoke. 'The Pendreighs have always been to my family the equivalent of the Greeks invading Troy. If they could not take us openly they would do it by stealth. And I, *I*, Mr Pendreigh, have always played the unwelcome role of Cassandra, warning my family of what you are up to: "Beware the Greeks even though they bring gifts". I should have known very well just what sort of skulduggery *you* were about!'

'Oh Margaret!' Susan looked shocked and, removing her spectacles, glanced agitatedly at her sister and sister-in-law.

'Skulduggery is a bit strong, Margaret.' Joe, his eyes rheumy with disbelief, looked at her placatingly.

'It is *not* strong Joe! Nothing is too strong for those Pendreighs! When I was a girl I ticked off Elliott Pendreigh in public and, nearly thirty years later, here I am once again ticking off his son who is up to very much the same tricks as his father was in those days. Pendreighs are always devious, always underhand. They are like that by nature. They do not come out and say "This, this and this". No, like the Greeks they employ subterfuge; they offer you a dagger under the guise of a gift, then they plunge it in your back when it is turned. Well, I can tell you now, I have not the slightest intention of letting Pendreighs succeed in their latest plot. I do not intend to be under the Gouldhurst umbrella, having to ask for this, and that. "Yes sir. Please sir. May I sir?" You may do what you like, Ruthven, but I should be out. I would never enter the doors of the Dunbar mills again. I know Harry Gouldhurst very well and he's a clever, accomplished man. But what Gouldhursts want is not what I want, not what Dunbars wants, and we shall oppose it, every one of us. Anyway, we shall outvote Harry Gouldhurst. We still have the majority of shares and, as for you, Ruthven Pendreigh, I move you are voted off the board this very moment. All those in favour please signify.'

'Oh Margaret, we must discuss this,' Juliet began but Margaret banged her hand on the table.

'No discussion. There is a motion on the floor. Do I have a seconder?'

Susan meekly put up her hand.

'Those in favour please.'

Susan, Mary, Juliet and Margaret raised their hands.

'Those against?'

Ruthven raised his.

'Abstentions?'

Joe Macallister diffidently put up a hand and Margaret frowned, quickly doing some calculations on her blotter. Then she raised her head.

'I declare the motion carried; four in favour, one against and one abstention. Mr Pendreigh, would you kindly leave the room?'

She stared at him without smiling and slowly, looking shocked, Ruthven got up, putting his papers together and placing them in his briefcase. As she saw his head bent, his crestfallen shoulders, she wondered bitterly how she could ever have contemplated falling in love with him again. Once more a man had proved what a treacherous race his was. She had let him court her, and her reward was this. She felt humiliated and angry, avoiding his eyes as he put his briefcase under his arm and came over to her.

'Margaret, I'm very sorry . . .'

'*I'm* very sorry, Ruthven. I'm absolutely disgusted you couldn't have discussed this with me before.'

'I knew how you'd react.'

'You were right! You should have realized my family would react as we did. Just because I don't give your son a place in the firm, as I said I would, you turn round and snap at my ankles.'

'That's not true.'

'It is. It's sheer spite!'

Margaret got up, her bosom heaving, and faced him.

573

She forgot she was in the Dunbar boardroom with the members of the board around her; she forgot she was the chairman of a company, a member of the Festival Committee, a woman about whom many people were beginning to talk and read of in their papers. She was called to serve on many committees, to advise, to lecture at home and abroad. There were profiles about her in business journals. But she forgot all this as she faced Ruthven Pendreigh in the boardroom that sunny August day. She remembered only a young girl standing facing his father in a marquee on a sunny day, not unlike this one, in 1919. And she remembered the man who, having held her in his arms, let her down and did not defend her.

'Your attitude to Russell has *nothing* to do with this.' From the expression on his face Ruthven looked as though he had divined her thoughts and she saw pain in his eyes; pain and anguish. 'You explained to me that William wanted to marry Yvonne and enter the business and that it would be awkward to have Russell at the same time. I was sorry, and so was he, but we quite understood. It would have been a difficult position. If you like, today I was simply warning you, hoping you would see sense. Harry Gouldhurst is going to give Russell a job in another firm and . . .'

'Oh, you're all being well taken care of aren't you?' Margaret's tone was cutting. 'The Welfare State has arrived as far as the Pendreighs are concerned. No more want or care; protection from the cradle to the grave. Well, we Dunbars are not like that. We are independent and we look after ourselves. I hope Gouldhursts smother you, Ruthven Pendreigh. I hope you disappear forever under their care and protection. I hope I never have anything more to do with you again!'

Margaret sat down abruptly, taking a large draught of water, and Ruthven, without saying another word, left the room.

'Well.' Margaret put down her glass. 'I needed that. I am sorry about all this. What a swine that man is!'

'I think you were over-hasty Margaret,' Mary intervened timidly. 'He looked very upset.'

'I've no doubt he looked upset! He's a snake in the grass, a traitor, the sort of person I despise from my heart. Now you realize we have a very serious situation on our hands? You know how I feel. How do you feel?'

They spent an hour telling her how they felt and what they felt; but all the time Margaret was looking anxiously at Joe. Her calculations showed that Joe held the fate of Dunbars in his hands. Apart from the forty percent sold to the public, the remaining voting shares had been even in the hands of the Dunbar family, Ruthven Pendreigh and Joe Macallister. Joe was Susan's father-in-law, the great-grandfather of the beloved Malcolm. Gouldhursts would no doubt make their offer attractive. Those who sold would nearly be millionaires, much richer than they were now, with no worries and with money to invest.

It was Joe who voiced this first. He said that he understood why Margaret was upset. She had worked and fought and everyone admired her. But she was at her peak. How much further did she want to go? She was respected by all who knew her, in commerce and outside it. Would it not be nice to accept the Gouldhurst offer when it was made, provided it was enough; to become very rich and yet retain a place in the business she loved? Harry Gouldhurst, whom they all knew, they agreed was a very nice man. He wasn't a crook. For once in her life Margaret would have all the cares of running a, by now, much extended business taken away from her. She could enjoy her flair and creativity. He urged them all to look at the offer when it came, consider it and if they thought it right, accept it.

'No!' Margaret cried passionately, rising from her chair. 'No, no, no!'

* * *

The takeover battle, for battle it became, for the newly constituted firm of Dunbar-Macallister raged for the next six months, from August 1948 to February 1949. It also captured the public imagination. From being a name well known in business circles only, Margaret became familiar to the world at large and, as happens to celebrities, her views were sought on all sorts of matters whether to do with the knitwear business or not. What did she think of the atomic bomb, of the moves to establish a Council of Europe, of Communist infiltration in the unions and the introduction of the last word in 'multilateral education', the comprehensive school? Women gossip columnists wanted to know her views on the Royal Family (should Princess Margaret marry a commoner?), what she thought of the 'New Look', sex before marriage and the teenage revolution. Was there a man in her life; if not why not, if so who was he? Pictures of her, elegantly dressed, were everywhere and her views on fashion were much sought after.

It was exhausting, unnerving, worse than she had ever expected; but it was exciting. It was challenging. Being a Dunbar she rose to the challenge and, by the very publicity she engendered, the small Dunbar David against the huge Gouldhurst Goliath, she began to win the public to her side so that Gouldhursts, soon out of their depth despite their acknowledged expertise, began to assume the stereotype of a wicked, grasping, greedy capitalistic uncle. Even the financial press supported Margaret and Gouldhursts' shares on the stock market fell rapidly. Harry Gouldhurst had never realized what he was in for when he took on a woman in a takeover battle. Meanwhile sales of clothes made by Dunbars soared, and so did the market price of its shares.

Although she applied herself with all her vigour to the battle, Margaret still went on with her plans for reorganization and rebuilding. Tom was appointed to the new board along with Peter Cartwright, Jamie Paterson and a newcomer John Mactavish. A member of the Mactavish family who had sold out before the war, a brother of Angus Mactavish who had been Cornet in 1923, he had bought heavily into the new Dunbar issue. Thus he had an interest in preserving the firm as it was, and represented those shareholders who felt the same way. Finally there was Joe Macallister, who was to play such a vital role. For the time being Susan too remained on the board because she held shares in trust for her son James and her grandson Malcolm.

In the middle of the winter Joe Macallister developed pneumonia and nearly died. Although Margaret seldom prayed, she prayed then because there was no doubt that the Macallister family, who had no interest in the business, would sell out if they inherited Joe's shares.

Also in the winter, in December, the marriage of Yvonne to William Murray had been solemnized in Branswick Parish Church. It was just the sort of large, extravagant wedding that Yvonne had dreamed of, with herself in white, her bridegroom and male guests in morning dress, and a bevy of young attendants clad in white silk. They went to stay with Yvonne's grandparents for their honeymoon, after weekending in Paris, and then came back to live in *Woodbrae* with Margaret, a temporary move which no one really regarded as satisfactory. Then someone had the idea of cutting off the top floor and making it into a separate flat, for which the permission of Fleur had to be sought and was quickly given.

To begin with, when the Gouldhurst offer was made, Margaret talked quite amiably to Harry Gouldhurst, telling him 'no', but it was a nice offer all the same. It was very civilized, they had drinks at the Ritz; but as the months passed and Gouldhursts felt themselves unfairly pilloried, it grew bitter and, with the illness of Joe, it reached a peak of recrimination and counter-recrimination. Many of those who had bought shares in Dunbars when it went public gladly sold them at double the price to Gouldhursts who, although they thus acquired a slice of the firm, still had nothing like the whole cake. Many people remained loyal because of the personality of Margaret and the impact her image of an embattled, brave Britannia made on the nation.

She was felt to be good for the country, to typify the British lioness at bay with teeth bared, protecting her cubs against the Barbarian hordes who swept in with American money and foreign techniques; though both Gouldhursts' money and techniques were as British as Margaret and Dunbars. It was just an idea, another wrong idea, that got about to Gouldhursts' disadvantage.

Finally in February the fateful board meeting was held in the boardroom of the Dunbar Mill, only this time the snow fell outside and *Woodbrae* on the top of the hill was obscured from view. Margaret hoped it was not an omen. There was only one item on the agenda: the rejection of the Gouldhurst offer. Margaret spoke first, followed by Tom and John Mactavish who, as became the brother of a man who had once been Cornet, painted a grisly parallel with the invasion of Scotland by the English in the sixteenth century and the resistance of the redoubtable, brave, but hopelessly outnumbered Scots.

Margaret listened to them, but once again her eyes were on Joe and on Susan sitting next to him, who had nursed him through his pneumonia and had spent many hours by his bedside, seeing him through the worst of his illness. The one thing Joe had steadfastly refused to talk about all the time, to anyone, was the Gouldhurst offer. He would bide his own time, he had said, and announce his decision in due course when all the fuss had died down.

Today his decision would be known. Margaret watched him nervously because half of the time he appeared fast asleep.

'Now,' she said at last, when John had finished his stirring peroration, 'have you anything to say, Joe, before we put it to the vote?'

Joe opened his eyes as though he had just woken from a deep and pleasing sleep. He looked a little like his great-grandson did when he opened his blue eyes each morning, as though he were aware of his place in the world, and satisfied with it. Joe was satisfied with life; he was an old man and, despite its tragedies, the death of Bruno among them, he had had a good life and now it was nearly over.

His very wrinkled hands with the large brown liver marks of age reached for a pencil, as a baby reaches for a toy, and he began to play with it. In his great age Joe resembled a child but he had not the mind of a child; it was still as acute and as unclouded as it had ever been.

'Aye, Margaret, I have something to say.' He played with the pencil, a smile on his lips, but his blue eyes looked straight at Margaret. 'I have this to say. I know the whole thing depends on me and you have all tried to court me and influence me one way or the other. Harry Gouldhurst has taken me to dinner, Ruthven Pendreigh to lunch – twice. You have said this, my family have said that. I must say I have enjoyed the spectacle of the battle from my seat high up on the hill, out of danger. I think you have enjoyed it too, Margaret, because you enjoy a fight.'

Margaret smiled but did not speak, slightly inclining her head as though to acknowledge he was not far off the mark.

'But, in my mind, above all, Margaret – and I address myself chiefly to you, because it has been your battle – has been this: what is the best for us? What is the best thing for *Dunbars*, for our families which have been united for many years by ties of blood, by the important bond of marriage. What is best for *you*, for your children, your newly married daughter and son-in-law, your young son

Charles? What is the best for Susan here looking after Malcolm, my great-grandson, the son of my granddaughter whom I so dearly loved?

'And it is this, Margaret and all you here, that influenced me more than anything else, for I am an old man and shall not live long. I have more money than I shall ever want; so I do not desire further wealth. What, I thought, can I give to the *younger* generation before I die? And then I thought, as I have so many times, of that young couple whom we saw married during the dark days of the war – my granddaughter Hesther to young Murdoch Dunbar. With Murdoch dead I thought, what point *is* there? Murdoch who, we all knew, was groomed to run the firm which bears the founder's name.'

Margaret closed her eyes. Now, she thought, she knew now, after all these months, what the old man was going to say. She leaned back in her chair to await the inevitable. Susan meanwhile was quietly sobbing into her handkerchief, moved to tears by the old man's words, by the memory of her dead daughter.

'Yes,' Joe continued, 'I thought of Murdoch and Hesther on that happy day – how fine they both looked, didn't they? – and soon came the news they were going to have a baby. How happy we all were. Little did we know that within a short time they would both be dead. That all that would be left of them would be that wee bairn, my dear great-grandson Malcolm, called after the grandfather he never knew; whom his father in his turn scarcely knew. What would my great-grandson want, I thought? What will be best for *him*? I will not live to see him grow up. But what would I like to say to him if I could say it, when the years roll by and he is a man?

'I would say this: "Malcolm, you come from two grand, fighting families: the Dunbars and the Macallisters. They have fought for their livelihoods and they have fought for their families. The Macallisters, as Laskeys, came over a

580

century ago from Poland because of the injustice there. They wanted freedom, independence. They have fought and the Dunbars have fought and, as Churchill said to us during the war, they never gave in." Would Malcolm, when he is a grown man, thank me if I sold his birthright for gold? For wealth? No. I want Malcolm to work as I worked. I do not want to bequeath mere riches to him, but no inheritance worth the name. Because the young grow idle and selfish with money; but if they can invest their talents in some enterprise they can have the best of both worlds, as I and my sons did, as Malcolm's grandfathers did.

'So although I think the offer a good one, and Gouldhursts good people, I have decided that Malcolm, when he grows up, will be like his great-aunt Margaret here – a fighter, in love with independence. I think he would want me to let the firm stay in the hands of the family, and so I cast my vote with you.'

As Joe, very tired, his voice failing, sank back in his chair, Margaret got up and, coming round to him, put her arms around his neck and embraced him. She had no need for words, nor any room in her heart for them.

CHAPTER THIRTY THREE

Hesther Dunbar Murray lay in her mother's arms utterly contented, at peace with the world. She'd cried a little when the pastor had poured water on her head, and her godmother Cathy Pendreigh had passed her quickly back to her mother who, in turn, gave her to her great-aunt Susan who had a way with babies.

But now, up at the house on the hill with family and friends swirling around, Hesther demonstrated once again the tranquillity and good humour which had been such a characteristic of her since her birth, three months before. She had the blue-green Dunbar eyes and red hair and Yvonne was happy because, such is the self-sacrifice of women and the vanity of men, women like their children to resemble their husbands; and the husbands are generally happy when they do.

The reception rooms of the house were packed and the terrace was full too, because it seemed as though all Branswick had been invited to rejoice in the christening of Margaret's first grandchild. The 'gentry' were there but so were several representatives from the mill, mixing with their betters in a way that would have seemed unthinkable in Margaret's youth. They still retained an air of deference, but it was not enough to obscure their enjoyment.

Marriage suited Yvonne, as she had known it would. She was not plump, but nor was she slim and she was very comely; she had not regained the figure she had before her baby had started to grow in her womb, but she was unconcerned about it. She would soon be starting another, so what did it matter? She and William liked domesticity, and children were an essential part of domestic life. She was not fashion-conscious like her mother and too much in love with her husband to be afraid of losing him. So she wore what she liked, a rather loose-fitting Paisley dress that she had worn as a maternity garment, and her black hair waved away from her vibrant, glowing face, falling to her shoulders in loose curls.

Yvonne gently rocked her baby in her arms, easing the soft, white cashmere christening shawl, specially made for her, away from her face as people came up to peep and stayed to admire and praise. But then they had to make way for others and, as the throng pressed in upon her, William anxiously hovered by her side to make sure she wasn't tiring herself.

When you saw them together, Margaret thought, their eyes first on each other and then on their baby, one was made fully aware of the life-enhancing power of love.

'It almost makes one envious,' she murmured to Susan, who stood by her side, and Peter Cartwright bent his head towards her so that he could hear too. 'That's not to say I'm jealous,' Margaret added quickly. 'But, yes, it is a sort of envy that they have what I didn't. I don't remember Yves and I appearing so harmonious at Yvonne's christening.'

'Oh you were!' Susan laughed and took a sandwich from a tray proffered to her by a passing waitress. 'I remember it was a lovely occasion. You must too Peter?'

Peter Cartwright's hair was now quite white and his stoop so pronounced that he seemed to have shrunk. It was almost impossible to recall the tall very handsome young man who had bent to peep at Yvonne twenty years before as he was now inspecting her baby. Peter had always been self-effacing, but so good-looking that people turned to stare. Now they only stared, if they remembered him, because he had changed so much. But as far as was known Peter was happy. He had sublimated his grief over Yves' death in his work and his friendship with the

Dunbar family. He was regarded as honorary uncle to its younger members and was one of Hesther's godparents.

'I remember it very well,' Peter said; 'but not for the reason you think. I was very jealous,' he murmured *sotto voce* so that only Margaret could hear. 'And I went and got utterly drunk afterwards.'

Margaret squeezed his arm, but her reply was lost in the noise made by the arrival of her son accompanied by a number of his young friends.

'I feel *terribly* old now that I'm an uncle,' he announced theatrically. 'But not as old as Mama says she feels now that she's a grandmother!'

'Charles!' Margaret assumed a reprimanding tone. 'You know that isn't true at all. I've never tried to conceal my age. After all, it's the one thing we can do absolutely nothing about.'

'We can *disguise* it, Margaret,' Peter said. 'But you have no need to. I am prematurely old and you are eternally young.'

Margaret, indeed, looked ravishing. There was no other word for it. She was dressed in white and navy, her calf-length dress with its swathed waistline accentuating her bust. A large navy blue cartwheel hat and high-heeled white shoes, handbag and gloves were perfect accessories. Her skin was delicately made up; her short hair curled below the brim of her hat. There was no trace of white in her hair but, when it did come, it would add to her distinction. Already she was thought of as something of a celebrity; a local girl who had not only made good but achieved nationwide eminence. Many said that her work on the Festival Committee would be rewarded with an honour, which would also show the establishment's tacit admiration for her stand against the takeover, the assertion of the nation's independent spirit.

For this was June 1951 and in May King George VI had opened the Festival of Britain from the steps of St Paul's

Cathedral. The Exhibition site on the South Bank in London with its many pavilions housed, it was claimed, all that was best in Britain in trade, the arts, science and industry. Throughout the nation similar displays and celebrations were taking place. It seemed somehow fitting, from Margaret's point of view, that she attained her own half-century in the year that commemorated the Great Exhibition of 1851 and also that it marked the birth of her first grandchild.

But the thought of her approaching fiftieth birthday in October did not seem to be the traumatic event she had anticipated, the sort of watershed that people liked to say it was. She felt younger than her age. She had worn well; she could allow herself now certain compromises that came with age: she was not so easily hurt, she did not dash around so much, she was not as fierce and she was certainly trying to be more tolerant of the mistakes of others. She was mellow. Mellowness suited her; it made her look softer and quite outstandingly beautiful for a woman of courage, poise and personality.

Margaret spent a lot of time in London, and several weeks of the year abroad. But when she was in Branswick she lived in the flat at the top of *Woodbrae*, from which she had a beautiful view of the valley, the town and the mill.

Six months after William's marriage Fleur had written from America to say she was not coming home, and wished him joy of the house. Everyone thought it a nice gesture on Fleur's part; a gesture of goodwill to repair the heartache of the past.

Margaret, however, did not intend to stay permanently in *Woodbrae* and was actively looking for another house, even if it meant leaving the hill where she had lived all her life. She and Yvonne were temperamentally explosive together and, although they took care not to get under each other's feet, there was too much tension in the house when they were both around. Yvonne's domesticity grated on Margaret. She couldn't understand how any woman, let alone her own daughter, could be content to be wholly absorbed by her husband, home and family.

'They're *terribly* happy, aren't they?' Susan had a wistful look in her eyes, as though sadly recalling the days of her own youth. Unlike Margaret, Susan did look her age. Her hair was more white than black; her figure had fallen victim to middle-age spread, which she did nothing to correct, and she dressed her age too – tweeds, skirts and Dunbar twin-sets. Her only pleasure now lay in her family; especially her grandson Malcolm.

'Terribly.' Margaret smiled at her sister who kept an anxious eye on Malcolm frisking in and out of the assembled company.

'Aunt Susan, *everyone's* happy.' Charles gestured around, swooping on a waiter with a tray of champagne. 'Mother?'

'Don't drink too much, darling,' Margaret murmured.

'Mother don't *fuss*,' Charles said, downing it at a gulp and, with a wink, reaching for another. She knew he provoked her deliberately, but she was always conscious of the Dunbar weakness. William only drank beer, and very little of it, but Charles, sixteen and at public school, was devilish. She was forever receiving notes from the head-master about one misdemeanour or another.

Charles was already very tall and well developed. His short black hair was brushed straight back from his head without a parting and his blue eyes were capable of the same penetrating gaze as his sister's. He moved easily, with a grace that uncannily recalled the man who had been killed in the war by the Nazis and whose Croix de Guerre Charles had framed on the wall of his bedroom. In fact it was astonishing how much Charles did, in fact, resemble Yves, whose memory he idolized. He was also particularly fond of his grandparents in France, who returned his affection.

Charles was an intelligent, handsome boy, attentive to his mother and sister, but already with an eye for young ladies. There were quite a few circling about, calculating on their fingers that, in a few more years, he would be a front runner in the Branswick marriage stakes which got going each year at the time of the Common Riding, when the nubile girls surveyed the eligible young men riding behind the Cornet up the Vertig hill.

Susan and Margaret were joined by friends from Edinburgh while Charles, glass in hand, stood contentedly surveying the crowded room. Everyone certainly looked happy. It was a lovely day and tables had been set on the terrace where strawberries and champagne were being freely dispensed. The ladies, able now to buy what they liked, or what they could, because clothes' rationing had ended, looked their best in day dresses draped to emphasize the bust, with large hip pockets, the hems twelve and a half inches from the ground. Their hats fitted closely to their heads with off-the-face lines, which, to many, looked like the return of the cloche only with the front brim turned upwards. Others wore large cartwheel-shaped hats in straw, which suited those experimenting with shorter hair. Stockings were of the sheerest silk, though some wore nylons they had managed to get from friends in America.

There were lots of children about, some as young as seven-year-old Malcolm who caused such consternation by running in and out among the guests; some younger, and some older like Charles. They were the new generation of Branswick citizens, the ones who would live on the hill with their families in future years. How many of them, some may have wondered, would still walk to work by then, or even have a mill to go to if the movement for mergers and acquisitions continued? But it was too nice a day to worry about the future. Indeed, no such worrisome thoughts crossed the mind of Charles Dunbar Lamotte, a young man poised on the threshold of life and excited by the thought of the prospects it offered him.

Susan reached out abruptly to waylay Malcolm as he ran helterskelter across the drawing room in pursuit of a young companion and pulled him sharply to her side.

'That's quite enough, Malcolm! You'll make yourself giddy.'

Peter leaned down and held out a hand. 'Come with me. I've got something very exciting to show you.'

'What?' Malcolm had his mother's curly black hair and some of her features, so that in certain moods Susan felt a pang of anguish when she gazed at him.

'Come, I'll show you,' Peter said, 'but only if you're good for the rest of the party.'

'Show me first. Then I'll promise.'

Imperiously Malcolm held up a podgy hand and everyone laughed as Peter firmly clasped it and led him away.

'Whatever can it be?' Susan wondered.

'I think Peter wants to give you a break. He'll think of something.' Margaret greeted one of the MacLeish cousins and then linked her arm through that of Charles who was taller than she. The doors onto the terrace were open, and the valley lay beneath them shrouded in greenery.

'Darling, let's go out onto the terrace. It's stifling in here. Susan?'

But Susan's back was turned and she was now talking to Cathy Pendreigh, Ruthven's daughter and the new baby's godmother. She was still called Cathy Pendreigh, though she had been married for two years to Alastair Turnball and lived with him in the Turnball house further down the hill. In these post-war years, with servants being non-existent because of full employment in the mills, many of the large houses were being turned into flats and the young marrieds were moving in with their in-laws.

'Mother, I'll escort you to the terrace,' Charles said

with a glance backwards to the room. 'But I'm going to leave you there. There's the most wizard girl over in the corner. Do you know her name?'

Margaret, following Charles's gaze, saw Jennifer Laidlaw who was the same age as Charles and at her old boarding school in Harrogate.

'It's Jenny Laidlaw. Surely you remember her, Charles?'

'*Jenny* Laidlaw,' Charles said incredulously. 'But last time I saw her she was about three feet high and very spotty.'

'Well, people do change you know,' his mother said sagaciously. 'You'd better go and have a word with her now. I see a number of other young men circling for the kill.'

'I'll ask her for tennis tomorrow.' Charles abruptly withdrew his arm from his mother's. 'You don't mind, Mother, do you?'

'Of course I don't, darling; but please don't propose just yet.'

'Mother, who's talking about *marriage*?'

Charles raised his eyes to heaven in a comic gesture of despair and went swiftly over to Jennifer who appeared, by the gratified expression on her face, to have been trying to bring about this very thing.

'He's a charmer,' Cathy Turnball said to Margaret. 'He's going to break any number of hearts by the time he's twenty. Jenny Laidlaw hasn't taken her eyes from him all afternoon. Have you seen Daddy, Mrs Lamotte?'

Margaret, who had been gazing at Charles and thinking of Hamish, not invited for this occasion, started and looked round. 'Is your father here?'

'He said he was coming. I think he wants to make it up with you.'

'There is nothing to make up.' Margaret, smiling at Cathy, imperturbably shook several more hands. 'I have a very short memory.'

Ruthven Pendreigh! She had known he was on the guest list. Even the sound of his name still affected her. She realized she had been subconsciously searching the crowd for a glimpse of his face, as she wandered towards the terrace door, anxious for that breath of fresh air, waylaid at every step by someone she knew.

'Mother-in-law, Aunt, won't you have more champagne?' William stepped in front of her and placed a glass in her hand. Then he solemnly raised his and toasted her. 'You're the loveliest woman in the room today.'

'Oh William! What about your wife?' She suspected she was blushing as she lifted her glass.

'*Woman*,' William said smiling. 'Yvonne would know what I meant. I still think of her as a girl.'

'I don't think she'd *like* to be thought of as one,' Margaret said gently, 'not in your eyes; but my daughter and I are not rivals. Thank you, though, for the compliment. You remember the last party we had here was for Yvonne's twenty-first birthday. How young I thought she was to be already a wife and an expectant mother! Though, it's true, I once thought of marriage at eighteen.'

'Really? I thought you had your sights all set on a career then?'

'Not at eighteen. Like Yvonne, I wanted to marry and live on the hill. But not for long!'

She still had Ruthven Pendreigh on her mind, and how different her life would have been had her fateful conversation with his father never taken place.

'You must tell me about it,' William raised a hand and looked over her shoulder. 'But not now, Yvonne wants me.' He quickly kissed Margaret's cheek and hurried to where his wife was beckoning to him.

'He's a lovely boy,' said Juliet Monroe, leaving a group of friends to join her sister. 'Everything we dreamed of – for Yvonne and the business. He's so steadying.'

Margaret looked with approval at the young bearded

590

Scotsman with his red curls and piercing blue eyes. She sometimes thought he looked like the embodiment of the Scots' hero Rob Roy, a true heir to Malcolm and Murdoch Dunbar, father and son, who had given their lives for their country. How strange it was that their strength had reappeared in the natural son of her weak brother Cullum and a Scottish mill girl.

'Yes, and I'm very fond of him too,' Margaret said in reply to her sister. 'Not only has he made Yvonne so happy, but he's doing very well in the business. He's taken to it like a duck to water and has a lot of good ideas. He has natural flair.'

'I think we're well set for the future – ' Juliet began. 'Oh there's Tom, I must have a word . . . ' She darted away and Tom, seeing her, came half way to greet his mother.

To everyone's relief Fiona had found a man who wanted to marry her and Tom and she were getting divorced. Until then Clare remained in London, where she was in charge of the London office, reopened and running to capacity with a large sales department and showrooms on the second and third floors. Clare was still timid about meeting the family, especially Susan. Time, Margaret supposed, would take care of that as well.

Time took care of everything. She turned, with this thought in her head, to stare straight into the eyes of Ruthven Pendreigh. She was so taken aback that she tried to pass by. But he put a hand out and took hold of her arm.

'Don't go, Margaret. Say hello.'

Although she had been looking for him, now that they were face to face she suddenly felt self-conscious and some of her old hostility for him returned. Still, she was surprised to hear herself say coldly, 'I'm surprised you came, Ruthven.'

'You mean you think I had a nerve?' He gave an

apprehensive smile. He looked extremely debonair in a dark blue suit, light blue shirt and dark tie. He had obviously been abroad for he was suntanned and his hair, now completely silver, was sleeked back, curling rather attractively just above his ears.

'Exactly.'

'Margaret, don't let's go on fighting all our lives. Can't you let bygones be bygones? I wanted to see you today and ask you this.'

'With a Pendreigh? No.'

'*Please*, Margaret. I've wanted so much to talk to you but you always scampered away after our Festival meetings.'

'That was because I had no wish to talk to you, Ruthven. What have we to say?'

'Plenty. My daughter and yours are best friends. We can't stay implacable enemies forever. All that nonsense is in the past. Look, what I did was business. You know that. You won and I'm glad. I really am. I wanted you to win.'

Margaret permitted herself a sarcastic smile and groped in her large white leather bag for a cigarette. He quickly took his case from his breast pocket and flicked it open in front of her. 'Two kinds, Virginia and Turkish.'

'Thanks.' She selected a Sobranie and he lit it for her. Looking into his eyes, so open and friendly, she suddenly wondered why she was still fighting. After all, she had won all the battles. What was it about Ruthven Pendreigh that provoked such strong reactions from her? She couldn't ignore him. He had never remarried, never taken a younger bride who would foist on him once again the burden of fatherhood. He was well thought of and spoken about and now on the board of Gouldhursts as well as the head of Pendreighs. Yes, he affected her. He was impossible to forget. Yet he was so . . . *infuriating*. 'Really? You *really*, truly wanted us to win?'

'Of course. I just told you at the time what Gouldhursts were up to. *I* couldn't influence them.'

'You sold them your shares.'

'That wasn't enough to influence the bid. I knew that Joe held the key and that Joe would back you. He admired you too much to let you down. If I didn't behave better it was because I didn't know what to do. I apologize for it now, with all my heart.'

'You might have told us about your hunch. You kept us on tenterhooks until the last minute.'

Mollified a little, Margaret allowed herself to relax, smiling her brilliant, special smile which still seemed to affect the men young and old. It came from the heart but it was still, to some extent, premeditated. It affected women too. It was a sign of forgiveness, of interest, and those who were its recipients felt as though they had been warmed by the sun.

It was a quality shared by the close members of her family, chiefly her son and daughter. Now at last she could unbend, be her old self with Ruthven, as she knew she so desperately wanted to. She was a lonely woman; happy and fulfilled, yes, and envied by many, but lonely too. She lived alone, travelled alone, worked alone. Even surrounded by people whom she loved and who loved her, she felt lonely, because a place in her heart was unoccupied: that special place that is kept for the love between a man and a woman. How nice it would be to share her life, and her bed, once again, after so many years, with a companion and lover.

As though he could read her mind, Ruthven moved imperceptibly closer and looked into her eyes. 'He enjoyed it. It was his last game. Joe loved games. Poor Joe.'

'No.' Margaret stepped back, unnerved despite her thoughts by the intensity of his expression. 'No, *not* poor Joe. He loved life but he had a good death, at a good age. It came swiftly and painlessly, in the night. That's how I'd like to go.'

'Not for a long time yet, Margaret.'

'I hope not, Ruthven.' The laughter suddenly seemed to spring out of her, as though its source were pure happiness. 'If only to fight more battles with you.'

'Not those kinds of battles Margaret, *other* battles.'

Was it a declaration? Margaret gazed at him in ill concealed astonishment. She wondered if the longing in his eyes were mirrored in hers. The implication was unmistakable. He was talking about the war between the sexes, and everyone knew the only way to resolve that. Companion and lover. Could he be both? If any man she had ever known could, that man was Ruthven Pendreigh – someone who had always attracted her, but whom she had resisted for so long because Dunbars had always come first and for too long Dunbars and Pendreighs had been at loggerheads. But could it be, was it remotely possible that, even after she had voted him off the board, Ruthven still loved her? Then she thought that, in all her fighting with Ruthven, there had been an undercurrent that was decidedly sexual. She never fought with other people as she did with him, hated them so much, was so loath to forgive. Had she been depriving herself, and him, of a much deeper, more fruitful enjoyment all these years? Why? But could one ever trust a Pendreigh completely? Or should one have, at *least*, a last try?

Finding her voice at last, she said, as lightly as she could: 'I'll think about it. I must go and see my granddaughter. I suppose you realize I *am* a grandmother?' She raised her eyebrows and smiled again, provocatively, putting one shapely leg in front of the other, aware of her aura, her individual brand of charm: above all, of her sex. Ruthven looked down at her legs and then his eyes travelled upwards, slowly, over her figure.

'I am a grandfather four times over. It makes no difference I assure you. One can still be young in heart. Looking at you now I feel like an undergraduate again.'

594

Margaret bowed her head, trying not to show him the sudden, almost overwhelming, extent of her happiness.

'Margaret, *please* say you'll come out with me. I have tickets for all the best concerts and plays for the Edinburgh Festival.'

'So have I.' She had to have one last try at resistance, if only for her self-esteem.

'Give them to your family and come with me. I'll ask you and ask you and ask you until you say yes.'

Margaret solemnly looked at him and thought that, before she lost him yet again, and perhaps finally, one of the battles she should at last allow him to win.

'Then I'll say yes now,' she said slowly as though to reinforce the double meaning of most of their conversation, 'and save you the trouble.'

Then she briefly, affectionately, touched his arm and moved to where Nan was standing alone by the window after talking to Cathy Turnball.

'How are you Nan?' she said stooping to kiss her. Now that they shared a granddaughter she felt that at last she could permit herself this intimacy.

Nan had always resisted her, always been cool, perhaps subconsciously blaming her for Cullum's failure to marry her before he met Fleur. She had been aghast when William brought Yvonne to see her and told her they were going to marry. She had made one of her rare journeys into Branswick to try and persuade Margaret to stop it. Margaret had laughed, asking Nan if she had any idea what sort of girl her daughter was? Margaret tried to be friends then; but it was useless. Nan went back to Homerton; to the cottage William had bought for her when the landlord put it on the market, the house where she had lived with Cullum.

She had gone to the wedding, but only for William's sake, saying she was unhappy with 'those people'. Now, although she was surrounded by 'those' people she looked more tranquil. She suffered badly from arthritis and walked with the help of a stick, although her face had hardly aged and she looked like the beautiful peasant girl Margaret remembered from all those years ago. The lines of age and experience had only added character to that strong, handsome face. Her hair was still thickly braided about her head and she wore a printed, rather shapeless cotton dress that bore the distinct mark of war-time utility.

'You look nice, Mrs Lamotte,' Nan said grudgingly.

'I was just thinking the same about you. You look lovely, Nan.'

Nan always used her surname, though Margaret begged her not to. It seemed to perpetuate the master/servant relationship which distressed Margaret but seemed to suit Nan, even though her son was married to Margaret's daughter.

'Ah, but you have such good skin. Yvonne is verra like you. Not only has she your skin, but your temperament too.'

'I don't quite know how to take that,' Margaret said, but when Nan didn't reply quickly continued, 'I wish you'd come and stay here from time to time, Nan. You could stay in my flat. I'm hardly ever here. Besides, I'm looking for a place of my own. Those two will be breeding again before Hesther is weaned. They seem set on a large family.'

'Aye, they do.' Nan's tone was lugubrious as though she entertained grave doubts about the wisdom of such a step. 'Strange how bent the young are on having children. I wouldn't have thought it was the world for it. You nevva know what the Russians will do, and that bomb . . .' Nan shook her head and looked anxiously towards the terrace door at the sky, as though she expected to see her worst fears instantly realized. 'The young don't seem tae learn, do they?'

'Hope springs eternal, Nan.'

'Aye.' Nan let her eyes rove over Margaret's face as though she were trying to convey, silently, some message. 'Still, things never turn out the way you expect.'

'No, Nan, they don't.'

Margaret levelly returned Nan's gaze, and then, instinctively, they both looked over to where the new parents, arms entwined, stood talking to a group of the young friends who, from now until old age, probably, would form part of their set. Nothing was going to alter in Branswick society, nothing. There would still be the parties and the luncheons, the sport, the coffee mornings and the gossiping. The rich were not quite so rich and the poor not quite so poor. Inevitably, with the mood of the post-war years, society would even out. But there would always be that difference, however slight, between the people who lived on the hill above Branswick and the ones who didn't.

That was what lay between her and Nan, an invisible gap created by class and money, or the lack of it. William had crossed that divide by marrying Margaret's daughter, but his mother would never join him. The marriage bond might have made her try, but she had never had that. She had never been a Dunbar for all the years she had lived with Cullum.

'I'll make a friend of you one day,' Margaret said to herself, studying Nan's rigid countenance, only her eyes betraying a softer emotion as she looked at her son and his first-born. 'I made a friend of Peter and I'll make one of you.'

'If you came when I was here,' she said aloud, 'you could help me look for a new place.'

A grin, very briefly, flitted on Nan's lips as though the preposterous nature of the idea was enough to make anyone smile. 'I canna come and stay Mrs Lamotte. I have the cat tae feed.'

Nan looked at her triumphantly, as though she had played a trump card, and Margaret was reminded how often people used helpless dumb animals as an excuse to prevent them doing something they didn't want to do. She could suggest that Nan could quite easily bring the cat; but then Nan would be sure to reply that the cat didn't want to come.

Despite her resolve to make friends one day, Margaret knew that Nan had always had a chip on the shoulder about the Dunbars; she always would. It was the price she paid for loving Cullum. Even though her son had married a Dunbar and her granddaughter was now a Dunbar, it would never make any difference to Nan – the resentment would always be there.

Margaret briefly grasped Nan's arm, smiled, and moved away, continuing her regal progress through the drawing room and back onto the terrace, chatting to the Laws and the Pendreighs, the Turnballs, the Hendersons, the Mactavishes and the new people who had come, like the Bullers and the Sutherlands. But nothing in Branswick ever really changed, the names remained largely the same and so did the people, the descendants of those who had gone before.

Momentarily finding herself alone, tired but surprisingly rather trembly with happiness, like a young girl with her first date, she sat on the balustrade at the edge of the terrace and looked down on the valley. Even on the christening day of her granddaughter the Dunbar mill was working in full production, three shifts a day, weekends included, frame after frame clicking away, knitting and trimming and binding.

She realized that even during her conversation with Nan she really only had one thing on her mind, one name in her head: Ruthven. It was of course premature to speculate about the situation that had so suddenly arisen in that crowded room between herself and Ruthven Pendreigh

598

(who, after all, could *trust* a Pendreigh?); but the Pendreigh house, below her now, was certainly most conveniently placed for someone who wanted to move but still stay on the hill.

It was especially convenient for someone, say like herself, who, ever since she was a little girl, had always risen early and flung aside the curtains to be sure that the Dunbar Mill was still there in its place by the side of the Drume, where it was joined by the Craigie.

The place where the rivers met, in the town where she was born.

ACKNOWLEDGEMENTS

I owe grateful thanks to the following people who were kind enough to assist me in my research for my novel: Alan Smith, Chairman of Dawson International Ltd, who gave me unlimited access to the companies in his group and ensured that facilities were available to me to find out anything I needed to know. His active participation was of the utmost help to me and I am indebted to him and his wife Alice for their immense kindness and hospitality. Bill McEwan, Managing Director and Graham Hayward, Marketing Director, of Pringle of Scotland, who cheerfully tolerated my intrusion into their busy working lives. Tommy Maden of Pringle of Scotland, who organized my stay in Hawick and looked after me so well, in addition to continuing to help me by answering any questions I put to him during the writing of the book. Mary Farries, secretary to Bill McEwan, who was good enough to entrust the Pringle archives to me. William Mactaggart, formerly Managing Director of Pringle, who went out of his way to meet me and help me with his reminiscences. Stuart Beaty, one time designer for Pringle, and his wife Moira, who entertained me and answered my many questions. Netta Anderson of Hawick. Donald Hartley and Jack Brown of Laidlaw and Fairgrieve, Selkirk. Bobby Lewis, Marketing Director, Graham Lennox, and Neville Barnes of Todd and Duncan Ltd of Kinross. Gordon Farquharson and Margaret Manzoni of the London office of Pringle who arranged a special fashion show for me. Toni Kent and Yvonne Allen, who talked to me about modelling and put me in touch with Michael Whittaker, whose reminiscences of the London fashion scene between the wars were invaluable. Evelyn Whiteside, formerly knitware buyer for Harrods Ltd. Jean Tyrrell, chairman of Sirdar Ltd, Wakefield. Nicholas Staveley of the International Wool Secretariat.

Finally special thanks to Margaret Pringle, formerly of the Doubleday London office, who gave me so much encouragement and help, and to my editors Patricia Parkin of Granada, London, and Kate Medina of Doubleday, New York, who carefully nursed the infant work on its path towards maturity and provided me with valuable suggestions for revision.

Nicola Thorne

BIBLIOGRAPHY

First of all I would like to thank Hugh Barty-King whose unpublished history of the knitwear industry in Scotland, *Scot Knit*, was made available to me and provided me with information I could only with difficulty have found elsewhere.

In addition I consulted the following works:

Blythe, Ronald. *The Age of Illusion*. London, 1963

Carter, Ernestine. *20th-Century Fashion: a scrapbook 1900 to today*. London, 1975

Cunnington, C. Willett. *Englishwomen's Clothing in the Present Century*. London, 1952

de Marley, Diana. *The History of Haute Couture 1850/1950*. London, 1980

Doyle, A. Conan. *The British Campaign in Europe 1914-1918*. London (N.D.)

Elstob, P. *Battle of the Reichswald*. New York, 1970

Jenkins, Alan. *The Twenties*. London, 1974

Jenkins, Alan. *The Thirties*. London, 1976

Laver, James. *A Concise History of Costume*. London, 1969

Longmate, Norman. *A History of Everyday Life during the Second World War*. London, 1971

Longmate, Norman. *The Doodlebugs*. London, 1981

Mowat, C. L. *Britain between the Wars 1918-1940*. London, 1955

Muggeridge, M. *The Thirties*. London, 1967

Seaman, L.C.B. *Life in Britain between the Wars*. London, 1970

Symons, J. *The Thirties: a dream revolved*. London, 1960
Wood, A. *Great Britain: 1900-1965*. London, 1978

Annual Register, *The*, individual volumes 1919-1951